THE HEART OF FIRE

Also by Michael J. Ward from Gollancz:

The Legion of Shadow

The Heart of Fire

The Eye of Winter's Fury

DESTINYQUEST

BOOK TWO

THE HEART OF FIRE

MICHAEL J. WARD

This edition first published in Great Britain by Gollancz in 2017

First published in Great Britain in 2012
by Gollancz
An imprint of the Orion Publishing Group
Orion House, 5 Upper St Martin's Lane,
London WC2H 9EA
An Hachette UK Company

3 5 7 9 10 8 6 4

A CIP catalogue record for this book
is available from the British Library

ISBN 978 1 473 22366 0

Typeset by Input Data Services Ltd, Somerset

Printed and bound in Great Britain by
CPI Group (UK) Ltd, Croydon, CR0 4YY

MIX
Paper from responsible sources
FSC® C104740

www.destiny-quest.com
www.orionbooks.co.uk
www.gollancz.co.uk

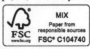

For the fans
Keep the fire burning

Once again, a big thank you to the team at Gollancz for making geek dreams come true – especially my editor, Marcus, who had the Herculean task of reading, editing and testing this labyrinthine gamebook. I owe him more than a few drinks (and payment for therapy bills) for surviving this one. I also want to thank my family, who have always had unquestioning faith in my 'weird and wonderful pastimes' and have supported me every step of the way. I hope they're as proud of this achievement as I am.

HERO DQ SHEET

NAME:		
CLOAK	HEAD	GLOVES
MAIN HAND	CHEST	LEFT HAND
TALISMAN	FEET	MONEY POUCH

SPEED	BRAWN	MAGIC	ARMOUR

HEALTH

HERO DQ SHEET

PATH: CAREER:

NECKLACE

RING

RING

SPECIAL ABILITIES:

SPEED

COMBAT

PASSIVE

MODIFIER

BACKPACK:

NOTES:

HERO SHEET

NAME:

CLOAK	HEAD	GLOVES
MAIN HAND	CHEST	LEFT HAND
TALISMAN	FEET	MONEY POUCH

SPEED	BRAWN	MAGIC	ARMOUR

HEALTH

HERO DQ SHEET

PATH: CAREER:

NECKLACE

RING

RING

SPECIAL ABILITIES:

SPEED

COMBAT

PASSIVE

MODIFIER

BACKPACK:

NOTES:

HERO DQ SHEET

NAME:

CLOAK

HEAD

GLOVES

MAIN HAND

CHEST

LEFT HAND

TALISMAN

FEET

MONEY POUCH

SPEED

BRAWN

MAGIC

ARMOUR

HEALTH

H E R O DQ S H E E T

PATH: CAREER:

NECKLACE

RING

RING

SPECIAL ABILITIES:

SPEED

COMBAT

PASSIVE

MODIFIER

BACKPACK:

NOTES:

HERO DQ SHEET

NAME:

CLOAK

HEAD

GLOVES

MAIN HAND

CHEST

LEFT HAND

TALISMAN

FEET

MONEY POUCH

SPEED

BRAWN

MAGIC

ARMOUR

HEALTH

HERO SHEET

PATH: CAREER:

SPECIAL ABILITIES:

SPEED

COMBAT

PASSIVE

MODIFIER

NECKLACE

RING

RING

BACKPACK:

NOTES:

HERO SHEET

NAME: Nevarin

CLOAK Shadow mantle +2 speed +3 brawn Vanish	HEAD Cowl of the Sabbat +2 speed +2 brawn Critical strike	GLOVES Demonhide gloves +1 speed +4 armour Rake
MAIN HAND Rune-etched blade (sword) +3 speed +4 brawn Bleed	CHEST Shrouded chestguard +2 speed +3 brawn Regrowth	LEFT HAND Morrowspike (dagger) +2 speed +3 brawn Piercing
TALISMAN Viper's fang +1 speed Trickster	FEET Spiral kickers +1 speed +2 brawn Knockdown	MONEY POUCH 100 gc

SPEED	BRAWN	MAGIC	ARMOUR
15	18	0	5

HEALTH 45

HERO DQ SHEET

PATH: **Rogue** CAREER: **Shadowstalker**

NECKLACE
Eye of rage
+1 speed
Savagery

RING
Spiked circle
+1 brawn
Thorns

RING
Band of ruin
+1 armour
Curse

SPECIAL ABILITIES:

SPEED Curse Knockdown

COMBAT Piercing Rake Shadow fury
Vanish

PASSIVE Bleed Thorns

MODIFIER Critical strike Regrowth Savagery
Shadow speed Trickster

BACKPACK:

Flask of healing +10 health 2 uses				

NOTES: Sample hero from 'The Legion of Shadow' for use in team battles. (Also available to download and print from www.destiny-quest.co.uk)

DQ

 Village, town or camp

 Easy quest

 Average quest

 Hard quest

 Hardest quest

 Team battle

 Boss monster

 Legendary monster

8
151
60
19
14
73
144
33
216
158
163
256
42
ACT 1: FENSTONE MOORS

ACT 2: TERRAL JUNGLE

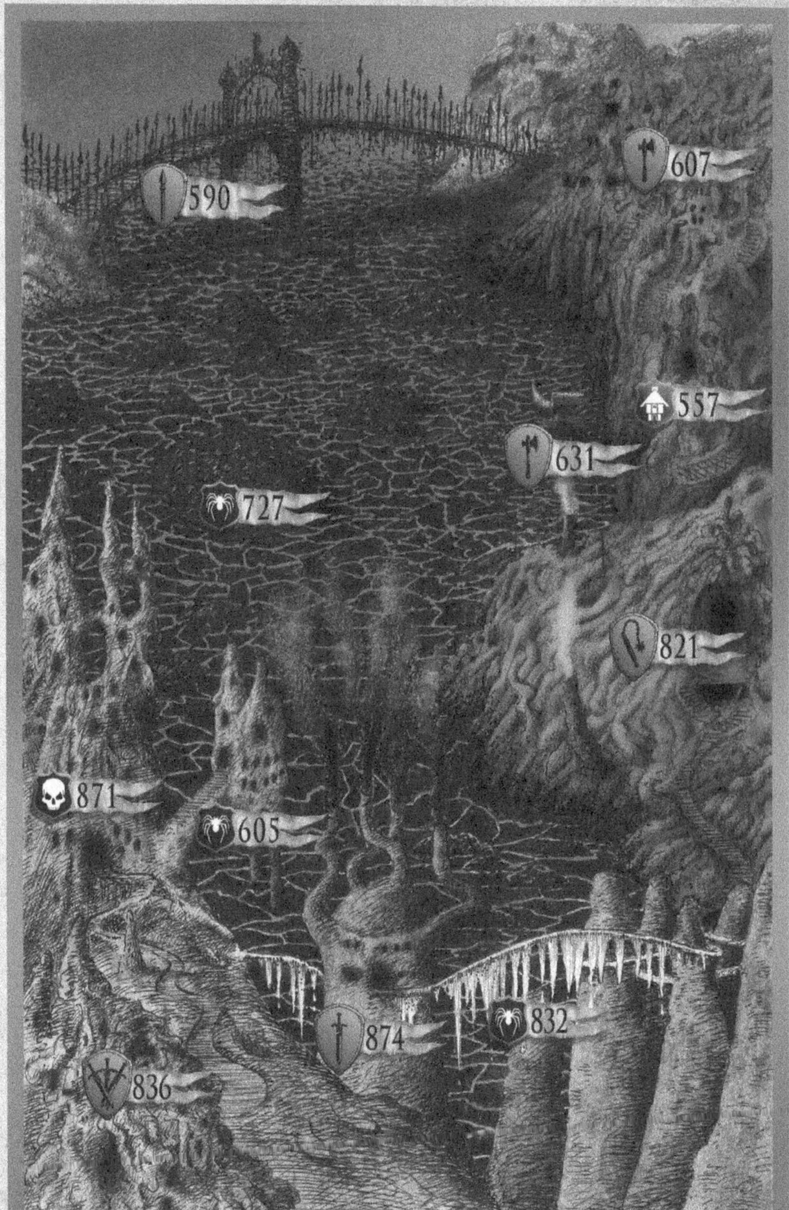

ACT 3: TARTARUS

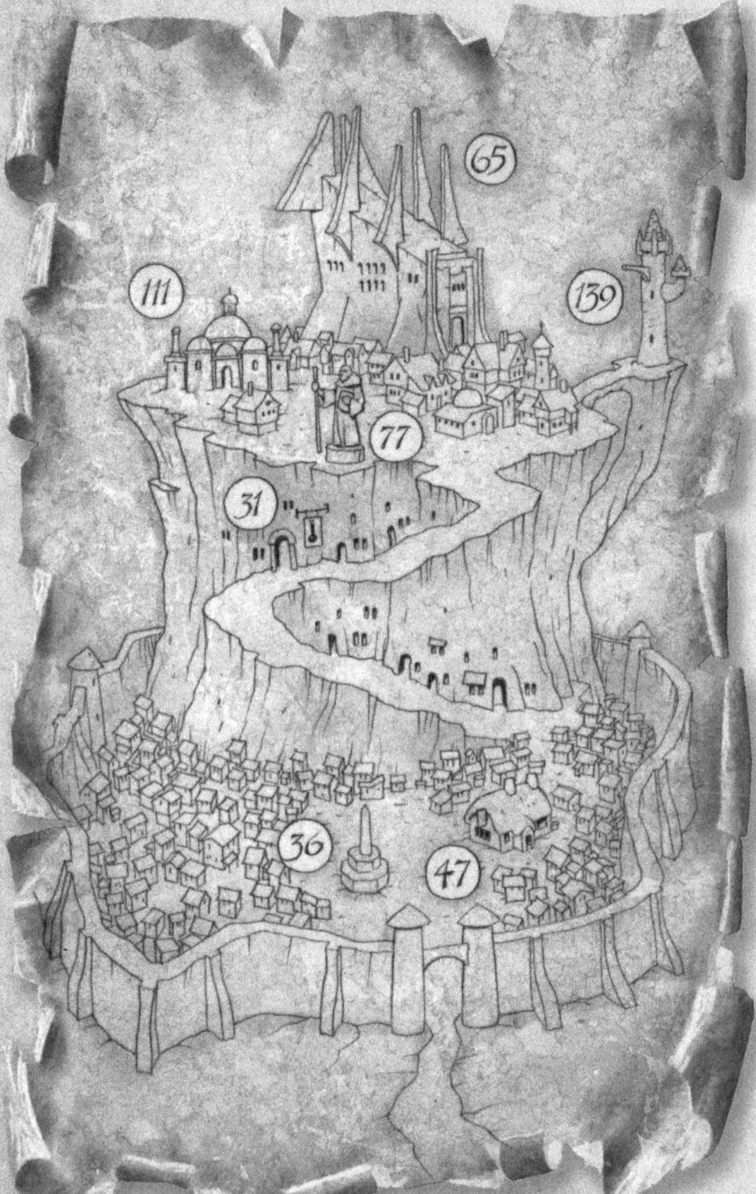
65
111
139
77
31
36
47

Second Dilain, Uttobre, 1387 of the Ascendant

Justinius Galt
Grand Inquisitor, High Warden of Durnhollow

To the venerable and most illustrious Justinius, by the grace of the One God, I present thee with this most urgent petition.

It is recorded in the archive of the Suprema Servorum, Prisoner 8311 hath been received for questioning at Durnhollow on the Fourth Ullir, Janar. The Prisoner is charged with murder and heresy.

Moreover, the records of the Sanctum Officium hold the principal report by holy confessor, Eldias Falks. In the wytchfinder's own words, delivered under divine oath in the presence of White Abbot Torque Marada, the suspect is further accused of false prophecy and wytchcraft. It is understood a calificador is duly assigned to the Prisoner to confirm these most unholiest of crimes from the lips of the guilty.

I hereby exercise the Right of Absolution, in accordance with the fifth clause of The Ninth Holy Writ and sealed with the King's Word, the law above the law. Prisoner 8311 is to be released from confinement and delivered forthwith to the capital under the vigilance of my trusted attendant, Virgil Elland. All records of this case, including those of thy calificador, will also be submitted to Virgil Elland.

Failure to comply with these wishes will result in thy subsequent excommunication. Should the Prisoner come to further harm whilst within custody of the Inquisition, I personally warrant that thy own freedoms and those of the calificador are duly removed. This is a truth, invested in me with the full authority of the King, Leonidas the First.

See thy work is done.

The Holy Light seal my words.

Avian Dale
High Seat of the Council,
Grand Master of the Dawn

DQ

Welcome to DestinyQuest!

'Another will follow; to break the chains of destiny and forge their fate anew – in fire.'
Cornelius the Prophet

Unlike ordinary storybooks, DestinyQuest puts *you* in charge of the action. As you guide your hero through this epic adventure, you will be choosing the dangers that they face, the monsters that they fight and the treasures that they find. Every decision that you make will have an impact on the story and, ultimately, the fate of your hero.

Your choices, your hero

With hundreds of special items to discover in the game, you can completely customise your hero. You can choose their weapons, their armour, their special abilities – even the boots on their feet and the cloak on their back! No two heroes will ever be alike, which means your hero will always be unique to you. And even better, you can take your hero into battle against your friends' heroes too!

Limitless possibilities, endless adventure

You can play through DestinyQuest multiple times and never have the same adventure twice. With so many options and paths to choose from, the monsters that you encounter, the people that you meet and the loot that you find will be different each time you play. There are numerous hidden secrets to discover, bonus items to collect and unique special abilities to unlock – in fact, every turn of the page could reveal something new for you and your hero.

Discover your destiny …

The next few pages will take you through the rules of the game, outlining the hero creation process and the combat and quest system.

Don't worry, it won't take long – and then your first DestinyQuest adventure can begin!

The hero sheet

Let's start with one of the most important things in the game – your hero sheet. This is a visual record of your hero's abilities and equipment. You will be constantly updating this sheet throughout the game, as you train new abilities and find better armour and weapons for your hero. (Note: The hero sheet is also available as a free download from **www.destiny-quest.com**.)

Attributes

Every hero has five key attributes that determine their strengths and weaknesses. These are *speed, brawn, magic, armour* and *health*. The goal of DestinyQuest is to advance your hero from an inexperienced novice into a powerful champion – someone who can stand up to the biggest and baddest of foes and triumph!

To achieve this, you will need to complete the many quests throughout the lands of Valeron. These quests will reward you with new skills and equipment, such as weapons and armour. These will boost your hero's attributes and give you a better chance of survival when taking on tougher enemies.

The five attributes are:

* **Brawn**: As its name suggests, this score represents your hero's strength and muscle power. A hero with high *brawn* will be able to hit harder in combat, striking through their opponent's armour and dealing fatal blows.
  Brawn is the main attribute of the warrior.

* **Magic**: By mastering the arcane schools of fire, lightning, frost and shadow, a hero can command devastating spells and summon fiendish monsters. Heroes that choose this path should seek out the staffs, wands and arcane charms that will boost their *magic* score, granting them even deadlier powers to smite their foes.
  Magic is the main attribute of the mage.

* **Speed**: The higher a hero's *speed* score, the more likely they are to score a hit against their opponent. A hero who puts points into *speed* can easily bring down stronger enemies thanks to their lightning-fast reflexes.
  Speed is the main attribute of the rogue.

* **Armour**: Whenever a hero is hit in combat, by weapons or spells, they take damage. Wearing armour can help your hero to survive longer by absorbing some of this damage. Warriors will always have a high *armour* score, thanks to the heavy armour and shields that they can equip. Rogues and mages will typically have lower scores, relying instead on their powerful attacks to win the day.

* **Health**: This is your hero's most important attribute as it represents their life force. When *health* reaches zero, your hero is dead – so, it goes without saying that you should keep a very close eye on it! Armour and equipment can raise your hero's *health* score – and there are also potions and abilities to be discovered, to help your hero replenish their *health* during combat.

Starting attributes

Every hero begins their adventures with a zero score for *brawn*, *magic*, *speed* and *armour*. These attributes will be boosted throughout the course of your adventures. All starting heroes begin with **30 health**.

Equipment boxes

The hero sheet displays a number of important boxes. These boxes each represent a location on your hero where they can equip an item. Whenever your hero comes across a new item in the game, you will be told which box or boxes on the sheet you can place it in. You can only have one item equipped in each box.

Backpack

Your hero also has a backpack that can hold five single items. On your travels you will come across many backpack items, including useful potions and quest items. Each backpack item you come across takes up *one space* in your backpack – even if you have multiple versions of the same type of item (for example, health potions).

BACKPACK:				
Healing +4 health (1 use)	Healing +4 health (1 use)	Stone tablet	Forest dew full heal (2 uses)	Miracle grow +2 brawn (1 use)

Special abilities

The special abilities box, on the right of your sheet, is where you can record notes on your hero's special abilities. Every hero has two special abilities, which they learn when they train a career. Items of equipment can also grant special abilities for your hero. All special abilities are explained in the glossary at the back of the book.

Paths and careers

Your hero starts their adventure as a simple traveller, with no remarkable skills or abilities. Once your hero has gained some experience, however, three paths will become available to you – the path of the warrior, the rogue and the mage. Your hero can only choose one of these paths, and once that decision is made, it can't be changed – so choose wisely. The chosen path will determine the careers and abilities that your hero can learn throughout their adventures.

Your hero's path and current career should always be recorded at the top of your hero sheet, and its special abilities should be recorded in the special abilities box on the right of your sheet. A hero can only be trained in *one career* at a time, but you can swap their career for another one, providing you have found the relevant trainer or reward item. When your hero trains a new career, all abilities and bonuses from the old career are lost.

Gold

The main currency in Valeron is the gold crown. These can be used to purchase potions and other special items whenever you visit a town, village or camp. More gold can be discovered by killing monsters and completing quests.

Quests and monsters

The kingdom of Valeron is a dangerous place, full of ferocious monsters, wild beasts and deadly magical forces ... bad news for some people perhaps, but for a would-be adventurer it means plenty of paid work! By vanquishing foes and completing quests, your hero will grow stronger and more powerful, allowing you to take on tougher challenges and discover even greater rewards.

The maps

The story is divided into three chapters – known as 'Acts'. Each of the three Acts has a map, which shows you the locations of all the different quests that your hero can take part in. To select a quest you simply turn to the corresponding numbered entry in the book and read on from there, returning to the map when you have finished.

Choosing quests

Each map will provide you with a number of different quests. Some quests are harder than others.

* **Spear quests**: These are the easiest quests to complete. Heroes with even the most basic of equipment will still emerge victorious.

* **Axe quests**: Heroes will find these tasks a little more challenging, requiring them to defeat numerous enemies to succeed.

* **Morning Star quests**: Things get a lot tougher with morning star quests. Monsters are more likely to have special abilities and higher attribute scores, meaning your hero will need to be fully prepared and equipped for the dangers they may face.

* **Sword quests**: These quests should only be attempted once you have completed the majority of spear, axe and morning star quests. Your hero will need to use everything they've got to overcome these tough challenges and triumph.

Quests can be done in any order you wish – although note that it is wiser to complete the easier quests before you attempt the harder ones. Once a quest has been completed, it cannot be revisited.

Legendary monsters

On each map you will also see some spider symbols. These represent 'legendary monsters': opponents that are tougher than your average foe. Only the bravest of heroes, who are confident in their abilities and have good gear from their questing, should seek out and battle these mighty opponents.

Team battles

The crossed swords symbol indicates an 'epic monster' – one that you will not be able to defeat alone! You will need to team up with another hero to help you battle these demonic entities and win their highly-prized treasures. (See advanced rules.)

Boss monsters

Each Act of the story has a final boss monster that must be defeated before you can advance the story to the next Act. These boss monsters are represented by the skull symbol on the map.

It goes without saying that these final bosses are no pushovers and should only be attempted once you have fully explored each map and completed most of the quests.

Towns, villages and camps

Every Act of the story has its own town, village or camp, which your hero can visit anytime between quests. They are represented on the map by the building icon. Simply turn to the corresponding page entry whenever you wish to visit. These locations can provide your hero with items to purchase, additional quests, hints and tips and even some career trainers.

It is always a good idea to visit these areas first, whenever you start a new map. The inns and taverns can be a great source of rumour and information regarding the challenges ahead.

Upgrading equipment

The primary goal of DestinyQuest is to equip your hero with better weapons, armour and equipment. These will boost your hero's attributes such as *brawn* and *magic*, and help them to survive longer in battle.

At certain times in the story you will be offered a choice of rewards for your hero. Usually this will be the result of killing a monster or completing a quest, but there are also many other ways of gaining rewards – some easier to find than others.

When you are offered a choice of rewards, you will be told how many items you may pick from the selection. It is up to you to decide which reward/s will be best for your hero. These rewards, such as rings, pieces of armour, weapons and necklaces, will commonly give boosts to certain attributes. Select your rewards wisely to boost the attributes that are the most essential for your hero.

When you have chosen your reward, you write its name and details in the corresponding box on your hero sheet. Make sure to update any attributes that are affected by the new reward. Remember, it is your decision what rewards you take. You can always ignore items if they don't interest you.

Replacing equipment

Your hero can only carry one item in each box. When you choose a reward and your hero already has an item in the corresponding box, the new item *replaces* the old one – and the old item is destroyed. When you destroy the old item, all attribute bonuses and abilities that it provided are lost, to be replaced by those from the new item.

Combat

Valeron can be a wild and dangerous place. Most of the creatures you encounter will be hostile and it will be up to you (and your hero!) to battle and defeat these monsters, to emerge victorious.

When you enter into combat, you will be given your opponent's attributes. These are usually *speed*, *brawn* (or *magic*), *armour* and *health*.

Some may also have special abilities that you will need to take note of.

The combat sequence

Combat consists of a number of *combat rounds*. In each round of combat you roll dice to determine who hits who and who takes damage. (Note: A die is considered to be a standard 6-sided die.) Once damage has been applied, a new combat round starts. Combat continues until either your hero or their opponent is defeated.

In each combat round:

1. Roll *2 dice* for your hero and add their current *speed* score to the total. This is your hero's **attack speed.**

2. Roll another *2 dice* for your opponent and add their *speed* score to the total. This is their **attack speed**.

3. The combatant with the highest attack speed wins the combat round. If both scores are the same, it is a stand off – the combat round ends (see step 7) and a new one begins.

4. The winner of the round rolls *1 die* and adds either their *brawn* score or their *magic* score to the total, whichever is highest. (Note: monsters will only have one or the other, not both.) This will give you a **damage score.**

5. The loser of the round deducts their *armour* value from the damage score. Any remaining damage is then deducted from their *health*. (If the damage score was 8 and the loser had an *armour* of 2, they would take 6 health damage.)

6. If this damage takes your hero's or your opponent's *health* to zero, they are defeated. If both combatants have *health* remaining, then the combat continues.

7. At the end of each combat round, any damage from passive effects (such as *bleed* or *venom*) are applied to each combatant. If both opponents still have *health* remaining, then a new combat round begins. Return to step 1.

Example of combat

Sir Hugo has awoken a slumbering serpent and must now defend himself against its venomous attacks.

	Speed	*Brawn*	*Magic*	*Armour*	*Health*
Hugo	4	7	1	5	30
	Speed	*Brawn*	*Magic*	*Armour*	*Health*
Serpent	6	3	0	2	12

Special abilities

Venom: Once you have taken health damage from the serpent, at the end of every combat round you must automatically lose 2 *health*.

Round one

1. Sir Hugo rolls 2 dice to determine his attack speed. He rolls a ⚃ and a ⚁ giving him a total of 6. He adds on his *speed* score of 4 to give him a final total of 10.
2. The serpent rolls 2 dice to determine its attack speed. The result is a ⚄ and a ⚅ making 11. The serpent's *speed* is 6, making its final total 17. The serpent has won the first round of combat.
3. A die is rolled for the serpent to determine its damage score. The result is a ⚅. Its *brawn* score is added on to this, to give a final total of 9.
4. Sir Hugo deducts his *armour* value from this total. This means he only takes 4 points of health damage (9–5=4). His *health* is reduced from 30 to 26.
5. Sir Hugo is also poisoned by the serpent's venom. He automatically takes another 2 points of health damage, reducing his *health* to 24.

Round two

1 As before, Sir Hugo and the Serpent roll 2 dice and add their *speed* to the result. Sir Hugo ends up with an attack speed of 15 and the serpent has an attack speed of 10. Sir Hugo wins.

2. Sir Hugo rolls a ⚄ for his damage score. He chooses to add on his *brawn* (which is higher than his *magic* score). His final total is 12.

3. The serpent has an *armour* value of 2, so takes 10 points of damage. The serpent is left with 2 *health*.
4. Because the serpent applied its venom special ability in the last round, Sir Hugo must now deduct another 2 points from his *health* – reducing it from 24 to 22.

Combat then moves to the next round, continuing until one combatant's *health* is reduced to zero.

Restoring health and attributes

Once you have defeated an enemy, your hero's *health* and any other attributes that have been affected by special attacks or abilities are **immediately restored** back to their normal values (unless otherwise stated in the text). In the above example, once Sir Hugo has defeated the serpent, he can return his *health* back to 30 and continue his adventures.

Using special abilities in combat

As your hero progresses through the story, they will discover many special abilities that they can use in combat. All abilities are explained in the glossary at the back of the book.

There are four types of special ability in DestinyQuest. These are: speed (sp), combat (co), modifier (mo) and passive (pa) abilities.

* **Speed (sp)**: These abilities can be used at the start of a combat round (before you roll for attack speed), and will usually influence how many dice you can roll or reduce the number of dice that your opponent can roll for speed. You can only use one speed ability per combat round.

* **Combat (co)**: These abilities are used either before or after you (or your opponent) roll for damage. Usually these will increase the number of dice you can roll, or allow you to block or dodge your opponent's attacks. You can only use one combat ability per combat round.

* **Modifier (mo)**: Modifier abilities allow you to boost your attribute scores or influence dice that you have already rolled. You can use

as many different modifier abilities as you wish during a combat round.

* **Passive (pa)**: Passive abilities are typically applied at the end of a combat round, once you or your opponent has taken health damage. Abilities such as *venom* and *bleed* are passive abilities. These abilities happen automatically, based on their description.

Damage score and damage dice

Some special abilities will refer to a damage score and others will refer to rolling damage dice. A damage score is when your hero rolls one die and adds their *brawn* or *magic* to the total (as in the previous combat example). This is the most common means of applying damage to your opponent. Some abilities allow you to roll damage dice instead. Damage dice are simply dice that are rolled for damage, but you do not add your *brawn* or *magic* score to the total. For example, the special ability *cleave* allows you to inflict 1 damage die to all your opponents, ignoring *armour*. You would simply roll 1 die and then deduct the result from each of your opponents' *health*. You do not add your *brawn* or *magic* to this total.

Using backpack items in combat

The outcome of many a combat can be decided by the clever use of backpack items, such as potions and elixirs. From restoring lost *health* to boosting your *speed*, never underestimate how useful these items can be in turning the tide of battle. However, you can only use *one* backpack item per combat round so choose wisely! Also note that every useable backpack item has a number of charges. Once these have been used up, they are gone forever.

Runes, glyphs, dyes and other special items

During your adventures, you will come across a number of *special* items that allow you to add attribute bonuses or additional abilities to the equipment you are already wearing. These items cannot be stored in your backpack and must be used *immediately* when they are found, to add their relevant attribute/ability to a chosen item. Each item of equipment can hold up to three of these special bonuses.

Death is not the end

When your hero dies, their adventure isn't over. Simply make a note of the entry number where you died and then return to the quest map. Your *health* is immediately restored back to full. However any consumable items that were used in the combat (such as potions and elixirs) are gone forever!

You can now do the following:

1. Return to the entry number where you died and try it again.
2. Explore a different location on the map, such as a town or another quest.

You can return to the entry number where you died anytime you wish. If you are having difficulty with a particular combat, then try a different quest, or purchase some helpful potions or items from a local vendor.

NOTE: In some quests, when your hero is defeated, there are special rules to follow. You will be given an entry number to turn to, where you can read on to see what happens to your hero.

Taking challenge tests

Occasionally, during your travels, you will be asked to take a challenge by testing one of your attributes (such as *speed* or *brawn*). Each challenge is given a number. For example:

	Speed
Climb the cliff face	*9*

To take a challenge, simply roll 2 dice and add your hero's attribute score to the result. If the total is the same as or higher than the given number, then you have succeeded. For example, if Sir Hugo has a *speed* of 4 and rolls a ⚁ and a ⚂, then he would have a total of 9. This means he would have successfully completed the above challenge.

Advanced rules: Team combat

Occasionally some monsters are just too powerful to overcome, even for your hero. To stand a chance of defeating these epic foes you will need to team up with your hero (or a friend's hero) from *DestinyQuest 1: The Legion of Shadow*. (A sample hero is provided at the front of this book.)

A team combat is shown on the map as a crossed swords symbol. These battles follow a slightly different set of combat rules to take into account two heroes fighting alongside each other against a powerful opponent.

The combat sequence

In each combat round:

1. Each hero can decide if they will *attack* or *support*. **If a hero attacks they roll for their attack speed as normal (using speed abilities if they wish)**. If one hero chooses to be a support hero, then they do *not* roll for attack speed. (See support hero, below.) One hero *must* attack in each round.
2. Roll *2 dice* for your opponent and add their *speed* score to the total. This is your opponent's attack speed.
3. **The combatant with the highest attack speed wins the combat round.** If the highest set of scores are the same (for a hero and their opponent), it is a stand off – the combat round ends (see step 6) and a new one begins. If two attacking heroes get the same score, then they can choose which hero will strike against the opponent.
4. **If a hero wins a combat round, they can roll for damage as normal against their opponent.** Damage is applied and the combat round ends (see step 6).
5. **If the opponent wins the combat round, then they strike against the hero who last dealt health damage to them** (this excludes passive effects, such as *bleed* and *venom*). **If no hero has caused health damage, then the opponent strikes against the hero with the highest armour**. The hero who is being attacked can use their combat and modifier abilities as normal. Their ally can also play any helpful modifier abilities (depending on the ability's description).

6. At the end of each combat round, any damage from passive effects (such as *bleed* or *venom*) are applied to each combatant. If opponents still have *health* remaining, then a new combat round begins. Return to step 1.

Support heroes

Heroes who choose not to attack during a combat round (see step 1) are referred to as *support heroes*. They can still be hit in combat if the opponent wins (see step 5), but by choosing not to attack they give their ally a chance to win combat rounds and apply abilities/damage. **A support hero can use modifier abilities on themselves or their ally as normal (depending on the ability's description).** This includes abilities like *heal* and *greater heal*.

* **Top tip:** Swap your heroes regularly, between attacking and support, to share out damage. Remember, an opponent always attacks the last hero to win a round and cause health damage – so your heavy hitters (such as mages and rogues) need to be careful that they don't become the sole target of the opponent's attacks. Swapping a hero into a support role, while their ally becomes the sole attacker, can be a vital strategy to control an opponent's aggression.

Passive abilities

If both heroes have the same passive effect (such as *bleed* or *venom*) then these abilities can *all* be applied to an opponent (providing each hero has met the criteria for applying that passive). For example, if both heroes have the *bleed* ability and both have done health damage to their opponent, then the opponent takes damage from each *bleed* effect (2 damage (1+1) at the end of each round).

Defeating and looting an epic monster

Providing one hero is still alive at the end of the combat, then both heroes are considered to have defeated the monster. This means that each hero can now choose one reward from those on offer. (NOTE: a hero can only choose a reward when they defeat the monster for the first time. If they fight the monster multiple times to aid other heroes then they cannot choose further rewards.)

Take your adventures online!

Join the DestinyQuest community at **www.destiny-quest.com** for the latest information on DestinyQuest books, hints and tips, player forums and exclusive downloadable content (including printable hero sheets, team combat rules and extra bonus quests!).

It's time to begin

Before you start your adventure, don't forget to check that your hero sheet has been fully updated. It should display:

* Your hero's name
* A zero score in the *speed, brawn, magic*, and *armour* boxes
* A 30 in your hero's *health* box

Now, turn the page to begin your adventure . . .

Prologue: The Great Escape

You are in free fall.

The black rock of the mountainside streaks past in a deadly blur. Your descent is fast – unstoppable. You can only watch, paralysed by fear, as the world tumbles through blue sky and earth. Then a wave of ash washes over you, turning bright day into a murky twilight.

Through the thickening dust, you see the ground spiralling up at an alarming speed; a pock-marked plain of splintered rock and fire-rimmed craters. Behind you, something rumbles and booms . . . then you feel a scalding heat at your back. For an instant the darkness becomes light as an immense ball of flame roars overhead, slamming into the ground and sending ash billowing across the hellish plain.

You spin and twist through the smoke, your broken body smashing off rock and stone as you tumble down the slope. You finally slam down hard onto baking hot ash, your exposed skin blistering on contact.

Gagging from the sulphurous fumes, you struggle onto your back, aware that the ground beneath you is shaking. From the dark sky falling stone beats against the earth, bouncing and rattling off your soot-streaked armour. Shielding your eyes against the barrage, you fix your gaze on the dark mountain. Through the ash you can dimly make out its summit, fountaining an endless column of rock and earth into the sky.

This is the end of the world.

And you are here to see it.

The ground shakes, a continuous and steady rhythm. You twist around, as you have done a hundred times before, to gaze upon your nemesis. It strides through the smoke, a shadow amidst the swirling red ash. An immense creature, impossibly large, with black wings and iron-tipped horns that blot out the broken landscape. Its charred body is crisscrossed with vivid veins of magma, pulsing with a hellish glow. And in its hand is a sword – a sword as big as the mountain itself, its serrated edge crackling with fire.

'NO!' Tears sting your eyes as the demon stalks towards you. You cannot see its face, but its gaze is inescapable: a single orb of crimson hatred, blazing hot like the sun.

'My journey is complete!' The demon snarls, flames rippling across its body. 'Ragnarok is remade!'

Scrambling in the dust for a weapon, your hands find only rock and earth. As you turn back, gripped by panic, you see the demon standing over you. It raises its mighty sword, the black metal inscribed with a thousand dark runes. Set into the crosspiece is a fist-sized gemstone, glowing with a piercing white light.

'Ragnarok is remade!' The demon turns the blade and then, with a roar as loud as the raging mountain, the beast plunges the sword into your heart . . .

'No!' You jerk backwards, flinching from the strike. The rattle of chains remind you that you cannot move your arms. You are a prisoner, bound within the four walls of a cell.

'Ragnarok . . .' you gasp.

In a corner of the room, a white shape is bent over a table. You hear the scratch of a pen on parchment. The noise is grating; each stroke setting your teeth on edge.

'The sword,' says a voice, cold and impassionate. There is a pause in the incessant scraping as the pen is lifted off the parchment. 'Tell me again what you saw. What is this . . . gem that you speak of?'

Already the vision is fading, replaced by a sickening wave of nausea. Once more you pull against the chains, struggling to break free, but the effort only brings you pain. You sag, hanging limp, your knees scraping against the hard stone floor.

'Answer me,' demands the voice.

You scowl at the thin, bald-headed man, his scarred scalp peppered by an occasional grey hair. A scholar, a librarian. Forever hunched over his writing table, forever asking questions. You count seven rolls of parchment resting against the wall. Each one, you know, will be covered in hundreds of neat lines; every word dragged from you, like a vulture constantly pecking away at a corpse in the desert.

'I'm done,' you mutter, letting your head fall against your chest. 'I'm done . . .'

'You're done when I tell you!' snaps the man. He stands suddenly, pushing the desk away. His hand goes to his belt, quickly unfastening the straps around a leather flask. 'More of this will make you talk.'

You flinch, knowing what is to come. The Elysium. A truth serum. It makes the visions stronger; more frequent. 'No, please, no more . . .'

There is a click of boot heels, echoing in the passageway. Two men appear at the bars of the cell. One is tall, dressed in a long grey coat. His face is hidden beneath the brim of his hat. Next to him is an inquisitor, a holy warrior, dressed in the white and gold armour of his order. The inquisitor produces a ring of keys from his belt. There is a rattling clatter followed by a grating squeal, as the cell door is unlocked and pushed open. The inquisitor stands back, his head bowed, as the stranger in the grey coat strides into the cell.

'What is this?' snaps the librarian, scurrying out of the man's way. 'I demand to know your purpose here!' His head jerks back and forth between the stranger and the guard, but he receives no answer.

Instead, the grey-coated figure halts, the heels of his boots snapping together in military fashion. He places a gloved hand inside a pocket and pulls out a letter. He holds it aloft, waiting for the librarian to take it.

'This better be good.' He snatches the document, scarred cheek pulling a crude sneer. There is silence as he unfolds the paper and begins reading.

'You can't!' he gasps suddenly, looking up in shock. 'By what right?'

The stranger removes his hat, revealing a gaunt face covered in vicious-looking welts. His left eye is missing entirely, the pulpy flesh covered by a gem-encrusted patch. He takes a step forward, placing a gloved hand beneath your chin and lifting it up. His one grey eye scrutinises you with interest.

'On Avian Dale's orders,' says the stranger, his voice deep and gravelly. 'This one is now my property.'

The librarian is struggling for words, his upper lip twitching. 'But you—'

'My name is Virgil Elland.' The stranger turns his head slightly, looking back over his shoulder. 'You know me?'

'I ... I do,' gasps the librarian, his eyes widening. 'You're a witchfinder. One of the king's confessors.'

Virgil grins, displaying a set of gold teeth. 'Once upon a time.' He leans towards you, his grip on your chin tightening.

'You caught this one, back in Tithebury – yes?' The librarian glares sourly at his back.

'No, that was another – Eldias Falks. I read his report.' Virgil leans back, following the length of your arms to the chains hanging above your head. 'A child was murdered.'

The librarian nods quickly. 'Edward Cooper. The miller's son.'

The man plants his hat back onto his head. 'Common criminals do not receive the attention of the inquisition.'

'Common!' The librarian snatches one of the rolled parchments, holding it out in front of the man. 'You know why this one is here. They claim to see the future – a prophet!'

Virgil ignores the proffered parchment. Instead, he plucks something from your arm. You feel a stinging pain, followed by a warm sensation running over your skin. You try and turn your head, but you are too weak to move.

'Ah, of course.' The witchfinder holds up a bloated leech. Scowling, he squashes it between his gloved fingers before sniffing the gooey residue. 'Elysium.'

'Yes, a necessary evil in these dark times.' The librarian's eyes dance shiftily. 'Any normal person would have died months ago, even with the leeches. But this one ... Their body doesn't fight it. It's almost as if it accepts it.'

'Interesting...' Virgil releases you, letting your head slump forward once again. 'Bring more leeches. I want this one clean. Two days, I'll be back for collection.'

He turns on his heels, revealing a vast array of pistols and rifles strapped across his shoulders. 'This one is very precious to me. Understand?'

'But what of the Lord Justice? I can't believe that...'

'It's taken care of.'

'But...'

'Avian Dale has made all the arrangements-'

The men's voices become distant. You struggle to focus but the room is blurring into a fevered haze. There is an echoing clang: the cell door closing. Then you are gone, adrift in another dream.

A rolling boom of noise.

You are thrown awake by a tremor, which has set the very walls to shaking. Still groggy from sleep, you struggle to bring your surroundings into focus. A cell; small and cramped. The desk in the corner has been overturned. Ink is spattered across the dusty floor.

Another thunderous boom.

Stone and dust rain down from the ceiling. Your chains rattle back and forth, forcing you into a swaying dance. From the passageway you hear raised voices and the clash of steel. Another explosion is followed by screams. Dust and debris billow down the passage. A woman's voice is raised above the din. You can't make out the words.

Stone crumbles and breaks around the edge of your cell. For a second, you are convinced you are still dreaming; you can't understand how the stone is moving, coming apart before your very eyes. Then you see tentacle-like roots, pushing up out of the ground, splitting the stone as if it was nothing but loose earth.

The cell door buckles as the stone shifts around it, filling the space with a thick cloud of dust. Unable to cover your face, you are seized by a coughing fit – the thick particles forcing their way to the back of your throat.

Eyes streaming, you watch as a dark shape moves towards you through the mist. For a moment you fear it is the demon from your dreams; the one that haunts your every waking moment. But this is a man.

He is short and wiry, dressed in half-tanned furs and rusted chainmail. As he steps closer, you see that his face has been painted: a black band cuts across the ridge of his nose, highlighting the whites of his eyes.

He mutters something in a guttural language, raising twin daggers that glow with an angry red light.

'Free me ...' you manage to choke, fixing him with a hard gaze. 'Free me.'

The man pushes his face close to yours. He sniffs you, then jerks back, his eyes widening with surprise.

'Old one.' His tongue struggles with the words, lisping through sharpened teeth. 'Old one.' In the distance, you hear another explosion. There is a rumbling crash as something heavy topples and smashes to the ground. The dust in the passageway grows thicker.

With a growl, the man swings his arms in a cutting motion. The weight that was pulling at your arms suddenly disappears, throwing you forwards onto your stomach. The severed chains rattle around you.

Weakly you try and rise, but there is no strength in your arms. You slump forward, your exhalation sending dust whirling before your face.

There is the scrape of boots as the man moves behind you. Strong hands take your shoulders and lift you up onto your knees. A gourd is pressed to your lips. You sup it greedily, the warm liquid washing away the dirt and dryness, and bringing fresh strength to your limbs.

When the gourd is taken away you are able to raise your hand to your lips, catching the last of the syrup as it drools down your chin.

'You owe me,' growls the man, thumping a fist against his chest. 'You owe the Wicca.'

Then he is gone – moving swiftly back into the cloudy maelstrom. You are left alone in the cell, as another explosion – more distant this time – echoes back through the subterranean rock.

Bodies choke the tight passageway. It is difficult to pick out anyone's allegiance, as each corpse is caked in a thick white dust. You stagger through the murky twilight, avoiding the side passages where the sounds of battle still rage. You flinch, drawing back against the wall, as one of the painted warriors races past you, heading back the way you have come. He pays you no mind, the hatchet he is carrying caked with blood.

You stumble onwards, your feet dragging through the loose rock and dirt. Then a sudden movement forces you to turn. An inquisitor looms out of the darkness. A jagged cut has bled down his face, mixing with the dust and coating his eyes in a bloody sludge. His first swing goes wide, but the second blow hits home – his sword punching into your chest. For a second, you both glare at each other down the length of the blade. Then white hot pain lances through your body, forcing out a gurgling scream …

Time blurs.

You stumble onwards, your feet dragging through the loose rock and dirt. A sudden movement forces you to turn. The inquisitor. Somehow, you already know how this encounter will end. His first swing goes wide, but the second blow you dodge, letting it slam into the wall, jarring the blade from the warrior's grasp. With a strength born from fear you kick back at your opponent, sending him tumbling back into the cell. His head thumps against a rock, drawing a muffled grunt. Then silence …

Quickly, you reach down and grab the inquisitor's sword:

Knight's folly
(main hand: sword)
+1 brawn +1 magic

As you continue down the passage, you find yourself pondering this sudden twist of fate. The inquisitor's blow had been fatal. You had seen it; felt it crush your ribs and pierce your lungs. But it had all been a vision – a glimpse of a possible future. As you gaze upon the sword, its magnificent blade glowing with holy scripture, you feel a newfound energy surging through you. Perhaps some of the Elysium is still in your bloodstream, heightening the strange powers that you have had from birth – the ability to see the future.

You have gained the following combat ability:

Prophecy (co): Use this ability when you have lost a combat round, to avoid taking damage from your opponent. You can only use this ability once per combat.

A set of stairs take you up into a torch-lined corridor. Your surroundings have become more opulent, with lines of fine tapestries covering the stone walls. The only sign that something is awry are the dusty footprints that track back and forth along the plush red carpet.

You find a side chamber, with several chests and bags resting at the foot of a bed. Aware that you are dressed in little more than a ragged gown, you quickly duck into the room and begin rummaging through its contents.

You find a backpack, 30 gold crowns and the following items, which you may take:

Plumed helm	Saddle blanket	Rider's jerkin
(head)	(cloak)	(chest)
+1 armour	+1 armour	+1 speed

Another corridor brings you out into a wide, vaulted hall. Its central pillars are carved into figures of warriors – both male and female – resplendent in decorative plate armour. They provide useful cover as a tight knot of inquisitors rush past, their armaments clattering noisily in the echoing chamber.

You break from cover, moving quickly towards the bright band of daylight seeping between a pair of arched doors. Several bodies lie amongst the shadows to either side, green-fletched arrows protruding from their chests. Without stopping, you slip through the doors and out to freedom.

The glare is almost blinding; the light of the pale sun reflected off the glistening snow. As you crest a hill, you look back at the place that once held you prisoner – a vast cathedral carved out of a spire of black rock. Durnhollow: the dungeon of the inquisition. You spit into the snow, before turning and heading down the wooded mountainside, into the valley below.

A narrow trail brings you to a well-worn track, carving its way through rolling hills. As you join the track, you see a procession approaching from the east; a group of dusty travellers, with carts and wagons piled high with belongings.

You wonder if they are fleeing some disaster, but as they near you see that several of the travellers are bedecked with garlands and crucifixes. Pilgrims, you suspect. You nod to one of the men, who is carrying a young girl on his shoulders. He smiles, then points ahead along the track.

'Look Aimee, we made it. That's Carvel, up there on the hill. We're following the path of the saints, just like I said we would.' He looks your way, offering you a grin. 'Are you headed our way, pilgrim? Come to pay your respects?'

You follow the child's gaze, towards a walled town perched on a plateau of rock. It promises you a new start; a safe haven from the prying eyes of the inquisition.

'Yes. Yes, I am.' You clasp the man's hand in welcome, before joining the procession.

'I'm Bernard. This is Aimee.' The girl giggles and waves. 'I'd say we made good timing; looks like this weather's gonna hold after all.' He frowns up at the heavy white sky. 'At least 'til we see the warmth of a tavern, eh?'

You peer sideways at him, offering a grin. 'I very much doubt that.' A moment later rain begins to fall, spattering off your helm and cloak. You raise your eyebrows. 'Told you so.'

Bernard gives a snort of laughter. 'What's this, we got our very own prophet?' He pats the legs of his little girl. 'See, Aimee. We come to the holy lands and find ourselves a prophet, just like the great Saint Allam. It's got to be a sign – a sign that our luck's changing.' He gives you a sly wink. 'What do you say, prophet?'

You keep your eyes set ahead, your hand gripping the pommel of your sword. For as long as you can remember, you have been hunted – running from town and village, with nowhere to call home. Will Carvel be any different?

'Tell me, Bernard. Do you believe that the future can really be foretold?' You glance up at the darkening skies. They promise a storm.

The traveller lowers his little girl to the track, helping her to fix her hood. 'I say it's up to the One God to decide our fate. None of our business is it, the future? Not unless you're a saint, like Allam.'

You nod, eyeing your reflection in the fast-forming puddles. A gaunt, pale figure; a stranger you barely recognise. 'Yeah, none of our business.' Your boot splashes down into the muddy water, obliterating the face staring back.

Your attention shifts to the welcoming lights of Carvel, blinking on the horizon. For now, you are happy to put thoughts of demons and dark mountains from your mind. The only future you want to see is a hot meal and a warm bed. 'Come,' you look to Bernard, gesturing towards the town. 'That tavern of yours is sounding like a very good idea.'

Turn to the first map to begin ACT 1 of your adventure. Choose where you want to visit by turning to the entry number displayed next to the shield. As a novice adventurer you may want to explore the town of Carvel (turn to 8) before embarking on one of the spear quests. Good luck!

1

You hand settles around something soft and velvety, clinking with coin. Excitedly, you withdraw your hand to find that you have discovered a purse of gold! (You have gained 10 gold crowns.) Suddenly you hear a grumbling, creaking sound coming from the tree. Stepping away, you see that the other holes have now closed up, locking away their treasures.

You may now try and climb the tree (turn to 96) or leave via the magic portal (turn to 46).

2

With your foe defeated you are free to examine the floating junk at your leisure. Amongst the trash you find an expensive-looking silver casket. Fishing it out of the muck, you open it up to find 30 gold crowns and a *black iron key* inside. (If you take the key, simply make a note of it on your hero sheet, it doesn't take up backpack space.) After pocketing your items, you wade through the stinking water towards the iron door. Turn to 409.

3

'I see you favour the magic arts,' nods Lazlo, glancing down at his charred clothing. 'My tailor will be less than impressed ... but I do know someone who would find your talents more to their liking.'

'Someone who can train me?' you ask hopefully.

'Ignatius Pyre. He is the tutor over in the mage tower. Take this and show it to his assistant.' He reaches into a pocket and produces a small iron badge. A symbol of a bat stands out in high relief on the surface. 'That is my personal seal. It will grant you an audience with the high mage – and he'll give you all the training that you need.'

You take the seal, thanking Lazlo for his kind assistance. (Make a note of the *prince's seal* on your hero sheet – it does not take up backpack space. Then turn to 182.)

4

You find yourself in a small rectangular chamber lined with shelves. Most are buckling under the weight of the many books and scroll cases that have been haphazardly piled on top of them. At the centre of the room stands a circular table, covered by a large sheet of parchment. A magical quill is moving diligently back and forth across the paper, scratching lines of script in a glistening black ink. The only other exit you can see is another door in the far wall, this time made of rusted iron.

Will you:

Search the book shelves?	323
Examine the parchment on the table?	362
Leave through the iron door?	46

5

The woman throws back her head and laughs. 'What local rumours would you like? That there's a caped vigilante, a vampire they say, preying on criminals and drinking their blood?' She sucks at the air, then puckers up her lips and blows you a kiss. 'Or that the prince in his merry ol' castle is hoping to woo every woman in Carvel?'

Her last comment draws a roar of laughter from the nearby patrons. The man next to you gives a snort. 'It's the Wiccans you need to watch. They're the ones what're causing all the trouble.'

The laughter trails off into angry mutterings.

You turn your head, raising an eyebrow. 'You know of the Wiccans?'

The man wipes the ale from his mouth. 'I know what everyone knows. This was their land, once. Then Allam and his army came and took it from them. They worship the old gods, the old magic, see. Allam didn't like that. They're still fighting for their lands now – but the church is having none of it.'

'Humph, what happens outside Carvel can stay outside Carvel,' sniffs the bar woman, tugging a cloth from her apron. 'Men and their quarrels. I'd like to knock some sense into all of 'em.' She rubs the cloth vigorously over the bar. 'Saints, Wiccans, they all as bad as each other.'

Return to 52 to ask the bar woman another question.

6

Your metal soldier charges into the paper monster, slashing it to shreds with diamond-sharp fists. Congratulations, you have chosen well and defeated papyrus. (Remove the *metal soldier* from your hero sheet.) Then turn to 208.

7

You duck beneath a crackling bolt of magic, bringing the butt of your weapon up across the woman's forehead. The blow should have stunned her, but instead she merely staggers away, hissing the words of yet another spell. As you ready yourself for a fresh barrage of magic, you are surprised when the woman throws up her arms, her gaze shifting skyward. There is a flicker of magic about her body and then she is gone.

You hear a flutter of wings and a deafening caw. Suddenly black feathers and yellow eyes rush at your face. With a cry you throw yourself backwards, slashing at the air. However, your desperate blows fail to connect with anything solid. For several moments you are fending off sharp talons and beating wings ... then the attack ceases.

Twisting around, you see a ragged-looking crow soaring away across the foggy moorland. A single black feather flutters down to land on the grass at your feet. You may now take the following item:

Crow feather
(talisman)
+1 magic

With the witch defeated, you are able to study the candles and runes more closely. Turn to 191.

8

The bustling gates of the town are clogged with carts and wagons. Two sombre-looking guards are doing their best to perform rudimentary inspections, poking through the newcomers' belongings and questioning their purpose in town. However, the tight-packed throng of animals and people make it easy for you to slip past the guards and into the town of Carvel.

Beyond the walls you are greeted by a ramshackle jumble of slate roofs and grey stone buildings, spread out around an immense outcropping of rock. A crooked lane winds back and forth along its face, leading up to a further huddle of buildings at its summit, their black outlines cutting a jagged silhouette against the storm-heavy sky.

All around you the cobbled lanes ring with noise, echoing back from the narrow streets and alleyways. Most of the people are pilgrims, but you also notice military-types – mercenaries and adventurers – bristling with weapons and armour. An occasional inquisitor pushes through the crowds, moving quickly on some urgent errand. You keep your head bowed, looking to blend in as best you can.

Will you:

Explore the lower town?	36
Follow the crooked street to upper town?	17

9

'Why not take a look?' Lazlo gestures to the shuttered window. Following his instruction, you slide off the bed and make your way across the room. 'I hope the view is to your liking.'

A cold wind ruffles your hair as you push open the shutters and lean out over the sill. For a moment your breath catches, a sickening wave of vertigo almost forcing you to lose balance. Gripping the sill, you steady yourself to take in the sight.

Carvel stretches below you like a tiny crescent of doll's houses, slate roofs sparkling with freshly-fallen snow. Across from you, the spires and domes of the church rise up from the stone plaza – an impressive building at ground level, but from this towering vantage point its beauty is easily surpassed by the sweeping vista of plains and mountains that stretch to the horizon.

'The castle,' you gasp.

You lean further over the windowsill to see the sheer black stone of the building dropping away to meet a distant courtyard below. You draw back, feeling giddy from the height. 'How did I get here?'

Lazlo joins you by the window, his eyes following a circling eagle. 'I have a secret entrance to this place, at the foot of the rock. Most of it, you'll find, is old dwarf tunnels and caves. Easy once you know your way …' He gives an involuntary shudder. 'And you can handle the bats. I hate bats.'

Will you:	
Ask him about the strange dream?	62
Ask about Carvel's 'masked crusader'?	39
State you wish to leave?	167

10

Nervously, you grip your weapons and approach the child. Although you fear the worst, there is always a chance that this child might have survived the strange blight that has affected the rest of the village. Your foot knocks into one of the wooden toys, sending it scraping and clattering across the floor.

The child's back straightens. For a moment, there is a heavy unsettling silence. You stand frozen, not even daring to breathe. Then the child spins around, hissing and snarling – its face drawing a shocked gasp from you. It is no human child – it is a goblin! The creature staggers towards you, wrinkled fingers raised, displaying sharpened claws. From its blank expression and shambling gait, it is clear that this creature is now a zombie like the others. You must fight:

	Speed	*Brawn*	*Armour*	*Health*
Ghastly goblin	2	2	1	20

If you manage to defeat this gruesome creature, turn to 20.

11

All of a sudden, you find yourself being tugged backwards off your feet, shoulders brushing past roots and earth. You land roughly on your back, aware that you have fallen inside an earthen passageway. As you look back towards the snarling wolf, you see the opening that deposited you here is starting to close. The wolf races forward, snarling and growling with anger. But its shoulders are too wide to break through the rapidly closing gap. Within moments you find yourself looking upon a wall of gnarly roots and dark soil – the opening nowhere to be seen.

Your first reaction is relief at having escaped the dire wolf. Then a cold dread settles over you, as you contemplate your new predicament.

You see that you are in a shadowy passageway. The air is moist and hot, reeking of mould and decay. A few metres ahead of you a torch rests in a sconce on the wall, spluttering blue-white flames that spark and hiss in the silence.

With no alternative you set off down the passageway, your ragged breathing echoing back from the damp walls. After several minutes, you find yourself stepping out into a wide circular chamber. Torches are interspersed along the rough-hewn walls, filling the space with dancing shadows.

Then you hear a noise. It starts out as a soft rustling, quickly growing louder into a slithering hiss. You spin around, looking for the source of the noise, but all you see are the shadows – bending, curling, winding about you.

Then a voice whispers in your ear. The words seem guttural, barely human. 'You do not know the Wiccan. You do not know our ways.'

You jerk sideways, batting the air next to you. But there is nothing to hit. The voice continues: 'I see your strength, old one. But your head is heavy. Filled with stones. I fill with memory.'

Suddenly the dancing shadows streak towards the centre of the room, where they billow upwards into a column of darkness. As you watch the column takes on shape, becoming a giant humanoid creature. It has no features, but the outline is clearly recognisable – a troll with muscular shoulders and arms, a broad chest, and a bow-legged gait. From its right hand the shadows distend outwards, forming a spiked club.

The voice whispers: 'My people's blood nourishes this soil. They have always known war; our lands forever overrun by the beasts from the dark.'

The troll stomps towards you, its club raised. Although the creature is made purely of shadow, you know instinctively that this foe presents a very real and deadly threat. You must now fight:

	Speed	*Brawn*	*Armour*	*Health*
Troll	0	1	0	15

Special abilities

- Regeneration: At the start of each combat round, the troll regains 2 *health*. Once the troll's *health* has been reduced to zero, it cannot heal. (Note: This ability cannot take the troll's *health* above its starting value of 15.)

If you defeat the shadow troll, turn to 67.

12

You find your eyes drawn to the grisly trophies that adorn the wall. The centrepiece is a stag's head, with enormous spiked antlers stretching across the ceiling. There is also a grey wolf, a brown bear and a ghost lynx's head. Each one has its mouth agape, teeth bared – their twisted visages as menacing in death as they must have been in life.

'It's an impressive collection,' you remark, leaning closer to the brown bear. You could almost fit your head inside its fanged jaws. 'Are you a hunter?'

'I am, yeah,' sniffs the shopkeeper. 'I sold a few of my best, but those are for keeps.'

'You sold this one?' you ask, tapping your finger on an empty plaque where you assume a head had once rested.

'That space is reserved,' growls the hunter. 'For the black shuck. A hellhound that stalks the western fens. I seen it only once – a terrible thing it was, the biggest hound you ever saw, with eyes of fire and a hide black as midnight. I'd give my right hand to get close to that one again.' He slams the point of his dagger into the counter, twisting it round with a cruel sneer.

If you have the *hound's head* turn to 305. Otherwise, you may ask to see the shopkeeper's wares (turn to 235) or leave the shop (turn to 199).

13

(If you have the word *mixer* on your hero sheet then turn to 328.)

A rope ladder has been strung over the side of the well shaft, offering a route down into the smoky depths. Steeling yourself for what you might find at the bottom, you slide over the side and start clambering down the ladder.

As you descend, the air grows thicker, reeking of brimstone and sulphur. When the ladder ends, you are forced to drop the last few feet, landing up to your waist in a sickening-looking sludge. You assume that this was once the well water, before it became poisoned.

Through the putrid yellow smoke you spy a circular side-passage leading through into a larger chamber. From inside you can hear the sound of glass smashing, accompanied by a series of dull-witted mutterings. Drawing your weapons you wade through the slime, cautiously emerging from the passage into the next room.

It appears to be a laboratory. Steps rise up out of the yellow sludge to a stone-paved platform. Here, a number of tables have been arranged in a semi-circle, covered with a complex array of scientific apparatus. A large creature is currently shuffling around the space, knocking over bottles and vials. You can't tell if it is human, undead or both – its body is swollen, covered in vile blisters and pustules. From its back, yellow tentacles writhe back and forth, their lengths covered in dripping slime.

The creature appears to sense you, twisting its head around to reveal bulging bloodshot eyes. Around its wobbling neck is a metal dog tag, engraved with the number thirteen. The monster emits an inhuman roar, then charges forward, flinging tables out of the way in its haste to clobber you. It is time to fight:

	Speed	*Brawn*	*Armour*	*Health*
Number 13	2	3	2	30

Special abilities

Unlucky for some: Each time you roll a ⚀ for your hero in this combat, you are hit by the creature's flailing tentacles. This automatically inflicts 2 damage, ignoring *armour*. If you have an ability that lets you re-roll dice, then you can use this to try and avoid the damage.

If you manage to defeat this grotesque creation, turn to 300.

14

Quest: King of the hill

Ahead, dark shapes loom out of the mist: a series of earthen mounds, carpeted with moss and heather. In the distance a solitary wolf howls. It is a sad, mournful noise, which seems perfectly in keeping with this drab and remote area of moorland.

The traveller had convinced you this was a good idea. 'Yeah, the barrows, my friend. If you're looking to get some fast treasure – get yourself suited and booted – then those ancient graves are just offering it up.'

As you gaze upon the eerie collection of mounds, many ringed by standing tablets of stone, you start to wonder if the traveller had been a little crazy.

'Well, I've come this far.' Gritting your teeth you trudge onwards through the high grass, into the thick veil of fog. You haven't gone far before the wind starts to pick up speed, beating about your body and ripping at your cloak. As you stagger back, losing ground to the onslaught, you suddenly sense the windstorm shift direction.

The mist is now whirling and twisting on the powerful currents, turning faster and faster until it has become a huge rippling tornado. Black lightning crackles around the funnel-shaped cloud as it spins furiously towards you. It is time to fight:

	Speed	*Magic*	*Armour*	*Health*
Raging storm	0	1	0	12

Special abilities

Celestial charge: Each time you deal damage to the raging storm, you are struck by the lightning and must lose 2 *health*.

If you defeat this strange apparition, turn to 25.

15

You take a gamble and push off from the tree, attempting to grab one of the thicker boughs further around the trunk. For a second you are free-falling through a frightening emptiness, then your hands grab a hold on the wood. Skilfully, you swing yourself up onto the branch, twisting your body around to sit astride it. From here you are able to shuffle back to the trunk, where you can now see a previously hidden set of handholds, carved to look like clumps of leaf mould. You clamber up this last distance in no time at all, flinging open the tree house door and pulling yourself up onto its polished floor. Turn to 425.

16

You make your apologies and move away, aware that a sudden hush has fallen over the room. 'I asked yer a question,' calls the woman, her gravelly voice cutting through the silence. 'I asked yer what yer gawping at!'

With a sigh, you turn back to the table. 'That coat,' you gesture with a nod of your head. 'I knew its previous owner. I was just … curious.'

'Curious, eh?' With a snarl the woman kicks over the table, sending pots and mugs flying. 'Come on boys, time to show this one what happens when yer bait the fish!'

There are screams and shrieks from the crowd as people scatter to a safe distance. 'No fighting!' bellows a voice from behind the bar.

Unfortunately, you don't have a choice – the ruffians run at you as a pack. You must fight:

	Speed	*Brawn*	*Armour*	*Health*
Bilhah the Fish	5	4	2	35
Ruffians	–	–	2	15

Special abilities

- Motley crew: The ruffians add 3 to Bilhah's damage score for the duration of this combat. If the ruffians are defeated, this bonus no longer applies.

In this combat you roll against Bilhah's speed. If you win a combat round, you may choose to strike against Bilhah or her ruffians. If Bilhah is defeated first then the ruffians will immediately surrender, winning you the combat.

If you defeat this cruel band of mercenaries, turn to **194**. If you are defeated, turn to **244**.

17

(If you already have the word *calling* written on your hero sheet, then turn to 31.)

As you make your way through the crowds, you suddenly start to feel faint. Someone knocks into you, sending you into a dizzying spin. There is an angry curse as you stagger into another pedestrian, who pushes you away, forcing you to lose your footing. You topple backwards onto . . .

Thorns.

You cry out in pain as their sharp points rip through your clothing. All around you, thick branches snake through the dark as if alive. A forest – pressing in on all sides, making you its prisoner. You struggle to free yourself as the barbed tendrils slash and cut at your flesh, but you are powerless; trapped. Then you see a beacon of light glowing through the wall of thorns; a pale radiance that beckons to you. With eyes fixed solely on the light, you find yourself floating towards it, the thorns parting for you like a curtain.

The light is everywhere now, pushing back the infernal forest and guiding you to safety ...

You awake to find yourself lying spread-eagled on your back. A crowd of people have gathered, muttering and gossiping to one another. One woman, with long blond hair and trinkets about her neck, is kneeling beside you. She offers you her water skin, which you take in trembling hands, greedily gulping down its contents.

'What happened?' you ask hoarsely, handing back the skin. 'I don't remember ...'

'I think you had a dizzy spell,' she smiles. 'I saw you collapse; no one else seemed that concerned about helping.' The woman nods to the nearby crowd, who are already starting to disperse.

Taking her hand, you stumble back to your feet. 'Perhaps it's the altitude,' she grins, flicking a stray hair from her eyes. 'Take it easy, okay?'

You thank the woman, watching as she heads back into the bustling throng, a sword swinging on each hip. Still shaken by your peculiar vision, it is some minutes before you are able to regain your composure. Write the word *calling* on your hero sheet, then turn to 31.

18

'That would be a pretty picture, wouldn't it?' The woman chortles. 'No, I think I'd remember a set of golden gnashers, sweetie. Though – come to think of it – we did have one witchfinder in, only two days past. He was asking questions about that Blight Haven, down south.'

You frown, urging her to say more.

'He didn't look well, pale and shifty, like all his kind ... and didn't stay long. Not welcome here.' Her hand strays to a crucifix hanging about her neck. 'I told him to stay well away from that village. It's cursed – haunted. Really, someone should've done something about it long ago, cleanse it or whatever those inquisitors do.' She releases a heavy sigh. 'Humph, let's not talk of such things. Spoils the mood, dearie.'

Return to 52 to ask the bar woman another question.

19
Quest: Curse of Crow Rock

The narrow street lurches dizzily from side to side, forcing you to cling to the nearest wall. You feel sick; every inch of your body burning as if on fire. Sweat stings your eyes, your head pulsing with pain. The guards thought you were just another drunk, thrown out onto the streets at closing time. But a passing pilgrim had taken pity on you, giving you directions to the local apothecary.

Letting go of the wall, you stagger onwards up the street. You focus on the lanterns hanging either side of a wooden door – its surface daubed with the symbol of a bottle.

A carriage rattles past, pulled by a team of horses. Their clattering hooves are loud as thunder in your ears. You cover them with your hands, stumbling dazedly towards the door. Several times you lose your footing and fall painfully to your knees. But you manage to drag yourself up, determined to find a cure for your malady.

Elysium. You know that your body is craving more.

You raise a trembling hand and knock on the door. There is a painful wait while you hug your cramping stomach, teeth grinding noisily together.

From inside you hear muttering, then a catch being released. The door creaks open far enough to reveal a woman's face. She is elderly, with tousled grey hair spilling out of a white bonnet. A small pair of spectacles rest on the end of her nose. After taking one look at you, she opens the door wide and gestures for you to enter.

The room is small and filled with various bottles and pots. Before you can speak, the woman is already moving towards a side room. 'What is it?' she asks hurriedly. 'I doubt I can help you.'

'Elysium,' you croak, closing your eyes as the room tips wildly.

The healer freezes mid-step, glancing back at you with a frown.

'It's a long story,' you wheeze, forcing back another wave of nausea. 'Please, I need your help . . .'

'Indeed.' The woman gestures for you to follow. 'My name is Anna. This way, please.'

You follow her into a dimly lit room, cut from the grey rock of Carvel's hillside. A pallet bed rests against one wall, where a male patient lies on sweat-soaked sheets. He squirms in a feverish delirium.

The rest of the room is dominated by a wooden table, covered in more bottles and containers. A curtain divides this room from another area, where you glimpse a stack of crates piled high to the ceiling. Each one has the symbol of a rose stamped on the side.

Anna is already selecting various bottles from her collection. 'Elysium is very rare and very expensive. Did you expect me to just have some lying around?'

You rest your back against the wall, clutching your arms to stop them shaking. 'I had no other choice.'

The woman adds a series of fine powders to a trestle bowl. 'I don't need to ask how you came in contact with such a devilish concoction.' After crushing another ingredient with a mortar she mixes the parts together, before pouring them into a bottle and adding a green-tinged liquid.

'You know, these ingredients aren't cheap.' Anna shakes the bottle, watching as the contents dissolve. 'One of these powders alone is five hundred gold crowns.'

You balk. 'I … I can't pay you … I …' Feebly, you try and locate your money pouch, hands grappling at your belt.

The woman watches and shakes her head.

'Enough. I knew you would not have the funds. So you can do me a favour instead, agreed?' She raises the bottle, which now contains a bubbling pale-green potion. 'This is not Elysium. But it is the next best thing. It will relieve your symptoms – your addiction. This potion is your true freedom.'

'I'll do whatever you ask,' you croak, reaching out for it. 'Please …'

Anna hands you the potion and watches intently while you drink its contents. The liquid tastes like sour apples with a hint of cinnamon. Once you have emptied the bottle, you feel your temperature starting to subside. The room has stopped spinning.

'Good,' smiles Anna, taking the bottle from you. 'Now, you're going to repay me by helping this man.' She nods to the patient, who is tossing and turning, gripped in a fevered nightmare.

'You couldn't cure him?' you ask, surprised.

'I need something first.' Her eyes wander to an object lying on the table. It looks like a charred and blackened piece of wood.

Will you:

Ask about her patient?	**115**
Ask about the strange object?	**92**
Ask about the crates in the other room?	**35**

20

With the goblin defeated, you search its body. You find 10 gold crowns and may take any / all of the following items:

Rusted knife	**Pilfered ring**	**Wishing well coin**
(main hand: dagger)	(ring)	(talisman)
+1 speed	+1 magic	Ability: charm
Ability: bleed		

You wonder what a goblin would be doing in such a village. Perhaps it came here to loot or seek shelter, but somehow it became infected by the zombie curse. It is a thought that sends a shiver up your spine. Will you suffer the same fate? Grimly, you turn away from the body and head back onto the landing. The light is still flickering from the room below, so you decide to investigate. Turn to 55.

21

'He was King Gerard's youngest son – born a weak and sickly child.' Lazlo gives a sigh, lowering his gaze. 'He was an embarrassment, to his father and to his twin brothers. Around court he was nicknamed the goose. A pale boy of timid nature – he hadn't much hope.'

The man's eyes rise to meet your own. 'Then he started to have dreams. Visions. As you can imagine, they embarrassed his father even more. Gerard was a great king, much loved by his men. He was an army man and his coffers were near empty from warring with the east. He was starting to lose the support of his court – a series of defeats to Mordland and there was talk of,' Lazlo flicks his wrist, producing a sliver of steel from the sleeve of his shirt, '... replacement.' He spins the blade in the palm of his hand. 'He was desperate – and in desperate times, what else can you do?' The blade stops spinning, its tip pointed in your direction. 'You call a crusade. He convinced the church that Allam was a holy prophet and sent him west with an army. Kill two birds with one stone – remove an embarrassment from court and take more land for the crown. For Gerard, it was the perfect solution.'

'How could you know this?' you ask, sounding sceptical. 'Allam is revered. Pilgrims flock to Carvel because of him. He was sanctified by the church.'

Lazlo gives a nonchalant shrug. 'That's just my opinion.' He slips the blade back into his sleeve. 'The outcome, I think you will agree, benefited the king and the church more than it did poor Allam.'

Will you:	
Ask what he thinks about prophets?	149
Enquire as to your whereabouts?	9
Ask about Carvel's 'masked crusader'?	39
State you wish to leave?	167

22

The tinker, a young woman in a grease-stained shirt and breeches, looks up from polishing a set of greaves. She smiles at you cheerfully. 'Good day, traveller. Might I interest you in one of my special deals?' The tinker turns and gestures to a rack of weapons and armour. 'Faith can only go so far in protecting us from the evils of this world. Oft times I prefer a good blade and some chain between me and my enemy. What d'you say?'

You peruse the items on offer, noting that many of them, despite the obvious 'spit and polish', have certainly seen better days. However, a few notable bargains catch your eye. The following are available for 100 gold crowns each:

Head splitter	**Silver streak**	**Inscribed mantle**
(main hand: axe)	(left hand: dagger)	(cloak)
+1 speed +2 brawn	+1 speed +1 brawn	+1 magic +1 armour
Ability: savagery	Ability: feint	Ability: iron will

After viewing the items, you turn back to the bustling streets of lower town. Turn to 36.

23

The blacksmith swings the mighty hammer as if it weighed no more than a roll of parchment. However, despite its obvious strength the creature is slow-witted and clumsy, the cramped room making it hard to benefit from the range of its weapon. Using the close quarters to your advantage, you step around the demon's ungainly attacks, hacking and blasting at the scaly body. At last, dripping with sweat from the intense heat, you finally fell the monster, bringing its mighty hammer crashing to the ground.

You may now help yourself to one of the following rewards:

Forger's hammer	**Dread forge gauntlets**
(main hand: hammer)	(gloves)
+2 brawn	+1 brawn +1 magic
Ability: pound	Ability: retaliation

You may also take the sheet of *enchanted iron* that the forger had been working on. (Simply make a note of this on your hero sheet, it does not take up backpack space). Keen to leave this sweltering heat behind, you are grateful to discover another portal tucked away inside an arched alcove. Without delay, you step through it – wondering what will await you on the other side. Turn to 46.

24

Dawn finds you out on the moors, frost still crisp on the ground as you trudge across the undulating hills. Joss sets a brisk pace, her bow slung over her shoulder, quiver resting at her hip. You can't help but marvel at her single-minded devotion – to have waited nearly a lifetime for the return of the tower, dutifully keeping her husband's memory alive when all hope must have been lost. With the tower's sudden reappearance, you can understand her urgency as she pushes through the coarse brush, barely stopping to draw breath.

Behind her is the paladin, Anse. He is now wearing a white surcoat over a padded blue jerkin. His silver crucifix hangs across his back, his other weapons bristling from the numerous belts and wraps about his body.

And rattling along at your side is Polk. The rugged warrior is struggling to keep up, huffing and puffing through his beard. A crossbow is cradled in his arms, loaded and ready for action. 'Are we there yet?' he gasps for the umpteenth time that morning. 'I swear, when this is over I'm retiring . . .'

You have stopped dead in your tracks, letting Polk trudge on for several paces before he looks around, confused. 'It seems we have arrived,' you reply, pointing ahead. Polk puts a hand over his eyes, squinting over the next rise.

'Well, would yer look at that.'

The tower is a monolith of black stone, cracked with veins of spitting fire. Its pointed spires stab through the clouds, looking like a giant hand of shadow grasping for the sun. In some parts, sections of the tower have crumbled away – but, rather than fall loosely to the ground, they hang suspended in the air, captured as if in a painting.

'I guess it didn't look like that when last you saw it?' ventures Polk, glancing sideways at Joss. The woman is speechless, gazing upon the black tower with fear and apprehension.

'I have to find my husband,' she breathes at last, starting down into the valley.

Silently, the rest of you follow, wondering what horrors you will find inside this malign-looking tower. Turn to 190.

25

As your magical blade slashes through the misty apparition, you see it recoil – the lightning flickering more angrily than before. Armed with the knowledge that this creature can feel pain, you continue to hack away at its whirling form, sending ribbons of mist spiralling away into the gloom. Soon the elemental is no more, the wind that created it dying down to an ineffectual breeze.

Keeping your weapon drawn you continue into the barrows, eyeing your surroundings warily. After several minutes, you see a series of oval hills looming out of the fog; burial mounds where the traveller insisted you would find ancient weapons and treasure. To your left, you notice one of the mounds has a ring of candles placed on top of it; their tiny flames flicker in the wind. To your right, you can see an opening in the side of one of the hills. It looks like it was once covered by a boulder, which has now been pushed aside.

Will you:

Investigate the candles?	40
Enter the open burial mound?	61

26

'This is actually for you.' Anna hands you the casket. 'It's Jolando's and he asked me to give it to you, as a thank-you for saving his life.'

The casket is plain, with no decoration or mark. It feels heavy in your hands. Opening it up, you find a black-bladed dagger inside, with a small leather pouch and an envelope tucked alongside it. If you wish you may now take:

Cutthroat's carver
(main hand: dagger)
+1 brawn +1 magic
Ability: bleed

The pouch contains 15 gold crowns; the envelope contains an iron key. You turn it over in your hand, looking for any clue as to its use.

'It's the key to Jolando's safe house,' says Anna. 'He will leave town for a while, until the troubles have died down. His safe house is now yours. I can give you directions.' (Make a note of the entry number 49. Anytime you are in Carvel and wish to visit the safe house, turn to that entry number.)

Will you:

Ask about what happened to the thief? 54

Ask about the statue above the door? 98

Thank Anna and leave? **Return to the map**

27

Malak's face lengthens into a scowl. 'The shroud is a place of demons and spirits – where the raw elements rule over all. It is the centre of everything, the meeting place of worlds.'

'And the old magic comes from this place?' you ask frowning.

Malak clicks his tongue. 'Yes, you fool. The dwarves were the first to commune with the spirits, binding their power into runes. Over time, they learned that they could summon more sentient spirits; those who would gift them greater powers.'

Malak raises his hands, summoning crackling flames to his fingertips. 'We have to learn control. If we don't, we can lose ourselves to the magic and then …' He snaps them closed, extinguishing the flames. 'Only with control can we understand true power. Not like those Wiccan fools who dabble freely in the darker magics; magics that will turn them all into gibbering demon spawn.'

Will you:

Ask about the Wiccans? 265

Ask about the testing? 213

Leave and return to upper town? 77

28

Damaris turns to face you. Taking your hand, she places it on one of the dark runes glimmering against her robes. 'Do you feel it?'

The rune tingles against your skin, pulsating with a powerful energy. 'The dwarves used runes,' you nod, appraising the other sigils that adorn her clothing. 'A way of binding spirits from the shroud to do their bidding.'

Damaris smiles. 'You know something of the art then. Yes, we are able to reach into the shroud, the ghost world, and commune with the spirits there. The minor spirits are easily bound. The demons, however … Well, they can prove more … wilful.'

If you have the word *duty* on your hero sheet, turn to 253. Otherwise return to 126 to ask Damaris another question.

29

You doubt you stand much of a chance against an opponent you can't even see. Instead you turn and run, splashing through the murky water towards the door. All around you various missiles are being flung through the air but miraculously, apart from some minor cuts and bruises, you manage to reach the door unharmed. You are even more grateful to discover that the door is unlocked. You push it open, the grimy water gushing around your legs as it spills out into the corridor beyond. There is a series of angry bangs and thuds coming from behind you. Quickly, you attempt to push the door closed, struggling against the force of the rushing water. It finally closes with a metallic clink, leaving the poltergeist to vent its fury alone on the other side.

After brushing the grime and dirt from your clothes, you take a moment to study your surroundings. The corridor is fashioned from black stone, smooth and without decoration. To your left, it continues for several metres before ending in a set of worn stairs leading up to a decorative wooden door. To your right there is an open metal grill, beyond which you can see a set of rusted stairs spiralling down towards the sound of buzzing, hammering machinery.

Will you:

Take the stairs up?	417
Take the stairs down?	382

30

A sudden jealous craving comes over you as you gaze upon the finely-jewelled sword. You take an angry step forward, demanding that the old man hand over his possessions.

'Ah, very good,' he snorts. 'The manners of a Wiccan and the smell of one, to boot. You know, you do look very threatening. Apart from your hands, which are shaking like leaves.'

You glance down, aware that that the man has a point – your whole body is trembling from exhaustion and the bitter cold. The man watches you with a thin smile. 'I suppose the test of good manners is to be patient with bad ones. Let's see. The sword is not my property, so I suppose you would not be stealing from *me*. Although its owner might take offence.'

He picks up the scabbarded sword and tosses it towards you. It slides across the wet ground to settle at your feet. If you wish you may now take:

Winter's fall
(main hand: sword)
+1 speed +1 brawn
Ability: silver frost

'Presumably you want gold as well.' His attention shifts to his pack. 'But I'm afraid we don't have a need for it on these . . . little ventures.'

'You said *we*,' you enquire suspiciously. 'You have a companion. Where did they—'

Suddenly you hear a bellowing roar coming from somewhere deep inside the rock. It is followed by someone's cry and a loud ground-trembling boom. The man smiles at your startled reaction then shrugs his shoulders, continuing.

'Are you planning on leaving now or do you want my clothes as well? This coat was tailored in Venetia; the lining is Lakrosa silk from across the Dune Sea.'

You ignore his banter, fixing your gaze on the dark rock. 'What was that noise?' you ask worriedly.

'What was what?' asks the gentleman, leaning over the cooking pot and taking a sniff of its contents. 'Ah, yes. The stew is ready. Would you like some tea? I brewed some earlier. Silver Grey, the finest.'

There is another monstrous roar, dislodging stone and dust from the rock walls. The man moves around the fire and settles down on a blanket, acting as if nothing untoward is happening. 'You can join me if you like,' he says, raising a cup of steaming tea to his lips. 'No sense in parting company when there is a good meal to share.'

Will you:

Join him by the fire?	187
Ask about the disturbance?	156

31

The cobbled lane bends back on itself as it winds crookedly up the face of the grey rock. Exposed to the elements, a fierce wind sweeps in from the rolling highlands to batter the awnings and signs hanging outside the buildings. These, you notice, have been cut into the rock itself, their interiors lit by flickering lantern light.

Most of the buildings appear to be hostels or homes, but there are also a few stores. One catches your eye; an apothecary, with an image of a potion bottle painted on its wooden door.

Will you:

Visit the apothecary?	120
Keep heading to upper town?	77
Descend to lower town?	36

32

You find yourself stumbling forward into a dusty attic, its sloping ceiling forcing you to stoop. Thankfully the tremors have now subsided, but their aftermath is still evident to see – boxes of junk have been thrown around and upended, spilling their contents across the floor. Of the child there is no sign, although you notice another glowing doorway at the other side of the attic.

Will you:

Stop and search the room?	108
Hurry through the portal?	440

33

Quest: Bullets over Blight Haven

You hurry across the barren moors, a chill wind at your back. With night fast approaching and the black clouds promising a storm, you are desperate not to spend another freezing night without adequate shelter. From the ridge you had spied a village, nestled at the foot of the valley. There had been none of the usual signs of life: no smoke from chimneys or flickering lights at windows. Nevertheless it had been a lucky find, offering a welcome alternative to a bed of hard ground and a damp cloak for warmth.

As you near the village, you pass through a copse of dark gnarly trees. A weather-beaten length of parchment has been nailed to one of the trunks. You immediately walk over, grabbing its edge to stop it flapping in the wind. The paper carries the seal of the king, a crown and a crook, marking it as an official document of the realm. The neat-flowing script has been inscribed in holy runes, making it impervious to the elements. The message reads:

Blight Haven

On Mindas Day, Beltaine, in the year 1385 of the Ascendant
The Holy Protectors, King Leonidas and Lord and Lady Justice
hereby decree that the village formerly known as Andor's Haven
is fated for termination and cleansing. Any person found on said land
will be considered a trespasser and punished in
accordance with The Seventh Holy Writ.

Cold rain starts to fall, spattering off the rocks and leaves. A distant crack of thunder sends a nearby crow to flight, cawing and screeching as it hurries away between the spidery branches. The storm is coming – and it makes your decision an easy one.

You rip the paper from its nail and toss it away into the mud. Fixing your gaze on the village, you continue down the wooded slope into the valley. No king's document is going to stop you from finding food and warmth this night. Turn to 100.

34

You fling open the chest and root through its contents, finding a number of war trophies and pieces of jewellery wrapped in linen. With your only exit closing rapidly behind you, there is no time to waste.

You may grab any two of the following items:

Blood iron knot	**Troll's bones**	**Chieftain's guard**
(necklace)	(backpack)	(head)
+1 armour	These might prove valuable	+1 brawn
Ability: charm	to the right person	Ability: might of stone

When you have made your choices, turn to 95.

35

Anna grabs the curtain and tugs it along the rail, covering up the crates. 'They are much needed supplies,' she explains hurriedly, looking slightly flustered for the first time. 'I'm lucky to have a benefactor who believes in what I do.' Anna glances over at her patient, wringing her hands with worry. 'There have been many casualties in this war . . .'

'War?' you ask in surprise. 'What war?'

The woman raises an eyebrow. 'The Church and the Wiccans. Neither will back down – the Wiccans want their lands back; their ancient sites. The Church wants to convert their people; make them change their heathen ways. Do you really see any solution other than war?'

Will you:

Ask about the patient?	115
Ask about the strange object on the table?	92
Ask what you need to do?	130

36

A crowded mass of bodies files through the streets and cobbled squares, where the endless cries of hawkers compete for attention. You are drawn to a row of stalls, where skewered lizards are being cooked over hot coals. Nearby, a woman is spooning stew into small wooden bowls. A cage of live rats hangs from a post beside her, making you wonder exactly what type of meat has made its way into the sloppy-looking gruel.

'Fancy some of me finest hot pot?' asks the woman, offering you a bowl.

Grimacing, you move on, your attention settling on a group of traders. One has a table, strewn with an odd assortment of objects. They appear to be charms and bracelets, made from woven straw and wood and what looks like . . . finger bones. Next to the charm-maker a tinker has set up shop, with a gleaming array of weapons and armour displayed on racks.

Behind them, a rickety-looking building leans over the street. A newly-painted sign sways in the chill wind, proclaiming it as 'The Pilgrim's Rest'. The image shows a rosy-faced woman, supping from a pewter tankard. Sounds of music and merriment drift out from the smoky interior.

Will you:

Examine the charm-maker's wares?	41
Investigate the tinker's shop?	22
Visit 'The Pilgrim's Rest'	47
Follow the crooked street to upper town?	17
Leave Carvel?	**Turn to the Act 1 map**

37

(Record the word *raven* on your hero sheet.)

The robbers clearly have no combat experience, their ragged clothing and crude weapons suggesting that this was not their primary choice of career. Your first blow sends the leader staggering back, your second severs his rake in two. Twisting around, you parry an incoming strike from behind, swinging your knee up to hit your attacker in the groin. He gives a gasp of pain – time enough for you to slam your elbow into his back, sending him sprawling into the mud.

You turn to your remaining assailant – the youngest of the three, barely old enough to be sporting his fuzz of beard. He clutches the wooden club tightly, holding it out before him like some magical talisman to ward you away. You take a quick step forward – and the boy's resolve crumbles. He drops the club and backs away, arms held out wide.

'We thoughts you were a Wiccan,' he begs, his voice breaking on the words.

'Should that make a difference?' you growl angrily.

'They took everything from us,' says the leader, the eldest of the three. He throws the broken stumps of his weapon into the mud. 'They burnt our farmstead to the ground. My wife . . .' He shakes his head, his words sticking in his throat.

You sheathe your weapons, then walk over to the robber who is still lying on the ground, groaning with pain. 'I find it hard to sympathise with those who would prey on travellers,' you reply harshly, offering a hand. The robber takes it and stumbles to his feet. He is a few years older than the boy, with broad shoulders and thick-set arms. This one, at least, might make a decent fighter – with some training.

'You're the first, honest,' says the youngest, looking around nervously. 'We've not had a decent meal for days. We got desperate . . .' He clutches his arms to his chest, shivering with cold. You notice that his clothes are torn and threadbare, caked in mud. It is a sorry sight – one that makes you marvel that they have managed to survive at all, out in this harsh wilderness.

Will you:

Ask them to tell you more about the Wiccans?	162
Ask about Raven's Rest?	319
Tell them to find charity some place else?	107
Give them a gift of 5 gold crowns?	326
Leave and continue your journey?	199

38

The woman plants her hands on her hips. 'Now, what you doing asking me about a place like that for, dearie? Look around you – this is a home of merriment and cheer; me very own church of joy. But that place … I know what it is. It's where the inquisition take those they don't like; those that don't play by their rules.' She dabs at her forehead with the back of her hand. 'You got a friend there, me dear? Someone you missing?'

You shake your head. 'No, I was just curious.'

The woman blows out her cheeks. 'I don't need to tell you this, dearie, I'm sure there's a smart head on those shoulders, but don't be prying into the affairs of the inquisition. Their way of answering ain't going to be as sweet as mine, if you get my meaning.'

Return to 52 to ask the bar woman another question.

39

'Yes, I do profess to having had a hand in some of the more … unsavoury clean up operations that have been going on in Carvel.'

'I heard rumours,' you add. 'Some masked vigilante … the stories sounded a bit …'

'Fanciful?' Lazlo raises an eyebrow. 'I did hear one story that I was actually a vampire – a fanged assassin, preying on the weak and vulnerable. That is one rumour I have now put paid to. Or should I say, you did.'

You frown. 'I did?'

'The margoyle,' he prompts with a grin. 'They normally don't come this far north and they certainly don't come near settlements.

But this one was ranging further afield, attacking pilgrims on the roads and even venturing into the town at the dead of night.' He winces, rubbing at his bruised face. 'I was able to guess at its lair. And that is where you found me. And the margoyle.'

'So the mask,' you enquire. 'That is a disguise?'

Lazlo nods. 'Of course. It wouldn't do for my dear father, the king, to know his son is running around the streets of Carvel, fighting criminals and hoodlums .' He sniffs, smoothing down his silken shirt. 'I'm not his favourite. My taste for the high life doesn't quite agree with him.'

Will you:	
Ask him about the strange dream?	62
Enquire as to your whereabouts?	9
State you wish to leave?	167

40

As you clamber up the hill you are surprised to hear an old woman, muttering and cackling to herself. You can't make out the words, but they sound like part of a chant or a rhyme.

At the top of the mound you see that an intricate pattern of runes has been burnt into the grass. A woman, old and hunched over, is hobbling around its edge, pulling black candles from a sack that she drags behind her. These are being placed in various chalk circles. Most of the candles are already lit.

At the centre of this bizarre display, a large hollowed-out pumpkin rests on a bed of stone. Two slanted eyes and a jagged mouth have been cut into one side, and a candle burns within it, giving off a ghoulish glow.

The woman sniffs the air, then suddenly whirls around, pointing a gnarled finger at you. She spits out a curse, her eyes narrowing to dark slits. Your first reaction is to raise your hands, to prove you mean her no harm, but the woman's scowl is a clear sign that she sees you as her enemy.

'Must finish the ritual,' she hisses. 'Sacred land must be protected!' She lunges forward, her long bony fingers crackling with magic:

	Speed	*Magic*	*Armour*	*Health*
Wiccan witch	0	1	0	14

If you defeat the deranged witch, turn to 7.

41

(If you have the word *bones* written on your hero sheet, then turn to 56.)

The weasel-faced trader makes the sign of the cross as you approach. 'Ah, the One God bless you, my friend. You walk in Saint Allam's footsteps. They say he stood on this very spot, to proclaim 'imself the reincarnation of Judah.' His eyes dart from side to side, then he leans over the table, stroking the band of charms around his neck. 'I tells you the truth, my friend. These charms are made from the finest of materials, none of that charlatan nonsense. Here, tell no one this …' He drops his voice to a whisper. 'I got it on honest word that these here bones are saint's bones, from out on the moors. You want a piece of the saints, right, to bring you good luck, yes?'

You view the unsavoury collection of charms and relics, noting the different-sized bones used in their construction. It seems unlikely that any of these bones could possibly have belonged to a saint. 'Isn't that *goblin*?' you ask, pointing to a short, stubby finger bone. 'And that one looks like a troll …'

The trader gives a heavy sigh. 'Yeah, I sees yer a smart one. Look, I've had ta diversify; times are 'ard, right? But might be some work in it for yer, if you fancy a bit of bone collectin'?'

Will you:

Examine the items on sale?	59
Ask about the 'bone collectin'?	70
Return to lower town?	36

42

Quest: The light and the dark

(Note: You must have completed the blue quest *Behind the mask* before you can start this quest.)

You leave the settlement of Raven's Rest, striking south along the well-worn track that will take you out of the moors and into the lands beyond – the grassland plains known as the Saskat Prairies. It is time to move on – something you have always been good at, aware that your strange powers can often draw the wrong kind of attention. The last few weeks have taught you that your gift, your ability to glimpse the future, has been changed somehow by your exposure to the Elysium. It has made you faster and more agile in combat, a second sight that always keeps you out of harm's way. As for the other visions, they come and go, but are always the same – a vast forest of thorns and some presence beckoning you from its darkest depths.

A light rain begins to spatter off your cloak as you make your way through the bleak hills. You will not be sorry to trade this wet and wintry northland for the warmer climes to the south. Lowering your head to the chill wind you pick up the pace, hoping to reach a settlement or inn before nightfall.

You slow when you hear voices ahead. Through the blanket of drizzle you see a covered wagon lying askew across the water-logged track. Your hands immediately go to your weapons, your quick eyes flitting between the three visible travellers: an elderly-looking man sat hunched on a boulder by the roadside, and a man and a woman talking by the wagon. All three are dressed in mud-splashed coats and hats; possibly pilgrims or trinket sellers.

The woman has already spotted you, her hands dropping to the long swords resting against her hips. Curtains of blond hair tumble out from beneath her wide-brimmed hat, framing a pale face dominated by piercing blue eyes. The man next to her appears to be weaponless, but the cuffs of his coat are long and wide, covering his hands. He stiffens, his eyes narrowing suspiciously.

You nod your head in greeting, approaching cautiously. It is the woman who drops her guard first, her face splitting into a wide beaming smile. 'Well, lookee here. If it isn't my woozy fainting friend.'

For a moment you frown, trying to place her. Then you remember – the woman who came to your aid when you first had your strange vision in Carvel. 'You're a long way from town,' you state, noticing that the man is still tensed, his posture emanating distrust.

He scowls. 'Someone else you courted with that tongue of yours?' he says, aiming his statement at the woman. She gives him a hurt expression, before lowering her eyes.

'The priest will come good,' she says. 'He wanted to help.'

You notice that the elderly man by the roadside has not looked up or shown any interest in the conversation. He is muttering to himself, wringing his hands together as if trying to rid them of something unclean.

Will you:

Ask what happened to the wagon?	274
Ask what is in the wagon?	223
Ask where they are travelling to?	178
Ask if you can help?	141

43

'You're no fun, no fun at all!' squeals the child. You hear angry thumping sounds, reverberating along the metal walls. You can almost imagine the child beating his fists in some juvenile frenzy. Then there is a grating squeal, coming from behind you. You spin around, to see one of the wall panels sliding open to reveal a glowing doorway.

'An exit at last . . .' you sigh with relief.

You step through. There is a bright flash of white light, accompanied by the dizzying sensation of movement, then you find yourself stumbling out into a small square room. A quick scan of your surroundings confirms you are back where you started, with the trapdoor opening in the floor ahead of you. You step around it, eager now to explore the noisy workshop below. Turn to 398.

44

With the pillars destroyed, the stone giants are weakened – making it easy for you to smash through their rock armour and extinguish whatever dark magic had once given them life. You may now help yourself to one of the following rewards:

Charged breastplate	**Rock fist**	**Stone spike**
(chest)	(left hand: fist weapon)	(main hand: dagger)
+1 brawn +1 armour	+1 speed +1 magic	+2 brawn
Ability: lightning	Ability: surge	Ability: critical strike
	(requirement: mage)	(requirement: rogue)

If you have the word *Wiccan* on your hero sheet, turn to 354. Otherwise, turn to 400.

45

The priest reins in his horse in a flurry of mud and water. 'You!' he sneers, raising his staff. 'At last, the One God delivers you to me.' A white fire leaps along the length of the staff, mirroring the fire that burns in his fanatical eyes. 'The bishop died because of you. And now you will pay!'

If you have the word *papal* on your hero sheet, turn to 282. Otherwise, turn to 315.

46

You emerge in a small square room made from riveted plates of iron. It is devoid of any furnishing or decoration, save for a giant metal wheel set into the floor. Your feet clang noisily on the metal panels as you step closer to examine it. The wheel is reminiscent of those you might find on a ship, with a series of spokes radiating out from a centre point, each one ending in a wooden handle. You assume that the wheel is meant to be turned – but for what reason, you cannot fathom. There does not appear to be any exit from the room, other than the door you used to enter.

Will you:

Turn the wheel clockwise?	385
Turn the wheel anti-clockwise?	320

47

It is difficult to get a sense of your surroundings, as the tight press of bodies and the hazy clouds of pipeweed obscure much of the cramped taproom. From somewhere to your left you hear drums and flutes, and an orator retelling a story about Saint Allam. Onlookers are clapping along to the rhythm, offering occasional hoots or boos at opportune moments in the story.

You head for the bar, passing a group of bedraggled travellers who are gathered in a corner. They look pale and shaken, their clothes grime-stained and weather-beaten. They are recounting their own story in hushed tones to a smaller gathering, who are all listening intently.

At the bar, a plump woman is serving drinks to the clamouring patrons. She is laughing and joking along with their banter as she hands over frothing mugs of ale. As you near, you realise that it is her face that adorns the sign outside the tavern.

Will you:

Speak to the tavern keeper?	52
Join the travellers?	63
Listen to the orator?	75
Leave and return to lower town?	36

48

You make short work of the headless horseman, while Eldias gives the skull a firm kick, punting it over the nearest building.

'And good riddance,' he growls.

You find 10 gold crowns and may now help yourself to one of the following rewards:

Highwayman's coat	**Ghost rider's spurs**	**Gloves of the night fiend**
(chest)	(feet)	(gloves)
+1 speed +1 magic	+1 speed	+1 brawn
Ability: fear	Ability: reckless	Ability: fiend's finest

With the way clear, you follow Eldias up the stone stairs that lead to the church. Turn to **168**.

49

Jolando's safe house is an elegant-looking mansion on the east-side of upper town. However, its outward appearance is sadly deceiving. Once past the front door the interior is an empty shell, crawling with rot and mould – and the occasional rat.

It appears that Jolando's belongings amounted to little more than a pallet bed, a chamber pot and a rusted old trunk. Opening it up, you discover that the trunk is empty – but this will provide a useful area for you to store items safely.

You may store any extra backpack items or items of equipment in the safe house during act 1. If you swap equipment (weapons, backpack items etc.) during a quest or while exploring Carvel, you may put the item you are replacing in your safe house by turning to this entry number. This will prevent it from being destroyed. You can only keep a maximum of four objects in your safe house:

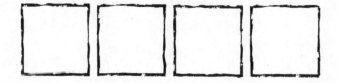

You can only re-equip items from your safe house when you visit this entry number *between* quests. When you are done, return to your previous entry number.

50

The armour and weapons are coated in dirt and grime, but it is clear that these were once prized treasures belonging to a great hero. With your only exit closing rapidly behind you, there is no time to waste.

You may grab any two of the following items:

Great divider	Shadow-dyed cloak	Trollskin gloves
(main hand: axe)	(cloak)	(gloves)
+1 speed +1 brawn	+1 magic	+1 armour
Ability: bleed	Ability: wisdom	

Once you have made your decision, turn to 95.

51

The sheet of parchment has a pattern drawn on it, with the words 'A stitch in time saves nine,' across the bottom. Next to the parchment are nine squares of cloth with the numbers one to nine stitched on them. This looks like some form of puzzle.

The pattern shows an arrangement of squares. You assume you need to place the nine pieces of cloth on the pattern, so that a number is in each square. There is only one of each number, so the pattern should finish up with the numbers 1 to 9 arranged within the grid. Then the symbols will give you a three digit number.

'Look Maxi! Someone wants to play!' The child's voice squeals with excitement. 'They think they're cut from the same cloth as me, but I bet they can't make me a number of three. Each stitch adds one or they'll come undone. Get it right and they'll run and run. So, what's my answer?'

If you are able to solve the puzzle then turn to the appropriate entry number. Otherwise, after much head scratching, you decide to give up on this foolish task. You leave the room via the half-open door. Turn to 391.

52

'Hello me dear, a new face round here if I'm not mistaken,' the woman looks up from the barrel tap, flashing you a toothy grin. 'I've a good memory for a face and a smile. So what's it to be, me sweet?' She slams the newly-filled mugs onto the bar, sending bubbles of froth floating through the smoky air. 'Don't keep a lady waiting, mind.'

Will you:

Ask about local rumours?	5
Ask what she knows of Carvel?	82
Ask what she knows of Durnhollow?	38
Ask if she remembers a witchfinder with gold teeth?	18
Turn your attention back to the taproom?	47

53

'Oh, that one.' You catch the flicker of a smile from beneath the man's hood. 'I sent her packing with the rest of her half-breed crew. I had to teach one or two of them a lesson, mind.' He tilts back his flask, emptying the last of its contents into his mouth. He screws up his face as he swallows. 'Yeah, don't you be worrying about them. They're barred from the coaching inn – no food or ale means they'll have moved on pretty swift.'

Will you:

Ask the vagrant to share his story?	127
Return to the town?	199

54

Anna lets out a sigh. 'Jolando was hired to steal a relic from the church vault. It should have been an easy enough task for someone with his skill. But when he arrived at the vault, someone else was already there . . .' The healer pauses, scratching her chin thoughtfully. Clearly she is still trying to make sense of the thief's words. 'He said it was a dwarf.'

Your eyes widen with surprise. 'I thought they were wiped out long ago, that they destroyed each other in their constant wars and bickering.'

'Well, not quite,' replies Anna. 'But none have been seen in Fenstone Moors for hundreds of years.'

'So, what happened?'

Anna removes her glasses, rubbing at her tired eyes. 'There was a struggle. Jolando tried to stop the dwarf from taking the relic. The noise drew the attention of the bishop, who discovered them both there inside the vault. Then the dwarf produced a staff – a charm – and broke it in two, releasing its magic. Both the bishop and the thief were struck by a curse. The dwarf escaped unharmed.'

'What do you know of this relic?' you ask, absorbed by the story. 'What does it do?'

'I don't know.' Anna shrugs her shoulders. 'Some inquisitors found it in a set of ruins to the south. They thought they were protecting it by bringing to Carvel – no doubt to take it apart and study. But the Wiccans believe it might be something powerful. A weapon that could help them win their war.' Anna drops her gaze. 'I should not have got involved in this. It's all getting too dangerous.'

Will you:

Ask about what is in the casket?	26
Ask about the statue above the door?	98
Thank Anna and leave?	**Return to the map**

55

You descend the stairs, worried that the creaking from the wooden boards will alert others to your presence. However, the persistent banging coming from the zombies outside has probably masked much of the noise. The front door gives a shudder as something heavy slams against it. You doubt it will hold for much longer.

Turning to the side door, you see that it is slightly ajar. Flickering shadows dance in the space beyond, cast by a lantern or a fire. Steeling yourself for what you might find, you push open the door, wincing as it gives a grating squeal. Turn to 347.

56

The trader rubs his hands together excitedly. 'So, yer got any of dem bones for me today?' If you have *goblin bones*, you can trade these in for 10 gold crowns each. If you have *troll bones*, you can hand these over for 20 gold crowns. If you have *giant bones*, the trader will give you 30 gold crowns. Remember to cross these items off your hero sheet once they have been traded in.

You may now view the charm-maker's wares (turn to 59) or continue exploring the lower town (turn to 36).

57

You notice that Benin does not have a pack with him, only the clothes on his back and a plain-wood staff. From his belt hang a number of pouches and gourds.

'I assume you're not here just for the sight-seeing?' you ask, looking around at the bleak landscape. 'Are you collecting herbs?'

Benin pretends to be brushing dirt from his robes, but you can tell he is deliberating over his answer. He finally gives a sigh. 'I'm on an errand for the church. You could say I got the short straw; I used to play in these hills as a child so I know them well.'

He avoids your questioning stare, squinting back towards the mountains, which rise like dark thorns against the rising sun. 'I don't have much time. Others are depending on me.'

Will you:	
Ask Benin about his magic?	80
Examine the remains of the creatures?	133
Continue on your journey?	157

58

Ahead of you, Eldias has already reached the stone well. The witch-finder has swapped his pistols for a pair of magical swords, which he spins in a rapid whirlwind of steel, slicing through the cadaverous monsters that stand in his way.

Wiping the rain and sweat from your eyes you hurry onwards, your gaze lifting to the church on the hilltop. Ghostly lights are flickering from within, the reverberating hum of the organ reaching a sinister crescendo.

Suddenly you are hit by something hard and powerful, which sends you sprawling backwards, sliding across the wet stone. Groggily, you lift your head, stars spinning before your eyes. It is some seconds before you can properly focus on the whirling colours and shapes that are lurching towards you.

It's something big – very big.

Rain is spraying off its broad shoulders, forming a cloak of sparkling droplets. It is a half-giant, nearly seven feet tall and almost half as wide, clutching a meat cleaver in one hand and a front door in the other. Its dull, blank expression makes it obvious that this is another zombie – that, and the gooey mass of innards that are hanging out of its bloated, diseased body. It is time to fight:

	Speed	*Brawn*	*Armour*	*Health*
Gutless	3	3	2	30

Special abilities

- Blood 'n' guts: The zombie's trailing guts can be a help and a hindrance. At the start of each combat round, roll a die. If the result is ⚀ or ⚁ then you get tangled up in its stringy guts and must reduce your *speed* by 1 for that combat round. If the result is ⚂ or more, then Gutless gets tangled up in his own guts, reducing his *speed* by 1 for that combat round.
- Undead: You may use your *ashes, holy water* and *holy protector* abilities against this zombie.

If you manage to defeat this loathsome creature, turn to 234.

59

'Forget these, let me show yer ma finer goods.' The trader pushes aside his grisly collection of bone charms. He then produces a leather case, which he opens out to reveal an exquisite set of necklaces and rings. This new collection is fashioned from wood and stone, inset with gems and carved with runes. 'See, I tells yer I ain't no charlatan. These are the real deal.'

You may purchase any of the following for 50 gold crowns:

Wanderer's wytchstone	**Puritan's band**	**Epona's blessing**
(necklace)	(ring)	(ring)
+1 magic	+1 brawn	+1 armour
Ability: charm	Ability: charm	Ability: charm

When you have made your decision, you may ask the trader about his job offer (turn to 70) or turn your attention back to the street (turn to 36).

60
Quest: Menace from the deep

Through the veil of falling snow, you finally catch sight of the logging camp – four stone cabins, arranged within a clearing. Behind them the forested hills give rise to the impressive Valhalla mountain range, their lofty peaks lost to the clouds.

'Be on your guard!' snaps the gruff voice of the captain as he marches to the front of the group, his boots crunching through the snow. He is a heavily-built veteran, muscles bulging beneath his leather tunic. He turns to look back at your rag-tag band, his eyes squinting in the bright light. With a grimace, he works a roll of tobacco around his mouth before spitting juice into the snow. 'Goblins are dangerous. Let's not have any foolish heroics . . . I'm looking at you, Vas.'

A shaven-headed woman, her features as hard and sharp as the mountains, gives a snort. She whispers something to her companion, a tall skinny man with a rat-like face. He sniggers, drawing out his broadsword with a ring of steel.

'Just another gobbo hunt,' he grins, patting the blade. 'When we get to see some real action, Cap'n?'

'Shut that greasy mouth of yours, Surl or I'll shut it for yer,' growls the captain, stabbing a fat finger in the air. 'I'm not having any talk back on this mission. You got that? Same goes for the rest of you noobs.'

You glance around at the gathering – a dozen mercenaries and adventurers, recruited from Carvel for what was described as a 'simple' mission. There have been reports of goblin raids from the north. The logging camp was attacked recently and, seeing a chance for some local fame and fortune, Captain Sanders has put together a group to investigate.

'Right, now move it,' he growls, turning and starting down the slope. 'And stay frosty, people. Surl, go scout. Vas, I want you out on that left flank.'

His two regulars move quickly and efficiently; the rat-faced man scuttling towards the camp while the woman hurries into the trees, a knife in each hand. They are soon lost from sight.

Shoving through branches, you arrive at the edge of the camp.

Surl is already waiting there, crouched beside an overturned cart. The camp is clearly deserted, its contents ransacked. You see boxes and crates smashed open, doors banging to and fro in the wind, sheets and clothing poking out of the snow.

'Don't smell no stinking gobboes,' says Surl, snorting and then spitting over his shoulder.

'I think we're too late,' sighs one of the group.

The captain turns and grabs the person who spoke, a boyish-looking mage in grey-woollen robes. 'Then you can join Surl and go search those cabins. Rest of us will stay 'ere. Now get moving.'

If you have the word *sure blade* written on your hero sheet, turn to 93. Otherwise, turn to 214.

61

You duck under the opening, to find yourself in a musty-smelling hollow. A thin shaft of light seeps through a crack in one of the walls, illuminating the thick stone slabs that have been used to support the earthen structure.

In the centre of the dark cave is a stone bed, carved with intricate runes. Around it you can see smashed pottery, a splintered chest and some scattered remnants of rusty armour. This place has evidently been looted by thieves.

You are about to leave, when you hear a wheezing groan close to your ear. Quickly you spin around, just in time to avoid the edge of an axe blade as it whistles through the air.

'Leave me in peace!' rasps a voice.

You watch with revulsion as a mould-covered skeleton, clad in tattered leather and chain, lurches out of the dark. As it swings its axe once again, you notice that the skeleton is wearing a glowing medallion around its neck. Perhaps this is the source of its unnatural life. You must now fight:

	Speed	*Brawn*	*Armour*	*Health*
Drust the defiled	0	0	0	14

If you manage to defeat the skeleton warrior, turn to 74.

62

'Yes, the forest of thorns.' Lazlo tilts his head to one side, regarding you with another smirk. 'You mentioned it quite a few times during your delirium. Have you been there? I must say, it is a place that … stays in the memory.'

'You mean it is real?' you ask, surprised. 'Where?'

'To the west of here, past the Pilgrim's Road – if road you could call it. The forest is old – and impenetrable. Many have tried to fell those trees, to clear a safe passage through. But all have failed.' He turns to gaze upon a large tapestry hanging on the far wall. It shows a young man in white robes leading knights across barren moorland. Shafts of sunlight break through the dark clouds to fall on his staff, which is raised before him. 'They say Allam had dreams … visions of that place. Some believe that was the very reason he was so eager to come to these forsaken lands, to find something … hidden away in that forest.'

'And what happened?' You reach for your throat, remembering the strange beast that attacked you in the dream.

'He had another of his grand visions,' shrugs the man, turning back. 'He took a handful of his best knights and went south. They were ambushed by stone trolls. Allam didn't survive.' He shakes his head, giving an amused snort. 'So much for being a prophet. He never saw his own death coming.'

Will you:

Ask what he knows of Allam?	21
Ask what he thinks about prophets?	149
Enquire as to your whereabouts?	9
Ask about Carvel's 'masked crusader'?	39
State you wish to leave?	167

63

'We just abandoned the camp,' sighs one of the men, as you edge into the circle of listeners. 'More than my job's worth to defend it from the likes of goblins.'

His nearest companion, whose arm is bound in a sling, scowls as he glares into his mug. 'They just came out of nowhere,' he mutters. 'We didn't stand a chance.'

You catch the eye of the man next to you, who has been listening to the story intently. 'What happened?' you ask, dropping your voice to a whisper.

He grimaces. 'Goblins come down from the mountains,' he says. 'Raided the logging camp at the end of the Pilgrim's Road. These men did the right thing, downing tools and making a run for it. Goblins are like wolves, cowardly until you face them as a pack .'

The wounded logger beats his fist on the table. 'Where was the inquisition anyway?' he growls. 'I thought they were meant to be protecting us.'

'Yeah,' sniffs the original speaker. 'Left my best sword behind too. Been in my family for as long as I remember. It better still be there, guarded by me sweetheart's smile – unless one of them stinkin' greenheads got it now.'

Write the word *sure blade* on your hero sheet. With your curiosity sated, you turn back to the busy taproom. Turn to 47.

64

As you approach the taproom, there is a commotion from inside. Suddenly two bodies come flying out of the open doors, tumbling and rolling through the mud. A large woman, wearing a dirt-stained apron, appears at the doorway, a skillet held menacingly in one hand.

'And that's the last time I'll tell you soaks,' she shouts, her chubby face flushed with anger. 'I'll have no fighting in my establishment.' She turns and re-enters the smoke-filled interior. Warily you follow her in, ignoring the drunken curses of the two men as they try and pick themselves up out of the dirt.

The common room of the inn is long and narrow, and full to bursting point. The noise is almost deafening – a discordant blend of laughter, shouting and bawdy singing. Between the crowded tables you spy a number of serving girls running back and forth, carrying platters of steaming food and clay mugs filled with ale.

Behind the bar, a giant of a man is rolling fresh barrels out of the cellar. Even stooped over, he is at least seven feet tall, his chest as wide as the barrels he is handling. The woman with the skillet pushes past him and disappears into a smoky kitchen, where the succulent aroma of meat and spices waft out into the common room – a welcome respite from the stench of sweat and unwashed bodies.

Will you:

Approach the bar?	248
Take a wander around the common room?	172
Leave the inn?	199

65

The strange-looking keep is surrounded by a high wall of stone, which looks to have been built more recently than the rest of the building. A wrought-iron gate provides a glimpse of the paved courtyard beyond, where you spy several carriages lined up outside the front steps.

Two guards move quickly to bar your way, crossing their halberds in front of you. Both are wearing white livery, displaying the outline of a black bat.

'Back off, commoner,' sneers one of the guards. 'Invitation only.'

Your eyes travel up the vast spear-head of rock to its wedge-shaped summit. There you can make out a crown of towers, stabbing even further into the murky clouds. 'Who lives there?' you ask. 'I never saw such a place before.'

'Prince Lazlo, you fool,' snaps the other guard. 'Now, back off – or this becomes a situation. And you really don't want a situation. Ain't that right, Bork?'

The other guard nods his head. 'Yeah, situations are bad. Real bad.'

Looking to avoid a 'situation' you bid the guards a hasty farewell. Turn to 77.

66

You back up against the nearest building and prepare to defend yourself. However, as the chaotic horde of undead draw in from all sides, you immediately start to regret your decision. There are too many of them for you to possibly defeat. You must now fight:

	Speed	*Brawn*	*Armour*	*Health*
Zombies	2	2	1	70

Special abilities

- Grappling hands: If the zombies win a combat round and roll a ⚅ for their damage score, then you must lose an item of equipment or a backpack item from your hero sheet. This item is immediately destroyed.

If you manage to survive to the end of the *fifth* combat round, turn to 203.

67

The troll is a formidable opponent, but its attacks are slow and clumsy. Your weapons quickly cut it down to size, reducing its body to shreds of shadow. As they curl away on the smoky air, the voice whispers in your ear once more: 'The dwarves taught us the runes. They gave us strength. Power. And so we conquered. Made these lands our own.'

The shadows start to wind and coil together, forming another shape. This one is human-sized, the outline hinting at heavy-plate armour. In one hand a warhammer materialises into being; in the other, shadows spread outward to fashion a shield.

'Then the eastlings came. Men with steel in their hearts; weapons of light and flame, and a false god to master us. But we Wiccans have no masters . . .'

The knight charges towards you, the warhammer crackling with dark magic:

	Speed	*Brawn*	*Armour*	*Health*
Knight	0	1	2	18

If you manage to defeat your shadowy foe, turn to 86.

68

'You really are wet behind the ears, aren't you?' The man shakes his head with a sigh. 'I suggest you wise up quickly to what's going on. The Wiccans have got themselves a new leader – some powerful dark warrior, who they say becomes a demon in battle. The inquisition had him under lock and key, but I hear he broke out. The Wiccans trashed the place.'

'Durnhollow?' you add quickly, your interest piqued.

'Yeah,' nods the map-seller. 'Hmm, you're not so ignorant after all, eh?'

'But what do they want, the Wiccans?'

The man rolls his eyes. 'See, I spoke too soon. Look, the Wiccans used to be all over these moors, this land was theirs, but then the king's army came. Naturally, the inquisitors didn't like what they saw; the Wiccans follow the old ways, see – the old magics. So the church tried to civilise them.' He snorts with derision. 'Like them wild lunatics could ever be civilised, cavorting with demons and drinking blood! I ask you! So most of 'em went south, but for some reason, they've come back – and they've come back fighting.'

Will you:

Ask about the prince?	101
Ask for more news?	137

69

Benin clasps your hand, shaking it firmly. 'Thank you once again, my friend. You have done a great service to the church. Here, I have something for you.' The priest removes a leather bag from his belt and hands it to you, grinning. 'I made these myself. Thought they might help you on your future expeditions.'

You open up the bag to find that it is lined with small pockets. Each one contains a clay potion bottle. You have gained the following items:

Pot of healing	Flask of healing	Pot of magic
(1 use)	(1 use)	(1 use)
(backpack)	(backpack)	(backpack)
Use any time in combat to restore 4 *health*	Use any time in combat to restore 6 *health*	Use any time in combat to raise your *magic* by 2 for one combat round

When you have updated your hero sheet, turn to 78.

70

'I gotta friend, out of town, who works the charms. They're genuine magic, I swears on me good 'ealth. But no one 'ere gonna buy 'em unless they think it's holy – unless they think they belonged to some great saint.' The trader scratches behind an ear with a grimy finger. 'Look, yer don't needs to do any fightin'. The moors are full of tombs and caves, and places where you find … well, dead stuff. Like bones.' He rattles one of the charms around his neck, which displays an unsettling array of teeth. 'So, youse bring me dem bones and I give yer me own kinda blessing – good honest gold. Deal?'

The trader offers out his grubby-looking hand. You shake it gingerly, agreeing to provide him with whatever you can find. (Write the word *bones* on your hero sheet.) You may now view the charm-maker's wares (turn to 59) or continue exploring lower town (turn to 36).

71

You leap over the rail of the ship, your attention focused solely on the cannon team. In alarm, you see that they are now turning the cannon to fire across the deck, heedless of whether they will hit friend or foe. Quickly, you charge towards them, dodging the pockets of battle that are already raging across the deck.

As you near, a larger goblin intercepts you, dressed from head-to-toe in rusted chain mail. He swings a club into your side, sending you reeling back against the mast pole. Behind the goblin, you see the gunner pushing an iron ball into the muzzle of the cannon while his spindly companion struggles to light the fuse using a tinder box.

You stumble to your feet, desperate to stop the cannon from firing – but once again, the armoured goblin is blocking your way, patting its mighty club with an ugly grin. You will have to defeat this brutish foe to have any chance of striking against the cannon team. It is time to fight:

	Speed	*Brawn*	*Armour*	*Health*
First mate	2	2	2	20
Cannon team	–	–	1	15

Special abilities

- Blast off: The cannon team will fire their cannon at the start of the *sixth* combat round. (See below.)
- Cowardly: If the first mate is defeated first, then the cannon team will automatically jump ship, winning you the combat.

If you win a combat round against the first mate, you can choose to apply your damage to the first mate or the cannon team. If the cannon team are *not* defeated by the start of the sixth combat round, then they will fire the cannon, wiping out everyone on board the ship! This means you automatically lose the combat.

If you defeat the dastardly goblins, turn to 205.

72

'They see things. The future,' says Murlic. 'But we not have Sanchen for long time. We stumble blind and in the dark. We hope that . . .' He stops to regard Conall darkly. 'We hope you tell us what to do.'

You take a step back in astonishment. 'I am no leader! I thought Conall . . . Damaris . . .'

Murlic sniffs with displeasure. 'They do not see. But you . . .' He waves a dirt-stained finger in your face. 'You see things. And you lead us out of dark. Yes?'

Will you:

Learn the pariah career (requirement: rogue)?	**302**
Explore the rest of the cave?	**485**

73

Quest: Behind the mask

(NOTE: You must have completed the green quest *Curse of Crow Rock* before you can start this quest.)

You hurry across the open moors, buffeted by wind and snow. How quickly the weather changes in this strange land. Only hours before you had been wandering through a tranquil forest, ringing with bird-song and the chatter of water over rocky stream beds. And then, as you trudged out into the wilder country, the skies had darkened and the snows had come. You considered turning back, to take shelter in the forest, but something – perhaps a wilful stubbornness not to surrender – kept you blundering onwards into the face of the storm.

After what feels like an hour, shivering and shaking from the cold, you spy a ridge of rock, cutting a grey line through the white haze. The sight immediately raises your spirits, promising you shelter to wait out the storm.

As you near, you see that the ridge is dominated by a single rocky bluff, which thrusts up out of the mist like a giant fist. Firelight dances at the base of the rock, flickering within its many pits and hollows. It appears you are not the only one to have come here for shelter.

You cautiously put a hand to your weapon before approaching. A jagged cleft runs down one side of the bluff, forming a natural overhang. Here you see two horses tethered to a finger of rock, shifting nervously in the chill wind. The cleft goes deeper and rises, forming a rocky shelf, where a small fire has been lit. A black-coated man with short grey hair is poking at the contents of a cooking pot. You catch a waft of stew and find your stomach knotting into a growl of hunger.

You step closer. The man looks up startled, his hand reaching towards his pack. There you see a scabbarded sword, its hilt gleaming with jewels. As the firelight shifts across his features you see that he is an elderly gentleman, with a neatly clipped moustache and beard. His appearance speaks of wealth and high class, a cravat and formal shirt visible between the collars of his coat. Mindful that both horses are still saddled, you quickly scan behind him, looking to see if he has company. It seems he is alone.

Will you:	
Ask what he is doing here?	117
Ask if his companion is lost?	136
Demand that he hands over his sword and gold?	30

74

Your final blow smashes through the skeleton's ribcage, sending it stumbling back into the nearest wall. Reaching out, you grab the medallion and yank it free. The moment the medallion is removed, the skeleton ceases its rattling throes and crumbles into a cloud of grave dust.

You may now take any/all of the following items:

Drust's medallion	Greenstone axe
(necklace)	(left hand: axe)
+1 magic	+1 brawn

Searching the rest of the chamber, you manage to uncover 5 gold crowns but little else of worth. Disappointed with your finds, you decide to leave the tomb. Turn to 215.

75

The performers appear to be a family. The wife is playing a flute, whilst the two sons beat a steady rhythm on their drums. The crowd cheer and gasp as the orator, a thin, balding man dressed in white robes, hops agilely onto one of the tables.

'Come,' said Allam, 'join my side! Swords are no good, to fight this tide.' He raises a wooden sword above his head, pulling an exaggerated frown. 'We must cast down our weapons to win this day. We must show our faith, to keep them at bay!' He tosses the sword aside as the drumbeat gets louder. 'I call upon your faith. Do you believe? Question all that you perceive?' He sweeps a hand across the crowd, his eyes sparkling with zealotry. 'What about you? You?' His finger stabs at various onlookers, who raise their mugs and call out, goading him on.

The drumming stops abruptly, the soft notes of the flute rising into a sonorous melody.

'Behold, the light! The One God's might! It will smite our foes with zeal!' With a flourish the orator throws up his arms, sending gold dust billowing into the air. Then he falls into a crouch, his expression serious. 'Our fists are now our hardened steel; our bodies the—' He throws a punch, losing his balance as his foot slips on a patch of ale. With a squeal, he falls backwards off the table, much to the amusement of the crowd. They are all clapping and stamping their feet, although it is clear that the mishap was not part of the show. However the performer skilfully recovers, springing back with a flurry of kicks and punches. 'Behold, my fists of light. With these fair hands, I will bring the fight!' Urged on by the crowd the orator continues to battle his unseen enemy, assuming various exaggerated poses to much cheering and applause.

The show continues, but your attention has already wandered back to the taproom. Turn to 47.

76

'An unfortunate mistake on my part,' says the witchfinder, his hungry eyes flicking to your wound. You step away warily. 'I'm sorry,' he smiles weakly, putting a hand to his mouth. 'I haven't ... I haven't taken blood. You don't have to worry.'

You frown, your grip still tight around your weapons. 'Isn't that what your kind needs – craves? It's what keeps you alive.'

The witchfinder leans forward, his pale eyes glimmering like stars in the lantern light. 'I am dying. Can't you see that? I have very little strength – my sight is ...' He clenches his fists, looking away; greasy strands of hair fall across his face. 'I cannot tell you what it is like; the hunger is ... indescribable. But I will not ... become a monster.'

Turn to **347** to ask Eldias another question. When you are ready to continue, turn to **340**.

77

Reaching the summit, you find yourself on a windswept plaza. Various stately-looking buildings crowd in on a wide paved square, dominated by a tall statue of a man. A group of pilgrims are kneeling before the statue, offering prayer. Two guards stand either side of it, watching the pilgrims warily.

To the left of the square, rising high above the buildings, is a church – a sprawling arrangement of golden domes and white towers, glowing with holy scripture. Such a building alone would be the talking point of most towns and cities, but your attention is already being drawn across the square, to the dark castle that juts out of the murky gloom. It is clearly dwarven, with sharp angles and points, making it look more like a vast stone arrowhead than a place of habitation.

Next to it, a narrow bridge leads out across a vertiginous drop to an outcropping of rock. There a single tower stands in eerie isolation, its cracked stonework patched with moss and ivy.

As you ponder your next move, you spot a man weaving between the crowds. An open satchel hangs at his side, filled with rolls of parchment. 'Keep to the path of the righteous!' he calls. 'Let Mendo's maps lead you to the light!'

Will you:

Examine the statue?	84
Explore the church?	111
Investigate the castle?	65
Cross the bridge to the tower?	139
Talk to the map-seller?	99
Leave Carvel?	**Turn to the Act 1 map**

78

You are about to leave when Benin takes your arm, leading you into a secluded corner of the nave. 'I spoke to the bishop,' he says, dropping his voice to a whisper. 'I found out what happened.'

You nod, urging him to say more.

'It was a *dwarf*,' he grimaces with evident distaste. 'I thought such vermin were wiped out long ago – by their pagan magics and constant warring.'

'Perhaps the bishop was mistaken,' you venture.

Benin frowns. 'I know the bishop. He is an honest man.'

'So, the dwarf was the one who cursed him? The one who made the charm?'

Benin nods. 'Both the bishop and your Wiccan thief were struck down with the curse. The dwarf escaped unharmed – and took the relic with it.'

'Seems a lot of fuss over some old artefact. What does it do?'

'I don't know.' Benin glances warily over his shoulder. 'It was discovered by a group of inquisitors, in some ruins to the south. They said the place was haunted – corrupted by old magic. The relic was brought here, to the church, so that our scholars might learn more about it, keep it safe.' He drops his gaze. 'Now it is lost to us.'

'But were there no clues?' you ask intently. 'Perhaps we can track this dwarf. Find out what happened?'

Benin sighs, then straightens, forcing a smile. 'You have already done enough for us. Thank you, my friend – but this is a matter for the inquisition now.' He gestures to the entrance of the church, implying your conversation is now at an end. Grudgingly, you decide not to pursue the topic. After bidding Benin farewell, you leave the church and resume your journey. (Return to the map.)

79

You descend a set of creaking stairs into the cramped crew's quarters. Several bunk beds and hammocks line the walls, with a table and bench nailed to the centre of the room.

You search the beds, looking for any clues that might explain what happened to the original crew. To your surprise, a few items have escaped the goblins' attention. The first is a note, which looks to have been torn out of a journal. It reads:

The storm is getting worse, I fear. Some of the crew want to turn back. For once I am in agreement – I don't see how we can navigate the Sisters in such weather. But Betsy is adamant. I think if any captain could, perhaps it is her. I will say another prayer to the One God. Let His light guide us to safety.

You also find a red bandanna hanging from a bed post and a small gold ring caught in the crack between two floor boards.

'Ugh!' shrieks one of your team. 'You gotta be kidding me!' You turn to see them backing away from a bunk bed. Resting on the lower mattress is a human hand preserved in a bottle of vinegar. 'Who would want to keep *that*?' they grimace.

If you wish, you may take one of the following items:

Marauder's bandanna	Motley band	Luke's left hand
(head)	(ring)	(talisman)
+1 brawn	+1 brawn +1 magic	Ability: high five!
	Ability: sneak	

Finding little else of interest in the crew's quarters, you head back to the deck. Turn to 159.

80

'I am a priest, devoted to the One God,' says Benin, proudly. 'My power comes from within – from my kha.' He glances around at the smoking circle of devastation. 'I prefer to use my powers for good – for healing – but there are times when more … direct measures are required.'

Will you:	
Ask Benin what he is doing here?	57
Examine the remains of the creatures?	133
Continue on your journey?	157

81

You are able to make sense of the complex runes and glyphs. They provide a powerful set of enchantments designed to punish unruly spirits. If you wish, you may take the following item:

Book of Binding
(backpack)
This ancient tome might
prove useful in the future

You find little else of interest amongst the other books and scrolls. You may now examine the parchment on the table (turn to 362) or leave the room via the iron door (turn to 46).

82

'What's there to know about Carvel, dearie?' The woman frowns, screwing up her face. 'It's the end of the road – the cross on the map – for those looking for some place better. Allam was the first, a prophet and a king's son. Brought the whole army here on some holy crusade. Well, he pops his clogs and now look what we got,' she nods to her boisterous clientele, who are currently singing a bawdy song about a barmaid and a saint. 'I followed one of them here; a simple man with dreams of making a new start. He didn't find what he was looking for, but I did.' She lifts up her hands, gesturing to her surroundings. 'I suppose love got me something worthwhile, in the end.'

Return to 52 to ask the bar woman another question.

83

You drop the bark shavings into the mixture and stir it around with one of the spoons. To your surprise the bark quickly dissolves into the liquid, giving off a pungent-smelling steam. As you continue to observe your creation, the mixture starts to change colour – going from green to brown, then to a bright golden-yellow. You hold it up, marvelling at the shimmering magic that seems to dance around the bottle. Could this be the cure? It certainly looks like you have created a powerful elixir of some description. You must now take:

Unknown elixir (1 use)
(backpack)
This could be the miracle
cure that Eldias needs

With your work in the laboratory complete, you hurry back to the church. Turn to 372.

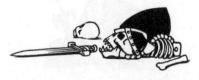

84

The statue shows a young man in his early twenties, dressed in long decorative robes. In his right hand he holds a staff; in the other a book. A marble plaque at the foot of the statue reads:

Saint Allam Medes
Third blood of King Gerard I
Pray for the soul of the prophet.
By his will and faith
the One God's light was brought to
the west.

One of the guards steps forward, his hand tightening around his sword grip. 'Not too close, stranger. No one touches the statue.' He scowls at the rows of pilgrims that are kneeling in prayer. 'Someone tried to deface it last week. A Wiccan disguised as a pilgrim. Trust no one.' He glares at you intently, until you move away from the statue.

Turn to 77 to continue your exploration of upper town.

85

You have chosen the path of the rogue. You may permanently increase your *health* by 5 (to 35). Make a note of this change on your hero sheet. Then turn to 182.

86

You smash through the shield, severing the shadow warrior cleanly in two. As you stagger back, breathing hard from the fight, you hear the voice once again in your ear.

'The Wiccan will endure. Our legacy will live on.'

The shadows wind their way across the stony ground. When they reach the far wall they creep up the cracked stonework, forming a doorway of midnight black.

'Your head is full of stones,' hisses the voice. 'Fill it with memory.'

You take a step towards the door. Suddenly the torches go out, throwing the room into freezing darkness. A second later they reignite, their blue radiance falling on a vast array of treasures. Somehow you have been transported to an ancient vault, beneath the hill.

There is the sound of grating, squealing rock. You turn around to see a short passageway, leading up to a circle of daylight . . . but, alarmingly, you see that the circle is growing smaller, threatening to trap you here forever. You realise that you have mere seconds to grab what you can from the Wiccan warrior's tomb.

To your left is a pile of weapons and armour. To your right is a long oak chest, inlaid with runes of iron.

Will you:

Search the weapons and armour?	50
Open the chest?	34

87

You emerge in a huge cavern, brightly lit by luminous mushrooms growing along the walls. It is hard to get a sense of scale, even with the light – the ceiling is lost from view, somewhere in the chill darkness above. The wind provides the only sound in this vast space, making an eerie moaning sound as it whistles between the rocks and channels.

Warily, the party progresses across the cavern. After a hundred metres you hear Surl making a disgusted grunt. His foot is caught in something green and sticky. As he tugs his foot loose, he pokes at the slime with his sword.

'What's this? he sniffs. 'Hey, we got some goblin snot!'

'Shut it,' growls the captain, eyeing his surroundings warily. 'I heard something . . .'

Everyone is silent, turning slowly on the spot. For a moment all you can hear is the murmur of the wind, then you hear something else – a skittering, metallic sound. It is hard to make out where it is coming from. Slowly, your eyes are drawn upwards, towards the dark ceiling . . .

Then you hear a cry from behind you. Spinning around, you manage to catch sight of the young mage being dragged into the air, kicking and flailing. He is lost from sight in seconds.

'What is it?' shouts Vas, falling into a crouch. 'I don't see—'

There is another scream, as one of the party is hit by something – it looks like a stream of green sticky goo. They are slammed back onto the ground. Then another streaks out of the dark, hitting the unfortunate mercenary and yanking them off their feet. You are about to run to their aid . . . then all hell breaks loose.

From above you, more gooey threads rain down from the dark. Several hit members of the group, who barely have time to register their shock before being tugged upwards by some powerful force.

'Move it!' bellows the captain. He raises his shield just in time to block one of the sticky strands. It splats across the face of the shield, which is ripped from his grasp and goes hurtling back up into the darkness. 'Give us some covering fire. Artillery!'

He races forward, the others following, while one of the remaining mages hurls a blazing ball of fire across the cavern. As the flames arch overhead, they illuminate the ceiling of the cave for the briefest of moments – and there, scuttling over the dark rock, is a swarm of giant insects.

'Ants!' shouts Surl. 'Bloomin' ants! Run!'

To dodge the gooey missiles you will need to take a *speed* challenge:

	Speed
Outrun the slime	10

If you are successful, turn to **186**. If you fail the *speed* challenge, turn to **281**.

88

You hand over the *household spirit*, much to Anna's delight. 'Oh, this is wonderful!' she gasps, clutching it tightly to her cheek. 'Oh, I never thought my dear twins would be reunited. Here, take one of my special remedies as a reward for your kindness!'

You may now choose one of the following:

Healing salve (2 uses)	Elixir of life (1 use)
(backpack)	(backpack)
Restores 2 *health* at the start of every combat round for one combat	Use any time in combat to restore your *health* to full

(You can now remove the *household spirit* from your hero sheet.) If you wish to view Anna's other wares, turn to 120. Otherwise, you may now leave the shop and head to upper town (turn to 77) or to lower town (turn to 36).

89

The woman stiffens at your question, looking personally insulted. Polk quickly intercedes. 'A fair question,' he proffers, nodding his head. 'Why would you risk your life for us? I asked *you* because you don't look like a mercenary lap dog. All of them out there,' he waves a thumb at the bustling taproom, 'got more space in their heads than a beggar's bank vault. You see, when we're talking the shroud,' he drops his voice to almost a whisper, 'we're talking treasure. Rare magic. Things you can sell on for a pretty penny or two.' His eyes flick to Joss. 'And sure, we're doing a good deed too.'

'But why not hire a whole band of mercenaries?' You frown, bunching your shoulders. 'Pay them for their muscle, not their wits.'

Polk glances at Anse – the two warriors share a knowing smile. 'And I thought you was bright, kid. Look, mercenaries talk. Once word got out that a tower – that's been missing for forty years – suddenly shows back up … every treasure hunter and thief in Valeron will be descending on it like flies on a meat wagon. And what's more, the inquisitors will soon have that place locked down when they get wind of it. So we have a narrow window of opportunity, see, get what I'm saying?'

Will you:

Ask about Anse's strange markings?	270
Ask about the shroud?	238
Agree to the mission?	24

90

'We are here to train the wayward flock,' he grins, showing off the gemstones embedded in his teeth. 'Old magic and the Church – it's an uneasy alliance we have. *They* favour the magic of the one – the magic that comes from within.' He prods your chest with a finger, then grimaces as he wipes his hand on his coat. 'But our magic comes from the elements; from the shroud.'

Malak's head lolls to one side, his eyes half-closed. 'You test my patience. Such things can be learnt from a book; go find a library and appease your ignorance there.'

Will you:

Insist he tells you more about the 'shroud'?	27
Ask about the testing?	213
Leave and return to upper town?	77

91

With the beast defeated you may now choose one of the following rewards:

Stone blood	Windbreaker	Dark vein bracers
(talisman)	(left hand: shield)	(gloves)
+1 armour	+1 speed +1 armour	+1 speed
Ability: heal		

Exhausted from the fight, you drop to your knees in the snow, your breath coming in fitful gasps. Behind you there is the crunch of booted feet. Someone kneels close beside you, putting a hand on your arm. You hear words being spoken but you cannot make them out … a white noise is roaring in your ears. Feeling dizzy, you sway backwards. The grip on your arm tightens. You see a face, eyes glinting behind the slanted holes of a black mask.

Then darkness takes you.

The forest is vast, stretching away in every direction as far as the eye can see. But not an ordinary forest. This place reeks of corruption, an all-pervading sense of doom that infects the very air, chilling your skin and gnawing at your soul. It is the trees. A warped and misshapen mass of thorny branches, twisted into unnatural shapes. There is some malign sentience to this forest, as if it is alive, a single creature with a single purpose …

You struggle through the wiry branches, aware that the thorns are ripping at your clothes, scratching at your skin. But you must keep moving. There is a darkness at your back and the light is ahead of you, promising freedom.

'Free me …' A voice in your head. A whisper.

At last you break out of the trees, stumbling into a clearing. The light is blinding, a radiant pillar of whiteness that rises up from the craggy earth into the star-lit heavens. Tired from your journey, you stagger and fall, dragging yourself across the ground towards the light. Somehow you know this is the reason you are here.

A voice, back in the forest, calls out. You can't make out the words but they sound like a warning. You ignore it, crawling onwards … ever onwards toward the light.

'Free me . . .' The voice in your head. Persistent. Commanding.

You manage to find your feet, stumbling into the light, hands held out blindly before your face. Then the light is gone. You feel powerful tendrils wrapping around your body. A snake-like face hovers before your own, its mouth widening to reveal yellowed fangs. You try and scream but there is no breath left in your body. The breaking, snapping sound is your bones, shattering like the dead wood of the forest.

In the distance, a lone voice calls.

You jerk awake to find yourself lying on a comfortable mattress, covered in thick blankets of fur. Bright sunlight filters through the shutters of a window, falling across the man who is watching you intently from the end of your bed. He is tall and handsome, his blond hair cascading across broad shoulders. The face, the smile, seem strangely familiar.

'Well, I see you have woken at last,' he smirks, rubbing absently at a bruise along his left cheek. Jewelled rings sparkle from his fingers. 'I was starting to wonder if Jeeves would have to sing to get you to rise. And trust me – that would be a last resort.'

'Who are you?' you ask hoarsely, pushing yourself up in the bed.

'I have a few names about town,' he grins. 'But Lazlo is my birth name. Will that suffice?'

Something of his manner pulls at a memory. Then realisation dawns. 'You were the masked man!' you exclaim, eyes widening.

Lazlo spreads his arms and takes a formal bow. 'Indeed I am,' he smiles impishly.

Will you:

Ask him about the strange dream? 62
Enquire as to your whereabouts? 9
Ask about Carvel's 'masked crusader'? 39

92

You go to touch the splinter of wood but Anna reaches forward quickly, knocking your hand away. 'Do not touch it!' she snaps angrily. 'Stay well away from it.'

'But it's just a burnt piece of bark,' you shrug. 'Does it have anything to do with him?'

The woman follows your gaze to the man lying on the bed. 'That … *bark* as you call it, is part of a very powerful charm. When it was broken it released a hex – a curse. This man will die in a matter of a few hours unless I break the spell.' She fixes you with a determined stare. 'It won't be easy – and I need your help.'

Will you:	
Ask about the patient?	115
Ask about the crates in the other room?	35
Ask what you need to do?	130

93

You remember the story you overheard in 'The Pilgrim's Rest' about the valuable sword that had been left behind. Seeing your chance to acquire this treasure, you quickly raise your hand, offering to join Surl and the mage. The captain nods then gives you a hearty shove, sending you staggering forward into the camp. 'Get to it then, runt!'

With weapons at the ready, the three of you search the cabins. It appears that everything – cupboards, shelves, chests – has already been rifled through and anything of value taken, including food. There are a few signs that a fight took place – sword nicks in a wall, a scorched area of floor and arrows protruding from a makeshift shield.

From outside, you hear the captain bellowing orders.

'Time to go,' growls Surl, sheathing his blade and hurrying out of the cabin. The mage scurries to catch up. You are about to follow, when you notice one of the beds at the end of the barracks has not been vandalised. It was probably missed by the goblins. You walk over to investigate, wondering if you might still have a chance to find the woodman's sword.

Above the bed hangs a painting of a brown-haired girl, holding a posy of flowers to her nose. As you step closer to inspect it, your eyes are caught by a leather strap protruding from underneath one of the pillows.

Will you:	
Investigate the painting?	109
Look under the pillow?	170

94

'Ah yes, our good friends – the zombies.' The witchfinder glances back towards the latticed window, where dark shapes are moving behind the glass. 'I've managed to piece together what happened here. It appears that the well water was poisoned.'

'Poisoned!' You blink back surprise. 'Why? Who would do that to an entire village?'

Eldias gives you a look from the corner of his eye. 'I've seen worse acts of revenge.'

'Revenge for what?'

The witchfinder gestures to the piles of papers and books. 'They discovered that one of their number was a vampire. His name was Rorus Satch, an unassuming man who liked to study herbs. He was just unlucky – met the wrong person. He was bitten.' Eldias leans his neck to one side, rubbing it with his hand. 'I know the feeling.'

'So he poisoned the well? Because they found him out?'

The witchfinder smiles. 'It was actually his apprentice. Who then fled the village. But I don't think it really matters now – do you?'

Turn to 347 to ask Eldias another question. When you are ready to continue, turn to 340.

95

Clutching your items you turn and race up the passageway, towards the shrinking circle of light. Just as it is about to close you throw yourself forward, hands grappling at the rotting roots and earth. You stagger through the hole, turning to watch as it snaps closed, leaving no trace of a secret passageway. Facing you is a solid mound, as nondescript as the others in the barrows.

Overcome with elation at your hair-raising escape, you give a whoop of joy, punching the air.

It is then you hear a wolf-like snarl.

Your heart skips a beat. Slowly, you turn on the spot, the stench of wet fur drifting on the wind. The giant dire wolf is watching you with its glittering amber eyes, spit drooling from its fangs. The beast has waited for you. And once again, there is no escape.

But something has changed in you now. After your ordeal in the burial mound you feel different – more confident in your abilities. You have the chieftain's treasures to aid you – fine equipment from a bygone age; from a bygone hero.

You fall into a battle stance, meeting its stare. For a brief instant the wolf's forehead wrinkles, as if displaying surprise at your sudden show of courage. Then its eyes narrow. Throwing back its head, the beast emits a knee-trembling howl – and then pounces in a savage blur of snapping teeth! It is time to fight:

	Speed	*Brawn*	*Armour*	*Health*
Dire wolf	1	2	2	20

If you manage to defeat this fearsome predator, turn to 106.

96

You study the trunk of the tree, noting its many stubs and protrusions, which will help you in your climb. With a route planned, you place one foot against the gnarled wood and begin your ascent.

Once you reach the halfway mark, you find yourself struggling to find adequate supports. Several times a hand or a foot slips, making your stomach reel as you glimpse the ground far below. If this is a replica of a real tree, then the craftsman was obviously a skilled climber. To reach the top you will need to pass a *speed* challenge:

	Speed
Tree hugger	10

If you are successful, turn to **15**. Otherwise, turn to **306**.

97

The steam escapes in hissing geysers from the newly-opened pipes. Virgil flashes you a gold-toothed smile. 'And here was me thinking you was all hot air ...'

Congratulations, you have solved the puzzle and improved your chances of defeating the fire sprites! Make a note of the keyword *wind breaker* on your hero sheet and the number 350. You may now examine the cogs and pulleys, if you haven't already (turn to **786**) or head up the stairs to the forge (turn to **601**).

98

'Oh, that,' smiles Anna, her mood suddenly brightening. 'It's dwarven – a household spirit. It's meant to bring good luck and prosperity.' She takes it down from the shelf, turning it over in her hands. 'A traveller gave it to me. I've done some research since and, apparently, they're always crafted in twos. Somewhere, there is the twin of this one. I would so dearly like to have the set.'

Anna proudly places the statue back above the door. 'He does look lonely up there, all on his own. Perhaps one day, I'll find the other.'

Will you:

Ask about what happened to the thief?	**54**
Ask about what is in the casket?	**26**
Thank Anna and leave?	**Return to the map**

99

The map-seller greets you with an exaggerated flourish. 'Mendo and his magnificent maps, at your service.' He rummages through his pack. 'Adventurer – yes, let's see. How about a map of Carvel, made by my own fair hand.' He takes out a roll of parchment and unravels it, revealing a detailed map of the town.

'Five gold crowns for the map – you won't find a better bargain.' He glances around at the nearby guards, then leans a little closer. 'Cross my palm with a little extra gold and maybe I'll share some gossip with you.'

Will you:

Purchase a map for 5 gold crowns?	250
Pay 3 gold crowns to listen to rumours?	140
Turn your attention back to upper town?	77

100

The grey-stone buildings of the village huddle close to the muddy track, each one as dark and silent as the next. You go up to the nearest house and bang on the front door. You wait and knock again, aware of the silence settling around you, broken only by the persistent drumming of the rain. Putting your face to one of the dirt-streaked windows, you try and see inside, but your eyes cannot penetrate the gloom.

You continue onwards, turning a corner to find yourself in the village square. At the centre stands a solitary well, its cracked stonework overrun with weeds and moss. Across the square a set of stairs wind up a dark finger of rock, leading to a church dimly visible at its summit. For a moment, you are almost sure you can hear organ music coming from within – then a gargling cry rips your attention away, to one of the side streets.

Something is shuffling towards you. A woman, in a mud-stained dress. Her blond hair hangs limp across her pale face, its tangled length matted with leaves and filth. Behind her you can see other figures, perhaps half a dozen or more, all sharing the same dishevelled appearance and shambling gait.

'You've got to be kidding me . . .'

You draw your weapons as the woman staggers closer. Her dull eyes are devoid of life, her skin almost translucent. A grey tongue lolls from her mouth as her jaw slowly cracks open, revealing rotted black teeth.

Then she gives a piercing scream – a hellish sound that turns your blood to ice. It is a call that is immediately taken up all over the village, ringing from every direction. It is joined by the patter of feet . . . running, scrambling, clattering over the stones. You start to back away, looking around frantically. Then you see them, spilling out of the side streets – more and more people, ragged and thin, snarling and howling like wild animals. They are closing in from all sides.

Will you:

Stand your ground and fight the zombies? 66

Look for shelter in a nearby building? 185

101

'Prince Lazlo?' The map-seller jerks a thumb in the direction of the wedge-shaped castle. 'The black sheep of the family – not too different to Allam, back in his day. Brought enough scandal already on the king's household with his womanising and gambling. Yeah, a real wild card. Why else do you think the king would send him out to this backwater? To keep him out of the way, that's what. At least here, Lazlo can do whatever he wants without making a fool of his betters.'

Will you:

Ask about the 'troubles'? 68

Ask for more news ? 137

102

The prince leads you briskly down a series of corridors, the dark stone walls crowded with tapestries. You glimpse a few rooms off to either side, each one an empty cobwebbed space devoid of furniture – devoid of life.

'I try not to spend too much time here, if I can help it,' states the prince, throwing open a set of double doors. 'I like to travel – see new places.'

You pass through a long draughty hall, filled with racks of weapons and polished armour. Your steps falter as you find your attention wandering across the sumptuous array of weaponry. 'This is quite the collection,' you gasp. 'Are these from your travels?'

When you receive no answer, you look back to see the prince waiting for you at the end of the chamber. You hurry to catch up.

'After you.' The prince bows, gesturing for you to step through the archway.

The next room is circular, lit by rainbow light shimmering through the stained-glass windows. Like many of the previous rooms you have seen, there is no furniture or decoration – only a set of stairs leading up to a raised dais. At the foot of the stairs is a wooden rack with swords, greatswords, daggers and poleaxes resting between its posts.

'What is this?' you ask, looking around warily.

'My games room,' smiles Lazlo, striding towards the stairs. He grabs a sword from the rack, testing its weight and balance. He grins, spinning the grip in his hand. 'Want to play?'

You follow him up the stairs, onto the stone platform. Drawing your weapons, you watch him carefully, suspecting a trick. The prince circles you, following the edge of the dais. 'One of my good friends made this for me,' he grins. 'A mage – Avian Dale.'

He utters a word of magic and suddenly the dais lifts up into the air with a grating rumble. You almost lose your footing as it ascends above the floor of the chamber, rotating slowly. Stepping to the edge, you look over the side to see that the platform is floating on a cushion of magic.

'Neat trick, eh?' The prince clicks his fingers. Suddenly, the air around you starts to crackle and hiss, charged with powerful magics.

'What's happening?' you ask, confused, struggling to keep your balance as the circle gives a sudden lurch.

'A lesson,' says Lazlo. His eyes glint mischievously. 'Be aware of your opponent – but be doubly aware of your environment.'

At that moment, veins of lightning crackle over the surface of the stone. Lazlo sidesteps them easily, moving to a clear space. You, however, are caught by one of the bolts. You give a startled cry as a sudden shock of pain lances through your body.

'I thought you were fast?' grins the prince, advancing across the circle. 'Now, let's see what you're really made of.' Your weapons clash, as the disc starts to spin faster, sending more crackling bolts across the stone. It is time to fight:

	Speed	*Brawn*	*Armour*	*Health*
Lazlo	5	4	2	40

Special abilities

- Shock treatment: If any combatant rolls a double for their attack speed (before or after a reroll), they are automatically hit by the lightning and must lose 4 *health*, ignoring *armour*.
- In a spin: If you win a combat round, roll a die. If you get a ⚀ or ⚁ then you have lost your balance and your strike misses its mark. You cannot roll for damage and the combat round ends. ⚂ or more and you can roll for damage as normal.

If you manage to defeat the prince, turn to 286. If you are defeated, turn to 261.

103

The archers are already in position, sending a shower of arrows towards your party. One of your number takes a shaft in the chest, flying back off the rocks and splashing down into the murky waters. After taking cover behind a boulder, you summon magic to the palms of your hands and prepare to fight back.

(In this ranged combat you must use your *magic* to determine your damage score.)

	Speed	*Brawn*	*Armour*	*Health*
Archers	2	2	0	20

Special abilities

- Ranged foe: You cannot use speed or combat abilities in this combat.

If you manage to defeat the goblin archers, turn to 258.

104

You add the ingredient to the liquid. However, it only takes a few minutes of stirring for you to realise that you have made a mistake. The liquid is now giving off a bitter smell, having turned lumpy and sour. You will need to start again.

If you wish to try and create another potion then turn to 361. Otherwise, you can leave the laboratory and visit the reverend's house (turn to 210) or the herbalist's cottage (turn to 224).

105

Your weapons and magic soon reduce this sorrowful creature to a pile of sawdust and tattered fur. Searching through the shredded remains you find one of the following items:

Grizzly mantle	**Sawdust 'n stitches**	**Maker's button**
(cloak)	(chest)	(talisman)
+1 brawn	+1 speed +1 armour	+1 speed
Ability: savagery	Ability: heartless	

There is a dull rumbling sound as the east wall slowly swings outwards, revealing a narrow stone passageway. You hurry through, eager to find your companions.

The passageway is short, ending in a rusty metal door. It has already been pushed open, leaving a yellow-brown stain where it has scraped across the stone. A can of oil rests on the floor next to it, which someone evidently used to help grease its hinges. There is still some oil inside. (If you wish you can take the *can of oil*, simply make a note of it on your hero sheet, it doesn't take up backpack space.) You pass through the open door, grateful that one of your problems has been solved, at least. Turn to 304.

106

Anticipating the wolf's savage attacks, you are able to dextrously weave between its snapping jaws and fearsome claws. The beast is powerful, but your attacks are faster and more precise. The battle is over in a matter of heartbeats; the wolf's blood-spattered corpse lies sprawled at your feet.

You may now help yourself to one of the following rewards:

Dire claw	Predator's pelt	Wolf bone vest
(left hand: dagger)	(cloak)	(chest)
+1 brawn +1 magic	+1 brawn	+1 speed +1 armour

With the beast of the barrows defeated you decide to return to Carvel, proudly displaying your newfound weapons and trophies. (Return to the map to continue your adventure.)

107

'We tried that,' sighs the leader, scratching the back of his head. 'Went to the church at Carvel. They were good to us – gave us money for food. But this one decides to go gamble it all away, don't he.' He waves a hand at the youngest boy who looks away ashamedly.

'I'm good at it,' he mutters. 'Not my fault the man cheated.'

The leader shakes his head. 'The church weren't interested then. So that's that – out on our own. Can't get no help or mercy from those inquisitors. They look at us like dirt . . .' He glances down at his ragged clothing. 'I suppose we *are* dirt.'

Will you:

Ask them to tell you more about the Wiccans?	162
Ask about Raven's Rest?	319
Give them a gift of 5 gold crowns?	326
Leave and continue your journey?	199

108

With one eye on the portal, which could disappear at any second, you set about searching through the scattered junk. There is very little of value amongst the musty-smelling odds and ends, but you do manage to uncover a velvet pouch containing 10 gold crowns. You also find a clay jar labelled 'extra-sticky glue'. The lid has become stuck tight. You will have to take a *brawn* test in order to open it:

	Brawn
A sticky problem	9

If you are successful, turn to 222. Otherwise turn to 165.

109

You lift the painting away from the wall, discovering that it is much heavier than it looks. Turning it over, you find an elegant short sword strapped to the frame. Tugging it loose, you hold your find up to the light. The hilt and guard are decorated with silver leaves, while the metal of the blade shines with a pale green lustre. You may now take the following item:

Sword of the dales
(left hand: sword)
+1 brawn +1 magic
Ability: heal

Outside you hear the captain's gruff voice, barking orders once again. Not wishing to be on the receiving end of a tongue-lashing, you quickly leave the cabin. Turn to 220.

110

You have chosen the path of the warrior. You may permanently increase your *health* by 15 (to 45). Make a note of this change on your hero sheet. Then turn to 182.

111

Six stone angels flank the double doors that lead into the church. As you pass through, into a wide circular nave, you find your footsteps faltering as you gaze in wonderment at the breath-taking vista before you.

Light falls in bright shafts from the crystals set into the ceiling, converging on a large fountain that sits at the centre of the nave. From its angelic statue, water tumbles out into channels, forming a series of interlinked waterways. Small bridges span the water, their intricate lattice work gleaming with a pale radiance.

Heading around the nave you see white-robed priests and acolytes in adjoining chambers, poring over scrolls or kneeling in prayer. A woven tapestry hangs across one wall, where a number of travellers are stood scrutinising the embroidered scenes. Nearby a man sits alone on a bench, his head held in his hands.

Will you:

Inspect the tapestry?	181
Talk to the man?	152
Leave the church?	77

112

With your obstacle removed, you are finally able to reach the gemstones. As you brush the dust from their jagged faces, you see that they are actually razor-sharp diamonds. (If you wish to take the *diamonds* simply make a note of them on your hero sheet, they do not take up backpack space.) With little else of interest in this chamber, you decide to leave.

Will you:

Leave via the stairs?	46
Return to the passage and try the wooden door?	4

113

You wonder if something interesting might be hidden inside one of these dark cavities. There are a number of holes to choose from. Roll a die. If the result is ⚀ or ⚁ turn to 1, ⚂ or ⚃ turn to 145, ⚄ or ⚅ turn to 233.

114

You add the ingredient to the liquid. However, it only takes a few minutes of stirring for you to realise that you have made a mistake. The liquid is now giving off a bitter smell, having turned lumpy and sour. You will need to start again.

If you wish to try and create another potion then turn to 361. Otherwise, you can leave the laboratory and visit the reverend's house (turn to 210) or the herbalist's cottage (turn to 224).

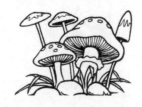

115

'He is known in these parts as Jolando: an assassin, a sword for hire.' Anna takes an oil lamp from the table and holds it closer to the man's face. You notice white scars cutting vivid lines across his cheeks and chin. 'This man is a thief . . . and a murderer.'

You step away, momentarily startled. 'This is an assassin and you would have me help him? Why?'

Anna places the lamp by the bedside. 'He was doing a job for the Wiccans. I made the contact myself.' She glances at you, nervously gauging your reaction. 'I happen to believe in their cause, as do many others in Carvel.'

You shrug your shoulders. 'You helped me; that is all that matters.'

Anna nods. 'That is good. I am putting a lot of trust in you.'

Will you:

Ask about the strange object on the table?	92
Ask about the crates in the other room?	35
Ask what you need to do?	130

116

Many of the male warriors are stripped to the waist, their muscled bodies displaying a dazzling array of painted patterns. A female notices you and strides over. Her lithe body is wrapped in thin bands of black cloth, leaving little to the imagination. Like the men, her pale skin is daubed with intricate designs.

'The runes make us strong,' she says, pointing to one of the women who is crushing berries and powder into a bowl. 'If you fight with us, Sanchen, then you become real Wiccan.'

Will you:

Learn the brigand career (requirement: warrior)?	446
Decline and explore the rest of the cave?	485

117

'Hopefully, about to fill my stomach with rabbit stew,' the old man replies. You flinch as he leans closer to his pack, his hand passing over the jewelled sword. But he doesn't take it. Instead, he simply lifts a pouch from a side pocket. 'Salt,' he grins, bouncing it in his hand.

Suddenly, you hear a bellowing roar coming from somewhere deep inside the rock. It is followed by a cry and a loud ground-trembling boom. The man hesitates for a second, glancing up at the rock behind him. Then he sets about adding salt to the stew as if nothing untoward has happened.

'What was that?' you ask worriedly.

'What was what?' asks the gentleman, stirring the stew. 'Would you like some tea? I brewed some earlier. Silver Grey, the finest.'

There is another monstrous roar, dislodging stone and dust from the rock walls. The man moves around the fire and settles down on a blanket. 'You can join me if you like,' he says, raising a cup of steaming tea to his lips. 'I plan on being here for a while.'

Will you:

Join him by the fire?	187
Ask about the disturbance?	156

118

'Stop gawping and get searching this ship,' barks the captain, glaring at the remnants of his rag-tag band. 'I want some answers to this sorry mess!' He stabs a finger in the direction of the poop deck. 'What yer waiting for, a cannonball up yer rear? Move it!'

You must now decide which search party you will join.

Will you:

Search the captain's cabin?	264
Investigate the crew's quarters?	79
Explore the cargo hold?	189

119

'My name is Polk,' says the bearded warrior, glancing back over his shoulder. 'And I'm the chatty one, trust me.' He stops next to the curtained alcove, gesturing to his full mugs. 'Any chance you could do the honours?' he asks. 'I think I spilled enough beer in this place already.'

You reach forward and pull back the curtain. Turn to 135.

120

(If you have the word *hallowed* written on your hero sheet, turn to 161.)

A bell rings as the door is opened, revealing a small room littered with crates and sacks. Squeezed in amongst the clutter rests a narrow table, covered in various pastes, liquids and powders.

An elderly woman appears from a side room, wiping her hands with a cloth. She is short and stocky, with long grey hair twisted into dreadlocks. 'I'm very busy,' she adds curtly, peering at you over her spectacles. 'Everything's labelled, so no need for dawdling.'

The following are available for 10 gold crowns each:

Pot of healing (1 use)	Pot of brawn (1 use)	Pot of magic (1 use)
(backpack)	(backpack)	(backpack)
Use any time in combat to restore 4 *health*	Use any time in combat to raise your *brawn* by 2 for one combat round	Use any time in combat to raise your *magic* by 2 for one combat round

If you have the *household spirit*, then you can hand this over. Turn to 88. Otherwise, you may now leave the shop and head to upper town (turn to 77) or to lower town (turn to 36).

121

You add the ingredient to the liquid. However, it only takes a few minutes of stirring for you to realise that you have made a mistake. The liquid is now giving off a bitter smell, having turned lumpy and sour. You will need to start again.

If you wish to try and create another potion then turn to 361. Otherwise, you can leave the laboratory and visit the reverend's house (turn to 210) or the herbalist's cottage (turn to 224).

122

The tunnel eventually becomes a ledge, overlooking a vast subterranean lagoon. Its banks are littered with the bodies of dead ant-men – most of them little more than charred husks. From across the waters you see torches flickering on the deck of a pirate galleon, its black masts rippling in the chill wind.

'Well, would you look at that,' grins the captain, scratching his stubbly chin. 'How'd that end up here? Must have drifted in from the sea.'

'At least they look like they're on our side,' says Surl, skidding down the slope to investigate. 'Woah, this is a lot of bugs!'

Suddenly there is a flash of light from the ship, accompanied by a loud bang. Something is hurtling towards you, whistling through the air.

'Cover!' shouts the captain, dropping to the ground. Everyone scatters as an iron cannonball slams down onto the muddy bank, throwing up a thick plume of dirt and sand.

'They fired at us!' shouts Surl, staggering back to his feet. 'Why'd they do—'

'Goblins,' growls the captain angrily. 'Can't you smell 'em?'

'But the waters,' pleads one of the party, a young warrior who looks dwarfed in his ill-fitting heavy armour. 'I can't swim. I'll sink like a stone.'

'We don't need to! Follow me!' To everyone's surprise the captain starts running, following the ledge around the far side of the cavern.

You scan ahead, to see that the ledge ends in a jumble of rocks that jut out into the dark waters. It is there that the pirate ship has run aground, its stern raised up on the rocks.

Another cannonball hums through the air, landing in the water with a thunderous splash. Its aim may have been off but it provides all the incentive you need to throw yourself into a sprint, following the captain. The others take your lead, hurrying towards the outcropping.

At last, after scrambling over the sharp rocks, you see the deck of the ship only metres ahead of you. The captain was right; it is crawling with goblins. One of their number, wearing a pirate's tricorn hat, is trying to issue orders to the chaotic rabble. Archers are scrabbling up the rigging, whilst another group are struggling to turn a cannon, to aim it towards the rocks.

The captain doesn't slow, flinging himself through the air to land on the deck. He then quickly sets to work with his axe, battering away the defenders. You hastily consider your options.

Will you:

Use your magic to blast away at the archers?	103
Jump onto the deck and fight the cannon team?	71

123

You push open the door, your breath escaping in a surprised gasp as you look upon your new surroundings. The room, if room you could call it, is domed and circular – and carved entirely from wood. Its single, curving wall depicts an intricate, almost lifelike scene, showing a cart laden with toys travelling through rolling hills. A line of children run after it, giggling and laughing. The painstaking sculpture continues across the floor, where leaves and grasses have been carved out of the wood – and there, seemingly growing from its centre, is a column of oak, sculpted to look like a tree. Branches spread out towards the lofty ceiling, where you see a children's tree house perched on its highest limbs.

Moving closer to the tree you notice holes cut into its side, forming gnarled nooks and crannies. They are large enough to put your hand inside. Across the other side of the room, a white portal shimmers against the carved backdrop, inviting you to continue your journey.

Will you:	
Climb up to the tree house?	96
Put your hand in one of the holes?	113
Leave via the portal?	46

124

As the knight topples to his knees a column of sunlight breaks through the fog, streaming over his glistening armour. A voice whispers in your ear – *I am delivered. May the maker forgive me.*

The knight's armour falls to pieces, rattling across the hard black rock. Of his body there is no trace, save for a faint blue shadow, which rises like smoke into the sparkling light.

Congratulations, you have defeated the ghostly knight. Searching the remnants of his armour, you find 50 gold crowns and one of the following special rewards:

Frostreaver's tongue	Phantom gauntlets	Graven chill
(main hand: sword)	(gloves)	(necklace)
+1 speed +2 brawn	+1 speed +1 armour	+1 brawn +1 magic
Ability: silver frost	Ability: curse	Ability: frostbite

If you have the words *fallen knight* on your hero sheet, turn to 276. Otherwise, with your opponent defeated, you decide to leave this bleak region. Return to the quest map.

125

'The prince is back in town for the All Saint's celebrations. Word is he's digging into his own coffers for this year's festivities – they're going to be the best ever. Street entertainers, fireworks … it's what the people need to take their mind off the troubles.'

Will you:

Ask about the prince? 101
Ask about the 'troubles'? 68
Ask for more news? 137

126

You ascend the stairs to the rocky ledge. Golden sunlight floods the walls and ceiling, pouring in from an opening to the east. As you approach, you see that the ledge juts out from the side of the dark mountain, affording you a breath-taking view of the moorlands below.

Damaris stands alone at the edge, the wind whipping through her long grey hair and ruffling the black crow feathers sown into her braids. 'I'm glad to see your strength has returned,' she says, her eyes remaining fixed on the view. 'Tell me, Sanchen. What do you see?'

You move to her side, scanning the verdant wilderness, which glitters with rivers and lakes. 'I see a beautiful land,' you reply truthfully. 'But a little cold for my tastes.' You shiver, pulling your cloak tighter around your shoulders.

The woman glances sideways at you. 'What you see is Gilglaiden. The land that was ours – the land that belongs to the Wiccans.' Damaris places a hand on your arm, her bright eyes sparkling in the fading light. 'You come to us at the time of the crossing, when the fate of our people will be decided.'

Will you:

Ask about the old magic? 28
Ask why they can't settle elsewhere? 212
Ask why the church is to blame? 426
Ask how you can help? 357

127

'You want to know how someone like me can end up here?' The man draws his sword. You gasp as the white-steel bursts into light, its inscribed runes glimmering in complex and dizzying patterns.

'You're an inquisitor?' you ask, both surprised and wary.

The man nods, resting the blade across his knees. 'This is a named blade. The inscriber who gave his life to imbue it called it "Faith". It was an honour for me to receive it – to wield it in battle.'

'It is indeed a fine sword,' you add encouragingly.

The blade's pale light catches the stranger's face. It is young and handsome – not the grizzled veteran that you had been expecting. 'I have failed the One God,' he sighs, bowing his head. 'I lost my brother ... not of kin, but of battle. We had fought many times together, took our vows together, helped each other through the testing.' His fingers trace the edge of the glowing blade. 'But nothing prepared me ... us ... for the Wiccans, what they can do. They have a dark power. Twisted. It is a mockery of everything that we believe in.'

You shift uneasily, waiting for him to continue.

'Myself and Gairn took justice into our own hands – tried to find their encampment so we could end this, make the roads safe again for the pilgrims. But *they* found us ...' He flinches, removing his hand from his blade. You notice a line of blood trickling from one of his fingers. 'They had magics that I had not seen before. Elemental and powerful ...' He takes a ragged, shaking breath. 'I fled like a coward. I knew we had no chance. I lost my ... faith. And Gairn. He wanders that place still, a restless spirit. Abandoned.' The warrior slides the blade back into its scabbard, extinguishing the light and returning the alleyway to its former gloom. 'He cannot move on ... neither of us can.' He blows out a sigh, tilting his head back to offer you a thin smile. 'And for that, I think I deserve another drink.'

(Record the words *fallen knight* on your hero sheet.) You sense there is little you can do for this disheartened warrior. Taking your pack, you wish him well, before heading back into town. Turn to 199.

128

Your choice was a bad one. The paper monster cannot be harmed by your soldier, for the thin body simply folds or crumples around the attacks, taking no damage. (Remove your soldier from your hero sheet. Then return to **444** to fight this monster yourself.)

129

Murlic glances towards the fire, where you see the hulking silhouette of Conall, the giant warrior, staring into the flames. 'Our last Sanchen said he would be king one day. Conall already bring clans together – Hannen, Blackmoor, Crow. We free him from Durnhollow after Church take him as prisoner. They think they defeat us by removing leader but we paid them back. Now Conall leads again.' Murlic spits into the dust with a sour expression.

'I sense you are not at ease with this?' you ask, watching closely for his reaction.

The Wiccan rogue sneers. 'He is lapdog to Damaris. That witch uses demon magic with no care. Conall too. Bad things . . .' He visibly shivers, running a hand through his grease-spiked hair. 'We have no choice but to follow. We have nothing left now – so we must fight.'

Will you:	
Ask about the Sanchen?	72
Learn the pariah career (requirement: rogue)?	302
Explore the rest of the cave?	485

130

'This man, Jolando, is the best in his field. He was contracted for a job – and it went wrong.' Anna's fingers brush against a set of daggers resting at the foot of the bed, half-wrapped in black cloth.

'An assassin,' you mutter beneath your breath.

'This wasn't about murder. He was retrieving an object from

the church; an ancient dwarven relic that was found out on the moors.'

'So, what happened?'

Anna takes one of her mixing spoons and uses it to prod the charred wood on the table. 'I don't know for certain. He came to me much as you did, feverish and delirious. He was clutching this . . . part of a charm. I believe it's responsible for his condition.'

You grimace at the blackened wood. 'So, where do I come in?'

Anna turns to a side table, covered in sheets of parchment. She takes a quill and begins making marks on one of the pages. 'I'll keep this simple. I need you to go to Crow Rock and kill a manticore.' Her hand makes another series of scrawls on the page. 'I need its blood to break the curse.'

You snort, shaking your head in disbelief. 'Kill a manticore? Why not throw in a dragon too – make it a little more challenging.'

Anna snatches up the paper and hands it over. 'This is not a time for humour.'

You take the parchment and hold it closer to the lantern light. The scrawls form a map, showing a route from Carvel to a series of rocks to the south-east. You look up, realisation dawning on you that she is being perfectly serious. Manticores are savage, bloodthirsty predators – known for preying on humans and other large animals.

'You owe me,' says Anna, as if reading your thoughts. 'And I need its blood.'

'Why a manticore?' you ask, folding the paper and sliding it into your pack.

The man gives a sudden cry as he twists and turns on the bed, his fingers forming claws as they fend off some unseen, nightmarish foe.

'Manticore's blood was one of the reagents used to craft that charm,' explains Anna. She takes a glass vial from the table and hands it to you. 'Whoever made it was serious about doing harm. And I doubt anyone in the church could have made such a thing . . .'

The vial is attached to a silver chain. You lift it over your head, letting it rest against your chest. 'I'll do what I can. I promise.'

Anna peers over her glasses. 'I know you will.'

After bidding the healer farewell, you head out of Carvel, its cobbled streets glimmering in the first light of dawn. Turn to **150**.

131

The map-seller drops his voice, glancing over his shoulder. 'You heard of the fanged crusader, right? He's preying on criminals in Carvel. At least two gangs have gone down in the last month and even the thieves' guild has broken up. He's a real vigilante.'

'And where do the fangs come in?' you ask, with a sceptical frown.

'Some of the guards got a good look. They say he can turn into a bat – a giant vampire bat. And it was taking bodies off into the night. A few pilgrims gone missing in the town lately, too.' The man shakes his head. 'Not sure if it's good or bad, but it all sounds very ugly to me . . .'

Will you:

Ask for more news?	137
Turn your attention back to upper town?	77

132

You pass down a short candle-lit corridor into a wide chamber, filled with the fragrant scent of incense and rose petals. Clearly someone has tried to make this space as homely as possible, covering the paved floor with sumptuous rugs and its high, grey walls with rich silk tapestries. Braziers burn in the far corners of the room, illuminating a bed of cushions. Slumped amongst them is a shrivelled husk of a man, his skeletal body poking bumps and ridges through his thin white robes.

As you enter, you hear him take a sharp rattling breath, his pale rheumy eyes roving back and forth. 'I thought I had only one today,' he wheezes. 'Come forward, child.'

You step closer to the frail man, noticing that he is staring vacantly past you. 'Good.' He leans forward, scratching at his bald pate with spider-long fingers. 'Now speak, child. You have passed the training. Are you ready to take the One God's light?'

You hesitate, not sure how to answer. The man is clearly blind and assumes you are another monk, come to receive the abbot's blessing.

Will you:

Answer yes (requirement: warrior)?	415
Answer no and return to the courtyard?	260

133

'What were they?' you ask, rummaging through the charred remains. If you wish, you may now help yourself to one of the following items:

Splintered claw	Warded wood
(main hand: fist weapon)	(ring)
+1 brawn +1 armour	+1 brawn +1 magic

Benin scowls as he prods at one of the tangled bodies with the end of his staff. 'It looks like Wiccan work to me. Old magic. Perhaps those savages are defending this area for some reason; wanting to frighten off inquisitive travellers like ourselves.' He lifts an eyebrow, regarding you with a mischievous smile.

Will you:

Ask Benin about his magic?	80
Ask Benin what he is doing here?	57
Continue on your journey?	157

134

You slice off the bulb and remove the outer leaves. You then take the main stalk and chop it into thin slices, adding these to the potion base. They spit and hiss as they sink into the milky liquid, releasing a pleasant lemony smell. What ingredient will you add next?

Will you:

Add meadowsweet?	104
Add white willow?	83
Add sagewort?	114

135

Quest: The toymaker's tower

The private area is bigger than you thought, the alcove actually serving as a low arch through into a separate dining room. Logs spit and fizz on an open fire, flooding the space with dancing shadow. At a round table a man is sat over a bowl of stew, picking at its contents with his spoon. A woman paces nervously around him, stopping and looking up as you enter.

'Who are you?' she asks with a flicker of irritation.

Before you can reply, Polk pushes past and plonks the mugs onto the table. 'I found your number four, Anse.' He appears to be addressing the man at the table, who raises his head. It is only when he leans back that you see his eyes are covered by a band of white cloth.

You take an awkward bow, acutely aware of the sudden silence. 'I can take my leave, if you prefer . . .'

Polk grabs you by the arm and ushers you over to the table. 'Bah, nonsense,' he grins, settling into a chair in front of a platter of steaming food. 'Like I says, I'm the chatty one.'

The woman gives a disparaging grunt. You pull out a chair to take a seat, studying her closely. She is elderly, her short-cropped hair peppered with grey. Her clothing suggests an outdoor type – layers of boiled leather, with a generous cut allowing for comfort and movement. A bow and quiver of arrows rest against the wall behind her.

'You are alone?' she enquires, toying with her necklace – an expensive trinket seemingly at odds with the rest of her make-do appearance.

'Yes,' you reply assuredly. 'Would you care to explain what's going on?'

Polk noisily clears his throat, gaining your attention. 'We're heading out at first light, to go and find a tower. It hasn't been seen . . .' he pauses while he downs one of the mugs, stopping only to wipe the froth from his beard, ' . . . in forty years.'

The man opposite, who Polk referred to as Anse, favours you with a tight smile.

'I don't understand,' you reply. 'How does a tower disappear and . . .'

'The tower is Jacob's,' snaps the woman, some private torment evident in her eyes. 'He was a toymaker – a master craftsman. As children, we used to crowd around his cart whenever it came into the village. He would always have little gifts for us ...' Her gaze shifts to the crackling log fire. 'My husband apprenticed with him. He spent most of his time in that tower; spoke little of his work, only that Jacob was studying ancient texts – Elven. He wanted to make his toys ... more special.'

You glance at Polk, seeing that the bearded warrior is supping on another mug of ale. He flicks his eyebrows at you. 'I sense this does not end well,' you sigh, turning back to the woman.

'There was talk of experiments,' she says with obvious distaste. 'And then, one day, the tower simply ... vanished.' Her hand returns to the necklace, fingers tracing a ring that hangs from its silver links. A wedding band, perhaps. 'I have waited forty long years.'

'So there you have it,' smiles Polk, slamming another empty mug onto the table-top. 'We're going to check out the tower and find out what's left ... ' He stops, aware that the woman is glaring at him across the room. 'Find out what happened to Joss' husband,' he corrects carefully.

'And why do you need me?' you ask, confused. 'Is this dangerous?'

Polk shifts nervously in his chair, hand reaching for his next mug of ale. 'Two things. You're number four because Anse here has a thing about numbers.'

You glance over at the man in the white blindfold. He has returned to picking meat out of his stew, placing the dripping morsels on a separate plate. It appears his sight is perfect, despite the blindfold he is wearing. You also notice that every inch of his visible skin, bar his face, is tattooed with white glowing lines of script.

'And point two?' you prompt, your eyes remaining fixed on the man's peculiar markings.

'We're dealing with the shroud,' sighs Polk, taking a noisy gulp of ale. 'And that means demons, or worse. You *can* fight, I take it?'

Will you:

Ask about Anse's strange markings? 270

Ask about the shroud? 238

Ask why you should risk your life? 89

Agree to the mission? 24

136

'Oh, we're not lost,' the man replies, with a knowing smile. 'We're exactly where we need to be.' You flinch as he leans closer to his pack, his hand passing over the jewelled sword. But he doesn't take it. Instead, he simply lifts a pouch from out of a side pocket. 'Salt,' he grins, bouncing it in his hand.

'You said *we*,' you enquire suspiciously. 'You have a companion. Where did they—'

Suddenly, you hear a bellowing roar coming from somewhere deep inside the rock. It is followed by someone's cry and a loud ground-trembling boom. The man flinches for a second, then proceeds to add the salt to the bubbling pot as if nothing untoward has happened.

'What was that?' you ask worriedly. 'Are they in danger?'

'What was what?' asks the gentleman, stirring the stew. 'Would you like some tea? I brewed some earlier. Silver Grey, the finest.'

There is another monstrous roar, dislodging stone and dust from the rock walls. The man moves around the fire and settles down on a blanket. 'You can join me if you like,' he says, raising a cup of steaming tea to his lips. 'I plan on being here for a while.'

Will you:

Join him by the fire?	187
Ask about the disturbance?	156

137

'More news is going to cost you,' grins Mendo, holding out his palm. 'Show me some of those shiny ones and we're in business.'

If you pay the 3 gold crowns, turn to **140**. Otherwise, you decide to continue your journey. Turn to **77**.

138

Eldias removes a gourd from his coat, plucking out the stopper with his teeth. He then moves swiftly to the window, pouring its contents along the floor. It looks like a fine black powder.

'What is that?' you ask with interest.

The witchfinder doesn't answer. Instead he snatches the lantern from the table, just as the window is smashed inwards by a pair of grasping hands. Through the shattered glass, you see white flashes of rainwater and an endless bobbing sea of heads . . .

Eldias overturns the table, scattering books and papers across the floor. He then moves around the table, ducking down behind it. He urges you to do the same.

You huddle down beside the witchfinder, confused as to what is happening. Eldias is breathing hard, his eyes feverishly bright. 'Listen to me,' he gasps. 'I am weak – I may not make it through this. But understand that the reverend must be stopped – at all costs.'

The door of the room buckles inwards, the chair that was holding it scraping across the floor. A swarm of hands appear through the gap, struggling to get through.

When you glance over at Eldias, you see that he is regarding you with a thin smile. 'You're a prophet,' he says, raising an eyebrow. 'And you're telling me you don't know how this will end?'

You shake your head. 'I sometimes see my own death, if that helps?'

Eldias is silent for a moment, the lantern flame mirrored in each of his ghostly eyes. 'Hmm, probably not.' He twists around, peering over the top of the table. 'Okay, my friend. Well, I'm no prophet but I always knew one thing . . .' He swings the lantern over his shoulder, sending it rattling through the air to smash against the far wall. 'I knew I'd go out in a blaze of glory.' He ducks down, covering his ears. You follow suit as an enormous, bone-jarring explosion sends glass, wood and plaster flying in all directions. Then Eldias is moving, vaulting over the table with a flint-lock pistol in each hand.

You follow behind him, coughing and choking on the thick smoke. Through the haze, you see flames licking at what is left of the wall. Most of it has been completely blasted away, creating a jagged opening leading out onto the village square.

Leaping over charred bodies and debris, the witchfinder unloads one bullet after another into the crowd of zombies. For a moment, you are captivated by the sight – his fierce countenance, the blazing guns, his cries of impassioned fury – he is like some avatar of vengeance, a living part of the very storm that surrounds him.

You hurry to the witchfinder's side, cutting and blasting your way through the howling, snarling masses of undead. But there are so many of them now, surrounding you, clawing at you, dragging at your clothes and armour. You must fight:

	Speed	*Brawn*	*Armour*	*Health*
Enraged zombies	2	2	1	25

Special abilities

- Back from the dead: When the zombies have been reduced to zero *health*, roll a die. If you roll ⚀ or ⚁ they rise from the dead once more, and regain 6 *health*. If the zombies are reduced to zero *health* a second time, then they will no longer rise from the dead.
- Undead: You may use your *ashes, holy water* and *holy protector* abilities against the zombies.

If you manage to battle your way through the first wave of undead, turn to 58.

139

You stagger across the bridge, head bowed to the fierce wind that seems intent on driving you back. Finally, trembling from the bitter cold, you reach the lonely tower, ascending the stairs to an open doorway.

Inside, you find yourself in a small stone chamber. A man sits behind a desk, slouched in a leather seat. As you walk over, the man looks up and sighs.

'This is the tower of mages,' he drawls, inspecting his fingernails. 'Are you wanting instruction in the magic arts?'

Before you can answer, the man slides off his chair and walks around the desk. His white hair is pulled back tight from his face, bound into a ponytail by a black ribbon. 'I am Malak Drake, secretary and understudy to the wise and great Ignatius Pyre.' He looks you up and down, his nose wrinkling. 'I should warn you, the testing is not easy – you wouldn't be the first to suffer,' he pauses while he stifles a yawn, 'irreparable mental and physical damage.' His heavy-lidded eyes settle on your own. 'Speak, then, or take your putrid presence elsewhere.'

Will you:

Ask about the mage tower?	90
Ask about the testing?	213
Return to upper town?	77

140

The map-seller greedily pockets the gold. 'So, do you want the good news, the bad news or the downright ugly news?'

Will you:

Ask for the good news?	125
Ask for the bad news?	184
Ask for the downright ugly news?	131
Continue exploring upper town?	77

141

'Well, that's mighty kind of you,' grins the woman, stepping forward and offering out her hand. 'I'm Bea – and this here is Brother Ventus.'

The man rolls his eyes. 'Judah's light, let's have no secrets.' He gives the woman an incredulous look. 'With a tongue as loose as yours, you should have been a bard.'

'Oh Vent, I know a good heart when I see one.' Bea gives you another of her open smiles. 'I believe the One God sent this one to us.'

Your eyes haven't left her male companion. 'You said "brother". Are you an inquisitor?' you ask nervously.

He raises an eyebrow, grinning for the first time. 'No, I'm a brother of the monastery.' He doffs his hat, revealing his shaven scalp. You also notice glittering inscriptions on the back of his hand.

'And him?' you gesture to the elderly man by the roadside. He is still muttering to himself, rocking back and forth in agitation.

Bea and Ventus exchange glances. The woman is silent, carefully guarding her words. The monk is about to speak when something catches his eye. His head snaps around quickly, surveying the surrounding moorland.

'They found us . . .' gasps Bea.

Black figures pepper the rocky hills, standing stark against the grey-white sky. You count possibly thirty or forty warriors, clad in furs and rusted mail. A troop approaches, striding towards you with a surly confidence. Their leader is a woman – her grey hair decorated with crow feathers and silver beads. Black runes glimmer against her tanned-hide robes. To her left is a giant of a warrior with great wide shoulders. In each hand he carries a mighty axe, their runes spitting and hissing as the rainwater splashes against the steel. To the woman's right is a short man, thin and wiry. The hood of his fur cloak is pushed back to reveal his war-painted face. As he bares his pointed teeth, you recognise him instantly – the Wiccan who freed you from the prison at Durnhollow.

Bea draws her swords, their inscribed steel dancing with white light. The monk tosses his hat aside, ripping open his coat to reveal padded brown robes. He lets the coat drop from his arms, his body immediately snapping into a battle stance. Magic flares around his inscribed knuckles, surrounding his hands in balls of white light.

The Wiccans come to a halt, showing neither fear nor surprise at this show of aggression. The woman smiles, her amber eyes sliding past the others to settle on your own. 'Sanchen,' she nods, her feathered hair flapping in the wind. 'We meet at last.' Turn to 296.

142

This is your opportunity to choose the path you wish to follow – the warrior or the rogue. The warrior is a master of weapons and armour. Although slow in combat, the warrior compensates for this with a hardy endurance and mighty strength. If you have a high *brawn* and *armour* score, then the path of the warrior could be for you.

If, on the other hand, you have a high *speed* and *brawn* score, then the path of the rogue may be more to your liking. The rogue is a master of speed and deception. Whilst weak and vulnerable in longer fights, the rogue excels in exploiting weaknesses and avoiding damage.

Will you:

Choose the path of the warrior?	110
Choose the path of the rogue?	85

143

Grateful that the glowing fungi is providing you with some light, you scramble up the steep passageway. Behind you, the walls ring with the clatter of weapons and the scraping of boots, as the rest of the group struggle to follow. 'So much for the stealthy approach.' You grimace.

Eventually the passage levels out, ending in another junction. To your left the tunnel widens, opening out into a large cavern. To the right the tunnel narrows, becoming a cramped space filled with stones and rubble. Something glints back at you from between the rocks – a pair of eyes. Then it is gone. You hear the pad of feet, followed by a hooting cry. *Goblins.*

Will you:

Head left into the cavern?	229
Head right, following the goblin?	363

144

Legendary monster: The black shuck

The fenlands stretch as far as the eye can see, bright pools shining like molten gold in the afternoon sunlight. Some might consider it a picturesque scene, worthy of a painting, but not the poor traveller forced to wade through it, cold and soaked to the skin, assaulted by an endless array of buzzing black flies.

You swipe them away, desperately scanning the distant hills for some sign of habitation. It seems the map you were given has led you astray. You drag it out of your pocket, picking the wet ends apart to peel it open. The inn is clearly marked, only a short walk from the track you were following. But that track had quickly turned into a forest, which in turn has led you to this foul-smelling, fetid marsh.

You are about to turn back when you glimpse a bright light on the horizon. For a second you consider it might be another lost traveller, but that hope is swiftly quashed. The light is moving towards you at incredible speed, flickering and smoking as it leaps from bank to bank. There is a black shape at its centre – a four-legged animal, wreathed in flame.

You fumble for your weapons as the beast closes in – a giant hound, covered in midnight-black fur. Around its shoulders and forelegs fire flickers from cracks in its skin, hissing and spitting as the beast's powerful claws splash through the muddy pools. There is no chance of outrunning this fearsome predator. It is time to fight:

	Speed	*Brawn*	*Armour*	*Health*
Hellhound	4	7	3	50

Special abilities

- Backdraft: Each time your damage score/damage dice inflicts health damage on the hellhound, you must take 3 damage, ignoring *armour*, from the flames that surround its body.
- Enraged: If the hellhound is still alive at the start of the fifth combat round, it goes into a savage frenzy, raising its *speed* and *brawn* by 1 for the remainder of the combat.

If you are able to defeat the monstrous demon hound, turn to 231.

145

You hand settles around something small and round. Excitedly, you withdraw your hand to find that you have discovered a ring, fashioned from three spiralling bands of wood. If you wish, you may take the following item:

The fellowship ring
(ring)
+1 brawn +1 magic
Ability: charm

Suddenly, you hear a grumbling, creaking sound coming from the tree. Stepping away, you see that the other holes have now closed up, locking away their treasures.

You may now try and climb the tree (turn to 96) or leave via the magic portal (turn to 46).

146

'Boom Mamba brings the boom!' A raggedy figure appears on top of one of the nearby walls, a staff held in one hand and a flaming skull in the other. The undead pay him no mind, until he tosses the skull into their ranks – and a second later there is a bright explosion, bones and mud sent showering in all directions. 'Skellies go boom!'

Then the figure is leaping towards the remaining undead, swinging his staff in a fast-moving blur. 'We move. Skellies don't stay dead for long.' He drives the end of his staff into the nearest warrior, shattering its ribcage. 'Follow me if you wanna live.'

The shaman springs onto the wall, unhooking another skull from his belt. After uttering some strange-sounding words, the skull ignites into flame. He tosses it at another advancing horde, blasting a sizeable chunk out of the earth and tossing blazing bones high into the air. Taking your chance you sprint for the wall, dodging the few stragglers that remain. There is another explosion to your left, accompanied by a screech of laughter.

'Eat flame, skellies!' The man shakes his staff above his head before turning and jumping down off the wall. You follow him as he weaves through the mist-shrouded ruins, changing direction constantly to avoid further crowds of undead. From the corner of your eye you see more of them shambling around inside the buildings – this entire region is a clearly a haven for their kind.

'Down here, we safe from skellies.' The man veers off to the right, heading into a narrow side-alley between two buildings. Runes have been painted on the walls and floor, pulsing with a faint purple light. 'Runes protect us. Skellies can't cross magic.' The man ducks through a doorway at the end of the alley. You follow close on his heels, curious to find out more about this peculiar mage. Turn to 342.

147

You rip loose your cloak and throw it through the air, watching as it settles over the top of the poltergeist's body. The creature gives an angry screech as it attempts to break free of the unwanted prison – but it is already too late for this ghostly nuisance. You are charging in, aiming for the kicking, punching limbs that are now revealed beneath your cloak:

	Speed	*Magic*	*Armour*	*Health*
Poltergeist	5	3	3	35

If you manage to defeat the poltergeist, you can reclaim your cloak. However you must lower one of your cloak's attributes by 1, due to the damage inflicted to it during the course of the fight. Then turn to 236.

148

As you approach, Bea looks up, a cold breeze brushing the blond hair from her face. 'Oh, lookee here – mended at last!' She jumps to her feet, sending her sword clattering noisily to the ground. With a beaming smile, she starts forward to give you a hug, then checks herself.

'Oh, I shouldn't … I … excuse me.' Blushing, the woman stoops to retrieve her blade. 'So … so clumsy of me, sorry. Not like me at all.' Bea forces a nervous laugh as she straightens, catching your eye and turning a deeper shade of crimson. Behind her on the bench, you see some tattered journals resting on an oil-skin bag. They look to contain a series of arcane markings.

Will you:

Ask Bea why she is acting so strangely?	330
Ask Bea about the books?	293
Return to the courtyard?	260

149

'Ah, prophets,' Lazlo's grin spreads a little wider. 'If you're Allam and also the king's son then you get the backing of the Church – you are proclaimed a hero and sent on a holy crusade. But if you're a commoner …' The man's grin fades. 'Well, the inquisitors don't take kindly to just anyone walking around, telling people they see the future.'

'Why?' You scowl angrily. Memories of your cruel treatment at Durnhollow are still raw in your mind. 'Do many people have such … visions?'

'If you're gullible enough to believe them,' he smiles. 'There are many false prophets in this world, proclaiming they know the destiny of our lives. People flock to them – they grow powerful, wealthy. They can become a threat. The Church doesn't like that. Understandable, I think you'll agree.'

You fall silent, reflecting on the strange dreams and visions you have had. Are they just the product of a childish imagination? No – you have already seen the things you have dreamed of come to pass. Aged eleven you foresaw the death of your older brother. You tried to stop it happening, but you were too late. He fell from the rocks … and because you had warned others, they thought you were the cause. You flinch, remembering the stones that were thrown at you, the angry faces, the accusations. Still just a child, you had fled the village …

Lazlo is watching you intently and appears to read your thoughts. 'I did know one man – a true prophet. His name was Jenlar Cornelius. He could see the future. And he could change it.'

Your eyes widen with interest. 'Where is he now?'

Lazlo pulls a grimace. 'Six feet under. I guess even a prophet can't cheat death when it comes knocking.'

Will you:

Ask what he knows of Allam?	21
Enquire as to your whereabouts?	9
Accuse him of being the masked crusader?	39
State you wish to leave?	167

150

The sky is bright and cloudless as you head briskly across the moors, aware that Jolando's life is in the balance. As you get nearer to the mountains the ground becomes steeper, frost crunching underfoot as you find yourself entering a forest of pine and larch.

You haven't ventured far before you hear a cry and the hollow thump of wood hitting wood. Drawing your weapons you hurry through the trees, emerging on a rocky hillside. A young man in fur-trimmed robes has his back against a tree, frantically fending off the attacks of some unusual creatures. They look like a haphazard clutter of twigs and branches, melded together into a vaguely humanoid form. Their arms end in splintered points, almost like sword blades, which are punching and slashing through the air. The man sees you and calls over desperately as his staff swings in a wide arc, smashing one of the creatures through its midriff. 'Traveller, your aid!'

Without hesitation, you move to join the attack:

	Speed	*Brawn*	*Armour*	*Health*
Sinister sprigs	0	0	1	12

If you manage to help defeat these bewitched creatures, turn to 179.

151

Boss monster: The forest of thorns

Above the town of Carvel, thunder claps and booms, filling the night sky with flickering ribbons of brightly-coloured light. It is All Saint's Eve and the celebrations have started, the fireworks casting staccato flashes over the distant rooftops and spires.

You stand alone on the hill, watching it all with the faintest hint of a smile. It is a comfort to know that there is still some semblance of joy and festivity in this cold, bleak land. You glance down at your hands, still throbbing with pain. Turning the palms over in the silver moonlight, you see the relic's runes branded deep into your blistered skin. A thin veil of snow begins to fall, the cold flakes kissing the smarting flesh and offering a fleeting solace against the persistent ache.

Someone calls your name from the foot of the hill. You glance around, to see your companions waiting at the edge of the forest. Misshapen branches stretch like a diseased growth across the marshy ground, intertwining their barbed limbs until it seems they have become a single living entity – some dark thing that exists for the single purpose of keeping others away. Indeed, you can understand why few would choose to come here. The Pilgrim's Road sweeps past it – deviating cowardly from its intended course. The woodsmen could not fell the dark trees of the forest and so the road was never able to push through to the coast. The forest has always remained, dark and silent, and untouched.

You head down the hill, fragments of your visions running through your head. You doubt this will end well – there is a nagging fear pinching at your stomach, but for some reason you feel compelled to see this through. That same desire is written on your companions' faces, coupled with their unwavering belief that you are the one to finally lead them through the forest, to discover its hidden secrets.

The relic rests on the back of a rickety cart, wrapped in fresh blankets. You can smell the acrid stench of burnt cloth. Since its retrieval from Duerdoun the strange relic has lost much of its unnatural heat, but it has still proved impossible for anyone else to touch. You feel expectant eyes watching you as you pull back the cloth and take the relic into your hands. The heat throbs against your raw palms. Shifting the grip, you feel the runes on its surface slide into the depressions burnt into your skin. Then its hammer-like head opens and bright light pours out across the marsh, glittering off the wickedly-sharp thorns that stretch before you.

At your approach the twisted branches recoil, creaking and shifting as they seek to draw away from the light. Within moments the noise of cracking limbs is almost deafening as the roots themselves drag their black bodies from the sodden earth, slinking back to the darkness as quickly as they can. You watch in stunned awe as a pathway is slowly revealed through the forest, framed by high walls of shifting, tormented trees. Holding the relic out, you start along this newly-revealed trail, your companions following. Turn to 196.

152

(If you have the *coat of many scales* turn to 209.)

The man looks up as you approach. His clothes are dirty, his appearance ragged. Clutched in one of his fists is a crumpled piece of paper. 'Look around you,' he hisses angrily. 'If you can't find charity here, then where can you find it?'

You take a seat next to him, asking the man to explain.

'I got nothing, not a coin to me name. But I got this.' He shakes the tattered roll of paper. 'It's me grandma. She sent it to me … before … before …' He breaks off, tears welling in his eyes. 'Gah, look at me!' Angrily, he rubs at his face with his dirt-blackened fingers.

'The village … I left to go east. I thought I could make it big in one of the cities. Things didn't go well; debts … you know. Had a few people leaning on me. Then a messenger found me – gave me this.' He unravels the paper. 'A letter from me grandma. Sounds like something happened in the village. Something bad. She wrote this to warn me, that if … if she weren't around no more, then her house and its belongings would be mine.' With a scowl, he crumples up the paper again. 'They call that village Blight Haven now. You know why?' He looks at you with bloodshot eyes. 'Everybody died. But they didn't stay dead … it's cursed, a place of evil.'

He shudders. 'The inquisitors don't do nothing; they say it's forbidden to go there. And what I'm owed …' He opens his fist, letting the ball of paper drop to the ground. 'Not worth the parchment it's written on.'

His attention strays to your weapons. 'Hey, you're an adventurer, right? You wouldn't be heading that way, you know, looking for a fight or whatever you people do?'

You shrug your shoulders. 'Perhaps.'

The man scratches his unshaven chin. 'There's a coat. Belonged to my grandfather. A coat of basilisk scales. If you should come across it, then you'd be doing me a real favour. Charity and all that.' He sneers at a passing group of priests. 'The Church doesn't care about us commoners no more. But you'll help, right? I may not get me rightful home, but that coat could get me out of a lotta trouble. I'll even give you a cut of the gold, too. What d'you say?'

You agree to do what you can.

'Thank you,' he grins, shaking your hand. 'My name is Joseph. I'll be waiting right here, just in case you come back.' He flashes you a mouth full of rotted black teeth.

You may now inspect the tapestry (turn to **181**) or leave the church (turn to 77).

153

Despite your best efforts, you cannot move the heavy stone slab. Frustratingly, you are unable to recover the gemstones. With little else of interest in this chamber, you decide to leave.

Will you:

Leave via the stairs?	46
Return to the passage and try the wooden door?	4

154

You leave the tower, following Dean Margo across the courtyard and back into the building of cells. After turning down several corridors, you find yourself entering a library. A number of reading tables are visible in the soft glow of candlelight. Seated at one of the tables is a monk, with spectacles perched on the end of his nose. He is scratching words onto parchment, listening intently to the figure sat opposite him: a ragged old man with streaked grey hair and dirt-stained clothing. He is rocking back and forth, wringing his hands together nervously. You recognise him as the man at the roadside – the one that the others had been so keen to protect.

Ventus stands by the table. When he sees you, he bows his head in greeting. The dean strides over, his long robes rippling out behind him. 'Do we have the information?'

Ventus winces, shaking his head. 'It's been difficult. Trying to get him to focus …'

The dean turns, fixing you with an unflinching gaze. 'This man is our weapon in the war against the Wiccans.' He points to the ragged traveller. 'He has a unique gift – one that will root out the truth.'

Will you:	
Ask about the traveller's gift?	429
Ask about 'the truth' they seek?	394
Ask about the war with the Wiccans?	491

155

The wicker man is brought crashing to the ground, its rune-painted wood splintering into plumes of dark magic. Elated with your victory, you and your companion search what remains of the strange creature.

Each hero finds 100 gold crowns and may choose one of the following rewards (heroes may choose the same reward if they wish to):

Harvester	Solstice	Garland of sacrifice
(ring)	(main hand: staff)	(head)
+2 brawn +2 magic	+1 speed +3 magic	+1 speed +2 brawn
Ability: regrowth	Ability: channel	Ability: atonement

Eager to leave this bewitched hilltop, you and your companion head back into the mist-shrouded forest. There you rejoin the road to Carvel, hoping that the warmth and merriment of an inn will ease the dark memories of this infernal night. (Return to the quest map to continue your adventure.)

156

'Oh, it's nothing to worry about,' he says, with no hint of mockery. 'The situation is well in—'

A man's pained cry echoes back from the rock. There is another dull boom followed by an ear-piercing shriek. You can't tell if the latter was human or something else.

'What's going on?' you insist, craning your neck back to take in the dark, high walls of the bluff.

'Extreme sports,' replies the old man, holding his tea cup to his lips. A sudden tremor sends more dirt and dust pluming into the cleft. The man's tea cup shakes in his hands, spilling tea down his coat. 'Oh, how bothersome,' he grimaces, putting the cup aside to brush at the stain.

You frown, confused by the man's actions. He doesn't seem remotely bothered by what is happening. 'Perhaps we should investigate,' you urge, stepping out of the way out of a falling rock. It is accompanied by an anguished roar and a series of hollow thuds – as if something large is beating against the ground. Each one sends a tremor through the rock walls, rattling the porcelain tea cups on their tray.

'Very well,' sighs the man, pushing himself to his feet. 'But I do assure you, my master is an expert at what he does.'

There is another wailing scream.

'Extreme sports?' you ask, with a quizzical frown.

'Just a little spelunking,' he proffers with a shrug. 'Cave diving ... he likes the adrenaline rush.'

Suddenly there is an almighty bang, as the side of the bluff explodes outwards, hurling rock and dust through the snow-drenched sky. Turn to 200.

157

'These lands are not as safe as they once were,' says Benin, resting his staff across his shoulder. 'May I suggest we travel together – at least for the time being? Where are you headed?'

'Crow Rock,' you reply, tugging the map from your pack.

Benin's eyes narrow suspiciously. 'Really?'

'You know of it?' you ask, noting his sudden change in manner.

'Of course,' he states briskly. He turns and points up the hillside, to where a series of boulders mark the start of a steep expanse of rocky scree. 'When I was growing up, the children used to dare each other to touch the rock.'

'Why – what's so special about it?' you ask, shielding your eyes against the brightening sun.

'Oh, you'll see.' With a smirk, Benin starts up the rock-strewn slope. You fall into step behind him, not entirely sure if you trust this strange traveller. Turn to 169.

158

Legendary monster: The restless knight

Rising out of the fenlands is a ragged bluff known as the 'Witch's Wold'. Its bleak hilltops are said to be haunted – by all accounts, a place to be avoided. And yet you find yourself deviating from the overgrown trail that would have taken you safely past them, your curiosity piqued by tales of ghosts and lost treasures.

As you rise higher into the hills the temperature drops suddenly, plunging you into a chill fog. The only visible landmark is an outthrust of rock, arching like a black finger across the marsh. Frost crunches underfoot as you make your way towards it, passing through a copse of dark stunted trees. The hard ground is littered with bones, sparkling with coats of ice. The remains of unfortunate travellers perhaps, although the spattering of rusted weapons and shields suggest a larger battle took place here.

You stumble onto the black rock, the mist shifting to reveal its summit. There, silhouetted against the broiling white clouds, is the figure of a knight, dressed for battle. His tattered cloak snaps back and forth in the wind – the only thing that moves in this still, bleak wasteland.

Your heart thuds in your chest as you advance closer, picking your way past the frost-covered boulders. The knight is watching you – of that you are certain - and yet you sense there are no earthly eyes within his winged helm, only a seething, angry darkness.

There is the scrape of metal as the knight draws his sword from its scabbard. The translucent blade glitters like a shard of crystal ice, its inscribed runes humming with magic.

I did my duty! How I could I have been so blind!

The words reverberate all around you, sharp and cutting as knives.

I dedicated my life. But I was betrayed! Betrayed!

The knight starts down the slope towards you, his movements eerily silent and weightless – like something trapped between worlds, in a dream perhaps, or a nightmare. Raising your weapons, you prepare to meet this ghostly knight in battle:

	Speed	*Magic*	*Armour*	*Health*
Gairn	5	5	4	50
Skeletons (*)	4	4	3	40

Special abilities

- Frost fire: Once you have taken health damage from Gairn, at the end of every combat round you must automatically lose 1 *health*.
- Corpse dance (*): At the start of the *fourth* combat round, Gairn raises the skeletons from the battlefield to help defend him. You must defeat the skeletons before you can return to attacking Gairn. (Note: during this phase, Gairn surrounds himself with a magical shield. All passive effects, such as *bleed*, are removed from Gairn. He is also immune to any further abilities, such as *thorns* and *fire aura*, until the skeletons are defeated and he drops his shield.)
- Book of Binding: If you have the *Book of Binding* then you may use it to weaken your enemy. If you win a combat round, instead of rolling for a damage score, you can use the book. This automatically lowers Gairn's *speed, magic* and *armour* by 2 for the remainder of the battle.

- Body of bone: The skeletons are immune to *bleed*.
- Undead minions: You may use your *holy water* and *holy protector* abilities (if available) against the skeletons.

If you manage to defeat this spectral villain, turn to 124.

159

The captain listens to everyone's reports with interest. It appears that the original crew were indeed pirates, smuggling and pillaging along the west coast. However, something must have happened to them out at sea as the entire crew have strangely disappeared, leaving their ship – the *Celeste* – to drift into this cave. The hold is flooded, but it looks to have contained a large number of explosives, some of which have been taken.

The captain looks around at the ragged corpses of the goblins. 'Somethin' must have really spooked them to want to hole up here as a last defence. Goblins hate water.' His gaze shifts to the far shore, where the banks are littered with the remains of the ant-men. 'I think I can guess why.'

Lowering the gangplank your party leaves the ship, crossing back to the rocks. As you follow the ledge around the cave, Surl spots the entrance to another tunnel. It winds deeper into the mountain, leading you through into another large cave. Turn to 229.

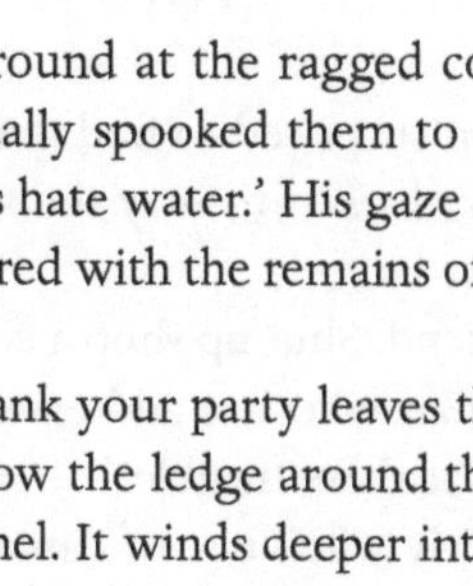

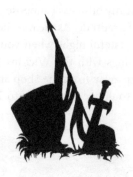

160

Amongst the piles of wind-scoured rock, you find a silver casket containing 50 gold crowns and one of the following items:

Squall	**Circle of storms**	**Bracers of frenzy**
(left hand: axe)	(ring)	(gloves)
+1 speed +2 brawn	+1 armour	+1 speed +1 brawn
Ability: savage arms set (requirement: brigand)	Ability: lightning	Ability: compulsion

When you have updated your hero sheet, turn to 239.

161

You push on the door, surprised to find that it is locked. As you step back, looking for any clues as to why the shop is closed, a passer-by calls over:

'She's gone, my friend. Shut up shop a couple of days ago.'

You turn to the man who has addressed you. 'What happened?' you ask worriedly. 'Was there trouble?'

The man shrugs. 'My wife's one of Anna's patients; I collect medicine for her every day. I turned up and Anna was packing her bags. She looked in a hurry – in a panic, I'd say. Gave me enough medicine for a month. I heard those inquisitors had paid her a visit. Don't know the ins and outs, none of my business I suppose.'

You offer a nod of gratitude. As the man heads away, your thoughts wander back to that fateful night when you came seeking Elysium. Perhaps Anna's dealings with the Wiccans have put her in danger. With a sigh, you step away from the shop and resume your journey. You may now head to upper town (turn to 77) or lower town (turn to 36).

162

'We knows to mind our own business; not get involved.' The leader breathes a heavy sigh. 'There was some battle, off in the moorlands. A Wiccan – a woman – came to our farm, begging for succour. She had a child. I suppose she got lost, separated. We took 'em in. What else could yer do? They were poor, desperate things, tired and hungry.'

The broad-shouldered boy snorts. 'Yeah, no one listened to me. I knew she were a witch. '

'You helped them?' you ask, puzzled. 'But you said—'

The leader nods. 'We gave them food and rest. A few days, we thought they'd be gone. But then . . . the others came.' He trembles at the memory, both fear and anger in his hard stare. 'Because we helped one, they thought we'd help them all. Grain, livestock – they wanted it all. Everything I worked hard for.'

'And they offered nothing in return?' you ask.

The leader falls silent. You look to the boys instead, searching for an answer. It is the youngest who finally speaks. 'Mother was ill. The healers at the church couldn't do nothing. But the Wiccans said they could. They had a mage – one of them druid types. She said she could give her life again – make her walk like she used to.'

'Enough!' the leader, who you assume is the father, snaps angrily. 'I won't be listening to it! I won't!'

You turn back to him, frowning. 'So you agreed – you let the druid heal her?'

'Heal?' The leader glowers, almost choking on the word. 'It were a curse. She became something else – one of their demon kind. It was out of control, destroyed the farm. Destroyed everything. And those Wiccans let it happen. They just watched it all burn. That *thing* is still there now. It ain't my beloved Dags no more.' (Record the word *duty* on your hero sheet.)

Will you:

Ask about Raven's Rest ?	319
Give them a gift of 5 gold crowns?	326
Leave and continue your journey?	199

163

Team battle (advanced): The wicker man

Outside Blight Haven there is a desolate hill, perpetually shrouded in a yellow-green mist. According to the ghost stories, whispered around the campfire, the inhabitants of this cursed village turned their back on the church, delving into witchcraft and devilry to try and save their people from the plague. In desperate times, people will resort to desperate measures.

The wicker man stands as dark testament to the bloody practices that took place in the village: a giant effigy of wood and straw, bedecked with wilted garlands and tattered carnival ribbons. A crowd of ravens caw and peck at the sack-cloth head, where a crude mockery of a smile has been stitched beneath the hollow eye sockets.

Bones litter the hillside as you clamber to its summit, a companion in tow. Some say many travellers and pilgrims were sacrificed here, to feed the wicker man's insatiable hunger. And where there is death, there is bound to be treasure.

The mist is thick, reeking of fetid marsh water. It curls in snake-like tendrils over the rooftops of the forgotten village, creeping around the wicker man and weaving between its skeletal frame.

A creak of wood. A scrape of limbs.

So the ghost stories were true, the wicker man has gained some semblance of life – infused by the demonic magics that were used to craft it. The giant lurches forward, its cage-like body falling open, ready for a fresh sacrifice.

Your companion's steps falter, their breath steaming in the cold.

Then you hear it. An angry buzzing sound – growing louder and louder. Suddenly, from out of the sackcloth head, a dark swarm of bees spill forth into the chill air. Then a wooden hand descends, snapping around you and lifting you up towards the cage. You beat and kick in an effort to get free, but there is no escaping your fate. You find yourself flung inside the creature's body, the door snapping closed behind you. Then the swarm of bees spiral into the cage, trapping you within a humming maelstrom of blinding, stinging death. It is time to fight:

	Speed	*Brawn*	*Armour*	*Health*
Wicker man	15	13	10	250
Bee cage	5	5	4	90

Special abilities

- Bee stings: The hero in the bee cage must suffer 4 damage at the end of each combat round, ignoring *armour*.
- Blood sacrifice: If the hero in the bee cage is defeated, then the wicker man's *speed*, *brawn* and *armour* are increased by 2 for the remainder of the battle.
- Broken magic: If the hero in the bee cage wins (reducing the bee cage to zero *health*) then the wicker man's *speed*, *brawn* and *armour* are lowered by 2 for the remainder of the battle.
- Straw and wood: The wicker man and bee cage are immune to *bleed*, *disease* and *venom*.

Special rules

- The fastest hero (based on *speed* score) fights the wicker man and the slowest hero fights inside the bee cage.
- Each combat round is fought separately between each pair of combatants. Abilities that damage more than one opponent (such as *ignite*, *cleave*, *thorns* and *fire aura*) can be used by a hero, and their damage applied to the other hero's opponent.
- If the hero in the bee cage defeats the bee cage they can join their ally against the wicker man, using the team battle rules for attack and support heroes . They also benefit from the *broken magic* rule (see special abilities above).
- If the hero in the bee cage is defeated, then the remaining hero must continue to fight the wicker man alone, using the *blood sacrifice* rules (see special abilities above).
- Once the wicker man is defeated, the heroes have won (even if the bee cage still has *health*).

If the wicker man is defeated, turn to 155.

164

The tunnel is littered with bones and rusted weapons. A quick examination reveals that they were once goblins. If you wish you may now help yourself to any/all of the following items:

Goblin bones	Bug splatter	Pot of speed (2 use)
(backpack)	(left hand: club)	(backpack)
These might prove valuable to the right person	+1 speed +1 brawn	Use anytime in combat to raise your *speed* by 2 for 1 combat round

After another hundred metres the passageway descends steeply, opening out into a wide chamber. Here the glowing fungi are joined by green-glowing crystals, sparkling from the rock face. Their light gives the cavern a sinister, eerie feel as you silently advance, eyeing the shadows for any sign of attack.

The skittering patter of feet is your first warning that you are not alone. Then a large rock smashes into the ground ahead of you, throwing up a thick cloud of dust.

'We're under attack!' shouts the captain. 'Form up! Form up!'

Surl and Vas rush to his side, the latter pulling a pair of pistols from her belt. The skittering sound gets louder and louder, echoing in the vast chamber.

Then you see them: a glittering swarm of black beetles moving swiftly across the ground, their abdomens glowing with a blood-red light.

'What are they?' cries Surl.

Another boulder explodes nearby, raining shards of sharp stone across the cave. The captain staggers, holding a hand to his side. 'Above us!' he growls. 'They got artillery!'

You look up to see one of the giant ant-men perched on a rock shelf. It is lifting up slabs of heavy granite and tossing them into the chamber.

'Someone get that thing!' snarls the captain, turning to face the oncoming swarm of beetles. 'Surl! Cover my back!'

Vas levels her pistols at the rock-flinging ant. 'I could do with some help here!' she calls.

Will you:

Climb onto the ledge and attack the ant?	290
Help the captain to fight the beetles?	327

165

Despite your best efforts, the lid is stuck fast and you cannot open it. A cursory glance towards the portal reminds you that you have more pressing problems – the doorway has started to fade. Not wishing to become trapped in the attic, you push through the remaining junk and step into the portal. Turn to 440.

166

Benin quickly rises to his feet, offering out his hand. 'My friend, you have made a remarkable recovery. The dean is a powerful healer; I see there is much I could learn from him.'

You take Benin's hand and shake it warmly. 'So what brings you here, so far from Carvel?' you ask, smiling. 'Have you freed the town of its sinners already?'

The priest laughs. 'If only that were true. Alas, I left because I believe this is where I belong. The inquisitors may be turning their backs on these troubles, but the monks … they believe the Wiccans must be stopped, before it is too late. When I heard I could be of use to the monastery, I left Carvel. I believe it is the One God's will – this is my test of faith.' Turn to 197.

167

You scan the room, eyes coming to rest on your belongings heaped on a plush chair. 'I should be going,' you state, crossing the room.

Lazlo watches you thoughtfully, as you strap on your belt and weapons. 'You know, defeating a margoyle is no easy task,' he says, folding his arms across his chest. 'You showed some skill back there at the bluff.'

'I saved your life, you mean?' You grin, sliding your arms into your backpack.

The prince nods and smiles. 'Agreed. But I can make you better.'

You start for the door. 'I'm fine, I'm a fast learner.'

Lazlo puts out a hand, to grab your arm – but you are quicker, anticipating the move and snatching his wrist. You grip it tightly, meeting his surprised gaze. 'I told you I was fast.'

'Your body might be – your wits, less so.' He glances down. You follow his gaze to the dagger he is holding in his other hand, resting against your stomach. 'I can train both. If you'll let me.'

You release his wrist, stepping warily away from the point of the dagger.

'Come,' smiles the prince, spinning the knife and sliding it back under his sleeve. 'I have something special to show you. I think you'll like it.' Turn to 102.

168

By the time you reach the top of the stairs the witchfinder is stooped over, gasping for breath. He waves away your attempts to help him.

'I'm fine,' he snaps hoarsely. 'I'll be even better when I find that cure ...'

Reminded of the urgency of the mission, you hurry towards the double-doors of the church. As you grab hold of the handles to push them apart, the building suddenly trembles with a loud peal of organ music. The doors fly open of their own accord, revealing a narrow nave lined with stone pews and flickering candles.

'What were you saying about theatrics?' You smirk, stepping through the arched doorway. Eldias follows behind, his sallow features twisted with pain.

'Beware the reverend,' he hisses through fanged teeth. 'I may not be able to help you.'

At the far end of the church you see an immense reed organ, its wooden pipes rising up to a mountainous peak. Sat at the organ, with his back to you, is a man with wild white hair. He throws back his head, cackling with delight, as his pale fingers play skilfully across the keys.

'Come! Come!' he spins round in the chair, the music ending abruptly. 'And Judah said unto his flock, let the sinners come to me; those who have forsaken the light. For here they will find peace everlasting.'

He rises up off the chair, sending dust motes dancing from his tattered robes. The man is clearly one of the undead, his green-tinged skin stretched tight over ridges of bone. His appearance draws you up short, halting your advance. Eldias slumps into one of the pews, head lowered, breath rasping in his lungs.

'Do you see them?' he gasps. 'Books, scrolls ... anything?'

You quickly scan behind the reverend, to where a set of stairs lead up to an altar. Piled on top of it are a number of leather-bound books, coated in dirt and cobwebs. 'I see them,' you whisper.

Eldias pushes himself to his feet. 'Then let's do this.'

A crack of thunder shakes the shattered glass in the windows.

'Ah, a witchfinder!' grins the reverend. 'The fist, the blade, the retribution of the One God.' He frowns, his eyes twinkling in the lantern light. 'But you have lost your way, haven't you? Fallen from the path of the righteous.' He raises his hands, leaning back to address the heavens. 'Come to me, my children of the night. Let us test this one's faith.'

You hear a gibbering, chattering sound coming from outside. It grows in volume, joined by the scrape of claws on stone. Fearful of what you will discover, you run over to one of the broken windows. At first you are met by an impenetrable dark, then a flicker of lightning illuminates the sea of bodies hurtling up the stairs to the church. They look like animals, running on all fours, but their faces are almost human – twisted into bestial shapes.

'Ghouls!' you cry out in horror.

Eldias draws his pistols, springing onto the back of the pew. 'Take out the reverend,' he orders, fixing his gaze on the doors of the church. 'I'll hold back this filth.'

You charge towards the undead priest, as the first of the ghoulish horde pour into the church:

	Speed	*Magic*	*Armour*	*Health*
Reverend	2	3	2	50

Special abilities

- Pest control: Eldias is shooting at the oncoming tide of ghouls. At the *end* of each combat round, roll 1 die. If the result is ⚀ or ⚁ then a ghoul has managed to get past Eldias and is now attacking you with its claws, inflicting 2 damage at the *start* of every combat round. (Note: You take 2 damage from each ghoul that gets past Eldias.) If the result is ⚂ or more, then Eldias has fended off the ghouls and destroyed any that are attacking you.
- Undead: You may use your *ashes*, *holy water* and *holy protector* abilities against the reverend.

If you manage to defeat the reverend, then any remaining ghouls are automatically destroyed. Turn to 218.

169

The journey becomes an exhausting climb over jumbled boulders and loose, skittering rock. With your map forgotten, you rely on Benin to lead the way through the makeshift valleys and channels, ascending ever higher into the cloud-tipped mountains.

At last, after clambering up yet another treacherous slope, you spy Crow Rock. It is an unmistakable landmark – a huge outcropping of grey limestone that has been weathered by the elements to take on the hunched shape of a brooding crow. Silhouetted against the sky it looks almost lifelike, as if at any moment it might take to the air, cawing and screeching across the plains.

'Now, do you see?' asks Benin grimly. 'This place has long been revered by the Wiccan. As children, we believed that the crow was real – that it came alive at night and hunted for prey.' He shivers, gripping his staff tighter. 'I suppose the legend does have a hint of truth.'

You follow Benin towards the rock. Beneath it, you can see the land falling away into a hollow canyon. It is then that the stench hits you.

'A monster has made its home here. But it is no stone crow.' Benin grimaces with disgust. 'And I suspect that's why you've come to Crow Rock. As have I.'

You cover your nose as the pair of you scrabble down the rubble into the basin-like depression. The ground is covered in gravel and dirt – and a graveyard of bones. Flies buzz over the carcasses of animals, while crows peck at the half-eaten remains. The stench is almost overpowering.

'The manticore,' you gasp, choking on the rancid air.

Benin points to a cave opening with his staff. 'That is its lair.'

'You don't seem afraid,' you croak, stepping over the shattered ribcage of some unknown creature. 'Manticores are savage – ferocious.'

Benin starts towards the cave. 'The errand I mentioned earlier – it ends here.' He looks back over his shoulder. 'Now, I suggest we work together or else it will be our corpses rotting out here in the cold.' Turn to 225.

170

You push aside the pillow, only to discover that the strap is actually a leather cord, attached to a small silver whistle. If you wish, you may now take the following item:

Silver whistle
(necklace)
Ability: faithful friend

Outside, you hear the captain's gruff voice, barking orders once again. Not wishing to be on the receiving end of a tongue-lashing, you quickly leave the cabin. Turn to 220.

171

You slice off the bulb and remove the outer leaves. You then take the main stalk and chop it into thin slices, adding these to the potion base. They spit and hiss as they sink into the milky liquid, releasing a pleasant lemony smell. What ingredient will you add next?

Will you:

Add meadowsweet?	**104**
Add white willow?	**310**
Add sagewort?	**114**

172

As you pass through the tightly-packed crowds, you see that most of the tables and benches are taken, filled with an odd mix of traveller, from pilgrims and young families to gruff-looking mercenaries and sell-swords.

If you have the word *Joseph* written on your hero sheet, then turn to 332. If you have *Dagona's locket*, then turn to 221. Otherwise, your brief scan of the room turns up little of interest. You now contemplate heading over to the bar (turn to 248) or leaving (turn to 199).

173

Your choice was a bad one. The paper monster cannot be harmed by your soldier, for its thin body simply folds or crumples around the attacks, taking no damage. (Remove your soldier from your hero sheet. Then return to 444 to fight this monster yourself.)

174

'I hope I managed to teach you something back there,' grins Lazlo, sliding his sword back onto the rack. 'Else my bruises will have been for naught.'

If you have a high *magic* score and wish to learn the path of the mage, turn to 3. If you have a high *brawn* score and wish to learn the path of the warrior or the rogue, turn to 142.

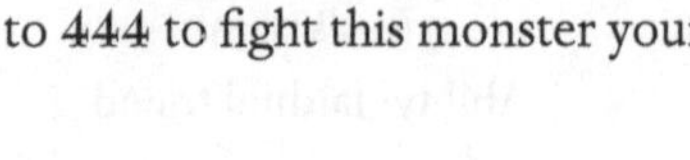

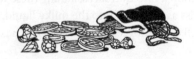

175

'Ah yes, that little problem.' Virgil begins pacing up and down, his boots clicking against the panelled floor. 'Cernos is a demon from ancient times – a demon prince, to be precise.'

'What's the difference?' you ask hoarsely, coughing to clear your throat.

Virgil continues pacing, the pistols and rifles bouncing at his back. 'He was an ordinary man, once – if the legends are to be believed – before he was gifted extraordinary powers by an Archdemon, transforming him into... what you saw in the forest.' His boot heels snap together as he comes to a halt. His gaze drifts to your wounds. 'Demons can pass their powers on to others, if they so wish.'

'How do you know this?' You frown suspiciously. 'How did you know we would be there – in the forest?'

The witchfinder tilts his head, gold glittering in his smile. 'Do you hold me accountable for all that has happened? Masterminding a prison break, before hounding your steps and driving you into the arms of your companions? Do you suspect that I remained in the shadows, putting the pieces in play and then watching and waiting for my perfect moment to pounce and save the day?' Virgil pauses, grinning through the expectant silence.

When you finally start to reply, the witchfinder holds up a finger, wagging it back and forth. 'You give me too much credit, prophet. Not all of us are gifted with visions of the future. As to your forest – it was dwarven magic. Created to keep the demon prisoner. An odd punishment, perhaps, but then it has been effective for several thousands of years. Now, sadly, Cernos is free – and he will seek to enact his revenge. He'll be following in his maker's footsteps – the Archdemon, Barahar.'

Return to 494 to ask another question, or turn to 433 to continue.

176

Searching through the vault, you find 200 gold crowns. You may also take any/all of the following:

Glyph of power	Rune of healing	Acheron's tower
(special: glyph)	(special: rune)	(main hand: wand)
Use on any item	Use on any item	+2 speed +4 magic
to add 1 *magic*	to add the special ability *heal*	Ability: might of stone

When you have made your decision, you leave the vault and exit the hall through the open doorway. Turn to 797.

177

'I am Sir Bastion,' proclaims the knight with gusto. 'You must have heard of me. My deeds in these lands often precede my good name.' He flicks a hand through his golden mane of hair. You spot the farrier rolling his eyes.

'I must admit, I have not,' you reply honestly.

The knight glares at you for a moment, then drops his shoulders, visibly deflating. 'Humph. I should have guessed as much – it's not for want of trying, I tell you. Unless I lower myself to become some pilgrim's bodyguard, there's no glory to be found in this ignoble marsh. I am positively wasted here.'

The farrier snorts, coughing noisily into the back of his hand. 'Sorry, just some dust,' he grins in apology.

'Why did you come here?' you ask, looking around at the ramshackle settlement. 'Is this really the place to find heroic adventure?'

The knight grimaces at a passing group of mercenaries. 'Granted, it is not what I expected. Dear mama used to tell me such wonderful stories of Saint Allam and his knights. They came west to find adventure and spread the word of the One God. I thought perhaps … here, at least, I might finally make a name for myself. Do something to be remembered.'

'There's always time,' you smile encouragingly.

The knight pats the neck of his steed. 'I fear this is not a place for honourable heroes – is it, Wilma? Scoundrels and mercenaries, perhaps. That's all I see.' He suddenly catches himself, quickly putting a hand to your arm. 'Present company excepted, of course.'

Will you:
Ask the knight if he wishes to accompany you? 356
Explore the rest of the settlement? 199

178

'The monastery,' says the woman, bouncing on her heels with excitement. 'I can't wait to see it. Heard so many stories about—'

The man clears his throat noisily, forcing her to silence. They exchange a look, then she lowers her gaze, her shoulders slumping. 'Ah yes. Not supposed to say, am I? My mouth runs away with me sometimes.' She turns away glumly.

'Indeed it does,' the man glowers angrily. He shoots you a scathing glance. 'There is nothing you can do here, traveller. So be on your way.'

Will you:
Ask what happened to the wagon? 274
Ask what is in the wagon? 223
Ask if you can help? 141

179

The creatures confronting you are fast, deadlier than they first appear, but they soon fall to your attacks. Leaping over their splintered remains, you hurry to aid the beleaguered traveller. However, it appears he is now on the top of the situation. Having fended off the remaining creatures with his staff, the man raises his palm and utters an arcane command. From his hand, a white light bursts forth – blinding and intense. There is an echoing crack of thunder.

You stagger back, trying to blink through the bright afterimage. When you are finally able to focus again you see that the area around him is charred and blackened, as are the broken bodies of the strange woodland creatures.

The man lowers his hand, which is still glowing with a faint residue of magic. 'Thank the One God,' he gasps, his shoulders slumping with exhaustion. He catches your eye and manages a crooked smile. 'And thank you, too. I thought I was a goner.'

He steps forward, offering out his hand. 'I'm Benin,' he grins. 'Don't worry, you're perfectly safe to shake it.'

Mirroring his grin, you take his hand in friendship.

'I wasn't expecting to run across anyone else in these woods,' he says, sounding grateful for his change of fortune. 'And certainly not these!' He kicks at the nearest pile of blackened wood.

Will you:	
Ask Benin about his magic?	80
Ask Benin what he is doing here?	57
Examine the remains of the creatures?	133
Continue on your journey?	157

180

'There was a man who once lived in this village – Rorus Satch. He was working on a cure for vampirism. He was looking for a way to cure himself.'

'How do you know all this?' you ask, bewildered.

Eldias cracks his knuckles. 'I found his apprentice. And after some persuasion, he was willing to talk.'

You glance over at the scattered papers and the overturned writing desk. 'And have you found the cure?'

The witchfinder shakes his head. 'This is not his house, but I have already searched there… everywhere. All his books, all his journals, have been taken.' He walks over to the desk and stoops down, plucking something from the floor. It is a painting of a man, held in a cracked glass frame. He holds it out to you.

Taking the picture, you tilt it towards the light. It shows a middle-aged man, thin and gaunt, with pepper-grey eyes and a thick mane of silver hair. 'Who is this?' you ask.

Eldias watches you, his jaw clenched. 'The reverend. The man I am here to kill.'

Turn to 347 to ask Eldias another question. When you are ready to continue, turn to 340.

181

The tapestry features a number of embroidered panels; each one tells part of the story of Saint Allam. Your own knowledge of the saint is scanty, having never had time for books in your youth. The woman beside you notices you scratching your head in confusion as you try and make sense of the scenes.

'You're not familiar with the story?' she asks. Before you can answer she is already pointing to one of the scenes, where Allam is depicted kneeling in a church, looking up at a bright light. 'That's Allam, the youngest of King Gerard's sons. He was given a message, a vision, that he must journey to the west.'

Her finger travels to an image of Allam riding at the head of a procession of knights. 'The king sent him west with an army, and a personal guard of his best knights. Those knights became the six saints.' The woman points to a further panel, where Allam is shown striking down a misshapen creature with a bolt of lightning. 'Their armies fought their way west, conquering the trolls and the goblin hordes. But those victories meant nothing to Allam. He was searching for something else – something he called "the True Light".'

'Did he ever find it?' you ask, scanning the many scenes.

The woman shakes her head sadly. 'They brought much to the west; they founded Carvel and brought the One God's grace to the pagan peoples. But Allam never found the True Light. Many think it is a myth, something he invented to keep up the morale of his forces. But he always believed in it – and we must believe too. These lands are special. That is why we come here.'

The woman moves closer to the final panel, where Allam is shown ascending into clouds on angel's wings. 'It's nearly two hundred years to the day that Allam was reunited with the One God.' She looks your way. 'You are staying for the All Saint's celebrations aren't you? I've heard it's going to be really something. The prince has promised—'

Her voice grows distant as your attention wanders back to the first image, of Allam kneeling before the bright light of the One God. Could it have been the same light you saw in your recent vision, guiding you through the forest of thorns?

You mumble a hasty 'thank you' to the woman before moving away.

Will you:

Talk to the man on the bench?	152
Leave the church?	77

182

Lazlo escorts you to the courtyard, where a group of servants are busy unloading crates from a series of wagons. Jeeves appears to be overseeing the operation, furiously scratching notes into a log book whilst hurrying between wagons, snapping at everyone's heels.

'Just some extra goodies for the All Saint's festival,' smiles Lazlo, noticing your look of bewilderment. 'Fireworks – the very best.'

'And those?' you ask, pointing to a pile of smaller boxes, each one carrying the stamp of a white rose.

Lazlo stops, glancing sideways at you. 'Yes, the white rose. It's the symbol of the cardinals from the White Abbey. Those are supplies for the war effort.'

'The war effort . . .' you repeat, confused. 'You mean, the Church's fight against the Wiccans?'

Lazlo winces, shifting uncomfortably. 'Look, I don't get directly involved. My supplies are medicinal – potions, cures. I make sure that they go to the right people . . .' He scratches nervously at the back of his neck. 'On both sides. That could get me into a lot of trouble. But I trust you are the sort to be discreet.'

You shrug your shoulders. 'I try and stay out of politics.'

Lazlo's grin returns. 'And those are wise words, my friend.' The prince nods to the guards at the gate, who move aside to let you pass. 'Good luck,' he smiles. 'I hope our paths cross again, one day.' Thanking Lazlo, you leave the castle and return to the bustling streets of Carvel. Turn to the map to continue your adventure.

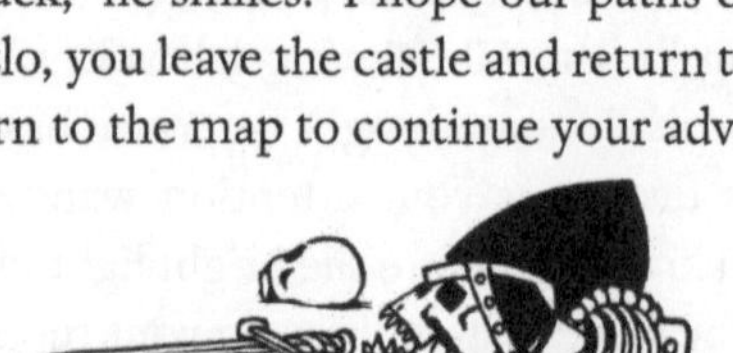

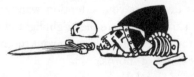

183

Your legs soon ache from your ascent into the mountains. After what seems like a lifetime you finally reach a ledge, banked with snow. Here the goblin tracks are clearly visible, leading into and out of a cave.

The captain slides his shield from his back and tugs his axe loose from his belt. You see the others similarly drawing their weapons, tensed and ready for combat. Surl, the party's tracker, creeps forward into the cave. The rest of you follow, unsure what you will find inside. Turn to 87.

184

'It's common knowledge that we got a war brewing in the east; been skirmishes with Mordland already. I dare say it won't be long before the king raises an army and announces another one of them holy crusades. Probably about time – bring some of the One God's light to that forsaken land.'

The map-seller's gaze falls on the domed church. 'But it's bad news for us. Inquisitors are being pulled back to the capital. The guards try their best, I know, but they aren't enough to handle the problems in Carvel. We need them around, not gallivanting off east where'll we never see them again.'

Will you:

Ask for more news?	137
Continue exploring upper town?	77

185

Frantically, you turn your back on the advancing zombies and hurry towards the nearest building, a two-storey cottage of grey stone and black wood. You try the front door but it is locked. With the screeching zombies closing in on all sides, you are left with only one choice. Turn to 227.

186

You dodge through the bombardment of gooey strands, following the others as they race across the cavern. Up ahead you see a flash of magic and the glint of steel. The captain and several of the others are fighting off a giant creature, which has appeared out of a side tunnel. It has the head and torso of a man, but the lower body and legs of a black ant. Both of its human-like arms end in serrated blades, which the creature is using to slash and hack at its attackers.

The captain lands a lucky blow, felling the ant-man. He puts a boot to its squirming body as he extracts his axe blade.

'Get moving!' he bellows. 'Into the tunnel!'

Within seconds you are all huddled in the tight space, breathing hard. Even the captain looks momentarily shaken.

'What was that?' gasps Vas, grimacing at the corpse of the ant-man.

'A massacre was what it was,' cries Surl, sounding panicked. 'That weren't no greenheads.'

You look around at the party. Of the original dozen, only half remain.

'Come on,' growls the captain. 'Keep it together, people.' He grabs your arm and pushes you forwards. 'You're tracker now. Get moving!'

Feeling more like bait than a valued member of the team, you find yourself leading the group deeper into the cave. After several hundred metres the tunnel widens, joining a much larger passageway which cuts left to right. A chill wind blows from the west, carrying with it a salty, stagnant odour. To the east the passage ascends steeply, heading deeper into the mountain.

Will you:

Take the east passage? 143

Take the west passage? 122

187

You squat down by the fire, your gaze fixed on the old man. There is no denying that the stew smells delicious – and you are famished. But you are not ready to trust him just yet. Your weapons stay at your side, where they can be easily reached.

'Ah yes, this a little more civilised, isn't it?' smiles the old man, spooning some of the stew into a bowl. As he hands it to you there is a bone-trembling roar, reverberating from somewhere deep inside the rock. You drop the bowl in surprise, spilling stew across the ground. Warily, you spring back to your feet, weapons in your hands.

'What's going on?' you insist, craning your neck to take in the dark, high walls of the bluff.

'Extreme sports,' replies the old man, holding his tea cup to his lips. A sudden tremor sends more dirt and dust pluming into the cleft. The man's tea cup shakes in his hands, spilling tea down his coat. 'Oh, how bothersome,' he grimaces, putting the cup aside to brush at the stain.

You frown, confused by the man's actions. He doesn't seem remotely bothered by what is happening. 'Perhaps we should investigate?' you urge, stepping out of the way out of a falling rock. It is accompanied by an anguished roar and a series of hollow thuds – as if something large is beating against the ground. Each one sends a tremor through the rock walls, rattling the porcelain tea cups on their tray.

'Very well,' sighs the man, pushing himself to his feet. 'But I do assure you, my master is an expert at what he does.'

There is another wailing scream.

'Extreme sports?' you ask, with a quizzical frown.

'Just a little spelunking,' he proffers with a shrug. 'Cave diving . . . he likes the adrenaline rush.'

Suddenly there is an almighty bang as the side of the bluff explodes outwards, hurling rock and dust into the snow-drenched sky. Turn to 200.

188

Ignoring the pillars, you focus your attacks on the giants, chipping away at their dense armour until some vital spot is revealed. It is a hard and gruelling battle, but your determination pays off – leaving you the victor. You may now help yourself to one of the following special rewards:

Shockwave	**Stone fury**	**Black peak**
(chest)	(left hand: fist weapon)	(main hand: dagger)
+2 brawn +1 armour	+1 speed +2 magic	+2 brawn
Ability: lightning	Ability: surge	Ability: deep wound
	(requirement: mage)	(requirement: rogue)

If you have the word *Wiccan* on your hero sheet, turn to 354. Otherwise, turn to 400.

189

The narrow hold is filled with stagnant-smelling water. Rotted food, splintered wood and the occasional drowned rat bob up and down on its briny surface.

Wading through the water, you head towards a set of crates that have been roped together in a thick netting. You take a knife and cut through the top ropes, before prising open one of the crates. Inside, resting on a bed of straw, is a circular metallic object.

'What's that?' asks Surl, leaning over to take a closer look.

Tentatively, you lift the object out of the crate. On one side of the disc, engraved in the metal, is the message: 'Handle with care!' A roll of touch paper dangles from its underside.

Surl's eyes widen. 'Oh! I know what that is! Explosives!' He blows out his cheeks, making an impressive-sounding 'boom'. 'Yeah, one of them could take off the side of this mountain.' He points to another area of the hold, where the ropes have been cut and some of the crates have been smashed open. 'Wonder if the gobboes got their hands on any?'

If you wish, you may take any/all of the following items:

Borehole charge	**The *Celeste*'s anchor**
(backpack)	(left hand: club)
The writing on the side states: 'Handle with care!'	+1 brawn Ability: pound

Finding little else of interest in the hold, you head back to the deck. Turn to 159.

190

Anse pushes on the black-iron doors, which grate and squeal in protest as they slowly slide open.

From inside the tower a searing heat rushes out through the widening gap, like a blast from a furnace. It is accompanied by a thunderous, reverberating boom, echoing from somewhere deep in the building itself.

'This is surely the moment when someone suggests we turn back,' says Polk meekly. He looks up at the cracked wall, sweeping away into the chill, white skies. 'Anyone want to suggest that now ... please?'

Joss is first through the doors, an arrow nocked to her bow. Anse follows close behind, moving with a silent and careful grace. You give Polk an apologetic frown, before drawing your weapons and reluctantly following the others.

'Just remember, I suggested it ...' mutters Polk, hurrying to bring up the rear. 'Just remember.'

As you enter the tower, several images of what you might find flash through your mind. An opulent entrance hall, perhaps, or a cold-stone chamber filled with dusty cobwebs and shifting shadows ...

And then your jaw hangs open, your footfalls slowing as you crane your head back, struggling to take in and understand what your eyes are seeing. Turn to 251.

191

Candles have been placed inside a series of chalk circles, marked across the hilltop. Three of the circles remain empty. You wonder if the witch meant to complete the ritual by adding more candles to these empty circles. Retrieving the witch's bag, you find a dozen candles and a tinderbox inside. Perhaps you could finish this strange ritual to see what happens …

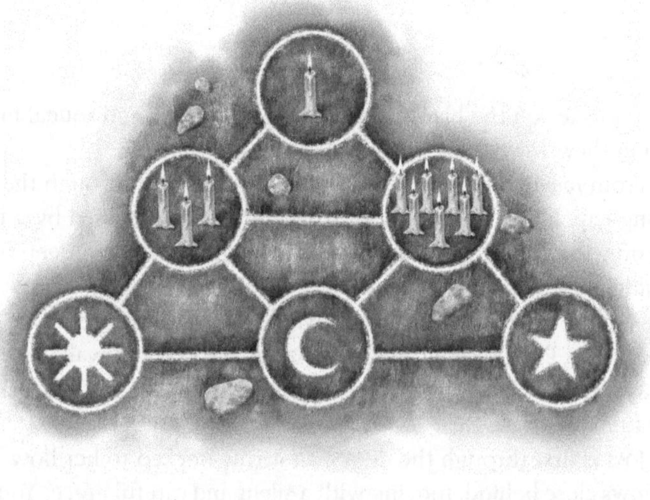

Decide how many candles you will place in the sun, moon and star circles. Take each of these individual numbers, in that order, to give you a three digit number. (For example, 5 candles in the sun circle, 2 candles in the moon circle and 3 in the star circle would give you the number 523.)

Then turn to the resulting entry number to see if you were successful. If you fail to solve the puzzle then you have no choice but to resume your journey. Turn to 215.

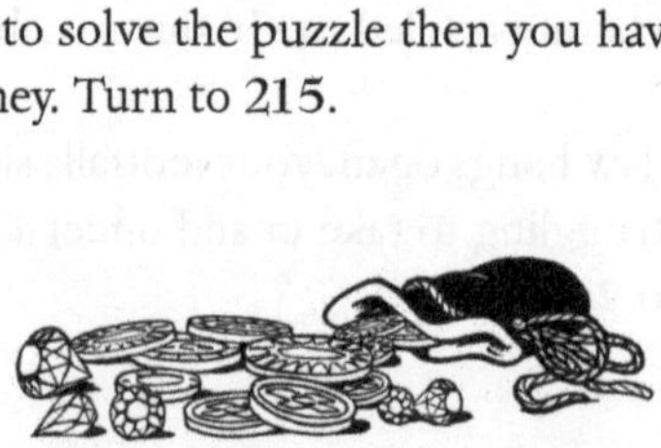

192

You take the leaves of the sagewort and grind them into a mushy pulp. This is then stirred into the liquid, turning it from white to a light-shade of green. The mixture has started to bubble and fizz. What ingredient will you add next?

Will you:	
Add meadowsweet?	104
Add white willow?	310
Add lemongrass?	287

193

The priest reins in his horse in a flurry of mud and water. 'My friend!' he gasps, his surprise mirroring your own. 'The One God shines on us this day.'

The feathered woman snarls, tugging a black wand from her belt. 'It seems you have already chosen your side, Sanchen.'

'No!' The cry comes from Benin, as the Wiccan witch aims the tip of her wand at you. There is a blast of cold, black fire – then you are falling backwards, screaming in agony. The last thing you remember is the rain, spearing down from the black skies, beating against your pain-wracked body. Then the light fades and a feverish darkness takes you. Turn to 338.

194

With the ruffians defeated, you are able to snatch the coat from the chair before the half-giant barman lumbers over and grabs you by the scruff of your neck. Despite your protests, the barman drags you out of the inn and throws you headfirst into the mud.

'Now don't yer come back until yer learnt some manners!' he bellows. 'The missus got a worse temper than me, I warnin' yer!' He starts to turn, then hesitates for a moment, before looking back with a smile. 'But good on yer. High time someone gutted that stinkin' fish.'

Congratulations! You have gained the following item:

Joseph's coat
(chest)
+1 speed +1 armour
Ability: many scales, charm

Inside a pocket, you also find 20 gold crowns. Remove the word *Joseph* from your hero sheet. After dusting yourself off, you contemplate your next move. You may talk to the knight and farrier (turn to 177), visit the equipment store (turn to 352), return to the inn (turn to 64) or leave Raven's Rest (return to the map).

195

You push open the door. It takes a few minutes for your eyes to accustom to the darkness. It looks as though the room was once used as a nursery. There is a wooden cot pushed up into one corner and a small bed beside it. A number of dolls and toys lie scattered across the floor.

You are about to leave and return to the landing, when your eyes catch on something lurking in the shadows: a child, small and hunched over, dressed in a leather vest and breeches. Its head is resting against the wall, its arms hanging limp at its side. You can faintly hear a sad, wet-sounding moan coming from its direction.

Will you:	
Approach the child?	10
Quietly leave the room and go downstairs?	55

196

The twisted vines pull back, revealing a diamond-shaped dais of black stone. Four large iron rings have been hammered to its four points.

From each, a thick chain trails through the fog to a set of manacles, that imprison a giant, hulking creature.

At first its body is obscured by wings, stretched taut to reveal the corded black veins that snake through the ridged membrane. Then, with a crack, the wings fold back and the creature shifts around, drawing astonished gasps from your companions.

It is a demon.

As it rises to its full height you find yourself teetering back, awestruck by its dark and fearsome majesty. It stands over eight feet tall, its broad shoulders covered in spiked plates of hardened skin. The rest of its body is scaled, the serrated edges rippling in the light, its chest heaving with deep, rumbling breaths. Two curved horns, over a metre in length, jut out from its temples, framing a pair of crimson eyes burning with a cruel arrogance.

'Was I not what you expected?' booms the demon, its commanding tone resonating through your very bones. 'Perhaps you had prayed for an angel.' The creature displays a curve of sharp teeth as it lazily flaps its wings. 'I led you here, prophet. Now you will free me. I have waited such a very long time...'

Before you have a chance to respond, you hear the sound of roots and limbs snapping behind you. One of your companions cries out a warning. You spin around to see the pathway closing, the thorn branches twisting and wrapping together into a solid wall.

'What's happening?' You glance back at the dais, wondering if this is some trick or spell of the demon's doing. He merely watches with a mocking smile.

Another cry from your companions. The thorns have started to rise up into the air, clumps of wet earth falling away from their writhing forms. In horror, you watch as the trees start to mould themselves into a single creature, a mockery of a human, with trunk-like legs and long, trailing arms. Within seconds the land to either side of you is reduced to a barren, featureless marsh – the trees having drawn themselves up into the dark skies to become a barbed colossus.

'Free me,' hisses the demon, shaking the manacles snapped tight around its wrists. 'You cannot defeat it. Orgorath is an ancient spirit, in thrall to the dwarves who made me their prisoner. You need me to defeat it!'

The forest monster throws back its head and lets loose a blood-curdling scream. Then it lumbers forward, its vine-like arms twisting into gigantic fists.

If you have the word *Wiccan* on your hero sheet, turn to 268. Otherwise, turn to 237.

197

Benin folds his arms, casting a critical eye over your trappings. 'I sense a powerful magic about you, but it is not focused, it lacks discipline. That will leave you open to … bad influences.' He pauses, his face twisted with indecision. 'Hmm, I suppose I could correct that failing – show you how to unlock your inner kha. Yes … perhaps then, you could truly serve the One God.'

Will you:	
Agree to become an acolyte (requirement: mage)?	487
Decline and return to the courtyard?	260

198

You match your enemy's speed, expertly dodging the bug's attacks and responding with your own. For the onlookers, the battle must be a frenzied blur – but for you, it is a dance, your heightened awareness alerting you to each of the creature's attacks a moment before they happen.

At last you sever the ant's head, sending it spinning away in a spray of slimy ichor. The rest of the body shakes and convulses, then topples over, leaving its spindly legs to twitch feebly in the air. You may now take one of the following items:

Assassin's veil	Green blaze	Mighty claw
(head)	(chest)	(main hand: fist weapon)
+1 magic	+1 speed +1 armour	+1 speed +1 brawn
Ability: vanish	Ability: haste	Ability: sideswipe

'How'd you do that?' asks Surl, his eyes wide with amazement. 'I've not seen anyone move like that.'

You shrug your shoulders, unsure how to respond. Since your body was introduced to the Elysium in the inquisitors' dungeons, your powers appear to have taken on a new form; your gift of prophecy becoming something more immediate and instinctive.

'I don't care what tricks you got hiding up yer sleeves,' growls the captain. 'We work as a team. And this team is moving. Now!'

Out of the original party, only yourself, Surl and Vas remain. Thankfully, you reach the other side of the cave with no further encounters. In the facing wall, a jagged hole leads through into another rough-hewn tunnel. Turn to **164**.

199

The Pilgrim's Road continues through the fenlands, taking you through dense thickets of mould-covered trees and over rickety bridges, to finally bring you to a clump of tumbledown buildings. They seem squat and ugly things, perched crookedly at the edges of the dirt track, their sloping roofs dripping with curtains of weed and fungus. If it wasn't for the bustling signs of life – solemn-clothed travellers for the most part – you would assume this place was a forgotten ghost town, left to rot away amidst the murk and gloom.

To your left is the only building of note in this ramshackle settlement, a coaching inn, which has evidently been extended over time to become a sprawling jumble of outbuildings and stables. The inn appears to be full to bursting point, and from the open doors of the main taproom you can hear an endless crescendo of boisterous laughter and song.

Across to your right, two armed men stand on sullen guard outside an equipment store. The sign above the door reads *Edgar's Essentials* – with a pair of deer antlers hanging lopsidedly over the faded lettering.

Further along the street, a farrier is shoeing a grey warhorse, while its rider – a tall man dressed in polished silver armour – holds onto the beast's reins to keep it steady. The knight catches your eye and nods his head in greeting.

Will you:

Enter the taproom of the coaching inn?	**64**
Talk to the knight and the farrier?	**177**
Investigate 'Edgar's Essentials'?	**352**
Leave and continue your journey?	**Return to the map**

200

A dark body is flung out of the ruptured hole, soaring high overhead with a hollering cry. You glimpse a tattered cloak and black clothing then it is gone, turning and twisting through the thick clouds of snow. The old man is on his feet in seconds, snatching a brand from the fire and hurrying out of the shelter. You follow, picking your way past the fallen boulders that now pockmark the snow-covered ground.

A few metres from the bluff, a gnarled rowan tree grows from the side of a rocky hummock. A man is now dangling from its branches like a yuletide decoration, his long cloak snagged on the thorny limbs.

'My lord!' The old man raises his brand, its flames guttering in the wind. 'What happened, sir?'

There is a loud rip, then suddenly the black figure is dropping, tumbling and bumping his way through the lower branches to finally land in a heap in the snow. He grunts, rubbing his side.

'Extreme sports?' you enquire once again.

The man in black looks up. You see that he is wearing a mask over half of his face, the nose piece giving him the appearance of a bird. He smoothes back his wet blond hair with a gloved hand.

'That could have gone better,' he grimaces. 'Jeeves, I do believe we have a problem.' He looks up at the old man, holding out an arm for assistance. He groans as he finds his feet, the tattered cloak parting to reveal the hilts of several knives.

'Indeed we do, sir.' Jeeves clucks his tongue, dusting the grey dirt and bark from the man's shoulders. 'This is the fifth costume in as many days. I'll have to get more cloth—'

The masked man waves him away. 'We've got bigger problems than my wardrobe, Jeeves.'

At that moment, the howling wind is joined by a bone-chilling shriek. It is coming from the bluff behind you. Spinning around, you gasp in horror at the monstrous creation that is now perched on the rock. At first, you mistake it for some devilish bird – its immense wings rising like dark sails from its shoulders. But this is no bird. Its body is humanoid, with thick arms and bowed legs. The head forms a sleek crest, fronted by red glowing eyes and a wide maw filled with fanged teeth.

'It's bigger than I expected,' states Jeeves, still sounding oddly detached from the situation. 'Not your usual margoyle is it, sir?'

The masked man gives an impatient sigh. 'No, Jeeves, not your usual margoyle.'

The beast takes to the air with another deafening screech, its giant form moving with a startling speed. Half-blinded by snow, you raise your weapons, ready to defend yourself. Then you see a cascade of glimmering steel flash past your shoulder. Knives. They strike harmlessly against the creature's stony skin as it sweeps in to attack. The man in black races forward to head it off, his hands moving in a blur as they send more knives flickering towards it. The beast bats them away with its wings, then swings one of its clawed fists in the warrior's direction. He tries to twist aside, but is struck by the full force of the blow and is sent tumbling backwards into the snow.

The beast turns to face you, its diamond-sharp fangs gnashing together. Up close, you can see the blood-red veins that crisscross its grey skin, pulsing with a demonic magic. Jeeves has already scurried away, to tend to his companion. You are now alone and must fight:

	Speed	*Brawn*	*Armour*	*Health*
Margoyle	3	3	3	50

Special abilities

- Stone blood: If the margoyle rolls a ⚃ or more for its damage score, its fangs latch onto you, sucking your blood. This causes damage as normal, but also raises the margoyle's *armour* by 1 (up to a maximum of 6) as the blood flows through its magical veins.

If you manage to defeat the margoyle, turn to 91.

201

Within minutes the earthen mound is littered with bones and chunks of pumpkin. You wipe the fleshy pulp from your blade, before searching what remains of the creature's body. You may now take any/all of the following items:

Pumpkin squash (2 uses)	All hallow's ring
(backpack)	(ring)
Use any time in combat to raise your *brawn* or *magic* by 2 for one combat round	+1 brawn

The witch must have been summoning this grisly guardian to help protect the burial mound. You set about breaking up the ritual area, extinguishing the candles and scuffing the chalk circles with your boot heel. Satisfied with your efforts, you leave the mound and head deeper into the barrows. Turn to 215.

202

'Stories, eh? I like stories and got a good head for 'em too.' He furrows his brow, tapping his chin as he thinks. 'Let's see – the latest one I got was from a ranger, stopped off here for feed for 'is horse. He said that there been a battle west of here, out on the Witch's Wold. Two of them inquisitors went at it against a 'ole band of wild men. It didn't end good. And now the place is haunted – very bad from the sounds of things.' He taps the wood of the counter with his knuckles. 'I can 'andle what's real and solid – that makes sense to me – but when we talkin' ghosts …' His metal teeth scrape together as they form a scowl. 'I prefer 'em to just stay in the stories, where they belong.'

To ask the barman about his teeth turn to 344, to explore the rest of the tap room turn to 172, or to leave turn to 199.

203

You are pressed against the building by the endless tide of bodies. With barely enough room to swing your weapons, you realise that you cannot possibly defeat so many enemies. Frantically, you look around for an opening, a means of escape, but the zombies form an impenetrable wall of snarling, snapping death. There is only one route left available to you now – up. Turn to 227.

204

The man chuckles as if there is some hidden joke to the question. 'I'm Bim Mamba. But when I start to mix up the special magic, I get the name Boom.' He spins the staff around skilfully in his hands. 'I make the boom skulls and the potions, but this is my favourite.' He aims the staff at the far wall, sending a bolt of magic crackling through the air. It slams into a wooden shield propped up against the rocks, shattering it to pieces. 'Boom stick. You like?'

Will you:

Ask what he meant by a 'spirit walk'?	462
Ask how he can help?	257

205

Congratulations! Your boarding party has managed to wrest control of the ship. The captain picks up the leader's pirate hat and turns it around thoughtfully. 'Nice bit of headwear.' He tosses it to Surl, who giggles with delight as he places it on his head.

You take a moment to search the bodies of the cannon team. You may choose up to two of the following rewards:

Goblin bones (backpack)	Rusted chainmail (chest)	Sailor's sandals (feet)
These might prove valuable to the right person	+1 speed +1 armour	+1 speed Ability: surefooted

When you have made your decision, turn to **118**.

206

You hurry through the portal. For a second you experience a lurching, dizzying sensation, like falling, then you find yourself stumbling forwards into a narrow stone passageway. The air is cold and musty, a stark contrast to the blazing heat of the courtyard. Sadly, there is no sign of your companions – you can only assume that the doors they chose must have taken them to different parts of the tower. And as for Anse … you hope that the paladin was able to escape from the fiery demon before it was too late.

Behind you is a smooth wall of black stone. With no other choice but forward, you warily advance along the passageway. As you progress, you become aware of a constant rumbling sound reverberating through the rock. Every so often there is a thunderous clunk, like something suddenly locking into place. Then the rumbling starts again. You wonder if it might be the tower itself, moving and rearranging itself in some strange fashion. It is a thought that brings little comfort.

After several hundred metres you come to a junction. Ahead, the passage ends in an archway, beyond which you can see a chamber filled with flickering lights. To your left, a smaller side passage leads to a plain wooden door.

Will you:	
Investigate the room with the lights?	318
Try the wooden door?	4

207

You stand over the beast's lice-ridden corpse, torn between pity and loathing for such an unfortunate beast.

'Give me space,' says Boom, tapping his staff against the ground. 'I need to get spirit.'

You step away from the body as it starts to decompose, quickly forming a foul-smelling yellow dust. From the shaman's staff there is a bright flash of light, then the dust sweeps up into the air, funnelling towards the staff. The runes glow for a second, then the dust is gone.

'That be good riddance to him,' grins Boom, his staff now surrounded with a sickly yellow aura. 'We got his power now.'

(By defeating Lycanth, the shaman's staff has gained the *infected wound* ability. Make a note of this on your hero sheet.)

If you are a warrior, turn to 232. If you are a mage, turn to 350. If you are a rogue, turn to 507.

208

The portal glimmers once again – and out steps your largest foe yet. It reminds you of the metal warrior that you first saw with the child when you entered the tower, but this one is bigger – a hulking monstrosity of iron plates, riveted together to form a cruel mockery of a human. From its metal gauntlets a set of buzz saws suddenly whirr into motion, spinning into a grey blur as the giant advances. You must fight:

	Speed	*Brawn*	*Armour*	*Health*
Ironclad	5	5	5	35

Special abilities:

Body of iron: Ironclad is immune to *bleed, thorns* and *thorn cage*.

If you have one of the following and wish to use it, turn to the relevant entry number: *metal soldier* (turn to 456), *paper soldier* (turn to

448), *rock soldier* (turn to 252). Otherwise, you must fight this opponent yourself. If you win, restore your *health* and turn to 228. If you are defeated, turn to 464.

209

Joseph stares at the coat open-mouthed. 'I don't . . . I don't know what to say. Can I . . . can I try it on?' You hold it open, letting him slide his arms into the sleeves. When the coat is finally on, he spins around on the spot, the coat-tails whipping through the air.

'This is amazing! My coat of many scales!'

You cough into your hand, interrupting his spinning and dancing. 'I thought your plan was to sell this. We're splitting the profits, aren't we?'

Joseph's enthusiasm deflates, his arms dropping by his side. 'I know. I just . . . I never owned anything this special before. Basilisk scales are second only to dragon scales in their worth. Can't I keep it?' (Remove the *coat of many scales* from your hero sheet.)

Will you:

Let Joseph keep the coat?	254
Insist that he sells it?	267

210

Stepping over the charred corpses of the zombies, you re-enter the reverend's home through the blasted wall. For a moment you scan the scorched papers and books that litter the ground. It could take hours to search through them all in the hope of finding a stray clue. You are about to leave and explore the rest of the building when your eyes catch on a section of the far wall. It would have been covered up by the writing desk, but that now lies on its side, revealing a patch of paint that is damp and peeling. A hairline crack runs across it, forming a square.

Intrigued, you walk over and kneel beside it. Yes – you can feel a breeze coming from between the cracks. It must lead through to a secret passage. Pushing on the square panel, you discover that it is loose. It slides back, revealing a damp, musty-smelling cavity. You duck down and crawl forwards, the rough stone grazing your hands. After several metres, the tight passage makes a right-hand turn, depositing you in a small room. Candles flicker in numerous alcoves set around the walls, the hot wax forming dripping beards over the grey stone.

The only item of furniture in the room is a metal reading stand, stood against the opposite wall. Resting on it is an open book, its pages grime-stained and crumpled. You quickly walk over to take a closer look. It appears to be a field guide or journal, covered in sketches and scribblings. Lifting it up, a loose piece of parchment slides out from between the pages. Intrigued, you hold the sheet closer to the candlelight. The writing is erratic, most of the rambling obscured by blots of ink. Only one section is clear – a list of ingredients to make a potion called elixir vitae. They are underlined several times, as if the writer was keen to stress their importance: *meadowsweet, lemongrass* and *white willow*. You stuff the sheet of paper into your backpack before leaving the reverend's home. (Make a note of those ingredients on your hero sheet, they might prove useful later.) You may now investigate the wishing well (turn to 13) or search the herbalist's cottage (turn to 224).

211

'My mother used to practise alchemy,' explains Benin. 'I know something of the art, enough for me to know where to look for answers.' He glances over at the manticore nervously. 'The church at Carvel has an extensive library; I was able to find a match for the charm in a dwarven tome. When the healers at the church couldn't save the bishop, I knew then I'd have to fall back on the old ways.'

He looks at you imploringly. 'The spell can only be broken by using the same reagents. And one of those is the blood of a manticore.'

The beast snorts, flapping its wings lazily. 'Now, aren't we a popular bunch?'

'Please,' begs the priest. 'We must find out who did this. The bishop will know more, once we cure him of this curse!'

Will you:

Let Benin take the blood he needs?	343
Argue that you need the blood instead?	259
Convince Benin to help you defeat the manticore?	280

212

'We tried,' replies Damaris, a remembered pain furrowing her brow. 'We went south, where the grasslands turn to dust. A hard land. The soil would not take our crops and the hunting was poor. We were starving, homeless. The creatures there, dust devils and sand goblins, preyed on our weak, harrowing us at every turn. In the end we had no choice but to return to the homeland, Gilglaiden. We are ready now – to do what we must to win it back.'

Turn to 126 to ask Damaris another question.

213

'To learn the path of the mage, you need to be tested – we need to know that you have the mental strength to control the magic, to stave off the temptations that will come your way.'

'What temptation?' you ask with interest.

'Our most powerful magics come from the essence of demons,' explains Malak. He reaches inside his coat and pulls out a pulsing blue orb. As he holds it aloft, lightning begins to flicker around it. 'This is my kha. It belonged to a demon once … but now I use it to draw power; to strengthen my magic. One day I will need to break my bond with it or else I will become the very demon I defeated to obtain it. Tell me,' Malak's lips curl into a scowl. 'Do you really think *you* can master such power?'

If you have the *prince's seal*, turn to 288. Otherwise, you may question Malak further (turn to 139) or return to upper town (turn to 77).

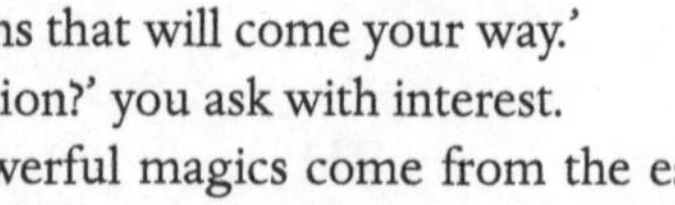

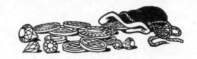

214

After a tense wait, Surl and the mage return to deliver their report. As with the rest of the camp, the cabins have all been ransacked. Anything of value, including food, has been taken. Turn to 220.

215

The fog has thickened once again, obscuring your surroundings. Picking a direction at random, you press on through the barrows, looking for tombs that might offer up their riches.

You haven't travelled far before you become aware of something following you. There is the sound of padded feet. And a low, guttural growl.

You spin around with weapons drawn, hoping to catch your pursuer. But there is nothing there, only a ghostly white mist. Another growl forces you to turn again. Your breath catches in your throat as you spot a dark shape moving towards you. The reek of damp earth and stagnant water grow stronger as the creature approaches, clawed feet crunching through the straggly grass.

Then the fog parts and you see it. A black-haired wolf of immense size, its gangly shoulders almost as tall as your own. For a moment, you are held by its glittering yellow eyes . . .

. . . and then you run.

Frantically, you sprint across the uneven ground, with no sense of where you are headed. The beast is following, close on your heels, its wet snarling the only sound in the grim silence.

Your foot catches on something – a root or a stone – and you find yourself flying forwards over the side of a steep hill. Unable to break your momentum, you tumble and slide through the damp grass, finally crashing down onto stony soil.

You barely have time to clamber to your feet before the wolf is upon you. The stench of death is almost overpowering as a shaggy head, full of glittering fangs, fills your vision. Somehow, you are able to push the beast away, dodging a swipe from its curved claws. Desperately you back away, hands shaking as you grip your weapons.

Then your heel hits against something hard. You can feel stone and earth pressing against your rear.

Grimly, you realise you are trapped against one of the mounds.

The dire wolf knows there is no escape. With frothy saliva dripping from its hairy jowls, the enormous beast rears back on its haunches and prepares to pounce. Turn to 11.

216

(If you have the word *raven* on your hero sheet, then turn to 199.)

They call it the Pilgrim's Road: a grand name for what is little more than a rutted dirt track, winding like a grimy smear through bleak hills and fenland. In places, it has become flooded with stagnant water, forcing you to splash through miles of weed-choked marsh, with only the occasional marker to signify that a road lies somewhere beneath.

The cold of the land seeps into your boots – into your bones. After a tiring trek through the cloying mud, you are grateful when the track finally begins to rise, taking you into hills crowned with straggly trees and black gorse. In the distance you see a ribbon of lights shining through the pale mist. A sign by the roadside reads: 'Raven's Rest – 1 mile'.

Before you can breathe a sigh a relief, you hear the snap of a twig to your left. There is a muffled curse.

Quickly, you draw your weapons, as the first of the robbers comes hurtling out of the trees – a bone-thin man wielding a rake. Behind him you see two others, similarly armed with make-shift weapons – one holding a wooden club and the other a rust-bladed hoe.

Will you:

Make them pay for their foolishness?	241
Try and reason with them?	37

217
Quest: The temple of Boom

You hack angrily at the wall of creepers, snarling and spitting like some enraged demon. It has taken only half a day for the jungle to reduce you to this. The searing humidity is unbearable, soaking you in sweat and grime. It pastes your hair to your forehead, running into your eyes, down your back, tickling your neck and arms. Then there is the noise – a chirruping, shrieking, jabbering crescendo. It comes at you from all angles, battering you with unfamiliar sounds. You've learnt to ignore it, concentrating instead on the wildlife you can see. Snakes and spiders have now become commonplace, as well as the multi-legged bugs crawling through the leaf litter, some disguised to look like twigs or rocks, barely distinguishable from their surroundings.

As you push on through the trees, your anger continues to build – anger at Virgil for sending you out here on this foolish mission, and anger at yourself for agreeing to it. To hunt a demon, of all things.

'How do you hunt a demon?' you growl crossly at no one in particular. It's not even as if there are footprints to follow or a path of burning devastation to mark the way – anything that would give a clue. Instead, you feel utterly alone and lost, hemmed in on all sides by the thick forest.

You stop at the banks of a sluggish river, its low-water level exposing tangled tree roots. Warily, you slide down to the muddy water and fill your canteen, taking thirsty gulps of the brackish water before tipping the rest over your head.

A flash of light. A grinning skull leers at you through a putrid green mist.

You stumble, blinking and gasping.

A pillar of stone. A courtyard, littered with bones. The winged demon strides past ruined buildings. He is staggering – wounded. One side of his body is burnt, the skin blackened and scarred. A runed-iron box is cradled against his chest and from it you can feel an intense heat – blazing like a sun.

When you open your eyes, you give a startled cry, seeing a grinning skull staring straight back at you. Your first instinct is to draw your weapons. Then you relax. The skull is simply a carving on the opposite bank of the river – part of a circular marker stone.

The demon is here.

Your heart beats faster. From your scars you feel a sudden, burning pain, which slowly grows in intensity, finally becoming an unbearable agony. You pull at your clothes, exposing your scarred shoulder. The blackened bruises have now spread, covering more of your skin in glittering dark scales. They give off a sickly-black smoke, reeking of brimstone.

For an instant your rage subsides, replaced by a creeping, unsettling horror. Virgil was right – you are becoming a demon. Your body is now infected by some dark magic and unless you defeat Cernos, you will become more like him; more like a monster.

The thought spurs you back into action, driving you into the murky waters of the river. You wade across to the opposite bank, your eyes fixed on the unsettling visage of the grinning skull. This is your first clue – your first step on the path to locating Cernos. Turn to 249.

218

The reverend falls to his knees, his life force ebbing away. 'No! No! You will never have my secrets!' He turns and, with the last of his strength, hurls a ball of green fire at the books on the altar. The fireball smashes into the stone, the books bursting into flame. He then slumps to the ground, his flesh withering away before your eyes. Within seconds, all that is left of the priest is a pile of bones.

Searching his remains, you find 20 gold crowns. You may also choose one of the following rewards:

Repentance	**Signet of sorrow**	**Spectral shawl**
(left hand: staff)	(ring)	(cloak)
+1 speed	+1 brawn +1 magic	+1 brawn
Ability: channel	Ability: suppress	Ability: vanish

When you have made your decision, turn to 275.

219

Somehow you are able to anticipate the monster's blows, allowing you to twist and dodge the buzzing blades and swinging chains. It quickly becomes obvious that the demon is indiscriminate in its attacks, swiping its saws through the air in a blind frenzy. Using this to your advantage, you weave between the wooden soldiers, blocking and parrying their clumsy sword thrusts, whilst the giant shreds them to pieces.

At last, after a gruelling battle, the demon lies dead – its whirring saws finally coming to a silent rest. Searching through the debris you find one of the following rewards:

Iron stompers	Lock jaw	Buzz saw
(feet)	(head)	(main hand: fist weapon)
+1 speed +1 armour	+1 brawn +1 armour	+1 speed
Ability: knockdown	Ability: slam	Ability: cleave

You also find a collection of nuts and bolts, glowing with some residue of magic. (If you wish to take the *nuts and bolts* make a note of these on your hero sheet, they don't take up backpack space.) When you have updated your sheet, turn to 412.

220

The captain chews thoughtfully on his roll of tobacco. 'I expected the goblins to have holed up here; that's what they normally do.'

Vas, the shaven-headed warrior, returns to the group. 'Snow's making it difficult but I found goblin tracks coming down from the mountains. An equal number of tracks are headed away south. They didn't stay here; must have moved on.' The woman thrusts her knives back into her belt. 'We gonna follow 'em? I didn't come all this way just to eyeball the scenery.'

The captain is silent for a moment, peering at the mountains through the thickening snow. 'We go north.'

There are gasps of surprise from the party. Surl voices what everyone is thinking. 'But the gobboes went south . . .' he says.

The captain leans forward, spitting a stream of juice into the muddy snow. 'They were in a hurry, fleeing from something – perhaps just a raiding party. Either way, our problem lies in that direction.' He lifts his burly arm, pointing a finger towards the grey mountains. 'I ain't running after a few goblins. There's gotta be more of 'em up there. You want to stop a flood, you go straight to the source.'

The captain trudges off through the camp. Surl and Vas exchange looks, then grudgingly fall into step behind him, leaving the rest of you to bring up the rear. Turn to **183**.

221

You spot the three farmers that had tried to rob you, sitting along one of the benches at the far end of the taproom. At first your eyes had passed over them, assuming they were just a group of gaudily-dressed nobles from some far flung city. But then you recognised the two boys; it is surely them, resplendent in tailored clothing, surrounded by a veritable feast of suckling pig and spiced potatoes. The boys are tucking into their food with gusto, whilst sharing jokes with some pilgrims on the next table. The father is supping his ale, his eyes fixed on a scabbarded sword resting on the table top.

'Well, your fortunes have certainly changed,' you smile, walking over to the table and gesturing to the succulent array of food.

The boys smile up at you, mouths full. The father stands, awkwardly rearranging his ill-fitting doublet. 'Me good friend, a pleasure to see yer.' He grins, sporting a gold tooth. 'Turns out me youngest was a better gambler than I thought. Please, will yer join us and share our food?' He gestures to the bench opposite.

You hesitate, reminded of your recent battle at the farmstead. Reaching into your pack, you lift out the locket that you found on Dagona's body.

The father gasps, his eyes widening. The two boys stop their eating as their attention shifts to the glittering chain and the broken-heart locket. 'Is that … Mother's?' asks the youngest, forcing his words around a mouthful of food.

'She is at rest,' you add gravely, handing the chain over to the father.

He takes it, his hands trembling as he lifts it up to his teary eyes.

'This . . . this is hers, yes.' He touches a similar chain that hangs around his neck, where you see the other half of the locket glittering in the lantern light. 'It is good to know that she won't suffer no more. Thank you.' (Remove *Dagona's locket* from your hero sheet.)

The man reaches for the scabbarded sword. 'I bought this . . . with half a mind to return to that cursed farm and do what . . .' He stops, shaking his head. 'I were a fool. I have not your courage. Take it. The blade is yours and good riddance to it.'

You may now take the following special reward:

Duty
(main hand: sword)
+1 speed +1 brawn
Ability: charm, faith and duty set

If you wish to decline the farmer's kind offer, he offers you 30 gold crowns instead. After sharing food and conversation with the family, you take your leave and head back towards the bar. Turn to 172.

222

You are able to prise open the lid, revealing the gooey white paste held inside. (If you wish to take the *extra-sticky glue* simply make a note of it on your hero sheet, it doesn't take up backpack space.)

As you pocket your item, you notice that the portal is starting to fade. Not wishing to become trapped in the attic, you push through the remaining junk and step into the white light. Turn to 440.

223

Both travellers speak at the same time.

'Nothing,' snaps the man darkly.

'Supplies,' says the woman, talking over him. She flinches, realising her error. 'Sorry,' she says bashfully.

You glance at the wooden crates, piled up in the back of the wagon. Most are plain, but you notice a couple carry the stamp of a white rose. The mark seems familiar – then you remember the crates that you saw being unloaded in the prince's courtyard in Carvel. 'The white rose,' you comment, nodding to the crates. 'That's the symbol of the cardinals from the White Abbey.'

The man shifts uneasily. 'I had you down as a traveller, not a scholar. Perhaps you best move on now – stick to the travelling part, not the nosing around part, eh?'

Will you:

Ask what happened to the wagon?	274
Ask where they are travelling to?	178
Ask if you can help?	141

224

The herbalist's cottage is not difficult to find. It is lies on the edge of the village, a little way from the other buildings. The garden outside is overgrown with weeds, the building itself a burnt-out ruin. Clearly, when the villagers discovered that Rorus Satch was a vampire, they didn't hesitate to put his home to the flame.

You doubt you will find anything in the house, but the garden might still have some herbs growing in it. If you have the *Handy Herbalist's Spotter's Guide* then turn to 351. Otherwise, you realise that your paltry knowledge of herbs is not going to be enough to identify what you need. Frustrated, you turn your attention back to the village. You may now investigate the wishing well (turn to 13) or search the reverend's home (turn to 210).

225

A short tunnel leads you through into a circular rock basin, open to the sky. The floor is littered with half-chewed bones and ragged scraps of cloth. Ahead of you, on a stone ledge, lounges an immense leonine creature. It is at least ten metres long from head to tail, its powerful white-skinned body rippling with muscle.

The manticore.

It is just like the stories you were told as a child: a savage predator with the body of a lion and the wings of an eagle. The beast's tail is scaled, tapering back into a barbed tip that drips with a deadly venom.

Your heart sinks when you see it, knowing that you could never defeat such a beast. From the skeletons lying around you, it seems many others have tried – and failed.

The beast is watching you through heavy-lidded eyes.

'Did you have a plan?' whispers Benin, his voice shaking. 'I assume you're an accomplished hunter, come to gain another trophy?'

You are about to answer, when the beast rises onto its forelegs, its immense wings snapping back from its broad shoulders. After giving a long yawn, displaying the largest set of canines you have ever seen, it shakes its shaggy mane from side-to-side, its neck bones clicking.

Then it speaks.

'Why are you here?' it asks, in a deep and sonorous voice – magnified a hundred-fold from the high stone walls.

Your shocked expressions draw a smile from the beast. 'I see you had been expecting a fight, not a conversation.' Its barbed tail flicks lazily from side-to-side. 'Sometimes, I do like to approach matters in a more … civilised way. Now speak – or a fight is what you'll get!'

Benin steps forward, bowing awkwardly. 'The … the bishop of Carvel has been the victim of a … a sinister attack,' he stammers. 'I know how to break the spell, but I need …' He pauses, nervously licking his lips. 'I need your blood to break the curse.'

It takes a moment for the priest's words to sink in.

'You as well?' you frown. 'I should have guessed …'

'What!' Benin exclaims in surprise. 'You're not a hunter?'

'I need the blood. I made a promise to someone.'

'To who?' he demands, his face suddenly flushed with anger. 'It's the thief, isn't it? The one who stole the relic!'

'Wait, I don't know …' you implore.

'The bishop is dying!' Benin shakes a clenched fist. 'He needs this cure.'

'And I'm helping a man who was attacked in *your* church,' you snap, losing your patience. 'A charm was used on him – and I need the blood or he will die.'

Laughter booms from the canyon walls. 'And do I have a say in this matter?' asks the manticore, flexing one of its enormous paws.

Its words bring you both up short.

'Then speak, great one,' says Benin, bowing once again.

'I know who made the charm,' snarls the manticore, 'and they are stronger than anything I have previously encountered.' The creature turns to display its left flank, where a jagged wound cuts across its white flesh. 'They took my blood for a ritual and I was powerless to stop them.' The beast settles back onto the stone ledge. 'But you two do not have such power, so I will offer you a choice instead.' The creature's mouth twists into a cruel smile. 'Decide who is most worthy to take a single drop of my blood – and you will have it.'

You are about to protest, when Benin spins to face you. 'I must have it!' he demands. 'The bishop must live!'

Will you:

Argue that you need the blood? 259

Challenge Benin to defend his claim? 240

Convince Benin to help you defeat the manticore? 280

226

'Ah, excuse me clumsiness,' says the bearded man. 'Not used to the confines of civilisation. I prefer more … open spaces, if you know what I mean.' He quickly adjusts his balance as someone else nudges past him, nearly upsetting his mugs once again. 'Ugh, would yer look at me. Could shoot a marsh rat at a thousand paces, but here I am struggling to hold a few cups of beer.'

You try and move past – only to find the burly man in your way again, his eyes fondly appraising your gear.

'Say, would you be looking for some work?' he asks hopefully. 'It'd help me out of a real pickle. Here, follow me – we got a private booth away from the crowd.' He raises a mug, gesturing towards the far wall where a tattered velvet curtain is drawn across an alcove.

Will you:

Follow the man (this starts a red quest)? 119

Decline the man's offer? 283

227

Desperately, you scrabble up the side of the building, putting your foot on the nearest windowsill and then jumping onto the sloping slate tiles above the door. A zombie makes a grab for you, screeching at the top of its lungs. You kick it away, watching as the body tumbles back into the crowd of snarling villagers. Then, after finding your balance on the sloping roof, you grab the edge of an upper-storey window and pull yourself up. To your relief you see that the window is slightly ajar. Gritting your teeth, you haul yourself up the rest of the way, wrenching your body through the opening.

You land in a heap on the dusty floor of a bedroom. It is dark and cold, your breath gasping out frosty clouds in the gloom. The deafening screams and shouts of the undead still ring in your ears. From below you hear banging – fists hitting against stone and wood. They are trying to break in.

You scramble to your feet and hurry through the door opposite. It leads on to a landing, with another room across from you and a set of stairs leading down to the ground floor. You notice a glimmer of light spilling into the hall. It is coming from one of the rooms below you.

Will you:

Inspect the other bedroom?	195
Descend the stairs to investigate the light?	55

228

You have defeated all three of the golems. The portal flashes into being and a chest appears, waddling forward on a series of spider-like legs. It trundles over to you then lowers to the ground, flipping open its lid to allow you to view the treasures inside.

You find 20 gold crowns and may help yourself to one of the following rewards:

Patchwork gloves	Torque of iron	Rock shoulders
(gloves)	(necklace)	(cloak)
+1 magic +1 armour	+1 brawn +1 magic	+1 armour
Ability: charm	Ability: rust	Ability: might of stone

The portal shimmers and then fades to nothingness. The only other exit from the room is the balcony. Thankfully, the remains of the metal warrior lie slumped in a heap underneath it. Using the warrior as a make-shift set of stairs, you sprint up its iron body and then make a jump for the bottom of the balcony. You manage to grab one of the rails, swinging a leg up to hook around another. Steadily, you raise yourself up over the side to land in a panting heap on the balcony floor. After brushing yourself down, you draw your weapons and head through the arch at the balcony's rear, determined to hunt down this elusive child. Turn to 289.

229

You have barely entered the cave before you sense that something is wrong – a cold tingle races up your spine. The others seem less perturbed, briskly marching forward, eyes scanning their new surroundings. As with the previous areas, the cave is lit by phosphorescent fungi, growing in clusters around a series of stone pillars. These pillars form a dense forest, obscuring the other side of the cave.

'Are we looking for ants or gobboes?' growls Sürl, his fingers clenching and unclenching around his broadsword.

'Both, you idiot,' snaps Vas, spinning her daggers in her hands. 'Shut up and keep watching.'

The party advances through the cave, taking a snaking path between the pillars of rock. You still can't shake your sense of dread – your sense that something very bad is about to—

There is a scream from behind you.

One of your party members grips their chest, looking down at a blossoming wound. You see green venom bubbling between their fingers. With a gargling cry, they drop to the ground dead. There is no sign of a weapon or even an attacker.

'What's happening?' growls the captain, turning on the spot. 'Spread out – talk to me. What you see?'

'I don't see nothing!' cries Surl, a hint of fear in his voice.

There is another squeal. You spin around to see someone else from your group toppling to the floor, venom pouring from a puncture wound. Then you catch it – from the corner of your eye. Some kind of green mist, moving fast. You hurry towards it, but in the poor light it is impossible to keep a track of.

'You see anything?' shouts Vas, backing up against a pillar. 'I thought I . . . there!'

You follow her gaze, to where the party's last surviving mage is standing. A green-skinned ant-man is looming behind them, its human arms mutated into sharp blades. With a single, precise movement, the ant drives one of its blades through the chest of its victim. You see a spray of venom, then the mage keels over, dead before they hit the ground.

In the blink of an eye, the ant-man has vanished.

'It's just picking us off,' whimpers Surl. 'It ain't fair!'

You sense something behind you, a subtle movement of the air. Your skin prickles . . . In a flash, you whirl around to find yourself face-to-face with the giant bug. It lunges forward, its venom-laced blades looking to run you through. It is time to fight:

	Speed	*Brawn*	*Armour*	*Health*
Assassin ant	3	2	2	35

Special abilities

- Venom: Once you take health damage from the assassin ant, you must lose 2 *health* at the end of every combat round.

If you manage to defeat this elusive predator, turn to 198.

230

You return to the armourer. 'Good timing,' he grins. 'These little beauties won't be around for ever.' He places a shield, a helm and a longsword onto his work surface. 'Had more scales than I thought,' he adds. 'So, I was able to craft this nice helm and blade too.'

You may purchase any of the following for 200 gold crowns each:

Dark-scale warhelm	Black heart	Midnight's edge
(head)	(left hand: shield)	(main hand: sword)
+1 speed +1 armour	+1 speed +2 armour	+1 speed +2 brawn
Ability: deflect	Ability: deflect	Ability: dominate
	(requirement: warrior)	

When you have made your decision, return to your previous entry number or turn to 36 to explore Carvel's lower town.

231

The beast's claws whip through the air, its yellowed fangs snapping at your body. It is a miracle that you are able to dodge the relentless assault and press your own attack. Finally, after a tiring battle, the hound's body slumps back into the fen water, marsh flies buzzing around its smoking muzzle. It isn't until you inspect the corpse and see the many scars that crisscross its massive body that you are reminded of the legend of the ancient hound that stalks these western fenlands. The locals call it the black shuck.

You may now help yourself to one of the following special rewards:

Hound master's tunic	Shaggy mukluks	Wildfire weave
(chest)	(feet)	(cloak)
+1 speed +1 brawn	+1 speed +1 armour	+1 magic +1 armour
Ability: sideswipe	Ability: haste	Ability: backdraft

As this is a creature of legend, there is a chance that someone might be willing to pay good money for a trophy. You set about acquiring the creature's head, which you place into a sack. (Make a note of the *Hound's head* on your hero sheet, it doesn't take up backpack space.) With your grim task complete, you head back into the forest, eager to leave this rank marsh to the flies. Return to the quest map to continue your adventure.

232

Amongst the putrid mould and clumps of animal hair, you spy a number of interesting items. Some appear to be from previous adventurers. As well as a pouch containing 20 gold crowns, you also find one of the following rewards:

Lice-ridden pelt	**Lycanth's teeth**	**Rusted bracers**
(cloak)	(ring)	(gloves)
+1 speed +1 brawn	+1 brawn	+1 brawn +1 armour
Ability: parasite	Ability: bleed	Ability: counter

When you have made your decision, you return to the courtyard. Turn to 510.

233

You hand settles around something large and smooth. Excitedly, you withdraw your hand to find that you have discovered a trinket box, shaped to resemble a love heart.

Opening it up, you are a little disappointed to find it empty. (If you wish to keep *the heart-shaped box* then make a note of it on your hero sheet, it doesn't take up backpack space.) As you turn back to the tree, you hear a grumbling, creaking sound coming from within. Stepping away, you see that the other holes have now closed up, locking away their treasures.

You may now try and climb the tree (turn to 96) or leave via the magic portal (turn to 46).

234

The undead behemoth topples backwards, crashing to the ground with a sickening crunch. After disentangling yourself from its gooey innards, you begin a hasty search for anything of value.

You find 10 gold crowns and one of the following rewards:

Cruel cleaver	**Doorman**	**Giant bones**
(left hand: cleaver)	(left hand: shield)	(backpack)
+2 brawn	+1 armour	These might prove
	Ability: slam	valuable to the
		right person

Once you have updated your hero sheet, turn to 262.

235

'So you must be Edgar,' you state, approaching the counter. The man gives you a fierce look, his thick brows knitting together with annoyance.

'Change of management,' he growls. 'Me name's Kam. Last owner squealed and ran.' He flips the dagger into the air, catching it deftly. 'I'm waiting on fresh supplies, so not got much in that would interest the likes of you, sell-sword. I guess you didn't come here for a fresh pair of boots or a rain hat, eh?'

You shrug your shoulders, staring past him to the empty shelves. 'Do you have anything at all?' you ask, in all seriousness.

With a grunt, the man turns in his chair. 'Margrit! Margrit!'

'Yes dear!' calls a woman's voice from a back room.

'Bring out the special deals; whatever we got left.'

You hear some banging and scraping, then the sound of creaking floorboards. A few moments later a short woman appears, carrying a jumble of objects in her arms. Unlike Kam, she is well turned out, her silver-grey hair tied back in a bun. She drops the items onto the counter, nods her head quickly in greeting, and then scuttles away into the backroom.

'So,' smiles Kam, his dirty fingers rummaging through the goods as if they were a pirate's treasure hoard. 'Do any of these beauties take your fancy?'

You may purchase any of the following for 80 gold crowns each:

Pilgrim's progress	Walking stick	Wolf's paw
(feet)	(main hand: staff)	(talisman)
+1 speed +1 armour	+1 speed +1 magic	+1 speed
Ability: surefooted	Ability: safe path	

When you have made your decision, you may ask Kam about his hunting trophies (turn to 12) or leave the shop and explore the rest of town (turn to 199).

236

A well-aimed blow sends the spirit screeching backwards into the murky junk-filled waters. When its body finally bobs to the surface, you discover that the fight is over – and the creature's floating corpse is now visible to the naked eye. It is a pitiful sight and one that makes you step away, grimacing with disgust. From the charred and blistered remains, you assume it was once a man, but some magic or fire has flayed most of the skin from his bones. Holding your breath, you search the corpse and find one of the following items, which you may take:

Grounded boots	Janitor's safety gloves
(feet)	(gloves)
+1 speed +1 magic	+1 brawn + 1 armour
Ability: insulated	

When you have made your decision, turn to 2.

'This place is cursed!' cries Benin, spinning his staff around to grip it with both hands. He glances at Ventus, his eyes narrowed to points of rage. 'We were fools to come here. All we have found are demons and corruption!'

Ventus drops into a battle stance, magic rippling across his fists. 'Faith hold your tongue, priest – we were brought here for a purpose and that purpose is clear. To end this evil once and for all!'

Bea draws her twin swords, the magic woven into their blades blazing with blue fire. 'The relic,' she shouts, swiping at one of the giant's enormous legs. Her blows send splinters of wood and slimy ichor spraying through the whirling snow. 'Use its magic!'

You raise the relic and charge forward, hoping to drive it into the creature's twisted body. But mud spatters into your eyes as one of its fists slams into the sodden earth. You stumble back, temporarily blinded – and fail to see the other fist whipping in behind you. Barbed tendrils strike your arm, sending the relic spiralling away into the marsh. By luck rather than the quickness of your reflexes, you are able to avoid the full force of the blow, tumbling over onto your back. Benin is less fortunate, however – the priest is picked up in the beast's barbed fist and carried high into the air. His screams are deafening, chilling you to the bone, as his body is crushed within the prison of thorns.

'No!' Tears blur your vision as you lurch back to your feet. Frantically, you scan the marsh for signs of the relic, but the muddy banks offer up no clues – clearly the relic's headpiece must have closed, hiding its bright light and making it impossible to see. Angrily, you turn back to the battle. Bea and Ventus continue to press their attack, but their blows seem ineffectual, the bewitched roots moving quickly to reseal any wounds. Grimly, you realise there is no escape – and worse, the thorn giant appears to have no obvious weakness.

'Free me!' insists the demon, shaking its chains. 'Your false god has forsaken you. I will not! Release me now!'

'Trust you?' You laugh bitterly. 'An imprisoned demon?'

'You were a prisoner once, prophet,' it snaps, crimson eyes staring you full in the face. 'We have much in common, you and I. But if you are too blind to see it, then go ... see what your puny strength can achieve.'

Readying your weapons, you charge back into the fray – hoping that, together, you and your companions will find a way of besting the thorn giant:

	Speed	*Brawn*	*Armour*	*Health*
Orgorath	5	5	4	80

Special abilities

- Deadly thorns: At the end of each combat round, you must automatically lose 3 *health* from the creature's barbed fists.
- Divine fury: Bea's enchanted swords add 3 to your damage score.
- Thousand fists: Instead of rolling for a damage score when you win a round, you can choose to use Ventus' *thousand fists* attack. This does 2 dice of damage to your opponent, ignoring *armour*. If you win the next round of combat, Ventus can apply his *thousand fists* attack again, applying 3 dice of damage. Each time this ability is used in a consecutive combat round, you can add 1 damage die, up to a total of 5 dice. Then the monk's ability is exhausted and can no longer be used in this combat.

If you are able to defeat Orgorath, turn to 308.

238

Polk leans forward, pushing his plate away and crossing his arms. 'Look, when Judah preached the teachings of the One God, he described two places – Heaven and Hel. One place all nice and welcoming like, and the other where all the bad people go to suffer eternal fire and damnation.'

The blindfolded warrior smiles with bemusement.

'Let me guess, the shroud is the second one?' you remark dryly.

The woman speaks up before the warrior can reply. 'The shroud is dangerous!' she snaps, her voice sharp and cold. 'When Jacob started his experiments he didn't know what he was doing, what powers he was playing with. He tore a hole in our world and dragged the tower and my husband – everything in it – to that … *other* place.' Her face hardens as she clenches and unclenches her fists, her own expression made menacing by the dancing flames.

'It is not unheard of,' nods Polk, speaking softly. 'A great discharge of magic – a bad event or happening – can rip away at the very fabric of our world. I've heard of whole towns, even cities back in the day, just disappearing, only to return – but different, twisted somehow.' He sighs, blowing out the whiskers of his beard. 'Nothing good comes of the shroud. I just hope,' the warrior's gaze drifts over to Joss, who is pacing up and down in front of the fire, 'we aren't too late.'

Will you:	
Ask about Anse's strange markings?	270
Ask why you should risk your life?	89
Agree to the mission?	24

239

The elemental has blasted a hole in the floor of the temple, revealing a hidden recess. Inside, wrapped in animal skins, is a heavy leather-bound book. Its yellowed pages are covered in hundreds of intelligible runes and glyphs. You may take this item if you wish:

Book of Alpha
(backpack)
An ancient Lamuri
spell book

When you have made your decision, you rejoin Boom in the court-yard. Turn to 510.

240

'This was some Wiccan curse, I know it!' snaps Benin furiously. 'The Wiccan have always been a threat to these lands; they prey openly on the pilgrims. My parent's caravan was attacked …' He breaks off, his jaw clenching. 'I lost my family to those savages; I was left with nothing ... The bishop was like a father to me; kind and generous. He taught me my skills – helped me to control my magic. My anger was channelled into something good.'

He breathes a heavy sigh. 'Last night, someone broke into the church vault. The bishop must have heard something and gone to investigate. I don't know what happened – a powerful relic was stolen, one that I know the bishop was keen to keep from the Wiccans. I found traces of a charm at the scene; I believe it released some kind of curse. He will die unless I can cure him.'

Will you:	
Ask Benin how he knows so much about charms?	211
Let Benin take the blood he needs?	343
Argue that you need the blood instead?	259
Convince Benin to help you defeat the manticore?	280

241

These vagabonds appear weak and poorly armed. Tired and ill-tempered from your journey, you decide to fight back:

	Speed	*Brawn*	*Armour*	*Health*
Roadside robbers	3	3	1	35 (*)

(*) Once you have reduced the robbers' *health* to 10 or less, turn to 278. If you are defeated, turn to 339.

242

'If it avoids bloodshed, then I will go with you,' you reply, taking a step towards the Wiccans. 'But I ask that you let these people go unharmed.' You gesture to the three travellers.

'No.' The feathered woman shakes her head. 'We want that one – and we won't leave without him. Conall ...'

The giant grunts and starts towards the elderly man, who is now humming to himself quietly. Ventus moves quickly to intercept the warrior. 'Lay one hand on him and . . .'

Suddenly, the loud blare of a horn reverberates across the moorland. It is followed by a hooting call from one of the Wiccans. Some kind of warning. They all turn as one, weapons leaping from scabbards and belts, as the first bright explosion rips into their ranks. Turn to **442**.

243

Your final blow sends the sniper toppling over the tower rail, his wailing screech cut off seconds later by an eye-wincing thud.

If you have a *brawn* of 12 or more you may rip the repeating crossbow from its moorings and use it as a weapon – gaining the following item:

Stormbound
(left hand: crossbow)
+1 speed +2 brawn
Ability: volley

At the foot of the tower, you search through the hunter's grisly remains. You find a purse containing 30 gold crowns, and one of the following rewards:

Lucky crown	**Sniper's jacket**	**Sniper scope (1 use)**
(necklace)	(chest)	(unique)
+1 speed	+1 speed +1 magic	Attach to a *head* item to
Ability: charm	Ability: focus	add +1 brawn

With the sniper defeated, you turn your attention back to the battle. Turn to **785**.

244

You wake to find yourself lying face down in a muddy puddle. A loud and insistent pain is pounding inside your head, reminding you of the blow that you took – a second before everything went black. With a grimace, you roll onto your side, wiping the grit and mud from your face.

'Pick a fight, did we?'

You painfully jerk your head around, squinting in the grey light. It appears you have been dumped in an alleyway, with only a stray cat and a vagrant for company. The latter is clad in a thick riding cloak, the hood pulled down low over their face. A hip flask is clutched in their grimy fingers, which you suspect is filled with a stronger beverage than just plain water. You can smell filth and beer, and leftover food.

'Yeah, something like that,' you wince, pushing yourself back to your feet. It is then that you notice your backpack, lying in the dirt right next to the stranger's feet. The cat is sniffing it with interest.

'Don't worry, I think they just took some gold,' says the vagrant, nodding to your pouch lying in another puddle of muck. You stoop down to retrieve it, annoyed that you have lost half of your gold. (Remember to update your hero sheet.) 'It could have gone worse, mind,' he remarks, noting your annoyance. 'I managed to save your pack.' He reaches over and takes one of the straps, then tosses it over to you. As his cloak shifts open, you catch a glimpse of a silver breastplate and the hilt of a sword.

'Shouldn't you be supping in more comfortable surroundings?' you ask with a frown. The cat gives a forlorn meow, as if in agreement.

The man snorts, then takes another gulp from his flask. 'I prefer my own company to that of thieves and scoundrels. And that's all you'll find in this town, save for the pilgrims – and they ain't much better.' He wipes his mouth with the back of his hand. 'Fools, the lot of 'em.'

Will you:

Ask what happened to Bilhah the Fish?	53
Ask the vagrant to share his story?	127
Return to the town?	199

245

You enter the chapel, your footfalls echoing back from the high stone walls. As you approach the kneeling priest, he turns and lifts back his hood to reveal a young, handsome face, framed by blond curls of hair. It is Benin.

If you have the keywords *hallowed* or *prevail* on your hero sheet, turn to 166. Otherwise turn to 197.

246

On the banks of the swamp you discover the remains of several unfortunate adventurers – their grey corpulent flesh bloated with swamp water. Quickly, you rifle through their belongings to see if there is anything worth salvaging.

You find a mouldy bag containing 20 gold crowns and one of the following items:

Preacher's coat	**Gravedigger's ring**	**Fingerless gloves**
(chest)	(ring)	(gloves)
+1 speed +1 brawn	+1 brawn	+1 speed +1 brawn
Ability: missionary's calling set (requirement: pilgrim)	Ability: underhand	Ability: crawlers

With your grim task complete, you return to the courtyard. Turn to 510.

247

You drop the bark shavings into the mixture and stir it around with one of the spoons. To your surprise, the bark quickly dissolves into the liquid, giving off a pungent-smelling steam. What ingredient will you add next?

Will you:

Add meadowsweet?	104
Add lemongrass?	287
Add sagewort?	114

248

You push through the smoky crowds, making towards the counter. As you near, your attention becomes fixated on the half-giant barman who is serving ale to the patrons. You wonder how one of his kind ended up working behind a bar in a backwater place such as this. Giants are renowned for their strength and endurance – and clearly this half-giant is missing none of those traits. He would be prized stock for the king's army or some mercenary outfit.

Your thoughts are suddenly interrupted as one of the patrons knocks straight into you, slopping ale down your front. It is a burly, middle-aged man dressed in brown tanned leathers. He shrugs his shoulders as way of apology, grinning through his thatch of beard. If you have the word *tower* on your hero sheet, turn to 263. Otherwise, turn to 226.

249

Only metres from the bank you discover a second marker, tangled in foliage. You pull away the creepers and leaves to reveal the sculpture of a fanged arachnid. Behind it, a cracked stone pathway winds away through the trees, leading further into the steaming jungle. You follow it without a second thought, relieved to finally have something solid underfoot instead of cloying mud and twisted roots.

After an hour, the path descends into a steep-sided ravine, its walls carpeted with moss and creepers. You advance warily, conscious of the green mist rolling in between the huddled trees, bringing with it a brooding, heavy silence.

As the fog starts to thicken, you are forced to feel your way forwards, gagging on the rotten air. Eventually the walls of the ravine drop away and you stagger out into an open clearing. Through the green haze, you see tall shapes stretching back into the distance

– some peaked and angular, others smooth and curved. Buildings, you quickly surmise. This must be some kind of settlement.

Then you hear the scrape and clatter of feet on stone. From out of the fog a line of figures is advancing towards you. For a moment you are hopeful it might be a welcome party, but then you notice the staggering, jerking movements and the bone-thin bodies.

Undead.

They continue to advance at a lumbering pace, giving you chance to size up the threat. The majority appear to be warriors, armed with spears and shields, whilst a smaller number are clad in tattered robes, their bodies crackling with magic. At the rear of the band a rotted corpse in a feathered headdress marches alone, wielding a staff carved in the likeness of a hooded cobra.

It is clear that you are hopelessly outnumbered, but with no other option than to flee back into the jungle, you decide to stand and fight:

	Speed	*Magic*	*Armour*	*Health*
Warriors	5	4	3	40
Mages	–	–	2	20
High priest	–	–	2	20

Special abilities

- Bone mending: At the end of each combat round, the high priest uses its snake staff to heal its cohorts. This restores 4 *health* to the warriors. (Note: This cannot take the warriors above their starting *health* of 40.)
- Dark fire: At the end of each combat round, take a *speed* challenge. If you get 12 or less, then your hero is hit by the mages' spells. This causes 5 damage, ignoring *armour*. If you get 13 or more, then you have avoided the attack.
- Body of bone: Your enemies are immune to *bleed* and *venom*.
- Undead minions: You may use your *holy water* and *holy protector* abilities (if available).

In this combat you roll against the warriors' *speed*. If you win a round, you can choose to strike against the warriors, the mages or the high priest. If the mages and/or the priest are defeated, their relevant ability no longer applies. To win the combat, you only need to defeat the warriors, reducing them to zero *health*. Once the warriors are defeated, any surviving undead (mages and priest) are also defeated.

If you manage to send these fiends back to the grave, turn to 314.

250

You have purchased a map of Carvel. You may view this map whenever you like by turning to the colour section of this book. This special map will allow you to 'fast travel' to any of the numbered entries, allowing you to visit locations more speedily than before.

If you wish to return to the map-seller, turn to 99.

251

You are standing in a huge open courtyard, its cracked stone floor spattered with rubble. The ground is warm underfoot, gouts of steam and black smoke spewing through metal grilles set into the rock. Around the edges of the yard the walls have been smashed apart, as if by some powerful explosion. Their fragments now hang suspended in the air like a haphazard jigsaw, forming stairways and platforms that float eerily against a backdrop of purest, darkest night.

'What happened here . . . ?' you rasp, almost frightened to speak in this strange place.

'The work of the shroud,' whispers Polk, turning slowly on the spot. 'Be on your guard. Trust nothing, no one.'

At that moment, you hear a peal of childish laughter. All eyes turn to an area of the crumbling walls, where a child sits on the edge of a fractured archway, kicking his legs back and forth in the empty space. He is wearing a patchwork cloak, which sparkles like stars against the black void. 'Look Maxi, someone came to play!'

Behind the boy, you can dimly make out a large shape. Its proportions look strange, almost a mockery of a human body. It isn't until it steps closer that you see it is made entirely of iron, the appearance mimicking that of an armoured knight.

'Where is my husband?' cries Joss angrily. 'What have you done with him?'

The boy titters to himself. 'You have to play my games. You want to play, don't you?'

Suddenly, the ground starts to shake. A torrent of angry flame bursts up through the metal grilles.

'Wait! No!' screeches the boy, hopping to his feet. 'Who left the furnace open? Who left it open?'

Then the floor explodes in a churning maelstrom of heat, as some gigantic fiery elemental rises up through the seared stone, its body a blazing expanse of sizzling, hissing magma.

'Summon the doors, Maxi!' cries the boy. 'We gotta close the furnace!'

A glowing doorway appears behind him. The boy runs into it, disappearing the moment he comes into contact with the glowing magic. You notice that several other doorways have appeared in other areas of the jumbled maze.

'We've got to get out of here!' shouts Polk. You spin around, only to find that the tower doors are nowhere to be seen – replaced by an endless void of black space.

'Trapped!' you gasp, turning back to the courtyard.

The fiery beast rears up into the air, its body forming two enormous fists of fire. Anse moves casually towards it, pulling his crucifix free from its restraints. With the flick of some hidden mechanism, a row of knives punch out from the cross-piece, its surface suddenly glittering with inscribed runes. The paladin shows no fear as he approaches the monster.

Then everything turns to chaos.

The beast's arms come crashing down, shattering the stone beneath its fists. You are thrown backwards by the resulting tremor, skidding across the ash and dust to the very edge of the shattered courtyard. Above you, Anse is springing from one floating platform to the next, using them to gain height. Silently, he springs into the air, his crucifix swinging around in a white-flaming arc. He connects with the beast's shoulder, eliciting a bellowing scream. Then the paladin is rolling across its back, seemingly impervious to the heat, and starts pummelling the other shoulder with his holy crucifix. The beast twists around, trying to bat him away.

'We have to run!' shouts Polk. 'Anse is buying us time!'

Already the portals have started to flicker and fade. Polk makes a dash for the nearest one. Without looking back, he steps through and disappears, the portal winking out of existence a second later. At the other side of the yard, Joss is scrambling from platform to platform, headed for the exact same portal as the boy. The glowing doorway has begun to shrink and fade, but the speedy ranger hurls herself inside just as it snaps closed, vanishing from sight.

'Get out of here!' shouts a voice in your ear. For a moment you are so startled you find yourself looking around for its source. Then your attention shifts back to the paladin, who has made a leap for one of the floating platforms. 'I said run!'

You realise that the voice must be Anse's.

The fire demon is now spitting balls of flame from its gaping maw. They smash into the rock walls, splintering them and sending showers of stone floating out across the strange black void. You spot two remaining doorways that you can still reach – one to your left on a cracked dais of rock and another to your right, glimmering between two pillars of stone. You realise that, unless you choose one of them quickly, they will disappear, trapping you here with this enraged demon.

Will you:

Take the left portal?	436
Take the right portal?	206

252

You send your rock soldier forward, confident that its hardened body will be able to withstand the metal monster's attacks. As you predicted, the buzz saws grate and spark as they try and cut through the rock, but they cannot penetrate it. With its blades bent and crippled, the metal warrior is forced to resort to punching and kicking – but to no avail. The rock soldier uses its own mighty fists to pummel its opponent's body into scrap metal. Congratulations, you have chosen well and defeated ironclad. (Remove the *rock soldier* from your hero sheet.) Restore your *health*, then turn to 228.

253

You briefly recount what happened to the farmers – and the curse that was inflicted on the farmer's wife. 'It was one of my apprentices,' says Damaris, wincing as she appears to recall the moment. 'Leena thought she could help, but the spell – the demon – was beyond her powers to control. We offered the husband and the boys sanctuary. But they turned against us. Understandable …' She shakes her head with regret. 'I'm sorry. It was an unfortunate end.'

Turn to 126 to ask Damaris another question.

254

'Oh yes!' A delighted Joseph gives another spin in his shiny, black coat. 'I'm going to be the talk of the town!'

'Just be careful,' you remind him. 'A coat like that might get you the wrong kind of attention.'

But Joseph isn't listening – he is already sauntering away towards the doors of the church, winking at the passers-by who are all staring at him in wonder.

You hope he doesn't wind up in more trouble. For now, you decide to focus on your own matters. Leaving the church, you return to upper town. (Make a note of the word *Joseph* on your hero sheet. Then turn to 77.)

255

All that remains of Umbra is a pile of rumpled clothing and a scatter of jewellery. You also spot the skeleton of an adventurer, propped up against one of the columns. Their mildewed vestments and tattered books of scripture suggest they had once been a missionary or pilgrim.

You find a pouch containing 15 gold crowns and one of the following rewards:

Stole of shadow	Spook chi	Cobwebbed capotain
(cloak)	(talisman)	(head)
+1 speed +1 brawn	+1 speed	+1 speed +1 brawn
Ability: steal	Ability: trickster	Ability: missionary's calling set (requirement: pilgrim)

When you have made your decision, you return to the courtyard. Turn to 510.

256

Legendary monster: Dagona the Damned

Crops wither in the fields, while the farm buildings burn, spitting showers of glowing embers through the red-black sky. Smoke is everywhere, whirling and snaking across the hellish landscape, like a living spirit come to relish in the fiery destruction.

'It's Wiccan magic,' the young pilgrim had warned, hurrying in the opposite direction. 'The farm is cursed – forsaken by our god! ' The second had been a priest, old and wrinkled. 'Please, pass by, child. Leave the fires to cleanse the land of its sin.' The last was a mercenary, armour spattered with rust and dirt. 'I saw a demon there,' he said, his voice shaking. 'You'd do well to keep going, just pass on by.'

Three warnings. Three chances.

But you did not deviate from your path, nor pass on by. Instead, you entered the blazing farmstead, determined to put an end to rumour – or a demon's life if that's what it takes.

'No more chances,' you reflect grimly.

Ahead is the ruin of the farmhouse. A broken shell, its roof beams and boards forming a giant, charred skeleton. And sitting hunched at the edge of one of the splintered floors is a sullen-looking creature. It is throwing stones into a heaped pile of ashes, tattered hair hanging over its soot-streaked face. There are remnants of a summer dress, clinging to its reddened skin, torn and bloodied.

As you approach the creature looks up, regarding you with smouldering coal-black eyes. Then its face creases into a mask of hatred, lips pulling back to emit a wailing scream. It is a horrible, teeth-grating sound that almost breaks your spirit and sends you running. But there is no escape – the creature is charging towards you, powerful strides driving it forward at speed. You draw your weapons and prepare to defend yourself. It is time to fight:

	Speed	*Brawn*	*Armour*	*Health*
Dagona	6	4	4	70

Special abilities

- Slash and burn: If Dagona wins a combat round, roll three dice and choose the single highest die result to use for her damage score.
- Ashes to ashes: Dagona breaths clouds of choking ash. If you roll a double for your hero's attack speed, you are caught in an ash cloud. You automatically lose the round even if your attack speed was higher. (If you have an ability that lets you re-roll dice, then you can use it to try and avoid this.)

If you manage to defeat this demonic fiend, turn to 301.

257

'Elders don't like me,' explains Boom, grinning once again. 'They want warriors to hunt and protect tribe. Not want me. I got smarts for magic – not strength of hunter. So elders give me spirit walk they know I never return from. I gotta kill great Mortzilla.'

You frown, the name being unfamiliar. 'You must kill this . . . creature before you can return to your tribe?'

Boom nods, still unable to keep a smile from his face. 'I been here for longest time. A hundred and seventeen moons. I try spirit walk but I fail. Mortzilla is a spirit, trapped here like all the others. Bad things happen here long time ago. Make cut in shroud.' He slices the palm of his hand through the air. 'Space between this world and shroud made thin like palm leaf. Let magic in and other things. Spirits from that other place.'

'And how does this help me?' you reply. 'I came here looking for a—'

'Demon, I know.' Boom's smile fades at last. 'I sees it with own eyes. It come here day ago. It hurt bad. Skin black from fire. You're too late, that demon gone south.'

You rise up from your seat, intending to leave immediately – but the shaman raises a finger in the air. 'Demon talk with Mortzilla. I find out why if you help me. Complete the spirit walk and I get all the answers, yes?'

Will you:	
Agree to help Boom Mamba?	399
Refuse his offer of aid?	483

258

Congratulations! Your party has wrested control of the ship from the goblins. The captain picks up the leader's pirate hat and turns it around thoughtfully. 'Nice bit of headwear.' He tosses it to Surl, who giggles with delight as he places it on his head.

You take a moment to search the bodies of the goblin archers. You may choose up to two of the following rewards:

Goblin bones	**Sniper's goggles**	**Goblin mittens**
(backpack)	(head)	(gloves)
These might prove valuable to the right person	+1 armour Ability: focus	+1 magic +1 armour

When you have made your decision, turn to **118**.

259

'I cannot go back on a promise,' you state, folding your arms stubbornly. 'My life was saved and now I must do the same for another.'

'Who?' snaps the priest. 'Is it a Wiccan? Was it the one who stole the relic from the church? That thing is dangerous! It's a weapon that needs to be protected, else it will endanger lives!'

'They stole nothing,' you add tersely. 'They went with the intention of taking it, but something happened; something went wrong.'

Benin snorts, shaking his head. 'So, you would put the life of a common thief over that of the bishop. I hardly think that is a fair decision.'

'Here, here!' grins the manticore, clapping its front paws together.

Will you:

Take the blood for yourself?	312
Challenge Benin to defend his claim?	240
Convince Benin to help you defeat the manticore?	280

260

You follow Ventus down a number of echoing stone corridors. Doors to either side afford glimpses of similar cubicles to your own, with pallet beds and kneeling stools. Eventually, you are led out into a wide open courtyard. For the first time you see the vast walls of the monastic buildings looming up into the clear blue skies.

'The dean's offices are over there,' says Ventus, pointing to a set of stairs leading up to a rectangular tower. 'I must attend to other matters in the library. One God guide your path, traveller.' The monk bows and then re-enters the building behind you.

As you cross the courtyard, you spot Bea sitting on a bench beneath a row of mullioned windows. One of her swords is resting across her knees, and she is scrutinising it with a thoughtful expression. An oil-skin bag is open next to her, with several tattered books scattered on top of it.

To your left you see an elaborate door, made from ivory and gold. It creaks open and a young monk appears, squinting in the light. You notice that he is rubbing the back of his hands, where branded sigils flash and sparkle with their own bright radiance.

To your right, an archway leads through into a columned hall. At its far end, a lone priest kneels in prayer before a statue of the prophet Allam.

Will you:

Ask the monk about his markings?	316
Talk to Bea?	148
Enter the chapel and speak to the priest?	245
Climb the stairs to the dean's tower?	291

261

It is a long and gruelling battle. Lazlo observes your performance with growing admiration, occasionally offering advice when he sees you overstepping a lunge or struggling with a parry. Eventually, exhaustion forces you to make a mistake, your wild swing going wide of its mark. Before you can recover, a sudden lurch of the disc throws you off balance. Lazlo catches you with the hilt of his sword, knocking you flat onto your stomach.

You are about to struggle, when you feel the point of his blade at your neck.

'Game over,' laughs the prince. He utters a word of magic, and suddenly the disc starts to lower itself back to the ground. 'Do not be downhearted,' he grins, helping you back to your feet. 'I saw much improvement in you. Like you said, you're a very fast learner.'

If you have a high *magic* score and wish to learn the path of the mage, turn to 3. If you have a high *brawn* score and wish to learn the path of the warrior or the rogue, turn to 142.

262

A body goes hurtling past you, kicking and jerking as it is consumed in yellow flames. You spin around to see Eldias fending off a crowd of zombies. One of his hands is glowing with a yellow-orange light, the glow caught in his dazzling eyes.

'I judge you!' he screams, rainwater pouring like a sparkling curtain from the brim of his hat. 'And I find you guilty!' The witchfinder sends another bolt of magic from his hand, slamming into two of the undead and sending them writhing through the air.

Then you feel hands wrapping around your legs. In horror, you realise that the half-giant is still moving. Its massive hands now have a hold of you, dragging you down to the rain-slick ground. As you try and fend it off, a group of zombies break away from Eldias, hurrying towards you, snarling and howling with hunger. From the corner of your eye, you see another group closing in as well.

You cry out to Eldias for help as the horde descend on you,

suffocating you in a tight press of stinking, rotting bodies. You will need to fend off their attacks until the witchfinder can reach you:

	Speed	*Brawn*	*Armour*	*Health*
Zombie horde	3	3	2	28

Special abilities

- Unstoppable!: You only need to fend off the zombie horde until Eldias can reach you. (See below.)
- All pile on!: There is very little room to manoeuvre. You cannot use special abilities or backpack items in this fight.

If you manage to survive to the end of the *fifth* combat round, turn to 335. (Special achievement: If you defeat the zombie horde within five combat rounds, turn to 367.)

263

You push past the clumsy traveller, settling into a space at the busy bar. After several minutes of waiting, you finally catch the bar man's attention. Turn to 364.

264

You follow Vas into the captain's cabin. Like the logger's camp, the place has been ransacked. Paintings have been slashed to ribbons, charts and maps have been torn apart – in one corner, a chair lies in broken pieces, its seat stuffing spilling out across the grimy floor – everywhere you look, the goblins have smashed and ruined whatever they could get their hands on.

'Goblins,' scowls Vas. 'Crazier than the captain.' She kneels down and picks up the remains of a tattered chart. 'This could be interesting.'

You help her clear a space on the table, so that the chart can be spread out. It appears to show the north and west coasts of Valeron, with various areas marked with red circles. Vas nods her head. 'Pirates.

These are prime spots for ambushing traders, especially army ships moving between Skardland and Beeches Fort.'

You move around the table to get a better look. As you do so, a loose panel in the floor buckles slightly under your weight. Intrigued, you take a closer look – pushing down on the panel with the heel of your hand. The other end lifts slightly, revealing a dusty cavity.

'Well, aren't you the detective,' grins Vas. 'What's in there?'

You reach into the space and pull out a heavy sack. Inside you find a small pouch of money, a golden compass and a highly-polished pirate's cutlass.

'Halves on the money,' smiles Vas. 'And I'll let you have first pick of the treasures.'

You are left with 10 gold crowns and may choose one of the following rewards:

Cutlass of the seven seas	**Betsy's second compass**
(left hand: sword)	(necklace)
+1 speed	Ability: safe path
Ability: parry	

With little else of interest in the room, you both head back to the deck. Turn to **159**.

265

'They learnt their paltry magic from the dwarves, back in the dark ages – back when we were all savages, with no wisdom or understanding.' Malak picks a stray hair from his silken cuff and flicks it away. 'They treated it like any other weapon – used it to crush their enemies.'

He snorts. 'I suppose they became civilised, in their own way. But where there is ignorance there is always danger.' He folds his arms, lifting his head back to peer at you down his nose. 'Did I mention the word ignorance yet again? How very ... apt. Now, if you would just crawl back to your little hole I can get back to my life.'

Will you:

Ask about the testing?	213
Leave and return to upper town?	77

266

A white light shoots out from the pages of the book, bursting into a cloud of sparkling dust as it breaks against your invisible opponent. As the glittering motes settle you see that they have revealed the poltergeist, shimmering around its humanoid body. The creature gives an angry screech as it tries to brush the dust away – but it is already too late for this ghostly nuisance. You are charging in, aiming your strikes with a deadly precision:

	Speed	*Magic*	*Armour*	*Health*
Poltergeist	5	3	3	35

If you manage to defeat the poltergeist, turn to 236.

267

You escort a dejected-looking Joseph to the lower town market where you are able to find an armourer who wants the scales to create a shield. After much haggling, you are able to secure a good deal. (You have gained 100 gold crowns.) Joseph pockets his own gold sulkily before heading off towards the nearest tavern. You doubt the gold will last long in his hands, but he's no longer your problem.

As you go to leave, the armourer stops you. 'Come back 'ere if you are interested in the shield I'm making. Going to be something really special.' Make a note of the entry number 230. Turn to that entry number at any time when you are in Carvel to view the armourer's goods. Turn to 36 to continue your journey through lower town.

268

Murlic spins his daggers, their green magic trailing through the snow-whipped air. 'Why are we fighting demons, witch?' he snarls at Damaris. 'You brought us here! How does this help save our people?'

Conall growls, baring his teeth. 'Hold your tongue, cur, or I cut it from your throat.'

'Enough!' Damaris raises her staff, its feathered head splintering into shards of dark light. 'Do not fear this aberration. It is a servant only – bound to do its master's bidding. It doesn't know why we're here. It doesn't care for motives. It is protecting the forest.'

Conall glares at the witch. 'Then give me the magic.'

Damaris points her staff at the giant warrior. Spears of darkness streak out from its tip, slamming into the brigand's bared chest. It ripples across his painted runes, flowing across his whole body. Then he starts to change. His muscles bulge as coarse black hair pushes out of his skin, spreading quickly to cover his broad shoulders and swollen arms. He howls with pain, throwing back his head, as an enormous muzzle pushes out of his face, settling into a grim scowl filled with glittering fangs.

The warrior has become a bear – a black shadow of fur and claw. With a bestial roar, the bear bounds forward towards the giant, swiping at the tangled roots with its leathery paws.

As if in answer, the thorn colossus brings its fists hurtling down through the air, ripping deep furrows in the earth. Conall is caught by one of the barbed limbs, blood splashing across his fur as he is sent sprawling back onto his haunches.

'How can we defeat it?' cries Murlic, torn by fear and indecision. 'It's too powerful!'

Damaris swings to face you. 'The relic,' she shouts. 'Use its magic!'

You raise the relic and charge forward, hoping to drive it into the creature's twisted body. But mud spatters into your eyes as one of its fists slams into the sodden earth. You stumble back, temporarily blinded – and fail to see the other fist whipping in behind you. Barbed tendrils strike your arm, sending the relic spiralling away into the marsh. By luck rather than the quickness of your reflexes, you are able to avoid the full force of the blow, tumbling over onto your back. Murlic is less fortunate, however – the rogue is picked up in the beast's barbed fist and carried high into the air. His screams are deafening, chilling you to the bone, as his body is crushed within the prison of thorns.

'No!' Tears blur your vision as you lurch back to your feet. Frantically, you scan the marsh for signs of the relic, but the muddy banks offer up no clues – clearly the relic's headpiece must have closed, hiding its bright light and making it impossible to see. Angrily, you turn back to the battle. Damaris has now summoned a group of earth golems, their bodies fashioned from mud and rock. They lumber forward, punching and battering at the giant – but their blows seem ineffectual, the bewitched roots moving quickly to reseal any wounds. Grimly, you realise there is no escape – and worse, the thorn giant appears to have no obvious weakness.

'Free me!' insists the demon, shaking its chains. 'Your pitiful magic will not prevail.'

'Free a demon?' you laugh bitterly.

'You were a prisoner once, prophet,' it snaps, crimson eyes staring you full in the face. 'We have much in common, you and I. But if you are too blind to see it, then go ... see what your puny strength can achieve.'

Readying your weapons, you charge back into the fray – hoping that, together, you and your companions will find a way of besting the thorn giant:

	Speed	*Brawn*	*Armour*	*Health*
Orgorath	5	5	4	80

Special abilities

- Deadly thorns: At the end of each combat round, you must automatically lose 3 *health* from the creature's barbed body.
- Earth golems: The magical golems inflict 2 damage to Orgorath at the end of each combat round. If you lose a combat round, you can sacrifice the golems instead of taking damage. This means the golems' damage ability will no longer apply for the duration of the combat.

- Furious roar: Instead of rolling for a damage score, you can use Conall's *furious roar* ability. This boosts your *speed*, *brawn* and *magic score* by 1 for the next three combat rounds.

If you are able to defeat Orgorath, turn to 308.

269

'I don't see we have much choice in this matter,' you reply grimly, your eyes ranging across their sizeable force. 'As you say, a fight would not favour us.'

'What?' Bea looks at you angrily. 'We can't surrender!'

'You do not speak for us, stranger,' snaps Ventus, his face twisting with derision. '*We* will lay down our lives if we must.'

The Wiccan woman nods. 'That is regrettable, but changes nothing. And what do you say, Sanchen?' She appraises your weapons with interest. 'Will you lay down your life for a Church that chose to imprison you?'

Bea shifts away from you warily. 'You were a *prisoner*?'

Suddenly, the loud blare of a horn reverberates across the moorland. It is followed by a hooting call from one of the Wiccans. Some kind of warning. They all turn as one, weapons leaping from scabbards and belts, as the first bright explosion rips into their ranks. Turn to 442.

270

'Holy inscriptions,' says Polk, his eyes suddenly lighting up. 'Paladins are anointed by the inscribers, as a means to ward away bad spirits … demons …' He gives a noisy belch as he settles back in his chair. 'It also makes them ruddy amazing at killing stuff. Which is useful.'

The man called Anse hasn't spoken. He simply lifts his stew bowl to his lips and takes a careful sip before setting it back down on the table. He gives a grunt of disgust and then pushes it away with a flick of his fingers.

'A paladin …' you gasp. The title is familiar to you – given to veteran warriors that have pledged their lives, and some say their souls, to fight for the One God. You glance past his shoulder, to where a set of weapons have been carefully laid out on a side table. Resting on the white cloth are several knives, two swords and a mace. And propped up next to them is a silver crucifix, almost a metre in length.

'He doesn't say much,' says Polk, grinning through his beard. 'But then I respect someone whose actions speak louder than words.'

Will you:	
Ask about the shroud?	238
Ask why you should risk your life?	89
Agree to the mission?	24

271

'You were lucky to have survived,' states the witchfinder firmly. 'Few, if any, recover from a demon attack – and I think we can both agree, it was not Cernos' intention to leave you alive.'

You scratch at the itchy scales on your shoulder, perturbed when one of them comes off in your fingers. 'What is happening to me? Is this a disease?'

Virgil is silent for some time. It isn't until you press him that he snaps out of his thoughtful reverie. 'No, not a disease,' he replies softly. 'You have a taint. And left unchecked, you will become . . .' He glances sideways at his companion, who remains silent by the window.

'Become what?' you ask tensely, turning the dark scale over in your fingers.

The witchfinder takes a deep breath, straightening his back and brushing down his grey coat. You can tell this topic has made him uncomfortable. 'We will do what we can,' he says, shifting his gaze to avoid your own. 'But not all wounds can be cured by a medic's tonics and balms.'

Return to 494 to ask another question, or turn to 433 to continue.

272

'A riveting display!' You twist around to see an elderly mage in a red silk robe, floating down from a high balcony. 'Really, I haven't seen such an admirable show of magic by a novice for a long time.'

'Ignatius Pyre!' you rasp, still panting from your exertions. 'What . . . what was *this*?' You look down to see the creature's body starting to decompose, releasing a sickening green smoke into the air.

The mage's grin remains fixed. 'Your movements were so fast, so agile. It was almost as though you were anticipating each strike. Fascinating.' He snaps his fingers and the door in the far wall swings open. 'Come. You have passed the test. Now your training will begin.'

You follow the mage up another set of stairs into a small room, which appears to be a study. A desk occupies most of the space, surrounded by boxes and shelves filled with books.

Wincing with discomfort, Ignatius lowers himself into a chair. 'Ah, that's better. Now stand before me. Good. Let's begin.'

The old man proceeds to instruct you in the finer points of magic, demonstrating through a number of simple mental exercises how you can channel your powers more effectively. Each challenge you are given, you complete quickly, drawing surprise and admiration from your tutor.

Congratulations! You have now learnt the path of the mage. You may raise your *health* by 10 (to 40). As you go to leave the tower, Ignatius leads you back to the room where you fought the fungus. Nothing remains of the creature now, save for a rotting patch of mould.

'Magic is a fickle ally,' explains Ignatius sadly. 'Even the best can succumb to the lure of a demon.' His rheumy eyes scan your face thoughtfully. 'There is something different about you, mage. I feel you will do great things. I will not confine you to these walls, but use your power wisely. Or else . . .' His eyes shift to the mould.

Heeding the mage's warning, you leave the tower and return to upper town. Turn to 77.

273

The bugs have been defeated, but you are the only one from your party left standing. Sheathing your weapons, you hurry to the captain's side. His breathing is laboured, teeth clenched tight against the pain from his wound. The bodies of Surl and Vas are sprawled nearby.

'Go on,' gasps the captain, gripping your arm. 'To stop the flood . . . you must go straight to the source. Find out. . .what is causing this.' He gives a shudder, his eyelids flickering. 'Avenge us . . .' Then his eyes darken and his hand goes slack, dropping to his side. Gently, you lower him back to the ground, before rising to your feet. Turn to 355.

274

The woman pipes up immediately. 'We came a cropper; well and truly stuck in a rut.' She taps the side of the wagon with her boot heel. 'Water here makes it impossible to spot the deep holes. Think our axle may have gone with the weight.' The woman pats her belly, grinning. 'Not mine, I hasten to add.'

Her companion continues to scrutinise you with predatory eyes. 'That hole was there by design,' he mutters. 'Probably the work of Wiccans.' He emphasises the last word, watching carefully for your reaction. 'This is their territory and, right here, we're sitting fools for an ambush.'

You notice that there is no horse or pony tethered to the wagon. The woman appears to read your mind. 'Oh, we sent one of our companions ahead to fetch aid. They won't be long now.'

Will you:

Ask what is in the wagon?	223
Ask where they are travelling to?	178
Ask if you can help?	141

275

You find Eldias sprawled on the floor, his back against one of the pews. The corpses of the ghouls lie all around him, in tangled piles of stinking, charred flesh. He appears unharmed, but his breath is little more than a rasping wheeze. You kneel at his side.

'The books, the journals . . .' You glance back at the altar, where the fire has burnt itself out, leaving behind a heap of ashes. 'I'm sorry.'

The witchfinder offers you a half-smile. 'I said I'd go out in a blaze of glory . . . the irony is not lost on me.' His voice trails off into a fit of coughing.

'I might have a healing tonic. Wait . . .' You remove your pack and start to rummage through your belongings. Eldias leans his head against the pew.

'Your potions won't work on me.' He nods to the window opposite. You see that the storm has abated and a pale shaft of moonlight is now flooding in through the shattered glass. 'I will await the dawn. I think it is a fitting end . . . of sorts.'

Moonlight catches on the witchfinder's fangs. Without blood to sustain him, Eldias is too weak to go on. Come the dawn, his body will turn to ash.

You rise to your feet, determined not to give up on the witchfinder. If the herbalist, Rorus Satch, was close to creating a cure, then surely he must have left some clues behind. Or perhaps the Reverend was hoarding more of the herbalist's possessions elsewhere in the village.

Will you:

Find and search the herbalist's cottage?	224
Return to the reverend's home ?	210
Investigate the wishing well?	13

276

You hear the clink of metal behind you. Spinning around, you see an armoured figure staggering through the mist. They are mumbling to themselves, stumbling from one boulder to the next in an effort to stay upright. You hurry toward them, concerned it may be a wounded traveller. But as you near, you recognise their silver plate armour and tattered riding cloak – and the reek of filth and beer. It is the vagrant inquisitor who you met in the alleyway.

He reels forward, losing his footing. You catch him as he knocks into you.

'Gairn, is it you?' he mumbles. His red-rimmed eyes struggle to focus.

'Your friend has found peace,' you state slowly and firmly, hoping that the drunken man will understand your words. 'I suggest you do the same.' You prise the hip flask from his fingers and toss it away.

The inquisitor looks up at you, his face going slack. 'You mean … the curse is lifted? He no longer …' He sways as he attempts to survey his surroundings. His eyes catch on the knight's armour, scattered over the rocks. His expression of confusion slowly turns to one of wonderment. 'Yes … he is at peace now.'

He shifts around to face you, grunting as he struggles to draw his sword. You back away, wary of his intentions. After several awkward minutes of fumbling, he finally yanks the blade free, its inscribed runes glittering with white light. Then, to your surprise, the warrior drops to one knee, bowing his head and offering out the sword.

'I am no longer worthy of this blade … take it. You have faith in your heart where I do not – its steel should sing in your hands now.'

If you wish, you may take the inquisitor's blade:

Faith
(left hand: sword)
+1 speed +2 brawn
Ability: immobilise, faith and duty set

If you refuse his kind offer, then the grateful warrior offers you a purse of money instead, containing 20 gold crowns. You thank the inquisitor and agree to accompany him back to Raven's Rest. Return to the map to continue your journey.

277

You return to the bar and ask after the bearded warrior named Polk. No sooner have you said the words then you feel a nudge at your back. Turning, you are surprised to see Polk watching you with a grin on his face. 'Good timing,' he nods, showing you the full mugs of ale in his hands. 'You still interested?'

You follow him over to the curtained alcove. 'Any chance you could do the honours?' he asks. 'I think I spilled enough beer in this place already.'

You reach forward and pull back the curtain. Turn to **135**.

278

The robbers clearly have no combat experience, their ragged clothing and crude weapons suggesting that this was not their first choice of career. Quickly, you despatch your first assailant, who is too slow to defend himself. The others, who seem little more than boys, halt their attack – their mouths going slack at the sight of their fallen companion.

'We thoughts you were a Wiccan,' says the youngest, barely old enough to be sporting his fuzz of beard. He clutches the wooden club tightly, holding it out before him like some magical talisman to ward you away. You take a quick step forward – and the boy's resolve crumbles. He turns and runs back off into the trees, his companion hurrying after him.

Sheathing your weapons you search the robber's corpse, wrinkling your nose at the reek of mud and sweat. He has no possessions or gold, other than a *broken silver locket* in a pocket of his breeches. (If you wish to take this item, simply make a note of it on your hero sheet. It does not take up backpack space.)

Hoping that the rest of your journey will be less eventful, you continue along the track, towards the welcoming lights of Raven's Rest. (Record the word *raven* on your hero sheet, then turn to 199.)

279

As you place the cloth pieces onto the pattern you hear a cackle of delight from the unseen child. 'Oh yes! They like to play games, Maxi!'

At first you look around with disappointment, having hoped that some form of reward would be forthcoming. Then you spot a wooden trunk resting underneath one of the arched windows. You don't remember it being there before. You hurry over, crouching down to push open the lid. Inside you find what appears to be a child's dressing-up clothes. Several of them glimmer with special enchantments. If you wish, you may take one of the following rewards:

Hat of stars	Medic's uniform	Barbarian chest wig
(head)	(chest)	(chest)
+1 magic +1 brawn	+1 speed +1 magic	+1 speed +1 brawn
Ability: charm	Ability: heal	Ability: fear

You also find a leather case that contains a number of blank sheets of parchment. You can't fathom their significance but decide to take them with you anyway. (Make a note of the *parchment* on your hero sheet, it doesn't take up backpack space.) As you close the trunk, your eyes settle on the half-open door that leads deeper into the tower. Determined to find the child and the rest of your companions, you head through it into the passageway beyond. Turn to 391.

280

Unwilling to make a decision, you turn to Benin. 'Why should we play this game?' you scowl, drawing your weapons. 'You said before, we need to work together.'

The priest does a double-take. 'Are … are you serious?' he hisses. 'Look at it!'

The manticore beats its enormous wings, lifting its body into the air. Then, throwing back its head, the beast gives a thunderous roar.

'I think it's too late for regrets,' you state grimly. 'You're a priest, right?'

Benin nods, his mouth hanging open as he stares at the beast's dagger-like claws.

'Good. Then say a prayer to that One God of yours!' Ignoring the sickening fear in your gut, you charge towards the beast. Behind you, Benin calls out the words of a spell, surrounding you in a shimmering halo of light.

'I gave you a choice,' snarls the manticore, its barbed tail whipping through the air. 'It appears you have chosen to die!' With a booming roar, the monster lunges. It is time to fight:

	Speed	*Brawn*	*Armour*	*Health*
Manticore	2	3	1	25

Special abilities

- Benin's blessing: Your hero's *speed, brawn* and *magic* are raised by 1 for the duration of this combat. After this combat, they return to their normal values.
- Holy healer: If your *health* drops to 8 or less, Benin heals you back to full *health* and removes any venom that you are currently inflicted with. This ability can only be used once.
- Venom: Once you take damage from the manticore, you must lose 2 *health* at the end of every combat round.

If you manage to defeat the Manticore, turn to 292.

281

You have almost made it to the other side when something heavy slams into your arm, tugging you backwards off your feet. Before you have a chance to register what is happening, you find yourself being lifted up into the air. Your right arm and chest have become covered in thick strands of green slime, which are now reeling you in, taking you higher and higher.

In alarm, you see that you are being dragged towards one of the waiting creatures. It has the head and torso of a man, but the lower body and legs of a black ant. The gooey tendrils are coming out of spiracles either side of its thorax . As you near, the ant-man snatches you out of the air with its hands. Then you are being moved, a bumping, jolting journey, filled with the incessant clicking of legs and chitinous plates.

You are pushed through a hole in the ceiling, the ant-man scurrying in after you. In the dim light, glowing from the gooey walls, you see a swarm of similar creatures dashing back and forth along a narrow cave. Some of them are carrying wriggling bundles, which you assume are your companions.

'Tchk zizzt food,' chitters one of the ants, who appears to be some kind of overseer. 'Tchk zizzt queen hungry. More food.' The bundles are being carried off down adjoining tunnels that wind away into darkness.

Suddenly you are being spun around, twisting fast through the air. You realise that your captor is seeking to wind more of the goo around you, sealing you in a bundle just like the others. Desperately, you tug a weapon free with your remaining hand and swing it in the direction of the ant. You hear a high-pitched screech. Again, you swing the weapon, half-blind as to where your blows are landing.

Suddenly, you find yourself being dropped to the ground. Quickly, you hack through the slime, freeing yourself from its sticky prison. The ant-man is dead, but the others are scuttling towards you now. The air hums with gooey missiles, as the angry creatures try and catch you in their netting. You must fight:

	Speed	*Brawn*	*Armour*	*Health*
Archer ants	2	1	1	20

If you defeat the archer ants, turn to 311.

282

'No, Benin!' Ventus appears at your side, breathing heavily. 'This one is with us. They are not a Wiccan.'

The priest snorts. 'Then you are fooled. This is a spy – they aid our enemy!'

You open your mouth to protest, but the feathered woman interjects. 'You owe us a debt, Sanchen. Murlic saved you from Durnhollow. If it wasn't for us, you would still be rotting in that cell.'

Ventus balls his fists, the tattooed inscriptions sparking and crackling with holy magic. 'Be gone, witch! This one does not court demons!'

'I think they can speak for themselves.' The woman fixes you with a cold glare. 'I am Damaris of clan Hannon. Come with me now and I will help you master your powers. Or remain here with these fools and let their preaching blind you with ignorance.'

Will you:

Agree to leave with Damaris?	315
Refuse the witch's offer?	396

283

'Ah, that's a real shame,' he sighs. 'I could have used you. Say, my name's Polk. If you come back this way and change your mind, then come find me. Chances are, I might still need you to make up the numbers. Always the bloomin' numbers.'

The man moves away, muttering through his beard as he struggles back across the crowded taproom. (Make a note of the number 277. You can turn to that number at anytime during Act 1 to start the red quest.)

Turning back to the bar, you raise your hand for service. Turn to 364.

284

The sound of rattling hooves alerts you to your next danger. Eldias moves beside you, tugging another flint-lock pistol from his coat. At first, the sound echoes all around you, making it impossible to discern its direction. You both spin on the spot, eyes scanning the darkest shadows.

Then you hear the whinny of a horse and a cackle of laughter. From between the buildings a skeletal steed races out into the square, hooves glowing with a spectral light. On its back is a black-coated apparition – a highwayman – with the head of a flaming skull. In one of its fists is a scythe and in the other a pistol.

'The reaper has come for you!' snarls the skull. 'Expect no mercy from the scythe of doom!' At that moment, the church organ thunders with a chilling refrain as a jagged bolt of lightning streaks down from the heavens, striking the blade of the scythe and bathing it in crackling energy. 'Your end is nigh!' The skull breaks off into a manic cackle of demonic laughter …

BOOM!

Which is abruptly cut short as the skull is blown back off its shoulders, rolling and bumping along the ground like a child's ball. There is a pained groan, then the headless body slumps off the horse into the mud. The riderless mount gives a terrified screech before galloping away as fast as its legs can carry it.

There is a breath of silence.

Stunned, you turn to see Eldias holding a smoking pistol. He gives a nonchalant shrug of his shoulders. 'What can I say. I hate theatrics.'

His smile quickly fades, however, when the devilish laughter rings out once again. The skull has lifted up into air, flames billowing from its eye sockets. The headless body staggers to its feet, swaying slightly as it finds its balance. Then, together, the two undead foes move to attack.

'Figured that'd be too easy,' grunts the witchfinder. You must now fight:

	Speed	*Magic*	*Armour*	*Health*
Headless	2	3	2	35
Flaming skull	–	0	2	20

Special abilities

- Searing skull: At the end of every combat round you automatically take 2 points of damage from the skull's flames. If the skull is defeated, this damage no longer applies.
- Head case: The skull is immune to *bleed*.
- Wrath of the witchfinder: Eldias adds 2 to your damage score in this combat.

If you win a combat round against Headless, you can choose to apply your damage to Headless or the Flaming skull. If Headless is defeated, then the skull (if still alive) is automatically defeated also, winning you the combat.

If you defeat the headless horseman, turn to **48**.

285

This demon must have been the farmer's wife – or what was left of her after the Wiccan's magic had run its course. Amongst the creature's smouldering remains, you spot a silver locket glittering in the firelight. You retrieve it from the ashes, wondering if it might be of significance to the farmer and his sons.

You have gained *Dagona's locket*. (Make a note of this on your hero sheet, it does not take up backpack space.) After pocketing the locket, you decide to leave the farmstead – hoping there is still time to find the family and inform them of what has happened. (Return to the map to continue your journey.)

286

You try and settle into a calm state where you are reading your opponent, anticipating his attacks. Lazlo is a skilled fighter, agilely dodging the lightning and constantly throwing you off balance with his feints. But few of his measured blows strike home.

It is a long and gruelling battle. Lazlo observes your performance with growing admiration, occasionally offering advice when he sees you overstepping a lunge or struggling with a parry. Eventually Lazlo makes a mistake, failing to dodge the lightning in time. He stumbles back, wincing with pain. Before he can right himself, a sudden lurch of the disc throws him forward. You dodge aside, sliding a leg between his own and tripping him over. He lands roughly on his stomach, with your foot resting on his back.

'Game over,' you grin, looking down at the defeated prince.

He releases his grip on his sword. 'A worthy victory,' he smiles. 'You fought well.' The prince utters a word of magic. The lightning ceases and the disc starts to lower itself back to the ground.

Lazlo gets to his feet, dusting off his shirt and breeches. 'I think you deserve a reward, don't you?' He nods towards the weapon's rack. 'Take whatever you like.'

The disc comes to a rumbling halt, allowing you to descend the stairs. The rack contains a fine array of weaponry, all sharpened and polished, ready for battle. If you wish, you may now choose one of the following items:

Knot of knives	Red mist	Jeeves' juicer
(chest)	(main hand: sword)	(left hand: dagger)
+1 speed +1 brawn	+2 brawn +2 magic	+1 speed +1 brawn
Ability: flurry	Ability: bleed	Ability: gouge

When you have made your selection, turn to **174**.

287

You add the ingredient to the liquid. However, it only takes a few minutes of stirring for you to realise that you have made a mistake. The liquid is now giving off a bitter smell, having turned lumpy and sour. You will need to start again.

If you wish to try and make another potion then turn to **361**. Otherwise, you can leave the laboratory and visit the reverend's house (turn to **210**) or the herbalist's cottage (turn to **224**).

288

Malak glares at the seal, his scowl deepening. 'Humph. You'd better follow me, then.'

The mage leads you up a spiral staircase to a small landing. Here, he unlocks a door and indicates that you should enter. Warily, you step through the doorway into the room beyond.

The first thing that hits you is the smell – dampness and rotting decay. The second thing to hit you is a giant fist, which sends you hurtling across the room. You crack into the far wall, slumping down to your knees with a groan of agony.

There is a bestial growl.

Looking up, you see a hulking creature shuffling towards you. Its entire body is a writhing mass of vines and roots, crawling with worms and other small bugs. Frantically, you edge around the wall, towards the open door where Malak is grinning at you.

'What is this?' you growl angrily.

'The last student,' he replies. Then the door is slammed closed, the rattle of a key confirming that you are now locked in. You circle the beast warily, looking for some sign of weakness – for some possible advantage. But you are constantly distracted by its writhing snake-like vines and the gooey sap running from the corners of its gaping mouth. Is this really what happens, when magic goes bad? It is time to fight:

	Speed	*Magic*	*Armour*	*Health*
Fungalus	4	4	12	30

Special abilities

- Sinister sap: At the end of each combat round the fungus belches out a globule of sap, which immediately moves to attack you. For each sap in play, you lose 1 *health* at the start of each combat round.
- Blast the bile: When you win a combat round, instead of rolling for a damage score, you can use your magic to destroy all the saps that are currently in play.
- Power pruning: When you win a combat round, instead of rolling for a damage score, you can use your magic to blast away at the beast's armour. This automatically reduces Fungalus' *armour* by 4 each time it is used. (Note: You cannot use *blast the bile* and *power pruning* in the same combat round.)

If you defeat the lumbering fungus then all saps are also defeated. You may restore any lowered attributes (such as *magic*) and then turn to 272.

289

The tower is starting to break apart. You can barely maintain your footing as you are thrown from one wall to the other. Cracks and fissures branch through the black stone. Behind you, a whole wall crumbles outwards, its stone fragments floating away into the inky dark.

Aware that time is running out you quicken your pace, making for a set of double doors at the end of the passage. Throwing them open, you find yourself in an immense stone hall lined with slender pillars. A red carpet cuts a wound through its centre, leading up to a high-backed chair. The child sits watching you, his pale fingers drumming against its arms.

'This is over!' you cry, reeling against a pillar as the ground lurches once again. 'Where are the others?'

'Right here,' sneers the boy. He makes a small motion with his head. You follow his gesture to the side of the room, where his metal knight stands in eerie silence. Gripped in his gauntleted hands is Joss, who is fighting to break free. She snarls and hisses like an angered cat, but her efforts seem in vain.

'Jacob! Stop this, let me go!' she screams.

The boy hops to his feet. 'I told you to be quiet,' he shouts, his voice shrill with irritation.

You shake your head in disbelief. 'You ... you are Jacob?'

The boy flashes you a dark look, filled with menace and loathing. 'Jacob is old and weak. I am not Jacob! Not any more!'

'Where is my husband, you monster?' Joss kicks her heels against the metal giant in a renewed effort to get free. 'You took him! You took him!'

The boy scowls. 'Adam. You always did have eyes for him – but you never cared for me. Never loved *me*.'

'What?' The woman's eyes go wide. 'You were jealous? You did all this for some childish revenge?'

'No.' The boy raises a finger. 'It was an experiment. And Adam volunteered for it. To see if it was possible to make the toys ... better.' He points towards the metal knight, his lips twitching with excitement. 'I made the greatest discovery. One that has confounded scholars since the dawn of our age. To take a soul – a human soul – and put it into the body of another. To give true life – to be a god!' He throws back his head, laughing triumphantly.

At that moment one of the walls explodes inwards, heat and flame washing into the chamber. They are accompanied by a ragged body, flying through the air. It lands in a roll, springing back to its feet.

'Anse!'

His clothes hang in scorched tatters from his inscribed flesh, their sigils glowing weaker than before. Breathing heavily, the paladin draws two knives from his belt, then turns to face the collapsed wall. For a moment, you see only darkness – then a flaming head swings into view. It is the giant fire elemental. The furnace.

'I suggest you run,' snarls the paladin, starting towards the beast.

The elemental drags its body through the charred hole, flames rippling over its cracked skin. The paladin charges forward, dodging the monster's blazing fists as he springs into the air, punching his knives into the molten body.

Meanwhile, the boy is chanting a spell. A portal flickers open above his head – and a white ladder starts to descend. Quickly, he snatches hold of it, clambering up the rungs towards the light. He pauses, sparing a brief glance at his metal warrior. 'Maximus. Kill her! Kill your foolish wife!' Then he disappears into the portal.

A scream draws your attention back to Joss. The metal warrior has flung her to the ground. She is sobbing, shaking her head. 'Adam? Is it you?'

The warrior's hands clench into fists. 'I obey my master …'

'No!' Joss scrambles to her feet, but she doesn't run. Instead, she stands there, trembling, tears streaming down her face. 'Did Jacob do this to you? What did he do to you, Adam?'

'New life,' booms the voice from within the metal helm. 'Jacob gives life. And Maximus gives death.'

The iron golem grabs Joss around the waist, lifting her up into the air.

'I still love you,' she cries, making no effort to break free. 'I will always love you, Adam.'

Another violent tremor rips across the floor, tearing out a deep trench. The gap quickly widens as its jagged edges crumble away, sucked down into a whirling vortex of darkness.

'The shroud is taking us back …' echoes the child's voice. 'We're going back!'

Will you:

Climb the ladder after Jacob?	477
Attack the metal warrior and free Joss?	484
Help Anse battle the fire elemental?	490

290

While Vas blasts away at the flying boulders, you quickly clamber up the rock face. You barely have time to pull yourself onto the ledge before the ant-man is upon you – a huge boulder raised above its head. It is time to fight:

	Speed	*Brawn*	*Armour*	*Health*
Bombardier ant	3	2	2	40

Special abilities

Bullet storm: If the ant wins a combat round, roll a die. On a roll of ⚃ or more, Vas has hit the boulder that the ant was holding, shattering it to pieces. This means it does not roll for damage and the combat round automatically ends. A roll of ⚂ or less and the ant rolls for damage as normal.

If you manage to defeat the bombardier ant, turn to 273.

291

The stairs bring you to a dark-panelled door. You knock and push it open, to find yourself in a large high-ceilinged room dominated by painted friezes along each wall. In the centre of the room is a desk and chair, looking excessively small and austere next to the vivid painted scenes.

Seated at the desk is a man in red robes. A cap rests on his shaven scalp, edged with gold and silver. He is poring over a pile of parchments as you enter, shaking his head and muttering to himself. It isn't until the door clicks shut behind you that he flinches and looks up.

'Ah yes, the traveller.' His dark eyes scrutinise you intently. 'The Wiccans believe you are a prophet. I see there may be some truth in their heretic notions.' He taps a finger at one of the papers on the desk. 'You were at Durnhollow. A prisoner of the inquisition, no less.'

You stiffen, instinctively preparing yourself to run. But the man merely chuckles to himself. 'You have nothing to fear from me. All I see before me is a tool. An instrument I can use.' He rises to his feet, his robes rustling about his broad body. 'I am Dean Margo. And I would like you to tell me about the forest of thorns.'

You strain to keep your face neutral. 'I don't know …'

'The visions,' the dean replies bluntly. 'I was able to retrieve these from Durnhollow – at great personal risk.' You glance down at the papers, several of which are scorched and tattered. 'I wonder if Allam had such visions – demons, swords, mountains of fire.'

You back away to the door. 'You have mistaken me for someone else. I do not …'

The dean raises a hand, silencing you. 'Enough. Come, follow me. There is something I want to show you.' Turn to **154**.

292

Somehow you are able to stay one step ahead of the beast's attacks, dodging its flailing claws and whip-like tail. A lucky blow from your weapon forces the manticore back against the canyon walls, where its wings catch on the jagged rocks. For a moment, it struggles to right itself – and a moment is all you need to drive your weapon home, ending the beast's life.

Exhausted, you step away from the manticore's body, watching as its black lifeblood trickles into the pits and crevices of stone. You remove Anna's vial from around your neck and collect a sample of the blood. Benin does likewise, using a small gourd.

With your grisly task complete, you eye each other warily.

'I'm sorry,' says Benin at last. 'To the One God, every life is sacred. I should not have chosen to judge you.' He glances down at the corpse of the beast. 'I had hoped for a different outcome to this, but what is done is done.'

Searching the manticore's cave, you find 10 gold crowns and the following items which you may take:

Goblin bones	Manticore's tooth	White mane
(backpack)	(left hand: dagger)	(head)
These might prove valuable to the right person	+1 brawn Ability: savagery	+1 brawn +1 magic Ability: charm

Together you leave Crow Rock and return to Carvel. It is midday when you finally reach Anna's apothecary. You fear that it may already be too late to save her patient's life. Record the word *prevail* on your hero sheet. Then turn to 329.

293

'Oh, these!' says Bea, grinning from ear to ear. 'They're inscriptions. I copied them down from the shrines of Saint Mary. She was one of Judah's disciples, the first pilgrim to spread the holy word across Valeron.' She hands you one of the battered journals from the pile. Flicking through its yellowed pages, you see that most of them are filled with a confusing mix of arcane glyphs, annotated scripture and hastily-scrawled maps. 'Mary's teachings provide the faithful with safe passage – for those pilgrims who would follow in her footsteps and seek out the shrines.' Bea lifts up her sword, revealing the inscriptions that are cut into the steel. 'They have many uses. These are to provide healing, whilst others . . .' She touches a necklace of charms that hang around her neck. 'These give me protection. Useful when walking the darker roads – as we pilgrims must.'

Will you	
Learn the pilgrim career (requirement: rogue)?	481
Return to the courtyard?	260

294

You are knocked to the ground by one of the tigris' powerful swipes. Before you can find your feet again the white tigris straddles you, his fists raised. Behind him you hear the roars and snarls of his pack, urging him to finish the battle. But, once again, a single voice rings out, clear and commanding.

'Hold your claws. This is not the place for killing.'

The white tigris grunts and then climbs off you. 'Skin not worthy of the Sheva. Take this one to marsh if that is your wish. We are done here.'

The white tigris depart in silence, heading back into the dark forest. Scar-face walks over and helps you to stand. His disappointment is evident on his ravaged face. 'I hoped you'd do better.'

'Me too,' you wince, putting a hand to your bruised rib.

The leader, Grey-hair, watches you from the rock shelf. 'We would still welcome you. The journey across the marsh has many dangers. Will you help us, bright claw?'

Will you:	
Agree to help?	**549**
Decline the offer?	**Return to the quest map**

295

'What business is it of yours?' she yells, kicking over the table and sending pots and mugs flying. 'Come on boys, time to show this one what happens when yer bait the fish!'

There are screams and shrieks from the crowd as people scatter to a safe distance. 'No fighting!' bellows a voice from behind the bar. Unfortunately, you don't have a choice – the ruffians run at you as a pack. You must fight:

	Speed	*Brawn*	*Armour*	*Health*
Bilhah the Fish	5	4	2	35
Ruffians	–	–	2	15

Special abilities

- Motley crew: The ruffians add 3 to Bilhah's damage score for the duration of this combat. If the ruffians are defeated, this bonus no longer applies.

In this combat you roll against Bilhah's speed. If you win a combat round, you may choose to strike against Bilhah or her ruffians. If Bilhah is defeated first, then the ruffians will immediately surrender, winning you the combat.

If you defeat this cruel band of mercenaries, turn to **194**. If you are defeated, turn to **244**.

296

Bea gives you a sideways glance, her hands flexing around her sword grips. 'Sanchen. You're a prophet?'

Your attention remains fixed on the Wiccans. The short man whispers something to the feathered woman, who nods and smiles. 'We should never have left you at Durnhollow,' she says with genuine regret. 'We have need of your powers, Sanchen. Old one.' She tilts her head, looking past you to the elderly man sat by the roadside. He is fumbling with one of the buttons on his coat, the rainwater dripping from the brim of his hat. 'And we want that one. The so called "secret weapon".'

'God's teeth,' curses Ventus, looking straight at Bea. 'Is there no one in Carvel who doesn't know?'

The pilgrim shakes her head quickly, her cheeks reddening. 'I was careful.'

'Not after a cup too many, dear,' grins the Wiccan woman. 'We have our eyes and ears, even in the towns.' She points to the elderly man. 'He is important. And he comes with us. Don't try and stop us. As you can see …' The woman gestures to her ragged band of warriors, all armed with brutal weapons. 'A fight would not favour you.'

Bea takes a step forward, raising her swords. 'I'll gladly put your steel to the test.'

The giant throws back his head and laughs – a deep, hard sound, both daunting and terrible. His ragtag soldiers follow suit, throwing curses and jibes in a guttural-sounding language.

With a bullish snort, the mighty warrior takes a step forward, beating the flat of an axe head against his chest. 'I am Conall. The freed man. Leader of the Wiccans. We take back the old lands. The kin lands. And we make you pay for our suffering in tears and blood!'

'Wait.' The feathered woman stops him with a commanding tone. 'Stay your hand, king in the making. Let our zealous friends here decide their fate.' Her eyes flick to you, the corners of her mouth twitching with amusement. 'What say you, Sanchen? The crows got your tongue?'

Will you:

Convince your companions to surrender?	269
Look for a peaceful compromise?	242
Draw your weapons and defy the Wiccans?	309

297

Amongst the piles of wind-scoured rock, you find a silver casket containing 50 gold crowns and one of the following items:

Storm riders	Shard of sky	Silver flight
(feet)	(ring)	(left hand: sword)
+1 speed +1 armour	+1 brawn	+1 speed +2 brawn
Ability: pagan's spirit set (requirement: pariah)	Ability: blind	Ability: charm

When you have updated your hero sheet, turn to 239.

298

With Shonac defeated, you race up the pathway to the next platform. As before, your way is blocked by another ghostly scene. A group of dwarves lie sprawled across the ground, spears and arrows protruding from their armoured bodies. Goblins scramble over them, snorting and hollering in glee. Then the scene blurs and shifts as one of their number is brought into focus – a female goblin, with jewelled trinkets and bone charms threaded through her tangled hair.

'Sarak Dun Garag Gar!' The shaman pulls a wand from her belt, dark magic flickering around its spiked headpiece. 'Gun Sark Virag Dor!' Her guttural words become a cat-like hiss as she raises the wand and sends a cascade of magic surging towards you. It is time to fight:

	Speed	*Magic*	*Armour*	*Health*
Rap Unzal	11	7	3	40

Special abilities

- Dem bones: At the end of each combat round, Rap Unzal heals 2 *health* from the magic of her bone charms.
- Ghost of a victory: You cannot use *cutpurse* or *pillage* to gain gold/ items from this combat.

If you manage to defeat Rap Unzal, keep a record of your *health* and remaining abilities, and turn to 533. If you are defeated (or reach the end of your twentieth combat round), then the wind demon has outrun you. Restore your *health* and return to 630 if you wish to tackle the challenge again.

299

The women are applying a thick coloured paste to the rock wall, using pieces of bark to quickly and skilfully craft it into shapes and textures. The last image shows some demonic-looking animal rearing up over the heads of two knights. Eva is adding the claws to its immense paws, scratching them into the paste with deft movements of her makeshift brush.

'What is this?' you ask with interest, leaning over to get a closer look at the two knights. They are cowering away from the mighty animal, their weapons discarded on the ground.

'We celebrate when spirits aid us,' states Eva, taking a step back to admire her work. 'Conall is blessed by spirits. He will be king one day – and wear the crown of all peoples.'

You look at the gigantic bear with its ferocious jaws and blazing red eyes. 'But this is a demon,' you reply tentatively. 'Conall is a man, I thought.'

The other women giggle to each other. Eva frowns at you. 'Conall is our champion. With Damaris, his strength is greater than a thousand demons.' She resumes her painting, while the other women continue to whisper and chuckle. (Return to 485 to continue your exploration of the cave.)

300

The creature staggers back, dislodging stones from the wall as it grapples to stay upright. While it is distracted, you step in and deliver the killing blow, watching as the diseased monster slides down the wall into the thick sludge.

With the beast finally defeated, you decide to search its remains. You find 5 gold crowns and may choose one of the following rewards:

Number of the beast	**Bile-coated boots**
(necklace)	(feet)
+1 brawn +1 magic	+1 brawn +1 magic

You also find a small pocket-sized book floating in the slime. Silver lettering on its cover spell out the title: *Handy Herbalist's Spotter's Guide*. This might prove useful, so you pluck it out from the sticky sludge. (Make a note of the book on your hero sheet. It doesn't take up backpack space.) Turn to 328.

301

The beast is fast and powerful, and yet somehow you are able to stay one step ahead of its attacks, expertly weaving between sharp claws and searing breath attacks.

After an arduous battle the demon is finally defeated, its blistered body exploding into a cloud of fine black dust. You may now help yourself to one of the following rewards:

Earthen embers	**Armbands of living flame**	**Grieving soul**
(talisman)	(gloves)	(ring)
+1 brawn	+1 speed +1 magic	+1 armour
Ability: cauterise	Ability: sear	Ability: fire aura

If you have the word *duty* on your hero sheet, turn to 285. If you are carrying the *broken silver locket*, turn to 313. Otherwise, you leave the farmstead and continue your journey. (Return to the map.)

302

Murlic hands you a second training dagger and then proceeds to teach you his technique. You discover that the Wiccan favour heavier daggers, adding their own weight to that of the weapon to deliver slow, punishing strikes. Murlic watches you, nodding with approval as you move through the stances. 'You make good fighter,' he grins.

If you wish, you may now learn the pariah career. The pariah has the following abilities:

Beguile (mo): You may use one of your speed abilities twice in the same combat, even if its description states it can only be used once.
Double punch (co): (requires a dagger in the main hand and left hand.) Use this ability instead of rolling for a damage score, to automatically inflict 2 damage dice plus the total *brawn* modifier of your two weapons to a single opponent. This ability ignores *armour*. You can only use *double punch* once per combat.

You may now ask Murlic about Durnhollow (turn to 129) or explore the rest of the cave (turn to 485).

303

A fatal blow extinguishes whatever infernal life this demon once had, sending its body flying apart in a spray of black ink. You spin away, covering your face as the liquid showers across the room, splashing over the floor and walls. As it settles you realise, with a grim sense of unease, that the ink blots are spelling out a familiar phrase:

paper, scissors, stone

In the distance you hear a child's laughter.

Quickly, you set about searching the remains of the dark demon. You find one of the following items, which you may take:

Quill of Aquila	Ink-blotted tome
(left hand: dagger)	(left hand: spell book)
+1 speed +1 brawn	+1 speed +1 magic
Ability: bleed	Ability: dominate

You also find an ink pot, which you fill with some of the magical ink. (Make a note of the *magic ink* on your hero sheet, it does not take up backpack space.) Your task complete, you cross the room to the iron door. To your relief you find it unlocked, its rusted hinges screeching in protest as you force it open. Turn to 46.

304

You find yourself in a corridor fashioned from black stone, smooth and without decoration. To your left it continues for several metres before ending in a set of worn stairs leading up to a decorative wooden door. To your right, there is an open metal grille, beyond which you can see a set of rusted stairs spiralling down towards the sound of buzzing, hammering machinery.

Will you:	
Take the stairs up?	417
Take the stairs down?	382

305

You deposit your grisly trophy on the counter. Kam's eyes widen with interest as he stumbles to his feet. 'It can't be ...' He lift's the beast's head, observing the smoke still billowing from its eyes and muzzle. The room steadily fills with the stench of sulphur. 'They say seeing is believing, but ...'

'So, what will you give me for it?' you ask confidently.

The burly hunter straightens. 'It's the black shuck all right.' He places the head carefully back on the counter, then proceeds to make a number of grunting sounds as he ponders the situation. 'Reckon, this'll cover it.' He takes a pouch of money from his belt and hands it to you with a hopeful grin.

You count out the grimy collection of coins. 'Forty gold,' you reply, making your disappointment evident.

'Okay, okay.' Kam blows through his moustache. 'You ever heard of the Colt Phoenix, kid? The fastest crossbow in Valeron.'

You shrug your shoulders. 'How does this help our negotiation?'

Kam reaches behind the counter and produces a small hand-crossbow. Its cross-piece is covered in runes, some of which are glowing with a fiery magic. A bolt already rests in the chamber. 'She's fast enough for you, kid. If you can handle her. Made a few modifications myself.' He straightens his arm, resting the bolt-head to your chest. He stares down the groove, grinning through his beard. Your heart skips a beat as you wonder what his next move will be. A heavy silence descends, broken only by the creak of the hunter's finger on the trigger.

Then, with a grunt of laughter, Kam spins the crossbow and offers it out to you. 'She's all yours, kid.'

If you wish, you may now take the 40 gold crowns and the following item:

Colt phoenix
(left hand: crossbow)
+1 speed +1 brawn
Ability: volley

If you do not want to take the crossbow, then Kam agrees to sweeten his bargain to 80 gold crowns instead. When you have made your decision, you thank the hunter and leave the shop. You may now explore more of Raven's Rest (turn to **199**) or return to the map to continue your journey.

306

Unable to progress, you clamber back down the tree – stepping through the magic portal to continue your journey. Turn to 46.

307

You march forward into the cave, determined to end this threat once and for all. The queen has clearly sensed you, lowering her head as if to charge.

'Tzzk chkk, my brood!' she snarls. 'Tzzk chkk, do not defile the eggs!'

With a deafening screech, the queen surges forward, breaking free of her silken egg sac. The ground trembles as she approaches, her spiked crown and bladed arms looking to spit you through. You must fight:

	Speed	*Brawn*	*Armour*	*Health*
Queen Bellona	3	2	3	40

Special abilities

- Pin cushion: Every time you cause health damage to Bellona, you must take 1 damage in return, ignoring *armour*.
- Look out for larvae!: Roll a die at the start of each combat round. If you roll ⚂ or less then one of the eggs has hatched, producing a larva. These maggot-like creatures may be small, but they are still deadly – and cause you 1 damage (ignoring *armour*) at the end of every combat round. (You must take 1 damage from each larva that is in play.)
- Bug blaster: If you have a *borehole charge*, you can use this item instead of rolling for a damage score. This will automatically inflict 10 damage to Bellona, ignoring *armour*. It will also lower Bellona's *armour* by 2 for the remainder of the battle. (Once the charge is used, you must remove it from your backpack.)

If you defeat Bellona, then any remaining larvae are also defeated. Turn to 381.

308

Dodging the jagged, razor-sharp fists, you pummel away at the beast's legs, combining your attacks with those of your companions to sever the vines and roots. Unable to heal fast enough, the beast stumbles and falls, the earth shaking as its giant body crashes down into the mud. Temporarily prone, the monster provides an easy target.

Leaping onto its chest, you slash and blast away at the twisted boughs until the beast is reduced to a blackened, scorched heap. With the giant defeated, you may now help yourself to one of the following rewards:

Briar star	**Bark skin binding**	**Bramble blade**
(ring)	(chest)	(main hand: sword)
+1 armour	+1 speed +1 armour	+1 speed +2 brawn
Ability: thorns	Ability: thorn armour	Ability: bleed

If you have the word *Wiccan* on your hero sheet, turn to 331. Otherwise, turn to 353.

309

(Make a note of the word *papal* on your hero sheet.)

You draw your weapons, moving to stand beside Ventus and Bea. 'All I see are thieves and brigands,' you reply, scowling. 'You prey on travellers and make these lands unsafe. I will not go with you – nor will we surrender.'

The feathered woman shakes her head, sighing with disappointment. 'You know nothing of us, Sanchen. And your ignorance will cost you dearly this day. Conall, get what we came for . . .'

The warrior grunts, then starts towards the elderly man, who is now humming to himself quietly. Ventus moves quickly to intercede. 'Lay one hand on him and . . .'

Suddenly, the loud blare of a horn reverberates across the moorland. It is followed by a hooting call from one of the Wiccans. Some kind of warning. They all turn as one, weapons leaping from scabbards and belts, as the first bright explosion rips into their ranks. Turn to 442.

310

You drop the bark shavings into the mixture and stir it around with one of the spoons. However, it only takes a few minutes of stirring for you to realise that you have made a mistake. The liquid is now giving off a bitter smell, having turned lumpy and sour. You will need to start again.

If you wish to try and create another potion then turn to 361. Otherwise, you can leave the laboratory and visit the reverend's house (turn to 210) or the herbalist's cottage (turn to 224).

311

'Tchk zizzt intruder!' chitters the overseer. 'Zizzt destroy!' Looking around, you see more of the creatures scuttling out of a side tunnel.

You cannot win this fight. Shaking with exhaustion, you turn to the larger ant-man. You sheathe your weapons, its mirror-like eyes reflecting your determined stare.

'Give it your best shot,' you growl.

The overseer's spiracles blast slime in your direction. You twist your body at the last possible moment, catching one of the strands in your hand. The ant reels you in quickly, its sharpened teeth clicking together hungrily. Only then does the creature's slow brain register your plan. Once you are in range, you throw yourself against the ant-man, wrapping your arms around its waist. Your forward momentum sends you both tumbling backwards, rolling across the ground . . . and straight through one of the holes in the floor.

The wind is a dull roar in your ears, the world spinning over and over in a dizzying blur. Then, you are jolted sideways. Out of instinct, the ant has fired a slime rope at the ceiling. Suddenly you are both swinging rather than falling, slamming against one of the walls where you finally let go.

Thankfully the drop is only a short one, the ant-man's sticky rope having slowed your fall. Landing on your feet you start sprinting for the tunnel, where you see the other survivors taking shelter. One of the party steps forward, a mage in black and gold robes. They throw a spear of fire through the air, which whistles past your ear and hits something behind you, filling the cavern with a high-pitched wail. Part of an ant's body crashes down nearby.

The mage grabs your arm as you reach the tunnel, pulling you in to safety.

'What was that?' gasps Vas, breathing hard.

'A massacre was what it was,' cries Surl, sounding panicked. 'That weren't no greenheads.'

You look around at the party. Of the original dozen, now only half remain.

'Come on,' growls the captain. 'Keep it together, people.' He pats you on the shoulder, a hint of admiration in his steely grey eyes. 'Come on, hero. You're tracker now. Get moving!'

Feeling more like bait than a valued member of the team, you find yourself leading the group deeper into the mountain. After several hundred metres the passage widens, joining a much larger tunnel which cuts left to right. A chill wind blows from the west, carrying with it a salty, stagnant odour. To the east the tunnel ascends steeply, heading deeper into the mountain.

Will you:

Take the west tunnel? 122
Take the east tunnel? 143

312

Your hand goes to the glass vial, hanging around your neck. 'I'm sorry Benin, but I made a promise – a promise to someone who saved my life.'

Benin's face contorts into a mask of rage. He raises his staff, its tip igniting with a blazing white fire. 'I cannot let you do this! I'll lose everything – everything! I won't let you take the bishop's life!'

You barely have time to draw your weapons, before the berserk priest is upon you:

	Speed	*Magic*	*Armour*	*Health*
Benin	0	2	1	18

Special abilities

Harm or heal: If Benin wins a combat round, roll a die. If the result is ⚀ or ⚁ then Benin heals 2 *health* instead of rolling for a damage score (this cannot take him above his starting *health* of 18). If the result is ⚂ or more, Benin rolls for a damage score as normal.

If you defeat the priest, turn to 333.

313

You spot a silver chain lying amongst the demon's smouldering remains. You retrieve it from the ashes, surprised to discover that it is the twin of the locket that you found on the robber's corpse. After brushing away the dirt and grime, you take the two broken halves and lock them together, forming a heart-shaped pendant.

You have gained the following reward, which you may take:

Dagona's heart
(necklace)
+1 brawn +1 magic
Ability: radiance

As the wind scatters the demon's ashes, you are left to ponder how a desperate robber came to be carrying the other half of this enchanted locket. (Return to the map to continue your journey).

314

As you smash through the endless horde, a berserk fury starts to take hold. One that you gladly welcome. Skeletons splinter and explode as you drive your weapons through their bodies, their clumsy strikes forever missing their mark as you dodge and weave, your prophetic sixth-sense allowing you to anticipate each and every move, keeping you one heartbeat ahead.

'Is that the best you can do?' you snarl, spittle flying from your lips.

Magic missiles arc through the green mist, zipping past you by scant inches. You howl and snarl like some unleashed beast, filling the sky with an endless rain of body parts.

Then it is over. You stand alone at the centre of a wide swathe of destruction.

Gasping for air, you stumble back, a sudden weariness dragging at your muscles. From beneath your clothing a sulphurous smoke curls into the air.

'What am I becoming?' You drop to your knees, looking down at trembling hands caked in blood and dust. For a brief moment, you wonder if they are still your own ... if this body is still your own, or whether it has become something else. An instrument of another power.

Then you hear a mournful wail, echoing through the mist. All around you the bones are starting to tremble and shake, as if still possessed of some dark life. You rise to your feet, turning slowly on the spot as you see the fragments start to lift up like marionettes, scraping and sliding against each other as they re-arrange themselves back into skeletal shapes.

Another screeching wail. You turn, to see more of the undead spilling out of the fog, their hollow eyes bereft of care or compassion. In desperation, you try and call on the strange power that aided you previously – struggling to find that core of fiery rage. But there is nothing there, save a dispiriting exhaustion. The skeletons close in once again. You raise your weapons and resign yourself to your fate, knowing that when you fall in battle you will become just like them – another undead warrior, haunting this remote and forgotten place. Turn to **146**.

315

'Traitor!' Benin levels his staff at you. A bolt of white flame sizzles through the air, slamming into your chest and lifting you into the air. You crash down in the muddy water, gasping for breath. From behind you, there is a thunderous explosion. For several moments your ears are ringing with white noise, then you hear horses whinnying and raised cries.

'Get the Sanchen,' shouts the feathered woman, from somewhere nearby. 'We're leaving this place.'

You struggle to move but your limbs are not responding. The last thing you remember is the rain, spearing down from the black skies, beating against your pain-wracked body. Then the light fades and a feverish darkness takes you. Turn to 423.

316

The monk raises his glowing hands, his round face breaking into a gap-toothed smile. 'I've waited years for my sanctifying. It's not often a white abbot comes here – I'm the last of my brothers to receive the blessing.' He proudly studies the inscriptions, emblazoned into his skin. 'Now I can complete my warrior training – so I can finally fight for the One God.'

'You choose not to use weapons?' you ask, patting those that hang at your side.

The monk smiles again. 'We follow the way of Saint Allam. He commanded his men to forsake their blades and trust in the One God. He gave them fists of light, to smite their foes with holy vengeance. That faith is what we keep alive, here at the monastery.' He clenches his fists, watching with delight as they spark and crackle with magic. 'Swords can be untrustworthy, they can dull and rust, be turned against you. But having faith in yourself … to be one with the power inside,' he glances up at you, a zealous pride brightening his eyes, 'that's something no one can take away.'

You glance past his shoulder, to the door of ivory and gold. You assume that the white abbot, who gave this monk his inscriptions, must be taking residence inside the building.

Will you:

Head through the door?	132
Return to the courtyard?	260

317

Eldias frowns as he listens to your accusation. 'Yes,' he nods, tilting his head to one side as he looks you up and down. 'I remember you. You look different: thinner, leaner. Less meat.'

'Is that all you have to say?' You glower angrily. 'I was made a prisoner of the inquisition. You know what happened to that child was an accident. I'm no murderer!'

Eldias waves at you dismissively. 'I was doing my job, what do you expect? I didn't hand you over because of what you did – I gave you to the inquisition because of what you are.'

'Then what am I?' you snap, glaring at him intently. 'Enlighten me.'

Eldias looks about to say something, then checks himself – choosing his words carefully. 'You were lost to some kind of vision when you attacked the boy. He was trying to help you; he was trying to give you water. He didn't know any better. You were not accountable for your actions. I know that.'

'You didn't answer the question.'

Eldias shrugs his shoulders. 'You could be many things. But I think you might be a prophet; someone who sees future events, glimpses possible destinies. It's a fine gift, but one that is also dangerous. You need to control it – you need to know how to use it.'

'Were you hoping the inquisition would teach me?' you reply petulantly. 'They had me chained in a cell while some clown filled me full of Elysium – they questioned me again and again and ...' You stop, aware that the banging outside has intensified. From somewhere close by you hear glass breaking. A window.

Eldias drops a hand to one of his swords. 'Well, you can either take your anger out on me or them,' he says. 'But I reckon your chances of survival are going to be considerably better with me at your side.'

Turn to 347 to ask Eldias another question. When you are ready to continue, turn to 340.

318

You pass beneath the archway, entering a circular room filled with rubble. Part of the ceiling and a wall have toppled inwards, offering an unnerving glimpse of the black nothingness beyond.

A number of glowing wisps are floating above the loose stones. If you have a potion in your backpack, you could tip out its contents and fill the empty bottle with some of these strange balls of light. This will replace your potion with the following item:

A bottle of wisps
(backpack)
The tiny glowing lights are
trapped inside!

If you do not have a potion in your pack, then you have no way of capturing the wisps of magic – they simply slip through your fingers each time you try and catch one.

Turning back to the room, you see that the only other exit is another archway in the north wall, where a set of metal stairs wind away into the tower.

Will you:	
Search through the rubble?	348
Leave via the stairs?	46
Return to the passage and try the wooden door?	4

319

'It can be a rough place,' the leader grunts disparagingly. 'Never used to be the case, but now too many mercenary types around. The travellers need 'em, for the protection. The roads ain't … safe.' He falls to silence, looking down at his feet.

'Yes, I had noticed,' you add tersely. 'Perhaps Raven's Rest will be more agreeable.'

The leader scowls, bristling. 'Yer gotta understand,' he glares. 'We lost everything. I saws you was alone . . . I thought . . . .' He shakes his head. 'It makes no matter, does it. We're just as bad as those Wiccans. Judge all you like.'

Will you:

Ask them to tell you more about the Wiccans?	162
Ask them if they have sought any help?	107
Give them a gift of 5 gold crowns?	326
Leave and continue your journey?	199

320

You put your hands to the wheel and push. For the first few seconds you find yourself grunting with exertion, your boots sliding across the metal floor as you struggle to move it. Then it gives a teeth-grating screech as it slowly begins to turn, grinding against the rust and grime that has gathered around its axle. After pushing it round a full turn, you hear a rumbling coming from your left, followed by a loud clunk. Glancing around, you see that a glowing portal has now appeared against the west wall. It looks similar to the doorway that you used to escape from the fire demon.

Will you:

Step through the magic portal?	416
Turn the wheel clockwise?	388

321

You chop up the leaves and root and add these to the potion base. The flowers are then crushed and mixed into the liquid, turning it from white to a light-shade of green. The mixture has started to bubble and fizz. What ingredient will you add next?

Will you:

Add lemongrass?	134
Add white willow?	121
Add sagewort?	114

322

'That's it! That's it!' You hear a childish peal of laughter, followed seconds later by a grating rumble. As you hurry towards the sound, you find yourself turning a corner to see one of the wall panels sliding open to reveal a secret room.

The interior is dark and dusty, the metal walls blackened with streaks of soot. Thick black ash covers most of the floor, dotted with debris. Against the opposite wall a ladder leads up to a metal gantry that circumvents the chamber, where a magic portal glows with a faint glimmering light.

You search through the ash, assuming there will be some reward hidden here. But all you find are the charred remains of wooden dolls, some broken tools and a rusted saw blade. Frustrated, you kick at a mound of ash in anger – and give a cry of pain as your foot hits something very hard.

Dropping to your knees, you scrape the ash away to reveal a soot-blackened box. Flipping open the lid you discover two compartments inside. One contains 20 gold crowns, the other a set of stonecutter's tools – a wooden mallet, a hammer, and a set of metal chisels. (If you wish to take the *stonecutter's tools* then simply make a note of them on your hero sheet, they do not take up backpack space.)

You climb up to the gantry and step through the portal. There is a bright flash of white light, accompanied by the dizzying sensation of movement, then you find yourself stumbling out into a small square room. A quick scan of your surroundings confirms you are back where you started, with the trapdoor opening in the floor ahead of you. You step around it, eager now to explore the noisy workshop below. Turn to 398.

323

One book immediately stands out from the others – a great thick tome bound in black leather. You reach up and take it off the shelf. Despite its considerable size, the book is peculiarly light. Cracking open the cover, you flick through its yellowed pages. Each one is covered in strange glowing runes, which seem to dance before your eyes. If you have a *magic* score of 5 or more turn to **81**. Otherwise, you cannot make sense of the arcane glyphs. Closing the book, you place it back on the shelf before contemplating your next action.

Will you:	
Examine the parchment on the table?	362
Leave through the iron door?	46

324

'Yes, I'm afraid my intention to chart the entire jungle has proved a trifle optimistic.' He taps his finger in the middle of the large blank circle that blemishes his map. 'This is what happens when you have to rely on others.'

'You haven't been into the jungle yourself?' you enquire.

'Cripes no!' he bristles with affront. 'I'm a man of learning. I'm far too important to risk on some dangerous and poorly-financed expedition. Could you imagine the heat with *my* boils?'

You grimace at the thought. 'Well, you've not done a bad job of it so far,' you smile weakly, changing the subject.

The scholar nods, looking over the rest of the map. 'Yes, I suppose the explorers from the university haven't been a complete waste. Shame I keep losing the little blighters. It really makes my work so much harder.'

Turn to **386** to ask the scholar another question or turn to **548** if you wish to leave and continue your journey.

325

You notice a number of items snagged in the weed-choked waters. Using Boom Mamba's staff, you are able to fish them out of the pool. As well as a pouch containing 40 gold crowns, you also find one of the following rewards:

Electrified vest	Conga kickers	Lightning whetstone
(chest)	(boots)	(talisman)
+1 speed +1 brawn	+1 brawn +1 armour	+1 speed
Ability: shock!	Ability: lightning	Ability: sure edge

When you have made your decision, you return to the courtyard. Turn to 510.

326

(Deduct 5 gold crowns from your hero sheet.)

You offer the gold to the leader. His first reaction is one of surprise, then his expression folds into a sceptical frown. 'Is this some game? A trick?'

'Father, please.' The youngest boy moves closer, greedily eying up the shining coins. 'We have to be more trusting.'

'Take it,' you insist. 'I can spare it – and perhaps the gold will get you some clothes and food. It'll certainly make the roads a little safer.' The last statement is accompanied by a wry grin.

The youngest looks to his father. 'Please?'

Reluctantly, the leader nods, reaching out and taking the gold. He catches your eye and offers you a grudging smile. 'I'm sorry. Things have been … hard. Not often a stranger offers us charity these days. Not without something attached to it, anyways.'

You retrieve your pack from the mud. 'Are you headed for Raven's Rest?' you ask, hoisting the pack onto your shoulders. 'We could travel together.'

The leader looks to his boys, then nods in agreement. 'It's a deal – Raven's Rest it is.' (Record the word *raven* on your hero sheet, then turn to 199.)

327

The swarm of beetles crash into you, a dark wave of clicking death. Desperately you try and bat them away, but their sharp pincers are everywhere, digging through your armour and stabbing into your flesh. In horror, you realise that these creatures are a giant form of tick, and they are trying to suck your blood! You must fight:

	Speed	*Brawn*	*Armour*	*Health*
Blood ticks	3	2	2	30

Special abilities

- Bombardment: At the start of each combat round, roll 1 die. If the result is ⚂ or less then you have been hit by one of the rock missiles and must take 2 damage, ignoring *armour.*
- Blood suckers: If the blood ticks win a combat round and cause health damage, then they heal themselves for 1 *health.*

If you manage to defeat these blood-sucking bugs, turn to 370.

328

Most of the laboratory was destroyed in the fight, but one table remains intact, covered in a vast array of alchemical equipment – potion bottles, mixing spoons, chopping knives, weighing apparatus. It is all the equipment you need to create your own potions. The only thing missing is the ingredients.

If you have the word *gatherer* written on your hero sheet, then turn to 361. Otherwise, you cannot proceed at this time. Write the word *mixer* on your hero sheet, then turn to 210 if you want to search the reverend's home, or turn to 224 if you want to investigate the herbalist's cottage.

329

You find Anna at Jolando's bedside. Quickly, she takes the vial from you and sets to work on the antidote. It appears you have arrived just in the nick of time. The thief's condition has worsened drastically. His face is now gaunt, the skin clinging to the bone. Occasionally, he gives a wheezing, rattling breath – the only outward sign that he is still alive.

Anna pours her concoction into a shallow bowl before moving to the man's side. You grab a blanket and use it to prop him up, while the healer tilts the bowl to his pale lips. He coughs and splutters on the sticky liquid, but it appears he has at least swallowed some of it. Anna seems satisfied.

'Now, we must wait,' she says. 'We should see an improvement in the next hour or so. Otherwise …' The healer shakes her head sadly.

You wait in the shop, surrounded on all sides by a multi-coloured array of potions, herbs and powders. However, your eyes keep returning to a small onyx statue set in an alcove above the front door. It looks like a bearded man with his hands resting on a large rotund belly. You make a note to ask Anna about its origin – you have never seen one like it before.

At last, Anna emerges from the side room. The healer looks tired, but she is smiling. Under one arm, she is carrying a small iron casket. You rise quickly to your feet, urging Anna to reveal the outcome.

'The antidote worked,' she nods, glancing back towards the side room. 'Jolando is sleeping now; he needs to regain his strength. But we were able to talk – briefly.'

Will you:

Ask about what happened to the thief? 54
Ask about what is in the casket? 26
Ask about the statue above the door? 98
Thank Anna and leave? **Return to the map**

330

Bea purses her lips as if trying to contain the words. Then they suddenly burst forth in an excited flurry. 'I'm not supposed to speak to you – but this is too exciting! You're a prophet, aren't you? That is why the Wiccans called you Sanchen. It's their word for their elders – those they believe have the sight. I don't trust they could ever have such a thing, not like the great Allam, blessed by the One God. But you, perhaps . . . yes, the Dean is very excited, very excited to have you here, if it's all true that is, and not just made up – not that you would make it up, but oh . . .' The woman finally draws breath, her words faltering. 'Look at me, I'm not supposed to have said any of that.' She glances down at her feet guiltily. 'I do go on so. Pretend I never said a word, that's the best.'

Will you:

Ask Bea about the books? 293
Return to the courtyard? 260

331

'Impressive, very impressive,' grins the demon, who has watched the entire fight with bemused indifference. 'But futile all the same.'

Damaris strides towards the dais, then drops to one knee, her head bowed. 'Great one. We follow the old ways, the old magic. We have endured much to come here.' She looks up at the demon, her feathered grey hair streaming in the wind. 'Why did the dwarfs imprison you, great one?'

The creature leans closer, wings flaring out from its spiked shoulders. 'My crimes are endless, witch. Do you know who I am?'

Damaris continues to study the creature. 'You are a demon prince.'

'I am Cernos,' nods the demon. 'I have been a prisoner here for thousands of your mortal years. I have served my time and now I desire freedom.' Its crimson eyes flick to you, its horned brow creasing together. 'Grant it or you will die here.'

Conall steps forward, his body now human once more. The glow from his painted runes casts dark shadows about his face. 'And do you know who *I* am, demon?' he snorts.

Damaris spins suddenly, flinching with irritation. 'Conall! You witless fool! Leave this to me.'

In a blur the warrior draws his twin axes, their crimson runes sparking to life. 'You forget yourself, Damaris. It is I who will be king.' His angry gaze passes between the witch and the demon. 'You think this one will kneel before me? I will not share my throne. Not with anyone.'

The demon tuts, lifting his eyes to stare past the warrior. 'Such matters are irrelevant.'

A familiar sound tears through the silence – of snapping, rustling, creaking wood. You turn slowly, a cold dread prickling your skin.

'No, it can't be!' gasps the witch. 'It still lives ...'

Indeed, the vines and branches are weaving themselves back together again, knitting the gaping wounds in the monster's body. With a deep, rumbling roar, the forest guardian levers itself back to its feet, towering above you in all its menacing glory.

'Your weapons cannot defeat Orgorath,' hisses Cernos. 'You either free me – or die.'

Will you:	
Free Cernos from his bindings?	475
Ignore Cernos' request?	406

332

A grimy-looking band of ruffians are huddled in a corner, tucking into plates of meat and gravy. Their leader, a grey-clothed woman in her forties, sits with her boots resting on the table top, supping noisily on a mug of ale. She has a sullen, pale complexion – her narrow face dominated by two bulging eyes and a wide greasy mouth. When one of her companions calls her 'the fish' you can see why it was an apt choice of nickname.

But there is something else, other than the woman's unsavoury appearance, that has drawn your attention – a spectacular black coat hangs from the back of her chair, its length fashioned from hundreds of scales, sparkling and flashing in the lantern light. Basilisk scales. You have only seen one such coat before and that was the one you gave to Joseph.

'What yer glowering at?' scowls 'the fish', thumping her mug down hard on the table. Her companions jump to attention, some with food still hanging from their mouths. As one, they reach quickly for their weapons, their mean-spirited eyes watching you intently.

Will you:

Ask the woman how she got the coat?	295
Apologise and leave?	16

333

Benin stumbles back, pressing a hand to his blood-soaked robes. 'I yield, enough!' Bright light flashes from his fingertips, knitting together his many wounds. The effort leaves him pained and exhausted.

'It . . . it is yours. Now take it,' he gasps.

You turn to the manticore, wondering if this strange creature will honour its deal.

'Come closer then,' it growls, offering out a paw. 'Take your blood and leave.'

You remove Anna's vial from around your neck and walk over to the beast. Warily, you meet its stare, expecting an attack – but the manticore merely watches you with a cold detachment, as if what is transpiring is of no consequence. Taking its paw, you prick the skin and catch a droplet of the beast's blood in the vial.

When you turn back, you see that Benin has already departed. There is a part of you that feels guilt for having deprived him of the cure he so desperately needed, but in the end you were left with no choice – Anna had saved your life, and she was counting on you.

With your mission now complete, you leave Crow Rock and return to Carvel. It is midday when you finally reach Anna's apothecary. You fear that it may already be too late to save the Wiccan thief. Turn to 329.

334

'Shonac was the first,' explains Scar-face proudly. 'A skin, like you. He was a Lamuri prince. Exiled from his kin. A brave warrior. One day he lassoed the last of the great tigers, Quan Mait. He beat it with his club until Mait shared its secrets. Then Shonac kill tiger to take its pelt – make Shonac as strong as the mighty Quan Mait.'

'So, Shonac was the first of your people,' you nod. 'If he was a warrior, then wouldn't he have chosen to fight the hunters – make them pay for what they are doing?'

Scar-face wrinkles his nose. 'Shonac taught us to choose our battles. We show claws to save our pack. Not lose it.'

Will you:

Ask about the name, Shara Khana?	358
Leave for the marsh?	722

335

You are pushed to the edge of exhaustion, your own cries of pain mingling with those of the zombies. For each adversary you beat back with your weapons and magic, there is another to take its place. At last your legs buckle beneath you, your weapons falling from numb hands, while all around you the zombies continue to close in, promising you a slow and painful death.

All of a sudden, the nearest zombie blows apart in a shower of body parts. You hear a cry and the sound of ringing steel. Something flies past your head – it might have been an arm. A zombie staggers and then falls on top of you, expelling black gunge from its mouth. The blade of a dagger protrudes from the back of its head.

With revulsion, you push the body away, to find Eldias standing over you. He sheathes his swords and then doffs his hat to you. 'Welcome to the party, my friend.'

Taking his hand, you stumble back to your feet, aware that you are now standing at the centre of a vast circle of zombie corpses. Eldias has saved your life. Still shaking from your ordeal, you retrieve your weapons from the rotted remains. Turn to **284**.

336

As the ogre topples to the ground you leap over the body, weapons cutting through the gang of goblins that have rushed in to attack. Despite your exhaustion you are able to fend off their knives and spears, forcing them to lose ground.

Then you hear a booming war cry from behind you, followed by the crunch of booted feet. The captain is now charging up the slope, his axe held high above his head. The rest of the party are close behind. A bowstring twangs and the goblin in front of you flies back, an arrow shaft in its chest.

There is a fleeting moment where the remaining goblins are frozen in situ, undecided whether to run or defend their position – then the captain and his men crash into them, hacking with weapons and blasting with magic.

The battle is over in seconds.

'Damn greenheads,' scowls Surl, kicking the nearest corpse. 'Got blood on me best breeches.'

Vas gives him a shove. 'They smell better than you, Surl.'

He feigns a hurt expression, then starts sniffing at his clothes with a worried frown.

'Nice work,' grins the captain, slapping you on the back. 'Okay, let's see what we got here.'

You search the bodies and find 10 gold crowns. You may also choose up to two of the following items:

Goblin bones	Flint knife	Tarsus boots
(backpack)	(left hand: dagger)	(feet)
These might prove valuable to the right person	+1 speed Ability: gouge	+1 brawn +1 magic Ability: surefooted

When you have made your decision, turn to **345**.

337

'Don't speak of it,' snarls the white tigris, his mean scowl chastising you. 'The marsh is cursed. Land of ghosts and bad spirits.'

Grey-hair shakes his head. 'Sheva, it is the only way. Skins will not follow us across the marsh. They speak of the grey and know her power.'

'The grey?' you ask, glancing sideways at Scar-face.

The younger tigris shifts uneasily. 'A Lamuri witch. She can stalk you both in flesh and in dreams. The marsh is her hunting ground and no one passes.'

'Beyond the marsh is the stone claws,' continues Grey-hair. 'What the skins call the cloud mountains. We cross stone claws and we find escape – from the hunters.'

The white tigris glares back at the leader defiantly. 'A coward's choice. But not ours. Shara Sheva are fighters. We do not run from skins!'

Will you:

Ask about the 'skins'?	555
Agree to help the Khana flee?	452
Agree to help the Sheva fight?	704

338

You awake to find yourself staring at a stone wall. A cold wind is gusting through a narrow window, sending light flickering across the grey slabs. With a groan, you roll onto your back, aware that something is constricting your chest. Looking down, you see bandages wrapped tight around your ribs. From beneath the dressing you can feel a hot, smarting pain.

Your attention shifts to your surroundings – and for a second your breath catches in your throat, convinced that you have been brought back to Durnhollow. The room is small – little more than a cramped cell – and austerely furnished, with only the straw pallet bed and a dripping candle for company. An arched wooden door stands half-open, beyond which you can hear the resonant echo of voices, chanting in unison. You try and rise but a sudden flash of pain drives you back against the bed. Then dark dreams take you once again, filled with black thorns and cackling demons.

When you next awake, you find yourself propped up by a pillow. Someone is leaning over you, tipping a clay cup to your lips. The mixture tastes sweet, like honey, as you gulp it down.

'Good, I see your strength returns.'

It is Ventus, the monk you met on the road. He is dressed in his familiar brown robes, padded with bands of leather. As he takes the cup away, you catch the sparkling white inscriptions etched into the back of his hands.

'Where am I?' you croak, wincing as you try and rise.

Ventus bows his head, his fingers making the sign of the cross in the air. 'The Monastery of the Risen Light. You are safe here.'

Memories suddenly come flooding back – the fight on the moors, the Wiccan woman with feathers in her hair. You glance down at your bandages, remembering the blast of magic from her wand. 'What happened to the Wiccans?' you ask, rubbing your aching side.

Ventus offers you a thin smile. 'Fireworks, of all things. A stray blast hit the wagon and one of the crates blew sky high. Must have been given to us by mistake – something meant for the Carvel celebrations. It was enough of a distraction to get you and,' he pauses for a moment, pressing his lips together, 'our charge to safety. Come,' Ventus offers out a hand, to help you stand. 'If you feel up to it, the dean would like to meet with you.' Turn to 260.

339

The robbers clearly have no combat experience, their ragged clothing and crude weapons suggesting that this was not their first choice of career. However, whether it is plain greed or hunger that drives them, the men manage to press their attack with a frenzied recklessness. You try your best to fend off all three of them, but you are already exhausted from your trek through the marshlands. One of the robbers manages to get in a lucky blow, striking you across the forehead with his club. There is little strength behind it, but it is enough to send you stumbling forwards onto your knees. Another blow lands across your shoulders, driving you into the mud.

'This ain't no Wiccan,' says one of the robbers. 'I thoughts it was one of them wild men.'

'I don't care,' growls another. 'Get their purse ... come on.'

You struggle to rise, desperate to defend yourself, but then something hard slams into your head, hammering you back into the mud – and into darkness. Turn to 360.

340

There are further bangs from the hallway. You hear splintering wood and the snarling cries of the undead. Grimly, you realise that the only way out of this room is through the small lattice window.

'Did you have a plan to escape?' you ask, moving quickly to the door and peering through the crack. You see clawed hands trying to tear their way through the front door.

When you look back, you see Eldias watching you with an intent expression. 'I need your help,' he says. 'The reverend of the village, Septimus Palatine, is one of the undead. But a very powerful one. The villagers turned on him when the first of their number fell to the poison. They were angry that the One God was not curing them of the strange curse – they blamed the reverend. I suppose it was no surprise he'd lock himself in that church.'

'But that's on top of the hill,' you gasp. 'We'll never reach it!'

There is the sound of snapping wood followed by a loud bang. You turn to see zombies spilling into the hall, clawing and grappling at each other to get through the doorway. Their waxy, yellow skin is slick with rainwater.

Eldias grabs the overturned chair and hurries to the door. Kicking it closed, he pushes the chair underneath the handle. Then he turns to you, his eerie pale eyes inches from your own. 'The reverend fell to the curse – but his magic has made him strong, different to the others. He is no mindless zombie. He is a powerful lich and he must be defeated.'

You shake your head frantically, as the door buckles and shakes. On the other side, you can hear the howling, shrieking mob. 'We'll never make it!'

Eldias grabs your shoulders, holding you tight. 'Listen to me! I think Rorus Satch, the herbalist, was close to discovering a cure for vampirism. I need that cure! But the reverend has all his books, all his learning. He is using them to grow more powerful. I must get to the church, but I can't do it alone.'

'But how will we defeat the undead?' you ask desperately.

Eldias opens out his coat, revealing an array of weapons and other strange items tucked into the lining. 'The witchfinder's motto,' he grins. 'Always be prepared! Come, take what you need, I cannot use these – they are as dangerous to me as they are to the zombies.'

If you wish, you may help yourself to two of the following items:

Sanctified ashes (2 uses)	**Holy water (2 uses)**	**Angelica wreath**
(backpack)	(backpack)	(backpack)
Scatter these to protect you from harm Ability: ashes	Use instead of rolling for a damage score to inflict 2 damage dice to an undead opponent ignoring *armour*	A woven ring of white flowered herbs Ability: holy protector

When you have made your decision, turn to **138**.

341

'Demons, always the demons.' The scholar looks at you suspiciously. 'Did Andos put you up to this? That boy's always pestering me for fanciful stories. Not good for young heads.' He gives a wistful sigh. 'I might devote a paragraph or two to it in my book. You'll just have to wait until then.'

He drums his fingers on the desk, humming to himself.

'A sneak peek?' you venture, hopefully.

The man gives a theatrical-sounding sigh. 'Okay, if you absolutely insist. I suppose one mustn't deny a thirst for knowledge, eh? Let's have a think … when it comes to demons, there is one name that keeps cropping up. Barahar. He was the last of his kind – a race of demons that once dwelled in the underworld.'

'An archdemon?' you suggest, remembering back to your conversation with Virgil.

'Yes, an archdemon – and he sounds quite the character,' the scholar chirps, as if discussing nothing more serious than the weather. 'Caused a bit of trouble in his day, laying waste to towns, villages, even whole cities. The Lamuri legends talk of a sword – Ragnarok. Anyone killed by that blade was bound to serve its master, even in death. As you can imagine, Barahar was good at the killing part; had a veritable army at his disposal.'

'Ragnarok?' You look away, suddenly struggling for air in the stuffy room. You can picture the sword from your vision at Durnhollow – the black rune blade, wielded by a demon. 'How was he defeated?' you ask hoarsely.

'The dwarves, apparently. They destroyed his sword and with it his power. A happy ending by all accounts – so, worry not – I don't think it'll be demons you'll be crossing paths with in the jungle.'

Turn to 386 to ask the scholar another question or turn to 548 if you wish to leave and continue your journey.

342

You find yourself in a long stone hall, its columned length awash with flickering candlelight. Several sections of the ceiling have collapsed inwards, allowing tangled curtains of liana to break through into the smoky interior.

The man scampers over the jumbled rock, towards a small scattering of belongings arranged within a circle of runes. It is an odd collection – a pile of skulls, some fruit partially wrapped in palm leaves, an assortment of clay pots and leather gourds, and a row of wooden staffs similar to the one he is holding.

'Be at home,' grins the man, gesturing to a moss-covered stone. 'You coming here was no simple chance. I waited for this long time.' He places his staff with the others, then proceeds to pick another from the line up. You notice various symbols have been carved into the wood.

'What were those undead?' you ask, eyeing the protective runes painted onto the stone. 'There were hundreds of them.'

'Dead Lamuri. My ancestors, bless their spirits.' He pats the carved wood against the palm of his hand. 'They don't mind being boomed I think – not themselves no more. Dead inside and out. Magic of this place keeps them here.'

You settle onto the stone seat, taking a moment to study your rescuer. The man is tall and lean, his scrawny body toned to rods of hard muscle. The smooth brown skin and sparkling eyes make him appear youthful, and yet his banded braids are peppered with grey and white. Of his clothing, there is not much to speak of – just a simple loin cloth and a necklace of charms.

'I sense you have questions,' he says, crouching down on the balls of his feet. 'You ask Boom Mamba and he answer. Then we go boom some more. We finish spirit walk – then I go home to elders. Boom Mamba hero – and I help you too.'

Will you:

Ask how he got his name?	204
Ask what he means by a 'spirit walk'?	462
Ask how he can help?	257

343

You remove Anna's vial from around your neck and offer it to the priest. 'Take it,' you insist. 'I cannot judge whose life is more worthy to save. But I trust that you speak the truth – and I will not come to blows over this.'

Benin is struck speechless.

'Hurry or I might change my mind,' you grin, shaking the vial.

The priest swiftly steps forward and takes the vessel from you, before turning to the manticore.

'Come closer, then,' it growls, stretching out one of its enormous paws. 'Take your blood and be gone.'

Benin stoops down and picks up one of the jagged bones from the ground. Then, taking the beast's paw in his hand, he pricks the skin with the tip of the bone. Black blood blossoms from the tiny wound, which the priest carefully collects in the glass vial.

With the deed finally done, Benin joins you in the tunnel.

'Thank you, my friend,' he smiles, placing a hand on your shoulder. 'The bishop will reward you, I promise. Now, come – we must make haste.'

Together, you leave Crow Rock and return to Carvel. (Record the word *hallowed* on your hero sheet, then turn to 359.)

344

'Ma height I owe to me father, but these lovelies . . .' He gnashes his teeth, the metal sparking as they grate together, 'I owe to a Skardland runt who 'ad me well and good in the pit. Knocked me out with a club the size of me head.'

'You were a gladiator?' you ask in awe.

The half-giant jerks a finger over his shoulder, to a magnificent broadsword hanging on the bar wall. Its blade is tempered black steel, inlaid with gold runes. 'I done the whole circuit and won the capital games. Got that off of the king 'imself.' He sniffs dismissively. 'Not much of a man if yer asking me.'

'And you gave it all up for . . .' You stammer over your words, worried you may cause offence.

The half-giant flashes a metal grin. 'I get yer. This ain't much, I know, but I do it for the missus. The ol' ball and chain.' He glances over his shoulder towards the kitchen, where you can hear a woman squawking orders over the rattle of pots and hissing steam. 'She's a good 'un – stands taller than anyone in my eyes.'

As you gaze at his sparkling teeth, you are reminded of the gold-toothed witchfinder who visited you in your cell at Durnhollow. Virgil Elland.

'Have you seen anyone else in these parts, with . . .' You nod towards his gleaming dentures.

'Wife said we 'ad one of them witchfinders in tuther day,' he replies, folding his arms. 'Was looking for someone but never gave much of a description. Think he was after one of them escaped loons from that dungeon up north.' His eyes suddenly narrow, suspiciously. 'Why yer ask?'

You quickly offer a non-committal shrug. 'Ah, old friend of mine – it's nothing.'

The half-giant nods slowly, not looking entirely convinced. 'Good. I don't want any trouble on ma doorstep, yer understand?'

To ask the barman about local rumours turn to 202, to explore the rest of the tap room turn to 172, or to leave turn to 199.

345

It appears that the goblins and the ogre had holed themselves up in a small defensible area. Opposite the slope, the entire wall has collapsed inwards, leaving behind an impenetrable mass of jagged rock. Apart from some cooking pots and a few gnawed bones, there is little else in the cave.

'Wait, I got something!' Surl is kneeling beside a wooden crate – or what is left of one. The lid has been smashed open, revealing a number of metal discs inside.

'Borehole charges,' grins Surl, lifting one up.

You notice the others backing away. The captain gives a snort. 'Put that down, Surl, or you'll blow the top off this mountain, and take us with it!'

'What are they?' you ask, watching as Surl lays it carefully onto the ground.

'Explosives,' grins Vas. 'Only the army have them. And maybe smugglers who got lucky.'

'Yeah, but how'd they end up here?' asks Surl, turning a broken piece of the crate over in his hands. 'You think the gobboes used them to cause that cave-in?'

'I don't think so, I know so,' growls the captain, starting back towards the slope. 'Come on. This is a dead-end – and you're giving me heart burn with all your rattling.' He spits a stream of tobacco juice at the wall. 'This place stinks.'

If you wish, you may help yourself to one of the charges:

Borehole charge
(backpack)
The writing on the side states:
'Handle with care!'

You follow the captain through the narrow tunnel and back to the junction. Ahead, lies the entranceway to the next cavern. Turn to 229.

346

Amongst the piles of wind-scoured rock, you find a silver casket containing 50 gold crowns and one of the following items:

Lost scriptures	Wind baton	Twister
(left hand: spell book)	(main hand: wand)	(cloak)
+1 speed +2 magic	+1 speed +2 magic	+1 speed +1 magic
Ability: Cistene's chattels set	Ability: windblast	Ability: confound
(requirement: acolyte)		

When you have updated your hero sheet, turn to 239.

347

You step into the room. A quick scan reveals a lantern resting on a table top, surrounded by books and piles of crumpled papers. Against the far wall, a writing desk has been overturned and a chair lies on its side.

Then you feel the cold kiss of a flint-lock pistol against your cheek. Someone is standing right beside you, just out of your eye-line. You can smell sweat and leather, and the faint hint of wood smoke.

Instinctively, you slam your elbow into their side, falling forwards as a bullet hums overhead, hitting a mirror in the far wall and sending fragments of glass showering in all directions. The room fills with the smell of brimstone and sulphur. You spin around, taking a kick in the chest. Still unable to focus on your attacker, you roll over – dragging yourself under the table as another bullet slams into the ground, creating a charred crater in the wood.

'Damn it . . .' hisses a voice.

You slide out from underneath the table, springing onto your feet and falling into a battle stance. At last, you are able to look upon your attacker. It is a man, dressed in an open black coat. The hilts of various swords and daggers are visible from his waist band. A battered capotain rests on his head, the brim shadowing his eyes. He is muttering to himself as he struggles to wrestle another pistol from a holster inside his coat. Catching your eye, he stops, his pale mouth twitching into a half-smile.

'I used to be faster than this,' he says hoarsely. 'You're no zombie.'

'So I'm lucky on both counts.' Your weapons remained raised. There is something familiar to you about this man.

'And you make enough noise to wake the dead.' He cocks his head in the direction of the front door – where the zombies are still banging to get in. You catch a glimmer of sharp canines, protruding from the man's gums. His skin is pallid, his hollow cheeks giving him a similar appearance to the undead outside.

'And what about you?' you ask warily.

'Well, a couple of gunshots has probably done it now . . .'

'I meant, are you . . . like those things out there?'

The man gives a sigh, then removes his hat, doffing it to you in greeting. His eyes are like pale discs, full moons shining in an equally white face. He grins, revealing his sharp canines once again.

'Eldias Falks . . .' you gasp, recognising the witchfinder who handed you over to the inquisition. The witchfinder who accused you of murder.

The man staggers over to the table, resting his palms on the surface to recover his breath. His movements appear sluggish and pained. 'I see my reputation proceeds me.' He meets your gaze with a half-cocked smile. 'But as you can see, perhaps I'm something of a disappointment; a shadow of what I once was.'

'You're a vampire.' You take a step back, glass crunching underfoot.

Eldias glares at you with his pale, unnatural eyes. 'A hazard of my profession, I'm afraid.' He licks his lips, his gaze falling to your arm. You look down to see a small shard of glass protruding from your skin. Blood has started to seep out of the wound.

Will you:

Reveal how you know him?	317
Ask about the zombies in the village?	94
Ask how he became a vampire?	76
Ask why he is in Blight Haven?	180

348

A preliminary search offers up little of interest. As you are about to turn away, you suddenly catch something sparkling at the corner of your eye. Dropping down onto all fours, you see a collection of gemstones scattered in the narrow space beneath a fallen slab of stone. You slide onto your stomach and attempt to push your shoulder into the gap, reaching out with your fingers to grab the stones. But, after much groaning and cursing, they remain tantalisingly out of reach.

The only way to get to the gems is to remove the stone slab. You can either push it away using *brawn* or blast it to pieces using your *magic*. Take a challenge test:

	Brawn/Magic
A rock and a hard place	12

If you are successful, turn to 112. If you fail, turn to 153.

349

Three glass pots catch your attention, filled with different fabric dyes. A label has been glued to the side of each one, written in a child's hand. If you wish, you may choose one of the dyes and use it on a *head*, *chest*, *cloak*, *feet* or *gloves* item that you are wearing:

Mighty monster metal	Putrid pixie puke	Slimy stringy snot
(special: dye)	(special: dye)	(special: dye)
Add 1 *armour* to an item you are wearing	Add 1 *magic* to an item you are wearing	Add 1 *brawn* to an item you are wearing

You may now examine the cloth scraps on the table (turn to 51) or leave the room via the half-open door (turn to 391).

350

Amongst the putrid mould and clumps of animal hair, you spy a number of interesting items. Some appear to be from previous adventurers, whilst others look worryingly part of the strange spirit that once inhabited this festering place. As well as a pouch containing 20 gold crowns, you also find one of the following rewards:

Braids of the outcast	Weirdstone	Silver bullet
(head)	(ring)	(necklace)
+1 speed +1 magic	+1 magic	+1 magic
Ability: fearless	Ability: focus	Ability: quicksilver

When you have made your decision, you return to the courtyard. Turn to 510.

351

Using the *Handy Herbalist's Spotter's Guide* you are able to recognise some of the rarer herbs and plants that might help you in making a cure. You pick these and stuff them into your backpack. Record the word *gatherer* on your hero sheet. You may now investigate the wishing well (turn to 13) or search the reverend's home (turn to 210).

352

Warily, you step between the guards, who both shoot you a mean glare from beneath their leather helms. You offer a thin smile by way of greeting, trying not to choke on the odour of ale and sweat emanating from their dirt-stained armour.

'Behave yerself or yer'll see the point of ma blade,' mutters one, his scowl revealing black-stained teeth.

'A point well made.' You smile thinly, glancing down at the man's rusty sword.

Ignoring his bemused frown, you push on the door and enter the shop. Inside, you find a dark, dingy room, devoid of furnishings save for a row of hunting trophies along one wall and a bear-skin rug spread across the slatted floor. Behind a counter, a grizzled man slouches in a high-backed chair, idly picking at his teeth with a dagger. His matted black hair and tangled beard give him a wild appearance, perfectly in keeping with his choice of decor.

Will you:	
Ask to see the man's wares?	235
Admire the hunting trophies?	12
Leave the shop?	199

353

'Impressive, very impressive,' grins the demon, who has watched the entire fight with a bemused indifference. 'But futile all the same.'

Ventus stalks towards the dais, his fists still bunched into balls of crackling light. 'Explain yourself, demon spawn. Why are you a prisoner here?'

The creature twists to face him, wings flaring out from its spiked shoulders. 'My crimes are endless. As is your ignorance. Clearly you know nothing of whom you address.'

Bea is crouched by Benin's side, tears tracking down her dusty cheeks. 'You are a monster!' she screams in anger. 'Do not trade words with it, Vent! Do not listen to it!'

Ventus continues to study the creature. 'You are a demon prince.'

'I am Cernos,' nods the demon. 'I have been a prisoner here for thousands of your mortal years. I have served my time and now I desire freedom.' Its crimson eyes flick to you, its horned brow creasing together. 'Grant it or you will die here.'

Ventus snorts, raising his fists. 'I don't see how you can stop us, demon.' His gaze moves to the runed manacles that bind the creature's wrists and ankles.

'Oh, it won't be me, brother of the light.' The demon lifts its eyes to stare past you. A familiar sound reaches your ears – of snapping, cracking wood. You turn slowly, a cold dread prickling your skin.

'No! It can't be!' Bea cries in desperation. 'That's impossible!'

The vines and branches are weaving themselves back together again, knitting the gaping wounds in the giant's body. With a deep, rumbling roar, the beast levers itself back onto its feet, towering above you in all its menacing glory.

'Your weapons cannot defeat Orgorath,' hisses Cernos. 'You either free me – or die.'

Will you:

Free Cernos from his bindings?	453
Ignore Cernos' request?	468

354

With the stone guardians defeated, you advance on the black temple. It is an imposing structure of spine-like towers, arched windows and high columns. The mist has receded, but in its place is a presence – thick and palpable. It pushes against you like an invisible hand, forcing you to grit to your teeth as you struggle onwards, your will matched against that of some unseen foe.

Murlic is the first to stumble, falling to his knees. 'I can't …' he mutters weakly.

You notice Conall staggering as if blind, his fists batting away at some invisible foe. Damaris has also stalled, gripping her staff with white-knuckled hands. You go to her aid but she puts out a hand to stop you. 'No … continue … if you can …' she gasps, struggling to draw breath.

Alone, you clamber up the stairs of the temple, crawling the rest of the way to finally reach its dark, imposing doorway. Turn to 419.

355

Across the other side of the cave is a deep fissure, cutting through the rock. As you approach, you see that it is edged with a thick black soot. You wonder if the goblins had created this, using the explosives. Perhaps they had intended to dig deeper into the mountain, looking for treasures. Instead they released a plague of bugs.

Ducking your head, you pass through the fissure into another vast cavern. The walls and floor are slick with a gooey slime. At the far side, glittering in the green glow from the rock crystals, is a gigantic ant. Unlike the others, this one is female. Black scales cover her segmented body, rising along her spine to form a black crown on her head.

'The queen . . .' you gasp.

From the back of the creature's black carapace a silken tube spits out a steady stream of eggs, which gather in an ever-increasing pile against the cave wall.

Hundreds of eggs.

You realise that this must be the source of the bug threat. However, as you gaze upon the queen's thick armour and monstrous, blade-like arms, you wonder if you have the power to defeat such a foe. Turn to 307.

356

'An interesting offer,' replies Sir Bastian, nodding with approval. 'If you are willing to agree to my terms then you have yourself a deal.'

'Terms?' you ask in disbelief, trying to ignore the sniggers coming from the farrier.

'Well, there's my repair costs,' sniffs the knight. 'For my armour. Not to mention feed for Wilma here. Oh, and I want first choice of any treasures that come our way. A fair deal, don't you think?'

You find yourself struggling for words, mouth agape.

'Indeed, I see the honour renders you speechless! To share in my adventures – to have the bards sing of Sir Bastian and his faithful squire. Forty gold crowns up front.' He extends his hand, beaming a broad smile. 'For a legend such as myself, it's an outright steal!'

'Yer can say that again,' smirks the farrier, tapping home another nail. He looks up from his work, frowning when he sees that you are actually contemplating the offer. 'Blimey, there's one born every minute,' he sighs, shaking his head.

If you wish to hire Sir Bastian then the knight will provide you with the following for 40 gold crowns:

- **For glory:** Sir Bastian will help you fight a legendary monster. If you are defeated then Sir Bastian will flee the combat and you will have to hire him again if you wish to receive further aid.

- **Man-at-arms:** Sir Bastian adds 2 to your damage score for the duration of the combat.
- **Wilma's wallop:** The knight's warhorse has a powerful kick. For each ⚅ you roll for your attack speed, Wilma hits an opponent with her hooves, doing 3 damage, ignoring *armour*.
- **A just reward:** If you defeat the legendary monster, Sir Bastian gets first choice of the treasures. When you are offered a choice of rewards, roll 1 die. ⚀ or ⚁ the knight takes the first item, ⚂ or ⚃ the second item and ⚄ or ⚅ the third item. You must then choose from the remaining two items.

Remember that Sir Bastian will only stay with you for *one* encounter. If you wish to use his services again you must hire him for 40 gold crowns. When you have made your decision, turn to 199 to explore more of Raven's Rest, or return to the quest map to continue your journey.

357

Damaris points to a black smudge on the horizon. You squint, trying to make out what it is. At first you assume it is some dark lake or patch of rocky scree, but then you see the golden sunlight catching on hundreds of sharp, barbed edges.

'The forest of thorns,' you gasp.

Damaris nods. 'There is something at its centre. Something ancient and powerful. I sense it is of the old magic – of the old times. And I believe that it could help us win this war.'

You glance at the witch, frowning. 'A weapon?'

Damaris shakes her head quickly. 'No, it is living, that much I can sense.'

'Then why not just . . . go there and find it?'

Damaris snorts. 'The forest is impenetrable. No blade or magic can fell those cursed trees.' She turns and raises her hand. There is a dull grating sound as a secret panel in the wall slides open, revealing a set of worn stairs. 'Come, follow me.' Turn to 497.

358

'We all Shara Khana,' states Scar-face, patting his chest then pointing to the rest of the pack in turn. 'Not have names like skins. We all pack. All Shara Khana. That is our name.'

You look back towards the rock shelf, where more members of the pack are appearing from the forest. It is a paltry gathering – only a dozen tigris, eight males and four females. The only child that you can see is the one you helped to save, still clutched protectively in their mother's arms. 'Is this all that is left of your pack?' you ask, bewildered.

Scar-face fixes you with his round, yellow eyes. 'Hunters take the rest. That is why we leave. To save Shara Khana. I believe that is what Shonac would do.'

Will you:

Ask about Shonac, the great spirit?	334
Leave for the marsh?	722

359

You are perched on the edge of a stone bench, glaring at the angelic statue opposite. The winged figure is beaming down at you with a radiant smile, arms open wide in welcome invitation. It doesn't really seem to belong in the cold, featureless corridor of the church.

It has now been several hours since you arrived back with Benin. The priest immediately retired to his chambers with a medic and another priest to prepare the antidote. Since then, you have heard no word regarding the cure or the bishop's condition.

Tired and frustrated, you finally get to your feet – preparing to leave. It is then that the double doors at the end of the passageway fly open and an inquisitor appears, striding purposefully towards you. He is dressed in thick plates of white and gold armour, a glimmering sword scabbarded at his side.

Panic rises in your stomach, your hands dropping to your own weapons. Your first instinct is to run – after all, it was the inquisitors who imprisoned you in their dungeon at Durnhollow, seeking to find answers to your strange prophetic powers. But you hold your ground, trying to relax your tensed muscles; trying not to look like a guilty escapee.

As the inquisitor nears, his sullen face creases into a broad smile. 'Come, the bishop will see you now.'

Breathing a sigh of relief, you follow the inquisitor back down the hall. The doorway leads through to a set of stairs that wind up to a short landing. There you are taken through another set of doors into a plush chamber, dominated by a four-poster bed. Propped up amidst a sea of pillows and blankets is a thin elderly man with wispy white hair. A tray with soup, bread and fruit rests on a table next to him.

As you enter, he claps his hands.

'Ah, praise be to the One God, here is our brave hunter – the kind soul who aided my dear Benin.'

'I am pleased to see you are well,' you smile, halting at the end of the bed. You bow your head in reverence, not entirely sure what the correct formality is for such meetings.

The bishop gestures to the far wall, where a stone altar is set beneath an arched window. A cloth has been laid across its surface and a priest is now carefully arranging a number of items on top of it.

'We have some small treasures from our vault that I can off—' His voice trails off into a fit of coughing. Another priest is immediately at his side, offering a cup of water.

The inquisitor takes your arm. 'The bishop is still unwell. Come, choose a reward and then we can leave him to his rest.'

You walk over to the altar and examine the three items. You may now choose one of the following:

Prayer beads	**Ivory spire**	**Cardinal's cappa**
(necklace)	(main hand: wand)	(cloak)
Ability: heal	+1 magic	+1 brawn +1 armour
	Ability: focus	

Once you have made your decision, the inquisitor escorts you to the main entrance of the church, where Benin is waiting for you. Turn to 69.

360

You awake with a thumping headache, your clothes soaked with rainwater and mud. Painfully, you try and sit up, every muscle of your body protesting. It takes several minutes for you to remember what happened, how you came to be here ... Then realisation dawns.

Quickly, you scramble to your feet. Your backpack has been emptied out onto the track, its contents lying scattered in various pools of mud. Fearful of what the robbers might have taken, you frantically take stock of your supplies and equipment.

To your annoyance, the robbers have made off with half your gold, one item of equipment and one backpack item. (You must remove these from your hero sheet.) Wincing with pain, you stuff your remaining gear back into your pack and hoist it onto your shoulders. Things could have gone worse, you reflect grimly. Perhaps the robbers had a conscience after all.

'Crazy land, crazy people,' you mutter, rubbing the bump on the back of your head.

Across the track, the wooden signpost points away into the thickening gloom: *'Raven's Rest – 1 mile'*. Hoping it will bring you better fortune, you set off in the direction of the settlement. Turn to 199.

361

You set out your plants and herbs on the table top. A few of the bottles already contain a milky-looking solution, labelled 'elixir base'. To make the cure, you will need to decide which ingredients you will use and in what order they will be added to one of the bottles.

Will you:	
Add lemongrass?	171
Add meadowsweet?	321
Add white willow?	247
Add sagewort?	192

362

The words on the parchment spell out the same phrase again and again: *paper, scissors, stone. paper, scissors, stone* ... As you stare at the dark lettering it starts to move, swirling into hypnotic spirals. You try and tear your eyes away, but you are mesmerised by the whirling currents, which drag you closer and closer to the parchment ...

Then, all of a sudden, the ink coalesces into a black fist which slams into you, throwing you backwards. You find yourself tumbling through the room, upsetting a shelf and sending books and paper showering across the floor. From the splintered remains of the table, a dark shape is starting to form, like threads of shadow being spun and woven together.

There is a sickening squelch. You feel something cold and wet running past your hand. Glancing down, you are horrified to see that the ink from the scattered pages is now running across the floor, moving in snakelike patterns towards the dark monster.

'I live!' thunders a voice, rattling the remaining shelves and sending more books toppling onto the floor. You watch with growing dread as rivers of ink spill out of their bindings, joining those that are already flowing into the monster, allowing it to grow bigger by each passing second.

You realise you must defeat this demon as quickly as possible, before it becomes an unstoppable giant! It is time to fight:

	Speed	*Brawn*	*Armour*	*Health*
Inkheart	5	4	3	35

Special abilities

- Back to black: Inkheart is growing all the time as the demon absorbs more ink into its body. At the end of each combat round, Inkheart raises its *brawn* by 1, up to a maximum of 8.
- Body of ink: Inkheart is immune to *bleed, thorns* and *thorn cage*.

If you manage to defeat this black-hearted villain, turn to 303.

363

You hurry after the goblin, the others following closely at your heels. By the time you emerge from the tight cleft into a larger cavern, your ears are ringing with the strange, hooting calls. They are now coming from the top of a steep slope, where you can discern shapes moving behind a row of boulders and rocks. At the foot of the slope, the ground is littered with piles of rotting corpses. From the spindly legs and shell-like carapaces, you guess they were once ant-men.

'Argh!'

You hear a cry behind you. Turning, you see that the captain's armour has got caught in the narrowing of the passageway. He is struggling to free himself, face reddening with the effort. Behind him, Surl is pushing and shoving in an effort to break him loose.

You spin back to face the slope. Something big is moving at the summit, grunting as it shifts its heavy weight against one of the boulders. You hear the scraping of stone, then suddenly – with a bellowing cry – the creature sends one of the boulders bouncing down the slope. The rock moves fast, barely giving you time to dodge aside, as it crashes into the cave below.

Already the creature has moved on to another boulder, preparing to send it tumbling down towards you. The goblins at the top of the slope are cheering and hooting, believing that you are done for. However, you have other ideas.

Weapons at the ready, you charge up the slope. The creature is an ogre, its thickly-muscled body covered in war paint. Before you are even halfway up, the ogre has pushed the next boulder in your direction. You roll aside, just in time – quickly scrambling to your feet to take on this deadly adversary:

	Speed	*Brawn*	*Armour*	*Health*
Konga	–	–	2	30

Special abilities

- Thick skinned: Konga is immune to *bleed*.

This encounter is played differently to a normal combat. To be able to strike the ogre you must first dodge three boulders to get to the top of the slope. To do this, roll two dice and add your *speed* score to the total. If the result is 7 or more, then you have dodged one of the boulders flung in your direction. Roll again to see if you dodge the second boulder and then the third boulder. If you do, you have reached the top and may roll for damage against Konga as if you had won a combat round.

If the result is 6 or less, then you have been hit by a boulder and must take 4 damage, ignoring your *armour*. You are also knocked back to the bottom of the slope and must dodge three boulders to get to the top again.

Once you have rolled for damage against Konga, the ogre's swinging fists send you back to the bottom of the slope. You must dodge another three boulders to before you can roll for another damage score.

If you manage to defeat Konga, turn to 336.

364

The half-giant plants his massive hands on top of the counter, his steely eyes glinting from beneath his protruding brow. 'So, what'll it be?' he grunts, cracking his neck muscles. 'Ma patience ain't as big as ma good looks now.' His subsequent smile presents an unsettling array of jagged metal teeth.

Will you:	
Ask about his 'good looks'?	344
Ask about local rumours?	202
Explore the rest of the tap room?	172

365

Quest: The dark interior

(You must have completed the green quest *The Temple of Boom* before you can start this quest.)

You stand at the canyon edge, ready for the next stage of your journey. Previous explorers have named this region the dark interior and now you can see why. From the rocky precipice the land drops away into a thick impenetrable mist, forming a silvery veil stretching from one side of the canyon to the next. Below it, hidden by the fog, there is a steaming jungle – unmapped and dangerous. Many have tried to navigate its tangled darkness, few have lived to tell the tale. Its reputation is not one you wish to test, but crossing the dark interior is the quickest and most direct way of reaching the southern jungle, where you hope to find the Lamuri city and the demon, Cernos.

It takes nearly half a day to navigate the steep canyon wall, using ledges and caves to work your way down through the mist to the jungle floor. As you descend, the air grows thick once again, settling around you like a heavy mantle. With it come the eerie hoots and cries of the wildlife, lying unseen amongst the cobwebbed trees.

You trudge onwards, scratching at the back of your scalp where the demon scales are now prickling along your spine. Your body is changing daily, not only in appearance – but also in other ways. It has been four days since you last ate a proper meal, but you feel no lack of strength or dizziness from fatigue. Your senses have also become heightened – sounds and shapes have taken on a sharper quality. Out here, far away from a society that would brand you a monster, your demon-side is fast becoming a welcome companion.

After several hours of trekking, the forest begins to show its own changes. The first is the smell – the fetid reek of decay – accompanied by the wet squelch of mud underfoot. Then you notice the trees start to thin, their listless sagging bodies covered in thick bands of fungus and mould. To the west the forest continues in this manner, its smell and murky appearance suggesting the start of a stagnant marsh. In the opposite direction the view is more favourable, where the ground rises steeply into a ridge of hills. There, you can just make out the angular silhouettes of ruined buildings jutting out through the curling mist.

Will you:
Head west into the marsh? 523
Head east into the ruins? 459

366

The white tigris is strong but also impatient – eager to show off to the rest of his pack. When he leans away, going for an overhead blow, you are ready to retaliate. As the claws come down you twist around the attack, thrusting an elbow into his side, then launching a follow-up blow to the neck. The tigris staggers back, startled – giving you just enough time to level a weapon at his chest. Sheva glares down angrily, contemplating a counter attack, but the leader of the Khana intervenes.

'You have your answer, Sheva,' he states, with more than a hint of satisfaction. 'Honour your word. You want vengeance – then bright claw was sent for this, with Shonac's blessing.'

Sheva snarls, then looks back at his pack. Their earlier gusto has been replaced by a reluctant admiration. Scar-face offers you a smile.

'So be it,' growls the white tigris, his green eyes burning fiercely. 'But if this a trick, then you will pay with blood … bright claw.' The last words are spat out with scorn.

'Your mind is set then, Sheva,' sighs Grey-hair. 'Shonac be with you.'

The white male grunts, then motions to his pack. Together they take their leave, while the Shara Khana watch their departure with a mix of sadness and relief.

'May your claws be sharp,' says Scar-face, tapping his chest with his paw. 'And your eyes sharper.' You echo his gesture, nodding a farewell to both Scar-face and his leader, before following the Sheva back into the forest. Turn to 527.

367

Panic overwhelms your senses, driving you into a savage frenzy. Desperately, you hack and slash at the clammy wet bodies that surround you until at last, exhausted and dripping with grime, you find yourself standing in a vast circle of undead corpses.

As rain drums against the rotting bodies, you spot a number of valuable-looking items lying amongst the remains. If you wish, you may now take any/all of the following:

Coat of many scales	Ghost cloth	Pot of speed (2 uses)
(backpack)	(cloak)	(backpack)
A dazzling coat made from basilisk scales	+1 armour Ability: charm	Use any time in combat to raise your *speed* by 2 for one combat round

Eldias has defeated the zombies that were attacking him. He sheathes his blades, stumbling back against the stone well to catch his breath. Turn to 284.

368

You cup your hands and take a tentative sip of the waters. Immediately the pain subsides, as a cool and refreshing sensation shimmers through your body. You sense that these waters have powerful healing properties.

Reaching into your pack, you take out your empty water bottle and sink it into the basin of water. You have now gained:

Saint's blessing (1 use)
(backpack)
Use any time in combat
to heal yourself to full *health*

If you are *hexed*, turn to 441. Otherwise, turn to 374.

369

Bill opens a trunk and lifts out a feathered staff, an ivory ring and a tanned leather cloak, faded by the sun. 'Don't let appearances deceive you,' he says, unfurling the plain-looking cloak. 'All these are enchanted – the ring and staff I found in that Lamuri city, Lanko Curzo.' He shudders with the memory. 'I'll never go back there, but if you're planning on making a visit, you might do well to have one of these.'

You may now choose one of the following special rewards:

Medicine staff	Ring of remedies	Hunter's burden
(left hand: staff)	(ring)	(cloak)
+2 speed +3 magic	+2 magic	+1 speed +2 armour
Ability: greater heal	Ability: cauterise	Ability: feint

Bill also hands you a purse, containing 100 gold crowns. After making your exchange, you bid the hunter farewell and leave. You may now explore the rest of the camp (turn to 744) or return to the quest map.

370

With the deadly swarm defeated, you turn your attention to the ant-man on the ledge. Vas is still firing bullets in its direction – one slams into its chest, producing a spray of black blood. The creature gives a shriek, teetering back on its bowed legs. Another bullet slams home, knocking the ant into the wall and forcing it to drop the boulder it was holding … right on its own head. There is a sickening, eye-watering crunch.

Vas spins her pistols, before sliding them back into their holsters. 'I still got it,' she grins. When she turns around, her smile quickly fades. 'Captain!' She hurries over to Surl, who is kneeling by the captain's side. The aged veteran is breathing hard, his teeth clenched against the pain from his wound. 'I can't go on,' he gasps, gripping Surl's arm.

'I ain't leaving you here,' he growls. 'Come on, Vas. Lift!'

Together, they place their hands under his arms and hoist the burly warrior to his feet. The captain looks haggard, sagging in their arms. 'You should leave me,' he rasps.

'It's not fatal,' says Surl, wincing as he looks down at the wound. 'We'll get you out of here.'

As they move away, the captain glances in your direction. 'To stop the flood ... go straight to the source. Find out ... what is causing this ...'

'Hey, enough crazy talk,' snaps Vas. 'We're done here. We're out!'

As they start back across the cave, you find yourself hesitating. Vas looks back, frowning. 'Tell me you aren't gonna play the hero?' She shakes her head. 'Well, you're on your own, fool.'

You wave them away, then turn back to the heaped mound of beetle bodies. The captain is right – there must be something deeper in this cavern network that is producing these strange creatures. Turn to 355.

371

Legendary monster: Kaala

Night-time is never a pleasant experience in the jungle. Even with a makeshift shelter to escape the worst of the rain, there are still the bugs to contend with. Every inch of your body feels like it is under assault – driving you to the edge of insanity with the constant scratching, itching, chewing ...

And so, after a hard day's travel, when the last thing you want to do is to spend another night in this rain-sodden, bug-infested place, a bright welcoming light is hard to ignore. You approach warily, having learnt that most things in the Terral Jungle are designed to lure and then eat you, but when you finally break from the trees, angrily brushing away yet another bug intent on chewing your neck, you see that the glow is coming from a set of crystal pillars, lining the walls of a narrow gully. Passing between them, you are led to the opening of a cave where more crystals grow out of the grey rock, bathing it in the same phosphorescent glow.

Shelter and light. It is almost too good to be true.

The cave turns out to be a tunnel, descending further into the rock.

Following it, you are brought to the banks of an underground pool, its perfectly-still surface mirroring the hundreds of crystals protruding from the ceiling and the cavern walls. Removing your pack, you prepare to strip off and take a dip in the inviting waters – eager to wash away the stink of the jungle.

As you unbutton your shirt, your hands brush against the demon scars, and the scales now growing around them. In the crystal light they appear like gemstones, coating your skin in the same blue glow as the rest of the cave. It is almost mesmerising, as you stroke the hard ridges, wondering how long it will be before your entire body is covered in this strange demonic armour.

A splash from the pool drags you from your reverie. You step closer to its edge, peering out across the sparkling water. Something is moving beneath the surface, its own body glittering like a trail of diamonds. At first, you are not sure if it is a trick of the light; this whole cave seems to have an hypnotic quality to it, the blue crystals bouncing light off hundreds of surfaces. But no, you are sure this is no trick – there is something down there in the pool, winding through its turquoise depths. You blink in an attempt to refocus. When you look again, it is gone.

You rub your eyes, wondering if tiredness is to blame.

Then the waters of the pool explode outward, drenching you from head to foot. You slip on the wet stones, crashing down onto your back as a set of fangs snap closed inches from your face. Shaking with shock, you scramble across the ground, eyes locked on the serpentine head rocking back and forth. The creature is huge – you can dimly see the coils of its enormous body winding in and out of the water, the white scales spotted with glowing sigils of magic.

The serpent gives a rattling hiss, its head continuing to rock from side to side. You find yourself gazing into bright white eyes that seem to grow larger and more intense, capturing the reflection of the blue crystals and dazzling you with their brilliance. It takes a supreme effort to break that entrancing gaze, as you reach for your weapons and prepare to take on:

	Speed	*Brawn*	*Armour*	*Health*
Kaala	10	7	6	100

Special abilities

- Look into my eyes: Make note of each time your hero rolls a ⚀ in this combat. Once you have rolled eight ⚀ results, Kaala has hypnotised you – and you automatically lose the combat. Abilities that let you re-roll dice can be used to change any ⚀ results. If you have the *golden mirror*, then you gain control of this ability instead, automatically winning once Kaala has gained eight ⚀ results.
- Lethal venom: Once you have taken health damage from Kaala, you must lose a further 6 *health* at the end of each combat round from the serpent's deadly poison.

If you manage to defeat Kaala, turn to 537.

372

It is only a few hours until dawn. Your skin tingles with the cold, frost sparkling in the moonlight. When you reach the church, Eldias has his eyes closed, his head slumped forward onto his chest. You fear that you might already be too late to save him. However as you approach, picking your way between the corpses of the ghouls, he lifts his head, giving a low groan.

You move to his side, kneeling to offer him the potion. His eyes flick open as you hold the mouth of the bottle to his fanged lips. There is a flicker of surprise on his face, then he greedily accepts the strange brew, gulping it down thirstily. Within seconds, there is nothing left – he has drunk the entire contents. (Remove the *unknown elixir* from your backpack.)

You lean back, watching him with concern, wondering if the concoction you created was indeed a cure, or something that might have done more harm. Eldias remains silent, his breathing still laboured, forming bright clouds in the chill air. Then, as the sky turns a blood red, brightening towards the dawn, you see him transform before your very eyes. His skin flushes with colour, the fangs sliding back beneath his gums. A blink of his eyelids reveals blue-grey eyes, filled with a sudden vigour.

Eldias forces out a wheezing laugh. 'I feel . . . I feel . . .'

He grips your arm, using it to regain his feet. As he lets go, he takes a moment to settle his balance, clenching and unclenching his fists. 'It can't be . . .' He shakes his head. 'I feel it. . . I feel it gone.'

It appears that the potion worked. The witchfinder has been cured of his vampirism. Together you leave the blighted village, as the rising sun finally breaks through the clouds.

'Thank you, my friend,' smiles Eldias, clasping your hand. 'I do not know how I can thank you; how to repay you. Perhaps . . .' He reaches inside his coat, producing a double-barrelled pistol and a thin silver dagger. 'I was given these when I completed my apprenticeship. Here, I think it's time they served a new master now.'

You may choose one of the following rewards:

Falk's firestarter	Stalker's stiletto
(left hand: pistol)	(main hand: dagger)
+1 speed +1 brawn	+1 speed +1 magic
Ability: headshot	Ability: silver frost

If you refuse Eldias' gift, then he offers you 20 gold crowns instead. When you have made your decision, you bid the witchfinder farewell, heading back into the frosty wilderness. (Return to the map to continue your adventure.)

373

'I've seen and heard a lot of strange things,' says Bill, scratching his cheek. 'I'm just here for the game hunting, mind – but I've crossed paths with plenty of treasure seekers. One was babbling he'd found a lost temple – where all the priests had turned to monkeys.' Bill pauses, then chuckles to himself. 'I'll put that one down to the jungle fever.'

'What about the Lamuri city?' you ask. 'You been there?'

The hunter's eyes widen. 'Lanka Curzo? Sweat and blood, what you take me for, a fool? That place is off limits – seriously.' He cuts his hand through the air, as if that is the end of the matter.

'I have to go there,' you insist. 'Why do you fear it?'

Bill flinches, as if from a blow. 'Me . . . fear?' He stabs a finger at you. 'Look, pal, I've stared down the face of carnosaurs and dracolichs and not batted an eyelid. When they sing of me after I'm gone, they won't ever say the Buckmaster,' he pauses, as if struggling with the words, 'that I fear.'

There is an uneasy silence as you eyeball each other. Clearly the hunter wants you to back down, but you are convinced he is hiding something. 'But you said it's off limits,' you reply, exaggerating a look of confusion. 'Is there something there I'm not meant to find?'

Bill glares at you, then shakes his head. 'By Judah, you're a persistent one. Well, I'll give you this much. Okay, I have been there – and I know others that have too. I've seen gardens of gold and caskets with jewels the size of your fist. I also seen other things – things I'd sooner forget.' He fumbles in his jacket, pulling out a stained sheet of parchment. 'Lanka Curzo is thousands of years old. The jungle moved in now – not much left but scavengers and things best left to the dark. You understand?' He pushes the piece of parchment into your hand. 'Explorer gave me that once. Made no sense to me, but he promised it led to riches. He died of the fever and I was happy to leave it at that. Maybe you have better luck, eh?'

You open out the parchment to find a series of maps and sketches of the city, and a name written underneath a drawing of a bird-like creature: *Quetzal Volax*. You thank the hunter, hoping that the information will prove useful in the future.

You may now continue exploring the camp (turn to 744) or leave and return to the quest map.

374

After bowing your head and offering a prayer to the One God, you leave the shrine and head back into the jungle. Turn to 500.

375

After an hour of trudging through the marsh, you find yourself at the edge of a stagnant lake. Sludge and grime coat its surface, belching bubbles of noxious gas into the air. At the centre of the lake you can see a small island, on top of which rests a wooden chest. The hazy fog makes it difficult to make out details, but it looks as though the chest is perfectly intact. You find it odd that someone would choose to leave their possessions here – and even odder that the chest shows no signs of decay, despite its soggy surroundings.

Will you:

Cross the lake to reach the chest ?	560
Ignore it and continue your journey?	586

376

Quest: Revenge of the tigris

Night falls and with it comes the rain, slapping against the leaves and filling the forest with streaming beads of water. Within minutes the path you were following has become a river, the mud swelling and pulling at your feet. You struggle up a bank, aiming to reach higher ground, the rainwater thumping against your face and into your eyes. Everything about this place – this environment – is hostile and unforgiving. You slide back into the muddy river, too exhausted to continue.

Then your body tenses as you catch a sound – something crashing through the undergrowth.

There is a raised call and the boom of a gunshot. You ready your weapons, scanning the dark forest. You see it all clearly, despite the lack of moonlight; another of your demonic powers.

You turn again, your gaze shifting past splayed leaves and knotted tree roots to finally halt on a pair of brilliant amber eyes. It is a creature you have heard stories about – children's tales of the tiger people that live in far-flung lands. You always thought they were the result of a fervent imagination, a bard's fanciful yarn. But one is staring back at you right now – a female, with orange and black markings. A baby is cradled in her arms.

She looks towards the forest, then quickly back at you – as if deciding her next course of action. Her posture and behaviour are of someone running scared. The tigris flinches and prepares to run again. Then you hear the wet splat of feet and two men emerge, slipping and sliding out of the undergrowth. One is dark-skinned and bare-chested, his thick arms banded with tattoos. A cruel-looking hunting knife flashes in one hand, a sputtering torch in the other. His companion is a thin weasel of a man, with shifty eyes and a pock-marked face. He levels his pistol at the tigris then sees you and his eyes narrow. Your presence draws both men up short.

'Outta our way!' snarls the weasel.

You hear a splash behind you. The tigris has taken flight again, her child held tight to her chest. The dark-skinned man gives a rumbling growl as he advances towards you. The weasel swings his arm around, aiming his pistol for your chest.

Will you:	
Attack the men?	521
Ask why they are hunting tigris?	437
Offer to help them?	570

377

The spear is broken – and with it your curse. (You must remove *the glaive of souls* from your hero sheet and update your attributes accordingly). However, part of the dark weapon still remains, which you may now take:

Runed rod
(backpack)
A splintered length
of black metal

The font's magic has also cured you of your hex. You can now access all of your abilities once again. When you have updated your hero sheet, you leave the pagoda and continue your journey. Turn to 668.

The bronze doors stand open, leading through into a circular chamber with a domed ceiling. Rows of stone chairs rise in tiers along the walls, giving it the appearance of a meeting room or assembly. The rest of the space is littered with grey statues. There seems no logic to their placement, as if someone had left them there in a hurry. Most are missing heads and limbs, a few are severed completely in two. As you walk around the strange display you notice that they are all dwarves, wearing plate or chain armour. Of those that still have their heads, their expressions seem tormented, caught in some instant between pain and death.

'Strange choice of décor.' You grimace, stepping over a dismembered head.

'They're not statues,' says Virgil in a low tone. He passes his blade's light across their twisted features. 'They were titans.'

You look back at Virgil, confused. 'You mean these were living dwarves?'

Virgil nods. 'Dwarves had rune magic, power over the elements. Their titan warriors could turn to stone – gave them the strength and armour of rock.' He gives a dismissive snort. 'Not that it appears to have done much good.'

Beyond the statues the floor of the chamber is scorched and shattered, as if some fiery weight had smashed against it. Where the stone is still intact, you notice a congealed pool of black grime spread through the dust. Virgil is already squatting next to it, prodding the dark matter with his finger. He tastes it and grimaces. 'Blood.'

You frown. 'Is it fresh?'

Virgil shakes his head. 'Mixed with something. A bone resin perhaps, or maybe mage oil.'

'The remains of a demon?'

Virgil's expression sours. 'No. This is part of a ritual . . .' You join him, scanning the strange array of marks. They originate from the same pool of blood, which has then been smeared across the stone in a variety of brushstrokes, forming an intricate pattern of runes.

'This is powerful magic,' says Virgil, flinching away. 'Dark magic. I didn't think the dwarves would resort to such measures.'

'Perhaps it wasn't the dwarves . . .' A shiver creeps along your spine as you eye the statues. They almost seem to be moving, their shadows stalking along the walls . . .

'Come.' The witchfinder's voice makes you jump. 'Let's keep going.'

You follow him through into the next chamber. It is a columned hall, dominated by a long table of blue-white marble surrounded by high-backed chairs. The table has been sliced cleanly in two, from one end to the other, its cleaved edges melted into glass hunks. Similar marks are evident along the walls and columns, where deep gouges have been taken from the stonework.

The rest of the room is strewn with rubble and cracked shards of pottery. Virgil reaches down and picks up a clay gourd. He shakes it, brightening when he hears a sloshing sound coming from inside. 'Dwarven spirits. Two thousand years old. Now there's a vintage . . .' He removes the stopper with his teeth and sniffs at the contents. He immediately jerks away with an expression of disgust. 'Humph, appears age has not been kind . . .' He tosses the gourd away, the clay shattering against a tumble of rocks.

Meanwhile, your attention has been drawn to the left-hand wall. Brushing away the dirt and grime, you reveal a stone panel carved with angular patterns. There is another beside it. You step away, realising that the whole wall is covered in neat rows of squares, forming a larger design.

'Dwarven treasure vault,' says Virgil, striding over. 'And it looks to be . . .'

You cut him off with a raised hand. 'Listen.'

The sound you detected is getting louder – boots crunching on stone, the clink of metal, muffled voices.

Drawing your weapons, you turn to face the doorway at the end of the hall. Three spindly creatures come marching out of it, jabbering to each other in a guttural language. They are clad in tattered leathers, their round glassy eyes reflecting the bright light from Virgil's sword.

'Goblins!' The witchfinder hurriedly reaches for a pistol.

The lead goblin stumbles to a halt, his two companions bumping into him with surprised yelps. You notice that the rear goblin, the larger of the three, is shouldering a patchwork sack. It rattles and clinks with loot as he thumps into the back of his skinnier cohort.

'Dorak Ka!' The leader gives a shocked cry of alarm, then spins around, pushing and shoving to get back through the doorway. The other goblins follow suit, jostling each other to escape, their shouts and yells and hasty footfalls echoing back from the passageway.

Will you:	
Chase after the looters?	620
Stay and investigate the treasure room?	805

379

The hound is a powerful and brutal adversary, but its eagerness to please its master is its undoing. The floor of the chamber is covered in dust and stone, making it slippery and treacherous. In its haste to attack the hound is frequently missing its mark or struggling to manoeuvre, making it easy prey for yourself and Virgil.

At last the hound's snarls turn to whimpers, as it flounders on its back, paws still feebly raking the air. You step in and end its life – drawing a hoarse gasp from the dwarf king. He rises from his throne, shaking with fury.

'Upstarts! Vermin! You are not fit to even look upon me!' He beats a hand against his chest, the runes on his plate flaring with a fiery-red light. 'I am Erkil Giantsbane, King of the Hammer and last blood of the titans.' Magic flickers around his fists, forming them into a stone sword and axe. He marches forward, wisps of smoke billowing from beneath his visor. 'These are my halls . . . this is my kingdom! Demons, be gone!'

The dwarf charges across the hall, moving with a swiftness that belies his heavy armour. The blows that follow rain down with equal speed, both sword and axe chopping and slashing in a deadly frenzy. It is time to fight:

	Speed	*Brawn*	*Armour*	*Health*
Erkil	13	10	10/28 (*)	120

Special abilities

Stone skin: At the start of the fifth combat round, Erkil casts *stone skin*. This encases his body in hard stone, raising his *armour* to 28.

- Chip away: Once Erkil has cast *stone skin*, if you win a combat round you can choose to lower his *armour* by 4 instead of rolling for damage. Each time Erkil's *armour* is lowered, you must take 4 damage from the flying shards of stone.
- Titan stone: Once Erkil has cast *stone skin*, he is immune to all passive damage effects, including *monkey mob*, *bleed*, *thorns*, *barbs* and *venom*.

If you manage to defeat this dwarven king, turn to **811**.

380

Congratulations! You have created the following item:

Self-published tome
(left hand: spell book)
+2 speed +3 armour
Ability: dark pact

If you wish to create a different spell book, you can start the process again (turn to **850**). Otherwise, you may now leave the chamber and continue your journey. Turn to **866**.

381

The queen ant has been defeated! Quickly, you set about destroying her eggs, putting an end to the bug infestation. You may now choose one of the following rewards:

Pins 'n' needles	**Crown of spite**	**Eye of the swarm**
(ring)	(head)	(necklace)
Ability: thorns	+1 armour	+1 magic +1 brawn
	Ability: curse	Ability: swarm

With your mission complete, you leave the caves and return to

Carvel. There, you deliver your report to the Church. It appears the goblins were simply fleeing their own caves, which had become overrun by ant-men. With the threat eradicated, the woodsmen should now be able to return to their logging camp. The Church awards you 20 gold crowns for your bravery. (Return to the quest map to continue your adventure.)

382

The stairs lead down into a small square room that reeks of sulphur and smoke. Shadows whirl and shift across the floor and walls, created by the huge-bladed fan whirring slowly in the ceiling. At the opposite side of the room the rusted stairs continue down into a large workshop, where you can see various worktables and pieces of machinery. You are about to make for it when you spot a metal trapdoor in the floor. You grab hold of the ring set into its centre and tug it open. The door panel comes off freely in your hand, revealing a hole swathed in darkness. There is no sign of any stairs or a ladder to help you down.

If you have *a bottle of wisps*, then you may use their light to help you explore this hidden place (turn to 401). Otherwise, you decide it would be unwise to expose yourself to dangers you cannot see. You decide to explore the workshop instead (turn to 398).

383

With the venomous Kaala defeated, you may now help yourself to one of the following rewards:

Eyes of the serpent	Mantle of the deceiver	Death rattle
(head)	(cloak)	(main hand: staff)
+1 speed +2 armour	+1 speed +3 brawn	+2 speed +3 magic
Ability: hypnotise	Ability: deceive	Ability: near death
		(requirement: mage)

Prising open the serpent's mouth, you tug one of its enormous fangs loose. You decide to take this as a trophy. (Make a note of Kaala's fang on your hero sheet, it does not take up backpack space.) If you have the glaive of souls equipped, turn to 430. Otherwise, return to the quest map to continue your adventure.

384

'Gaia is old spirit. Very powerful.' Boom plants his staff at the edge of the swampy crater. 'Watch roots. They are real danger.'

'What roots?' you ask, your head snapping around sharply.

'Them . . .'

Suddenly, a geyser of mud erupts from the centre of the pool. You duck, covering your head as wet clumps of weed and dirt shower around you. Then something hard hits you in the stomach, driving the wind from your lungs. It is accompanied by the unsettling sensation of wet, muddy limbs wrapping around your waist and legs. They grip with a strength like iron, dragging you forwards off your feet. Desperately you try and grapple for a hand hold, but your fingers find only mud, gouging trenches as you are pulled into the swamp.

You twist around, concentrating on freeing your weapons. All around you the air is alive with whipping, snake-like roots. They are coming from the centre of the pool, where a giant toad-like head has surfaced.

'I start ritual. Stay calm. It'll be all right.' Boom Mamba places both hands on his staff and begins chanting.

'Stay calm?' you sputter angrily, wrestling to free yourself from the tangled roots.

Then the creature's mouth yawns open, presenting an immense chasm of foul-stinking darkness. For one horrible moment you ponder your fate – being dragged down into those fathomless, watery depths. Then fear gives you strength. You raise your weapons and begin hacking at the constricting roots, determined not to become this monster's next meal. It is time to fight:

	Speed	*Brawn*	*Armour*	*Health*
Gaia	5	4	4	55
Roots	–	–	1	20(*)

Special abilities

- Feeding time: The roots are slowly dragging you towards Gaia's gaping maw. If they are not defeated by the end of the third round of combat, then Gaia will swallow you up! You automatically take 15 damage (you may use *armour* to absorb some/all of this) before you are spat out. The roots then heal back to full *health* (or new roots are created, if the others were defeated) and the process begins again: you have three combat rounds to defeat the new roots before you are dragged inside Gaia's worm-filled mouth once more. This cycle repeats for the duration of the battle.

If you win a combat round against Gaia, you can choose to attack Gaia or the roots. Once Gaia is defeated, the combat is automatically won.

If you manage to defeat this fearsome elemental, turn to 516. If you are defeated, you may return to 510 to choose a different foe to battle.

385

You put your hands to the wheel and push. For the first few seconds you find yourself grunting with exertion, your boots sliding across the metal floor as you struggle to move it. Then it gives a teeth-grating screech as it slowly begins to turn, grinding against the rust and grime that has gathered around the axle. After pushing it round a full turn, you hear a rumbling coming from your left, followed by a loud clunk. Glancing around, you see that a glowing portal has now appeared against the north wall. It looks similar to the doorway that you used to escape from the fire demon.

Will you:

Step through the magic portal?	395
Turn the wheel anti-clockwise?	405

386

You follow Andos through an opulent-looking hall, into a small windowless backroom. Books and crates crowd in around a rickety writing desk and stool – and a single sad-looking candle that provides the only source of light. From the reek of stagnant water and the various buckets and mops resting against the far wall, you suspect that the man has hired out the mansion's broom cupboard. Andos drops his books in an unceremonious heap on the floor, wincing as he rubs his aching shoulders.

'Some tea, Andos,' scowls the scholar irritably, waving him away. 'Then back to cataloguing. And see if you can't get some driftwood – knock up a shelf or two.'

The youth gives a dispirited mumble, before leaving to attend to his master's needs.

The scholar tuts, shaking his head. 'Youth of today. No respect for their elders.' He perches on the stool, rifling through the charts and maps on the desk. After some time, you wonder if he has simply forgotten you are there.

'Your charts, sir,' you enquire, shaking the crumpled papers that you are holding.

The man looks up with a start. 'Oh yes – yes. Just file them away.'

You look down at the disorderly jumble of books and crates. Following the youth's lead, you drop the charts and scrolls onto the nearest pile.

'Good, now ... let's see.' He lifts up a tea-stained chart, which appears to show a partial map of the jungle. 'I hope you're made of brighter stuff than the last lot of miscreants. I know the university is cutting costs but...' He blows out his cheeks 'Seen more sense in a howler monkey.'

Will you:

Ask about the man's studies?	583
Ask about the unfinished map?	324
Ask what he knows about demons?	341
Ask if you can help?	565

387

A sudden thought occurs to you. Opening your pack, you retrieve the heart-shaped object and offer it out to the creature.

'My heart!' The bear hugs the object to its torn chest. 'The toymaker promised me a new one. He hasn't forgotten me after all.' The sad-looking creature turns and shuffles back across the room, muttering to itself as it fondly strokes the object. (You can remove this item from your hero sheet.)

You have now gained the following special ability:

Bear hug (1 use): Instead of rolling for a damage score after winning a round, Cuddles will come to your aid. The bear inflicts 3 damage dice to a single opponent, ignoring *armour*. This ability can only be used once, and only during this quest.

There is a dull rumbling sound as the east wall slowly swings outwards, revealing a narrow stone passageway. The bear continues to shuffle back and forth, attention focused on its new present. Seeing your chance to escape this peculiar cell, you head immediately into the passage.

After only a few hundred metres, you come to a rusty metal door. It has already been pushed open, leaving a yellow-brown stain where it has scraped across the stone. A can of oil rests on the floor next to it, which someone evidently used to help grease its hinges. There is still some oil inside. (If you wish you can take the *can of oil*, simply make a note of it on your hero sheet – it doesn't take up backpack space.) You pass through the open door, grateful that one of your problems has been solved, at least. Turn to 304.

388

You shift position, putting your weight behind the wheel to turn it in the opposite direction. As it revolves, screeching and squealing and setting your teeth on edge, you see that the previous portal has faded away. There is a repeated series of rumbles followed by a booming thump. Then a different portal appears, this time against the north wall.

Will you:

Step through the magic portal?	395
Turn the wheel anti-clockwise?	405

389

The man looks up as you approach, offering you a grin filled with sharpened teeth. 'Old one,' he bows his head, then gives the sparring child a kick in the back of the leg – throwing him off balance. 'You stretch too far,' he growls. 'Keep feet closer. Watch enemy.'

The boy looks up at him, angrily spitting words in their strange guttural language.

The warrior scowls, cuffing him with the back of his hand. 'You learn like others, Fran. Go, your weakness angers me.' He takes the polished training daggers, watching as the teary boy scampers back to his friends – a ragged band of children with dirty, scowling faces.

'He don't see reason for training,' he spits. 'Soon, we may all need to fight.'

'I owe you my thanks.' You smile, offering out a hand in friendship. 'You saved my life. Gave me my freedom.'

The rogue looks down at your hand, momentarily confused. Then he slaps one of the training daggers into the offered palm. You are surprised at its heaviness – its tip weighted more than the handle. He notes your surprised reaction. 'I am Murlic. I teach you to fight, if you want. Fight Wiccan way.'

Will you:

Learn the pariah career (requirement: rogue)?	302
Ask about Durnhollow?	129
Explore the rest of the cave?	485

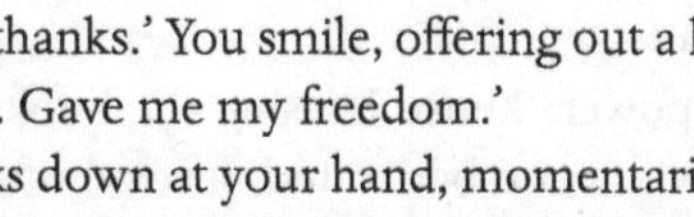

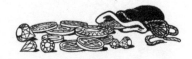

Andos rifles through the books, a sinister smile creeping across his face. 'Yes! These are the books –*The Negra Lumaris*. Their knowledge is mine at last!'

'Andos?' You back away, perturbed by his strange behaviour. 'Is something wrong?'

He snarls, baring his teeth. 'Andos is merely my servant, fool!' The boy swings back his arm, drawing crackling bolts of energy from one of the open books. It pools around his fist, the glow reflected in his maddened eyes. With a beast-like roar he hurls the ball of magic in your direction. You leap aside just in time as the missile punches into the ground, throwing up a column of sand and smoke.

'You cannot defeat me,' snarls the youth, circling you with a menacing sneer. 'I am Xenos the ever-living – and now you have granted me the power of the ancient Lamuri!'

Quickly, you spring back to your feet and prepare to fight:

	Speed	*Magic*	*Armour*	*Health*
Xenos	12	9	9	65

Special abilities

- Knowledge is power: Xenos is using the books to help boost his *magic*. If you win a combat round, instead of rolling for damage you can choose to destroy one of the three books. This automatically lowers Xenos' *speed, magic and armour* by 1. You may repeat this in future rounds, until all three books are destroyed.

If you manage to defeat this magical entity, turn to 438.

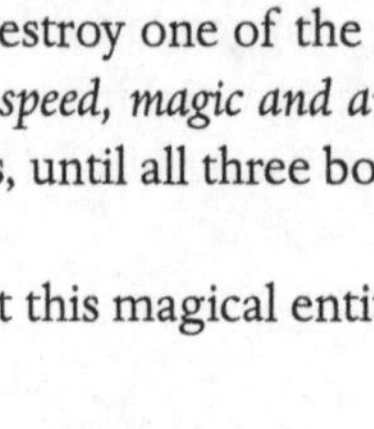

391

At the end of the passageway you see the strange child watching you, his patchwork cloak wrapped tight around his scrawny shoulders. Behind him is a glowing portal, identical to the others you have used to travel around the tower.

'You are good at my games,' grins the boy, scratching at his chin. 'But my best game is yet to come. It's my favourite!'

'Where are the others?' you demand angrily, striding towards him. 'Enough of your games!'

'Ah, can't tell you that,' he smiles.

Suddenly, the passageway starts to shake violently, throwing you to your knees. The child looks around in confusion. 'No! The tower ... it's starting again ... It wants to take us back!'

'Back where?' you yell over the rumbling din. 'You mean the shroud?'

The child doesn't answer. Instead he turns and runs, disappearing through the glowing portal. You stagger after him, determined not to let him escape. Turn to 32.

392

Dark shapes lumber towards you through the white haze. At first their size and form is deceptive, their angular appearance and broad shoulders suggesting plate-armoured knights. But as they close on your position, you realise that they are actually immense statues fashioned from onyx and crystal. They stand over ten feet tall, their giant hands chiselled flat into hammer-like fists. As they near, black lightning starts to flicker about their mighty limbs, charging the air and making the hairs on the back of your neck prickle.

Then, as one, they rush to attack, the ground shuddering and breaking beneath their anvil-sized feet. You draw your weapons, dodging the first set of whirling fists to fly in your direction. Weaving beneath your opponent's legs, you launch a desperate chain of attacks against its black-stone hide. But each blow is turned away by the hard rock, leaving mere scratches rather than deep wounds.

'The pillars,' one of your companions shouts above the din of battle. 'The runes are the source of their strength!'

You must now fight:

	Speed	*Brawn*	*Armour*	*Health*
Stone giants	5	4	12	35
Runed pillar	–	–	3	10
Runed pillar	–	–	3	10
Runed pillar	–	–	3	10

Special abilities

- Charged: Each time your damage score/damage dice cause health damage to the stone giants, you take 2 *lightning* damage in return, ignoring *armour*. If you have the *insulated* ability you can ignore this damage.
- Pound those pillars: For each runed pillar you destroy, the stone giants' *armour* is reduced by 4. When a pillar is reduced to zero *health*, it explodes, inflicting 6 damage to your hero. You can use *armour* to help absorb this damage.
- Enchanted rock: The giants and pillars are immune to *bleed, sear, thorns, thorn cage* and *fire aura.*

If you win a combat round against the stone giants, you can choose to apply your damage to the giants or a runed pillar (unless you have an ability that lets you strike more than one opponent). Once the stone giants are defeated, you have automatically won the combat.

If you able to overcome these mighty guardians, turn to 44. (Special achievement: If you are able to defeat the giants without destroying a single pillar, turn to 188.)

393

As the last chain is broken, the demon blurs forward with lightning speed. Unable to dodge aside in time, you are hit in the stomach by a fist of claws. The blow draws an agonised scream from your lips as your body is wrenched upwards, your legs kicking feebly in the air. Your nose fills with the sharp odour of blood and brimstone. Then you are being flung backwards as a blue-black shape hurtles past you, wings flapping through the air.

'Now, Orgorath. You are mine!' bellows the demon.

You hear a scream; one of your companions. Then you crash down onto the snow-crusted mud, your own wheezing breaths thundering in your ears. You lie for some seconds, choking on each agonised gasp. A cacophony of noise breaks over you – ripping, snarling, tearing. A shower of severed roots and branches go sailing through the night air.

You struggle to lift your head, to see what is happening, but the movement only brings a fresh spasm of pain. As you kick and squirm in the mud, your fingers brush against something cold and metallic. You manage a glance sideways, to see the relic lying next to you.

The ground trembles. A dark shadow moves into view, blocking out the blood-red moon with a frightening silhouette of horns and spikes.

'Cernos,' you gasp.

Your hand goes for the relic – but the demon is faster. A cloven hoof smashes down on the headpiece, staving in the metal panels. Then it descends again, accompanied by a hissing growl.

From the point of impact, a white light explodes outwards. Blinding. Impenetrable.

You blink, trying to focus – to see beyond the spots of pain and the bright brilliance that surrounds you.

'Dwarven fools,' booms the voice of the demon. 'They hand me the very thing I desire most – the heart of fire.'

As colours swim and merge together, you see Cernos standing over you, a bright gemstone gripped in one of his fists. Smoke billows between the clenched fingers, where the skin boils and blisters. But the demon shows no sign of pain.

'My time here is at an end,' he bellows, raising his other hand and summoning black flames to his palm. 'As is yours.' Turn to **418**.

394

'Allam had a chronicler – one of his knights,' explains the dean. 'Not a scholar, but someone who saw the value in recording the prophet's visions. It was not an ordered record, more a random collection of scrawls on whatever was to hand – parchment, animal hide, cloth, bandages ... it became a vast store of knowledge about Allam. There were thousands of records in the end as the prophet became more ... susceptible ... to the visions.'

The dean's words only serve to confound you more. 'What does this have to do with him,' you gesture to the dishevelled traveller, 'or the Wiccans?'

The dean grins. 'Allam was fixated on the forest of thorns. He couldn't penetrate it – no blade or magic was capable of cutting a path through those sorcerous trees. And yet, he firmly believed something lay there, at its centre.'

You are suddenly reminded of your own strange visions – and the ghostly voice beckoning you to the centre of that malign place. 'Go on.'

'For some reason, Allam headed south instead. His men were beset by stone creatures – some say trolls, but I believe they were of a darker magic. Allam and his followers never made it back from that expedition.'

'And you want to know why?'

The dean nods. 'Allam was looking for something on that expedition – something that would get him inside the forest.' He looks over to the monk, seated at the table. His quill is struggling to keep up with the vagabond's ramblings. 'The only way of knowing why Allam went south was to read the chronicles – to discover the vision that led him there. The chronicles are a sacred document; they cannot be copied or borrowed. They reside in the cathedral in the capital, under constant guard. Ventus' mission was to get our friend to the chronicles. His ability – his gift – would help us find out what Allam was after.'

Will you:

Ask about the traveller's gift? 429
Ask about the war with the Wiccans? 491
End the conversation? 496

395

The portal deposits you in a long narrow chamber of rusted metal. An ochre-tinged light filters through grilles in the ceiling, illuminating knee-deep sludge and the assorted junk bobbing on its surface. You cover your nose from the stench, guessing that this is some kind of waste area. Floating in the slimy water are scraps of metal, tattered cloth, wood shavings, broken tools, and some things you prefer not to identify. Looking over your shoulder, you see that the portal has closed behind you – trapping you in this foul-smelling chamber. Thankfully, there is a door at the opposite end. As you make your way towards it, you suddenly hear a splash followed by an angry hiss. Then something hits you in the back, sending you sprawling into the water. You twist around, just as another object comes flying towards you, missing your head by scant inches.

You stagger to your feet, frantically scanning your surroundings for the source of your tormentor. But you can't see anything – only bobbing piles of trash. Then a squelching movement behind you forces you to spin, as a sheet of battered metal lifts itself out of the water. There is an angry snarl as the metal is flung through the air. You duck beneath it, barely having time to recover before another length of metal is hurled in your direction. Quickly you draw your weapons, sidestepping the missile as it clangs against the far wall.

There is no sign of any visible enemy. You can only assume it must be a poltergeist – an angry spirit intent on using you for target practice!

Will you:

Attempt to fight the poltergeist?	414
Make for the door as quickly as possible?	29

396

The feathered woman snarls, tugging a black wand from her belt. 'You dishonour the blood of the Sanchen!'

'No!' The cry comes from Ventus, as the Wiccan witch aims the tip of her wand at you. There is a blast of cold, black fire – then you are falling backwards, screaming in agony. The last thing you remember is the rain, spearing down from the black skies, beating against your pain-wracked body. Then the light fades and a feverish darkness takes you. Turn to 338.

397

'I am a shadow, a nothing,' replies the witchfinder, tugging the brim of his hat lower over his eyes. 'I was once a king's hound, the embodiment of his justice, his divine retribution. I have killed demons in their scores, vampires, witches, pagans … the dark things of the underworld that would seek to make these lands their own. I have given my soul and body to that life – to that duty. But now. . . .' He raises a gloved hand, turning it over in the slanting beams of light. 'I cling to what I have left. My humanity.' He catches your eye, his fingers curling into a fist. 'When the darkness comes, that's all we have left.'

Return to 494 to ask another question, or turn to 433 to continue.

398

The workshop is a huge, rectangular hall, the furthest reaches obscured by smoke. It is hard to fathom how such a vast space could exist inside the tower; clearly some magic or enchantment must be at play here. Despite its size, the hall is full to bursting point with workbenches and machines, the latter a chaotic mishmash of saws, blades and other mean-looking cutting tools. Many of these are in operation, chopping or shaving logs of wood which are being fed into the machine by iron grappling claws attached to chains.

As you step warily between the deafening, screeching equipment, you spot store rooms off to either side of the chamber. Packed inside each of these is rank upon rank of wooden soldiers, all standing still and silent, their features almost lifelike.

Just as you are about to take a closer look, a shower of sparks draws your attention to a nearby worktable. It has started to rise up off the floor, lurching from side to side as if suddenly possessed of some demonic life force. Behind you, another table is scraping across the ground. You duck just in time as it lifts up above your head, fast-spinning blades missing you by scant inches. Panic starts to grip you, as you realise the whole workshop is now shifting and spinning, surrounding you in a dizzying maelstrom of snake-like chains and buzzing saws.

It is difficult to make sense of what is happening. It isn't until you back up to the foot of the stairs, hugging the ground while blades spin overhead, that you realise the workshop is actually a single, huge creature. The tables are its arms and legs, jointed by chains – and the whirring blades are its deadly armaments, bristling from its many limbs. Finally, as you watch with mouth agape, an iron claw swings onto its shoulders, giving the monster a grinning visage of gnashing metal teeth.

And then, as one, the wooden soldiers start to advance, shuffling towards you from out of the storerooms. Your immediate instinct is to run, but the saw monster has other ideas. A set of blades slice down from above, cutting through the metal walkway in a shower of bright sparks. Your only escape route has been closed off. You have no other option but to fight:

	Speed	*Brawn*	*Armour*	*Health*
Saw	5	4	3	40
Soldiers	–	–	1	25

Special abilities

- Spinning saws: Roll a die at the end of each combat round. On a roll of ⚀ or ⚁ you are caught by the deadly buzz saws and must take 4 damage, ignoring *armour*. If you roll ⚂ or more, the toy soldiers are caught instead, and must take 4 damage. (If the toy soldiers have already been destroyed, ignore a result of ⚂ or more.)
- Stabbing swords: At the end of each combat round, if the toy soldiers are still alive, then you must take 2 damage, ignoring *armour*, from their wooden blades.
- Wood and metal: Saw and the soldiers are immune to *bleed*.

If you win a combat round against Saw, you can choose to apply your damage to Saw or the wooden soldiers. If Saw is defeated, the soldiers are also automatically defeated.

If you manage to overcome this saw-wielding fiend, turn to 219.

399

'Good, follow me and I explain on the way.' Boom pads over to the doorway, carrying only his carved staff. You hesitate before following, wondering how a single staff will help defeat the hordes of undead.

'Surely we need more weapons?' you protest, as you emerge in the narrow alley.

'Don't be worrying about skellies. We go deeper into ruins so they not follow. They not like the bad spirits.'

Before you can reply, the shaman has shot out from the mouth of the alleyway, heading quickly across the open plaza. You struggle to keep up, the pea-green mist making it difficult to navigate the shambling groups of undead. Several times you almost run into the deadly creatures, but you manage to weave aside just in time to avoid their snatching hands and stabbing spears. Thankfully, by keeping on the move, the undead are unable to catch you.

'I got a plan to defeat Mortzilla,' says Boom, perching for a moment on a vine-covered wall.

He sounds barely out of breath, while you are panting and gasping in the stifling heat.

'What's the plan?' you croak dryly, wiping the sweat from your eyes. 'Tell me it doesn't involve more running . . .'

He gives a hooting laugh. 'We almost there. Listen. Mortzilla not harmed by weapons of this world. Too powerful a spirit. But the spirits of his world . . . they can do him harm.'

The shaman leaps off the wall, landing, rolling, and then springing back to his feet. 'We use the boom stick,' he shouts, waving the staff. 'It eat the spirit energy. Then we use it against Mortzilla. Make him go boom!'

You slide down off the wall, joining him at the centre of a circular courtyard. Beyond the shifting veil of mist, you see a series of buildings – mostly ruined and overgrown. As Boom promised, the undead have not followed.

'See this,' the shaman displays his rune-carved staff. 'This will hold magic of three spirits. You defeat spirits and I put them into boom stick. Once we got three, we go pay Mortzilla a visit.'

You nod, squinting in the ghoulish light. 'And where are the spirits?'

'There be five,' he grins, displaying the number with a raised hand. 'They inside the temples. But remember, we needing only three. Choose and we go boom them.' Turn to 510.

400

With the stone guardians defeated, you advance on the black temple. It is an imposing structure of spine-like towers, arched windows and high columns. The mist has receded, but in its place is a presence – thick and palpable. It pushes against you like an invisible hand, forcing you to grit your teeth as you struggle onwards, your will matched against that of some unseen foe.

Bea is the first to stumble, falling to her knees. 'I can't . . .' she mutters weakly.

You notice Ventus staggering as if blind, his fists batting away at some invisible foe. Benin has also stalled, gripping his staff with white-knuckled hands. You go to his aid but the priest puts out a hand to stop you. 'No . . . continue . . . if you can . . .' He gasps, struggling to draw breath.

Alone, you clamber up the stairs of the temple, crawling the rest of the way to finally reach its dark, imposing doorway. Turn to 419.

401

The trapped wisps provide just enough light for you to see by. Leaning over the hole, you can make out a metal floor several metres below. Deciding to take the risk, you slide your legs over the edge of the opening and drop down.

You find yourself in a narrow passageway, your shoulders brushing against the warm metal walls. Beneath your feet grey smoke spirals up through the meshed floor, carrying a noxious-smelling stench. Choosing a direction at random you head along the passage, your footfalls clanging and echoing noisily in the claustrophobic space.

After several hundred feet you come to a symbol, marked out on the floor in what looks like grime and oil. As you ponder what it might mean, your eyes catch some words daubed on the wall. They read:

Seeing is believing
Ignorance is blind
Turn around bright eyes
Tell me what you find
☆△☾

Three symbols are drawn underneath the words, one of which matches the shape you are standing on. Turning on the spot, you notice that the floor is divided up into square grilles, forming a maze. Some contain numbers, others have been left blank. You wonder if this is some type of puzzle.

Then you hear a child's voice, echoing through the walls. 'Someone's come to play! Tell me the number or here you'll stay!'

'What number?' you growl angrily, scratching your head in confusion.

(The following diagram is a top-down view of the maze you are standing in. The dark blocks represent walls and the square grilles represent the floor panels.)

If you are able to solve the puzzle, then speak your answer and turn to the corresponding entry number. Otherwise, frustrated and angry by this child's silly games, you demand to be let out of the maze. Turn to 43.

402

(If you have the word *explorer* on your hero sheet, turn to **515**.)

You put out a hand to greet the scholar. In his haste the man knocks straight into you, dropping his charts and scroll cases onto the dusty promenade. You offer an apology, stooping down to help retrieve his belongings.

'Flaming flummoxes!' The man pats at various pockets, finally hoisting a pair of spectacles onto the end of his nose. He glares down at you with his widened, magnified eyes. 'Wait, you're the new one, aren't you? How bothersome – not sure we have the room. But then, you won't be around long. We'll get you started straight away. Follow me. Keep up, Andos.'

He hurries off again, leaving you clutching the various charts and scrolls. As the ginger-haired youth stumbles past, he leans around his pile of books and gives you an apologetic smile. 'He's like that all the time. I think it's the heat.'

'What are all these for?' you ask, walking beside him.

'His lordship's studies,' Andos replies. 'Our last place fell down. Again. So, we're moving. Again.'

The scholar turns down a side path, which winds back through the trees to a more secluded area of the beach. Here you find a large two-storey building of white stone – a veritable mansion compared to the others you have seen.

'This belongs to the harbourmaster,' says the youth. 'Price we paid for a room, you could have bought the king's palace five times over Rip off, if you ask me.'

'Stop dilly-dallying!' snaps the scholar, removing his straw hat to fan his bright red face. 'Let's get those things safe inside – then we can get you briefed and started.' He disappears inside the house. Andos gives you a pitying look before staggering after him. Turn to 386.

403

Amongst the creepers and brambles, you spy an object resting on the stone. It looks like a cone-shaped seed, pulsing with a golden light. You may now take the following item:

Elder seed
(talisman)
+1 magic
Ability: druid career

As you step out from the hollow tree, you realise that you feel different. Something has been awakened inside you, a vibrant force that throbs with energy and life. Looking around, you see glimmering lines cutting across the floor of the cave. They pulse with an ancient magic, as old as the land itself. Ley lines. You realise that the roots of the elder tree are tapping into these lines, greedily sucking at the magic to nourish and sustain itself. It is an appetite you now share – your body filled with a constant craving for this raw energy, to fuel your newfound powers.

The druid has the following abilities:

Thorn cage (co + pa): Instead of rolling for a damage score, you can cast thorn cage. It automatically encases one opponent in a cage of thorns, inflicting 1 damage die (ignoring armour). It also inflicts 1 point of damage to the same opponent at the end of each combat round for the duration of the combat. *Thorn cage* can only be used once per combat.

Ley line infusion (co): Call on the fickle powers of nature to aid you. Instead of rolling for a damage score, roll 1 die. If the result is:

⚀ Both you and your opponent take 1 die of damage, ignoring *armour*. Roll separately for each.

⚁ or ⚂ You are healed for 5 *health* and your opponent takes 1 die of damage, ignoring *armour*.

⚃ or ⚄ You are healed for 8 *health* and your opponent takes 1 die of damage, ignoring *armour*.

⚅ You and an ally are both healed for 8 *health* and your opponent takes 1 die of damage, ignoring *armour*.

You can only use *ley line infusion* once per combat, and you cannot alter the outcome of your die rolls.

When you have updated your hero sheet, turn to 476.

404

Benin strides over to the creature. He makes a quick inspection of the body before turning away in revulsion.

'Ooh, what is it?' asks Bea, her voice shrill in the echoing chamber.

'A dwarf I think,' replies Ventus, wrinkling his nose. 'And I suspect he was guarding that . . .' The monk crosses the room to a large stone casket, set within a circle of runes. They still pulse with a faint glow, but at a gesture from the monk they crackle and spark, and then fade to nothing. 'This is what Allam was seeking.' He raises a glowing fist into the air. With a roar, he brings it down hard, shattering the stone lid. 'Agh, no!' Ventus suddenly staggers backwards, covering his face.

'A curse!' cries Bea, cowering behind her raised arms.

You can feel it from where you are standing. A fierce heat washing through the chamber. But whereas the others seem to be driven back by its intensity, you find yourself unmoved. Instead, you cautiously advance, much to the surprise of Benin.

'Stay back!' he cries in warning. 'The magic . . . it will burn you!'

You are already standing over the casket, looking down at a hammer-shaped object resting on a bed of glowing coals. Somehow you can feel the heat prickling against your skin, but there is no pain. You reach into the casket and take hold of the hammer, your hands settling around the grip. You smell burning flesh as your skin comes into contact with the super-heated metal, but it feels distant – like you are looking down at someone else's body, not your own. You lift the relic, admiring the intricately carved head-piece.

Suddenly, the panels that encase the head of the relic snap open and a bright white light pours forth, filling the room with dazzling radiance. You lift the object above your head, holding it aloft like a torch, as its light blazes like the heart of a sun.

'By Judah, it's the light of the divine!' gasps Bea, bowing her head with reverence.

Benin seems less sure, squinting as he struggles to focus on the glowing centrepiece. 'It's powerful … very powerful,' he remarks. 'Allam believed it was the key to the forest.'

Ventus removes his cloak, gesturing for you to wrap the relic within its folds. 'Then the forest is our next destination,' he asserts. 'At last, we will finish what Allam started all those years before. Let the One God guide us on the true path.' (Congratulations, you have retrieved the relic from Duerdoun. Return to the quest map to continue your journey.)

405

You shift position, putting your weight behind the wheel to turn it in the opposite direction. As it revolves, screeching and squealing and setting your teeth on edge, you see that the previous portal has now faded away. There is a repeated series of rumbles followed by a booming thump. Then a different portal appears, this time against the west wall.

Will you:

Step through the magic portal?	416
Turn the wheel clockwise?	388

406

Without a second thought, Damaris strides over to the first restraint and brings her staff down hard, shattering it to pieces.

'Stop!' Conall looks back over his shoulder, his eyes bulging beneath his protruding brow. 'The demon is a trickster! Its words are lies!' He spins on his heel, stalking towards her.

'Wait!' You hurry to head off the warrior, positioning yourself between the two feuding Wiccans. 'Damaris, wait – there has to be another way?' you plead.

The witch ignores your protests, continuing to smash through the remaining restraints.

'You betray me for a demon!' Conall lifts his runed axes, preparing to strike you out of the way. 'This is the end of us! The end of you, witch!' Turn to 393.

407

Your choice was a bad one. The rock monster smashes your soldier to pieces, stomping over the battered remains as it continues to advance. (Remove your soldier from your hero sheet. Then return to 427 to fight this monster yourself.)

408

Legendary monster: The fisher king

The high walls of the gorge amplify the roar of the nearby waterfall, plunging down from out of the mist to crash amongst the boulders and churning, white-frothed water. After hours of trekking in the wretched jungle heat, you are grateful to have found this oasis of life. You throw aside your pack and drop to your knees, cupping your hands in the chill waters and gulping it down as if each swallow could be your last.

After taking your fill, you find yourself studying your reflection. The face staring back is as thin and haggard as when you first fled Durnhollow. You lean closer, pulling away your collar to view the dark patch of blue-black scales. Every day, every hour, there seems to be more of them – spreading over your body like a disease.

You quickly sink your hands into the water, scattering the reflection as you draw more water to your lips.

It is then that you hear the sound . . .

Since trekking through the jungle, you have become accustomed to the noise – the croaking frogs, the hoarse, jabbering shrieks of the monkeys, the incessant buzz of the midges and flies. But occasionally a sound will stand out from the rest, competing for attention.

This is one of them. A breathy, rasping noise that suddenly rises in pitch, becoming a series of clacking, rattling wails. You look back up the river, to where it widens into a pool. There, squatting on one of the rocky islands, is a frog-like humanoid. The sunlight catches on its glistening, rainbow-oiled skin and the rusted prongs of the trident clutched in its spindly hands. The creature looks agitated, its throat bulging as it continues to emit a chorus of guttural caws.

You edge away from the water, slowly lifting your pack onto your shoulder. Your plan is to turn and make a run for it, back into the jungle. But you hesitate – your gift of prophecy flashing through the images of your death like pictures in a flipbook.

Suddenly the creature gives a single, gargling cry, then launches forward on its bowed legs. You drop your pack and fumble for your weapons as the frog descends on you with a startling speed. One of its legs catches you in the chest, sending you tumbling backwards. You fall into a roll, dodging the trident as it slams down with force, striking sparks from the stone. Then you are back on your feet, trying to gain distance.

The frog leaps again, a spear of red shooting out from its mouth. Before you can register what is happening you are being dragged across the rocks, your body entangled in a long, sticky tongue. You try and sever it, but a sudden jerk throws you forward, your feet flailing out from under you. In desperation, you swipe at the creature's legs, bright blood fountaining from a wound. The frog hops away, its tongue snapping back into its mouth.

Seizing your chance, you rush forward to press your attack – but the frog somersaults over your hasty swing, hopping to a nearby boulder then back to its island. With another gargling screech it spins to face you, beckoning you to follow. It is time to fight:

	Speed	*Brawn*	*Armour*	*Health*
Fisher king	8	6	5	80

Special abilities

- Jump around!: There are three islands in the pool – one to the north, one in the centre and one to the south. At the start of each combat round, decide which island you are going to jump to. Then roll a die to find out where the fisher king has jumped to – ⚀ or ⚁ the north island, ⚂ or ⚃ the centre island and ⚄ or ⚅ the south island. If you end up on the same island, then you can continue combat as normal, rolling for attack speed etc. If you are on different islands, then you cannot attack – and the fisher king immediately uses his 'tongue lashing' ability.

- Tongue lashing: Take a *speed* challenge. If you get 13 or less, then your hero is hit by the frog's sticky tongue, pulling you over onto its trident for 6 damage, ignoring *armour*. If you get 14 or more, then you have avoided his tongue attack. Once the *speed* challenge is complete (and any damage applied), the combat round automatically moves to the passive phase.

If you manage to defeat your island-hopping foe, turn to **575**.

409

You push open the iron door, the grimy water gushing around your legs as it spills out into the corridor beyond. After brushing the grime and dirt from your clothes, you take a moment to study your surroundings. The corridor is fashioned from black stone, smooth and without decoration. To your left it continues for several metres before ending in a set of worn stairs leading up to a decorative wooden door. To your right, there is an open metal grill, beyond which you can see a set of rusted-iron stairs spiralling down towards the sounds of buzzing, hammering machinery.

Will you:	
Take the stairs up?	417
Take the stairs down?	382

410

You leave the horses and continue on foot, clambering up the sheer slope to reach the causeway. Ventus leads at the head of the party, the white light from his fists helping to push back the lingering shadows of dawn. Behind him strides Benin, the priest. Since leaving the monastery, he has rarely spoken – his demeanour one of grim silences and thoughtful reflection. You and Bea bring up the rear, the pilgrim's chatter always seeking to lighten the mood.

'I don't think Duerdoun would make my top ten list of pilgrim spots,' she says, screwing up her face with distaste. 'First I thought it was just the smell. But now I think it's the dust. And the rocks. And the bones. A lot of bones. And that awful smell. . . . Oh, did I mention that already?'

As you pull yourself up onto the stone causeway, you get your first glimpse of the place known as Duerdoun. Your first impression is one of jagged black teeth, stabbing through the morning mist. The teeth are actually needles of rock, lining both sides of the causeway – some still intact, others broken and crumbling. They stretch away into the curling mist, to where you can dimly make out a temple-like building, carved into the side of a dark mountain.

'What was it used for?' you croak, choking on the black dust thrown up by the wind.

'It was an entrance way to a dwarf city,' explains Ventus, looking back over his shoulder. 'A place overrun with goblins and demons. It was sealed long ago – with good reason.'

Benin stops abruptly, raising a hand. You note his concern as the needle-like pillars either side of you start to glow with silvery-white runes. Bea draws her twin swords, falling into a crouch as their inscriptions dance with magic.

'There is evil here,' growls Ventus, his narrowed eyes scanning the swirling mist. 'Do not lose faith.' Turn to 392.

411

Once again, your concentrated attacks bring down the thorn colossus. Amongst its barbed remains you spy the following item, which you may carefully retrieve:

Providence
(necklace)
+1 brawn +1 magic
Ability: faith

Breathing heavily and aching from your wounds, you glance over at your companions, seeing that they are equally exhausted from the fight. The demon, however, remains unimpressed.

'Are we learning yet?' it asks in a mocking tone.

You struggle to answer, each lungful of air burning like fire. 'We're better than you think we are,' you manage to pant.

'No. You are not.' The demon shakes its head, dark scales scraping like knives. 'You are a disappointment to me.'

One of the charred roots lying next to you starts to twitch and shake. Then it slides away across the churned mud to join the other tentacle-like vines that are starting to coil together again, healing the giant monster.

Bea falls to her knees, sobbing. 'No … I can't do this. Not again …'

Something within Ventus snaps. The monk strides forward, his face a bitter storm of fury. 'I will be damned for this,' he bellows, bringing his fists down on the first of the demon's restraints. Both you and Bea race to his side.

'What are you doing? Stop!' Bea tugs on the monk's robe, but he ignores her protests. He moves around the dais, smashing his inscribed fists into the remaining iron rings.

'Yes,' snarls the demon, its breath quickening with excitement. 'At last!' Turn to 393.

412

At the other side of the hall you see the child watching you, his patchwork cloak glimmering amidst the curling smoke. Behind him is a glowing portal, identical to the others you have used to travel around the tower.

'You are good at my games,' grins the boy, scratching his chin. 'But my best game is yet to come. It's my favourite!'

'Where are the others?' you demand angrily, striding towards him. 'Enough of your games!'

'Ah, can't tell you that,' he smiles.

Suddenly the whole room starts to shake, rattling the metal walls. The child looks around in confusion. 'No! The tower … it's starting again … It wants to take us back!'

'Back where?' you yell, as debris starts to shift and slide across the hall. 'You mean the shroud?'

The child doesn't answer. Instead he turns and runs, disappearing through the glowing portal. You hurry after him, determined not to let him escape. Turn to 32.

413

Bill walks you over to the giant. 'He's yours for forty shinnies – and I'd say it's a good deal for that amount of muscle on your side.' The hunter nudges you, then points to the tree-sized club, resting next to one of the huts. 'Just remember – when he swings that ol' thing, keep your head down, pal. Wouldn't want to lose that pretty face, now.'

If you wish to hire Nelson, then the giant will provide you with the following, for 40 gold crowns:

- Big game hunter: Nelson will help you to fight a legendary monster. If you are defeated then Nelson will wander back to camp and you will have to hire him again if you wish to receive further aid.
- Nelson's column (mo): The giant's mighty club will add 3 to your damage score for the duration of the combat.

- Suicide swing (co): If you win a combat round, instead of rolling for damage as normal, you can use Nelson's *suicide swing*. Roll six damage dice. All ⚄ and ⚅ results are inflicted on your opponent. All results of ⚃ or less are inflicted on your hero. This damage ignores *armour* and cannot be avoided. This ability can only be used once per combat.

Remember, Nelson will only stay with you for *one* encounter. If you wish to use his services again, you must hire him for 40 gold crowns. When you have made your decision, you may explore the rest of the camp (turn to 744), or return to the quest map to continue your journey.

414

You charge forwards, your heightened reflexes helping you to dodge the barrage of flying debris. However, finding your opponent is proving to be more difficult. Your weapons repeatedly slash through empty air, a ghostly snigger always audible a second later from a different area of the chamber. The poltergeist is fast-moving and impossible to hit. You will have to resort to some other method of defeating it.

If you have the *Book of Binding*, you can try and use its powers to trap the spirit (turn to 266). If you wish to use your cloak (and risk damaging this item), you could use it to try and cover the poltergeist, in order to see it better (turn to 147) – or you could simply make a dash for the exit (turn to 29).

415

'Then kneel before me,' the old man rasps. 'And keep your hands steady. I am weary, as is my patience.' You quickly follow his instruction, kneeling beside the cushions and offering out your hands. The man fumbles at his side, producing a short metal rod from a pouch at his belt. He lifts it up before his pale sunken eyes, his lips twitching into a thin smile. 'Now, this will hurt …'

As the rod touches your flesh, you feel a hot searing pain punching through your body. It forces you to jerk backwards with an anguished cry. 'Hold still!' The abbot maintains a tight grasp on your wrist, his grip unnaturally strong for such a frail man. 'Suffering is part of faith.'

He continues to drag the rod across your skin, etching lines of holy script into the sizzling, blistered flesh. You can only watch, teeth gritted against the pain, as your hands are slowly covered by a bright white light. Turn to 502.

416

You find yourself in a small dank room, its walls and ceiling dripping with rust-coloured water. It has the appearance of a cell, with a barred window in the far wall and a pallet bed set underneath it. The mattress has been slashed to pieces, sawdust and cloth covering the floor. You also spot tufts of fur amongst the sodden debris.

A creature is shuffling back and forth across the room, head hung low. As your boot scrapes against the wet stone, the creature looks up suddenly. It is a bear – or some peculiar imitation of one – with a pointed black muzzle, round fluffy ears and buttons for eyes. It walks perfectly upright, its proportions almost human.

'My heart. Did you bring me my heart?' rasps the creature, its words burdened with pain and sorrow. It shifts around, revealing the gaping cavity in its chest. The fur has been torn or shredded apart, sawdust stuffing hanging loosely from the wound. 'He promised me a heart,' the bear moans sadly, shuffling towards you. 'All I ever wanted was a heart.'

If you have the *heart-shaped box* or *Dagona's locket*, turn to 387. Otherwise, turn to 434.

417

The centre of the door is carved to resemble a needle and thread, surrounded by a circle of nine stars. From somewhere in the distance you hear the faint echo of a child's laughter, followed by a woman's lingering scream. Worried that your companions are in danger you push open the door, keen to continue your search.

The room beyond is a high-vaulted chamber. White light pours in shafts through narrow arched windows, falling on a sumptuous array of fabrics, hanging from wooden frames. To one side of the room there is a large table, covered with scraps of cloth and what you assume are patterns, drawn out on parchment. Opposite is a row of shelves, with various pots and urns jumbled on them. A plain wooden door in the east wall stands slightly ajar, leading through into another passageway.

The child's laughter rings out once again. You turn on the spot, trying to discern its direction. 'Play my games!' titters the voice. 'Paper, scissors, stone! Paper, scissors, stone!'

Will you:

Examine the scraps of cloth?	51
Investigate the row of shelves?	349
Leave via the open door?	391

418

You lie in the mud, paralysed by fear and pain, as the demon prepares to end your life. For a fleeting second, you remember a vision from your time at Durnhollow: a black mountain erupting with fire. You, lying on your back amidst the flames and ashes while a demon stands over you, a huge runed blade gripped in its scaled hands.

You blink past the image, stiffening in horror as you realise that Cernos is that very same demon. But in this grim reality, there is no sword . . . only a fist full of dark fire.

A gunshot tears through the night. The demon flinches, staggering back slightly. Another gunshot follows, this one clearly connecting with something vital. The demon snarls in pain, whipping around to face its unseen tormentor. Gritting your teeth, you try and lift your head, struggling to gain a view of the battle.

'You are weak, Cernos,' cries a man's voice, edged like cold steel.

Swallowing back your nausea, you glimpse a man in a long grey coat and a broad-brimmed hat. He is striding purposefully towards the demon, unloading bullet after bullet into its scaled chest. With a final heart-stopping roar, the demon launches itself into the air, its huge wings beating a grey-black blur. The gunman fires another salvo, watching as the creature soars away into the night.

Wood and stone crunch beneath the stranger's boots as he holsters his pistols and walks casually towards you. When the man's shadowed face finally swings into view, you catch the glimmer of gold teeth, flashing in the moonlight. Then your strength gives out – and you let yourself fall back into the mud, and the cold, painful dark. Turn to 494.

419

Once inside the temple, you find that the debilitating presence has lifted. You can only assume that it was some spell or enchantment worked into the causeway, to turn back unwanted visitors.

Warily, you draw your weapons and advance slowly down the black-stone passage. It soon opens out into a vaulted chamber, its runed stonework illuminated by a huge shard of crystal hanging from the ceiling. The tip of the crystal points to a raised dais, where an upright sarcophagus breaks through the pale light. Concentric circles of runes radiate out from its base, carpeting the tiled floor in pulsing sigils of dark magic.

You catch the rustle of cloth and a serpentine hiss. As your eyes grow accustomed to the crystal's radiance, you see something moving within the confines of the sarcophagus.

'You did well to make it this far,' rasps a gravelly voice. A squat figure steps out from the stone coffin. The light makes it hard to pick out features, but you get the impression of a short deformed human, huddled in a cloak. A hood is pulled low over their face, its trim decorated with a band of shifting runes. 'Not even the great Allam could walk the causeway of Duerdoun.'

'Who are you?' you demand, trying to maintain a confident tone despite the sickening fear gripping your stomach.

'The custodian,' spits the voice. 'The sworn defender of the key. I lost it once – but never again!'

'You mean the relic?' you ask uncertainly. Then realisation dawns. 'Wait! You were the one who broke into the church vault – the one who cursed the bishop and the thief!'

You glimpse jagged sharp teeth, leering from the darkness. 'I had an errand – one of great import. The inquisitors took it before I could return. It matters not, they have already paid the price.'

'Why is this relic so important?' you persist. 'What does it do?'

The figure throws back its arms, revealing scaled hands twisted and misshapen into claws. 'These matters are not of your concern, youngling. You will soon join the other witless thieves who tried to steal my charge – who now serve *me* in eternal damnation! '

There is a flash of dark light, then the figure is gone. Behind you, there is a sudden rush of wind. Something slams into your back, blowing you forwards into the chamber. As you land in a roll, the runes on the floor suddenly spit and hiss, their dark glow turning to a bright blood red. You rise just in time to see the squat figure running at you, a sword gripped in one hand and a talon-like wand in the other. From beneath the cowl, two serpent-like eyes glitter with malice.

You must now fight this deadly adversary:

	Speed	*Magic*	*Armour*	*Health*
Custodian	5	4	3	50
Forty thieves (*)	5	5	2	40

Special abilities

- Reanimator: (*) As soon as the custodian is reduced to half his *health* or less, he immediately summons the spirits of his previous enemies to attack you. While you fight these forty thieves, the custodian takes refuge in the stone coffin, healing 2 *health* at the end of each combat round (this also removes any passive effects he is currently inflicted with). During this phase, the custodian cannot be attacked. You must defeat the thieves before the custodian will rejoin the fight with his restored *health*. (Note: the custodian cannot raise his *health* beyond its starting value of 50.) The *reanimator* ability can only be used once.
- Hex of pain: At the end of each combat round you must lose 1 *health* from the magic runes etched into the floor of the chamber.

If you are able to defeat this deadly foe, turn to 493.

420

The three ancestral spirits whirl around the shattered weapon, remaking it anew. If you are a warrior, turn to **461**. If you are a rogue, turn to **526**. If you are a mage, turn to **514**.

421

Bill opens a trunk and lifts out a sun-faded jerkin and a pair of muddied boots. 'Don't let appearances deceive you,' he says, noting your look of disappointment. 'Both these are enchanted – got me out of a few scrapes.' He places them down on the hammock, then continues over to the window. 'If neither of them take your fancy, then I suppose I could always talk to Nelson, see if he'd be up for parting with his club. I'd wager you have the strength for it.' He glances back at you, grinning through his beard. 'And the lunacy.'

You may now choose one of the following special rewards:

Nelson's column	**Safari cams**	**Bug grinders**
(main hand: club)	(chest)	(feet)
+1 speed +3 brawn	+1 speed +2 armour	+1 speed +2 brawn
Ability: knockdown	Ability: vanish	Ability: compulsion

Bill also hands you a purse, containing 100 gold crowns. After making your exchange, you bid the hunter farewell and leave. You may now explore the rest of the camp (turn to **744**) or return to the quest map.

422

The cramped room is awash with a feverish red light, emanating from the open forges ranged along the walls. At the centre of the room is a black anvil, where a hulking brute is beating at a sheet of metal with a giant hammer. It looks like an ogre, but its skin is black and scaled, its crimson eyes glowing as bright as the forge fires.

The creature senses you, looking up from its work with a rumbling growl. Then it lifts the hammer across its broad shoulders and starts to advance. It is time to fight:

	Speed	*Brawn*	*Armour*	*Health*
The Forger	4	3	4	40

Special abilities

- Flame wrapped: At the start of each combat round, roll a die. If the result is ⚂ or less then a flame sprite leaps out from one of the furnaces, wrapping itself around the hammer and imbuing it with fire. This adds 1 to the Forger's *brawn* each time.
- Knockdown: If you suffer health damage from the Forger, you are knocked off your feet, lowering your *speed* by 1 for the next combat round.

If you manage to defeat this monstrous foe, turn to 23.

423

You awake to find your arms and legs bound in wraps of cloth. Everything is moving, swaying – you are being carried or dragged through a forest. You catch the smell of pine and the sound of boots sliding on loose stone. You try and turn your head, but the constant swaying makes you feel sick. Closing your eyes, you slip back into tormented dreams, filled with grasping thorns and dark demons.

When next you wake, you are shivering. The cold must have woken you. Above your head there is a low ceiling of rough-hewn rock, pockmarked with fissures. Struggling to recall what happened, you push yourself onto your elbows, surprised to see bandages wound tight around your chest.

The rustle of cloth. A scuff of a boot.

You look around to see a girl – around ten years old. She is dressed in filthy-looking rags, her bright eyes narrowed as she glares at you from the shadows.

'Sanchen,' she whispers, chewing at the ends of her pony tail.

A quick glance at your surroundings confirms that you are in a small cave – part of some larger underground network. A narrow shaft of light breaks through a cleft in the ceiling, illuminating your makeshift bed and a table covered with ointments and poultices. As you rise to your feet, the girl gives a squeal and runs off, taking flight down a side tunnel. You hear voices, then footsteps. A woman appears, ducking to enter the cave. Her blond hair is braided, her simple dress smeared with clay and dirt.

'You are awake,' she says, talking slowly and in a thick accent. 'The spirits favour you.'

'Where am I?' you croak, wincing as you try and stand.

The woman moves to your side, offering support. 'You came with Damaris. You're the Sanchen. Our guest of honour. If your strength has returned, then you should join us.'

Memories suddenly come flooding back – the fight on the moors, the Wiccan woman with feathers in her hair. You glance down at your bandages, remembering the blast of magic from Benin's staff. 'You … you're a Wiccan?' you ask, startled.

'My name is Eva.' She smiles. 'Come. Damaris wants to speak with you.' Turn to 485.

424

The witchfinder frowns, as if the question has caught him off guard. 'You mean the female and the warrior?' He shrugs his shoulders, as if the matter is of no consequence. 'They fled the field of battle, both of them – assumed you were dead I think, and with two demons ripping shreds out of each other, I don't entirely blame them.'

You shake your head, the full weight of what happened suddenly crashing down around you in a jumble of frightening, confusing memories. 'They were hoping to find answers – something to help with their war. They never guessed …' You choke on your words, torn by grief. 'A demon … the forest was a prison. The custodian tried to warn me.' You meet the witchfinder's gaze. 'What will happen now? To Carvel? To the moorlands?'

Virgil brushes your concern away with a nonchalant snort. 'The Church and the Wiccans … that is not a squabble to be solved by the likes of you or I. Besides, we have greater concerns now. Their bickering has only served to put the entire world in danger. By opening up the forest, they have released a most terrible evil – one that must be stopped before it is too late.'

Return to 494 to ask another question, or turn to 433 to continue.

425

The tree house has a low ceiling, which you discover quite quickly when you knock your head several times on its slanting beams. Reminding yourself that this was built for children, you stoop your shoulders in order to explore the interior. In the middle of the room is a tree-stump table, surrounded by stools and benches. You spot three names carved into the surface of the table – *Jacob*, *Joss* and *Adam*. The last name has been crossed out. At the other side of the room is a trunk. You open it up, to find a childlike stash of odds and ends inside. Most of these are toys, like wooden soldiers or balls and hoops, but you also discover some potions and ointments, which you may take:

Mother's medicine	Jacob's special mix	Secret brew
(2 uses)	(2 uses)	(1 use)
(backpack)	(backpack)	(backpack)
Use any time in combat to heal 4 *health*	Use any time in combat to raise your *speed* by 1 for one combat round	Use any time in combat to raise your *brawn* by 2 for one combat round

With nothing else of interest in the tree house, you climb back down the tree – stepping through the magic portal to continue your journey. Turn to 46.

426

Damaris scowls, her fists clenching at her side. 'They came from the east, with their swords and their pride and their infallible faith. They had no care for my people or the old magic. If we didn't renounce our ways and worship their false god then they imprisoned us, or put our homes to the torch. Our most sacred sites were destroyed or defiled.

Those of us that didn't surrender were forced to flee – to become what you see now, stragglers with no place to call home.' Damaris takes a deep breath, calming her anger. 'If you poke a hive for long enough, you're going to get stung.' She glares at you defiantly. 'We intend to be the swarm that brings them to their knees.'

Turn to 126 to ask Damaris another question.

427

A portal flickers into being and from it an immense creature steps out into the chamber. Fashioned from chunks of black rock, the giant has a roughly humanoid appearance, its stumpy arms ending in boulder-sized fists. With a grating rumble, it stomps towards you, an angry fire burning from its hollow eye sockets. You must now fight:

	Speed	*Brawn*	*Armour*	*Health*
Rocco	5	4	4	35

Special abilities

Body of rock: Your opponent is immune to *bleed*.

If you have one of the following and wish to use it, turn to the relevant entry number: *metal soldier* (turn to 460), *paper soldier* (turn to 451), *rock soldier* (turn to 407). Otherwise, you must fight this opponent yourself. If you win, you must continue with the *health* that you have remaining (turn to 444). If you are defeated, turn to 464.

428

Damaris strides over to the creature. She makes a quick inspection of the body before turning away in revulsion.

'The dwarf ...?' asks Murlic, keeping to a safe distance.

The witch nods, her eyes scanning the rest of the chamber. 'Once perhaps ... ah, I believe that is what we came for.' She crosses the room to a large stone casket, set within a circle of runes. They still pulse with a faint glow, but at a gesture from the witch they crackle and spark and then fade to nothing. 'I've broken the weaves.' She puts her hands to the heavy lid. 'Conall.'

The giant warrior moves to her side, putting his immense strength to the task. The rumbling of stone is magnified a hundred-fold, as the lid is slowly pushed back. At last the interior is revealed – and both Damaris and Conall stagger backwards, covering their faces.

You can feel it from where you are standing. A fierce heat washing through the chamber. But whereas the others seem to be driven back by its intensity, you find yourself unmoved. Instead, you cautiously advance, much to the surprise of Damaris who is cowering behind her raised arms.

'Stay back!' she cries in warning. 'The magic … it will burn you!'

You are already standing over the casket, looking down at the hammer-shaped object resting on a bed of glowing coals. Somehow you can feel the heat prickling against your skin, but there is no pain. You reach into the casket and take hold of the hammer, your hands settling around the grip. You smell burning flesh as your skin comes into contact with the super-heated metal, but it feels distant – like you are looking down at someone else's body, not your own. You lift the relic, admiring the intricately carved head-piece.

'What is it?' snarls Murlic, backing away to the edge of the chamber.

Conall is urging Damaris to do the same, but the witch pays him no mind, her amber eyes wide and staring. 'It's powerful … very powerful …' she gasps.

Suddenly, the panels that encase the head of the relic snap open and a bright white light pours forth, filling the room with dazzling radiance. You lift the object above your head, holding it aloft like a torch, as its light blazes like the heart of a sun.

'This is demon magic!' growls Murlic, shading his eyes.

Damaris is uncommonly quiet as she regards you with a mixture of awe and fascination.

'This will take us into the forest,' you state, looking up at the relic. 'This is the key.'

Damaris removes her cloak, gesturing for you to wrap the relic within its folds. 'Then the forest is our next destination,' she asserts. 'We should prepare. What we find there will change the course of this war. Of that, I am certain!' (Congratulations, you have retrieved the relic from Duerdoun. Return to the quest map to continue your journey.)

429

'Dustin was only a child when he was brought here – a monk found him wandering the Pilgrim's Road. Since then, the monastery has sheltered him; protected him from a world that would label him an outcast.' The dean looks fondly on the old man, who is now tapping the sides of his head, making childish whining noises as the scribe urges him to continue. 'They wouldn't know he was special. It took Dustin only a week to read all the books in this library ...'

You glance around at the endless rows of dusty tomes. There must be hundreds and hundreds of books packed inside the library. 'That's impossible,' you snort, shaking your head. 'It would take a lifetime and even then ...'

The dean smiles. 'That's only part of his gift. Dustin can recount every word – from any book, from any page. He remembers everything he sees. He doesn't always understand it – but he sees the words. He sees the numbers. He remembers *everything*.'

Will you:

Ask about 'the truth' they seek?	394
Ask about the war with the Wiccans?	491
End the conversation?	496

430

The accursed spear quivers and shakes, its runes suddenly emitting a blood-red glow. From the corpse a spectral light rises up into the air, forming the ghostly shape of a serpent. Then it sweeps towards the spear, spiralling around the blade and shaft. The runes flash and spark as the spear continues to tremble – then, with a rattling hiss, the spirit-light is gone, absorbed into the weapon's dark runes.

Congratulations, you have gained *the spirit of the serpent*. (Make a note of this on your hero sheet.) You may now return to the quest map to continue your adventure.

431

With Anse's help you are finally able to extinguish the elemental's fury. Among its smouldering remains, you discover one of the following special rewards:

Furnace fire	Firewalker's boots	After burn
(main hand: wand)	(feet)	(ring)
+1 speed +1 magic	+1 speed +1 brawn	+1 armour
Ability: sear	Ability: turn up the heat	Ability: turn up the heat

You turn back to the hall, intending to help Joss, but the chasm has expanded, cleaving the hall in two. As the violent seizures continue to shake the chamber, more of the stone breaks away – reducing the hall to a series of crumbling islands. There is no sign of Joss or Maximus – or the ladder that Jacob used to escape. Turn to 469.

432

'Watch the shadows,' warns Boom Mamba, his eyes sliding sideways from pillar to pillar. 'Umbra is a shadow spirit. Fastest of them all.'

You advance warily along the promenade, moving from bright sunlight to cool shadow as you pass each of the columns. The shaman has held back, crouching down next to his staff. 'I start the enchantment – so we trap Umbra when he die.' He closes his eyes, mumbling words in a strange tongue.

Then you catch something blurring at the corner of your eye – a cloaked figure moving impossibly fast. It hops from one shadow to the next, making barely a whisper of noise. It is closing quickly on the shaman, black claws distending from its fists.

Shouting for the spirit's attention you charge forwards, trying to head it off. But as you swing your weapons, you find yourself hitting only air – until your wild swing takes a clump of stone out of one of the pillars.

A rustle of movement to your side.

You twist just in time to parry the shadow spirit's attack. Then it has gone again, flitting away from one pillar to the next. As you scan the ever-shifting shadows, you realise that this will prove a challenging battle. It is time to fight:

	Speed	*Brawn*	*Armour*	*Health*
Umbra	6	5	4	60

Special abilities

- It's behind you: At the end of each combat round, roll a die. If the result is ⚂ or less then Umbra has shifted behind you delivering a devastating backstab attack. This causes 10 damage to your hero (you may use *armour* to absorb some/all of this damage).

If you manage to defeat this elusive trickster, turn to **480**. If you are defeated, you may return to **510** to choose a different foe to battle.

433

You spot your weapons and belongings in a corner of the room. Wincing against the pain, you slide your legs off the bed, your eyes starting to sting from the incense burning on the nearby table.

'I have to go . . .' you insist, pulling away the rest of the blankets.

'No,' states Virgil firmly. He looks to his companion. 'Would you leave us, Modoc?'

The tattooed man bows, before crossing the room to the single exit. When he opens the door a blast of sand and dust billows into the room, carried on a hot wind. You glimpse a barren plain, scattered with gorse and weathered rock. Then the man steps out and closes the door behind him.

You look back at the witchfinder uncertainly. 'Are you holding me prisoner?'

He folds his arms. 'I'll get to the point. And I suggest you listen. Cernos has gone south. I can't be sure what his motives are – but he is headed into the Terral Jungle. And that is where I am sending you.'

'Sending me?' you retort angrily.

'I said listen!' snaps the witchfinder. 'There's a connection now, between you and the demon.' He gestures to your scarring. 'And that makes you the perfect demon hunter.'

You start to protest but Virgil halts you with a raised palm. 'Most prophets are also empaths. You are susceptible to the thoughts and impressions of others, picking up on emotions ... ideas. I won't deny you have some talent at seeing future events – but what led you to that forest was the demon itself. Like Allam before you – the demon can impress upon you its own thoughts, guiding you, making you see what it wants you to see.' The witchfinder walks over to a desk, where a pile of papers lie scattered next to a leather bag. 'I daresay your own powers resisted it at times ... but now, you and the demon have a link. And that will help you to find Cernos and discover his intentions.'

Virgil grabs the leather bag, his eyes falling on one of the sheets of parchment. 'I have secured you passage on a merchant vessel. It is heading south to Sheril and will be calling at the Emerald Isle on the way – your destination.'

'Don't I have a say in this?' you snap irritably. 'What if I just told you to—'

'Ah, I wouldn't do that if I was you.' Virgil tosses the leather bag onto the bed. 'You see, part of the demon is inside you now. Given time, you will start to change ... to become just like him. A demon.'

Your eyes widen in horror.

'But you can save yourself. Defeat the demon and take its heart. With it, Modoc will be able to do the necessary enchantments to halt the ... changes.'

You take the bag and lift it onto your lap. 'And what is this?' you ask, your anger having frayed to a surly resentment.

'Some items to help you on your way. Sadly, I cannot accompany you – I must travel east to the capital and speak with the council. Avian Dale will need to know what happened. Then I will rejoin you, if I can – hopefully with aid.'

'Avian Dale?' The name sounded familiar. 'He was the one who wanted me released. From Durnhollow.'

Virgil nods. 'He's had his eye on you for some time.'

You look up. 'I'm nothing special.'

'Oh really?' He raises an eyebrow. 'Visions of the future don't make you special? Look, Avian is one of the good guys, trust me. A powerful mage – and not someone you want to get on the wrong side of. Understand?'

You glance down at the bag. Opening it up, you discover a purse and a number of leather gourds inside. You have gained 30 gold crowns and may take any/all of the following:

Snakebite shake	**Gourd of healing**	**Elixir of invisibility**
(1 use)	(1 use)	(1 use)
(backpack)	(backpack)	(backpack)
Use any time in combat to remove one *venom* effect from your hero	Use any time in combat to restore 6 *health*	Special ability: vanish

You close the bag with a sigh of resignation. 'I don't have a choice in this, do I?'

'No,' replies the witchfinder firmly. 'But remember this – Cernos is weak. The dwarven runes that were branded into his irons will have drained him of much of his power. He'll have gone to ground, regaining his strength, waiting for his moment – and that gives you a chance.' He offers out his hand. 'May the One God protect you.'

You ignore his gesture, pushing yourself off the bed and back onto unsteady feet. You wait for the pain and nausea to subside before fixing him with a determined stare. 'So, when do I get started?' (Turn to 773 to begin Act 2 of your adventure.)

434

The bear lifts one of its big padded paws and points it at your chest. 'The toymaker promised me a heart. If you won't give it to me, then I'm going to take yours!' With a fearsome roar the creature lunges forward, claws looking to rip out your heart. It is time to fight:

	Speed	*Brawn*	*Armour*	*Health*
Cuddles	5	3	3	40

Special abilities

- Piercing claws: The bear's attacks ignore your *armour*.
- Bleed: After Cuddles makes a successful attack that causes *health* damage, you must take a further point of damage at the end of each combat round.

If you manage to defeat this heartless teddy bear, turn to 105.

435

'Sweet child,' echoes a woman's voice, soft and seductive. 'Your memories were ... most nourishing ...' You spin around, to see a black hooded figure swathed in shadow.

'Who are you?' you demand angrily, squinting in the murky half-light.

The woman pulls back her hood to reveal a hideous, monstrous face. The flesh is white and scaly, like a fish, swollen outwards to form a wide, sucker-like mouth. 'I have fed on your mind, prophet,' whispers the voice in your head. 'Now I will feed on your flesh!' If you have the word *scars* on your hero sheet, turn to 673. Otherwise, turn to 572.

436

You hurry through the portal. For a second you experience a lurching, dizzying sensation, like falling, then you find yourself stumbling forwards into a narrow stone passageway. The air is cold and musty, a stark contrast to the blazing heat of the courtyard. Sadly, there is no sign of your companions – you can only assume that the doors they chose must have taken them to different parts of the tower. And as for Anse ... you hope that the paladin was able to escape from the fiery demon before it was too late.

Behind you is a smooth wall of black stone. With no other choice but forward, you warily advance along the passageway. As you progress, you become aware of a constant rumbling sound reverberating through the rock. Every so often there is a thunderous clunk, like something suddenly locking into place. Then the rumbling starts again. You wonder if it might be the tower itself, moving and rearranging itself in some strange fashion. It is a thought that brings little comfort.

After several hundred metres you come to a junction. Ahead, the passage ends in an archway, beyond which you can see a room bathed in firelight. To your right, a smaller side passage leads to a plain wooden door.

Will you:	
Investigate the room?	422
Try the wooden door?	123

437

'You born yesterday, fool?' the dark-skinned hunter scowls. 'Tigris are worth good bounty back in the capital. Skin, bones – they'll take it all. And better alive.'

The weasel quickly wipes the wet hair from his eyes, circling you warily. 'We don't wanna lose her, so get on yer way. That babe is worth more than anything you could dream of – and as for her, might skin the spiteful beast, make her pay good for this.' He pats his leg where a bandana scarf has been used to poorly bind a wound. 'I ain't going back to the buckmaster empty-handed, so you either move or I swear I'll blow yer outta the way.'

Will you:	
Attack the men?	521
Offer to help them?	570

438

A well-timed blow sends Andos tumbling backwards, giving you a chance to turn your attention to the spell books. Within moments, they have been reduced to shredded ribbons.

'No!' Andos crawls towards them, trying to catch their remains as they are lifted up on the breeze. You stand over him, your weapons raised.

'Leave him be, Xenos! You are defeated!'

The boy's body suddenly goes into spasm, a white foam drooling from the corners of his mouth. Then he drops to the ground, twitching and pale. You kneel by his side, putting a hand to his shoulder.

'Andos? Can you hear me?'

Suddenly, he lurches forward, coughing and spluttering.

'What happened to me?' he gasps, wiping spittle and sand from his chin. 'You beat me up!'

'No, I freed you, Andos.' You lift up the torn cover of one of the books. 'There was some demon or spirit inside you – they were using you to get to these.'

The boy sits up, his ginger hair matted with dust. 'Bloomin' 'eck, that'll teach me. I've felt odd for days – all started when I borrowed Runtis' eye piece. I used it to read some of them inscriptions, on a rock at the other side of the isle. Then I got the headaches and . . .' He plucks one of the charred papers out of the air, studying its strange runes with a puzzled expression. 'I suppose I owes you an apology. Never meant for all this to happen.'

'Do you still have the eye piece?' you ask with interest. 'Perhaps I can safeguard it.'

'Yeah, yeah – take it, I don't want it!' The boy reaches into the pocket of his breeches and pulls out a golden-rimmed monocle. He stuffs it into your hand before clambering to his feet.

'I better get back before old misery-guts sees I'm gone.' After casting a frightened glance around the clearing, he scarpers into the forest.

You sit down to examine the monocle. If you are a mage, turn to 622. Otherwise, after much head-scratching, you accept that its power is beyond your understanding. Thankfully, Yootha at the trading post is willing to offer you 100 gold crowns to take it off your hands. When you have made your decision, return to the quest map to continue your journey.

439

You unwrap the grisly trophies and hold them out for the hunter. Bill picks up the jaguar paw, turning it over to inspect the long yellowed claws. 'The mighty Gheira, eh?' He shakes his head in bewilderment. 'And you've got more?' He looks down at the spider's eye and the snake fang. 'Anansi and Kaala. Never thought I'd see the day. Here, come with me.'

The hunter leads you into his hut, where a number of trunks and baskets are piled up next to a hammock. He takes a key from his pocket and moves over to the nearest of the trunks. 'I'm a man of my word. And I promised you gold and treasure. So, let's see what we got . . .'

If you are a rogue, turn to 499. If you are a warrior, turn to 421. If you are a mage, turn to 369.

440

You emerge in a small room with a square pedestal at its centre. Resting on it is a gold staff and a roll of parchment. As you step towards it, you hear a child's laughter coming from above. 'Time to play my favourite game!'

Glancing up, you see the boy is now standing on a balcony. He is raised up on tiptoe in order to see over the railing.

'Paper, scissors, stone!' he calls excitedly.

A sudden tremor causes the tower to shake, its foundations groaning as if in pain. The boy's grin is suddenly replaced by a petulant frown. 'No, not yet! I want to play!'

There is another quake, more extreme this time, shaking flakes of mortar loose from the walls. With a shriek the boy turns and hurries away, disappearing from sight.

With no other choice, you quickly examine the objects on the podium. Unfurling the scroll, you see that it contains a simple message: *Use the staff and follow my rules. Create your warriors, with the following tools:*

Soldiers:	Materials:
Metal	*nuts and bolts, enchanted iron, can of oil*
Paper	*parchment, magic ink, extra-sticky glue*
Rock	*stonecutter's tools, diamonds, extra-sticky glue*

You pick up the staff, seeing that it has a number of glyphs carved into its length. When you pass your hand over these, they flicker with magic. You reread the message, realising that the boy wants you to create a set of magical soldiers using certain materials. If you have the relevant materials to create a soldier, then you can craft it – watching with surprise as the staff brings your silent automaton to life. Make a note of the warriors that you are able to make (you must also remove the relevant materials from your hero sheet).

When your work is done, turn to 427.

441

By drinking the *saint's blessing*, you may also remove your hex. This will give you access to all of your abilities once again. However, if you are carrying the *glaive of souls* this weapon will automatically shatter and you will no longer be able to use it. Turn to 374.

442

First there is confusion. Then chaos. Through the rain and smoke you see brown shapes hurtling across the hills, moving with unnatural speed. There is the crunch of bones and the flash of magic as they collide with the Wiccans. One warrior goes flying past you, smashing into the side of the wagon. A smoking hole has been punched straight through their rusted armour. You glimpse a bald-headed man in brown robes go blurring past, his glowing fists smashing into another warrior and sending them flying backwards, as if they had been hit by the force of a hammer.

'Just in time,' grins Ventus. The monk springs into the air, his body twisting around to deliver a kick to the Wiccan giant. Conall staggers back, swiping at the air with his axes. But he is too slow – the monk has already slipped behind him, delivering a flurry of punches that lift the giant off his feet. With a roar he crashes down onto his stomach, rolling to parry the next incoming attack.

Meanwhile, Bea has sped forward, charging the rogue with the pointed teeth. He ducks and darts, moving gracefully around her strikes, his glowing daggers seeking to reach past her guard.

Another explosion sends clots of earth showering into the sky.

The Wiccans are already falling back as the monks spill through their ranks like a fast-moving river, their glowing limbs spinning and twisting in an endless blur of light. The feathered woman strides towards you, her expression as cold and bleak as the moorland. 'Tell me prophet, do you see how this will end?'

You shake your head, taking a step back. 'I'm no prophet.'

'Liar!' she snaps. 'What have the visions told you? Tell me!'

You continue to protest. 'I have seen nothing! Nothing that makes any sense …'

Suddenly, there is a clatter of wheels on the track. You both turn to see a cart rattling towards you. Several riders are galloping ahead of it. Their leader is a young man in white robes, his hands gripping a pale staff. You recognise him instantly.

'Benin!'

If you have the word *hallowed* or *prevail* on your hero sheet, turn to 193. Otherwise, turn to 45.

443

Quest: City of the damned

Your weapons blur, cutting a bright latticework of magic as they cleave through bone and sinew. The groans of the undead ring in your ears, their ancient sword blades clattering off your armour. The mob is endless, but you have no fear – only an impatient anger, driving you onwards with unyielding fury.

The demon is here and nothing will stand in your way.

A sword whips down, cutting through your clothing and hitting the hard scales beneath. They are like diamond now, turning the blade and wrenching it from the undead's grasp. For a moment you glare into his face, your battle-crazed eyes holding each other's stare. Then you bring your weapons down, smashing through the mouldered bones – aware that this is not a warrior you face, but a craftsman, the cloth of his tunic decorated with geometric designs. What magic, what curse, would drive him and his people to become such monsters?

You break from the throng of bodies, your powerful blows severing spines and slicing through bone. Since passing the perimeter walls the undead have assailed you every step of the way, swarming like ants from the ruined buildings – but, as always, they are slow and uncoordinated, most left trailing behind as you maintain a fast pace, determined to catch up with . . .

A flash. Clawed hands smash through pottery. Stones are hurled against a wall, shattering into jagged fragments. The shadow of a demon wavers in the half-light.

You stagger, caught off guard by the staccato images. Blind, you blunder into the path of an armoured champion, his tarnished breastplate sagging off his rotten body. Clutched in his hands is a bronze broadsword, which he brings around in a mighty blow.

Magic blasts against a door, breaking it from its frame. Dust plumes from the ceiling, obscuring the passage beyond.

You parry the blow, metal clanging against metal. The force sends a painful jolt through your body, throwing you sideways. A hand grasps you around the throat, nails digging into the scaled skin.

A throne room. The mosaic tiles are broken – shattered. A statue of a woman. Beautiful and delicate. 'Nephele,' cries a voice. Guttural. Hoarse. The claws strike the statue, severing the head clean from its shoulders.

You blink, trying to clear your head – struggling to focus on the battle. The champion has his sword raised, ready to bring it down. More hands are grappling at you, trying to drag you back into their midst . . .

'Where is it?' Eyes rove back and forth. 'The key! Where did they put it?'

The sword comes down, the warrior emitting a hoarse gasp, bones scraping and creaking with the effort.

A balcony, high above the ruined city. 'Foolish dwarves! They can't keep me from my birth right.' A pause. 'What? Get out of my head, prophet! You should not have come here. You are not fit to carry my blood!'

A fresh wave of anger surges through your body, sparking something deep inside – something bestial and savage. You wrestle free, twisting away as the sword comes down. It all seems to happen in slow motion, as if time has become distorted. Everything sharpens into focus – the dust motes dancing through the air, the bristly hairs on the arms of the undead warrior, the sun glinting off his dented helm. Then time speeds up, rushing in once again, as you smash your weapons straight through his armour, punching through to the other side.

Then you are running, feet gliding over the white sand of the courtyard – sand that must have been hauled here from some distant beach. You leap into the air, alighting on a curved wall, then leap again, to land amongst the tangled undergrowth of an enclosed garden. The wailing cries of the undead continue to echo across the ruined city – their scrabbling hands at the wall testament to their frustrated efforts to reach you. Turn to 568.

444

The portal reappears, releasing another creature into the chamber. Your eyes follow as it tumbles across the ground, its body looking like a crumpled mass of parchment. The instant it rolls to a halt the odd creation springs into the air, unfolding itself into a paper-thin warrior. Instead of hands, it has curved paper scythes, looking as wickedly sharp as any knife. You must now fight:

	Speed	*Brawn*	*Armour*	*Health*
Papyrus	5	4	3	30

Special abilities

Body of paper: Papyrus is immune to *bleed*.

If you have one of the following and wish to use it, turn to the relevant entry number: *metal soldier* (turn to 6), *paper soldier* (turn to 128), *rock soldier* (turn to 173). Otherwise, you must fight this opponent yourself. If you win, you must continue with the *health* that you have remaining (turn to 208). If you are defeated, turn to 464.

445

'Sweet children,' echoes a woman's voice, soft and seductive. 'Your memories were ... most nourishing ...' You both spin around, to see a black hooded figure standing in the shadows.

'Who are you?' you demand angrily, squinting in the murky half-light.

The woman pulls back her hood to reveal a hideous, monstrous face. The flesh is white and scaly, like a fish, protruding outwards into a lipless sucker-like mouth. 'I have fed on your minds,' whispers the voice in your head. 'Now, I will feed on your flesh!' If you have the word *scars* on your hero sheet, turn to 463. Otherwise, turn to 505.

446

The female warrior takes up one of the bowls, then gestures for you to remove your clothing. Feeling somewhat bashful, you raise your hands and back away – but the disapproving stares from the other warriors forces you to reconsider. Not wishing to offend, you remove your armour and watch as the female dips her fingers into the bowl and proceeds to paint the glimmering runes across your skin.

If you wish, you may now learn the brigand career. The brigand has the following abilities:

War paint (mo): The runes on your body give you greater protection and strength. You may raise your *brawn* or *armour* score by 3 for one combat round. You can only use *war paint* once per combat.
Pillage (pa): Each time you win a combat, roll two dice and automatically receive that amount of gold as a reward. This is in addition to any other gold or treasure you might receive.

After thanking your fellow warriors, you turn your attention back to the cave. Turn to 485.

447

As your blows rain down on the giant, Black Patch runs in behind, his sharp claws slicing across the back of the hunter's legs. With a groan of pain the giant staggers sideways then topples forward, no longer able to support himself. He crashes through one of the wooden huts, the splintered wood staking him like a bed of nails.

Searching the body, you find 50 gold crowns and one of the following rewards:

Nelson's column	**The nosepicker**	**Scarlet hunter**
(main hand: club)	(left hand: wand)	(left hand: dagger)
+1 speed +3 brawn	+2 speed +2 magic	+2 speed +2 brawn
Ability: knockdown	Ability: bleed	Ability: critical strike
(requirement: warrior)		(requirement: rogue)

With the giant defeated, victory is now looking assured. Turn to 466.

448

Your choice was a bad one. The metal monster cuts and dices your soldier to pieces, stomping their remains into the ground as it continues to advance. (Remove your soldier from your hero sheet. Then return to 208 to fight this monster yourself.)

449

The monkey temple has bested you. Remember, you can attempt this difficult challenge at any time during Act 2 of your adventure. If you wish to try to assault the temple again, turn to 596. If you wish to continue your journey across the dark interior, turn to 667. If you have already completed the dark interior, you may return to the quest map instead.

450

The accursed spear quivers and shakes, its runes suddenly emitting a blood-red glow. From the corpse a spectral light rises up into the air, forming the ghostly shape of a spider. Then it sweeps towards the spear, spiralling around the blade and shaft. The runes flash and spark as the spear continues to tremble – then, with a screeching cry, the spirit-light is gone, absorbed into the weapon's dark runes.

Congratulations, you have gained *the spirit of the spider.* (Make a note of this on your hero sheet.) You may now return to the quest map to continue your adventure.

451

You send your paper soldier forward. The rock monster attempts to smash it with its mighty boulder-fists, but the paper soldier simply folds beneath the blows, rising up again afterwards to press its attack. You notice that its paper cuts are not penetrating the beast's rock armour, but your soldier is holding its attention, allowing you to move behind it and deliver a fatal, killing blow. Congratulations, you have chosen well and defeated the rock monster. (Remove the *paper soldier* from your hero sheet.) Then turn to 444.

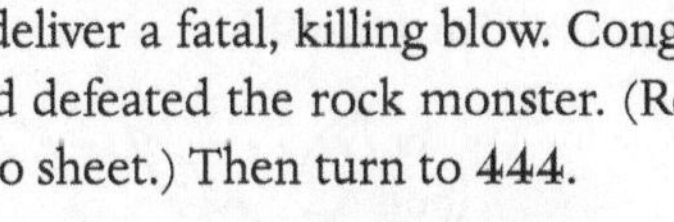

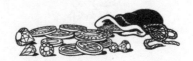

452

The white tigris grunts, turning his back on you. 'This skin not worthy of the Sheva. Take this one to the marsh. We are done here.'

The white tigris depart in silence, heading back into the dark forest. Scar-face walks over and places a paw on your shoulder. 'You kin now. I believe the great spirit, Shonac, sent you to fight for us.'

The leader, Grey-hair, watches you from the rock shelf. 'We welcome you to Shara Khana, bright claw. The journey across the marsh has many dangers. Prepare yourself, we leave at first light.'

Will you:

Ask about the name, Shara Khana?	358
Ask about Shonac, the great spirit?	334
Leave for the marsh?	722

453

You believe that the demon speaks the truth – without its aid, the thorn monster will continue to regenerate, wearing you and your companions down with its relentless attacks.

'I will be damned for this,' you bellow, bringing your weapons down on the first of the demon's restraints. Ventus and Bea race to your side.

'What are you doing? Stop!' Bea pulls on your sleeve, trying to drag you away. You ignore her protests, moving quickly around the dais to smash the remaining iron rings.

'One God protect us,' growls Ventus. 'Hold now! This is madness!'

'No,' snarls the demon, its breath quickening with excitement. 'This is your salvation!' Turn to 393.

454

Bertie shakes his head sadly. 'Them pictures are those that have gone missing – out in the jungle. A few of 'em were explorers, looking for lost cities and treasure, but the rest are just kids – eager for adventure. Come here with their backpacks and a compass and think they can just go off in the jungle like it's some walk in the woods.' He jerks a thumb towards the assortment of faces, all beaming back at you with innocent smiles. 'Those come from the families. They get likenesses done, just in case anyone finds them . . . like there'd be anything left to find.'

You can't help but be concerned by the sheer number of missing persons displayed on the board. Bertie pushes his hat back to wipe at his brow. 'I knows what brings them here – and what leads them where they shouldn't.' He glances around quickly, then beckons you to step closer. 'There's a story amongst the backpackers, more a legend they say, about a place they call "the cove". It's meant to be paradise, secluded – perfect white beaches, coral reefs, clear blue waters, you get the picture. There's meant to be a map that shows the way. You need the map to find it – and that map gets passed on, from traveller to traveller. Sounds simple, don't it? You find the map, you find paradise. But you see, I ain't never met anyone who ever saw it with their own eyes. Like I says, it's just a legend.' He glances back at the board with a sigh. 'It's a shame, but least I make 'em pay up before they leave. Just a precaution, mind.'

Will you:

Ask what services he can offer?	625
Bid farewell and continue to your journey?	571

455

Your weapons and magic blast away at the knight, reducing the monster back to its starting state – a mound of dirt and armour, writhing with maggots.

Using the tip of your weapon, you poke through the fetid remains. You find 30 gold crowns and one of the following items:

Grub's glory	**Maggot finger**	**Coif of waning**
(main hand: sword)	(necklace)	(head)
+1 speed +2 brawn	+1 magic	+1 speed +2 armour
Ability: crawlers	Ability: wither	Ability: dominate
	(requirement: mage)	

Not wishing to tarry here any longer, you leave the hilltop and return to the mire. Turn to 375.

456

Your choice was a bad one. The metal monster cuts and dices your soldier to pieces, stomping the remains into the ground as it continues to advance. (Remove your soldier from your hero sheet. Then return to 208 to fight this monster yourself.)

457

You crawl forward to take one of the eggs. However, the moment your hand passes over the nest you hear a loud screech from above. A shadow falls across the ledge, growing bigger by the second. Frantically, you twist around to see a giant bird swooping in to attack. It is time to fight:

	Speed	*Brawn*	*Armour*	*Health*
Quetzal	7	6	5	40

Special abilities

- Razor beak: The quetzal's attacks have the *piercing* ability and ignore your *armour*.

If you manage to defeat this bird of prey, turn to 509.

458

You notice a number of items snagged in the weed-choked waters. Using Boom Mamba's staff, you are able to fish them out of the pool. As well as a pouch containing 40 gold crowns, you also find one of the following rewards:

Shocking scales	**Rain dance**	**Lightning loafers**
(gloves)	(ring)	(boots)
+1 speed +1 magic	+1 armour	+1 speed +1 magic
Ability: shock!	Ability: Call of nature set	Ability: lightning
	(requirement: druid)	

When you have made your decision, you return to the courtyard. Turn to 510.

459

The ruins are eerily quiet, the only sound coming from your heart hammering against your chest. It is some minutes before you realise you have been holding your breath since arriving here – the air is sickly-smelling and heavy with decay.

You quicken your pace, wishing to return to the jungle as soon as possible. However, you are brought up short by a peculiar sight – a pillar of stone rumbling towards you. Its angular body is made up of three rotating cubes, each engraved with a different animal icon. As the totem continues to thunder closer, you realise that it has you in your sights – and it isn't slowing. It's time to fight:

	Speed	*Magic*	*Armour*	*Health*
Totem	7/6 (*)	5	–	–
Snake cube	–	–	5	25
Spider cube	–	–	5	25
Jaguar cube	–	–	5	25

Special abilities

- Power cubed: While all three cubes have *health*, the totem can roll 3 dice for its damage score (adding its *magic* as normal). Once a cube is destroyed, this ability no longer applies.
- Snake cube: While the snake cube has *health*, the totem has the *venom* special ability. Once inflicted with *venom*, you will continue to take damage even if the snake cube is destroyed.
- Spider cube: While the spider cube has *health*, the totem has a *speed* of 7. Once the spider cube is destroyed the totem's *speed* is reduced to 6 for the remainder of the combat.
- Jaguar cube: While the jaguar cube has *health*, the totem inflicts 2 damage at the end of every combat round, ignoring *armour*.
- Enchanted rock: The cubes are immune to *bleed, lightning* and *venom*.

In this combat, you roll against the totem's speed. If you win a combat round, you can choose to direct your damage against one of the cubes. Once all three cubes are reduced to zero *health*, you have won the combat.

If you manage to defeat this totemic terror, turn to 621.

460

Your choice was a bad one. The rock monster smashes your soldier to pieces, then continues to stomp towards you. (Remove your soldier from your hero sheet. Then return to 427 to fight this monster yourself.)

461

There is a bright flash of light and suddenly you find yourself looking upon a spear of purest gold, its runed blade flickering with a spectral light. You reach out and put a hand to the weapon, feeling its power course through your body, filling you with the magic of the ancestors. If you wish, you may now take:

Ancestral spear
(main hand: spear)
+2 speed +3 brawn
Ability: spirit hunter career

By equipping this item, you automatically learn the spirit hunter career. (Note: As soon as the *ancestral spear* is unequipped or you learn a new career, you lose the abilities associated with the spirit hunter career. If you do not take the spear, then you must leave your main hand equipment slot blank until you can find a new weapon.)

The spirit hunter has the following special abilities:

Spirit mark (co + mo): When your damage score causes health damage to an opponent, you can also mark them with an ancestral rune. In subsequent combat rounds, the mark allows you to increase your damage score by 2 against this same opponent for the remainder of the battle. Allies also benefit from this modifier. *Spirit mark* can only be used once per combat.
Spirit ward (mo): Cast this spell any time in combat, on yourself or an ally, to raise *armour* by 6 for one combat round. *Spirit ward* can only be used once per combat.

The font's magic has also cured you of your hex. You can now access all of your abilities once again. With your work here done, you leave the pagoda and continue your journey. Turn to 668.

462

'Spirit walk is test. We all get spirit walk in my tribe to prove we one with the ancestors. It prove we better than them.' His fingers trace one of the runes carved into the staff. 'Elders choose spirit walk for us when we come of age. They give me the hardest spirit walk. I not go back till it done or Boom Mamba shame family, shame ancestors. I not want to bring shame.'

Will you:

Ask how he got his name?	204
Ask how he can help you?	257

463

As you back away from the witch, your foot knocks into something. You glance around quickly to see Scar-face spread-eagled on his back, a knife wound to his chest. Lying next to him is a black-bladed dagger, still glistening with blood.

'No!' You step away from the body, your eyes fixed on the dagger. It is the same one from your dream ... the one you used to kill Virgil. 'I didn't mean ... I didn't know it was him!' you protest.

Scowler gives a roar of anger, spinning on the demon. 'Witch! I make you bleed!'

The woman's laughter rings in your ears. 'Oh yes. Remorse. Fear. Anger. All my favourite appetisers!'

Scowler drops onto all fours and charges the robed creature. Determined not to lose another of your companions, you draw your weapons and enter the fray. It is time to fight:

	Speed	*Magic*	*Armour*	*Health*
Succubus	10	5	9	80

Special abilities

- Mental daggers: You must lose 2 *health* at the end of each combat round.
- Delirium: If you take health damage from the succubus' damage score, you are immediately inflicted with delirium. If you win a combat round, roll a die. If the result is ⚀ or ⚁ then your attack misses its mark and you cannot roll for damage. If the result is ⚂ or more, you can roll for damage as normal.
- Revenge of the tigris: Scowler adds 2 to your damage score for the duration of this combat.

If you manage to defeat the succubus, turn to **585**.

464

You awake to find yourself lying on your back. Above you, white clouds drift by at a leisurely pace, while a chill wintry breeze rustles the stems of long grass.

Somehow, you are back on the Fenstone Moors.

As you rise groggily to your feet, you knock into a bottle lying in the grass. It is empty but looks to have contained a healing tonic. You turn around to see Anse standing on a nearby hill. His gaze is levelled on something in the distance. Joining him, you see the tower in the valley below, surrounded by broiling black cloud.

'The others!' You gasp, looking to Anse. 'Polk, Joss . . .?'

The paladin shakes his head, his eyes unreadable behind the band of white cloth. 'It was too late for them,' he whispers at last. He pats you on the shoulder, then turns and walks away.

You stand alone, watching as the tower is finally engulfed by the maelstrom. There is a pulse of dark light, then everything seems to implode inwards, as if pulled back into some other space, leaving behind an empty moorland. There is no evidence, no trace, that the tower was ever there. (Record the word *tower* on your hero sheet.)

Return to the quest map to continue your adventure.

465

With the spider queen defeated, you are free to search her lair. Amongst the webbed skeletons you find a pouch of gold (you have gained 100 gold crowns) and a book of strange runes, bound in leopard skin. You may now take the following item:

Book of Omega
(backpack)
An ancient Lamuri
spell book

If you are a rogue or a warrior, turn to **840**. If you are a mage, turn to **685**.

466

You step warily through the smoke, hunting for your next enemy – but all you find is charred debris and bodies sprawled in the dirt. Just as you begin to wonder if you are the only one left, a crack of thunder shatters the silence.

A gunshot.

It is followed by a wet-sounding snarl, filled with fury – and pain. Then another blast of gunfire brings silence once again.

You hurry in the direction of its source, your feet knocking into the body of a tigris. A smouldering hole has been punched straight through the beast's chest. It is the Sheva leader – his scowl of defiance still fixed on his face.

Boots crunch through the wreckage. A black-bearded hunter comes to a halt on a pyre of broken wood, his body silhouetted by the bright flames licking at his back. He holds a double-barrelled shotgun in each hand, their gaping nozzles still steaming with black smoke.

He spits out a half-chewed cigar, before eyeing you up with an amused frown. 'Well, lookee here.' There is the clink of metal as he levels his guns at you. 'Now, I ain't one to stand in judgement over another soul,' he says in a slow, gravelly drawl. 'I guess yer had ya reasons for helping these savages, I see that. But yer can't change the world, hero. There ain't nothing here but the law of the jungle. Survival of the fittest.'

You feel the sweat trickling down your cheek as you stare into the gun barrels, judging distances, angles, timings ... your strange gift of prophecy flicking through the outcomes of this battle. Most end in your defeat ... most, but not all.

'The law of the jungle,' you smile thinly, edging closer. 'Survival. The new replaces the old. You've had your time old man. Leave these lands – let the tigris live in peace.'

The man gives a throaty chuckle. 'Yer think *I'm* your problem? I'm just the delivery boy, pal. You want to point the finger then start with the king – and all them other rich hogs with more gold than sense. They like those tigris hides back in the cities.'

You edge closer, hands tightening around your weapons.

'And don't you be forgetting the games,' he continues. 'Tigris know how to fight. Guess yer can see that for yerself . . .'

The hunter takes his eyes off you for an instant as he gestures to the ruined compound. That second is all you need – you dive forward, rolling across the ground as a shotgun flares, spewing a storm of metal slugs at the spot where you were standing.

When you leap back to your feet, you find yourself standing eyeball-to-eyeball with the leader. Up close you can see his scars, like a spider's web of ice glistening against his weathered skin. They remind you of your own scars – from the demon.

'New replaces the old,' you grin.

Then you are both spinning and twisting in a savage dance of knives, guns and magic. It is time to fight:

	Speed	*Brawn*	*Armour*	*Health*
Bill	9	8	8	90

Special abilities

- Buckshot barrage: At the end of each combat round, Bill fires his shotguns. Take a *speed* challenge. If the result is 15 or more, you dodge the bullets. If the result is 14 or less, you must take 10 damage. You can use *armour* to absorb this damage.
- Animal attraction: If you have the *rhinosaur pheromone*, you can use it instead of rolling for a damage score to coat Bill in its powerful scent. If the rhinosaur has been freed from its cage, it will immediately attack the hunter. For the remainder of the combat, Bill must take 4 damage at the end of each combat round, ignoring *armour*.
- Survival of the fittest: You no longer benefit from the *strength in numbers* ability if you have it.

If you manage to defeat this veteran hunter, turn to 479. Otherwise, turn to 664.

467

The girl opens three baskets, lifting each of the snakes out in turn. The first is a medium-sized snake, with jagged bands of black and silver dancing along its body. 'Meet the fer-de-lance,' says the girl proudly. 'One of my younger snakes, a little churlish at times, but his brashness has its uses – this one won't shirk away from a thing. You'd make a great team.'

The girl offers out the next snake, which is smaller, its dark-green skin flecked with yellow. Behind its eyes is a raised crown of bone. 'The monarch viper is all about finesse – don't judge on size, her little poison cocktail can take down a troll … or bigger. Quick, clean and efficient.'

'And that one?' you ask, peering into the last basket.

The girl hesitates, her lips pursed. 'Hmm, this one might be a challenge. Zusha is a bushmaster, one of the deadliest killers in the Terral Jungle.' She carefully lifts out the snake, its thick grey body instantly coiling around her waist. 'Zusha likes to hug – and squeeze the life out of her victims. And you too, if you don't show her the right respect. Isn't that right, Zushi-wushi?' She tickles the snake under the chin, eliciting a long rattling hiss as the pale forked tongue flickers back and forth. 'So, do you fancy working your charm on any of these?'

The fer-de-lance is available for 150 gold, the monarch viper is 300 gold and the lesser bushmaster is 500 gold.

Fer-de-lance	**Monarch viper**	**Lesser bushmaster**
(left hand: snake)	(left hand: snake)	(left hand: snake)
+1 speed +2 brawn	+2 speed +2 brawn	+2 speed +3 brawn
Ability: venom	Ability: venom	Ability: constrictor
(requirement: venommancer)	(requirement: venommancer)	(requirement: venommancer)

You thank the girl for sharing her exotic collection of snakes. Turn to **571** to resume your journey.

468

'Have faith!' bellows Ventus, raising a glowing fist into the air. 'The One God tests us – and we will not be found wanting.' He sprints towards the giant, throwing his body into a spin as he kicks and punches at its enormous legs. Bea joins him, her magic swords hacking at the enchanted wood.

'Fools!' hisses Cernos. 'You are weak! Children fighting mountains with stones.'

As the giant's shadow sweeps over you, you start to wonder if the demon speaks the truth. But it is too late now – your beleaguered companions need your aid. It is time to fight:

	Speed	*Brawn*	*Armour*	*Health*
Orgorath	5	5	4	40

Special abilities

Deadly thorns: At the end of each combat round, you must automatically lose 3 *health* from the creature's barbed fists.

If you manage to defeat Orgorath a second time, turn to **411**.

469

'We go!' Anse grabs you by the arm and starts running for the edge of the island of floor. You instinctively pull back, fearful that he may have lost his mind, but the paladin is strong, dragging you with him. At the last moment, he jumps into the nothingness, putting a hand to the necklace dangling around his neck. A crucifix. You cling to him tightly as a chill wind roars in your ears, ripping and tearing at your clothes. There is a burst of bright light and then ...

You find yourself lying on your back. Above you white clouds drift by at a leisurely pace, while a chill wintry breeze rustles the stems of long grass.

'The Moors ...' You sit up quickly, looking around.

Anse stands several metres away, his sightless gaze fixed on the dark tower. It is steadily falling to ruin amidst a storm of whirling chaos.

'The others!' You gasp, hurrying to his side. 'Polk, Joss . . .?'

The paladin shakes his head, his eyes unreadable behind the band of white cloth. 'It was too late for them,' he whispers at last. He pats you on the shoulder, then turns and walks away.

You stand alone, watching as the tower is finally engulfed by the maelstrom. There is a pulse of dark light, then everything seems to implode inwards, as if pulled back into some other space, leaving behind an empty moorland. There is no evidence, no trace, that the tower was ever there. (Record the word *tower* on your hero sheet.)

Return to the quest map to continue your adventure.

470

You place the rune stone into the cavity (you may remove this item from your hero sheet). There is a dull click as it slots into place – the five glyphs suddenly lighting up with a red glow. The light continues to brighten, spreading out from the glyphs to form a glittering pattern of criss-crossing lines that cover the stone. Then there is a grating rumble as the lid draws back of its own accord, revealing the container's hollow cavity.

The tigris back away, looking uncertain. 'Dwarf magic not good,' sniffs Scar-face, covering his face with the back of his paw. 'Smell worse than bats.'

Unperturbed by your companion's reaction, you lean over into the stone treasure chest. Inside, you find a small casket containing 100 gold crowns and one of the following rewards:

Onyx blade	Hammerhead	Shaper's stone
(backpack)	(head)	(ring)
A crescent-shaped blade for a mighty weapon	+1 speed +2 armour Ability: charge (requirement: warrior)	+1 magic +1 armour Ability: might of stone

After examining the items, you rejoin the others and continue into the opposite tunnel. Turn to 513.

471

Following Andos' instructions, you discover a hidden trail that leads you through the forested hills. It eventually widens into a sandy clearing, where the youth is waiting for you.

'Did you get the books?' he snaps, fixing you with an intent glare. 'You've kept me waiting for quite some time.'

If you have *The Book of Alpha, The Book of Omega* and *The Book of Enigma*, turn to 390. Otherwise, you vow to return when you have tracked them down. Return to the map to continue your journey.

472

You clamber up the last section of the wall, pulling yourself across stones and gravel to the edge of a rocky bluff. As you take a moment to catch your breath, your eyes settle on the forest below – and the crumbling ziggurats of a Lamuri city, protruding above the treetops.

The southern jungle.

And there, in the distance, is an immense black volcano, its dark form brooding and ominous against the white haze. It immediately tugs at a memory, reminding you of the black peak from your vision at Durnhollow – the mountain that rained fire.

Congratulations, you have successfully navigated the dark interior. If you have the word *explorer* on your hero sheet turn to 817. Otherwise, you may now return to the quest map to continue your adventure.

473

With the venomous Kaala defeated, you may now help yourself to one of the following rewards:

Eyes of the serpent	Snake-skin coat	Slither steps
(head)	(chest)	(feet)
+1 speed +2 armour	+2 speed +2 brawn	+1 speed +2 brawn
Ability: hypnotise	Ability: deceive	Ability: charm

As a rogue you may also take one of Kaala's enchanted scales. This unique item will reward you with the venommancer career:

Kaala's scale
(talisman)
+1 speed
Ability: venommancer career (see below)

You must have *Kaala's scale* equipped if you wish to learn the venommancer career. As soon as this item is unequipped or you learn a new career, you lose the abilities associated with this item/career.

The venommancer has the following abilities:

Snake strike (pa): (requires a snake in the left hand.) Before the first combat round begins you may automatically inflict 2 damage dice to a single opponent, ignoring *armour*. This will also inflict any harmful passive abilities you may have, such as *bleed* and *venom*.
Toxicology (pa): You are immune to all *delirium*, *disease* and *venom* effects.

Prising open the serpent's mouth, you tug one of its enormous fangs loose. You decide to take this as a trophy. (Make a note of *Kaala's fang* on your hero sheet, it does not take up backpack space.) If you have the *glaive of souls* equipped, turn to 430. Otherwise, return to the quest map to continue your adventure.

474

Using your chosen reagents you craft a clawed wand, its gnarled fingers gripping the coal-black heart of a phoenix. If you wish, you may now lay claim to:

Scriva, nimbus of nightmares
(left hand: wand)
+3 speed +4 magic
Ability: curse, sear
(requirement: mage)

If you wish to craft another item, turn to 755. Otherwise, return to the map to continue your adventure.

475

You believe that the demon speaks the truth. Without its aid, you will not be able to defeat the guardian of the forest.

'Time to put your words to the test, demon.' You bring your weapons down on the first of the iron restraints.

'Stop!' Conall looks back over his shoulder, his eyes bulging beneath his protruding brow. 'The demon is a trickster! Its words are lies.' He spins on his heel, stalking towards you – but Damaris intervenes, whipping her staff around to aim it at the warrior.

'Do not stop us, Conall. Or I will end you right here.'

Conall draws up short, frowning at the witch through his matted strands of dark hair. 'You betray me.'

'No, you fool. You betray yourself,' she snaps. 'We need the demon. Can't you see that?'

Ignoring your companion's bickering, you continue to move quickly around the dais to smash the remaining restraints.

'I am your king!' Conall lifts his runed axes above his head, preparing to strike the witch. 'This is the end of us! The end of you!'

'No,' snarls the demon, its breath quickening with excitement. 'This is your salvation!' Turn to 393.

476

You rejoin Damaris and recount what happened. When you have finished, there is a moment of silence as the woman stares at the ancient tree, lost in thought. Then she gives a disgruntled snort. 'Duerdoun. I should have known.'

Before you get a chance to ask, Damaris has turned away, starting up the winding stairs that lead back into the mountain. You hurry to catch up.

'Duerdoun is a dwarf site, to the south,' she explains at last, once you are halfway up the long stairs. 'We avoid it – mostly ruins now, but it has become a haven for dark things, ancient magic best left alone. The relic that surfaced recently must have been taken there. We need to find it if we hope to get inside that forest.'

You are already struggling to recall many of the things that were shown to you in your vision, but you can still picture the strange artefact in perfect detail; an ornate warhammer, with a head fashioned from panels of gold and silver.

The climb is exhausting, your legs burning from the exertion. Even Damaris has become silent, her attention focused solely on navigating the narrow stairs. Finally, you feel a cool breeze brushing against your face. Having reached the top, you find yourself back on the ledge, overlooking the moors. The sky is now a deep blood-red, shot through with purple. 'We leave at first light,' states Damaris, her stoic expression cast in crimson hues. 'I suggest you prepare yourself, Sanchen. Duerdoun will be... unforgiving.'

Record the word *Wiccan* on your hero sheet. If you wish, you may now return to the map. When you are ready to continue this quest, turn to 489.

477

You follow Jacob up the ladder. As you pass through the glimmering circle of light, you feel a cold sensation prickling along your skin. Gripping the rungs tightly, you continue to ascend – until a cracked stone floor comes into view. You drag yourself onto it, aware of the whirling maelstrom of black cloud thundering above your head. Angry bolts of lightning arc through the hellish sky, illuminating the tower battlements.

You stagger to your feet, glancing around for any signs of the child.

Then something heavy strikes you across the back. You are flung against the crenellated wall, the world lurching in a dizzying blur. There is an angry hiss as you are hit again.

'Just die!'

Desperately you try and crawl away, while trying to get a fix on your attacker. It is a wiry man with bedraggled grey hair spilling over his gaunt face. A patchwork coat, grimy and soot-stained, hangs loosely off his scrawny shoulders.

'Jacob!' you gasp, realising that this must be the toymaker – transformed back to his old self.

'Don't stop me!' he snarls, looking like some wild animal. His eyes are bulging, drool dribbling down his chin. 'I want to go back. I want to go back to the dark place. I want to be young again!'

He is holding a gnarled wooden cudgel, which he raises above his head, ready to bring down in a savage blow. You fumble for your weapons – but there is no need. There is a dull thud as the man lurches forward, his mouth gawping open in astonishment. His rheumy eyes lower to the crossbow bolt protruding from his chest, its shaft painted with blood. The tower gives another violent shake, throwing the frail man off balance. With a shriek he pitches over the side of the low wall, disappearing into the swirling cloud.

You look around for your rescuer, your eyes settling on Polk, who is clambering over the side of the battlements, his clothes smoking and torn. He drops to the ground with a pained groan, his crossbow clattering next to him.

'Polk!' You rush to the warrior's side. 'Are you wounded? We have to get out of here!'

The warrior shakes his head, his eyes flicking to the blood seeping through his jerkin. He nods to his pack, leaning forward so that you can remove it from his shoulders. 'Take the box,' he whispers. 'The toymaker's box . . .'

You open the pack to find a wooden box wrapped in an oily sheet. Lifting it up, you see that a scene has been intricately carved on the lid, showing a cheerful man driving a cart filled with toys. When you look back at Polk you realise that the life has left his eyes, his head slumped against his chest.

Throwing caution to the wind, you flip open the lid of the box . . .

There is a flash of crimson as something bursts out, rippling like fire. You drop the box, stepping away as an immense bird, fashioned from paper, streams up into the sky. Its tail feathers sparkle with magic as they stream out behind it, rippling in the dark wind. Driven by pure instinct, you leap into the air and grab hold of the tail, letting it lift you up off the tower roof and into the storm. Everything goes black – and frighteningly cold – but you keep a determined grip on the strange bird.

Then the clouds are gone and you feel the warmth of sunlight beating against your face. Below you, the Fenstone Moors stretch as far as the eye can see – a verdant green wilderness, pockmarked with boulders, ridges and sparkling pools of water. It is a most welcome sight.

The phoenix spirals towards the ground, skimming the hills of windblown heather. You are finally low enough to let go, landing in a crumpled heap amidst the long stems of grass. Twisting around, you watch as the black clouds swallow the cursed tower, its walls and spires breaking up into clouds of rubble. There is a pulse of dark light, then everything seems to implode inwards, as if pulled back into some other space, leaving behind an empty moorland. There is no evidence, no trace, that the tower was ever there.

Lying next to you is the smoking remains of the toy master's box. You scramble over to retrieve it, finding an identical wooden box resting inside. Opening it up, you discover a purse of gold (you have gained 20 gold crowns) and a ring fashioned from black onyx. You may take:

Black hole

(ring)

+1 brawn +1 magic

Ability: dark pact

Shouldering your pack, you give the now-empty valley a last wary glance, before turning and heading back towards Raven's Rest. (Record the word *tower* on your hero sheet.) Return to the quest map to continue your journey.

478

There is a cry from up ahead. Two figures are wrestling with each other – then there is a crack of magic as one is blown back, crumpling against the wall. As the dust and smoke start to settle, you get your first glimpse of the two combatants. If you have the word *Wiccan* on your hero sheet, turn to 665. Otherwise, turn to 740.

479

Your weapons sear through the gun barrels, your magic blowing the hunter backwards across the ground. As he skids to a halt he reaches for a pistol, struggling to free it with trembling hands. You advance towards him, ready to dodge the shot – but it never comes. Suddenly, you hear a snarl from behind you – then a striped shape dives past, barrelling into the hunter and sending the pistol skidding away across the ground. You avert your eyes as the tigris finishes off the hunter.

Black Patch rolls away from the body, breathing hard. You note several wounds marking his striped white fur. You kneel by his side, as the tigris works to focus on you with his pale, green eyes.

'Sheva win this day,' he gasps. 'Shonac would be proud of battle. Now we hunt … together …'

His body jerks and then stiffens, the light of his eyes finally dimming. You rise to your feet, surveying the wasted compound. Yes, a victory has been claimed, but at what cost?

You search the remains of the hunter. You find 50 gold crowns and one of the following rewards:

Leather long arms	**Buckmaster's jerkin**	**Dark vine pith**
(gloves)	(chest)	(head)
+1 speed +2 brawn	+3 brawn +1 armour	+1 speed +2 armour
Ability: sure grip	Ability: cunning	Ability: thorns
	(requirement: warrior)	(requirement: mage)

White Cloak is standing on the edge of the compound. She is the only tigris to have survived the battle. You join her – and for a while, nothing is said. You both watch the flames as they consume the last of the wooden fort.

'They will return,' you say at last. 'There will always be hunters here.'

White Cloak shifts her gaze to the jungle. 'I am last of Sheva. My kin are no more.'

'What will you do now?' you ask. 'Will you rejoin the Khana – try and cross the marsh to the mountains?'

White Cloak shakes her head, her whiskers bristling. 'No. This is my land. I stay. And I will find new kin and bring them together. Make new pack.' The tigris glances sideways at you, her teeth bared in a smile. 'Will you join me, bright claw?'

You return a grin, but raise a hand in refusal. 'I have my own hunting to do.'

White cloak faces you, beating a bloody paw against her chest three times. 'Then Shonac be with you, bright claw.' You watch as she bounds away into the trees, disappearing like a ghost back into the jungle. (You may now restore your *health*. Return to the quest map to continue your adventure.)

480

At last you manage to corner the spirit against one of the pillars, thrusting your weapons into its black form. With a pitiful whimper its cloaked body crumples to the ground, then begins to melt – forming thick droplets of liquid-darkness.

You hop out of the way as the dark water races across the cracked stone tiles, towards the foot of the shaman's staff. The liquid smokes and sparks, and then disappears – seemingly absorbed into its glowing runes.

'You did it!' laughs Boom Mamba, shaking his fist in the air. 'Fear my boom stick, Mortzilla!'

(By defeating Umbra, the shaman's staff has gained the *shadow shift* ability. Make a note of this on your hero sheet.)

If you are a warrior, turn to 556. If you are a mage, turn to 534. If you are a rogue, turn to 255.

481

'Oh, how exciting!' Bea claps her hands together excitedly. 'I do love passing my teachings on to others, so they might do the same – that's what Saint Mary wanted us to do, after all.'

The pilgrim proceeds to teach you a basic set of inscriptions that will provide healing and protection. Using a metal tool, its length glowing with holy script, Bea shows you how to carve these into your possessions. As you scratch the designs into the steel of your weapon, you sense some part of yourself flowing through the tool and into the glowing inscription. It leaves you feeling faint and nauseous.

'Don't worry,' smiles Bea. 'You'll get used to it. They only draw on a small part of the inner kha. Nothing close to what the abbots have to endure, I promise you.'

If you wish, you may now learn the pilgrim career. The pilgrim has the following abilities:

Charm offensive (co): For each item with the *charm* ability that your hero is wearing, you can add 2 to your damage score. (If you had four items with *charm*, you could add 8 to your damage score.) You can only use *charm offensive* once per combat.
Blessed blades (mo): (requires a sword in the main hand and left hand.) You can heal yourself anytime in a combat for the total *brawn* modifier of your two weapons. You can only use *blessed blades* once per combat.

Thanking Bea for her time, you return to the courtyard. Turn to 260.

482

Although smoke is quickly obscuring the battle, you decide that the sniper could still present a worrying problem. If you are using *brawn* for this battle, then you will need to climb the ladder of the lookout tower to reach him. This means that in the first round of combat, the sniper automatically wins and can apply damage – you cannot use special abilities in this round. If you are using *magic*, then you may fight the combat as normal:

	Speed	*Brawn*	*Armour*	*Health*
Sniper	9	6	5	60

(Note: You cannot heal after this combat. You must continue this quest with the *health* that you have remaining. You may use potions and abilities to heal lost *health* while you are in combat.)

If you defeat the sniper, then turn to 243. If you are defeated, turn to 664.

483

Another grin spreads across the shaman's face. 'You not want to fight spirits? They got treasure. We not the first to come here. Many, many brave warriors try to beat this place but they all fail.' Boom's eyes flick to the staff in his hands. 'None have a boom stick.'

You shake your head, concerned that time is slipping away. 'I must pursue the demon. I can't let him get ahead of me.'

'So, you know where he went?' asks Boom, raising a dark eyebrow.

You reply with a sullen glare.

'I didn't think so. You not find demon by running around without the answers. Mortzilla has answers. And we make him talk with my boom stick.'

You still look unconvinced. With a sigh, Boom straightens and walks over to you. 'Hold this.' He hands you his staff, then proceeds to remove his necklace of charms from around his neck. 'Without this I am nothing. I carve life into charms. Tell story of where I come from.' He exchanges the staff for the necklace, letting you observe the silver and bone fragments dangling from its coils. Each fragment is covered with tiny lines of symbols, almost unreadable with the naked eye.

'Ya keep this as trust yes? Give it back when we complete spirit walk.'

You look again at the intricate script on the charms, finding it almost impossible to imagine the care and patience needed to complete such work. This is a rare and personal gift that you have been entrusted with. You have gained the following item:

Mamba's memory stones (2 uses)
(backpack)
Use any time in combat to
restore 4 *health*

You realise it would be wrong not to repay this shaman's trust. 'Ok,' you nod grudgingly, your fist clenching around the necklace. 'I'll help you.' Turn to 399.

484

You make a quick decision – and charge towards the iron golem. The creature lets go of Joss, raising its fists to meet your attack. Sharpened blades spring out of the metal gauntlets, shining in the hellish light.

'No!' Joss screams and runs at you, a crazed look in her eyes. She grabs you by the arm and tries to pull you away. 'No! Don't hurt him! Don't you dare hurt him!'

The iron golem strides forward, knocking her out of the way. Joss sprawls onto her back, a fresh cut bleeding from her lip. 'Don't hurt him! Please. It's Adam!'

You hesitate, distracted by the ranger's words. But the iron golem is now charging in, spiked fists raking the air. 'Me Maximus. Maximus gives death.' It is time to fight:

	Speed	*Brawn*	*Armour*	*Health*
Maximus	5	5	15	40

Special abilities

- Dismantle: If you win a combat round, instead of rolling for damage you can choose to lower the golem's *armour* by 3. You can do this as many times as you wish, lowering its *armour* by 3 each time.
- Body or iron: Maximus is immune to *bleed, thorns* and *thorn* cage.

If you are able to defeat this mighty warrior, turn to 498. If you are defeated, turn to 464.

485

Eva leads you into a vast cavern. A fire burns at the centre, its thick columns of black smoke spiralling up through the holes and fissures in the high ceiling. Amongst the shifting firelight you see dozens of Wiccans. Some are basking in the warmth of the fire, singing or humming along to a musician who is eking out a sad tune on a fiddle. Others are attending to various chores about the cave – tanning hides, sharpening weapons, mending clothing. It seems that this is part of a thriving community. Side tunnels snake off into other sections of the cave system.

As you glance around the cavern, you see the rogue who saved you from Durnhollow. He is teaching a young child to fight, offering advice as he watches them thrust and pivot with wooden stumps for weapons. Elsewhere, a line of warriors are having their bodies painted with coloured dyes. Eva takes your hand and points to a set of carved stairs, leading up to a shelf of rock.

'Damaris waits for you there.' Bowing her head, the woman leaves your side, joining a group of women who are daubing paint on the wall of the cave, adding to a long frieze of colourful scenes.

Will you:

Speak to the rogue?	389
Examine the painted warriors?	116
Take a closer look at the frieze?	299
Climb the stairs and speak to Damaris?	126

486

'This is Baba,' smiles the girl, raising her arm so that you can get a better look at the purple-scaled serpent. 'Look Baba, we have a customer.' The serpent's wedge-shaped head twists around, regarding you with black, glassy eyes. Then it lunges forward with a sharp hiss, its fanged jaws stretched wide. You step away, hands raised defensively.

'Oh, don't be frightened,' giggles the girl. 'I think she likes you.'

'Really?' you splutter, maintaining your distance.

'Well, she's been a little bad-tempered today; she gets that from her mother.' The girl kneels beside one of the larger baskets, carefully lowering the agitated snake back inside. 'Perhaps one of the others will be more to your liking.' She pauses, studying you thoughtfully. 'Yes, the fer-de-lance – or even the monarch. Hmm, we've got some options to play with. If you have the time, that is.'

If you are a venommancer turn to 467. Otherwise, you swiftly decline the offer and resume your journey. Turn to 571.

487

'Everyone is born with an inner kha – a soul,' explains the priest, tapping the centre of your chest. 'But very few know how to truly open up to their kha and draw on its power. Judah taught us this – that the holy light is a gift from the One God; a gift inside each and every one of us.'

With Benin's help you discover that you can concentrate on this point of force within yourself, carefully nurturing it from the faintest embers into a steady white flame.

'Good. An impressive start ...' Benin removes a silver necklace from around his neck and hands it to you. 'Here, this will help you to channel that energy – to do the work that the One God wills.'

You may now take:

Benediction
(talisman)
+1 magic
Ability: acolyte career

Using the talisman, you discover that you are able to summon the flame more easily. With practice the flame quickly becomes a fire, which finally bursts into a raging torrent of white heat, flowing through your body and filling it with power.

The acolyte has the following abilities:

Bless (mo): This ability can be cast at any time on yourself or an ally to heal 6 *health* and increase one attribute (*magic* or *brawn*) by 1 for the remainder of the combat. *Bless* can only be used once per combat.
Last rites (pa): Once an opponent has 15 or less *health*, you can instantly cast this spell to lower your opponent's *speed* and *armour* by 1 for the remainder of the combat. *Last rites* can only be used once per combat.

Thanking Benin, you leave the chapel and return to the courtyard. Turn to 260.

488

'I brought you south – to the Saskat prairies,' explains Virgil. 'Not an easy journey with the roads such as they are.' He scratches at his chin with a gloved hand. 'I had to get you to Modoc as quickly as possible in order to,' he pauses, his eyes studying your impressive scars, 'preserve you.'

'Preserve me?' You glower, trying once again to push yourself up. 'You make me sound like a museum exhibit.'

The witchfinder chuckles. 'Well, you are a rarity and incredibly precious to us – be grateful that makes you worth the effort. Besides, we have need of your powers.'

Turn to 494 to ask another question, or turn to 433 to continue.

489

You leave the horses and continue on foot, clambering up the sheer slope to reach the causeway. Damaris leads the way, a feathered staff held out before her, its pale light helping to push back the lingering shadows of dawn. Behind her towers the giant, Conall, his twin axes crossed at his back. You and Murlic bring up the rear, the rogue hissing curses beneath his breath.

'We should not have come here,' he growls, casting scathing glances at his surroundings. 'Duerdoun is cursed. A place of evil.'

As you pull yourself up onto the stone causeway, you get a glimpse of the place known as Duerdoun. Your first impression is one of jagged black teeth, stabbing through the morning mist. The teeth are actually needles of rock, lining both sides of the causeway – some still intact, others broken and crumbling. They stretch away into the curling mist, to where you can dimly make out a temple-like building, carved into the side of a dark mountain.

'What was it used for?' you croak, choking on the black dust thrown up by the wind.

'It was an entrance way to a dwarf city,' explains Damaris, looking back over her shoulder. 'A place overrun with goblins and demons. It was sealed long ago, like most of their great holdings.'

The giant makes a rumbling sound, deep in his chest. You note his concern, as the needle-like pillars either side of you start to glow with silvery-white runes. The warrior draws his axes, falling into a crouch as their own runes flash into being.

'This is not good,' sighs Murlic, his narrowed eyes scanning the swirling mist. 'This place does not want us here.' Turn to 392.

490

Anse frowns when he finds you standing at his side.

'You have a thing for numbers,' you remark, thinking back to the conversation in the taproom. 'I'm guessing two are better than one, right?'

The fire giant rears up before you, revealing the many wounds that scour its molten skin. Anse has clearly been busy – his previous attacks have seriously weakened the monster. Perhaps you have a chance to defeat it after all. It is time to fight:

	Speed	*Magic*	*Armour*	*Health*
The furnace	5	4	2	70

Special abilities

- Fury of the furnace: You must take 3 damage at the end of each combat round from the creature's intense heat. This ability ignores *armour*.

- Holy vengeance: Anse adds 3 to your damage score for the duration of this combat.

If you are able to defeat this enraged elemental, turn to **431**. If you are defeated, turn to **464**.

491

The dean's face hardens. 'They are a disease, a plague on this land, corrupted by demons and foul magics. We have chosen to end this – to stand alone against their evil and purge it from existence.'

Ventus flexes his inscribed fists, sending white sparks dancing across his knuckles. 'Indeed, the Wiccans are stronger now,' he adds with derision. 'The tribes used to be disorganised, unruly. But lately they have become united under a single figurehead. They call him Conall – the giant we met on the moors. A puppet, some believe, for that dark witch and her own schemes.' He shakes his head. 'Who leads them doesn't matter – they will strike and it will be soon.'

Will you:	
Ask about the traveller's gift?	429
Ask about 'the truth' they seek?	394
End the conversation?	496

492

The scholar inspects the map with his bespectacled eyes. 'This is … perfect,' he gasps. 'A most splendid job. A first!'

'And the reward?' you query, as the scholar starts to turn away.

'Oh yes, how bothersome. Let's see.' He unfastens a purse of money from his belt and carefully counts out twenty gold crowns.

'It was a hundred,' you remind him, with a polite smile.

Tutting to himself, he proceeds to hand over the rest of the gold. (You have gained 100 gold crowns.) You pocket the gold, shaking your head with disappointment. 'Not much, is it? I did risk my life out there. Those cannibal monkeys …'

The scholar rolls his eyes. 'Bloomin' mercenaries. Okay, accompany me back to my office and I'll give you something more . . . scholarly for your efforts.'

You follow him down to the beach, where a ragged-looking tent has been set up beneath a clump of trees. 'Take your pick,' he says, gesturing to the crates and books scattered across the sand. 'Now, if you'll excuse me – I've got a book to write!'

You may choose one of the following as a reward:

Bogglespiff's digest	**Scholar's seal**	**The don's cuffs**
(left hand: spell book)	(ring)	(gloves)
+2 speed +2 magic	+1 magic +1 armour	+1 speed +3 brawn
Ability: insight	Ability: confound	Ability: sideswipe

After thanking the scholar for his generosity, you return to the harbour. Turn to **571** to continue your journey.

493

The runes dim and then fade as the wounded creature attempts to crawl back to the stone coffin. You watch the futile scrabbling with contempt. Planting a boot on its side, you push it over onto its back. The face beneath the hood is not human – it is covered in blue-black scales, marred by deep scars. The thing hisses from its lipless mouth.

'It must stay . . . in the forest . . . you don't . . . understand . . .'

You kneel beside the dying creature, leaning closer to catch its last wheezing gasps.

'The forest . . . the forest is . . . a . . .'

Its breath rattles in its lungs as the deformed body shakes and convulses. Then the creature lies still, its yellow eyes staring sightlessly past your shoulder. As you rise to stand, you hear footfalls echoing in the passageway behind you. A second later and your companions file into the chamber, looking shaken but unharmed. Searching the creature's body, you find 30 gold crowns and one of the following rewards:

Twilight sceptre	Dawnlight	Hood of the night fiend
(main hand: wand)	(left hand: sword)	(head)
+1 speed +2 magic	+1 speed +1 brawn	+1 brawn +1 armour
Ability: wither	Ability: blind	Ability: fiend's finest set
(requirement: mage)		

You also find a small stone figure in one of the creature's pockets. It is carved to resemble a laughing dwarf, its enormous belly bulging over its squat legs. If you wish to take the *household spirit* then simply make a note of it on your hero sheet, it doesn't take up backpack space.

If you have the word *Wiccan* on your hero sheet, turn to 428. Otherwise, turn to 404.

494

You race through a fog-shrouded jungle, following something dark and elusive. Whatever it is, it stays just out of sight, winding between the dense tangle of trees. As you run faster, so does your quarry – leading you ever deeper into the steamy forest. And then, in a heartbeat, the dream shifts, becoming grey-stone corridors, swathed in cobwebs and vine-like creepers. They are never-ending, forming an endless, disorientating maze. And still the creature eludes you. Breathing heavily, you start to slow . . .

Then you see it, lurking in the shadows. A flicker of purple light picks out its misshapen body. You go to draw your weapons, but they have gone; your clawed hands scrapes against empty sheaths. Instead you back away as the creature steps out into the light. Its twisted frame is swaddled in grey cloth, embroidered with strange runes. As it lifts back its cowl, you give a gasp of horror as you look upon your own face staring back at you. Slowly, it opens its mouth – your mouth – revealing a dazzling array of glittering fangs.

'There is no escaping your fate,' the beast-like you snarls. 'No escaping what you are!'

'No!' you shake your head, looking for a route of escape. 'This is not real . . .'

'Demon!'

With a snarl the creature leaps across the passageway, its fangs closing around your throat. You scream as you are flung backwards, your head bursting with hot searing pain . . .

You are jolted forward, sucking at the air. It is hot and dusty, forcing you to choke. Something cold is suddenly held to your lips – you greedily gulp down the refreshing water, feeling it ease your sore throat and swollen tongue.

Words are spoken, but you don't recognise the dialect. You feel a hand, firm but reassuring, pushing against your chest, forcing you back down onto the bed of soft pillows. Then a sudden panic drives you forward again, as you realise you can't see – everything has remained dark. Your hands go to your eyes, where you feel a cloth or bandage restricting your vision.

Angrily, you tug it away.

For a moment you are blinded by light, forcing you to squint against the pain beating in your head. A shape moves at your side, edging away. You follow it, trying to focus on the details, struggling to make sense of what is happening.

'Where am I?' you croak, barely recognising the sound of your own voice.

'Safe.' A dark figure leans over you. Gold teeth sparkle in the brightness.

You jerk away instinctively, your hands grappling over fur blankets. To your left, sunlight streams in bands through a shuttered window. A man leans next to it, watching you with dark eyes. The slatted light picks out the bones and feathers sewn into his tanned leathers. Groggily, your attention blurs back to the other figure – the one with gold teeth. The witchfinder is watching you with a thin smile.

'Welcome to the land of the living,' he says, his gold smile broadening.

You try and slide up the bed, desperate to put distance between yourself and that malign-looking face, but you are brought up short in a fit of coughing, the pain from your chest and shoulders almost overwhelming.

'What happened to me?' You pull away the blankets to gaze down at your naked torso. Ugly red scars cut deep furrows through the skin, moving up from your stomach in jagged parallel lines. The scars end at your left shoulder, where you notice the skin blackening as if bruised, forming patches of reptilian-looking scales. You screw up your eyes as you prod the scaly-looking flesh.

'You were lucky,' states the witchfinder, his one steely eye flitting to the man by the window. 'And for that, you have Modoc to thank. The finest healer in all of Valeron.'

The stranger bows his head in greeting. A band of sunlight dances across the runes and sigils tattooed into his blood-red skin.

You look back at the witchfinder, begging for answers. He appears to read your mind, folding his arms and flashing you another gold-toothed smile. 'I am Virgil Elland. I imagine you have some questions for me, prophet?'

Will you:	
Ask about your whereabouts?	488
Ask who he is?	397
Ask about the demon?	175
Ask about your wounds?	271
Ask what happened to your companions?	424

495

You pull back the curtain of lianas and enter the interior of the pagoda. The smell that hits you is almost overpowering – a sour reek of mould and decay. A quick glance at your surroundings confirms that every inch of stone, from the floor to the arched dome ceiling, is covered in scabs of thick, yellow fungus.

'Lycanth's lair,' whispers Boom Mamba, pointing to the far side of the musty-smelling space. 'Spirit of rot.' At first, you assume the shaman is mistaken – it looks to be nothing more than a heap of mould, crawling with maggots. But then it moves, lifting up off the ground on bowed, hairy legs. A single bloodshot eye blinks in the darkness of its crusted hood, below which a wolf-like muzzle sniffs at the air. Then the beast gives a gargling howl of rage, its mouth distending into a row of jagged fangs. You quickly step forward to protect the shaman, as the creature advances. It is time to fight:

	Speed	*Brawn*	*Armour*	*Health*
Lycanth	5	5	4	55

Special abilities

- Miasma of decay: At the end of each combat round you must automatically lose 3 *health* from the cloud of stench that surrounds your foe.
- Disease: Once Lycanth's damage score inflicts health damage to your hero, you must automatically lose an additional 2 *health* at the end of each combat round.

If you manage to defeat Lycanth, turn to 207. If you are defeated, you may return to 510 to choose a different foe to battle.

496

'This is it!' The monk at the table snatches up the still-wet parchment, waving it in the air. He points to the ragged traveller, who is still muttering to himself, rocking back and forth in agitation. 'Listen, listen!'

Everyone crowds around the table, craning forward to hear the man's words. 'Causeway of stone … where the pillars rake the sky. Causeway of death to the black place, the dark place … temple … where the light is prisoner. The holy light of the God. The One God …'

You look to the others in confusion, the man's words making little sense. However, they seem to have struck a chord with the dean. He takes the parchment from the monk, his eyes quickly scanning the spidery writing. 'Duerdoun. I should have known. It's Duerdoun.'

'The dwarf ruins,' gasps Ventus. 'Why would Allam go to that place? It is evil – cursed.'

The dean crumples the parchment in his fist. 'He went there to find answers. And we must do the same.' He spins on Ventus. 'You should leave at first light. Do not delay.'

Ventus bows. When he rises, his gaze meets your own. 'I could do with your aid, traveller. Few here would be willing to walk the causeway of Duerdoun.'

Before you can respond, the dean strides forward, placing a firm hand on your shoulder. 'If it is your wish, then I suggest you prepare. Say your prayers and gather your blessings. Duerdoun will test the faith of even our strongest.'

If you wish, you may now return to the map. When you are ready to continue this quest, turn to **410**.

497

The witch raises a hand, summoning a pale green light to her palm. She leads the way as you descend deep into the mountain. 'We thought that the traveller we found might have had some answers. The monastery was working hard to keep his movements a secret from us.'

'You mean the elderly man by the roadside? He looked a little crazy to me.'

'He was,' she replies curtly. 'Which is why we decided to release him. He mumbled scripture and stared at walls. There was nothing to be gleaned from him. I cannot fathom why the monastery held him in such high regard. Ah, here we are.'

The stairs bring you out on a narrow ledge, overlooking a vast cavern. Its floor dips away to form a basin, where black roots twist and snake across the stony ground, radiating out from an ancient tree at its centre. Directly above the web of branches, a shaft of golden light breaks from the ceiling, shimmering over the tree's gnarled boughs and coating it in dripping leaves of light.

'That is an elder tree – one of the sacred guardians that protects this land. We keep it alive … as best we can.' Damaris leads the way around the ledge, to where a sloping path leads down into the crater. She stops at its edge, craning her neck back to look at you. 'You are a Sanchen. The spirits will speak to you.'

Damaris points to a cleft in the side of the tree. 'You are of this world and the next, Sanchen. You can tread where we cannot. Now go.' She places the palm of her hand against your back and pushes you out into the maze of roots.

You step warily between them, noticing that several of the thicker roots seem to be trembling and shifting, as if alive. A constant creaking sound accompanies your advance. On reaching the cleft you duck your head and pass through, pushing past grey and mottled fronds, to find yourself standing inside the hollow trunk. The golden beams spill through its upper limbs, forming a curtain of coruscating light. Standing within this magical radiance is a woman. She beckons you with a delicate hand, her long pale fingers sparkling with jewels.

As you approach, you can't help but marvel at the woman's timeless beauty. Her skin is perfectly smooth, her golden hair cascading about her shoulders in shimmering ringlets of light. Mesmerised, your eyes drift across the curves of her gown, woven from a myriad of leaves and flowers, to finally settle on the bright sword hanging at her waist.

The woman does not speak. Instead she simply takes your hand ... and suddenly, your eyes jolt open as your mind is assaulted with images. You can't tell if it is the future or a dream that now races through you, but you see yourself standing on a causeway of cracked black stone. There are pillars of splintered rock and a circle marked with runes. A heavy lid is being pushed aside. A warhammer rests on a bed of glowing coals. Your hand reaches out to touch it ...

Light surrounds you. A blinding white light. It leads the way – you lead the way – passing through the forest of thorns, towards the voice. The voice that beckons you from the dark.

Then you are stumbling back, frantically sucking in air as you gasp for breath. When you are finally able to recover, you see that the woman and the light have gone. In their place there is nothing but a weathered old stone, coated with creepers and brambles. If you have chosen the path of the mage, turn to 403. Otherwise, turn to 476.

498

The iron golem drops to its knees, rocking back and forth dizzily. Then, with a mournful-sounding groan, it slumps backwards, its metal body ringing against the cracked stone.

You may now help yourself to one of the following rewards:

Gratuitous maximus	Defendus maximus	Adam's core
(main hand: sword)	(left hand: shield)	(talisman)
+1 speed +1 brawn	+1 speed +1 armour	+1 brawn
Ability: fatal blow	Ability: deflect	Ability: iron will

Overcome with grief, Joss throws herself on the crumpled body of the fallen golem. 'Adam!' she cries, beating at its metal chest. 'Don't you dare leave me. Don't you dare!'

You move to her side, putting a hand to her shoulder. 'We have to go.'

'No!' The word is spat out like venom. Joss turns and pushes you away, her face twisted with rage. 'You killed him! You killed my Adam!'

You shake your head, backing away. 'There was no choice . . .'

Suddenly, you hear a grating rumble coming from behind you. Sparing a glance over your shoulder you see the chasm has now expanded, cleaving the hall in two. As its crumbling edges slide away from each other, you see a yawning whirlpool of darkness below. It is starting to suck everything towards it – dragging the broken hall down into some infernal abyss.

'We have to get out of here!' you cry, moving towards Joss.

The woman backs away, still quivering with rage. 'You— You killed him! How could you?' With an inhuman scream, she springs at you. The ground lurches, throwing her off course – her momentum taking her kicking and screaming over the edge of the chasm.

'Joss!' You try and grab hold of her, but it is too late. The woman tumbles away through the black void, rapidly becoming just another floating speck that is caught up in the fast-spinning currents. (Make a note of the keyword *blood debt* on your hero sheet.)

The floor starts to tip dangerously. You try and scrabble for some kind of a hand hold to stop yourself slipping away. Then you see a pair of white boots walk into view. You look up to see Anse standing over you. The paladin is breathing heavily, but appears to be unharmed. 'Time to go,' he says, offering out his hand. You take it, holding onto him for support as you struggle back to your feet. Turn to 469.

499

Bill opens a trunk and lifts out a blue crystal dagger and a black-bladed cutlass, its hand-guard embedded with rubies. 'If these beauties don't take your fancy – and you have the way about you – perhaps this might interest you instead.' He flips open a basket with the toe of his boot, revealing an emerald-scaled snake, coiled on a bed of straw. 'A taipan. The true king of the jungle.'

You may now choose one of the following special rewards:

Emerald taipan	**Crystal dagger**	**Ebon cutlass**
(left hand: snake)	(main hand: dagger)	(main hand: sword)
+2 speed +3 brawn	+2 speed +3 brawn	+2 speed +3 brawn
Ability: venom (requirement: venommancer)	Ability: gut ripper	Ability: piercing

Bill also hands you a purse, containing 100 gold crowns. After making your exchange, you bid the hunter farewell and leave. You may now explore the rest of the camp (turn to 744) or return to the quest map.

500

You decide to make for the river, hoping it will provide an easier and more navigable route through this tangled forest. Thankfully, it isn't long before you find yourself crunching across its pebbled shore – the roiling, murky water rushing past at speed, carrying logs and other debris downstream.

As you head along the river, you see a ramshackle cabin at the edge of the treeline. Next to it is a raft and paddle, pulled up onto a bank of gravel. You approach, suddenly excited by the prospect of some friendly company. However your steps soon falter when you hear angry mutterings coming from inside the cabin, punctuated by outbursts of high-pitched, manic laughter.

Will you:

Knock and enter the cabin?	638
Steal the raft and head downriver?	512
Sneak past and continue on land?	703

501

The climb is harder than you anticipated, but with patience and perseverance you finally reach the ledge. You pull yourself onto the overhang to discover a smaller shaft sloping away into the rock. Intrigued by your find, you drop onto all fours and squeeze through the narrow gap. After several minutes, you find yourself facing a dead end – where the skeleton of an explorer rests with his back against the rock.

You crawl over to the body and search the remains. As well as a purse containing 50 gold crowns, you also find any / all of the following items:

Coronado's pride	**Snakebite shake (1 use)**	**The untouchables**
(cloak)	(backpack)	(gloves)
+1 speed +1 magic	Use any time in combat to	+1 speed +2 brawn
Ability: reckless	remove one *venom* effect	Ability: shunt
	from your hero	

You also find a crumpled map, tucked into the pocket of his dirt-stained jerkin. It looks to have been torn in two, the half you are holding showing a trail to a section of coastline. Without the other half, it makes little sense to you. (You may take *Coronado's map* if you wish – simply make a note of it on your hero sheet. If you also have *Frobisher's map*, then keep a record of this entry number and turn to 606.)

There are no apparent clues as to why the explorer crawled into this space – perhaps to escape the skitters, you surmise, or to rest after suffering a wound. Whatever led him here, that knowledge died with him. You place the compass in the skeleton's outstretched hand, then head back to the ledge.

There is no sign of the others when you climb down into the cave. Quickly, you hurry along the tunnel they took, but it soon branches into an infuriating maze. You call out, but the only answer is your own voice – echoing back – each call more desperate than the last. You follow the twisting tunnels, taking one turning after the next, but each choice always seems to lead back to the cave. Grey-hair was true to his word – the tigris have continued onwards and left you behind, keeping their passage a secret. With no chance of catching them up, you head back through the caves and into the forest. Return to the quest map to continue your journey.

502

Tearful with pain, you rub at the smarting inscriptions that have been branded into your skin. The abbot seems indifferent to your suffering. 'Words are more powerful than weapons, child. Use them wisely.'

If you choose *not* to equip a main-hand or left-hand item, then your 'bare hands' provide you with the following:

Inscribed fist	**Inscribed fist**
(main hand: fist)	(left hand: fist)
+1 speed +2 brawn	+1 speed +2 brawn
Ability: knockdown	Ability: pound

You may also learn the monk career. The monk has the following abilities:

Focused strike (co): (requirement: fist or fist weapon in each hand.) Use *focused strike* to ignore your opponent's *armour* and apply your full damage score to their *health*. This ability can only be used once per combat.
Meditation (co + pa): Instead of rolling for a damage score, you can cast *meditation*. This automatically heals 1 *health* at the end of every combat round for the duration of the combat.

The abbot dismisses you with a wave of his hand. You rise and leave the chamber, returning to the courtyard. Turn to 260.

503

A tremor throws you off balance, your final blow landing wide of its mark.

'You saw your death!' snarls Virgil, his eyes burning with a zealous rage. 'And I will deliver it!' He swings Ragnarok, its arc sending a whirling torrent of crimson magic washing across the balcony. The ground bursts open at its passing, rock and stone disintegrating to dust. The wave slams into you . . . armour folds, bones crack and splinter. It beats against you with the fury of a hurricane, trying to lift you off your feet. In the distance you hear a roaring sound, growing louder and more insistent . . . building in tempo. A jet of lava spirals up past the balcony, hanging in space for a single heartbeat then dropping back to the lake in a shower of droplets.

'Die!' Virgil's second swing sends another flood of magic in your direction.

All you see is crimson light, then you are sent hurtling backwards across the lake of lava. Such is the power of the blast that it drives you straight into the opposing wall, smashing through the rock and out the other side. Dust is everywhere – and you are falling.

A dry wind whips at your face, tearing at your clothing. Rocks streak past. Everything becomes a fast-moving blur. The mountainside spins into sight only to sweep away again, replaced by dazzling sunlight and blue skies. Then you are looking at the plain below, pockmarked with craters. *My vision. This is my vision* . . . You try and beat your wings, to slow your descent, but there is no response. They flap uselessly against your back, torn and shredded.

Then the sun is gone, its light snuffed out. It is as if a great shadow has stretched across the dome of the world.

When the sky rolls back into view all you can see are dark clouds, lit by flecks of blazing rock. The deep rumble has now become a thunderous, earth-splitting roar. A moment later a black wave of ash washes over you, obliterating everything. Turn to 558.

504

You take a moment to admire the view, adding the details to the scholar's map. Make a note of the key word *west view* on your hero sheet. Then turn to 756.

505

You hear the scuffing of feet on stone. Turning, you see Scar-face standing in a doorway, his fur matted with mud and dust. He nods in greeting. 'We stand together, bright claw.'

The witch lurches towards you, her black robes rustling across the stone. 'Unfortunate you are still alive, tigris, but no matter. Together, you will make a most splendid feast.'

Scar-face and Scowler exchange a silent look – then they both spring forward as one, claws raking the air. You immediately follow their lead and charge into the fray:

	Speed	*Magic*	*Armour*	*Health*
Succubus	10	5	9	80

Special abilities

- Mental daggers: You must lose 2 *health* at the end of each combat round.
- Delirium: If you take health damage from the succubus' damage score, you are immediately inflicted with delirium. If you win a combat round, roll a die. If the result is ⚀ or ⚁ then your attack misses its mark and you cannot roll for damage. If the result is ⚂ or more, you can roll for damage as normal.
- Revenge of the tigris: Scar-face and Scowler add 4 to your damage score for the duration of this combat.

If you manage to defeat the succubus, turn to 519.

506

The face sinks back into the marble. An instant later and there is a dull scraping sound as the door trembles and then begins to lift up, sliding into some hidden recess. A small chamber is revealed, lined with stone shelves filled with books and carved tablets. A small desk and chair occupy one corner, fashioned from the surrounding rock. Resting on the table is a note, scrawled on parchment, and a glowing crystal ball.

Will you:

Read the note?	852
Examine the crystal ball?	659
Search the shelves?	711
Leave?	858

507

Amongst the putrid mould and clumps of animal hair you spy a number of interesting items. Some appear to be from previous adventurers. As well as a pouch containing 20 gold crowns, you also find one of the following rewards:

Hair of the wolf	**Lycanth's teeth**	**Feral falcate**
(cloak)	(ring)	(left hand: dagger)
+1 speed +1 brawn	+1 brawn	+1 speed +2 brawn
Ability: cunning	Ability: bleed	Ability: pagan's spirit set
		(requirement: pariah)

When you have made your decision, you return to the courtyard. Turn to 510.

508

Whoever searched the room previously clearly had something specific they wanted to find – as, amongst the wraps of linen, you discover several bundles of gold and jewellery that any common thief would have quickly pocketed. You find 100 gold crowns and a sickle-shaped dagger, encrusted with gems. If you wish, you may now take:

Ceremonial dagger
(main hand: dagger)
+2 speed +2 brawn +2 magic
Ability: bleed

If you haven't already, you can inspect the pyramid model (turn to 581) or leave and continue your journey (turn to 563).

509

With a squawk the bird goes spinning away through the mist, its bright red feathers trailing in its wake. Turning your attention back to the nest, you contemplate whether one of these eggs might prove valuable. If you wish you may take:

Quetzal egg
(backpack)
A large, oval,
red-speckled egg

Before you leave this precarious ledge, you take a moment to admire the view. If you have the word *explorer* on your hero sheet, turn to 518. Otherwise, you continue your ascent of the canyon wall. Turn to 472.

510

According to Boom Mamba, you will need to defeat three spirits in order to power his totemic staff. Once his staff has absorbed three spirits, you will be able to take on the powerful Mortzilla.

You take a moment to study the five buildings that surround the courtyard. To the north-east is a domed pagoda, shading a rectangular pool of murky water. To the north a similar pagoda has been engulfed in thick jungle foliage, its pillars and roof draped with clinging lianas. To its left a large temple has fallen to ruin, and between its mouldering remains a whirling column of air is visible, twisting and weaving like a devilish serpent. To the west there is a raised promenade, lined with two rows of circular pillars. They cast lengthy fingers of shadow across the cracked paving, where something moves – flitting from one shadow to the next. Finally, to the south, there is a gaping space where you assume a temple had once stood. The land has now sunk into a wide crater of muddy swamp water. Only the tip of a rooftop remains visible – everything else has been sucked down into the stinking mire.

Will you choose:	
The pool of water?	552
The overgrown pagoda?	495
The ruined temple?	573
The pillared plaza?	432
The swamp crater?	384

Once you have defeated three spirits – no more – turn to 525.

511

You have discovered rare Lamuri treasures that have been locked away for thousands of years! You may now choose up to two of the following rewards:

Cope of rituals	Embalming razor	Fyre fiend
(cloak)	(left hand: dagger)	(ring)
+1 speed +2 brawn	+2 speed +2 brawn	+1 armour
Ability: heal	Ability: blind strike	Ability: fire shield

You also find a bronze coffer, containing 100 gold crowns. Having looted the vault you return to the main chamber, where you take the sloping ledge up to the open doorway. Turn to 595.

512

You drag the raft into the river and clamber aboard. Within seconds the churning waters have swept you up, sending the raft bobbing and spinning crazily down the river. Desperately you try and steer the craft using the paddle, as sharp rocks and other snagged debris whip past at an alarming speed. You must take a *speed* challenge:

	Speed
River rapids	13

If you are successful, turn to 718. Otherwise, turn to 653.

513

The tunnel quickly branches into a confusing maze of side passages and shafts. Thankfully Scar-face and Scowler seem certain of their route, moving with an easy confidence as they lead you through the maze. At last, after what feels like hours of travel, you feel a cool wind brushing against your face. It carries with it a brackish, stagnant odour that reminds you of the fenlands outside Carvel.

A few twists and turns later and you see daylight ahead. You follow the tigris out of the caves and into the brightness. At first the light is blinding, your eyes having become accustomed to the dark. Then your surroundings slowly blur into focus.

A jumble of rocks spill from the mouth of the cave, leading down to the sun-kissed waters of the marsh. They stretch away into the dawn mist, lapping around islands of wind-tussled grass. Overhead a flock of birds wheel through the haze, their bright plumage sparkling like embers of fire, whilst below frogs and crickets beat their lively chirruping chorus – as if to welcome you to their home.

The marsh. The domain of the Lamuri witch.

'Doesn't look too dangerous to me,' you smile, glancing at Grey-hair.

The elderly tigris rumbles with dissent. 'Do not fall for charm. The witch of the waters is a deadly foe. Her claws tear at mind, not … just. . .body.'

The tigris' words drawl, his face becoming an unclear smudge of orange and black.

You scrub a hand across your eyes as you struggle to focus. The dappled light is misting your surroundings, making everything vague and indistinct.

'What's happening . . .?' You stagger forward drunkenly. When you try and steady yourself, you discover your arms won't move – they are being held back, high above your head. You feel cold iron biting into your wrists.

'A marsh,' says a voice, cold and impassionate. You hear the scratching of a pen on parchment. The noise is grating; each stroke setting your teeth on edge. 'Describe it again. I need to know more.'

You blink, the wash of colours suddenly solidifying into the grey walls of a cell. A thin bald-headed man sits opposite you, hunched over a desk. He is surrounded by rolls of parchment.

'No ... this isn't real!' you gasp, pulling against your restraints. 'I was in the forest ... the caves ...'

The librarian looks up from his work, his pen lifting off the page. 'No. You were experiencing a vision. A possible future.'

Desperately you look around, searching for some clue – some flaw in this dream – to prove that it is not real. But the musty smell of the cell, the bitter cold of the iron manacles, the pain in your aching joints – all of it feels horribly real.

'This is a dream,' you insist through gritted teeth. 'The Lamuri witch. This is her work ...'

The man leans forward, his eyes suddenly bright with interest. 'Yes, the witch. The tigris mentioned her. Tell me more. Do you see her now?'

'No!' You pull at your chains, feeling them rub painfully against your bleeding sores.

The librarian settles back, looking disappointed. 'Perhaps more Elysium.'

'No.' Tears fill your eyes, a solid lump forming in your throat. 'Please ... this isn't real. I was in the jungle ... the Terral Jungle.'

'Good. Good.' There is a scrape of a chair as the librarian gets to his feet. He walks over, untying a leather gourd from his belt. 'This will take you back. Make you see again.'

He lifts up your chin, pouring the thick milky liquid into your mouth. You gulp it down thirstily, your body craving its sustenance – dulling out the pain. 'Yes,' you smile, your eyes fluttering closed. 'I see again ...' Turn to **547**.

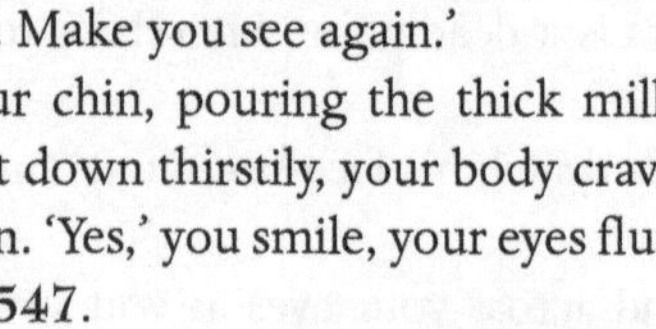

514

There is a bright flash of light and suddenly you find yourself looking upon a rod of purest gold, its length flickering with magical energies. You may now take:

Ancestral stave
(main hand: staff)
+2 speed +3 magic
Ability: overload, focus

The font's magic has also cured you of your hex. You can now access all of your abilities once again. With your work here done, you leave the pagoda and continue your journey. Turn to 668.

515

You step aside, dodging out of the scholar's path. He glances sideways at you, continuing on for several paces before halting suddenly.

'Wait a second. It can't be!' He starts patting his robes, in search of his spectacles.

'Still on the move?' You grin, looking back at Andos. The youth gives you an exasperated glare.

'Argument with the harbourmaster,' he glowers.

'A-ha!' The scholar finally locates his spectacles. Hurriedly, he pushes them onto his nose, looking you up and down with an impatient frown. 'Well? Do you have it? Where is it? Come on, let me see!'

If you have the words *north view, east view, south view* and *west view* on your hero sheet, turn to 492. Otherwise, your map is incomplete. Vowing to return at a later date, you beat a hasty retreat. Return to 571.

516

You break free of the roots, concentrating your attacks on the toad-like monster. After a furious barrage, the elemental gives a booming, snorting roar, spewing weed and black bile from its mouth. Then it slumps down into the water, its black glassy eyes sliding closed.

You wade to the shore, where Boom is completing his ritual. The staff has started to glow, its runes flickering with magic. Turning, you watch as the elemental's body collapses into a thick black sludge, which slides across the water towards the staff. The shimmering runes spit and hiss as the sludge congeals around the shaft, before disappearing inside the enchanted wood.

'That's a powerful spirit,' nods the shaman, struggling to maintain a grip on the trembling device. 'We gonna boom good with this!'

(By defeating Gaia, the shaman's staff has gained the *earth fist* ability. Make a note of this on your hero sheet.)

If you are a warrior, turn to **528**. If you are a mage, turn to **544**. If you are a rogue, turn to **246**.

517

With your foes defeated, you continue up the last stretch of stairs to the temple's summit. There, set underneath a small pagoda, is a sparkling throne of gold – and slouched across it is a black-haired monkey with a circlet of precious gems resting on his brow.

Standing either side of the throne are two guards, their long snouts striped with white and red bands. They glance at their leader, who nods with an imperious boredom – flicking his fingers at you as if warding away a fly. The two guards respond instantly, springing forward at an incredible speed. It is time to fight:

	Speed	*Brawn*	*Armour*	*Health*
Mandrills	9	6	8	50

Special abilities

♥ Feral frenzy: At the end of every combat round, the mandrills raise their *speed* by 1 (up to a maximum of 14).

(Note: You cannot heal after this combat. You must continue this challenge with the *health* that you have remaining. You may use potions and abilities to heal lost *health* while you are in combat.)

If you manage to defeat these savage guards, turn to 650. Otherwise, you have failed to assault the temple. Restore your *health* and turn to 449.

518

You take out the scholar's parchment and add the details to the map. Make a note of the key word *east view* on your hero sheet, then turn to 472 to continue your ascent.

519

The succubus is a powerful adversary, blasting you with her dark magics while her mind-numbing powers sap at your strength. Scar-face is the first to fall, his blow missing its mark and leaving him open to the creature's magic. The ensuing bolt of fire spears the tigris as surely as any steel, dropping him to the ground with a mournful cry. Scowler tries to retaliate, bounding off a broken column to strike from the air. But the witch is faster, spinning around and catching the tigris in her pale, scaly hands. She hurls the tigris back against the wall, following up with a blast of magic that sends the broken body smashing through the rock and out across the misty swamp.

Alone, you are forced to defend yourself against the witch's onslaught, giving ground to her powerful magics. Then, when all seems lost, you find some hidden reserve of strength – a bitter fury that floods through your body, helping you to shrug off her debilitating spells. The witch senses this change, pausing in her attack.

'Demon blood!' the voice whispers.

Then you fly forward, driving your weapons into her tattered robes. There is a deafening shriek as a black wind pours out of the wound, blowing you backwards. You tumble over onto your stomach, looking up in time to see the creature's mildewed robes flutter to the ground. There is no sign of a body, only a thin maggot-like worm, dragging itself across the stones. You clamber to your feet, marching forward to drive your weapons into its weakened form. There is a piercing, eldritch screech. Then there is silence …

At last, the succubus' power has been broken – and the marsh is now safe for the Shara Khana to cross. However, it feels a hollow victory, knowing that your tigris companions gave their lives to achieve this end. Turn to 748.

520

'My late husband was an historian,' explains Yootha, scrutinising her painted nails. 'I never had time for such pursuits myself, of course, but I did like the tales he used to bring home – of exotic lands and daring adventure. That's how he won me over and convinced me to come here. The Terral Jungle, of all places! He was always very persuasive, my Stan. A man you could trust.'

The woman sniffs, dabbing at the corners of her eyes. 'Sorry, where was I? Oh yes, the jungle. Stan became quite obsessed with it and the Lamuri. Found out about their lost city when studying the Dwarves. Apparently, they had close relations in times past – shared their ways, their magic. And, some say, the gift of immortality.' Yootha rolls her eyes. 'Such nonsense. The Lamuri city is a cobwebbed ruin, given over to the jungle. Didn't stop my beloved Stan though. He believed in the myth, that somewhere in those ruins lies the secret of ever-lasting life.'

'You said "late" husband,' you state carefully. 'I take it … he wasn't successful?'

Yootha distracts herself by adjusting her flower display. 'Things live. They die. That's the natural order of the world. Go looking for anything different and you're a fool. Now, did you want to buy something?' (If you have the word *restless* on your hero sheet, turn to 634.)

Will you:

Ask to see Yootha's specials?	593
Ask to view the Lamuri artefacts?	612
Thank Yootha and continue your journey?	571

521

In order to buy time for the tigris to escape, you charge the two hunters. Weasel pulls the trigger of his pistol – his grin fading fast when it makes a dull, wet-sounding click. You kick the weapon out of his hands, spinning around to meet the other hunter's thrusting blade.

'Blast it!' The weasel draws a pair of skinning knives, before lurching into the fray. You must fight the hunters as a single enemy:

	Speed	*Brawn*	*Armour*	*Health*
Hunters	9	7	4	50 (*)

* Once the hunters have been reduced to 15 *health* or less, turn to 532.

522

You rummage through the thief's pack, finding several of your own pilfered belongings amongst his pots and jars. Finally your hand settles around what you assume is the snake antidote, its parchment label helpfully displaying a snake and a cross.

The thief is now wracked with convulsions, choking for air. You kneel by his side, tilting his head and pouring as much of the antidote into his mouth as you dare. Most of it spills over his chin, but the wet-gargling sound suggests some of it might have been taken.

After several tense minutes, the convulsions ease – and the thief's limbs slacken, dropping by his side. At first you fear the worst, but then his eyelids flutter open, a wolfish grin spreading across his lips.

'Thief's luck,' he says.

You rise and step away – not completely trusting this back-stabbing assassin. But the thief makes no move to attack. Instead, he sits up, arching his shoulder blades. 'Blasted snake. Never saw it coming.' He stumbles back to his feet, then catches the heat of your suspicious glare. For a moment, his eyes do their customary flick, shifting from the balcony to the exit – calculating his options. Gloved hands drop to his knives. Then he bristles with surprise. His scabbards are empty.

You reveal your hands, holding his weapons.

There is a moment of silence, then you both laugh – the tension of the moment dispelled.

'Take your book.' You nod to the lectern. 'I'm here to hunt a demon, not become a scholar.'

Quito quickly takes the book, stuffing it into his pack. He makes to leave and then hesitates. 'Know this of Quito – he will always honour a debt.'

If you are a rogue, turn to **753**. Otherwise, turn to **701**.

523

The ground soon becomes a treacherous mire, the wet earth sucking hungrily at your boots. Thankfully, it isn't long before you spy a hill rising out of the sump. You clamber up its side, hands sinking through the wet soil and detritus. On reaching the summit, you notice pieces of armour scattered throughout the murk. They are rusted and covered in a film of green mould, but their intricate design and gilt-edging suggest they once belonged to a proud knight.

You crawl closer to the nearest piece, a plate chestguard embossed with a golden dragon. As you reach out to take it, the armour suddenly shudders and moves. At first you wonder if it is some forest animal sheltering beneath the plate. But then the earth starts to bulge outwards, lifting the armour with it. The other pieces are also starting to move, rising up on mounds of rotten detritus. They rattle and scrape together, quickly settling themselves around a parody of a knight, its body fashioned from rotted earth.

A choking wail comes from inside the plate helm, expelling maggots and beetles out of the grille of the visor. You scramble back in revulsion, readying your weapons, as the strange knight raises his fungal-covered blade and moves to attack. It is time to fight:

	Speed	*Brawn*	*Armour*	*Health*
Grub knight	6	5	4	55

Special abilities

- Grappling grubs: Each time you cause health damage to the grub knight, roll a die. If the result is ⚂ or less, you are showered by nasty grubs which crawl into your clothes and armour. This lowers your *speed* by 1 each time.
- Disease: Once the grub knight's damage score inflicts health damage to your hero, you must automatically lose an additional 2 *health* at the end of each combat round.

If you manage to defeat this decayed knight, turn to **455**.

524

Desperately you look for some sort of advantage, whilst the guards' sweeping blows continue to beat you back into the tangled garden. Then a plan comes to mind. Weaving between the next wave of attacks, you bait the guards to follow you – swiping at their golden limbs then back-stepping away. As the statues lumber after you, they quickly become entangled in the roots and creepers, staggering drunkenly as they seek to find their balance. Whilst they are distracted you move behind them, striking at their exposed backs. The runed armour sparks and hisses as the guards' magic quickly dies, their bodies becoming statues once again, frozen in situ.

With the guards defeated, you may now take one of the following rewards:

Wings of gold	**Burnished knuckles**	**Corroded pendant**
(head)	(main hand: fist weapon)	(necklace)
+1 speed +1 armour	+2 speed +2 brawn	+1 speed
Ability: time shift	Ability: fatal blow	Ability: rust
	(requirement: warrior)	

Pushing through the foliage, you rejoin the path and enter the ziggurat. Turn to **715**.

525

'The boom stick is ready. Let's go!' The shaman points to a narrow side-street, overshadowed by crumbling temples. 'Now we go boom the big one.'

Halfway along the street Boom pauses, kneeling down beside a rock. He moves it aside, then slides his fingers into the cracks of the paving stone beneath. With a grunt, he lifts it up to reveal a hollowed-out cavity. He reaches inside, his tongue worming inside his mouth as he struggles to locate what he is looking for.

'Gotcha!' He tugs out a hooped strap of leather, with over a dozen clay vials threaded along its length. 'This my back-up,' he grins, putting his head and arm through the strap so it rests across his shoulder. 'Take no chances.' Snatching up his staff the shaman continues down the street, the vials on his make-shift bandolier clinking together as he runs. Turn to 616.

526

There is a bright flash of light and suddenly, you find yourself looking upon a sword of purest gold, its crescent blade flickering with magical energies. You may now take:

Ancestral blade
(main hand: sword)
+2 speed +3 brawn
Ability: piercing, bleed

The font's magic has also cured you of your hex. You can now access all of your abilities once again. With your work here done, you leave the pagoda and continue your journey. Turn to 668.

527

The forest is beginning to awaken after the storm, the chirruping, warbling shrieks of the wildlife starting to ring out through the rain-dripping trees. As you follow the tigris through the steaming forest, you take time to study your companions more closely. They number only fifteen, four females and eleven males. You suspect their pack has been whittled away by the hunters, their rare pelts prized across Valeron, their fighting prowess demanded in the games and arenas.

After an hour of trekking north, through thick forested hills, the Sheva halt. The leader is discussing something with one of his pack, a younger male – more slight in build than the rest – his face distinguished by a black stripe over one eye. The others are glaring at you as they wait patiently. You sense that they don't completely trust you – yet. One of the females, however, saunters over. You have named her White Cloak on account of her having fewer markings than the rest of her kin. She offers a half-smile as she looks you up and down with her bright, green eyes.

'I will believe the great spirit Shonac sent you to us,' she says, her words ending with a catlike purr. 'This day we join claws and make the hunters bleed.'

You glance past her shoulder, to where the leader and Black Patch are now gathering together several of the others. 'They scout camp,' explains White Cloak. 'Before we strike.'

Will you:

Ask about the name, Shara Sheva?	566
Ask about Shonac, the great spirit?	542
Join the scouting party?	576

528

On the banks of the swamp, you discover the remains of several unfortunate adventurers – their grey corpulent flesh bloated with swamp water. Quickly, you rifle through their belongings to see if there is anything worth salvaging.

You find a mouldy bag containing 20 gold crowns and one of the following items:

Stoneguard chest	Thunder	Mud-sliders
(chest)	(main hand: axe)	(feet)
+1 speed +2 brawn	+1 speed +2 brawn	+1 speed +1 brawn
Ability: might of stone	Ability: savage arms set (requirement: brigand)	Ability: unstoppable

With your grim task complete, you return to the courtyard. Turn to 510.

529

Team battle (advanced): Issakhar

(Note: You must have completed the red quest *City of the damned* before you can start this challenge.)

The lava fields break at the foot of the volcano, becoming a series of steep-sided gorges. The ground is hard and cracked, the loose slate making the going slippery and treacherous. Occasionally you spy low-lying clouds of vapour, drifting over pools of water. They bubble and steam, belching sulphurous gas into the hot, smoky air.

You soon lose all sense of direction, your path determined by the ever-branching maze of valleys and gorges. One such valley eventually brings you to a narrow corridor, with angular slabs of stone set on either side. Even through the misty haze, it is clear that these are not natural formations – they have been placed here for a purpose.

You examine the nearest stone. Each of its faces has been carved with runes, their stylised patterns reminding you of those you saw at Duerdoun and amongst the Lamuri ruins.

'Dwarven.'

A man's voice catches you by surprise. You swing around, your weapons hissing from their scabbards. But there is no one there.

'I suppose this is something of a paradox.'

You spin again, eyes scanning the lines of stone. 'Who's there?' you growl impatiently. 'Face me!'

A shadow moves at the corner of your eye. You snap around, to see a black-cloaked figure step out from behind a carved stone. The hood of the cloak is drawn up to conceal his face.

'Would I be here if it wasn't for what you said – what you saw?' The stranger waves a spidery finger in the air. 'So, so, so perplexing. Am I as much a puppet in this as you, I wonder? Ah, the schemes of gods and monsters . . .' The man shakes his head, mumbling to himself.

'Show yourself!' you snarl, taking an angry step forward. After trekking across the barren lava flats for the last two days, you are not in the mood for tricks or conversation.

The man raises two pale hands to his hood, then pushes it back. For a moment you struggle to place the familiar features – a gaunt, hollow face, scars raking across the bald pate; a few tufts of grey hair protruding like spines from the pulpy flesh. Then recognition dawns, hitting you like a blow to the stomach.

It is the librarian from Durnhollow.

'That's impossible!'

You know you should feel anger – a desire for revenge for the tortures you were put through – but your mind is racing with too many questions. How could he have found you? How could he have known you would be here?

The visions.

'You . . . you listened to it all,' you croak hoarsely. 'Why? Why would you do this?'

'I'm here because you need me,' he replies, the scar on his left cheek tugging at his smile.

You stare at him, baffled. In your head you can hear the echo of that voice, scratching at your mind, tearing at your thoughts, torturing you in that cell for hour upon hour. 'I should kill you,' you reply darkly, hands tightening around your weapons. 'You have a lot of guts coming here. After all that—'

The man raises a hand for silence. 'I am not who you think I am,' he states firmly. 'My name is . . .' He stops, his body suddenly flinching with shock. 'No!' he hisses. 'Stay away! Stay out of this, fool!' He beats at the side of his head, as if looking to rid it of some nagging nuisance. 'Do not interfere. You want your fr, free, freedom, don't you?' His body continues to twitch and tremble. You notice a purple light flickering along one of his arms, glowing through the material of his clothing. 'Enough! We do what he says. I am in control now!'

'What's going on?' you ask hesitantly, fearing the man has gone completely insane.

He grimaces, still torn by some inner conflict. 'I am . . . Lorcan,' he manages to gasp. 'Yes, Lorcan.' He repeats it louder, as if by uttering the name it will keep his inner demons at bay. 'And we're here to kill a monster.'

'Cernos?' you ask, your eyebrows lifted with interest.

'No.' The man gestures impatiently to the corridor of rock. 'Not Cernos. A drake.'

You scowl peevishly. 'Then I don't have time for this.'

Lorcan mirrors your irritation. 'Listen. Unless you're going to sprout a pair of wings, the valley ahead is the only way to reach Tartarus. And it's guarded by an ancient evil from the time of the dwarves. Cernos is already ahead of you, but my wards will slow him down.'

You open your mouth to protest, but the retort dies swiftly. 'I suppose I have no choice . . .'

'We always have a choice,' he replies, a sudden mischief lighting his eyes. 'Come, let us do this quickly. Follow me.' He turns and starts away, pulling his cloak tight around his shoulders. As you watch him depart you notice a golden staff strapped to his back, glimmering with magic.

'And if I choose not to follow?' you state obstinately, holding your ground.

There is no response. The man – Lorcan – has already disappeared into the mist, his footfalls echoing back from the valley walls. *Of course*, you glower to yourself, *he already knows I will follow – as he knew I would be here, trekking through the lava fields*. Resigned to your fate, you hurry after the scribe, determined to drag more answers from him – by any means necessary. Turn to 662.

530

Next, you must decide what type of paper you wish to use. One set has been made with a light-coloured wood that sparkles with spots of silver. The other set has a bitter smell, the paper infused with flecks of dark crimson. If you wish to choose the *silver wood paper*, turn to 856. If you would prefer to use the *blood leaf paper*, turn to 719.

531

You have discovered rare Lamuri treasures that have been locked away for thousands of years! You may now choose up to two of the following rewards:

High priest's sceptre	Gilded chasuble	Fyre fiend
(left hand: staff)	(chest)	(ring)
+2 speed +2 magic	+2 speed +2 magic	+1 armour
Ability: resolve	Ability: channel	Ability: fire shield

You also find a bronze coffer, containing 100 gold crowns. Having looted the vault you return to the main chamber, where you take the sloping ledge up to the open doorway. Turn to 595.

532

A black body flies out from the undergrowth, slamming into the weasel and sending him screaming into the jungle. You hear a savage roar and the sickening sound of claws rending through flesh. You stagger back, as does the dark-skinned hunter, both of you drawn out of your own private battle by this new threat.

A male tigris bounds back into the clearing, powerful legs driving it into the other hunter. They crash together, going down into the watery mud. A knife flashes, slashing into the beast's side – but the creature shows no pain, its claws and jaws delivering a decisive end to the fight.

The head snaps up, golden eyes glaring at you. Three scars run down the tiger man's face, revealing pale flesh between the orange, rain-soaked fur. For a moment, you are caught between running and fighting – but neither choice seems to offer an appealing outcome. Instead, you lower your weapons in submission.

The tigris straightens to his full height, over eight feet tall, and steps towards you. 'You help Shara Khana,' he growls in an abrupt tone. 'You friend of pack.' He retracts his claws, beating a paw against his chest three times.

The foliage to your right rustles as it is pushed aside – and the female tigris reappears, the baby still clutched protectively in her arms. Her fanged mouth curls into a shy smile.

'Skin good,' growls the male, staring at you intently. 'You join us – come to pack den.'

You look back to the female, wondering if this is some kind of trap – but she nods her head, smiling fondly. 'You saved our lives,' she says, glancing down at her baby. 'Come. Meet with Shara Khana. We give thanks.'

You meet the male's brilliant gaze and give an answering gesture, beating your chest three times. He grins with approval, then strides over to join the mother. 'We move before blood scent brings other predators.' Turn to 559.

533

As soon as you deliver the killing blow the phantom scene dissolves, leaving the way clear for you to continue. You stumble dizzily towards the next pathway, bent double by the throbbing pain stabbing between your shoulder blades. Virgil appears at your side, shouting something – a warning, or perhaps encouragement. The words seem distant … distorted.

He grabs your arm, half-carrying, half-pulling you along the winding pathway. The floor and walls are now shaking, plumes of dust raining down from above.

'Do you see the top?' you gasp, struggling to focus.

All of a sudden, Virgil shoves you aside. You go staggering on all fours, aware that you have reached another platform. There is a croaking roar, accompanied by the rattle and clink of chains. You look up to see a giant lizardman towering above you, strings of drool hanging from its fanged teeth.

The creature swings back its thick, bulging arms, letting a pair of chains, attached to each wrist, snake through the air. For a second, the distended links hover above its head, then the lizardman brings them down with a ferocious force. You roll aside, leaving one to whip across the ground, sending cracks branching through the stone. The other catches Virgil across the shoulder, hurling him back against the wall.

Dazed, he slumps to the ground, blood seeping from his re-opened head wound.

The lizardman comes at you again, in a blur of teeth, scales and scything chains. Unless you defeat it quickly, the dark demon will catch up with you, plunging everything into darkness. It is time to fight:

	Speed	*Magic*	*Armour*	*Health*
Fengz	11	7	3	40

Special abilities

- Whirling chains: At the end of each combat round you must automatically take 4 damage, ignoring *armour*.
- Ghost of a victory: You cannot use *cutpurse* or *pillage* to gain gold/items from this combat.

If you manage to defeat Fengz, keep a record of your *health* and remaining abilities, and turn to 712. If you are defeated (or reach the end of your twentieth combat round), then the wind demon has outrun you. Restore your *health* and return to 630 if you wish to tackle the challenge again.

534

All that remains of Umbra is a pile of rumpled clothing and a scatter of jewellery, all reeking of dark magic. You also spot the skeleton of an adventurer, propped up against one of the columns. The mildewed white robes and cross-shaped pendant suggest they had once been a priest.

You find a pouch containing 15 gold crowns and one of the following rewards:

Seal of shadows	Umbra's cowl	Black pearl rosary
(ring)	(head)	(necklace)
+1 magic +1 armour	+1 speed +1 magic	+1 magic
Ability: veil	Ability: trickster	Ability: Cistene's chattels set
		(requirement: acolyte)

When you have made your decision, you return to the courtyard. Turn to 510.

535

To climb up to the ledge you will need to take a challenge test, using *speed* or *brawn* (whichever is your highest attribute):

	speed/brawn
Rock climb	16

If you succeed, then turn to 501. Otherwise, after several attempts and more than a few scratches and scrapes, you decide to leave and catch up with the others. Turn to 513.

536

Using your chosen reagents you craft a cruel black-bladed knife, its barbed length crackling with dark energies. If you wish, you may now lay claim to:

Mortis, shard of doom
(left hand: dagger)
+2 speed +5 brawn
Ability: bleed, lightning
(requirement: warrior/rogue)

If you wish to craft another item, turn to 755. Otherwise, return to the map to continue your adventure.

537

You avert your eyes from the serpent's hypnotic gaze, concentrating your attacks on its white-scaled body. After a tiring fight the snake finally gives a hissing gasp, then slumps back into the crystal waters, its crimson blood slowly spreading out across the glittering pool.

If you are a rogue, turn to 473. If you are a warrior or a mage, turn to 383.

538

There is a brief moment of calm as you stand motionless, muscles tensed, eyes fixed on the wave of shrieking creatures that are sweeping towards you. Avian continues to advance, arms outstretched to either side, blades glowing in his fists. Against this hellish backdrop he cuts a gallant figure, his embroidered cloak snapping back from his broad shoulders, runed armour glowing with arcane power. A light of hope amidst the darkness …

Then the moment is gone, and chaos descends. The furies break around you, biting and snapping, raking the air with their clawed feet. Avian is lost from sight – and yet the relentless thud of bodies crashing down around you is a sure indicator that his blades are making fast work of this grotesque flock. You follow his example, stabbing and blasting through the maelstrom, relying on sheer instinct to guide your blows. It is time to fight:

	Speed	*Magic*	*Armour*	*Health*
Furies	11	7	3	100 (*)

Special abilities

- Endless assault: At the end of each combat round, roll a die. On a ⚀ or ⚁ result, more furies join the battle, raising their *health* by 4. This can take them above their starting value of 100. Once the furies have been reduced to zero *health* this ability no longer applies.
- Fury of the swarm: At the end of each combat round you must take 2 damage, ignoring *armour*, from the furies' raking talons.

If you manage to overcome this nightmarish swarm, turn to 790.

539

Congratulations! You have created the following item:

Self-published grimoire
(left hand: spell book)
+2 speed +3 magic
Ability: surge

If you wish to create a different spell book, you can start the process again (turn to 850). Otherwise, you may now leave the chamber and continue your journey. Turn to 866.

540

You turn away from the thief, not wishing to view his final, pain-wracked moments. Instead, you focus on the book that Quito was so keen to claim. Its pages are covered in hundreds of intricate symbols and pictures, each one a breath-taking work of art. This is a rare and priceless Lamuri treasure.

If you wish, you may now take:

Book of Enigma
(backpack)
An ancient Lamuri
spell book

Once you have made your decision, you leave the chamber and resume your journey. Turn to 731.

541

You grab the vial and twist open the stopper. Virgil watches you with a gold-toothed grin. 'I knew you'd make the smart decision. Now drink up.'

In a single motion, you tip back the contents. The sour milky taste makes you want to gag, but you force yourself to swallow.

It takes a few seconds for the euphoria to hit. When it does you feel like liquid fire has been shot through your body. It rips along your veins, blazing beneath every pore of skin, twisting your stomach with its coils of flame. The empty vial drops from your nerveless fingers. You hear it smash, somewhere in the distance ... You struggle for breath. Smoke clogs your lungs, stifling you, suffocating you.

Then you are falling. You are dimly aware of arms reaching out to catch you, but you pass straight through them like a wisp of smoke, falling, falling, burning ...

You are being dragged across stone, blood streaking through the dust. Thump, thump as your limbs bounce at your side. There is a voice, weak and strained, begging for mercy. It is not your own. Someone else. The dark shape of the demon drags you through the cave, glittering with crystals. In the distance, you hear a howling ... a whispering. Voices. Ragnarok.

A giant sword, black and cut with runes, has been driven into the skeleton of some malign beast. There is blood ... everywhere. You can smell it, an acrid iron smell. A circle of crimson marks the ground – beating with life with each tortured scream.

The screams of a man, spread-eagled across the face of a black obelisk. Its scoured channels are awash with blood and the glint of magic. Avian Dale. The witchfinder's companion ... His screams become louder, as he bucks and twists to free himself.

A black door. Four runes. A charred claw is moving across them, muttering, wondering which one to choose, which one is safe. It opts for the crescent-shaped rune – and the door grinds open, revealing a vast chamber.

Shelves. Fashioned from the rock. You see dusty books and scrolls, and tablets of stone. The air is grey and cold. Something is moving along the aisles. A ghost. Muttering to itself. Lost. It cannot complete its task. Misery and death stalk the shadows ... nimble hands reach into your pack. An impish laughter and the patter of feet.

Then you are falling once again. The mountainside spins, blurring into an infinite blackness. An immense fireball streaks past. It explodes against the ground, spattering the hills with pools of magma. Another blast of flame. You are rolling and tumbling through hot ash. Cernos strides towards you, the hellish sword held tight in his fist. You look upon his face, one eye burning bright.

Flicker.

Virgil's face. One eye burning bright. The other patched with gemstones.

Flicker.

Cernos. His lips curl back, revealing gold teeth.

Flicker. Flicker.

The faces change, so fast that one becomes transposed on the other.

'My journey is complete!' the demon/Virgil snarls. 'Ragnarok is remade!'

Then all of a sudden you are jolted forward, your chest heaving and gasping. Everything is blurred, swimming in a haze. You can dimly make out Virgil – his eyepatch glittering with gemstones. He grips you tightly, shaking you. 'You're back! You're back! It's all right.' He leans away while you cough and splutter.

'What did you see?' he asks intently. 'Tell me what you saw.'

You take a moment to recover yourself, then recount what you remember. Little of it makes sense, especially the image of Virgil as a demon. You decide to omit that part, no longer sure if you can trust your companion.

When you finally describe Avian, imprisoned on the black obelisk, the witchfinder clenches his jaw. 'We won't let that happen. Come.' He holds out a hand to help you up. You stare at it woozily, your head still clouded with Elysium. Noting your hesitation, Virgil flashes you an apologetic grin. 'No more Elysium. I swear.'

You take his hand, pulling yourself to your feet. When he finally lets go you stagger uncertainly, your vision blurred. 'I fear the damage may already be done . . .'

For the remainder of this act, you must now suffer the following penalty:

Elysium soaked (pa): Every time you use a modifier ability in combat, you must roll a die. On a ⚀ result the ability fails. You cannot try to use the ability again until the next combat round. If the result is ⚁ to ⚅ then you can use the ability as normal.

Once you have updated your hero sheet, return to the quest map to continue your adventure.

542

'Others distrust you,' states White Cloak, shifting closer. 'But they forget Shonac was a skin like you. He was a Lamuri prince. Exiled from his kin. One day he lassoed the last of the great tigers, Quan Mait. He beat it with his club until Mait share its secrets. Then Shonac kill tiger to take its pelt – make Shonac as strong as the mighty Quan Mait.'

'So, Shonac was the first of your people,' you nod. 'What else do you know of the Lamuri?'

White Cloak wrinkles her nose. 'They all dead – yet some still walk like they have breath. Their rock dens stink of bad magic. We stay away from Lamuri. Stay in trees where it safer.'

Will you:

Ask about the name, Shara Sheva?	566
Join the scouting party?	576

543

With an ear-piercing shriek the princess's body rises up into flickering motes of light, leaving her crystal armour to topple to the ground. The motes swirl together, forming a woman's face – serene and beautiful. It is Nephele as you remember her, the princess of the Lamuri.

'You freed me . . . death has freed me . . . .'

Then the smile turns to a bitter scowl. The eyes become hard, merciless. 'Destroy Cernos! You must stop him from taking the sword!'

Her sudden anger surprises you. 'He was your lover. You defied your father for him . . .'

'He is not my Cernos. Barahar remade him – filled his heart with fire, not love. It burns only with vengeance. You must stop him!'

The face shimmers and then fades.

Virgil kneels beside the empty armour. 'I told you, never reason with a demon. . .' He lifts up a runed gauntlet, the glowing crystals still pulsing with magic. 'Witches, doubly so.' He tosses you the gauntlet. 'This magic is tainted, but I doubt that will worry the likes of you.'

If you are a warrior, turn to 818. If you are a rogue, turn to 723. If you are a mage, turn to 787.

544

On the banks of the swamp, you discover the remains of several unfortunate adventurers – their grey corpulent flesh bloated with swamp water. Quickly, you rifle through their belongings to see if there is anything worth salvaging.

You find a mouldy bag containing 20 gold crowns and one of the following items:

Gravedirt girdle	Armbands of attraction	Broken blade
(chest)	(gloves)	(main hand: dagger)
+1 speed +1 magic	+1 speed +1 magic	+1 speed +2 magic
Ability: parasite	Ability: confound	Ability: bleed

With your grim task complete, you return to the courtyard. Turn to 510.

545

Virgil gives a weak moan, his back arching as he comes awake. You go to help him but Lorcan grabs hold of your arm, halting you in a vice-like grip.

'I should have left him to die,' he states, meeting your questioning frown. 'He will betray you, before the end.'

You pull away, breaking his hold. 'I would question *your* loyalty first. Why are you here – why help us at all?'

Lorcan looks about to speak but he suddenly flinches instead, his body going rigid. Beneath his face you can see the muscles twitching, as if they are going into spasm.

'Are you ... all right?' You start toward him, putting out a hand for assistance.

Lorcan knocks it away, his face twisting into an uncharacteristic scowl. When he speaks, his voice seems frailer, stuttering over words.

'I must go back, back . . . the Nevarin says too much. Do not break the weave . . . all threads, yes. All threads.' He tugs the staff loose from its harness.

'No!' As he brings the staff around, you catch it in your hand, feeling a shiver of cold race along your arm. 'I'm not letting you go!'

Lorcan's scowl becomes something more bestial, almost evil. 'Don't touch the staff . . . staff . . . STAFF!' His other arm rises up, its runes flaring as they strike you across the face. For a second all you can hear is white noise, then you are rolling across the island in a cloud of ash. There is a flash of golden light from the edge of your vision. Angrily you twist around, knowing already that you are too late. The stranger has vanished.

Virgil shifts onto his elbows, looking around in confusion. 'Wha . . . How'd we get here?' He pats at his head, scowling when he discovers his hat is missing.

'It's a long story,' you reply, picking yourself up. For a moment, your eyes stray to the scorched, smoking earth where Lorcan had been standing. 'More questions than answers,' you grumble beneath your breath.

Virgil looks around dazedly at the mounds of rubble. One hand continues to pat absently at his head. 'Blasted demons . . .'

You walk over, offering out your hand with a dry smile. 'Don't worry. We'll find the hat . . .' (Return to the quest map to continue your adventure.)

546

You slice cleanly through the arratoch's neck, its wailing scream cut short as its carved face smashes into the ground, exploding into a thousand jagged pieces. These broken remains join the rest of the smoking rubble that now litters the accursed bridge.

Amongst the debris, you spot one of the following items, which you may take:

Angel's despair	Sentry shoulders	Helm of reflection
(talisman)	(cloak)	(head)
+1 speed +1 armour	+2 speed +2 armour	+2 speed +2 armour
Ability: dirge	Ability: heavy blow	Ability: deflect
	(requirement: warrior)	(requirement: mage)

With the guardians defeated you hurry after Avian and Virgil, who are already in hot pursuit of Cernos. Turn to 762.

547

You find yourself seated on a rock, overlooking the marsh. The rest of the tigris are resting nearby, talking in hushed tones. Grey-hair and Scowler stand apart from the group, discussing something with serious expressions. Scowler shakes her head, but Grey-hair presses on – evidently trying to convince her of something.

You push yourself to your feet and approach the two tigris. Grey-hair turns as you approach.

'Bright claw, you look troubled.'

You realise you are rubbing at your wrists, which have started to throb with a dull pain. 'It is nothing,' you reply, dropping them to your sides. 'Has a decision been made?'

Scowler snorts and walks away, standing alone to look out over the marsh.

'Yes. The marsh is too dangerous to cross,' sighs Grey-hair. 'I decide Khana stay here until safe. You and scouts go ahead. Once the witch dead, we all come.' He glances over his shoulder, to where Scar-face is hugging the mother and young cub. You guess they must be family and Scar-face has told her the news. When the young tigris turns away, you can see the pain in his eyes.

'This is not to their liking,' you state solemnly.

Grey-hair scratches at his whiskers. 'Pack long feared this place. No one ever return.'

Scar-face walks past in silence, beckoning to Scowler. The female nods, then together they start off into the marsh without another word.

'Look after my cubs,' says Grey-hair, placing a paw on your shoulder. 'May Shonac keep your claws sharp – and eyes sharper.' Turn to 735.

548

As you leave the mansion you see Andos waiting outside, chewing nervously on a fingernail. He jumps as you approach, then quickly peers past your shoulder to check you are alone.

'Here, wait up.' He beckons you over. 'Survive your meeting then? Better you than me but then Rotten-Runtis thinks I'm a right dolt – making me shift books and make his smelly tea. I was one of the best mages in my year, before I got shunted off on this dead-end farce with that stinking old misery guts.' He kicks his heels into the sand, his already-red face turning a shade more crimson. 'He thinks I don't study, but I do – and I found out things in his library. Things he never told me about.'

After another check to see if anyone is around, Andos leans in closer. 'The Lamuri were some of the greatest mages that ever lived. They had three books that they kept all their spells in. Together they're called *The Negra Lumaris*. The dark enlightenment. If you find them, then I'll give yer something real special. I got access to stinky-grump's possessions – and he has a Dwarven eye-piece. Powerful and very old. You wear it and you can understand anything – translate runes, decipher glyphs. I used it myself a few times.'

'What do you intend to do with these … books?' you ask dubiously. 'They sound dangerous.'

Andos shakes his head quickly, his forced laugh failing to put you at ease. 'Oh, they're nothing much – just mage-stuff, really. Thought they might make me look good – impress the university. They could be my ticket out of this horrid place. Can you blame me?'

Andos gives you directions to a clearing in the forest. You agree to meet him there for the exchange. (Make a note of the number 471. When you think you have found all three books, turn to that entry number any time between quests to receive your reward.) Return to the quest map to resume your journey.

549

Scar-face walks over and places a paw on your shoulder. 'You are kin now. I believe the great spirit, Shonac, sent you to fight for us.'

The leader, Grey-hair, beats his chest three times. 'We welcome you to Shara Khana, bright claw. Gather your strength, we leave for the marsh at first light.'

Will you:

Ask about the name, Shara Khana?	358
Ask about Shonac, the great spirit?	334
Leave for the marsh?	722

550

You have discovered rare Lamuri treasures that have been locked away for thousands of years! You may now choose up to two of the following rewards:

Sol shield	**Golden greaves**	**Fyre fiend**
(left hand: shield)	(feet)	(ring)
+2 speed +2 armour	+1 speed +2 brawn	+1 armour
Ability: radiance	Ability: charm	Ability: fire shield

You also find a bronze coffer, containing 100 gold crowns. Having looted the vault you return to the main chamber, where you take the sloping ledge up to the open doorway. Turn to 595.

551

The two severed heads crash to the ground in a spray of black blood, leaving the beast's scaled body to sink beneath the turbulent waves. Exhausted from the battle you lean against one of the rocks, your eyes seeking out Lorcan. The man is barely out of breath, his wounds healing instantly as purple light flares from the runes branded into his arm.

'Now for my favourite part,' he grins, walking over to the nearest drake head. 'The spoils of war.' (Each hero may now help themselves to one reward.) For warrior rewards, turn to 745. For rogue rewards, turn to 770. For mage rewards, turn to 761.

552

'This is Boogaloo, the water spirit.' The shaman raises his staff and points it towards the pool of dark water. 'Weaken it and we get spirit's power.'

You approach the edge of the pool, your eyes cautiously scanning the layer of dirt and weeds floating on its surface. Seeing nothing untoward, you lean in closer . . .

Suddenly a huge worm-like head bursts out of the water, filled with hundreds of spine-like teeth. You twist away, managing to dodge the snapping jaws – but in saving yourself, your foot catches on a water-slick stone, plunging you into the foul, stagnant pool. Through a flurry of bubbles, you see a long grey body coiling around you. Then you break the surface, gasping for air.

'Watch yourself!' shouts Boom Mamba. 'That thing – it's 'lectric!'

You have no clue what he means, until the creature's skin lights up with a bright coat of magic, sending painful jolts through your body. Recovering quickly, you suck in a big lungful of air before ducking back down beneath the fetid waters. It is time to fight:

	Speed	*Brawn*	*Armour*	*Health*
Boogaloo	6	4	3	50

Special abilities

- It's 'lectric: At the end of each combat round you must automatically take 2 damage plus 1 for each point of *armour* you are wearing. (If you had an *armour* of 4 you would take 6 damage per round). If you have the *insulated* ability you can ignore this damage.

If you defeat Boogaloo, turn to 577. If you are defeated, you may return to 510 to choose a different foe to battle.

553

The steamy haze makes the going more difficult than you anticipated. Several times you misplace your footing or your fingers slip on the smooth, slick rock. However, with patience and determination, you manage to complete the climb, joining Virgil on the bridge. Turn to 749.

554

Manoeuvring while in flight proves more difficult than you anticipated. Numerous times you are knocked to the ground by the wyrm's flailing head or by a deluge of pulpy missiles. Nevertheless, your persistent blows have succeeded in weakening it. When the wyrm breaks off to regurgitate more of its stomach's contents, you grab hold of the chain ladders and use them to gain height.

Once you are above the wyrm you leap off into space, weapons reversed in a downward strike. The wyrm rears back, its jaws stretching open to fire its pulpy missiles. But it is a second too late. You drive your weapons between its eyes, then flip away as blood and brains spew forth from the gaping wound. Its body twists in a spasm of pain, then its head crashes to the ground in a storm of paper and dust.

At last, the giant wyrm has been defeated. From its pulp-spattered remains, you may now help yourself to 100 gold crowns and one of the following rewards:

Gullet scales	Patchwork pulp	Wyrmhole
(necklace)	(cloak)	(ring)
+1 speed +1 armour	+2 speed + 2 brawn	+1 magic
Ability: charm	Ability: slick	Ability: vortex
		(requirement: mage)

If you have the word *spooks* on your hero sheet, turn to 691. Otherwise, you find nothing else of interest in the room, so decide to leave. Turn to 842.

555

'We try to talk, then we try to fight, but they keep coming, spreading like a disease across the forest.' Grey-hair's shoulders slump, looking as old as his years. 'They hunt us and take us away from den homes. We have lost many – pack brothers, sisters, young cubs.'

The white tigris clenches his paws. 'And that is why we must fight, Khana! We are the hunters of the forest, not them! Flee to the marsh and death will follow. Sheva are not cowards. We will show our claws!' There are roars of approval from his pack members, whilst the other tigris have fallen into a rebellious silence.

Will you:

Ask about the marsh?	337
Agree to help the Khana flee?	452
Agree to help the Sheva fight?	704

556

All that remains of Umbra is a pile of rumpled clothing and a scatter of jewellery. You also spot the skeleton of an adventurer, propped up against one of the columns. The mildewed white robes and cross-shaped pendant suggest they had once been a priest.

You find a pouch containing 15 gold crowns and one of the following rewards:

Shade's mantle	Nocturnal leathers	Pious halo
(cloak)	(chest)	(ring)
+1 speed +1 brawn	+1 speed +2 brawn	+2 brawn
Ability: trickster	Ability: savagery	Ability: seraphim's symbols set (requirement: monk)

When you have made your decision, you return to the courtyard. Turn to 510.

557

(You must have completed the orange quest *The Abussos* before you can access this location.)

Following a crude goblin map scrawled onto animal hide, you find yourself standing outside a ruined building at the corner of two streets. Something had once been written over the doorway – possibly a sign. But it is so faded with age that you can't make out any of the symbols. With a sigh you tug open the iron door, which comes away loose in your hands. Awkwardly, you lift it up and put it against the wall, then step inside.

The interior is much as you expected. The ground is covered in rubble and bits of broken glass. What had once been rows of shelves now lie smashed across the floor. In one corner the ceiling has collapsed, allowing thin rays of ashen light to illuminate the cobwebs and dust motes floating in the air.

'So much for treasure maps,' grunts Virgil, kicking at a stone. 'We're wasting time.'

'You're right, this is a dead end.' You pick up what looks like a tattered, dirt-stained blanket. Somehow it has survived all these years, but is riddled with mould and smells like a sewer. You toss it away with a grimace.

'Er ... do you mind,' says a voice right next to your ear.

You spin around, so abruptly that you almost lose your balance and fall over.

Much to your surprise, there is no one there.

'Virgil, did you hear something?' You glance over your shoulder to see that the witchfinder has left the building and is now waiting for you outside.

Cautiously, you begin searching between the rubble and broken shelves, looking for someone who might be hiding.

'Can I help you? Are you looking for something in particular?'

You twist around again. 'Who's there?' you shout. 'Show yourself!'

'I would suggest you calm down.'

You feel something touch your arm. You look down to see a white gloved hand hovering in mid-air... With a cry you knock the limb away, back-stepping to the nearest wall. As you go to draw a weapon you hesitate, wondering if your eyes are playing tricks on you.

Gliding across the room are a pair of white gloves and a black bowler hat. 'Welcome to my humble establishment,' says the disembodied voice. 'I am the proprietor, Mr G H Claypole. How can I help you?' The gloved hands spread themselves wide in a welcoming gesture.

You realise that you are looking at the shopkeeper, or what is left of him. Mr Claypole is a ghost.

'You're a little tall for a dwarf,' you remark, puzzled. 'How did you get here?'

'I came from the shroud, slipped through a space – a doorway, if you like. I've been here for...' He pauses, while his gloved hand scratches at an invisible chin. 'Substantially longer than I planned. But no mind, you've made my journey worth its while. And how did you find yourself here, pray tell?'

'I followed a map; I thought it might lead to ...' You stop yourself, glancing around at the broken remnants of the building, suddenly feeling more than a little foolish 'A stash of weapons, armour ... something useful.'

'Of course!' says the ghost, clasping his hands together. 'I have everything you might need, for a price of course.'

'But there is nothing here,' you implore.

You are met by an angry tut. 'Not in plain sight, mortal. I keep them in a vault of runes. Protects them from the living and the dead. Now, I sense your need is urgent, so what would you like to see?'

Will you:	
Purchase potions and elixirs?	609
Purchase runes and glyphs?	799
Purchase weapons and armour?	682
Purchase crafting reagents?	849
Leave the haunted shop?	**return to the map**

558

You jolt awake, coughing and spluttering. From the dark sky, falling stone beats against the earth, bouncing and rattling off your soot-streaked armour. Shielding your eyes against the barrage, you fix your gaze on the mountain. Through the ash you can dimly make out its summit, fountaining an endless column of rock and earth into the sky.

The crunch of feet alerts you to the approaching demon. It strides through the smoke, a shadow amidst the swirling red ash. Its charred body is crisscrossed with veins of fire, pulsing with a hellish glow. And in its hand is a sword – a rune-blade, its serrated edge crackling with magic.

My vision.

Tears sting your eyes as the demon stalks towards you. 'Virgil … What have you done?'

The demon snarls. 'My journey is complete! Ragnarok is remade!'

You scramble for a weapon, clawing through the dust and rock, but they have landed out of reach. When you turn back, the demon is standing over you, the dark sword raised. 'One of us will change the future.'

'Indeed I will.'

The voice comes from behind you. An arrow of purple light slams into the demon, sending it reeling backwards. As it tries to stand, another bolt blows it away into the mist. The sword rattles to the ground.

You struggle to rise, bewildered by this sudden change of events. A black-cloaked stranger strides past, a bright staff of gold resting across his shoulder. The wind tugs at his cowl, exposing his features for the briefest of moments. A bald head, gaunt face, weasel-like eyes. A scar curves along their cheek, turning their upper lip …

It is the librarian from Durnhollow. The man who drugged you and then questioned you. The man who brought you to the edge of ruin.

'How … how did you get here?' You struggle weakly to stand.

'You told me everything, remember?' He raises a hand, sending currents of magic coursing towards the sword. 'I'm here for Ragnarok. Nothing more.' The pale flesh of his arm reveals three branded serpents. They writhe and twist as if alive, glowing with an alien magic.

'You … you used me … used Cernos … to get the sword.'

The librarian glances at you, the air still rippling around his hand. 'I must do what the voice tells me. Ragnarok is part of the plan. The plan to return …' His magic curls around the sword, enfolding it within an invisible prison.

'No! I can't let you take the sword. It must be destroyed …' You tense, ready to spring. He reads your intention, his expression darkening.

'I saved your life, fool – if life you can call it. Do not try to stop me – or I will end it just as swiftly.'

The sword drifts through the air to hover at his side. He then raises the golden staff, its end panels flipping open to form the petals of a flower. 'Remember, I am Lorcan. I am the one who saved you. The future is now yours, prophet.'

There is a bright flash of golden light – then he is gone. And the sword with him.

The ground shakes violently, throwing you sideways. Only metres away the rock is torn asunder, ripping out a jagged fissure. From its depths, a bright sludge of lava spews forth in a glutinous mass.

You quickly find your feet, lurching from side to side as the world continues to shudder in its death throes. From behind you there is a thunderous crashing din, followed by a fierce wash of heat. You dare not look back, to see the scale of devastation. Instead, you simply press on. The demon lies nearby, crumpled body steaming with purple smoke.

A sudden tremor knocks you to the ground.

Forced to crawl, you scramble over the rocks to reach the demon's side. 'Virgil . . .?' The librarian's magic has blown a hole in his chest, exposing an ugly mass of bone and tissue. He lies twisted, arms outstretched as if reaching for something. Your eyes trace the line of his body, to the golden sphere lying in the dust.

A beacon stone. Identical to the one that Virgil placed inside you, to summon himself and Avian to the volcano. He had another . . .

Your hand closes around the sphere, thumb resting on the switch. 'Freedom . . .' The word has a bitter ring to it now, tainted with lies – tainted by what you have become. A demon. As Cernos was before you. 'All I ever wanted was freedom . . . .'

Your eyes stray to the witchfinder. The man who betrayed you. In the end, he lost himself to his anger and his rage. He took Ragnarok, believing it would rid the world of evil.

There are many steps on the path of darkness. I pray you find deliverance before its end.

You press the switch, just as a violent earthquake rips open the ground.

For a second you are falling, then a soft white light envelops you . . . Turn to 831.

559

The tigris move swiftly through the jungle, weaving agilely between the gnarled roots and walls of liana. Often they resort to running on all fours, leaping and bounding over obstructions or springing off fallen trees. The babe clings to the mother's shoulders, looking neither alarmed nor concerned by their speedy flight. Perhaps this is what they are used to – forever running, forever trying to outrun the hunters.

As the rain finally starts to slow you break out of the tangled undergrowth, your feet thudding into banks of wet sand. A river stretches to your right, already swollen with the rainfall. Its sparkling waters churn and roil, pitching a constant stream of forest debris along its course.

Ahead, a group of tigris are standing underneath a shelf of rock. By their animated gestures, it looks as though an argument is taking place. Two sides seem to have formed – on the one side, a pack of white-furred tigris, and on the other a larger group with black-and-orange markings, similar to your companions.

Scar-face slows, putting his arm around the young mother and her cub. A sudden silence falls as the two packs of tigris halt their exchange and turn to watch. Before anyone can speak, the air rings with a ferocious roar. One of the white-furred tigris with black stripes and green eyes springs forward, muscles rippling in his powerful arms.

'You bring a skin here?' he snarls.

'Hold, Sheva. This one not like others. Helped us; helped Shara Khana.'

'We not take help from skins,' growls the white tiger. The rest of his group edge forward in an aggressive stance. 'Khana grow weak. Hunters take your spirit.'

Scar-face leaps forward to face off against the white, his long tail whipping back and forth in agitation. 'I'll show you spirit, Sheva!'

'Hold your claws,' booms a voice.

Both of the tigris stiffen, looking back to the rock shelf where a larger orange has stepped forward. A thick mane of grey hair grows around his throat and shoulders. You suspect that this is their leader – or one of them at least – a leader accustomed to being followed. This Grey-hair glares at the white tigris. 'If we hope to cross the marsh, then we need fresh claws.'

'Marsh is the coward's way,' growls the white, making a face and spitting on the ground. 'I told you. We lost too many. Shara Sheva fight now.'

'Please, no.' The mother speaks up for the first time, addressing the grey-haired leader. 'They are strong. I tried to find a better way—' She pauses, glancing sideways at Scar-face. 'We tried to find better way,' she corrects. 'But hunters have pack lands and spread like shadow. Old dens not safe.'

Grey-hair grunts softly. 'I told you this. Better you see it with your own eyes.'

The white gives a rumbling growl. 'No one ever crosses marsh. Sheva fight now, before we all gone.' His green eyes regard you with utter disdain. 'Would this one lend its claws; turn steel against its own kin?'

'No,' implores Scar-face. 'The marsh is the better way. We flee across the mountains – find new dens. Join Khana – we need more claws.'

Will you:

Ask about the marsh?	337
Ask about the 'skins'?	555
Agree to help the Khana flee?	452
Agree to help the Sheva fight?	704

560

You wade out into the lake, the noxious stench of the water making you gag. It isn't until you pull yourself up onto the island, your clothes dripping with slime and pond weed, that you see the effect the polluted water has had on your equipment. The slime contains some kind of acid that has eaten away at the metal and leather, whilst leaving yourself unharmed. (You must immediately lower the *brawn*, *magic* or *armour* of two items of equipment by 1.)

At last you are able to inspect the chest. Up close, you can now see that the wooden panels are etched with runes. You cannot fathom their purpose, but suspect they might be protecting the wood from the effects of the swamp. Eager to see what is inside, you put a hand to the lid. Suddenly the runes flash into life, their spidery patterns glowing with purple light. Then there is a loud crack of magic. You feel yourself being flung backwards, your surroundings blurring into a white tunnel. Another deafening crack – and you are tumbling across rocks and stone, the sounds of the jungle rushing in to envelop you once again. Turn to 574.

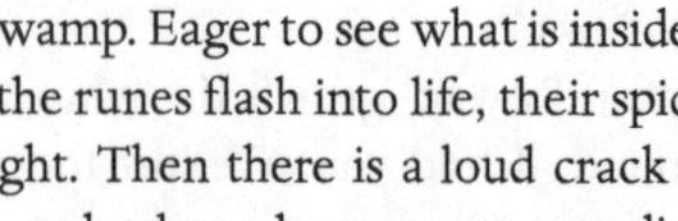

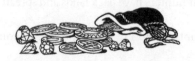

561

In your haste, you misjudge a handhold and slip, your legs scrabbling desperately against the rough wall. For several heart-stopping seconds, you are holding on with one hand. Then the loose rock crumbles and you find yourself falling. By luck rather than judgement, you manage to grab a jagged outcrop. It breaks your fall, but one of the straps on your backpack comes loose, swinging itself free of your shoulder.

When you finally make it back onto the bridge, sweating and shaking from your experience, you discover that you have lost one of your prized items. (You must remove one backpack item from your hero sheet.) Turn to 749.

562

Your weapons and magic shred through the raging elemental, weakening it and slowing its momentum. 'That's it!' Boom Mamba races into the centre of the ruins, lifting up his glowing staff. The wind snakes around him, now little more than a gust of whirling grit and sand. There is a flash from the staff's runes as the wind is drawn inwards, swirling and spinning into its glowing headpiece.

Then it is gone. Boom cracks a smile, his face shining from the blue light swirling around the staff. 'Zephyr is in the boom stick now. We gonna blast Mortzilla good with this!'

(By defeating Zephyr, the shaman's staff has gained the *wind guardian* ability. Make a note of this on your hero sheet.)

If you are a warrior, turn to 160. If you are a mage, turn to 346. If you are a rogue, turn to 297.

563

The stairs descend into cramped passageways, where the air is cold and musty. You sense you are now underground, as evidenced by the occasional root or creeper pushing between the tight stone slabs. Again, every stone here is covered in carvings; but these have taken on a more sinister tone, the images depicting bloody sacrifice and demonic entities.

Turning down another passage, you notice alcoves cut into the walls. Each one contains a linen-wrapped corpse, bent over in a crouched position. Some are wearing headdresses, others have clay animal masks fixed over their skulls. Pots and bowls have been arranged around each corpse – perhaps for offerings, or part of some after-life ceremony.

Another turning brings you to a junction. To the left the passageway ends in a stone door, which stands slightly ajar. To your right the passage becomes a set of worn stairs, rising past carved pillars of bronze.

Will you:	
Take the left passage?	599
Take the stairs?	889

564

You count nine hounds, tearing across the bridge – each an immense and powerful predator, shimmering with heat and flame. Virgil coolly raises a pistol and fires, discharging a bullet at the leader. It gives a savage roar of pain, its head thrown backwards by the force of the blast. The creature's momentum carries it forward, its broken body bouncing and sliding across the ground. The witchfinder leaps over the smouldering corpse, dropping another of the beasts with his second pistol. As the rest of the pack close in, he quickly trades his smoking weapons for two thin-bladed swords – their white steel glowing with holy inscriptions.

'Come and be judged!' Virgil dives into the pack, his swords cutting dizzying trails through the air. You hurry to join him, your own weapons burning bright with magic. It is time to fight:

	Speed	*Brawn*	*Armour*	*Health*
Hounds	11	7	5	90

Special abilities

- Pack attack: If you roll a double for the molten hounds' attack speed, you must take 4 damage, ignoring *armour* from their swiping claws. This ability deals damage in addition to their usual damage score.

- Molten skin: You automatically take 2 damage at the end of each combat round, ignoring *armour*, from the hounds' flames. If you have *fire shield* you can ignore this ability.
- Body of flame: The molten hounds are immune to *backdraft, fire aura, sear* and *searing mantle.*

If you manage to defeat these fiery fiends, turn to **783**.

565

'Well, you look better turned out than the others, so for once I'm optimistic.' He holds up the unfinished map, with the blank space at its centre. 'This area is known as the dark interior. Yes, predictable name, but that's geographers for you. It's a cratered valley that few, if any, have fully navigated. I've sent four explorers there now and none have had the good will to return.' He pauses, as if mulling over the matter. 'They might be dead, I suppose.'

You nervously clear your throat. 'So, you want me to complete your map?' you assert, hoping to get the conversation back on track. 'And for this, I get a reward?'

The man puts a finger to his ear. 'I'm sorry, did you say ... reward? The university not paying you enough already for this little holiday?'

'I'm not from the university,' you reply firmly, folding your arms. 'But if the price is right, I'd be willing to do what I can.'

The scholar picks up his sunhat and starts fanning himself. After much muttering and grumbling, followed by several long minutes of uncomfortable silence, the man finally nods his head. 'Humph, very well then. Fifty gold crowns up front, to help purchase any essentials you might need. I'll double that on your return ... *if* you return, that is.'

Your eyes are drawn to the gaping white circle on the map. It suddenly looks unsettlingly large. 'You can trust me,' you reply, holding out a hand for the money.

The scholar gives you 50 gold crowns. Make a note of the word *explorer* on your hero sheet, then turn to **548**.

566

'We all Shara Sheva,' states White Cloak, patting her chest then pointing to the rest of the pack in turn. 'Not have names like skins. We all pack. All Shara Sheva. That is our name.'

Your eyes scan the small gathering. 'Do we really have enough?' you ask candidly. 'The hunters will be well-armed.'

White Cloak's eyes narrow with affront. 'Each Sheva worth ten of their skins. Shonac's spirit burns in our hearts, not theirs. By sun fall, they will hunt us no more.'

Will you:

Ask about Shonac, the great spirit ?	542
Join the scouting party?	576

567

The stone plugs slide down over the outlets of lava, cutting off their flow to the forge. Virgil nods his head with approval. 'Our hot-tempered friends aren't going to like that . . .'

Congratulations, you have solved the puzzle and improved your chances of defeating the fire sprites! Make a note of the keyword *fire quencher* on your hero sheet and the number 350. You may now examine the pipes, if you haven't already (turn to 692) or head up the stairs to the forge (turn to 601).

568

Ahead, a stone ziggurat cuts an impressive shape against the bright-azure sky. You sense the demon has been this way – his taint, the pall of ancient evil, hangs heavy in the air.

You make an immediate beeline for the structure, pushing through the garden's unruly vegetation. At last, scratched and bleeding from the many thorns and needles, you break out onto a paved causeway. It leads straight to the base of the ziggurat, where an open doorway provides access inside. However, your presence here has not gone unnoticed.

Two gold statues stand guard, either side of the path. They are fashioned to look like armoured warriors, with winged helms and runed breastplates. Each statue is armed with an immense halberd, with a crescent-shaped blade almost a metre in length. The moment you set foot on the path the guards jerk into life, then proceed to move with deliberate strides towards you. It is time to fight:

	Speed	*Brawn*	*Armour*	*Health*
Golden guards	9	9	8	70

Special abilities

- Scything blades: Each time you choose to play a speed or a combat ability, roll a die. On a result of ⚃ or less you are caught by the guards' halberds. This causes 4 damage, ignoring *armour*. It also stops you from using your ability until the next combat round. ⚄ or more and you avoid damage, allowing you to use your ability as normal.
- Knockdown: If you suffer health damage from the guards' damage score, you are knocked off your feet, lowering your *speed* by 1 for the next combat round.

If you manage to defeat these deadly sentinels, turn to **524**.

569

You notice a number of items snagged in the weed-choked waters. Using Boom Mamba's staff, you are able to fish them out of the pool. As well as a pouch containing 40 gold crowns, you also find one of the following rewards:

Tremor stick	**Sanctified scale**	**Lightning whetstone**
(main hand: spear)	(necklace)	(talisman)
+1 speed +2 brawn	+1 armour	+1 speed
Ability: shock!	Ability: seraphim's symbols set (requirement: monk)	Ability: sure edge

When you have made your decision, you return to the courtyard. Turn to 510.

570

'You're wasting time,' you reply, raising your voice above the incessant thunder of the rain. 'I'll help you. For a cut of the prize.'

The two hunters exchange looks. Weasel scowls and looks about to argue, but his friend lowers his knife and starts towards the forest. 'I had enough of this place already,' he grunts. 'Let's get this done. Save the rest for camp.'

The dark-skinned hunter leads the way, moving quickly through the rain-dripping foliage, his spitting torch streaking its own trail behind him. He stops occasionally, checking a muddy imprint or a bent leaf stalk, then changes direction, heading deeper and deeper into the claustrophobic jungle.

Suddenly, without warning, a black body flies out from the undergrowth, slamming into the weasel and sending him screaming into the jungle. You hear a savage roar and the sickening sound of claws rending through flesh. You stagger back, as does the dark-skinned hunter, both of you momentarily shaken by the suddenness of the attack.

A male tigris bounds back through the trees, its powerful legs driving it into the other hunter. They crash together, going down into the watery mud. A knife flashes, slashing into the beast's side – but the creature shows no sign of pain, its claws seeking to rake through the hunter's leather armour. Quickly, you race forward, swinging your weapons and knocking the tigris away.

The beast rolls over, then springs back onto its hind legs, golden eyes glaring at you with a fierce defiance. For a moment, you are caught between running and fighting – then the tigris pounces. You must fight:

	Speed	*Brawn*	*Armour*	*Health*
Tigris	9	6	4	70

Special abilities

- Revenge of the tigris: Your opponent fights with a fierce

determination, keen to defend his fleeing pack mates. The tigris rolls three dice for damage and chooses the highest single die result to use for his damage score.

- Bleed: After the tigris makes a successful attack that causes health damage, you must take a further point of damage at the end of each combat round.

If you manage to defeat this savage opponent, turn to 678.

571

As you head along the sea front, you see a group of sailors hoisting bamboo cages onto the largest of the merchant vessels. You edge closer, to try and get a look inside one of the cages, but a bare-chested brute with thick hairy arms shoves you away.

'Move on or I'll be using yer as bait,' he growls. From the unsettling array of knives and pistols at his belt, you decide to heed his warning.

Further along the promenade, one building in particular catches your eye. Its entrance-way is fashioned from a giant turtle shell, raised up on stilts to create a sheltered awning. Behind it a wooden shack extends back into the trees, painted in a gaudy assortment of rainbow-coloured hues. Small, pig-like creatures are scurrying around the entrance, snorting and squealing as they nip and chase each other. A sign dangling from the arched-shell reads 'Yootha's Trading Post'.

Next to it is an altogether less flamboyant building – a rickety lodge topped with a sagging roof of palm fronds. An elderly man is sat on its veranda, soaking his feet in a bucket of water. A pirate-hat rests lopsidedly on his balding head. 'Hey there, need somewhere to stay?' calls the man, splashing his feet in the water. 'Only 1 gold crown a night at Bertie's hostel. And the cockroaches come free.'

As you contemplate his special offer, your attention is drawn to a tract of beach, where a collection of cages and baskets are resting on the sand. A young dark-skinned woman with oil-braided hair and sparkling jewellery is pacing in front of her wares – calmly handling the giant snake that rests across her shoulders. 'Looking for something more exotic?' she asks, offering you a playful smile.

'I've told you again and again,' snaps a voice behind you. 'Don't use the mosquito repellent on the parchment. Not the parchment!' You turn to see a grey-robed man in a straw hat, hurrying along the promenade. He is clutching a number of charts and scroll cases to his chest. A scrawny youth with a tangle of ginger hair is struggling to keep up, his sunburnt face craning around a tall pile of books. 'Hurry up, those are priceless works!' snaps the man, kicking up a dust cloud as he quickens his pace.

Will you:	
Visit the trading post?	**578**
Visit the hostel?	**594**
View the exotic pets?	**486**
Talk to the scholar?	**402**
Head into the jungle?	**Turn to the Act 2 map**

572

You hear the scuffing of feet on stone. Turning, you see Scar-face standing beneath a ruined arch, his fur matted with mud and dust. He nods in greeting. 'We stand together, bright claw.'

The witch lurches towards you, her black robes rustling across the stone. 'Unfortunate you are still alive, tigris, but no matter. Together, you will make a most splendid feast.'

You ready your weapons and prepare to fight:

	Speed	*Magic*	*Armour*	*Health*
Succubus	10	5	9	80

Special abilities

- Mental daggers: You must lose 2 *health* at the end of each combat round.
- Delirium: If you take health damage from the succubus' damage score, you are immediately inflicted with delirium. If you win a combat round, roll a die. If the result is ⚀ or ⚁ then your attack misses its mark and you cannot roll for damage. If the result is ⚂ or more, you can roll for damage as normal.

- Revenge of the tigris: Scar-face adds 2 to your damage score for the duration of this combat.

If you manage to defeat the succubus, turn to 591.

573

The column of wind roars through the ruined spaces of the old temple. 'This one angry spirit! Watch yourself!' Boom Mamba ducks behind a wall of rubble as the howling vortex blasts through a stone column, heading straight for you.

'We have to fight that?' you gasp, staring in horror at the rapidly-advancing gale.

Boom shifts into a crouch behind his staff, fingers tightening around its runes. 'Zephyr is spirit of air. Take courage. Weaken it and then we take into boom stick, yes? Give us its power.'

'But how do I—'

The wind smashes into you like a solid fist of rock, lifting you off your feet and sending you hurtling across the courtyard. You crash down onto your back, skidding through the dust as the howling wind bellows overhead. Then it is twisting away, gaining distance ready for another strike. Frantically, you scramble to your feet, fear and adrenaline helping to block out the pain. After retrieving your weapons you spin around, ready to defend yourself, as the head of the wind-snake rushes in once again. It is time to fight:

	Speed	*Magic*	*Armour*	*Health*
Zephyr	5	4	3	50

Special abilities

- Slipstream: If you win a combat round, roll a die. If the result is ⚂ or less you are caught in the zephyr's slipstream and are sucked inside its whirling coils. Instead of rolling for damage, your hero takes 4 damage instead, ignoring *armour*. If your result is ⚂ or higher, you may strike against your opponent as normal.
- Body of air: Zephyr is immune to *bleed, disease* and *venom*.

If you manage to defeat Zephyr, turn to 562. If you are defeated, you may return to 510 to choose a different foe to battle.

574

Clambering to your feet you discover that you are standing on the outskirts of a set of ruins, shrouded in a pale mist. After dusting yourself down, you decide to enter and explore them further. Turn to 459.

575

The frog proves a frustrating opponent, effortlessly avoiding the majority of your attacks. But each lucky wound you manage to inflict saps away at its agility, weakening your opponent and slowing it down. Finally the frog starts to back away, limping towards the waterfall. Weakened by loss of blood, the frog misses its footing and slips – giving you the opening you need to step in and deliver the final blow.

Searching the creature's remains, you find one of the following rewards:

Sea spray garland	Hunting fork	Fisher's friend
(necklace)	(main hand: spear)	(ring)
+1 speed +1 magic	+1 speed +3 brawn	+1 brawn
Ability: wave	Ability: skewer	Ability: hooked
(requirement: mage)	(requirement: warrior)	(requirement: rogue)

Stepping past the body, you clamber up the slippery rocks and pass underneath the waterfall. As you suspected, there is a cave here – a treasure trove of objects, all tangled up in nets of vine. There are also a number of skeletons caught up in the netting, both animal and human, and a golden crown sparkling on one of the rocks.

You may now take one of the following as an additional reward:

King of the pond	Kiss of a princess	Enchanted boots
(head)	(ring)	(feet)
+1 speed +2 magic	+1 brawn +2 health	+1 speed +1 armour
Ability: overload	Ability: charm	Ability: heal
(requirement: mage)		

Searching the remains of the other unfortunate adventurers, you find 50 gold crowns and a crumpled map. It looks to have been torn in two, the half you are holding showing a secret trail through the jungle. A name has been scrawled at the bottom, followed by a date: *Frobisher. 4.11.1362.* Without the other half, it makes little sense to you. (You may take *Frobisher's map* if you wish – simply make a note of it on your hero sheet. If you also have *Coronado's map*, turn to 606.)

Finding little else of interest in the cave, you leave and continue your journey. Return to the quest map.

576

You offer to join the hunting party. The Sheva leader scowls, ready to object – but Black Patch intervenes. 'Bright claw think like them,' explains the younger tigris. 'Skin knows skin, like we know tigris.'

The other members of the party rumble their displeasure, but the leader appears to be considering his companion's words. He finally gives a swift nod, ignoring the answering snarls of dissent as he leads the way into the trees.

As if to prove some point, the tigris set a punishing pace, running on all fours to cover the ground quickly. You struggle to keep up, forced to clamber and hack through the undergrowth while they bound agilely over it. At last you catch up with them at the edge of a rocky escarpment. Black Patch has climbed up onto a nearby tree, balancing on a growth of liana to get a better view.

Dropping onto your stomach, you slide forward to join the others. Through the misty dawn, you see a fort-like compound occupying the valley below. Each of its wooden walls ends in a fortified lookout tower, manned by guards. Inside the compound itself you spy several huts, a tent and some cages filled with large and ferocious-looking beasts. The main gates to the compound are open, as a series of carts clatter out onto a cleared track that cuts into the forest. On the back of each cart are a crowd of smaller cages, containing captured tigris. You spot members of the Sheva and Khana pack, as well as other tigris with less familiar markings.

You can feel the tension and rage from your companions. The leader starts to rise, his claws extended. If he had his way, he would charge in right now … but Black Patch advises caution. 'Look,' he snarls, pointing to the carts. 'Skins go with cages.'

Sure enough, a line of hunters are marching alongside the carts, armed with blades, pistols and crossbows. You count over a dozen – leaving only a skeleton crew back at the compound, including an eight-foot giant and a burly, black-bearded hunter bristling with weapons. The latter is barking orders, gesturing impatiently at the slow-moving procession.

'We strike their wood den,' growls the Sheva leader, baring his teeth. 'Attack when they weak. Take off head of pack. Then rest fall.'

'But our kin,' ventures Black Patch nervously. 'We must free them, then we strike with many claws. Or we lose them to skin lands. We not see again.'

The leader scowls. 'That is not our way. Those that fall we leave. They are lost to us.'

'But they are claws!' implores Black Patch. 'They would fight with us!'

You glance at the leader. He is scratching at the earth, torn with indecision. 'What say you, bright claw?' he grunts, his eyes remaining fixed on the compound. 'How should Sheva win this day?'

Will you:

Attack the camp? 617

Ambush the convoy? 632

577

The carcass of the creature bobs to the surface of the pool. Then it begins to shimmer and fragment into bright shards of blue light. There is a flash from the totem as Boom Mamba raises it above his head, absorbing the light into its glowing runes.

'We got the power of Boogaloo!' declares Boom Mamba, hopping up and down with glee. 'You do good! Mortzilla will be quaking in fear.'

(By defeating the water spirit, the shaman's staff has gained the *Boogie's booster* ability. Make a note of this on your hero sheet.)

If you are a warrior, turn to 569. If you are a mage, turn to 458. If you are a rogue, turn to 325.

578

You pass through a curtain of beads into a small, stuffy room lined with shelves. As you head towards the counter, you glance at some of the peculiar items on display – a jar containing pickled eels, a monkey-skull candle-holder, a snake-skin umbrella, a necklace of curled fingernails …

Behind the counter, a tall skinny woman is arranging flowers in an old boot. Her black hair rises up off her narrow brow in a mountainous peak, decorated with beads and shells and scraps of netting. It gives her the appearance of something that was just hauled in on the last fishing boat.

'Ooh, what we got here? You don't look the usual sort,' she smiles, fluttering her long, glittery eyelashes. 'Got a serious air about you, you have. Like someone who means business.' She puts her flowers to one side, brushing her hands against her black silk gown. 'So, to business then. I'm Yootha Finsbottom – think of me as your personal shopper. You won't leave here empty-handed or disappointed. That's my rules.'

Your eyes stray to the collection of jars and bottles on the shelves behind her, as well as a wooden trunk wrapped in iron chains. 'If you're going jungle-side then I have a few little Yootha specials to keep you safe and sound. Or if it's a souvenir you're after, then may I suggest a genuine Lamuri artefact? Rare and collectible. I'll cut you a good deal on those. No-one says Yootha isn't fair.'

Will you:

Ask to see Yootha's specials?	593
Ask to view the Lamuri artefacts?	612
Ask about the jungle?	520
Thank Yootha and continue your journey?	571

579

Boss monster: Cernos the demon

The canyon narrows, angling steeply into a tunnel of dark rock. At its end, two carved faces glare at you with flat, expressionless eyes. Dwarves, you assume, from the cropped beards and flabby jowls. The crowns on their brows curve upwards, forming a high archway cut into the side of the great volcano.

You stride into the chamber beyond – a vast alien hall, its vaulted ceiling glittering with veins of silver. For a brief moment, your steps falter as you struggle to take in the craftsmanship of your surroundings. There are no lines or fractures, no customary marks from a stonecutter's tools – the walls are as smooth as glass, reflecting the sparkling light and magnifying it a hundred-fold.

'Cernos!' Your footfalls echo as you march towards the demon. He is facing an immense door, its surface covered in a dazzling array of runes. The demon has put aside his iron casket – and now fumbles with something at the centre of the door. He stops when he hears you approach, his head cocked to one side.

'You are a tiresome nuisance,' he growls. 'How many lives do you have, prophet?'

He turns to face you, his crimson eyes glittering balefully in the torchlight. 'I gave you a gift, not a punishment.'

You break into a run, weapons flying into your hands. 'Then consider this a return, Cernos!'

The demon gives an incredulous laugh. 'Oh, so now you think yourself my equal?'

He springs forward, moving with a speed that belies his colossal frame. You crash together, snarling like dogs, trading blows in a frenzied blur that would leave any onlooker dizzy. For several seconds you have the upper hand, your weapons hammering against the demon's scales. Then a burst of pain flares in your chest. A claw has swept in under your guard, taking you in the ribs and lifting you off your feet. You roll and tumble, coming up hard against the rock wall. The demon moves in quickly, giving you little chance to recover. With a crack of his wings, he leaps into the air, drawing his hooves together, ready to slam them down …

You see your death, played out in slow motion – the ribcage shattering in an explosion of bone; fragments lancing through your heart and lungs – your life extinguished in a blood-spattered instant. Then the vision is gone. Time shifts back to the present. You whirl aside, dodging the deathblow … The demon's hooves smash harmlessly into the ground.

'Too slow, Cernos!' You scramble back to your feet, weapons raised. 'I see the future, remember?'

The demon swings around, his half-burnt face creased with fury. 'Tell me then, fool – do you not see *my* destiny? I am Barahar's heir! Ragnarok will be mine!' He throws up his arms, the air bending and shifting around his scaled fists. 'All will serve me in damnation!'

A tremble runs through the stone, shaking the walls and rattling your teeth. Then dark magic streaks across the room, gouging great chunks out of the ground. The fragments of rock hurtle towards the demon, folding themselves around his arms to form a brutal set of gauntlets.

'Tell me – what future do you see now, prophet?' Cernos spreads his wings, their vastness obliterating the light. Then he surges forward once again, his rock-encrusted knuckles splintering into razor-sharp spines. It is time to fight:

	Speed	*Brawn*	*Armour*	*Health*
Cernos	10	9	10	85
Rock fists	–	–	10	40

Special abilities

- Rock fists: While Cernos has the *rock fists* ability, he adds 2 to his attack speed and rolls 2 dice for his damage score.

- Body of rock: The rock fists are immune to *barbs, bleed, disease, piercing, thorns, thorn cage* and *venom*.

If you win a combat round, you can choose to strike against Cernos or his rock fists. Once the rocks fists have been destroyed, Cernos no longer benefits from their ability.

If you manage to defeat Cernos, turn to 698.

580

Survival is a powerful motivator, driving you to feats of strength and savagery that you didn't know you were capable of. Your weapons are soon forgotten as you roll through the mud, ripping and biting at the panther, caught up in your own dark rage. Finally, with arms snapped tight around the panther's neck, you squeeze and twist, listening to the bones crack – and the creature give its last, gargling gasp.

You slide out from underneath the panther's body. Only then do you notice your hands, glistening with blue-black scales – each finger ending in a sharp yellow talon. You stare at them in horrified amazement, realising that the demon curse – the transformation – is happening far quicker than you could ever have imagined. You have now gained the following special ability:

Demon claws (pa): For every double that you roll for attack speed (before or after a re-roll), your hero automatically inflicts 4 damage to their opponent. This ability ignores *armour*.

After retrieving your weapons, you turn back to the body, which is already crawling with bugs. It is only fitting that you take some token of this momentous victory before the forest reclaims this infamous predator. If you are a warrior or a rogue, turn to 729. If you are a mage, turn to 714.

581

The stepped pyramid looks like some kind of puzzle or magical device. Each tier has a circular depression, designed to hold one of the clay tablets. The first three tiers have already been filled, but the fourth remains empty. The script above the hole reads 'volax'. You glance around at the remaining clay tablets, strewn across the floor. Most of them have been smashed but three are still intact, displaying icons of animal deities.

Will you:	
Choose the jaguar?	759
Choose the bird?	725
Choose the snake?	767

582

Your decision made, you turn away from the hole and prepare to take on the bridge guardians. The arratoch lunges forward on its serpentine body, splitting the air with its shrieking barrage. Avian spins his staff, sending bolts of magic hurtling towards its malign face.

'We have to silence the arratoch!' he yells.

'I think we got bigger problems!' Virgil nods towards the charging stone giants. Spinning his blades, he moves to head them off before they can reach the mage.

For a second you hold back, sizing up your three opponents. Then with a clamouring battle cry, you hurl yourself into the fray. It is time to fight:

	Speed	*Brawn*	*Armour*	*Health*
Olum	11	8	9	50
Atum	11	9	7	50
Arratoch	–	–	5	35

Special abilities

🛡 Brotherly love: Once one of the golems (Olum or Atum) is defeated, the remaining golem goes into a fit of rage. This raises their *speed* by 2 and *brawn* by 4 for the remainder of the combat.

- Arratoch alarm: While the wailing arratoch still has *health*, you must lower your *brawn* and *magic* by 2 at the end of each combat round. Once the arratoch is defeated, your attributes are immediately restored.
- Body of rock: Your opponents are immune to *bleed, disease, piercing* and *venom.*
- Companions' courage: Your may add 2 to your damage score for the duration of this fight.

In this combat, choose one of the golems to attack. If you win a combat round, you may strike against your chosen golem or the arratoch. If you lose the combat, your chosen golem will strike against you. Once you have defeated both golems (Olum and Atum), you win the combat (the arratoch is automatically defeated).

If you manage to overcome these fearsome guardians, turn to 546.

583

'Ambition, plain and simple,' he replies, peering over the rim of his spectacles. 'Fifteen years I've been waiting for funding for this endeavour. Always overlooked – always some excuse. Now I think they sent me here just to get rid of me!' He chortles, looking smug at his attempt at humour.

'Funding for what?' you press, glancing around at the books and scrolls.

'Didn't they bother to tell you?' he splutters. 'Send you out here with no clue. Judah save us. Listen – no one to date has written the definitive work on the Terral Jungle. Yes, yes – I know we have a few sketchy journals from the odd explorer – raving with fever for the most part and offering nothing of any academic quality. But this will be a proper scholarly account. That is why I am here. To pen my masterwork – the one I'm remembered for.' He lifts his chin up proudly in the air. 'Runtis Bogglespiff. A name never to be forgotten.'

Turn to 386 to ask the scholar another question or turn to 548 if you wish to leave and continue your journey.

The demon raises a fist into the air, his clawed fingers still gripping the black runestone. Bolts of magic crackle from its surface, lancing across the room to play along the walls and ceiling. 'The dwarves built this citadel,' he bellows, lifting his head to survey the twisted canopy. 'And its magic will serve me now.'

All around you the smooth black stone swells and undulates, like waves on an ocean. Even the branches are moving, threading themselves together to form a dark, writhing mass.

'Stop this!' you beg hoarsely, your eyes dragged from one shifting horror to the next.

The demon laughs – cold and mocking. 'I have the key to Tartarus.' He shakes the black runestone, gripped in his palm. 'With the heart of fire, I will free Ragnarok and then I will have my revenge!'

Desperately you draw your weapons, lunging forward to strike – but Cernos spins aside, striking you across the back and sending you crashing to the ground. Then he launches himself skywards, his huge wings beating through the dusty air. You watch helpless, pinned to the ground by the violent tremors, as the demon soars through the chaotic maelstrom of moving stone, leaving you behind to face this, his latest trap.

The chamber has become a living entity – a giant chitinous creature, supported on hundreds of spidery legs. With a final deafening crunch the beast drags its rear from the palace foundations, the ensuing upheaval sending fractures branching through the stonework. You stagger to your feet, aware that the ground is starting to crumble away, the entire building collapsing into dust.

Forced onto a precarious span of rock, you realise there is no hope of escape. The beast is scuttling towards you, its entire belly ripping open into a fang-filled maw. It is time to fight:

	Speed	*Brawn*	*Armour*	*Health*
Sitadell	10	7	8	60

Special abilities

Rock bluff: At the end of each combat round, Sitadell casts a 'rock bluff' spell increasing its *armour* by 2. If you win a combat round, instead of rolling for damage you can remove the spell, reducing Sitadell's *armour* back to its starting value.

Body of rock: Your opponent is immune to *barbs, bleed, disease, fire aura, piercing, thorns, thorn cage* and *venom*.

Once Sitadell has been reduced to zero *health*, it begins to transform once again. Keep a note of your remaining *health*, then turn to 672.

585

The succubus is a powerful adversary, blasting you with her dark magics while her mind-numbing powers sap at your strength, making your movements sluggish and weak.

Scowler falls quickly, her blow missing its mark and leaving her open to the creature's magic. The ensuing bolt of fire spears the tigris as surely as any steel, dropping her to the ground with a mournful cry.

'You cannot defeat me!' snarls the voice in your ears. 'This marsh is mine!'

Alone, you are forced to defend yourself against the witch's onslaught, giving ground to her powerful magics. Then, when all seems lost, you find some hidden reserve of strength – a bitter fury that floods through your body, helping you to shrug off her debilitating spells. The witch senses this change, pausing in her attack.

'Demon blood!' the voice whispers.

Then you fly forward, driving your weapons into her tattered robes. There is a deafening shriek as a black wind pours out of the wound, blowing you backwards. You tumble over onto your stomach, looking up in time to see the creature's mildewed robes flutter to the ground. There is no sign of a body, only a thin maggot-like worm, dragging itself across the stones. You clamber to your feet, marching forward to drive your weapons into its weakened form. There is a piercing, eldritch screech. Then there is silence …

At last the succubus' power has been broken – and the marsh is now safe for the Shara Khana to cross. However, it feels a hollow victory, knowing that your tigris companions gave their lives to achieve this end. Turn to 748.

586

As you head deeper into the marsh, you start to notice droplets of green slime glistening on the ground. Everything around them is blackened and dead, as if the slimes themselves are responsible for sucking the life out of the land. You give them a wide berth, particularly when you see several start to tremble and convulse as you get near.

Eventually the boggy ground gives way to a series of craters, filled with bubbling slime. You pick your way between them, finally coming to the edge of a larger depression. At its far side you see a withered-looking tree shuffling back and forth, its roots dragging its wasted body through the blackened ash. From its bark and twisted boughs, green sap drips like tears onto the ground. You ponder if the tree is the cause of this corruption, its blighted sap slowly destroying the forest around it. Drawing your weapons, you march down into the crater. As you do so, the tree lurches around, its trunk splitting open into a jagged mouth. From its depths comes a gurgling roar – then it starts to shamble towards you, claw-like roots ripping through the dead soil. It is time to fight:

	Speed	*Brawn*	*Armour*	*Health*
The weeper	7	5	4	60

Special abilities

- Septic seepage: At the end of each combat round, the tree oozes a slime to attack you. This causes 1 damage at the end of each combat round, ignoring *armour*. A new slime is released each round, increasing the damage by 1 each time.

If you manage to fell this blighted tree, turn to 709.

587

If you have the word *explorer* on your hero sheet, turn to 623. Otherwise, you find little else of interest in the monkey temple. To head back into the ruins, turn to 667. If you have already completed the dark interior quest, you may return to the quest map.

588

You race over to the weapon crates, hoping they might contain something useful. However, as you begin to prise open one of the lids you sense a movement behind you.

'Thieving scum!' A pair of bone-bladed swords cut through the air. Their aim and angle are perfect – intending to cleave you through with a single blow. But your instincts are quicker than any falling blade. You spin aside at the last moment, hearing the sound of wood cracking beneath the weight of the swords. 'Hey, where'd they ...?'

Before your attacker can register what has happened you have slipped behind them, delivering a firm kick to their back and sending them flailing into a pile of boxes. 'Used to slower prey?' you smirk.

The hunter springs to his feet, snarling like one of the beasts in the cages. He is an ugly-looking man, clad in sweat-stained leathers and a battered fedora. 'Yer fight for them stinking savages,' he growls, advancing towards you. 'That the case, yer can join them – I'll add yer head to ma other trophies!'

You must fight:

	Speed	*Brawn*	*Armour*	*Health*
Zambezi	9	7	6	60

Special abilities

- Sniper fire: The sniper on the watch tower is firing bolts into the fight. Roll a die at the end of each round. If the result is ⚂ or less, you are hit and must lose 3 *health*, ignoring *armour*. If the result is ⚃ or more, then Zambezi is hit instead.

(NOTE: You cannot heal after this combat. You must continue this quest with the *health* that you have remaining. You may use potions and abilities to heal lost *health* while you are in combat.)

If you manage to defeat this dangerous hunter, turn to 780. Otherwise, turn to 664.

589

Weakened by your onslaught the immense giant comes crashing down, its chorus of skulls taking on a pitiful wail. You raise the staff and bring it down hard onto the bulbous, saggy flesh, pouring all of the trapped spirits' power into the blow.

Then something unexpected happens. Mortzilla begins to fade, its body dissipating into whirling tendrils of purple light. You stumble back, still gripping the staff, as the magic rushes into the pulsing runes. The staff shakes and bucks in your hand, then the purple light is gone ... and you find yourself lying on your back, staring up at the green clouds of slow-moving mist.

You glance over to see that the staff has been transformed, its length now twisted into a spear of wickedly-sharp barbs, ending in a crescent blade. The thing is ugly and evil-looking – glowing with black light. You scramble away from it, sensing that it is somehow alive, throbbing with the dark spirit of Mortzilla.

A cry forces you to spin, your eyes coming to rest on Boom Mamba. The shaman lies on his side, both hands pressed to his stomach. Blood trickles into the cracks of stone.

You hurry over, kneeling by his side. The shaman struggles to focus with pale, feverish eyes.

'You did it. You did ... the spirit ... walk.' Even in pain, he still manages a weak smile.

'Do you have any healing tonics?' you ask, glancing at the vials sewn into his bandolier.

The shaman shakes his head. 'I'm done for. This is my time.'

You look back to the twisted black spear. 'You said Mortzilla would have answers. What happened, the staff ...?' When you meet his gaze, you see shame written there – and then realisation dawns. 'You lied. Cernos never spoke to the spirit, did he? You just wanted me to help you – to complete the spirit walk.'

The shaman gives a wheezing gasp, blood coating his lips. 'You only one who could use the boom stick. Only a demon.'

You shake your head. 'I'm no demon. You're mistaken.'

Boom Mamba's smile takes on a sad quality. 'It was me. I spoke to your demon friend. I told him what he want to hear. In return, he help me finish the staff. So I could do spirit walk at last.'

'Cernos helped you? Why?' A cold bitterness creeps into your voice.

'He knew you be coming.' Boom's eyes flutter closed, his breath rattling in his lungs. 'He knew I make you help … perhaps he not think you have strength. Perhaps he think you not live to defeat the spirits.'

You blink and stare, unable to respond, your thoughts mired in a million unanswered questions. After swallowing a deep breath, you take hold of the shaman's arms, gripping him tight, willing him to stay alive just a moment longer. 'Tell me what you told Cernos. What was he looking for?'

'The key … key to Tartarus,' he rasps. 'Dwarf city … sealed after the fall …'

'Where is it?' you insist, aware of the harsh, cutting tone to your words. It shames you, but you know you must find this demon – at all costs. 'Tell me where the key is.'

'Taken south … Lamuri city …' Boom's eyes open, a grin still playing on his lips. 'You do good … you give best boom ever … ancestors favour … you'. Then the shaman's smile fades and his chest heaves its last breath.

You stand as if in a dream, still bewildered by what has happened. If what Boom says is true, then Cernos has played you like a puppet, knowing you would agree to aid the shaman. But did the demon think you would get this far? Is Mortzilla's black spear his final trick? You step towards the evil-looking weapon, aware that it is now humming to itself, the air around its purple runes popping with dark energies.

Will you:

Risk taking the black spear?	602
Leave the ruins and continue your journey?	629

590

Quest: The bridge of screams

The colossal walls of the volcano sweep away from its bubbling basin, forming a hollow cone of midnight black. Its many cracks and crevices bleed an endless river of molten rock, spilling over ledges and along weathered channels, to feed the shimmering lakes of fire. Like some tormented monster, the magma spits and hisses with fury, venting great torrents of fizzing steam into the air.

But this natural spectacle pales into insignificance next to the dwarven city. Where you had been expecting twisted streets and tumbledown houses, its appearance is something far more alien. It puts you in mind of a gigantic candle, melted and hardened to the side of the volcano. Waxen walls gleam in the firelight, dripping with hundreds of spiralling columns, towers and arcane structures, connected to each other by narrow bridges and vertiginous ledges. You twist around, mouth agape, as you follow the chaotic expanse extending almost the full circumference of the volcano.

It would be a sight worthy of the epic sagas … but like Duerdoun, this place has a profound sense of wrongness. You not only feel it – you can see it. Across the sculptured walls, twisted black shapes scramble over each other like flies. At this distance it is impossible to tell if they are human, animal or something else entirely. Occasionally, vague sounds echo back from those smoky heights. Screams, wails, sobbing…

And then there is the bridge.

Its vastness stretches out before you, spanning an immense lake of steaming magma. The rock is featureless and black, smooth as glass. Low walls run either side, lined with hundreds of grinning skeletons, staked on dark spears of rock.

You look to Avian, struggling for words, your gut twisted with fear and revulsion. The mage is kneeling next to something carved haphazardly into the stone at his feet. He traces it with a finger, his own expression paling.

'What does it say?' you rasp.

'It's dwarven,' states Avian plainly. His finger tracks back across the angular writing as he steadily translates it. 'Abandon all hope, those who enter …'

Your eyes flick to the staked skeletons, contorted into agonised shapes.

'Wise words.' Virgil moves past you, his brow raised as he studies the city. 'This place is clearly riven. Perhaps we should reconsider ...' He looks back at Avian. 'Barahar met his end here. Ragnarok was broken. What makes you think Cernos can make it through?'

'I'm afraid we can't go back.' Avian raises his staff, its tip blossoming into a sphere of white light. Somehow its radiance seems to push away the heat and the pervading sense of dread. 'Much rests on the success of this mission. Yes, Virgil, Tartarus is indeed riven – and as such, will likely be infested with anomalies. There will also be the spirits of Ragnarok to contend with. We must stay together and remain strong. Fear will make us weak.'

Will you:

Ask what 'riven' means?	645
Ask about magic anomalies?	891
Ask about Barahar?	882
Ask about Ragnarok?	865
Continue your journey?	766

591

The succubus is a powerful adversary, blasting you with her dark magics while her mind-numbing powers sap at your strength, making your movements sluggish and weak.

Scar-face falls quickly, his blow missing its mark and leaving him open to the creature's magic. The ensuing bolt of fire spears the tigris as surely as any steel, dropping him to the ground with a mournful cry.

'You cannot defeat me!' snarls the voice in your ears. 'This marsh is mine!'

Alone, you are forced to defend yourself against the witch's onslaught, giving ground to her powerful magics. Then, when all seems lost, you find some hidden reserve of strength – a bitter fury that floods through your body, helping you to shrug off her debilitating spells. The witch senses this change, pausing in her attack.

'Demon blood!' the voice whispers.

Then you fly forward, driving your weapons into her tattered robes. There is a deafening shriek as a black wind pours out of the wound, blowing you backwards. You tumble over onto your stomach, looking up in time to see the creature's mildewed robes flutter to the ground. There is no sign of a body, only a thin maggot-like worm, dragging itself across the stones. You clamber to your feet, marching forward to drive your weapons into its weakened form. There is a piercing, eldritch screech. Then there is silence ...

At last the succubus' power has been broken – and the marsh is now safe for the Shara Khana to cross. However, it feels a hollow victory, knowing that your tigris companions gave their lives to achieve this end. Turn to **748**.

592

For defeating Ixion, you may now help yourself to one of the following special items:

Ixion's shackles	Circle of sacrifice	Chained heart
(feet)	(ring)	(necklace)
+2 speed +3 magic	+1 magic	+1 speed +1 magic
Ability: immobilise	Ability: penance	Ability: channel

If you are *hexed* then you have gained an extra reward, turn to **808**. Otherwise, return to the quest map to continue your journey.

593

'You're a bold one – a fighter,' remarks Yootha, her eyes roving over your possessions. 'But fancy weapons and armour don't impress around here.' She reaches for the nearest shelf, taking down two bottles and a small leather pack. 'This is the jungle, honey; you've got the heat and the snakes ... not to mention the blood-sucking leeches, the killer ants, the cannibal monkeys, the jaguars, the spiders, the ...' She stops herself, putting a hand to her mouth and stifling a horsey-sounding laugh. 'Oh, listen to me. Don't want to get you worried now.' She pushes the bottles and pack in your direction with a sly wink.

You may purchase any of the following items for 25 gold crowns each:

Snakebite shake	**Traveller's tonic**	**First aid kit**
(1 use)	(1 use)	(1 use)
(backpack)	(backpack)	(backpack)
Use any time in combat to remove one *venom* effect from your hero	Use any time in combat to restore 6 *health*	Use any time in combat to remove one *bleed* or *delirium* effect from your hero

When you have made your decision, you may ask to see the Lamuri artefacts (turn to **612**), ask about the jungle (turn to **520**) or continue your journey (turn to **571**).

594

As you approach the hostel-owner, you notice a board attached to one of the veranda posts. A dozen sheets of parchment are pinned to it, showing individual portraits of different people.

'I'm Bertie,' says the elderly man, grinning up at you with red gums and a single, yellow tooth. 'They once called me Black Beard, the scourge of the seven seas.' He pats his pirate hat smugly.

'And what happened to the beard?' you ask, frowning at his remarkably hairless chin.

'Made a promise to a young lassie,' he sighs. 'I shaved it off for a kiss. And it never grew back. I suspect foul play.' He feels along his chin, making an ugly grimace. 'Mermaids, pah! Never trust anyone that's got more flippers than legs. That's my motto – you'd do good to listen.'

Will you:

Ask what services he can offer?	625
Ask about the people on the noticeboard?	454
Bid farewell and continue on your journey?	571

595

You emerge on a narrow bridge, spanning a dried-up river bed. On the other side the bridge ends in a raised rectangular courtyard, its stepped walls covered in impressive carvings. As you make your way along the bridge, you hear a distressed cry coming from up ahead. It sounds like someone in pain.

Quickening your pace, you hurry into the courtyard to discover the aftermath of a battle. Over a dozen bodies lie sprawled across the dusty stones, most lying in twisted contortions of agony. All are undead – dressed in gold helms and breastplates. The groaning is coming from the far side of the court, where one of the undead appears to be still moving. It squirms on its stomach, clawed fingers grasping for the dagger protruding from its back. As you pass the other bodies you see that they all have various puncture wounds, oozing a thick green poison. This does not look like the work of a demon.

You silence the distressed undead, then study your options. To your left, another bridge leads to a pagoda-style shelter, where a series of statues are arranged around a circular font. To your right, a similar bridge leads through into another ziggurat, this one taller than the last.

Will you:

Enter the ziggurat?	626
Cross the bridge to the pagoda?	613

596

Intrigued by this strange temple, you make the decision to fight your way to its summit. However, you have barely placed a foot on its lowest step before another jagged stone comes hurtling through the air, staggering you as it cuts across your chest. It is closely followed by a veritable hailstorm of missiles as the squirrel monkeys pelt you with whatever debris comes to hand. You cower beneath the onslaught, forced to rely on your armour to soak up the bludgeoning hits.

As you stumble onwards, determined to reach the summit, the

black-faced monkeys spring forward to bar your way. Several are clutching fan-shaped leaves which appear to have been stiffened by some type of resin, turning them into sharp knives. Their leader, scarred and battle-worn, throws up his arms, baring his teeth in a fanged snarl. You sense this is a signal of some kind – as there is a sudden halt in the stone rain as the squirrel monkeys scamper higher up the stairs. Then, with a blood-chilling howl, the langurs press their attack, their leaf daggers cutting ribbons from the mist. It is time to fight:

	Speed	*Brawn*	*Armour*	*Health*
Langurs	10	4	6	40
Squirrels	–	–	2	30

Special abilities

- Leaf blades: The langur's attacks cause *piercing* damage, ignoring your *armour*.
- Angry mob: Take a *speed* challenge at the end of each round. If you get 16 or less then your hero is hit by the squirrel monkeys' stones, taking 5 damage, ignoring *armour*. If you get 17 or more then you have avoided the stones. If the squirrel monkeys are defeated this ability no longer applies.

In this combat you roll against the langurs' speed. If you win a combat round, you can choose to apply your damage to the langurs or the squirrel monkeys. If you defeat the langurs, any remaining squirrel monkeys will automatically flee, winning you the combat.

(NOTE: You cannot heal after this combat. You must continue this challenge with the *health* that you have remaining. You may use potions and abilities to heal lost *health* while you are in combat.)

If you manage to defeat the first wave of defenders, turn to 687. Otherwise, you have failed to assault the temple. Restore your *health* and turn to 449.

597

You hurry into the tent, wondering if there might be vital supplies here that you could use. However, as your hand reaches out to pick up one of the bottles a whip cracks around your wrist, jerking you backwards.

'Look but don't touch, honey.'

A woman is standing at the mouth of the tent, her tanned skin covered in snake tattoos. She flicks her wrist, dextrously releasing the whip. You see that it is made from strips of bark, wound tight around a leather grip. 'Hmm, you're a little bald for a tigris.'

Before you can retort, the whip cracks again. You sidestep quickly, the edge of one strip nicking blood from your cheek.

'Still, that's a nice skin you're wearing, little cub,' she grins, looking you up and down. 'Mind if I take a piece, just as a memento, hmm?' The whip cracks again, accompanied by the woman's mocking laughter. You must now fight:

	Speed	*Brawn*	*Armour*	*Health*
Perez	9	6	6	70

Special abilities

Bark whip: For each [⚀] result you roll for your hero's attack speed, before or after a reroll, you must automatically take 4 damage, ignoring *armour*.

(NOTE: You cannot heal after this combat. You must continue this quest with the *health* that you have remaining. You may use potions and abilities to heal lost *health* while you are in combat.)

If you manage to defeat this whip-cracking fiend, turn to 720. Otherwise, turn to 664.

598

You withdraw your weapons, watching as thick welts of blood soak through the archer's tunic, staining it a deeper shade of red. A soft whimpering comes from her lips, then she slides to the ground, her accusing stare forever frozen in death.

You kneel beside the woman's corpse, your eyes flicking to the wedding band glittering around her neck. Whatever demon of rage had finally consumed Joss, you pray that she can now find peace.

You may now help yourself to one of the following special rewards:

Sanguine surcoat	Crimson cover	Scarlet sabatons
(chest)	(head)	(feet)
+2 speed +4 magic	+2 speed +2 brawn	+2 speed +3 brawn
Ability: dark pact	Ability: bleed	Ability: haste
(requirement: mage)	(requirement: rogue)	(requirement: warrior)

If you are a rogue, turn to **846**. Otherwise, turn to **855**.

599

You slip past the door to emerge in a small cobwebbed chamber. A gold sarcophagus rests open on a stone bed, its top piece overturned and lying on the ground. It is surrounded by the skeletal remains of adventurers and tomb robbers.

Inside the sarcophagus lies a linen-wrapped corpse, with runic stones sewn into the cloth. As soon as you enter, gagging on the rotting air, the corpse jerks into life, its hands scrabbling to find purchase on the sides of its coffin. Then, with a choking gasp, the corpse starts to rise, its head snapping around to glare at you between its mouldy bandages.

'Trespasser!' it wheezes. 'You defile the hall of sacrifices!'

The runes flare with magic, surrounding the mummified corpse in a flickering cloud of dark light. Too late, you realise you have awoken a lich – a powerful undead mage. You quickly draw your weapons, determined not to become the next skeleton to adorn its tomb. It is time to fight:

	Speed	*Magic*	*Armour*	*Health*
Lich	10	9	10	90

Special abilities

- Rune master: Roll a die at the end of each combat round:
  ⚀ or ⚁ The lich heals 4 *health*. This cannot take the lich above its starting *health* of 90.
  ⚂ or ⚃ The lich strikes you with lightning. This causes 1 damage for each point of *armour* you are wearing.
  ⚄ or ⚅ The lich curses you, reducing your *speed* by 2 in the next combat round. If you are *hexed*, you are immune to curse and may ignore its effects.

If you manage to defeat this undead mage, turn to 666. You can flee this combat at any time by leaving the tomb and returning to the cobwebbed tunnels, turn to 889.

600

Congratulations! You have created the following item:

Self-published grimoire
(left hand: spell book)
+2 speed +3 magic
Ability: dark pact

If you wish to create a different spell book, you can start the process again (turn to 850). Otherwise, you may now leave the chamber and continue your journey. Turn to 866.

601

Virgil leads the way, taking the stairs two at a time. As the forge comes into view, you see the sprites gathered around a circular hearth, its flames heating the underside of an immense black cauldron. The pot jumps and lurches in an effort to free itself from the flames, the iron chains that bind it rattling and clinking with each sudden movement.

The larger guardian points a glowing finger in your direction, hissing something to its fellow sprites. They respond instantly by charging forward, their thin bodies blazing with fury. While its minions move to attack, the larger sprite turns and dives into the cauldron, sending waves of molten liquid lapping over its sides.

'We must hurry!' gasps Virgil, drawing his pistols. 'Their leader will grow more powerful the longer we delay!'

You must defeat the four deadly sprites before you can take on their leader. (Keep a record of the number of combat rounds it takes you to complete this combat.) It is time to fight:

	Speed	*Magic*	*Armour*	*Health*
Fire sprite	11	6	4	40 (*)
Fire sprite	11	6	4	40 (*)
Fire sprite	11	6	4	40 (*)
Fire sprite	11	6	4	40 (*)

Special abilities

- Blistering heat: At the end of every combat round, each surviving sprite automatically inflicts 1 damage, ignoring *armour*. If you have the *fire shield* ability you can ignore this damage.
- Fan the flames: When a sprite is reduced to 20 *health* or less it immediately returns to the cauldron to regain its strength (unless its *health* is zero). Roll a die:
  ⚀ or ⚁ The sprite regains 10 *health* and increases its *magic* by 3.
  ⚂ or ⚃ The sprite regains 5 *health*.
  ⚄ or ⚅ The sprite increases its *magic* by 3.
  Each sprite can only visit the forge once.
- Body of flame: The sprites are immune to *backdraft, fire aura, sear* and *searing mantle*.
- Forge master: If you have the word *fire quencher* on your hero sheet, the fire sprites start with 30 *health* instead of 40. If you have the word *wind breaker* on your hero sheet, you can add 2 to the result of the *fan the flames* ability (the maximum result being 6).

In this combat, choose one of the sprites to attack. If you win a combat round, you may strike against your chosen sprite (or multiple sprites if you have an ability that lets you do so). If you lose the combat, your chosen sprite will strike against you as a single opponent.

If you manage to defeat these high-spirited sprites, turn to 792.

602

As your hands settle around the shaft of the spear you cry out in alarm – you feel some ancient evil reaching forth, grabbing you and pulling you down into the weapon's darkness. You try and release your hands but they are stuck tight to the runes, which are leeching your energy, tugging at your very being. In desperation, you attempt to lock wills with the dark entity, calling on every last reserve of mental strength to push the force away.

Then, all of a sudden, you feel a change. The barrier you were pushing against starts to recede, drawing itself back to whence it came. Warily, you lift up the spear, realising that the spirit's attempt to take you over has failed. However, in touching the spear, you have become *hexed*. The effects are as follows:

Hexed (pa): You can only use a maximum of *eight* special abilities in a combat (including modifier and passive abilities). No more than eight abilities can ever be played in one combat – you get to choose those that are activated/used and those that are not – even those that would ordinarily happen automatically. You must remain *hexed* until you find a cure for your affliction.

If you wish, you may now equip and wield the black spear of Mortzilla, the *glaive of souls* (NOTE: this item can only be equipped if you are *hexed*. If you are cured, the item will break and must be removed from your hero sheet):

Glaive of souls
(main hand: spear)
+2 speed +2 brawn +2 magic
Ability: vampirism

You leave the ruins and head back into the jungle, aware that Cernos now knows you are tracking him – and that the demon may have further traps in store for you. Return to the quest map to continue your adventure.

603

You swing your legs over the hole and drop onto the stairs. There is a sickening squelch as your boots sink into something wet and slimy. Holding your breath, you descend the stairs into the fetid darkness, the glow from your enchanted weapons providing a weak light to see by.

At the bottom of the stairs you find yourself in a windowless passage, running parallel with the bridge. The air is heavy with the sour reek of detritus. Avian joins you, the bright radiance from his staff throwing your surroundings into starker detail.

Bones cover the floor, piled in mounds against the walls. Some hang from the ceiling like grisly mobiles, dangling on cords of green slime. Virgil gives a dissatisfied snort as he reaches the foot of the stairs.

You advance along the passage, squinting into the shadows that squirm beyond the circle of light. Boots crunch through bone and dust, sending fragments clattering and skittering in the grim silence.

Avian puts a hand on your arm, bringing you to a halt. You are about to glance his way when your eyes catch on the crooked shape shambling in the dark. A voice whispers, hoarse and rasping, like an old man's.

'Who's that trip-tapping on ma bridge?'

You hear the ring of steel as Virgil draws his weapons.

'I smells yer, little ones. I smells yer tasty blood . . .'

Avian steps forward, raising his staff. Its brilliance extends out, across the clutter of bones, to the skeletal shape moving towards you. In life, you assume it was once a troll, its elongated skull bristling with curved tusks. But what it is now, you are less sure. Mottled fronds of fungus hang from its shoulders and ribcage, forming a tattered coat of foul-smelling decay. The growth extends along one of its bony arms, thickening into a club-like appendage.

'We's be hungry, yes . . .' rasps the creature, snickering with wheezy laughter. 'Been so long . . .'

The troll raises his arm, the monstrous club scraping the ceiling of the passage. As the light illuminates the growth's underside, you give a gasp of horror. The fleshy club is punctuated with hundreds of tiny mouths, all silently opening and closing with needle-like teeth.

'Come 'ere little ones. Ya gonna feed da shiny fings!' The undead monster swings his club, its many glittering mouths drooling with voracious delight. It is time to fight:

	Speed	*Magic*	*Armour*	*Health*
Nergal	10	8	10	100

Special abilities

- Hunger strike: Each time you take health damage from Nergal, his club's jaws latch onto you – leeching the life force from your body. Roll a die. If you roll a ⚀ you have broken free of the jaws and the combat round continues as normal. If the result is ⚁ or more, the club heals Nergal for 4 *health*. You must then roll again to try and break free – raising your chances by 1 each time. (On the second roll, you would break free on a ⚀ or ⚁ result, then a ⚀ to ⚂ result, and so on.) Each time you fail the roll Nergal heals 4 *health*. On the sixth roll, you automatically break free. (Note: this ability cannot take Nergal above his starting *health* of 100.)
- Unstoppable feast: If you lose a round, you cannot use any combat abilities for the remainder of the round.
- Companions' courage: Your may add 2 to your damage score for the duration of this fight.

If you manage to defeat the undead troll, turn to 724.

604

The tunnel breaks off into a series of natural shelves, forming a raggedy staircase to the cave below. For now, the skittering sound has stopped, replaced with the grunts and scrapes of the tigris as they pick their way down the slippery ledges.

The female scout pauses near the bottom, her scowl still evident on her face.

'Smell bad,' she hisses. 'Danger.'

Scar-face nods, extending his claws. 'Spiders?'

Scowler shakes her head, sniffing at the air. 'No, worse.'

Then, all of a sudden, lights start to wink on one by one – sweeping across the ceiling of the cave like a mantle of stars. It is both beautiful and eerie, the light quickly flooding the cave with a soft, white glow. The tigris glance at one another, looking for answers.

You cover your eyes, squinting towards the bright lights. Some have started to move, the skittering sound evident once again. It starts as a few points darting around each other, then all of a sudden they move as one, sweeping like a bright wave across the ceiling and down the nearby wall. The sound is almost deafening as the light streams over the rocks, picking out black furry bodies and spider-like legs.

'What are they?' you shout above the skittering din.

'Trouble,' growls Grey-hair, putting his back to one of the rock shelves.

The creatures rush towards you, some clambering over others in their haste. It isn't until they near that you see that the lights are actually phosphorescent globes, dangling from their stalk-like antennae; perhaps some lure used to capture insects and other animals. However, right now they look like they are after bigger prey. You draw your weapons as the first of the strange creatures springs at you, its entire body yawning open into a fang-filled mouth. You must fight:

	Speed	*Brawn*	*Armour*	*Health*
Skitter	9	–	4	15
Skitter	9	–	4	15
Skitter	9	–	4	15
Skitter	9	–	4	15

Special abilities

- Snapping frenzy: At the end of each combat round, you must automatically lose 1 *health* for each skitter that is still alive.
- Pile on!: The skitters do not roll for damage. Instead, each time you lose a combat round, roll a die. If the result is ⚁ or less a new skitter joins the battle (with the same stats as its companions). If you roll ⚂ or more nothing happens. (Note: You cannot use avoidance

abilities, such as *confound, prophecy* and *vanish,* to stop a new skitter entering the battle.)

In this battle you choose a skitter to attack, rolling against its speed. If you win the round, you must apply your damage to your chosen skitter (or multiple skitters if you have an ability that lets you do so). If you lose a combat round, see the *Pile on!* special ability above.

If you manage to defeat the skittering swarm, turn to 655. Otherwise, turn to 640.

605

Legendary monster: Garm and Erkil

You come to an imposing hallway of flame-red stone, lined with pillars etched with runes. Against the far wall a stepped dais leads up to a twin set of thrones, one of pure white marble and the other of black obsidian. The white throne has been shattered, its winged back lying in chunks across the ground. Its darker opposite is perfectly intact and seated on it is a plate-armoured dwarf, his gauntleted fists gripping the arms. He looks up as you approach, his dark visor leaning forward.

At the base of the dais, reclining on its forepaws, is a giant hellhound. It reminds you of the molten hounds that you encountered on the bridge, with blackened skin and veins of fire. But this one is twice the size, and twice as mean.

'I guard these halls,' booms a deep voice, made louder by its echoing resonance. 'I stayed true to my vows. I will not desert my throne.'

Between the plated armour there is nothing but an eerie, unsettling darkness. You realise that this must be a ghost – a death knight, bound by magic to defend these sacred halls. 'Garm!' The dwarf motions to his hound, who stretches lazily before rising. 'Send these devils back to the shroud!'

The hound gives a nonchalant yawn, belching a bright stream of fire from between its fanged teeth. Then it advances, powerful muscles bunching and rippling with every stride. It is time to fight:

	Speed	*Brawn*	*Armour*	*Health*
Garm	14	10	11	100

Special abilities

- Molten skin: You automatically take 4 damage at the end of each combat round, ignoring *armour*, from the hound's flames. If you have *fire shield*, you can ignore this ability.
- Dogged determination: Once Garm is reduced to 30 *health* or less, he goes into a frenzy. This raises his *speed* by 1 and his *brawn* by 4 for the remainder of the combat.
- Body of flame: Garm is immune to *backdraft, fire aura, sear* and *searing mantle.*

If you manage to defeat this slavering brute, restore your *health* and abilities, then turn to 379.

606

When the two maps are placed side by side, they chart a hidden trail, passing through the Grey Mountains to a narrow strip of coastline. You are suddenly reminded of a rumour you heard back on the Emerald Isle, of a secret backpackers' paradise – of white beaches and sparkling, turquoise waters. Could this be one of the mysterious maps that leads to this fabled location? If you wish to follow the secret trail, turn to 721. Otherwise, make a note of the entry number – you can turn to it at any time during Act 2, to discover the map's final destination. (You may now return to your previous entry number.)

607

Quest: The Abussos

(NOTE: You must have completed the green quest *The bridge of screams* before you can start this quest.)

You lead the way through the opening, emerging in a smooth-lined passageway of black rock. It climbs steeply, curving around into a tight spiral. Virgil draws his inscribed swords, their blades flaring into bands of white light. You flinch back from the sudden glare – your eyes more attuned to the darkness.

He gives an apologetic shrug. 'We don't all have demon blood,' he says dryly.

You sense he didn't mean it as a compliment.

The tunnel continues to climb. Only a few cracks and fissures mar the perfectly smooth stone. Eventually it levels off, widening into a more-spacious corridor.

'How did the dwarves do this?' you ask, running a hand along the flat, even walls.

'Geomancy,' he replies, scowling around the word. 'Old magic. The dwarves could shape rock and stone, as easily as working clay. The king's architects have been known to use it, on occasion.'

You glance back, raising an eyebrow. 'It can't be all bad, then?'

The witchfinder glares at you intently. 'The rock is sanctified afterwards, inscribed with holy script. The architects are warded from any demon taint. There is a difference …'

As you continue along the corridor you pass a number of side passages and vertical shafts, all blocked by fallen rock. Several have solid webs netted across them, as if the stone had been drawn out of the walls and woven together, forming an impenetrable barrier.

'Someone wanted to cut off their escape,' states Virgil, peering down one of the closed-off shafts.

'Or stop someone getting in,' you reply with uncertainty.

After another hundred metres, the main corridor becomes blocked by sharp-edged boulders. You give one of the slabs a tentative push, but it doesn't give, weighted down by the debris snagged on top of it. Admitting defeat, you turn back to Virgil. 'Looks like the main bridge was the only way in …'

'Not the only way. Here.' Virgil has his swords raised, their light illuminating a dwarven rune, etched into the stone. 'Touch it.'

'Why me?'

Virgil rolls his eyes, then taps it with the hilt of one of his inscribed swords. It gives an angry hiss, sending sparks trailing into the dusty air. 'I don't think it likes me.' He gestures impatiently towards the rune.

You reach out with a scaled hand, your claws clinking against the stone as you press your palm into the rune. Its angular lines glow with a sickly-looking yellow light. A second later, a scraping and groaning comes from the wall behind you. You swing around to see a rectangular slab sliding backwards, its edges tracking through the dust and dirt.

'You're right, we don't all have demon blood,' you grin.

Ignoring the witchfinder's glare, you step into the newly-discovered tunnel. It rises sharply towards a narrow doorway, smooth walls reflecting the shifting light from the chamber beyond. Turn to 801.

608

You search through the grisly remains of the golem, wondering if there is anything of value that can be salvaged. Amongst the charred bones and magic-imbued flesh, you find one of the following special rewards:

Blood thorn	**Mesh of sinew**	**Gore mask**
(left hand: dagger)	(cloak)	(head)
+2 speed +5 brawn	+2 speed +4 brawn	+2 speed +3 brawn
Ability: gouge	Ability: dark pact	Ability: mangle

When you have updated your hero sheet, turn to 877.

609

The hat and gloves float off towards the back of the shop. They disappear through a small doorway, returning a few minutes later with two large leather cases. The ghost places them on the dusty counter, then flips them open. Secured inside are a number of jars and bottles.

You may purchase any of the following for 40 gold crowns each:

Flask of healing	Elixir of swiftness	Pot of cleansing
(1 use)	(1 use)	(1 use)
(backpack)	(backpack)	(backpack)
Use any time in combat to restore 10 *health*	Increase your *speed* by 4 for one combat round	Use any time to remove the *hexed* curse from your hero(*)

(*) If *hexed* is removed, you will be unable to use or equip any items that have a *hexed* requirement. Any items already equipped must be removed from your hero sheet.

If you wish to make further purchases, return to 557. Otherwise, you thank the ghostly proprietor and resume your journey.

610

A blazing comet of purple light streaks overhead. It slams into the giant's chest, sending fire and shadow rippling across the island. You blink, trying to adjust your eyes to the glaring inferno. There is something at its centre – the silhouette of a man. Weapons flash and spark, runes igniting in angry ribbons of light. Then the stranger is backflipping away, moving with a startling grace and poise, the air swelling and flowing around his body.

He lands next to you, his cloak and armour still steaming with sulphur. Purple sigils flash along his arm, forming an intricate pattern of entwined serpents. The sudden glow illuminates the stranger's face. Lorcan. The thin, bald-headed librarian from Durnhollow.

'You really did grow a pair,' he grins, peering over your shoulders.

Before you can reply a dark shadow passes overhead – the rock giant lurches forward, its massive feet crunching through the stone. Lorcan narrows his eyes, seemingly unfazed by the size of his opponent.

'Time to dance, my friend.' He springs forward, matching the giant's roar with one of his own. You must now fight the following team battle alongside a hero from *The Legion of Shadow*:

	Speed	*Brawn/Magic*	*Armour*	*Health*
Krakatoa	15	15/5	16	180

Special abilities

- Molten flares: At the end of each combat round, each hero must take damage equal to Krakatoa's current *magic* score. This damage ignores *armour*. (NOTE: You can use abilities such as *confound* and *disrupt* to lower Krakatoa's *magic*.)
- Krakka's KO: If a hero takes health damage from Krakatoa's damage score, they are stunned and cannot attack in the next round of combat. If they are the only hero remaining, then the combat is automatically lost.

If you manage to reduce Krakatoa to zero *health*, then you may enter phase two of this combat. Keep a note of your remaining *health* and abilities, then turn to 793.

611

The room's features are relatively intact, the only signs of damage being some smashed stone tablets lying across the ground. The main feature of the room is a marble slab, with square depressions carved into its surface. Hanging above the marble is a metal cross-piece, supporting a row of grooved shelves. A simple chain system allows the cross to be lowered onto the marble.

'Strange looking torture device,' you comment grimly.

Virgil has moved over to a small table, covered in blank sheets of parchment. 'Hardly. It's a printing press.' He holds up a sheet of paper, turning it over in the light from one of his blades. 'Dwarves recorded their lore onto stone or clay. The Lamuri must have taught them this craft.'

You notice a set of shelves, stacked with rectangular plates of bronze. You pull one out, seeing that its surface is covered in raised dwarven script. Bottles of ink are lined up along one of the lower shelves.

Virgil opens his hand, letting the paper flutter to the ground. 'Alas, we're not here to print books. We should keep moving.' He crosses the room to a pair of black iron doors. They stand open, revealing a plain corridor leading through into another chamber.

If you have the *mind's eye* equipped, turn to **895**. Otherwise, you find little of interest in the room, so decide to leave. Turn to **866**.

612

Yootha crouches down beside the chest. Removing a pin from her hair, she places it inside the lock. After a series of quick prods and twists, the chains fall away onto the floor. 'Come round and have a look, lovey,' she says, flipping open the lid. 'These aren't the fakes you'd pay a fortune for back home; these are straight from the Lamuri city itself. Means you can pay me a fortune instead.' She titters to herself, then playfully flicks her wrist at you. 'Just a little Yootha joke. I said I'd do you a deal. Three hundred gold each – and that's just giving them away.'

You peruse the objects: a feathered spear with a bronze head, a cloak of coarse black hair and a collection of dried, crusty parchment bound in crocodile skin. You may purchase any of the following for 300 gold crowns:

Wangimbo	**Chibacha**	**Abracabamba**
(main hand: spear)	(cloak)	(main hand: spell book)
+2 speed +2 brawn	+1 speed +2 health	+2 speed +2 magic
Ability: impale	Ability: gorilla rage	Ability: blink
(requirement: warrior)		(requirement: mage)

When you have made your decision, you may ask to see Yootha's specials (turn to 593), ask about the jungle (turn to 520) or continue your journey (turn to 571).

613

There are five statues supporting the domed ceiling of the pagoda, each depicting a different animal deity. Their gaze is directed towards the stone font set into the centre of the floor. You approach it cautiously, sensing the powerful magics radiating from the runes around its edge. The top of the font is cast from a plate of bronze, with a large circular hole in its middle. You lean over, peering down into the cavity – drawing back instantly when you feel an icy cold wind brush against your face. If you have the *glaive of souls* equipped, turn to 706. Otherwise, unable to fathom the purpose of this strange device, you decide to leave. Turn to 668.

614

The land dips, taking you into a dark valley filled with eerie shrieks and wails. The jungle here is thick, the tree canopy obscuring the sky and plunging you into a sombre gloom. After an hour of clambering over roots and rotten mounds of earth, you hear the rushing thunder of a river to your right. If you are an acolyte, monk or pilgrim, turn to 751. Otherwise, turn to 500.

615

Congratulations, for defeating Erkil while *hexed* you have won the following rare item:

Blood-sworn crown
(head)
+2 speed +3 armour
Ability: iron will, blood-sworn set
(requirement: hexed)

Once you have updated your hero sheet, return to the quest map to continue your journey.

616

You sight the creature above the rooftops ahead. It is moving laboriously slowly, its hulking form a mass of writhing purple tentacles.

'That's . . . Mortzilla?' you ask with a sudden pang of dread.

'Yeah, the spirit trapped between here and next place,' explains Boom. 'That's why only the staff can harm him.'

You round a corner, entering a wide plaza overgrown with weeds. Ahead of you is the spirit known as Mortzilla. The gargantuan beast lurches forward on a single pair of stalk-like legs, their fragility at odds with the enormous body of tentacles they are required to support. Its head looks like a similar afterthought – just a small funnel-shaped protrusion, balancing on a thin stem. Where it widens into a flat face, you see the fleshy surface pitted with dark holes. It isn't until the beast nears that you see the human skulls peering out from the circles of darkness – hundreds and hundreds of them.

'That *thing* is your spirit walk?' you gasp, backing away in horror. 'Your elders must have really hated you . . .'

Boom Mamba turns and throws you the staff. You catch it as a reflex action, your brow creasing with confusion. 'Use the boom stick,' he says. 'Spirits help you to defeat it.'

Your eyes widen. 'Me? What about you?'

Boom tugs one of his vials free, removing the stopper with his teeth. Then he points. 'I gonna keep them busy.'

Suddenly the world is plunged into darkness. You look up to see a dense mist spreading out from the creature, obscuring the sun and the green-tinged sky. As the strange fingers of fog start to rush closer, you suddenly realise what Boom was referring to. It isn't a fog at all – it is thousands of black, ghostly bodies streaking through the air. And they are headed straight for you.

Boom throws back his arm and flings the vial. It spins through the air and then explodes, sending concussive waves of magical energy billowing through the swarm. The spirits caught in the blast are torn to ribbons – but as they fall, hundreds more sweep in to take their place.

You raise the staff and follow Boom into the dark maelstrom, dodging the ghostly claws and talons that reach out of the blackness. Your focus is the monster itself.

As another explosion rips through the spirit cloud, a piercing sound fills your ears – like a million voices screaming as one. You lift your eyes to the monster's face and realise that the sound is coming from the skulls – a dirge-like wail that saps at your courage.

'Use the boom stick!' shouts a voice over your shoulder. 'Before it's too late!'

You grip the staff in both hands and prepare to take on:

	Speed	*Magic*	*Armour*	*Health*
Mortzilla	5	5	4	60

Special abilities

- Shadow shroud: Mortzilla is immune to your special abilities. In this combat, you can only use the abilities absorbed by your rune totem (see below). You can still use backpack items as normal (such as potions).
- Screaming skulls: At the end of each combat round, you must lower your *speed, brawn* and *magic* by 1. Once your attributes have reached zero, they cannot be reduced further.

In this combat, your totem abilities (you should have a total of three) do the following:

- Wind guardian (sp): You may add 2 to your attack speed for the duration of the combat.
- Infected wound (pa): If your damage score causes health damage to your opponent, they must lose a further 3 *health* at the end of every combat round, for the duration of the combat.
- Shadow shift (co): You can use this ability instead of rolling for a damage score to backstab your opponent. This causes 6 dice of damage, ignoring *armour*. You can only use this ability once.
- Earth fist (co): You can use this ability instead of rolling for a damage score to cause 2 dice of damage, ignoring *armour*, and reduce your opponent's *armour* score to zero for the remainder of the combat. You can only use this ability once.
- Boogie's booster (mo): Use anytime in combat to instantly restore

your attributes (*speed, brawn* and *magic*) back to their starting values. This ability can be used twice.

If you manage to defeat this nightmarish apparition, restore any lowered attributes then turn to **589**.

617

Black Patch returns with the other Sheva, then together you plan your attack. The compound is lightly defended – but even so, the walls of the fort are high and staked, ending in four lookout towers, with a guard in each. You also notice that two of the towers have a repeating crossbow, capable of shredding anything that gets within range. You glance back at the tigris and start to wonder if the Khana pack were right to flee to the marsh.

But the Sheva have one big advantage – you.

'Fire,' you smile, showing them the sparks you can create with your tinderbox.

Half an hour later and you are skirting the far side of the compound, where the forest grows closest to the walls. Black Patch and White Cloak keep watch, while you attempt to set sparks to the kindling you have placed next to the wooden wall. It takes several attempts – but soon smoke starts to rise from the smouldering embers. You move on to a different section of wall, repeating the exercise. Then you head back into the forest and wait.

It takes an excruciating amount of time, but soon you hear calls of alarm as one of the walls suddenly goes up in flames. You slink back to the front of the compound, away from the fire, to see several of the Sheva scouts climbing the front wall. Their claws make short work of the height, dropping down on the other side. More cries follow – including a gargling scream. Then the rest of the Sheva emerge from the forest. One of the crossbows in the towers swings around, firing a rain of bolts in their direction. But the barrage misses its mark as the tigris surge forward, towards the slowly opening gates.

'Wood den is open,' grins White Cloak. 'Now, we make skins bleed!'

The female tigris leads the way, bounding from the cover of the trees and heading for the opening gateway. You follow, drawing your weapons, with Black Patch at your side. Turn to 669.

618

You must now decide if you want to take the raft and use it to navigate the fast-flowing river (turn to 512) or whether you would prefer to keep to the river's banks, following the edge of the forest (turn to 703).

619

Glancing down one of the side aisles, you notice an open doorway leading through into a darkened chamber. Metal tips protrude from holes in the door lintel, suggesting a raised barrier or portcullis. You suddenly remember back to the crystal ball and the room you saw in your vision. This is the secret cache that you unlocked using the crystal.

Excited by your find, your hurry along the passage to investigate the storeroom. Turn to 671.

620

You give chase to the goblins, following them into a set of labyrinthine passages. The dark tunnels wind and twist, constantly intersecting with other shafts and corridors, until you have lost all sense of direction. Your only guide through this infuriating maze is the goblins, who lead you on a serpentine path, taking you ever deeper into the black rock.

At last you sight a red glow, filtering through a crack in the wall. You squeeze through, finding yourselves at the top of a sloping ledge. Below you, through the fingers of mist, you can see the magma lake and its tiny islands, bobbing on the surface.

'There!' Virgil pats your shoulder and points. The three goblins are now scurrying down the rock, the flickering light stretching their shadows into dark, sinister giants. The larger goblin is lagging behind his companions, the bag of loot slowing him down. Virgil takes aim and fires. The goblin staggers. He takes another few steps then flops forward onto his stomach, his loot bag clunking down on top of him.

When you catch up with the goblin, you see a pool of black blood oozing around his body. You lift up the sack, seeing that the bullet has gone straight through.

'Hope I didn't damage the goods,' says Virgil, holstering his pistol. 'Let's see what the goblins found.'

You crouch down, tipping the bag's contents onto the ground. Most of the items appear to be junk: broken shards of pottery, a few chipped gemstones, some chunks of iron and silver. However, a few pilfered treasures catch your eye. You may take any/all of the following:

Onyx blade	**Rune of healing**	**Illumanti circlet**
(backpack)	(special: rune)	(necklace)
A crescent-shaped blade for a mighty weapon	Use on any item to add the special ability *heal*	+1 speed +1 armour Ability: confound (requirement: mage)

When you have made your decision, turn to 820 to continue your pursuit of the remaining goblins.

621

You smash the pillar down to size, its last vestiges of dark magic trickling away into the ruins. Searching the rubble, you find one of the following rewards:

Totem mask	**Rubrica's cube**	**Stone walkers**
(head)	(backpack)	(feet)
+1 speed +2 brawn Ability: might of stone	A baffling puzzle designed to frustrate	+1 speed +1 magic Ability: might of stone

If you wish to follow the escaped magic, turn to 733. If you would rather press on through the ruins, turn to 764.

622

Intricate dwarven runes are carved into the monocle's gold frame. When you wear it, you discover that you can understand any language or script, including the most complicated of glyphs. This is a powerful artefact indeed – and one that will help you to unlock new levels of power.

You may now equip the following item:

The mind's eye
(talisman)
+1 magic
Ability: scholar career

The scholar has the following abilities:

Tome raider (pa): Using the monocle you are able to unlock the hidden secrets of the arcane. You may automatically add 2 *magic* to each spell book in your possession.
Bright spark (mo): Your powers are amplified, allowing you to re-roll any dice for your damage score for the duration of the combat. You must accept the result of the re-rolled dice.

As soon as the *mind's* eye talisman is unequipped or you learn a new career, you lose the abilities associated with the scholar career.

If you do not wish to keep the monocle, then Yootha at the trading post will offer you 100 gold crowns for it. When you have made your decision, return to the quest map to continue your journey.

623

Most of your surroundings are obscured by cloud, but to the north you are afforded a breath-taking view of the forest. You take out the scholar's parchment and hastily add to the map, noting the rotten marsh to your left and the ruins stretching over the hills to your right. Make a note of the key words *north view* on your hero sheet.

You may now head back into the ruins to continue your journey. Turn to 667. If you have already completed the dark interior quest, you can return to the quest map instead.

624

Next, you must decide what type of paper you wish to use. One set has been made with a light-coloured wood that sparkles with spots of silver. The other set has a bitter smell, the paper infused with flecks of dark crimson. If you wish to choose the *silver wood paper*, turn to 863. If you would prefer to use the *blood leaf paper*, turn to 795.

625

'Yer don't want to be lugging all that gear around with you out in the jungle. Travel light as yer can. I got a locker out back – keep your swagger safe. I even give yer your own master key, so no funny business. Honest word.' The man's face splits into another gummy smile. 'Just 10 shiny ones and that stash is yours. If yer got any belongings back home yer want shipped in, then I can get that arranged . . . grease a few palms, you get me meaning.'

If you wish, you may purchase a locker for 10 gold crowns. You may store any extra backpack items or items of equipment in the locker during act 2. If you swap equipment (weapons, backpack items etc.) during your adventure, you may put the item you are replacing in your locker by turning to this entry number. This will prevent it from being destroyed. You can only keep a maximum of four objects in your locker:

You can re-equip items from your locker, whenever you visit this entry number between quests. If you had a previous safe house in

Carvel, you can have your items transferred to your act 2 locker by paying 30 gold crowns.

When you have made your decision, you may ask Bertie about the noticeboard (turn to **454**) or continue your journey (turn to **571**).

626

You enter a low-ceilinged room, filled with broken burial urns and anointed linen wraps. Someone has clearly been through this room with a mind to searching it – smashing through whatever they could get their hands on. You are reminded of your earlier vision of the demon and wonder if this was the room that you saw being ransacked.

To the left, an arch leads through into a smaller antechamber, where you can see a model of a stepped pyramid resting on a pedestal. It is surrounded by broken clay tablets. Straight ahead, a set of stairs lead down into darkness.

Will you:	
Search through the debris?	508
Inspect the pyramid?	581
Leave and continue?	563

627

There is a rumbling, cracking sound as a narrow section of the wall starts to slide backwards, revealing a hidden chamber. To your relief, you find that it is stacked high with treasures – from sparkling gold caskets to rune-forged weapons.

If you are a warrior or rogue, turn to **777**. If you are a mage, turn to **176**.

628

You hand over the *quetzal egg* (you can remove this item from your hero sheet). Bill studies it with an ever-widening grin. 'Oh yes, perfect find. And still in one piece. Bet it tastes good fried up with some bread, eh?' He slaps you on the shoulder, guffawing. 'Nah, just joking with you, friend. This will hatch into something far more valuable – they're prized by mages. I even heard of one teaching a quetzal to talk! Hah!' He fishes in his pocket for some gold. 'Here, there's a hundred crowns for your trouble.' (You have gained 100 gold crowns.) You may now explore the rest of the camp, turn to **744**, or leave and return to the quest map.

629

Although tempted, you manage to resist the lure of the powerful weapon. Your instincts tell you that it is an evil thing – and one that is best left alone. Turning your back on the black spear, you start away across the courtyard. On the spot where the great spirit Mortzilla was finally slain, you discover a rare treasure glinting back at you. If you wish, you may now help yourself to one of the following:

Screaming skull	**Zilla bling**	**Wish bone**
(talisman)	(ring)	(necklace)
+1 speed +4 health	+1 magic +4 health	+1 brawn +4 health
Ability: charm	Ability: charm	Ability: charm

Your decision made, you leave the Lamuri ruins and head back into the jungle. Return to the quest map to continue your adventure.

630

In the following series of encounters you must outrun the wind demon, Nyx. You have 20 combat rounds to fight your way to the top of the Abussos. Keep a track of each separate combat you fight and how many combat rounds have passed. Once you reach the end of the twentieth combat round, Nyx has caught up with you and you will have failed the challenge.

After each combat, keep a track of the *health* and abilities that you have remaining. You can only use/activate each ability once during the course of this challenge (even those that would normally happen automatically, such as *thorns* and *bleed*). You decide which abilities are used in each combat. Good luck! Turn to **815** to begin the challenge.

631
Quest: The rune forge

(NOTE: You must have completed the green quest *The bridge of screams* before you can start this challenge.)

You hurry across the magma lake, hopping from one island to the next. The dwarven forge looms tantalisingly close, rising up on a wedge-shaped plateau of crumbling rock. Its centre-piece is the black anvil, its shoulder and heel picked out by the flickering light from its runes. Next to it, a blazing hearth casts towering shadows against the dark face of the mountain, its firepot rattling and shaking as if alive. Occasionally, molten fire spills over the cauldron's rim, spattering the black rock with golden droplets of lava.

'Over here!' Virgil sweeps ahead of you, his scorched coat-tails flapping against his boots. He veers to the left, leading the way along a serpentine outcropping. It winds past the lip of the plateau, leading you round to a series of jagged sills that form a natural staircase up to the forge. At the foot of the stairs you can see a group of fiery sprites dancing and cajoling around a circle of smoking rubble. There are five of them, their scrawny humanoid bodies made entirely of flame.

Sensing your approach, the sprites scramble together like a pack of startled animals, their blazing heads twitching nervously from side-to-side. Behind them, a larger creature sits crouched atop a ruined column. It shares the same devilish appearance as the other creatures, but is broader of shoulder, its head crowned by a ring of forked flame.

Undaunted, Virgil fires his guns into the group. The sprites scatter, screeching and hollering. One is caught by a glowing bullet, its body exploding into wisps of smoke. The rest make for the stone stairs, running on all fours.

The crowned leader clenches his fists, spitting a furious stream of embers. *'Back, go back. We are the masters here, mortal!'*

Virgil swaps guns for swords as he strides towards it.

'Leave this place,' he commands. 'Or be purged by the holy fire of the One God!'

The witchfinder crosses his swords, making the sign of a crucifix. The carved inscriptions along each blade flare with a cold white light.

The larger sprite answers with another snarl, before leaping down from its perch and racing after its fleeing companions. When you catch up with Virgil, the witchfinder has lowered his weapons, a thoughtful frown knitting his brow.

'They must have been rune spirits, bound to the forge,' he grunts. 'Somehow, it must have become damaged – weakened. They've managed to free themselves.'

'Then it's high time they learnt their place.' You start towards the stairs, but Virgil slaps your arm with one of his blades, its cold sting bringing you up short.

'Wait. That larger demon is powerful. I'd advise we proceed with caution.' He turns from the stairs and points to a section of the ridged wall, where some alien-looking contraption has been built into the rock. One half is made up of a series of pulleys and chains, mounted into carved channels; the other is a confusing maze of pipes, their loose couplings leaking geysers of whistling steam into the smoky air. 'We could work on disabling the forge,' states Virgil, sheathing his blades and extinguishing their light. 'Just a temporary measure – but might help to even the odds. What do you say, fancy getting your hands dirty?'

Will you:

Examine the pulleys and chains?	786
Investigate the network of pipes?	692
Head up the stairs to the forge?	601

632

Black Patch leads the way through the jungle, to a spot ahead of the procession of carts. Here the cleared track is narrow, penned in on both sides by heavy undergrowth. A prime location for an ambush. However, as you crouch in waiting, you spot a problem.

Several hunters are hurrying ahead of the wagons, waving towards a high ridge of grey rock. The dirt track switches back, along its side, to a cave-like opening mid-way to the summit. Other hunters are standing guard outside, waving back at their companions. You notice the spiked teeth of an iron portcullis protruding from the stone above them.

'Where does that lead to?' you ask Black Patch.

'To death,' grunts the tigris plainly. 'Once gate closed, never see again. Take tigris all way to coast.'

You look back to the track, where the carts have started to clatter into view, pulled along by giant blue lizards. Although slow-moving, the carts are heavily fortified with iron plates and spiked rails, and guarded by hunters. You realise that the carts will need to be disabled one by one, before they reach the cave.

Black Patch raises a paw in the air, his curved claws sliding out of their sheathes. 'For the Sheva!' He cries. 'Shonac guide our claws!' There is an answering roar from the jungle, then the tigris surge forward. Drawing your weapons you follow them onto the track, ready to take on the defenders and free as many of the captured tigris as you can. It is time to fight:

	Speed	*Brawn*	*Armour*	*Health*
Defenders	9	5	–	–
Cart 1	–	–	6	15
Cart 2	–	–	6	15
Cart 3	–	–	6	15
Cart 4	–	–	6	15

Special abilities

- Going, going, gone: You must stop as many carts as possible from entering the mountain. Each cart you destroy (i.e. reduce to zero *health*), will allow you save more tigris to aid you in your attack on the camp. Keep a record of the number of combat rounds you have fought. At the *end* of the second combat round, Cart 1 will enter the mountain (if it hasn't been destroyed). At the *end* of the fourth, Cart 2 will enter the mountain, with the remaining carts entering the mountain at the end of the sixth and eighth combat rounds.

- Built to last: The fortified carts are immune to *barbs, bleed, demon claws, disease, fire aura, thorns, thorn cage* and *venom*.

In this combat, you roll against the defenders' speed. If you win a round against the defenders, you can choose a cart to attack. Once a cart is reduced to zero *health*, it has been successfully destroyed, freeing its captives. If a cart enters the mountain (see *going, going, gone*) then it has successfully escaped – and its captives cannot be freed. If you lose a combat round then the defenders strike against you as normal. (Note: You cannot use 'strike back' abilities in this combat, such as *confound, retaliation* and *sideswipe*. Damage can only be applied to a cart if you win a round.)

Once the four carts have either been destroyed or have escaped, turn to 646. If you are defeated, turn to 656.

633

Legendary monster: Gheira

Branches whip and crack as you hurtle through the jungle, the giant panther snapping at your heels. You know you have little chance of outrunning this fearsome predator, but since taking flight into the undergrowth you realise that you have no choice – to stop now will spell certain death.

A lapse of concentration and your foot clips a log, tipping you forwards. The beast barrels into you, its hot spittle splashing against your neck.

You hear something ripping.

The panther's claws have found purchase, its weight on your shoulders forcing you to stagger. Then your pack comes loose. The buckles snap open – and suddenly the weight is gone as the panther and your backpack go tumbling away. You crash onwards through the trees, not wishing to slow, your arms batting desperately at the clinging branches and leaves. Suddenly the ground dips, throwing you out onto a steep slope. Before you can change course you find yourself skidding and bouncing towards the edge of a ravine. You try and slow your momentum, grappling blindly to find a root or a vine – but the earth quickly gives way to a frightening nothingness.

You kick and flail, falling through the mist.

Then you hit something. Soft and buoyant, pitching you back into the air. The world spins over, rolling in a blur. You bounce again, tumbling head-over-heels, to finally land with a painful thump in a dark pool of mud. Above you, the white cap of a giant mushroom sways back and forth. There are more behind it, growing out of the side of the canyon. The nearest one shudders again as an object hits it with force, then your half-mangled pack splashes down a few feet away.

You start to rise, but catch yourself.

The low rumbling snarl is your first and last warning that you are not alone. Spinning around, you catch a glimpse of round, yellow eyes and sharp dagger-like canines, bright against a vastness of midnight black. Then the giant panther pounces! It is time to fight:

	Speed	*Brawn*	*Armour*	*Health*
Gheira	9	7	6	75

Special abilities

- Bleed: Once you have taken health damage from Gheira, you must lose an additional point of *health* at the end of each combat round.
- Blood thirst: At the start of each round that you are inflicted with *bleed*, Gheira increases its *brawn* by 1, up to a maximum of 12. If *bleed* is removed from your hero, Gheira reverts back to his starting *brawn* of 7.

If you manage to defeat Gheira, turn to **580**.

634

You hand over the pendant that you found in the wood cabin. Yootha glares at it in shock, then carefully takes it into her shaking hands. 'My … my Stan,' she gasps, stroking the silver boot. 'Where … where did you … find it?'

You hesitate, stumbling over the words to convey what happened. It seems Yootha can sense your discomfort, reading her husband's fate in your eyes. She raises a hand to stop you. 'It is all right. I do not need to know.' She places the pendant in the pocket of her dress, then gestures to the cluttered shelves. 'Please, choose something from my shop – anything you like. You deserve it for bringing him home.' She pats her pocket tenderly, giving a tearful sigh.

You may now choose one of the following:

Shrunken hand	**Monkey brain**	**Conch shoulders**
(left hand: fist weapon)	(head)	(cloak)
+2 speed +1 brawn	+1 speed +2 magic	+1 speed +1 armour
Ability: sideswipe	Ability: disrupt	Ability: time shift

If you don't wish to take any of the items, then Yootha offers you 40 gold crowns instead. When you have made your decision, return to 520.

635

The end of the passageway is blocked by a hill of bones, reaching from floor to ceiling. Thankfully, a jagged crack in the left-hand wall glimmers with crimson light, offering a way back out into the volcanic chamber. Virgil peers through the hole, twisting his head to view the side of the bridge.

'We can climb out this way,' he states, squeezing his body through the crack. 'Let's hope things have quietened down topside.' He disappears from view, the sound of grunting and cursing drifting back from the narrow hole.

You follow the witchfinder's lead, adjusting your weapons and pack so that you can pass through the opening. On the other side, you see that the cracked stone provides sufficient hand and foot holds to climb back up onto the bridge. Virgil has already reached the top. There is a tense moment as you wait for a response, fearing that the bridge guardians may still be patrolling – then his face reappears, his gold teeth flashing a grin. He signals for you to follow.

To climb the side of the bridge, you will need to take a *speed* challenge:

	Speed
A bridge too far	20

If you are successful, turn to **553**. Otherwise, turn to **561**.

636

You trudge back through the marsh, the journey proving easier without the witch's nefarious magic to contend with. At last you rejoin the Khana pack, who are waiting on the rocks outside the cave. Grey-hair moves to meet you, tapping his chest softly three times – the gesture of tigris pride and welcome. No words need to be spoken; your eyes drift to the mother and the young cub, both looking expectant – waiting for Scar-face's return. Grey-hair nods, taking a deep breath.

'We know Khana would pay the price for freedom. Few could have done what you did – to match claws with the witch and defeat her. The Khana owe you a debt of gratitude.' The elderly tigris looks out across the marsh, its steaming mist suffused with a golden light. 'The hunters will not follow us here. We can now cross to the stone claws and find new dens – safe dens – to start Khana anew. I have nothing to give … but this.' The tigris lifts his paw. Resting on it is a circular disc of bone, carved with a magical rune. 'I hope it keeps you safe, bright claw.'

If you wish, you may now take:

Khana's pride
(talisman)
+1 speed +1 armour
Ability: sideswipe

You say your farewells to the Shara Khana before heading back through the caves. Return to the quest map to continue your adventure.

637

For defeating Krakatoa, you may now help yourself to one of the following special items:

Kraka's casing	Blackrock shoulders	Hellslide halberd
(chest)	(cloak)	(main hand: spear)
+2 speed +4 armour	+2 speed +4 brawn	+2 speed +6 brawn
Ability: thorn armour	Ability: retaliation	Ability: impale

When you have made your decision turn to **651**, if you still need to choose rewards, or **545** to continue.

638

The cabin door creaks open, revealing a squalid space filled with rotted, mouldy blankets, decaying fruit and the half-eaten remains of various animals – most of which are now riddled with flies and maggots. Sat on the edge of a bed is an elderly man, bone-thin and dressed in rags. As you enter he springs to his feet, pulling a rusty-looking knife from his belt.

'Leave me be! Leave me be!' he hisses. You note the ashen tone to his skin and the gaping wounds across his scalp, exposing torn flesh and hunks of brain. This man is clearly one of the undead – and also deranged. Before you have a chance to react to the man's protests he is upon you, his blackened teeth reaching for your jugular. You must fight:

	Speed	*Brawn*	*Armour*	*Health*
Mad man	7	–	3	40

Special abilities

- Maddened rage: If the mad man wins a combat round, he rolls four dice to determine his damage score.

If you manage to defeat this wild maniac, turn to **648**.

639

You take the vial – and crush it in your fist. The milky liquid runs between your scaled fingers, dripping onto the ground where it is greedily absorbed by the ash. Opening your hand, you let the remaining dust sift away on the warm currents of air.

'There is your answer.'

The witchfinder gives a dismissive snort, shouldering past you in anger. 'I pray you don't live to regret that, demon.'

Your eyes drop to the wet mound of ash, now fizzing and steaming with the Elysium. There is a strange comfort in not knowing the future; being blind to how all this might end. *I won't be made a prisoner of, not again* ... You turn to watch Virgil as he strides away across the bridge, your suspicions mounting that he is not all that he seems.

'Hurry up,' he snaps, glancing back over his shoulder. 'We have double the work to do, thanks to you.'

For the remainder of this act, you must now suffer the following penalty:

Broken trust (pa): If you wish to use Virgil's *blessed bullets* ability, you must roll a die. On a ⚅ result, you can use the ability as normal. If the result is ⚀ to ⚄ then the ability fails. You cannot try to use the ability again, or use a different combat ability, until the next round.

Once you have updated your hero sheet, return to the quest map to continue your adventure.

640

You awake to find yourself lying on a bed of grass, your wounds bound by palm leaves and vines. A sickly scent wafts up from the makeshift bandages, where a thick poultice seeps around the edges. It seems that the tigris are not without some skill with herbs and natural remedies, which may well have saved your life.

Surprised to feel no pain, you lever yourself into a sitting position. There is no sign of the tigris, nor any message of fond farewell. You are reminded of Grey-hair's words before you left the river: 'If you fall, bright claw, we leave. That is our way. We move on – you understand?'

True to his word, Grey-hair has left you behind. You have no hard feelings – your wounds would only have slowed them down, and the dangers they face are many. After retrieving your pack and weapons, you start back through the forest. Return to the quest map to continue your adventure.

641

Your final blow smashes the creature against the corridor's remaining wall, shattering its spine and sending jagged cracks rippling through the stonework.

With the Terral devil defeated, you may now take one of the following rewards:

Devil's incisor	**Rodent's scratchers**	**Roughpelt moccasins**
(left hand: dagger)	(left hand: fist weapon)	(feet)
+2 speed +2 brawn	+2 speed +2 brawn	+1 speed +2 armour
Ability: fatal blow	Ability: piercing	Ability: dominate
(requirement: rogue)	(requirement: warrior)	(requirement: mage)

You have not forgotten Quito's betrayal. Determined to catch up with the wily thief, you hurry through the bronze doors. Turn to 676.

642

You grab the wounded creature and hurl it against the metal bars. The dark runes flash with magic, sending bolts of lightning crackling over its scrawny body. You cover your nose, backing away, as the imp slumps to the ground – its purple skin blackened to charcoal.

Virgil joins you, holstering his pistols. 'And I thought revenge was best served cold.'

You kneel beside the creature's smoking remains, cutting its bags and pouches loose with your weapon. Amongst its possessions you find 50 gold crowns and the following items, which you may take:

Flask of healing (1 use) (backpack)	Elixir of swiftness (1 use) (backpack)	Deft hands (gloves)
Use any time in combat to restore 10 *health*	Increase your *speed* by 4 for one combat round	+1 speed +2 brawn Ability: stun, steal (requirement: thief)

If you left any items in the hollow of the travellers' shelter whilst exploring the dark interior (act 2), then you discover these inside the imp's bags. You may now retrieve these items, if you wish, and add them to your backpack. When you have updated your hero sheet, turn to 696.

643

Legendary monster: Anansi

Sometimes you just can't stop yourself. Curiosity is a dangerous thing and it seems you weren't the first to venture into this earthy burrow, looking for treasure. As you brush aside the cobwebs you see the bones and skulls of other wayward travellers glinting back at you from the dark. You know you should turn back – that would be the sensible option – but your stubborn steak once again rises to the fore, taking you ever deeper into the warren.

Your enchanted weapons illuminate the ridged walls, which curve round in a tight spiral, to finally converge on a black abyssal hole. Its rim is covered in hundreds of skeletons, their bones wound tight in silken strands, twisted into anguished, tortured shapes.

Then you hear the shuffling, scratching sound, getting louder and louder, echoing all around the cave. Suddenly black hairy legs thrust out from the hole, thick as tree trunks. They scrabble across the rocky ground, dragging a huge black body into view. It is led by a pair of glittering fangs and a gruesome crescent of red glowing eyes.

You are frozen in horror as the immense spider pushes itself out of the hole, then rears up on its back legs, displaying a crimson underbelly. As you prepare to take on this fearsome enemy, you can't help but wonder if you will become the next skeletal statue to adorn this spider queen's lair. It is time to fight:

	Speed	*Brawn*	*Armour*	*Health*
Anansi	11	7	5	80

Special abilities

- Leaping attack: At the end of every combat round, Anansi will use her leaping attack. This attack does 15 damage, less the value of your hero's *speed*. (If your hero has a *speed* of 8, they would take 7 damage). This ability ignores *armour*.
- Necrotic venom: Once you lose *health* from Anansi's damage score (i.e. her ordinary attacks), she automatically inflicts you with necrotic venom. This venom does 2 damage at the end of each round and also lowers your *brawn* and *magic* by 1 each round. Affected attributes cannot be restored until the end of the combat, even if the venom is removed.

If you are able to defeat this multi-legged horror, turn to 465.

644

Not wishing to put your faith in an old and rotted bridge you skirt the edge of the gorge, looking for an alternate means of crossing. However, after nearly an hour of clambering over rocks and knotted roots, you see no other hopeful signs of navigating the gorge. As you peer over the edge at the raging river below, you contemplate whether jumping might be an option – then you catch sight of a narrow ledge below, winding down the face of the gorge. If you hadn't been looking over the side you would have missed it. Elated at your find, you carefully lower yourself onto the ledge and start inching your way along it, trying to ignore the sound of the crumbling rocks skittering down the sheer walls. Turn to 658.

645

Avian walks over to one of the staked corpses, passing the light of his staff over its splintered remains. 'Our world and the shroud are separated by an invisible wall, a barrier. It keeps us safe and the demons out.' He tilts his head, meeting the gaze of the lopsided skull grinning down at him. 'Terrible acts of violence … of magic … can weaken that wall – cut through it, like a knife. That leaves an open wound. Sometimes they heal, but often they are left to bleed. It means bad things can pass between.' The mage looks back at you with a heavy sigh. 'I'm talking spirits, demons. And worse.'

Return to 590 to ask another question, or turn to 766 to continue your journey.

646

For attempting to rescue the tigris, you have gained the following special ability:

Strength in numbers (mo): For each cart that was successfully destroyed (freeing its tigris captives), you may increase your damage score by 1 when attacking opponents in the hunter's camp.

(Special achievement: If you managed to destroy all four carts, turn to 697). Otherwise, turn to 686.

647

Cernos rocks back on his hooved feet, blood oozing from a myriad of wounds. With effort he raises his blackened face, lips curling back from his teeth. He sucks in a deep breath, then looks about to speak …

But his words are silenced by a bright barrage of magic. Avian has his white staff pointed at the beast, his face cold and impassive as he sends wave after wave of magic spilling from his staff. Cernos is slammed back against the stone door, pinned there by each successive blast.

Then the magic ceases, leaving a howl of pain echoing around the chamber.

The demon is left a smoking ruin. And yet – there is still life there, beating beneath the ravaged flesh. Pitifully, Cernos gropes for the iron casket, pulling it protectively towards his chest.

'What were you thinking, demon?' demands Avian, advancing with his staff raised. 'Tartarus was sealed by the dwarves. They feared what had been awoken by Barathar's magic. That place should stay in darkness . . .'

Cernos spits a stream of blood in answer, then drags himself back to his feet. 'Too late, mage,' he growls. 'You're too late.'

His free hand moves behind him. You notice a circular device carved into the stone – forming part of a central beam that partitions the door into two separate panels. Resting inside the device is the key that Cernos retrieved from the Lamuri city. He twists it sharply, eliciting a dull click.

Suddenly the two panels of the door rattle aside, sliding into hidden wall cavities. The demon tugs the key loose, then backs through the open doorway. 'This is my destiny . . .' he growls through broken lips. 'I will have Ragnarok!'

The cavity where the key had once rested flickers with a pale light, then the door panels start to grind closed.

'No!' Virgil lurches into a sprint, loosing bullets from his pistols. Twin sprays of blood fountain from the demon's chest. Then the stone panels meet with a thunderous boom – and Cernos is lost from sight.

The witchfinder skids to a halt, glaring angrily at the circular panel. 'He took the key!'

Avian joins him at the door, his eyes roving across the runed patterns. 'These are powerful wards. I'm afraid I'll need time.'

Virgil holsters his pistols with a sigh. 'We're not going anywhere.' He tilts up the brim of his hat, revealing the hard planes of his narrow face. 'Knock yourself out.'

The mage proceeds to tap his staff against the different runes, observing the flashes of light that ripple from each point of contact. His constant head-shaking suggests that his examination is not achieving the desired results.

You watch in quiet frustration. Since they arrived, neither Virgil or his staff-wielding companion have shown you a shred of interest. After all that you have been through in the jungle, you had been expecting more of a hero's welcome. Eventually, your anger boils over. Snatching up the metal ball, you call out for attention. 'Hey! Does anyone remember me?'

Virgil turns his head, his gem-studded eye-patch catching the silver light. 'This is not the time . . .'

'Oh, am I surplus to requirements now?' You stalk towards him, shaking the ball in your fist. 'Care to tell me what *this* is? I don't remember agreeing to carry your little toys!'

Avian continues to study the runes. Virgil merely grunts. 'I wasn't even sure it would work. That's an Elven beacon stone. You could be more grateful . . .'

'Grateful?' Your voice rises by several octaves as you hurl the ball at the nearest wall. Virgil winces as it smashes like glass, sending splinters tinkling across the ground. 'What am I?' you snarl. 'Just an experiment to you? I had Cernos . . . I was about to take his heart! Then that ridiculous ball starts flashing and-'

The witchfinder raises a gloved hand. 'I'd cool that anger of yours. The demon-blood is volatile.' His steely gaze takes in your transformation. 'Soon, you will—'

'Become like him! Say it! I'm becoming a demon – the very monster I was sent here to kill! '

'Look, we'll find Cernos,' replies Virgil coolly. 'He won't have got far.'

You gesture wildly at the two men. 'And this is what you call aid? Did you not think to bring an army?'

Avian addresses you for the first time, speaking over his shoulder. 'The beacon would not transport so many. Besides, you can't lead an army into Tartarus . . .' He taps another rune. All of a sudden, the whole spiral of markings flash with a brilliant red glow. The mage leans away, then steps back – waiting for the runes to settle back to their dormant state. 'Ah, this is impossible!' he mutters angrily. 'The weaves are too complex. I've never seen their like before.'

Virgil removes his hat and scratches at his close-cropped hair. 'And Cernos had the key . . .'

As you study the markings on the door, you are reminded of the dwarven device from Duerdoun which led you through the forest of thorns. You turn over your palms, revealing the grooved runes that were burnt into the flesh. An idea forms – a desperate one, but it might be possible.

'Out of my way.'

You walk over to the door. Avian turns in surprise. 'Don't tell me you're serious . . .'

Ignoring the mage, you stoop to examine the circular device. There is a line of runes spiralling around to a missing section at its centre, where you assume the key was meant to be inserted. You place your hands, palm outwards, into the cavity – feeling the scarred tissue fit around the subtle depressions in the rock. Then you twist your hands, moving them slowly – rotating them to the left as Cernos had done with the key. The rock moves with you, the runes flickering to life with a soft glow. A second later there is a click, followed by a deep rumbling. The doors start to open.

Avian gives a snort of disbelief. 'Unbelievable!'

Virgil plants his hat back on his head, a wolfish grin spreading across his face. 'We're in!' He tugs a pouch loose from his belt and tosses it to you.

'What's this?' You ask, snatching it out of the air.

'It's a doggy bag,' he replies, his grin widening further. 'You looked hungry.'

You open the bag and look inside. You may now take any / all of the following items:

Flask of healing	**Elixir of swiftness**	**Rune of fortune**
(1 use)	**(1 use)**	(special: rune)
(backpack)	(backpack)	Use on any item
Use any time	Increase your *speed*	to add the special
in combat to	by 4 for one	ability *charm*
restore 10 *health*	combat round	

With your hands absent from the device, the doors start to close.

'It's time to move!' shouts Avian. 'Come on!'

Quickly, the three of you hurry through the doorway – making it through with only seconds to spare. However, celebration is far from anyone's mind. Ahead of you lies Tartarus, the infamous city of the dwarves. Until now its gate has been closed for thousands of years, sealing away its secrets . . . and its past.

You draw back in horror at the gruesome sight that lies before you. 'One God have mercy, what happened here?' You struggle for breath, your mouth dry from the suffocating heat.

'Ragnarok,' states Virgil grimly. 'That's what happened.'

You may now turn to 590 to begin the Act 3 green quest, The bridge of screams.

648

The man puts up a fierce fight, but he is weak and malnourished. Your repeated blows soon silence his bestial snarls. Stepping over the body, you scan the contents of the cabin. Resting on the bed is a leather cord with a pendant attached to it, shaped like a boot. You lift it up, discovering that the boot contains a small inscription on one side: *Walk proud. Forever. Yootha*. If you wish to take the pendant, make a note of the word *restless* on your hero sheet.

You quickly scan the rest of the squalid mess, doubting there is anything here that would warrant your interest. However, as you move to leave, your foot knocks into a basket jutting out from under the bed. You stoop to examine it, finding a variety of brightly-coloured mushrooms packed inside. They look freshly-picked and succulent. If you wish to try the mushrooms, turn to 814. If you would prefer to leave the cabin, turn to 618.

649

Using your chosen reagents you craft a runed stave, its jewelled headpiece raging with elemental fury. If you wish, you may now lay claim to:

Occulus, eye of pain
(main hand: staff)
+2 speed +5 magic
Ability: focus, lightning
(requirement: mage)

If you wish to craft another item, turn to 755. Otherwise, return to the map to continue your adventure.

650

As the last mandrill hits the floor the monkey king leaps straight out of his seat, alighting on the back of his throne. Raising his fist in the air, he mutters some arcane gibberish – and suddenly a long red staff appears in his hand, its gold end-pieces crackling with magic. You charge forward, your weapons sweeping down to smash through the staff – but the monkey somersaults away, your blows ringing harmlessly against the gold throne.

Twisting around you see the monkey is now whirling the magic staff above his head, creating a tornado of swirling light. It quickly surrounds him in a bright halo, his body becoming a dark shadow that starts to expand – growing larger and larger.

When the staff stops and the tornado subsides, you find yourself facing a giant monkey – now grown to ten times his normal size. As you back away, trying to comprehend this sudden change of events, you see the monkey make a peculiar gesture, pinching the side of his chest. Then you realise he is actually pulling tufts of hair loose and scattering them across the stones. Wherever the hairs land there is a flash of magic – and a small monkey rises up out of the ground, long-limbed and black like a spider. Within seconds you are surrounded by a dozen of the spindly creatures, which immediately leap straight at you, snapping and biting. You struggle to bat them away, their combined weight threatening to drag you to the floor. But these spider-monkeys are merely a distraction. Through the chaos of grappling bodies, you glimpse the giant monkey stomping towards you, his staff raised to strike. It is time to fight:

	Speed	*Brawn*	*Armour*	*Health*
Hanuman	10	6	4	50(*)
Spider monkeys	–	–	2	18

Special abilities

- Clinging claws: The spider monkeys are clinging onto you in order to slow you down. You must reduce your *speed* by 1 for the duration of this combat. If the spider monkeys are defeated this ability no longer applies.

- Monkey magic: The king's power comes from his staff. Once he is reduced to zero *health* the combat is not over – the king is merely weakened and he must now be disarmed. From now on, when you win a combat round, roll a die. If the result is ⚂ or more, you have disarmed him – winning you the combat. Otherwise, your attempt failed and you must win another combat round to try again. Hanuman can still attack as normal if you lose a round.

In this combat you roll against Hanuman's *speed*. If you win a combat round, you can choose to apply your damage to Hanuman or the spider monkeys. If you manage to disarm Hanuman (see monkey magic), the spider monkeys are also automatically defeated.

If you manage to defeat the monkey king, turn to 737. Otherwise, you have failed to assault the temple. Restore your *health* and turn to 449.

651

The last elemental crumbles to dust, its broken runes fizzing weakly. Lorcan sheathes his weapons and steps away, his eyes roving across the lake of magma. You notice the golden staff resting in a harness against his back – the staff he used previously to escape.

'I suppose I should offer you my thanks.' You watch him closely, still wary of his sudden reappearance. 'Twice now. I'd say this is becoming a habit.'

Lorcan cracks his knuckles. 'I do what I'm told. Nothing more.' He glances around, then nods towards the smoking rubble. 'We should salvage what we can – may as well take something from this experience other than bruises and platitudes.'

(Each hero may now help themselves to one reward.) For warrior rewards, turn to 637. For rogue rewards, turn to 830. For mage rewards, turn to 873.

652

As soon as you near the foot of the stairs the four warriors come alive, their rigid bodies snapping into battle-ready stances. For several heartbeats there is silence – broken only by the flames, crackling and spitting in the braziers – then the four warriors surge forward with shrieking hollers, their swords igniting into blazing torches of flame. It is time to fight:

	Speed	*Brawn*	*Armour*	*Health*
Sun maiden	10	10	8	30
Sun maiden	10	10	8	30
Sun maiden	10	8	6	25
Sun maiden	10	8	6	25

Special abilities

- Searing blades: You must automatically take 2 damage at the end of every combat round from each surviving sun maiden. This ability ignores *armour*.

In this combat, choose a maiden to attack. If you win the combat round, you must strike against your chosen maiden (or multiple maidens if you have an ability that lets you do so). If you lose the combat, your chosen maiden will strike against you as a single opponent. Once you have defeated all four maidens, you win the combat.

If you manage to defeat these four fiery maidens, turn to 699. You can flee this combat at any time by leaving the ziggurat and heading through the open doorway. Turn to 595.

653

You soon lose control of the raft as you are buffeted through the chaotic tumult of logs and stone. Finally the raft crashes against a line of rocks, splitting through its base. You cling to the wood, almost willing it to stay together, but it is too late – the raft breaks apart, pitching you into the churning waters.

For the next few minutes you are tumbling in darkness, dimly aware of the forest debris whipping past. Then you break above the surface, grateful to see a river bank blurring by within arm's reach. Quickly you grab hold of a tree root, using it to steady yourself against the rushing force of the water. Then you slowly pull yourself up onto the bank.

You lie there panting, shaken by your ordeal but glad that you are still alive. After taking a few moments to recover and catch your breath, you set off again – following the banks of the river. Turn to 703.

654

The phoenix implodes, drawing heat and flame into the centre of its body. There is a bright flash, then the spirit is gone – vaporised into wisps of smoke. No trace of the phoenix remains, save for a single glowing feather, which drifts down to land at your feet. You stoop to retrieve it, noticing that its crimson fronds are beaded with glistening tears.

You may now take any/all of the following items:

Phoenix tears (1 use)	**Phoenix feather**
(backpack)	(backpack)
Use any time in combat to restore 6 *health*	A fiery feather from a phoenix's plumage

With the ghostly spirit defeated, you decide to leave and head up the stairs. Turn to 775.

655

It is a fierce and desperate battle as you struggle to beat back the relentless tide of snapping fangs. Thankfully Scar-face comes to your aid, his claws and teeth ripping through the bodies and making short work of the remaining creatures.

Exhausted, you turn to look at the carpet of bodies that surround you. There must have been over a hundred of the strange creatures. Thankfully, everyone survived the encounter – only a couple of the tigris have minor wounds.

Scar-face picks up the nearest body and stabs his claws into its back, ripping open the black-furred carapace. You grimace with disgust as he proceeds to scoop out the white pulpy flesh. 'This looks good,' he smiles, taking a taste. 'Want some?'

If you wish you may now take any/all of the following:

Skitter sausage (2 uses)
(backpack)
Use any time in combat to raise your *brawn* or *magic* score by 2 for one combat round

Skitter legs (2 uses)
(backpack)
Use any time in combat to raise your *speed* score by 2 for one combat round

After a brief rest the party continues across the cave, making for a tunnel in the far wall. As you are about to follow, something on the ground catches your eye. You hurry over to investigate, stooping down to take a closer look. It turns out to be a golden compass, rare and valuable – but its glass face has been smashed and the needle bent. On the back of the compass an inscription reads: *My dearest Sebastian. May your heart always point you in the right direction. Ellie.* You wonder what could have happened to Sebastian, to make him drop such a prized object.

You look up to see a ledge, jutting several metres above the tunnel opening. The pitted wall to either side offers a number of potential hand and foot holds, providing you with a means of reaching it. Grey-hair looks back, as the others head into the tunnel.

'Let it go, bright claw. We keep moving.'

Will you:
Stay behind to climb the rock wall? 535
Leave with Grey-hair? 513

656

You awake to find yourself lying next to the dirt track, your wounds bound by palm leaves and vines. A sickly scent wafts up from the makeshift bandages, where a thick poultice seeps around the edges. It seems that the tigris are not without some skill with herbs and natural remedies, which may well have saved your life.

Surprised to feel no pain, you lever yourself into a sitting position. There is no sign of the other tigris. You are reminded of the Sheva leader's words at the compound: 'Those that fall we leave. They are lost to us.'

True to their word, the tigris have left you behind. You have no hard feelings – your wounds would only have slowed them up, and the dangers they face are many. After retrieving your pack and weapons, you start back through the forest. Return to the quest map to continue your adventure.

657

Exhausted, you sag back against the rocks, watching as the seawater rushes in around the three bodies, leaving bloody smears across the sand. These three old crones must have once been sirens, luring sailors to this cove to prey on their remains. The maps were just another part of their seductive game, tempting travellers with false tales of paradise. At least you have finally put paid to their dastardly schemes.

For defeating the sirens, you may now choose one of the following rewards:

Comb of sailors' fingers	Eye of a kraken	Shawl of skulls
(main hand: fist weapon)	(talisman)	(cloak)
+2 speed +2 brawn	+1 speed	+1 speed +2 armour
Ability: disease	Ability: greater heal	Ability: purge
		(requirement: mage)

You follow the crones' footprints back to a small cave. As you expected, it is full of bones and other gruesome trophies. Not wishing to stay any longer than necessary, you quickly rummage through the contents. You find several pouches of gold (you have gained 100 gold crowns) and the following items, which you may take:

Snakebite shake	Flask of healing	Kalamari cocktail
(1 use)	(1 use)	(2 uses)
(backpack)	(backpack)	(backpack)
Use any time in combat to remove one *venom* effect from your hero	Use any time in combat to restore 10 *health*	Use any time in combat to raise your *speed* by 2 for one round

The putrid stench finally forces you back out of the cave. Return to the quest map to continue your adventure.

658

Halfway to the bottom of the gorge you pass an opening in the rock wall. Its angular shape and smooth edges suggest something man-made rather than a natural feature. You also notice several strange markings cut into the stone around its edge, but they make little sense to you.

Will you:

Investigate the hollow?	695
Continue along the ledge?	689

659

As you gaze into the depths of the crystal ball, a scene starts to form in your mind's eye. You are looking down on a store room filled with stone tablets. At its centre is a podium, fashioned from sculptured bands of black and red granite. Resting on it is a small carved statue. In the far wall there looks to be a doorway, but it is blocked by a row of metal bars.

You put your hands to the crystal, surprised to discover that it is warm to the touch. As you continue to hold them there, the scene in your head starts to change – the metal bars flash with magic then lift up into the ceiling, leaving the doorway open and the secret cache accessible. (Make a note of the key word *barrier* on your hero sheet.)

Will you:	
Read the note?	852
Search the shelves?	711
Leave?	858

660

You sever the creature's wings, dropping it to the ground. As the drecko scrabbles in vain to defend itself, you step in quickly and deliver a killing blow.

You may now help yourself to one of the following rewards:

Fang of the fearless	Rainbow-skin brassard	Brightscale hauberk
(main hand: dagger)	(gloves)	(chest)
+2 speed +1 brawn	+1 speed +1 magic	+2 brawn +2 armour
Ability: deep wound	Ability: regrowth	Ability: radiance
(requirement: rogue)	(requirement: mage)	(requirement: warrior)

Shaken by your ordeal, you decide to leave the rest of the jungle beasts safely behind bars. Turn to 466.

661

The benches are set in two rows, the aisle way between them leading through to an open balcony. There, silhouetted against the bright haze, is a stone lectern. An open book rests on its slanted arms, the yellowed pages rustling back and forth in the breeze.

A grunt of pain draws your eyes to the foot of the pedestal. Quito is laid on his back, fingers grasping for his bag. His whole body is shaking as if gripped by some terrible fever. You hurry to his side, spotting a black snake – no longer than your arm – winding away between the pews.

'Bla … black taipan,' stutters the thief. His arms are now drawn into his chest, his limbs set rigid. 'Antidote in … pack.' He makes a feeble nod towards his bag. You immediately put a foot to it, nudging it well out of reach.

'And why should I help you?' you ask, scowling. 'I wasn't aware camaraderie was part of your code. Remember when you tried to stick me with a dagger, then feed me to a rat?'

The thief's neck arches back, his throat clicking dryly. 'I need … book. Thought you … here for it … also.'

You glance up at the spell book, lying open on the lectern. 'Worth risking your life for, eh?' You gesture to the man's rigid limbs, which have now gone into spasm, entering the final stages of the poison. 'And you assume I'm the forgiving sort?'

Will you:

Use the antidote and help the thief?	522
Let him die and take the book?	540

662

The valley widens into a bowl-shaped canyon, dominated by a vast pool of water. Sulphurous smoke crawls across the lake's surface, an occasional belch of bubbles rising up to spout boiling steam into the air. You find the stranger, Lorcan, standing at its banks. As you move to join him you spot a number of carved rocks arranged around the pool. The largest has been smashed in two, but the others are still intact, shielded by cones of magic.

You look back at the bubbling pool, then at Lorcan. 'So, this great monster we're supposed to defeat. Did you forget to send the invite?'

Suddenly, the waters rush up in a broiling explosion of steam and smoke. You glimpse scaled skin and bright, crimson eyes.

Lorcan sweeps back his cloak, revealing elaborate armour and weapons humming with magic. 'Concentrate on the shrines,' he shouts above the roar of crashing water. 'I can re-weave their magic, but you need to break the drake's protective shields.'

You barely hear his words – your attention is rooted on the two reptilian heads swaying above you. As one, they open their gigantic maws and suck in the seared air with a keening cry. Then a torrent of fire streaks past their rings of teeth. You both race in opposite directions as the flames slam into the ground, super-heating the stone to shards of black glass.

You spin around, catching Lorcan's crazed expression. 'The shrines!' he snarls, dodging the monster's snapping heads. 'It's our only chance!'

You must now fight the following team battle alongside a hero from *The Legion of Shadow:*

	Speed	*Brawn*	*Armour*	*Health*
Issakhar	15	12	14	450
Fire shrine	–	–	7	30
Water shrine	–	–	7	30
Air shrine	–	–	7	30
Lightning shrine	–	–	7	30

Special abilities

- Headstrong: At the end of each combat round, both heroes must take 5 damage from the drake's fiery breath. This ability ignores *armour*. (If a hero has *fire shield*, then they are immune to this damage.)
- Deadly bite: Once a hero takes health damage from Issakhar's damage score, they are automatically inflicted with *bleed* and *venom*, taking 3 damage at the end of every combat round.
- Fire shrine: If the fire shrine is activated (see below), then all heroes are immune to the drake's flames and no longer suffer damage from the *headstrong* ability.
- Water shrine: If the water shrine is activated, each hero restores 2 *health* at the end of each combat round for the duration of the combat.
- Air shrine: If the air shrine is activated, the hero with the lowest *speed* may increase their *speed* by 4 for the duration of the combat.
- Lightning shrine: If the lightning shrine is activated, both heroes' weapons are imbued with lightning. This adds 1 to each die rolled for damage score, for the duration of the combat.
- Magic shrines: The shrines cannot be harmed by *barbs, bleed, disease, fire aura, thorns, thorn cage* and *venom*.

In this combat, one hero must be attacking Issakhar at all times. If a hero chooses to attack the shrines, they do not need to roll for attack speed – they automatically win and may roll for damage as normal. When a shrine has zero *health* it has been activated, and the above benefits apply. Abilities that strike multiple opponents, such as *cleave* and *black rain*, can be used to apply damage to all opponents (shrines and Issakhar).

If you manage to defeat this ancient beast, turn to 551.

663

The accursed spear quivers and shakes, its runes suddenly emitting a blood-red glow. From the corpse a spectral light rises up into the air, forming the ghostly shape of a panther. Then it sweeps towards the spear, spiralling around blade and shaft. The runes flash and spark as the spear continues to tremble – then, with a distant, echoing howl, the spirit-light is gone, absorbed into the weapon's dark runes.

Congratulations, you have gained the *spirit of the panther*. (Make a note of this on your hero sheet.) You may now return to the quest map to continue your adventure.

664

You jolt awake, coughing and choking on wood smoke. Then you feel a flash of pain shooting along your spine. Frantically, you push the charred wreckage from your body, gingerly testing the movement in your legs. Thankfully nothing is broken – most of the pain is coming from your back and head.

You lever yourself into a sitting position, dizzily surveying the smoky wasteland. Most of the compound is now a soot-blackened ruin – and of the tigris and hunters there is no sign. Many bodies litter the ground, one of them being the Sheva leader. It is hard to determine if there was a victory here – both sides have suffered heavy losses.

After salvaging a health potion to ease the pain, you retrieve your belongings and start back through the forest. Return to the quest map to continue your adventure.

665

Murlic is lying on the ground, his half-painted face speckled with blood and dust. Standing over him is the monk, Ventus. White balls of magic pool around his fists as he prepares to drive them into the defeated Wiccan.

Your foot knocks into a broken sword hilt, sending it clattering over the loose rock. Both combatants freeze, looking in your direction.

'Sanchen!' wheezes Murlic, struggling for breath. 'Save me.'

The monk scowls, glaring at you with contempt. 'Do not try to stop me, bright claw.'

Will you:	
Attack Ventus and save Murlic?	862
Stand by and let Murlic die?	822

666

The magic stones burn with a fierce light as they seek to heal the lich and maintain its magics. However, they cannot keep pace with the ferocity of your attacks, each blow ripping through the rotted bandages and splintering the brittle bones beneath. With their magic finally spent, the runes flicker and then die, leaving the lich to crumble to the ground – finding its own death at last.

For defeating the lich, you may now take one of the following rewards:

Mortal coil	**Shredded drape**	**Last breath**
(main hand: sword)	(cloak)	(ring)
+2 speed +2 brawn	+1 speed +2 armour	+4 health
Ability: reaper	Ability: channel	Ability: regrowth
(requirement: rogue)	(requirement: mage)	(requirement: warrior)

If you are a mage, turn to 778. Otherwise, you decide to leave the tomb and head up the stairs. Turn to 889.

667

The ruins end at a deep ravine, crossed by a raggedy-looking rope bridge. You take comfort that someone has at least provided a means of crossing – although, after studying the rotted wooden slats, most of which are missing, and the thin vines holding it all together, you start to wonder if this bridge is really a disaster waiting to happen.

Will you:

Cross the rope bridge?	684
Look for an alternative route?	644

668

You cross the courtyard, stepping around the corpses of the poisoned undead. Ahead looms the second Lamuri ziggurat. You wonder what secrets it holds – and whether it will bring you any closer to discovering the whereabouts of the demon. Turn to 626.

669

Inside the compound, it is already a scene of chaos. The fire has spread fast, obscuring much of your surroundings in a thick black smoke. Roars and screams fill the air, whilst indistinct bodies rush back and forth, many locked in ferocious combat.

Quickly, you assess your options. On your left is what appears to be a weapons cache; spears and crossbows are stacked up next to a series of crates, some of which have been broken open, spilling bundles of arrows across the ground. Behind them is a canvas tent, the flaps pinned open to reveal a table covered in bottles and flasks.

'Watch out!' A body hurtles out of the smoke, knocking into you.

As you swing around, ready to strike your attacker, you are surprised to see it is White Cloak.

'High tower!' she snarls.

Something tears past your shoulder, thumping into the dirt. It is followed by another series of thuds as the ground where you were standing is peppered with crossbow bolts. You look up to see a hunter in the nearest lookout tower – already loading another set of bolts into his repeater.

Will you:

Attack the sniper?	482
Investigate the weapons cache?	588
Search the supplies tent?	597

670

The tower is supported by two gargantuan columns of rock, rising up on either side of the bridge. An arched beam connects them mid-way along their length, its centre-piece a circle of runed stone. As you approach the circle starts to tremble violently, its surface wrinkling and swelling as if something behind is struggling to get free.

Avian raises his staff. 'Back, arratoch. We mean you no harm. We seek safe passage into your makers' city.'

The contortions become faster and more erratic, the unseen force hammering and punching at the stone until it has beaten out a cruel-looking face.

'Your city has fallen, arratoch. The twin thrones lie empty; the sworn kings have gone. Let us pass. I free you from your oath.'

The face crumples into a scowl. *What speaketh you of oaths and kings?* Its malign visage cranes forward on a long snake-like neck. *Barahar remade me. Only demons have dominion here!* The creature's mouth cracks open, and from its depths comes a wailing high-pitched scream. You stumble back, covering your ears.

'What is it?' you cry.

'An alarm!' shouts Virgil. 'It's summoning guards!'

The twin columns start to swell and ripple, as if the rock has become clay. It flows into invisible channels, rapidly forming itself around the contours of two giant-sized warriors. They have the appearance of dwarves, with grooved beards and runed armour – and moulded into each of their fists is a giant double-headed axe. Within a matter of seconds the newly-fashioned guards are stomping onto the bridge, leaving gaping hollows in the rock behind them.

Avian casts his eyes around desperately, then hurries over to a section of the ground. He taps his staff against it, revealing a glowing rune etched into the stone. 'Here!' he shouts, struggling to be heard over the shrieking guardian. 'We can go underneath them!'

You rush to Avian's side, as he taps the ground again. The glyph and the surrounding stone spark with magic, then disappear as if they were just an illusion. The resulting hole reveals a set of stairs, leading down to a lower platform. Avian jerks back as if startled, wrinkling his nose. A second later, you catch the stench drifting up from the hole – stagnant and rotting.

Virgil turns away, shaking his head with disgust. 'What smells bad, usually is bad.'

Avian tugs your arm, then gestures to the hole. 'Your decision – but decide fast!'

Will you:	
Descend the stairs?	603
Fight your way past the guardians?	582

671

You enter a small store room, stacked high with clay and stone tablets. At its centre is a podium, fashioned from a complex weave of red and black granite. Its top-piece is a pair of hands, cradling a carved stone idol.

Searching through the tablets you discover that most are simply historical records, written in a combination of dwarvish and common. However, you do manage to uncover a number of useful runes and glyphs. You may now choose one of the following rewards:

Rune of wisdom (special: rune)	Rune of nightmares (special: rune)	Glyph of life (special: glyph)
Use on any item to add the special ability *wisdom*	Use on any item to add the special ability *fear*	Use on any item to add 2 *health*

Virgil is standing next to the idol, tilting his head to inspect it. 'This is carved from the heart of a rock demon.' He leans away, his nose wrinkling as if from a bad smell. 'And still strong with magic.'

Intrigued, you walk over and examine the idol. It is carved to resemble a dwarf, with a ring-braided beard and a coat of runed mail. The surface is pitted black stone with glowing veins of red crystal. If you are a mage, you can unlock the idol's power by turning to 750. Otherwise, you return the idol to its podium. After a final check of the room's contents, you resume your journey. Turn to 842.

672

The beast rears back, its black-stone body reshaping itself into another horrific image – an immense worm, its mouth a circular chasm of diamond-hard teeth. It sweeps down through the dust and smoke, smashing through the rocky pinnacle with its cannonball head. (You must fight this next stage of the combat with the *health* you have remaining. Your abilities are restored and can be used again, as normal.)

	Speed	*Brawn*	*Armour*	*Health*
Sitadell	11	7	10	40

Special abilities

- Wrath of the worm: At the end of the eighth combat round, Sitadell will have destroyed the entire rock you are standing on, plunging you to your death. This automatically loses you the combat.
- Body of rock: Your opponent is immune to *barbs, bleed, disease, fire aura, piercing, thorns, thorn cage* and *venom*.

If you manage to defeat Sitadell, turn to 683. If you are defeated, this battle must be restarted from an earlier point. Restore your *health* and return to 584.

673

As you back away your foot knocks into something. You glance around quickly to see Scar-face spread-eagled on his back, a knife wound to his chest. Lying next to him is a black-bladed dagger, still glistening with blood.

'No!' You step away from the body, your eyes fixed on the dagger. It is the same one from your dream ... the one you used to kill Virgil. 'I didn't mean ... I didn't know it was him!' you protest.

'Oh, it's a little late for excuses!' The woman's laughter rings in your ears as the robed creature advances. 'Remorse. Fear. Anger. All my favourite appetisers!'

Desperately, you ready your weapons and prepare to take on this nightmarish opponent. This fight will be more difficult without the aid of your tigris companions:

	Speed	*Brawn*	*Armour*	*Health*
Succubus	10	5	9	80

Special abilities

- Mental daggers: You must lose 2 *health* at the end of each combat round.
- Delirium: If you take health damage from the succubus' damage score you are immediately inflicted with delirium. If you win a combat round, roll a die. If the result is ⚀ or ⚁ then your attack misses its mark and you cannot roll for damage. If the result is ⚂ or more you can roll for damage as normal.

If you manage to defeat the succubus, turn to 717.

674

Using your chosen reagents you craft a trinket of purest midnight, its fathomless depths flickering with the spirit of an imprisoned phoenix. If you wish, you may now lay claim to:

Fade, splinter of shadow
(talisman)
+1 speed +4 health
Ability: charm, trickster

If you wish to craft another item, turn to 755. Otherwise, return to the map to continue your adventure.

675

The thief turns down a side aisle, its mocking laughter taunting you to follow. As you skid round the corner, you hear the imp's merriment turn to a screech of pain. The thief is lying on its back, shaking its head as if stunned. In front of it the passage ends in an iron portcullis, barring access to the room beyond. Runes have been carved into the black metal, several of which are still glowing with a soft red light.

'Nowhere to run?' you grin, brandishing your weapons.

The imp flips back to its feet. With an angry hiss it lunges forward, a black curved dagger spinning into each of its palms. It is time to fight:

	Speed	*Brawn/Magic*	*Armour*	*Health*
Imp	(*)	(*)	9	60

Special abilities

- Steal your glory: The imp's *speed, brawn* and *magic* match your own. The imp will use the highest damage attribute (*brawn* or *magic*) when rolling for damage score.
- Vanishing trick: The protective runes have weakened the imp, stopping it from using its teleport ability. However, if the imp is still alive at the start of the sixth combat round it will have regained its power and will use it to escape – automatically losing you the combat.

If you manage to defeat this devious scallywag within five rounds, turn to 642. Otherwise, turn to 829.

676

You find yourself in a rubble-strewn hall. A set of stairs curve away to another storey of the building, but the way is blocked by fallen stone. The only remaining exits are an archway to your right, leading through into a brightly-lit room filled with stone benches, and a blasted hole in the far wall, where the twisted remains of a bronze door lie crumpled amongst the charred debris.

Will you:	
Investigate the lecture room?	661
Head through the blast hole?	731

677

A bright column of sunlight is being focused down the shaft. The mirror stands directly beneath it, but the light is falling past onto the surface of the stone plinth. You walk forward to inspect the mirror, discovering that the top stone is loose from the base and can be rotated.

Without hesitation, you turn the mirror so that the beam of sunlight is correctly hitting its surface. The angle immediately redirects the beam, channelling it towards the centre of the double doors, where a carving of a blazing sun starts to glow. A second later and there is a rumbling, grating sound from behind the wall – then the doors slowly turn inward, revealing a secret chamber. Turn to 688.

678

After a tiring battle the tigris is finally defeated. You push its heavy body off your own to find the hunter staring down at you, his rain-slick knife dripping with blood. For a moment, his expression is unreadable and you wonder if your life is once again in danger – but then the hunter breaks into a beaming smile, tucking his knife in his belt and offering out a hand.

'I'm Jerem,' he says. 'You fight well.'

Taking his hand, you struggle back to your feet. 'Your friend …' you state, glancing back towards the forest.

Jerem, shrugs his shoulders. 'His luck ran out, that's all.' He looks down at the corpse of the tigris. 'Come, help me get this one back to the boss. Would have been better alive, but still – not a bad night's work. Young male. Shara Khana pack.' He catches your eye, flashing another smile. 'Boss will be very impressed.'

If you wish, you may now help yourself to one of the following rewards

Bloodied claws	Tracker's chestguard	Tigris paw
(main hand: fist weapon)	(chest)	(talisman)
+2 speed +2 brawn	+1 speed +2 armour	+1 speed
Ability: rake	Ability: critical strike	Ability: evade

Jerem takes his knife and disappears into the undergrowth, returning moments later holding a staff of cane. After stripping away the stray leaves, he quickly sets about tying the animal's wrists and ankles to the rod using vines. Then Jerem takes one end, directing you to take the other. Together, you lift up the carry-beam with both hands, the corpse of the tigris dangling between you. 'Camp's not far,' says Jerem. 'Let's go, before more tigris come.' Turn to 744.

679

Congratulations, for defeating Nephele while *hexed* you have won the following rare item:

Blood-sworn gauntlets
(gloves)
+1 speed +4 brawn
Ability: unstoppable, blood-sworn set
(requirement: hexed)

Once you have updated your hero sheet, return to the quest map to continue your journey.

680

You hesitate, not wishing to pick a side in the fight – unsure whether anything you are witnessing is real or part of some elaborate fantasy.

'What are you waiting for?' splutters Benin. 'The Wiccan are our enemy!'

You shake your head. 'No, friend. This is not what it seems . . .'

'Wise move,' growls Murlic – suddenly speaking with a guttural, female voice. 'You are strong, bright claw.'

'No!' Benin shrieks with rage, fists clenching at his side. 'You were supposed to kill her!'

Suddenly your surroundings start to blur, sweeping into ribbons of ochre light. Then you lurch forwards, as if pushed by some invisible hand, to find yourself inside a ruined building, its roof open to the misty marshland sky.

Where Murlic had been standing there is now a female tigris. She is panting heavily, looking exhausted. 'The witch,' snarls Scowler. 'We must fight her together!' Turn to 445.

681

Virgil slays the last of the spectres, its sickly-green body reduced to tattered shreds. The dwarf staggers back, clutching at his wounds. There is no blood, only a thick black slime, oozing between his rotted fingers.

'You betray me . . .' spits the dwarf. 'Let Barahar take you and be damned!'

He dives past you, looking to grab one of the potion bottles from the table. But you are faster – your weapons swinging round to catch him mid-step. The dwarf gives a shriek, then his body explodes in a black shower of ash and slime.

'A death long overdue . . .' Virgil picks a string of gloop from his coat, flicking his fingers in an attempt to get rid of it. 'Told you it'd be messy.'

You walk over to the bottles, intrigued to discover what the dwarf was after. You may now take one of the following items:

Spectral slime (1 use) (backpack) Use any time in combat to heal 10 *health*	**Molech Tov's cocktail (1 use)** (backpack) Use instead of rolling for a damage score to inflict 6 damage, ignoring *armour*, to all opponents

If you have the key word *clean up* on your hero sheet, turn to **752**. Otherwise, turn to **847**.

682

The hat and gloves float off towards the back of the shop. They disappear through a small doorway, returning a few minutes later carrying a shimmering grey cloak. The ghost places the cloak on the dusty counter, then pulls it open to reveal the items that were wrapped in its folds – an ivory-and-gold shield and a wide-bladed dagger.

You may purchase any of the following for 450 gold crowns each:

Cloak of the undying	**Light-forged bulwark**	**Doom's harbinger**
(cloak)	(left hand: shield)	(main hand: dagger)
+2 speed +3 health	+2 speed +4 armour	+2 speed +5 brawn
Ability: greater heal	Ability: defender	Ability: doom
	(requirement: warrior)	(requirement: rogue)

If you wish to make further purchases, return to **557**. Otherwise, you thank the ghostly proprietor and resume your journey.

683

As the worm dives towards you, intending to smash through the stone, you throw yourself into the air, tumbling across its ridged back. The worm bucks and squirms, flinging you free, its own purchase on the rock slipping away.

You fall together, reeling through the dust and smoke – the jagged remains of the building blurring past you.

Suddenly the worm's gaping maw spirals into view. There is little you can do to slow your momentum. The worm lunges, swallowing you whole. For the next few seconds you are sliding through darkness, the rough walls of the beast's belly ripping at your armour. You strike out with your weapons, but the hard rock jolts them from your grasp. As you continue your hellish descent, the walls start to close in … seeking to crush you to pulp.

Then a miracle occurs. From the scaled skin on your arms barbed spines burst forth, punching through your clothing. At first, they spark harmlessly against the walls – but once they flare with dark magic, they start to slice through the rock. You sight daylight – a thin sliver which quickly widens.

At last you are free, tearing yourself out of the beast's stomach and hurling yourself into the smoky air. You smash through walls and floors, your diamond-hard skin taking the brunt of each impact. Then you finally crash down into a courtyard, the impact blowing a vast crater across the earth.

There is a moment's reprieve, before an immense shadow obliterates the sky – dropping at speed.

The worm.

As its stone body nears the ground it starts to break up, becoming fragments of razor-sharp obsidian. You dive for cover, sheltering behind a carved pillar as the shards rain down, hammering their points deep into the rock.

Then there is silence.

You slump against the pillar, exhausted from the fight. But you find little comfort in your escape. You look down at the hooked spines, bristling along your arms. Your demon-side has saved you once again. But at what cost?

You have gained the following special ability:

Demon spines (co): When your opponent's damage score causes health damage, you can immediately retaliate by inflicting 1 damage die back to them, ignoring *armour*. You can only use *demon spines* once per combat.

You retrieve your weapons before searching through the debris. Amongst the remains of the worm you find one of the following rewards:

Stone of the Sitadell	**Obsidian shard**	**Prickle pair**
(talisman)	(necklace)	(gloves)
+1 speed	+1 speed	+1 speed +2 brawn
Ability: disrupt	Ability: piercing	Ability: barbs
(requirement: warrior)	(requirement: mage)	(requirement: rogue)

Beyond the ruins the jungle continues south until it meets a vast wasteland of orange-grey rock, shimmering in the heat haze. You clamber up onto a nearby ridge to get a better view of the barren plateau. It presents many days of arduous travel, but such matters quickly pale into insignificance next to the one landmark that has remained a constant these last few days: the colossal black volcano. Even at this distance you can feel its formidable presence; its air of inescapable doom.

You sense that is where Cernos is now headed: to find the dwarven city of Tartarus and recover the demon-sword, Ragnarok. (Return to the quest map to continue your adventure.)

684

Appearances can be deceiving. Stepping out onto the ramshackle bridge, your stomach gives a dizzying lurch as it sways alarmingly from side to side. But, after taking a moment to balance yourself, the bridge soon settles into a rhythmic swaying, allowing you to take your first cautious steps out across the gorge. The wood creaks and groans beneath your weight, the tightly-wound vines squeaking in protest, but miraculously the bridge holds – much to your relief, as you glimpse the raging river thousands of metres below.

After a knee-trembling crossing, you finally make it to the forest at the other side. Relieved to be back on solid ground, you give the gorge a triumphant glare, before heading into the trees. Turn to 614.

685

Searching the cave, you also discover one of the following rare treasures:

Spinneret of shadows	Widow's weave	Anansi's hood
(left hand: wand)	(chest)	(head)
+2 speed +3 magic	+2 speed +3 magic	+1 speed +3 magic
Ability: webbed	Ability: weaver	Ability: webbed

Before you leave you help yourself to a trophy, to celebrate your victory over the spider. (Make a note of *Anansi's eye* on your hero sheet, it does not take up backpack space). If you have the *glaive of souls* equipped, turn to 450. Otherwise, return to the quest map to continue your adventure.

686

The surviving tigris have already dashed into the jungle, heading for the compound. You understand their eagerness for revenge, but you worry their headstrong attack – even with their superiority of numbers – may still fail to overcome the compound's sturdy defences.

As you break out of the trees you see the tigris have already started their attack, and put paid to many of your concerns; several of the compound's walls have been breached and one side of the fort is already ablaze. Sounds of battle ring out from the compound as the hunters rally to defend their camp. Turn to 669.

687

You have no idea how long the battle has raged, but when the attacks finally stop coming you see that the ground is now littered with bodies. The few remaining squirrel monkeys rush for cover, wailing and howling like mourners at a funeral. Their cries bring fresh enemies to the stairs, seeking to halt your ascent of the monkey temple. Turn to 754.

688

The hidden room is clearly some sort of vault, containing the temple's treasures. Many of these are of little interest: clay tablets covered in indecipherable script, urns and pots possibly used for ceremonies, and some rotted sets of clothing looking like they once belonged to a sect of priests.

However, amongst these artefacts you spot some valuable-looking items. Brushing away the dirt and cobwebs, you inspect your finds. If you are a warrior, turn to **550**. If you are a rogue, turn to **511**. If you are a mage, turn to **531**.

689

Reaching the bottom of the ravine, you decide to follow the course of the river. After a short trek, you see a ramshackle cabin at the edge of the treeline. Next to it is a raft and paddle, pulled up onto a bank of gravel. Eager for some friendly company at last, you approach the cabin. However, your steps falter when you hear angry mutterings coming from inside, punctuated by outbursts of high-pitched, manic laughter.

Will you:

Knock and enter the cabin?	638
Steal the raft and head downriver?	512
Sneak past and continue on land?	703

690

You are about to turn back when you hear a screech from up ahead. It sounded like a woman's voice, raised in alarm. As you pass around a series of shell-covered rocks, you spy an old woman perched on a boulder. She is crouched down, her tattered dress hanging off her wrinkly, weathered skin.

'I smells it! I smells it!' The woman swings around, her face almost entirely hidden by a curtain of matted grey hair. 'Muireal! Gorma! Come quick! It's over here!'

You hear the sound of feet crunching through the sand, then two women, equally old and frail-looking, emerge from the trees. They are both cackling with delight.

'What is this?' you ask in bewilderment, looking from one woman to the next. 'Are you survivors?' You nod towards the wreckage. 'Was your ship attacked?'

The first woman fumbles in her ragged dress, then pulls out a pulpy white object. She rests it on the palm of her hand, turning it to face you. In horror you realise it is a giant eyeball, with goo-covered tendons still hanging from its back. 'Oh, I sees it! Lovely! Tasty!' giggles the crone, moving the eye up and down.

'Yes, fine strong bones!' gasps the tallest of her companions – adorned in skulls and other grisly artefacts. 'Been a while, dear sisters; travellers not as dependable as the sailors.'

The third tugs a comb from her tangled grey hair. You grimace with revulsion when you see it is made from human finger bones. 'Oh, I do miss my sailors,' she croons, stroking the ghoulish comb. 'Since you lost your singing voice, Ceana, I suppose we must take what we can.'

'Blame me,' hisses the first, turning her magic eye to view her companions. 'You took my teeth, Muireal. And my eyes!'

'I made the maps, didn't I?' pouts Muireal, fanning herself with the comb. 'Without them we wouldn't get a morsel.'

'Shut it, dearies!' snarls the one with the skulls. 'This one's getting jumpy – and we ain't getting any younger!'

Before you have a chance to flee, the three women spring at you, hissing and snarling like starved animals. You must fight:

	Speed	*Magic*	*Armour*	*Health*
Gorma	11	8	6	40
Muireal	10	7	8	30
Ceana	10	6	6	40

Special abilities

- Shawl of skulls: Gorma is immune to all passive effects, such as *bleed, disease* and *venom*.

- Comb of sailors' fingers: Once you suffer health damage from Muireal, you are automatically inflicted with *disease*, losing 2 *health* at the end of each combat round.
- Eye of a kraken: At the end of each combat round, Ceana heals her two sisters, restoring 4 *health* to each. This cannot take Gorma or Muireal above their starting *health*. Once Ceana is defeated, this ability no longer applies.

At the beginning of each combat round, choose the siren that you wish to fight, rolling against their attack speed. If you win the combat, you must direct your damage against your chosen siren (unless you have an ability that can strike more than one opponent, such as *cleave*). If you lose the combat, the chosen siren strikes back as a single opponent, rolling for a damage score as normal.

If you manage to silence the siren sisters, turn to 657.

691

The ghostly servant appears in the doorway, clapping his hands together in glee. *'At last, Pondicut's Beneficiary Substitutionary Perambulations!'* He floats above the cluttered sea of books, heading straight for a black-leather bound tome. After tugging it loose and tucking it underneath his spectral arm, he floats over to another book, singing its title with euphoric delight.

By defeating the wyrm you have helped the ghost to retrieve some of his missing books. (Make a note of the key word *clean up* on your hero sheet.) You leave the spectral servant to continue his blissful book hunt, heading out of the archway and continuing south. Turn to 842.

692

The pipes branch and interlace, forming a convoluted network of conduits stretching the full height of the rock wall. They appear to be carrying super-heated air from a duct in the ground to a similar pipe attached to the forge bellows. On various sections of the piping, wheels have been attached to the couplings to allow the pipes to be turned, altering or cutting off the flow of air.

'These help to heat the forge,' says Virgil, wiping the sweat and grime from his brow. 'Anything we can do to lower the temperature will make it harder for those demons to heal.'

Will you:

Attempt to shut off air to the bellows?	705
Examine the cogs and pulleys?	786
Head up the stairs to the forge?	601

693

You sever the creature's wings, dropping it to the ground. As the drecko scrabbles in vain to defend itself, you step in quickly and deliver a killing blow.

You may now help yourself to one of the following rewards:

Fang of the fearless	**Rainbow-skin brassard**	**Brightscale hauberk**
(main hand: dagger)	(gloves)	(chest)
+2 speed +1 brawn	+1 speed +1 magic	+2 brawn +2 armour
Ability: deep wound	Ability: regrowth	Ability: radiance
(requirement: rogue)	(requirement: mage)	(requirement: warrior)

The tigris have seen off the rest of the drecko. Only one of their pack was lost in the fight – the unfortunate male who was carried away in the first attack. The tigris honour their lost comrade with a brief silence, heads bowed and paws clenched at their sides. Then their leader, Grey-hair, beats his chest three times. There are answering gestures from the rest of the pack, before they resume their march – expressions hard and resolute. Turn to 702.

694

'Good! Follow me!' The witchfinder drags you with him, through the twisted cell door and out into the passageway. 'The Wiccans will provide all the distraction we need.'

'But where are we going?' you ask, stepping around the rubble that chokes the tight corridor.

'We're getting out of here,' snaps Virgil impatiently. 'Come, this way.' He deviates down a side-passage, his magical blade lighting the way through the murky gloom. Turn to 478.

695

You duck your head and pass through the opening. As your eyes quickly adjust to the gloom, you find yourself in a cobwebbed cave. Carved into the far wall is a low rock shelf and, above it, several alcoves – a couple of which contain bone trinkets. At first you suspect this might be a shrine to some forgotten spirit or god, but on closer examination of the shelf you see names carved into the stone. Some are unreadable but a few seem more recent – *Frobisher, Coronado, Finsbottom* ... This cave is clearly a traveller's shelter, the rock shelf acting as a raised bed. You are also reminded of the custom whereby the last traveller always leaves a gift for the next visitor to find – a way of providing aid to fellow adventurers.

Will you:

Search the cave for supplies?	757
Leave and resume your journey?	689

696

You walk over to the bars, being careful not to get too close to the humming runes carved into the black iron. Peering past them you can see a small rectangular store room, stacked high with stone tablets. There is also a podium, fashioned from a complex weave of red and black granite, cradling a carved idol.

Sadly, there is no obvious mechanism or means to raise the barrier. Virgil pats you on the shoulder, sensing your obvious frustration. 'Some things are best left alone…' He touches one of the bars with the tip of a blade, eliciting an angry flicker of magic from the runes.

Admitting defeat, you give the room a last covetous glare, before following Virgil back to the main aisle. You continue to head east, until you reach another large chamber. Turn to 842.

697

As a special reward for freeing all of the tigris, you may now choose one of the following items:

Cart wheel	**Brazen bar**	**Captive's collar**
(left hand: shield)	(left hand: staff)	(necklace)
+2 speed +1 armour	+2 speed +2 magic	+1 speed
Ability: roll with it	Ability: knockdown	Ability: bleed
(requirement: warrior)		

Once you have made your decision, turn to 669.

698

A well-aimed strike punctures one of Cernos' wings. The follow-up blow takes the demon across the chest, hurling him back against the runed door. He scrabbles to find his feet, looking battle-weary for the first time. Black blood seeps between his charred scales.

'I am defeated,' he rasps, struggling for breath. 'I yield.'

You glare at the demon, knowing the trickster for what he is. This creature would never surrender …

And you are proved correct – the demon's expression changes in a heartbeat, flaring into a vicious snarl. He lunges forward, his dagger-sized claws slashing for your throat. Any lesser opponent would have been cut down in those fatal seconds … but not you.

You turn aside as the demon hurtles past, bringing your weapons around in a spinning arc. They slice through the demon's remaining wing, gouging a strip across his back. As your weapons complete their circle, you see more blood spatter across the cratered ground.

The demon tries to recover but, wrong-footed by your strike, he falls – collapsing onto his back with a grunt of pain. You stride towards the prone beast, your face darkened by fury.

'It's over, Cernos.'

The demon's eyes go wide. 'Indeed, it is . . .' His gaze flickers over the spines protruding from your arms, and the black scales rippling across your chest – visible beneath your shredded armour. 'Barahar's blood . . .' He nods with grudging admiration. 'You are truly becoming a demon prince.'

'I am becoming nothing!' You snap. 'I can stop all this . . .' You point the tip of your weapon at Cernos' chest. 'At last, your heart will serve some good in this world.'

As you draw back to deliver the final blow, a sudden jolt of pain lances across your torso. You stagger back, surprised to see a white light flashing beneath the surface of your skin. 'What . . . what is this?' Another burst of pain drives you to your knees. You drop your weapons, putting your hands to the smarting wound. 'Is this some trick, devil?'

Cernos looks equally confused. 'Strange magic,' he hisses. 'There's something buried there.'

You plunge a clawed hand into the scaly flesh, whimpering with pain as you gouge out the glowing object. It is a small metal ball, covered in bright sigils. The moment you hold it within your palm, the light winks out.

Before you can gather your senses a fist comes down, slamming into your cheek. For the next few seconds you are reeling in a daze, spitting blood and broken teeth. Then something cold reaches around your throat. When the dizzying nausea finally passes, you open your eyes – to see Cernos' cruel visage inches from your face, his clawed fingers gripping you tight.

'Never take your eyes off the prize, prophet.' He draws back his other hand, the leathery skin creaking as it folds into a fist. . .

But the blow never lands. Instead, the cave blossoms with a piercing white light. You hear a man's cry – then the crack of a flint-lock pistol. Cernos goes tumbling back in a shower of blood. Another crack and a bullet whistles past the writhing demon, blowing chips out of the far wall.

You twist around to see two figures silhouetted by the bright light. Their sharp profiles mark one as wearing an open coat and a broad-brimmed hat; the other is armoured in sculptured plate, a long cloak whipping back from their shoulders.

'Told you it would work, Avian.' The figure with the hat marches forward, holstering his smoking pistols and drawing a fresh pair.

'Indeed, Virgil, you're full of surprises.' His companion raises a polished white staff, its headpiece crackling with magical energies. 'And I would say our timing, as always, is impeccable.' Turn to 647.

699

When you finally come to a halt, breathing fast from your exertions, four bodies lie crumpled around you. You gaze upon the serene expressions carved into the golden masks, and wonder if the maidens are now at peace, or whether their spirits will be forever damned to haunt this dark place.

You may now help yourself to one of the following rewards:

Sun blaze	**Burnished breastplate**	**Maiden's mask**
(main hand: sword)	(chest)	(head)
+2 speed +3 brawn	+3 brawn +2 armour	+1 speed +2 magic
Ability: sear	Ability: blind	Ability: sear
(requirement: rogue)	(requirement: warrior)	

With the guards defeated, you approach the double doors and push them open. They creak against an age-old crust of dirt and sand, slowly revealing a small chamber beyond. Two flickering torches illuminate another set of doors in the opposite wall – this time fashioned from stone and dressed in more elaborate carvings. Directly in front of them is a plinth, with a golden mirror resting between a sculptured pair of hands. It is currently turned to face you, catching your reflection on its polished surface.

Above the mirror, cut into the low-ceiling, is a short rectangular shaft leading up to daylight – and at its top is another identical mirror, sparkling in the afternoon sun. If you have the word *sun seeker* on your hero sheet, turn to 677. Otherwise, turn to 779.

700

You twist the numbered dials, each one locking into place with an encouraging click. As the last dial catches on some hidden mechanism, the container starts to vibrate softly. Suddenly its pyramidal lid flips open, revealing a hollowed cavity. You tip the container over, letting its contents spill into your hand. As well as a few sparkling jewels and some gold (you have gained 100 gold crowns), you also discover a rune stone. You may now choose one of the following rewards:

Rune of meditation	**Rune of protection**	**Rune of fortune**
(special: rune)	(special: rune)	(special: rune)
Use on any item to add the special ability *channel* (requirement: mage)	Use on any item to add the special ability *iron will*	Use on any item to add the special ability *charm*

Pleased with your finds, you pocket the gold and jewels, before turning your attention back to the forge. turn to 755.

701

Quito throws you a purse of gold, before shouldering his bag and heading down the aisle. (You have gained 80 gold crowns.) As you watch him leave, a sudden thought occurs to you.

'Hey, who is the book for?' you ask, with interest.

'Raolin Storm,' he calls back. 'A mage suffering from an unfortunate affliction – too much money.' He glances back over his shoulder. 'Don't worry, I'm his perfect antidote.' After a departing wink he re-enters the hall, disappearing from sight. If you are a venommancer, turn to 885. Otherwise, you leave the chamber and resume your journey, heading through the blast hole. Turn to 731.

The forest starts to thin, quickly becoming bare hills strewn with hummocks of moss and lichen-covered boulders. A mile further in and a grey-white wall looms out of the haze – a limestone cliff, marking the boundary of an impassable plain of bluffs and ridges.

'We pass under rock,' states Grey-hair, pointing to a ragged crack in the cliff-side. 'Caves take us to marsh.'

Scar-face leads the way into the narrow crevice. Your shoulders brush against the sharp walls that loom close on either side, as if conspiring to keep you from advancing further. You squeeze through the tight spaces, trying to ignore the creeping sense of claustrophobia that threatens to overwhelm you. You take comfort in the occasional glimpse of daylight high above, but these become less frequent as you descend deeper, the tunnel eventually bringing you out into an underground cave.

It is pitch black and yet you can clearly make out the crowns of stalagmites protruding from the pitted ground. Once again, you are thankful for the strange powers that you have inherited from the demon.

Eventually the cavern dips, splitting into two tunnels. One winds away to the north, where a sickly smell wafts on a faint breeze. To the east is a wider tunnel which twists away, out of sight. Your sharpened hearing picks out a skittering sound coming from that direction, like many feet tapping across stone.

Scar-face looks back at the pack, waiting for a decision.

Grey-hair leans towards you. 'What do your instincts say, bright claw?'

Will you:

Suggest taking the north passage?	807
Suggest taking the east passage?	604

703

After an hour you see the dim grey of the canyon wall looming above the treetops. Your journey is nearly at its end. Quickening your pace, you leave the river and plunge back into the forest, making for the canyon. Once again the going is slow and arduous, hacking your way across the muddy, uneven terrain, but at last – insect-bitten and smarting from a multitude of minor scrapes – you stumble out onto a boulder-strewn slope, the high canyon wall only metres away from you.

Now a fresh challenge presents itself – getting to the top. As you walk along the wall, you notice a few areas that look climbable, with hand- and foot-holds and a few crumbling ledges. You also spot a cave a little further ahead, with skulls and bone-charms hanging from poles either side of the opening.

Will you:

Enter the cave?	867
Climb the canyon wall?	776

704

The tigris nods, a fleeting smile revealing his canines. 'You think you strong enough to fight with Shara Sheva?' He turns away, raising his arms to the boisterous growls and snarls of his pack. 'Skins think they better than us!'

The tigris swings around, lashing out with both paws. You twist sideways just in time, the sharp claws missing your chest by mere inches.

You draw your weapons, backing away in confusion. 'Wait, I offered you aid . . .'

Sheva prowls around you, squaring his shoulders. 'To fight with Sheva, you show your claws. Else you're worm-meat for the marsh.' His words break into a thunderous roar, as he flies forward in a blur of tooth and claw. You must now fight:

	Speed	*Brawn*	*Armour*	*Health*
Sheva	8	7	4	50

Special abilities

- Cat's speed: Sheva rolls 3 dice to determine his attack speed. Your hero's special abilities can be used to reduce this number, if available.
- Bleed: After the first time Sheva makes a successful attack that causes health damage, you must take a further point of damage at the end of each combat round.

If you manage to defeat this powerful predator, turn to 366. Otherwise, turn to 294.

705

The steam is flowing from one end of the pipes to the other. Your goal is to stop the air from reaching the outlet, which feeds the bellows. In order to achieve this, you can turn any *two* of the dark-coloured pipe tiles clockwise by 90 degrees. By turning two of the tiles, it is possible to stop any of the steam reaching the outlet.

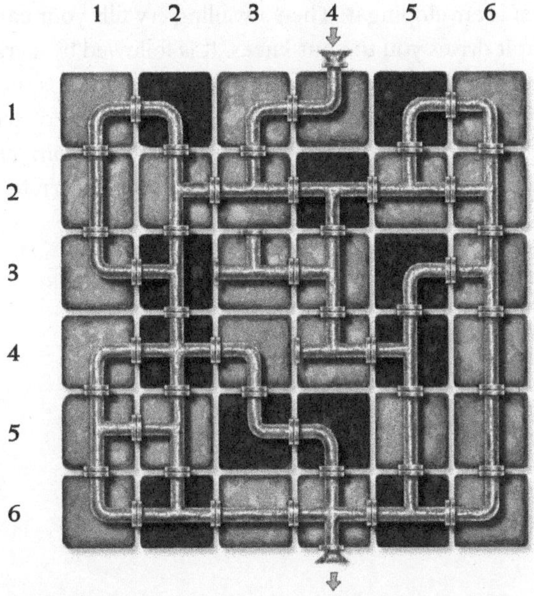

Each tile has a numbered reference. The row numbers give a tens value and the column numbers give a units value. For example, the first dark tile on the top row would be represented by the number 12. The dark tile on the second row would be 24. Decide which two tiles you need to turn, then add together their two numbers. This is your answer. Turn to the paragraph number that matches your total to see if you were correct.

If you are unable to solve the puzzle, then you have no choice but to leave the pipes and concentrate your efforts elsewhere. You may now examine the cogs and pulleys, if you haven't already (turn to 786) or head up the stairs to the forge (turn to 601).

706

The black spear starts to tremble and shake, pulled by some invisible force towards the magical font. You tighten your grip, struggling to maintain a hold, but the power is too strong. The spear is wrenched from your hands, drawn through the air to hover above the dark hole.

You watch dumbfounded as blue fingers of magic creep out of the font's inky depths, wrapping themselves around the spear. Metal grates and squeals as the spear continues to shake, fighting against the magic that is enveloping it. Then a wailing cry fills your ears, so deafening that it drives you to your knees. It is followed by a crack, as the spear breaks – releasing a black cloud of magic, which is sucked down into the font, the cry fading to silence within a matter of seconds.

If the spear contained the *spirit of the panther, the spirit of the spider* and *the spirit of the serpent*, turn to 420. Otherwise, turn to 377.

707

You spring at Virgil, taking him by surprise. Grabbing his arm, you attempt to wrest the blade from his grip. With a snarl, the witchfinder cuffs you with the back of his hand. You stumble back, knocking into the desk and sending it crashing onto its side.

'Fool,' growls the witchfinder. 'I was trying to save you.'

'You're not real,' you shout back defiantly.

You notice the black roots, which have broken through the stone, start to snake and wind around Virgil's legs. Too late the witchfinder looks down, realising his predicament. You charge forwards, ducking beneath his sword swipe and tugging a dagger from his belt.

'You will regret this, prophet!' he spits.

You drive the dagger into the man's chest, stepping away from the body as it topples to the ground, the black roots unravelling and slinking back into the stone. Virgil spits blood as he glares at you in anger.

'Why?' he asks fiercely.

You cling to the dagger, feeling its weight – the sticky blood oozing between your fingers. 'This is just a dream,' you reply, sounding less certain than before.

The witchfinder shudders then lies still. For several minutes you are frozen in situ, gazing down at the body. Something isn't right, but you can't work out what. You struggle to remember how you got here, what you were doing before this all happened. The broken manacles hang heavy around your wrists, rubbing against the blistered sores. The rust, the chains, the metal – all of it is perfect, exactly as you remember it.

'It can't be real,' you gasp, letting the dagger fall from your hands. It clinks across the ground, settling next to the dead witchfinder. Horrified by what you might have done, you hurry out of the cell, desperate to find answers (make a note of the word *scars*). Turn to 478.

708

Congratulations, for defeating Nephele while *hexed* you have won the following rare item:

Volcanist's handwraps
(gloves)
+1 speed +4 magic
Ability: melt, volcanism set
(requirement: hexed)

Once you have updated your hero sheet, return to the quest map to continue your journey.

709

Dodging the corrosive sap, you hack and blast at the withered bark, each blow causing more of the green slime to ooze from the tree's innards. It is a tiring battle, the noxious odour making you feel nauseous – but at last you stand victorious over the felled tree, its broken body slowly sinking into its own slime.

Amongst the tree's dark roots you spy a number of glittering treasures. As well as a casket containing 50 gold crowns, you also find one of the following rewards:

Forest cuirass	**Weeper's blooms**	**Tangle knot**
(chest)	(gloves)	(ring)
+2 brawn +2 armour	+1 speed +2 magic	+1 brawn +1 magic
Ability: thorn armour	Ability: call of nature set	Ability: barbs
(requirement: warrior)	(requirement: druid)	

If you are a brigand, druid or pariah, turn to 734. Otherwise turn to 804.

710

The moment your hand touches the rune, red lightning arcs across the face of the door, sending you reeling backwards in pain. Clearly you have chosen the incorrect rune, and have triggered some hidden trap woven into the magic of the door.

You have been inflicted with the following curse:

Curse of frailty (pa): You must lower your *health* by 5 until you next roll a double in combat.

Return to 871 to choose another rune.

711

There is a vast number of books and tablets neatly arranged on the shelves, but all are written in an unfamiliar script. However, when you tug one of the books loose from its shelf you discover that it is in fact a small stone chest. You flip open the lid to reveal a hollow cavity filled with gold. (You have gained 100 gold crowns.) Further searching reveals nothing of interest.

Will you:

Examine the crystal ball?	659
Read the note?	852
Leave?	858

712

The cracks in the platform start to widen, branching from one end to the other. Beneath your feet you can feel the stone vibrating as the wind demon rumbles ever closer, devouring everything in its path. Virgil wipes the blood from his eye, stumbling into a run. He tugs your arm, pulling you along with him. The pathway continues to circle upwards, taking you past more of the strange glowing scenes.

On the last platform a dwarf warrior is pacing angrily, resplendent in plate armour. He stands four feet tall, his spiked pauldrons towering an extra foot above his head. 'No!' He stops and turns, his finger stabbing at some invisible accuser. 'I were set up! I'd never disgrace the twin thrones.' He takes a step forward, teeth clenched tight. 'The Illumanti are corrupt! Their magic's what's done this! You don't believe me – then you're cursed like they are!' In a berserk fury he snatches a hammer and a shield from a crossed rack. When he turns to face you, there is a maddened gleam to his ghostly eyes.

'You … you murdered my drakes,' growls the warrior. 'Their blood is on your hands!'

With a murderous cry, the dwarf charges, his hammer sweeping around in a vivid crescent of green fire. It is time to fight:

	Speed	*Magic*	*Armour*	*Health*
Acheron	11	7	4	45

Special abilities

- Wall of steel: When you roll for damage, roll an equal number of dice for Acheron. If the digits of any dice match your own, the dice are removed from play.
- Ghost of a victory: You cannot use *cutpurse* or *pillage* to gain gold/items from this combat.

If you manage to defeat Acheron turn to 738. If you are defeated (or reach the end of your twentieth combat round), then the wind demon has outrun you. Restore your *health* and abilities, then return to 630 if you wish to tackle the challenge again.

713

As you light the last candle, the ground begins to tremble and shake beneath your feet. You quickly back away from the scorched markings, tugging your weapon free.

Then you hear the sound of crumbling earth. The pumpkin head has started to rise up off the ground, supported on a pair of dirt-covered shoulders. In horror, you realise that the creature is struggling to free itself, dragging first one arm and then the other out of the soil. Its long clawed fingers rake the earth as it crawls forward, slowly pulling the rest of its skeletal body free from the mound.

The creature kneels and then stands, clods of sodden earth falling from its dark bones. For a moment, it regards you thoughtfully, wobbling on bony heels. Then with a sudden lurch, the pumpkin staggers towards you, flames billowing from its jagged mouth. You must fight:

	Speed	*Brawn*	*Armour*	*Health*
Jack o' Lantern	0	1	1	15

If you manage to defeat this magical guardian, turn to 201.

714

With the mighty black panther defeated, you may now help yourself to one of the following rewards:

Cape of the savage	**Bad tooth**	**Waxen wilds**
(cloak)	(ring)	(gloves)
+1 speed +2 magic	+2 magic	+1 speed +2 magic
Ability: primal	Ability: disease	Ability: surge

You may also take *Gheira's paw*, as proof of your victory (make a note of this on your hero sheet, it does not take up backpack space). If you have the *glaive of souls* equipped, turn to 663. Otherwise, return to the quest map to continue your adventure.

715

Entering the ziggurat is like stepping into another world. After the heat and humidity of the jungle, you find the air here is cold and dusty – the quiet solemnity reminding you of being inside a church. The four sheer walls slope upwards towards a point of light high above, suggesting that the entire ziggurat is a hollow structure. Torches spit magical flames from rusted iron braziers; one set at each corner of the room. You wonder how long those flames have been lit – and to what purpose. This city is thousands of years old, a cursed ruin left to crumble away. No one lives here anymore, except for the forsaken souls shambling amongst the debris.

And yet, this place still feels alive. Perhaps the Lamuri are not yet ready to be forgotten.

The building's vast age – its alien nature – is evident all around you. On every slab of rock there are hundreds of intricate carvings. The script makes little sense to you, a combination of runic symbols and pictures, possibly recording events or the beliefs of a lost people.

Across from the entrance a flight of stairs leads up to a raised platform, where a pair of bronze doors are set into the wall. Four figures stand sentinel at the foot of the stairs, their postures rigid, their eyes unmoving. Unlike the statues outside, these appear to be undead. Their bodies are rotted to bone, but their burnished breastplates and golden facemasks still shine as if they were forged yesterday. Each of the four warriors, who appear female from their gold-banded skirts, is holding a sword and shield to her chest.

Against the right-hand wall a sloping ledge rises up to an open doorway, leading back out into bright sunlight.

Will you:	
Approach the stairs?	652
Leave via the side exit?	595

716

For defeating Erkil, you may now help yourself to one of the following special items:

Titan-forged hauberk	Garm's whistle	Cornerstone boots
(chest)	(necklace)	(feet)
+2 speed +3 armour	+1 speed +1 magic	+2 speed +2 armour
Ability: thorn armour	Ability: packmaster	Ability: insulated

If you are *hexed* then you have gained an extra reward, turn to 803. Otherwise, return to the quest map to continue your journey.

717

The succubus is a powerful adversary, blasting you with her dark magics while her mind-numbing powers sap at your strength. The onslaught is endless, forcing you to lose ground to the witch's fury.

'You cannot defeat me!' snarls the voice in your ears. 'This marsh is mine!'

Then, when all seems lost, you find some hidden reserve of strength – a bitter fury that floods through your body, helping you to shrug off her debilitating spells. The witch senses this change, pausing in her attack.

'Demon blood!' the voice whispers.

Then you fly forward, driving your weapons into her tattered robes. There is a deafening shriek as a black wind pours out of the wound, blowing you backwards. You tumble over onto your stomach, looking up in time to see the creature's mildewed robes flutter to the ground. There is no sign of a body, only a thin maggot-like worm, dragging itself across the stones. You clamber to your feet, marching forward to drive your weapons into its weakened form. There is a piercing, eldritch screech. Then there is silence …

At last the succubus' power has been broken – and the marsh is now safe for the Shara Khana to cross. However, it feels a hollow victory, knowing that your tigris companions gave their lives to achieve this end. Turn to 748.

718

The raft is buffeted through the chaotic tumult, but somehow you manage to keep it on course, avoiding the majority of the obstacles flung your way. Finally the river starts to slow, until you find yourself paddling through calmer waters, the thick forest rolling by on either side.

You start to relax, settling into a calm rhythm of strokes – until you spot the pair of yellow eyes glittering above the waterline. You draw in your paddle, leaving the raft to glide closer – hoping that you can pass unharmed. But as you near, the eyes dip below the surface.

A dark shadow flows quickly beneath your craft. A heartbeat. Then there is a thunderous crash as something drives up underneath you, smashing through the raft and sending you tumbling into the water. For several seconds, you are blinded by air bubbles, then you see the huge reptilian body whipping towards you – its long jaws open wide. It is time to fight:

	Speed	*Brawn*	*Armour*	*Health*
Alligator	7	6	5	60

Special abilities

- Death roll: If the alligator rolls a ⚅ for its damage score, it goes into a death roll – spinning you wildly around in its powerful jaws. The alligator may roll another die to add further damage. If a ⚅ is rolled again, it may roll another dice – and so on.
- Drowning: At the end of every combat round you must automatically lose 2 *health*.

If you manage to overcome this powerful predator, turn to 742.

719

After brushing ink over the bronze plates, you lower them onto the paper. When you lift up the cross-piece, you are pleased to see that the parchment is now marked with your chosen sigils. Your book is almost complete; all that remains is to bind the loose pages. If you wish to choose a *binding of black iron*, turn to 806. If you would prefer to choose a *binding of drake scales*, turn to 876.

720

You search the hunter's corpse, finding 30 gold crowns and one of the following items:

Bark whip	Jade teeth	Net of snares
(left hand: whip)	(main hand: fist weapon)	(cloak)
+2 speed +2 brawn	+2 speed +2 brawn	+1 speed +1 magic
Ability: bleed	Ability: rake	Ability: immobilise
	(requirement: warrior)	

With the hunter defeated, you quickly scan through the available supplies. You may take up to two of the following items:

Rhinosaur pheromone	Flask of healing (1 use)	Hunter's net (2 uses)
(backpack)	(backpack)	(backpack)
The pungent aroma of male rhinosaur sweat	Use any time in combat to restore 10 *health*	Use at the start of a combat round to reduce your opponent's *speed* by 2 for that round

As you step from the tent, you hear a wailing cry from above. Looking up, you see the sniper topple from the watch tower. A tigris follows him over the rail, her sharp claws whipping around to dig into the wood – slowing her fall. It is White Cloak. The agile tigris springs back to the ground, her eyes already scanning the battle for her next prey. Turn to 785.

721

The sun has sunk low in the sky, its reddish glow fanning through the treetops. You contemplate making camp, aware that this is now your third day trekking across the forested mountain slopes. But you sense you are getting close to the trail's end. The warm wind now carries a hint of the sea, whilst the cawing gulls have become a more frequent sight, reeling overhead.

You decide to make a final push – a decision that soon rewards you, as the dirt of the forest gives way to soft white sand. Elated that your journey is finally at an end, you race down the slope onto the beach. At first, it is everything you imagined: a hidden cove of clear-blue water, sheltered by a chain of coral reefs. The beach itself stretches away to either side, forming a perfect crescent, its undulating dunes hugged by swaying palms and barnacled rock.

Paradise. And yet, something isn't right.

There is wreckage on the shore. Fragments of wood and rusted metal. And the remains of a ship's mast bobbing on the waves. Gulls are pecking at bones, whilst other scavengers – rats and wild-looking dogs – sniff hungrily through the debris. You stride warily along the beach, sand crunching underfoot as you survey the dead bodies. They have been stripped to their bones, their few belongings now lying strewn across the beach. You wonder if some of these were other travellers – like yourself – who came looking for paradise, but found something else instead. Turn to 690.

722

You trek through the muggy dawn – a silent procession, winding between the towering trees of the forest. Scar-face leads the way, accompanied by a female pack member, her face permanently twisted into a scowl. Occasionally she glances back at you, teeth bared. You sense that not everyone is happy with you joining the pack.

Grey-hair walks at your side, his head constantly turning from side to side as he silently regards his surroundings. Little has been said since leaving the river – the tigris have proved to be a taciturn people, content to watch and listen rather than give voice to their thoughts. Knowing of the dangers that lurk here in the forest, perhaps silence is a wise defence.

Just before midday, Scar-face makes the first warning signal – raising a paw to halt the procession. The female tracker is scraping something from the groove of a tree. She holds it out to Grey-hair, who moves to inspect her find. You peer past his shoulder to see a collection of jelly-like eggs.

'Drecko,' snarls Grey-hair, his claws sliding out from his paws as he regards the tree tops. You notice that the rest of the pack is now hugging the ground, looking up through the shelves of foliage.

Then you hear a hacking cry from the trees behind you. There is an answering call from deeper in the forest. Quickly, you ready your weapons, trying to catch sight of whatever has spooked the tigris.

'There!' hisses Grey-hair, pointing.

You see a dark shape gliding across a thin patch of sky. It has black, webbed wings and a scaled body. It disappears into the canopy as another series of guttural calls breaks the brooding silence.

Several tense minutes pass, all eyes remaining on the trees. You are about to relax, believing that the tigris are being overly cautious, when suddenly the first of the beasts swoops down from above. You catch sight of a bone-crested head and curved talons. Then one of the tigris is snarling and screeching as it is grabbed in the creature's jaws and lifted up into the air. More of the creatures glide in from the opposite direction, their wings casting long shadows across the ground. One of them closes in on you, looking to snap you up with its needle-like teeth. It is time to fight:

	Speed	*Brawn*	*Armour*	*Health*
Drecko	8	6	8	50

Special abilities

- Winged predator: It is difficult to outmanoeuvre this agile combatant. You must lower your *speed* by 1 for the duration of this fight.
- Delirium: After the drecko makes a successful attack that causes health damage, you are immediately inflicted with delirium. If you win a combat round, roll a die. If the result is ⚀ or ⚁ then your attack misses its mark and you cannot roll for damage. If the result is ⚂ or more, you can roll for damage as normal.

If you manage to defeat the drecko, turn to 693. Otherwise, turn to 640.

723

For defeating Nephele, you may now help yourself to one of the following special items:

Cape of the unseen	Abandoned hope	Shiver spine
(cloak)	(main hand: dagger)	(left hand: snake)
+2 speed +3 brawn	+3 speed +4 brawn	+2 speed +3 brawn
Ability: coup de grace	Ability: gut ripper	Ability: frostbite
		(requirement: venommancer)

If you are *hexed* then you have gained an extra reward, turn to **838**. Otherwise, return to the quest map to continue your journey.

724

Avian blasts the troll off its feet. As it scrabbles through the bones, struggling to right itself, you leap onto its ribcage and bring your weapons down – slicing through the growth-like club. The grisly appendage goes sailing away in a sickening spray of foul pestilence.

'No!' hisses the troll, raising the severed stump to its hollow eye-sockets. 'My pretty! My treasure! My shiny fing!'

You swing your weapons again, watching with a grim satisfaction as the troll's skull leaves its shoulders, rattling away to join the rest of the bones littering the passageway. The body gives an agonised spasm, the legs kicking in the slimy dirt, then it lies still – dust motes swirling like carrion flies over its tattered remains.

For defeating Nergal, you may now help yourself to one of the following rewards:

Bone rot	Troll tusks	Nergal's splinters
(left hand: club)	(head)	(gloves)
+2 speed +3 brawn	+2 speed +2 armour	+1 speed +2 armour
Ability: leech	Ability: charge	Ability: rake
(requirement: warrior)		(requirement: mage)

When you have made your decision, turn to 635.

725

You place the bird tablet into the hole. There is a sharp click as it slots into place, followed by a scraping rumble as the final tier of the pyramid rises up. Resting on top of it is a small bronze urn. If you wish, you may take:

Bronze urn
(backpack)
A decorative burial urn
containing ashes

If you haven't already, you can search the main chamber (turn to 508) or leave and continue your journey (turn to 563).

726

You scoop up a rock and charge at the rogue. For a split second Murlic's eyes widen in surprise, then his familiar scowl returns. He swipes his daggers through the air, cutting angry red trails towards your chest. The blow would have hit you, and possibly ended your life there and then, but a blast of black magic slams into his side, blowing him back into the opposite wall.

As his smoking body slides to the ground, he fixes you with a contemptuous glare. 'Foolish cur … it's the witch …'

Suddenly your surroundings start to blur, sweeping into ribbons of ochre light. You hear a woman's laughter – cold and shrill – reverberating all around you. Then you lurch forwards, as if pushed by some invisible hand, to find yourself standing in a ruined building. A female tigris lies sprawled at your feet, blood pooling around her broken body. It is Scowler. Turn to 435.

727

Legendary monster: Ixion, the wheel of pain

The tortured screams carry across the churning waves of the lava sea. You spin around, eyes roving across the floating fragments of rock. At first, you don't see anything untoward – then, between the banks of steaming mist, you catch what looks like a giant wheel, bouncing and lurching through the lava. As it circles around your island, you realise that your eyes are not deceiving you – it is a wheel, one made of metal, with serrated spikes protruding from its outside edge.

The screams are coming from some poor victim, bound to the wheel's spokes. His arms and legs are manacled, his head held back by a cruel metal collar. He writhes and squirms in pain, his skin already blackened and charred, stretched taut over thin bone. By all reason he should be dead, fried to cinders – and yet some dark magic is keeping him alive, his tormented visage emitting an endless stream of wails and curses.

You glance at Virgil, his gem-studded eyepatch gleaming in the heat.

The witchfinder slides his pistols from his coat. 'Let's put this devil out of his misery.'

The wheel flips up on a viscous wave, spinning through the air towards your island. You scramble aside as it comes crashing down, its jagged spikes ripping deep furrows into the black rock.

'Fools!' The charred man leans forward, pulling against his restraints. 'There is no escape. No escaping the pain!' From his mouth comes a rippling torrent of flame, its edges flickering with ghostly skulls. You cover your face from the heat as the wheel screeches past, missing you by a hair's breadth. As it circles around to make its next pass, you draw your weapons and prepare to take on this hellish wheel of pain. It is time to fight:

	Speed	*Magic*	*Armour*	*Health*
Wheel	14/12	11	12	100
Ixion	–	–	5	35

Special abilities

- Rolling, rolling, rolling: The wheel picks up speed when it is charging and then slows down to turn. Its speed alternates between 14 and 12. In the first combat round, the wheel has a *speed* of 14, in the second, 12 – and so on.
- Purging flames: While Ixion is alive, you must take 6 damage, ignoring *armour*, at the end of each combat round. If you have *fire shield*, this is reduced to 2 damage.

In this combat you roll against the wheel's speed. If you win a combat round, you can choose to apply your damage to the wheel or Ixion. Once the wheel is reduced to zero *health*, Ixion is also automatically defeated.

If you manage to destroy this tumbling torture-chamber, turn to 888.

728

You search through the grisly remains of the golem, wondering if there is anything of value that can be salvaged. Amongst the charred bones and magic-imbued flesh, you find one of the following special rewards:

Blood diamond	**Tendon rope**	**Gloves of the firmament**
(ring)	(necklace)	(gloves)
+2 magic	+1 speed +1 armour	+1 speed +4 magic
Ability: bleed	Ability: greater heal	Ability: resolve

When you have updated your hero sheet, turn to 877.

729

With the mighty black panther defeated, you may now help yourself to one of the following rewards:

Untamed will	**Back to the wild**	**Hunter's heart**
(main hand: dagger)	(cloak)	(necklace)
+2 speed +2 brawn	+1 speed +2 brawn	+1 speed
Ability: piercing	Ability: fearless	Ability: savage call
(requirement: rogue)		(requirement: warrior)

You also take *Gheira's paw*, as proof of your victory (make a note of this on your hero sheet, it does not take up backpack space). If you have the *glaive of souls* equipped, turn to 663. Otherwise, return to the quest map to continue your adventure.

730

Blood and gore spatter in all directions as your weapons cleave through the demon's body. Unable to reform itself, the creature gives a gurgling screech before collapsing into a thick pool of steaming slime. Wafting away the noxious vapours, you spy a number of valuable treasures bobbing on the surface.

You have gained 200 gold crowns and one of the following rewards:

Glutton's robes	**Wastrel's guise**	**Fortune's seekers**
(chest)	(head)	(gloves)
+2 speed +4 magic	+2 speed +2 brawn	+1 speed +4 brawn
Ability: leech	Ability: blind	Ability: unstoppable
(requirement: mage)	(requirement: rogue)	(requirement: warrior)

With the demon defeated, you help Virgil to destroy the gate. Once the runes have been broken and the portal closed, the witch-finder turns on you angrily.

'Demons!' he spits. 'Next time, I suggest you listen to my counsel. Their art is murder and deceit.' He glowers at your scaled flesh. 'Just be grateful I do not choose to judge you, demon.'

He spins on his heel and marches away, his boots squelching through the slime. You glance back at the gate, wondering if there is a ring of truth to the witchfinder's words – the demon blood courses through your veins. With every hour, you feel yourself changing ... becoming more like them.

There are many steps on the path of darkness. I pray you find deliverance before its end.

Angrily, you push Virgil's warning from you mind. Cernos is the key to your freedom, and you don't intend on letting him escape. Turn to 872.

731

You clamber over the charred rubble to find yourself in a vast windowless hall. Wherever your eye falls there are bones, blackened and scorched. It would appear that a great battle was fought here – a terrible conflict where many lives were lost. You tread through the grisly wasteland, trying to piece together what happened. Black scars rake the walls and floor, as if some fire or heat was passed over them. Across the ceiling you notice similar trails and the occasional impact crater, where something must have been hurled against the stone with great strength.

Thousands of bones.

In some places they form steep mounds, pitched against the walls in waves of tangled death. You cannot guess at how many bodies – how many lives. What were they defending? What was so important that they would sacrifice themselves in this way? You pass through the hall, arriving at a set of stairs. Again, great chunks have been taken out of the walls, and the ceiling has been blown open, exposing a jagged window of daylight. You ascend the stairs, finding yourself in another rubble-filled passage. You pick your way carefully over the loose rock, noticing more skeletons trapped amongst the debris.

Finally you come to a grand hall, its architecture different to that you have seen before. The stone is obsidian, melted and then moulded like clay to form sweeping lines and curves. There are no edges, no carvings, simply smooth rock rising up into a forest of curling branches. It has the feeling of something alive … and very old.

At the far end of this immense chamber is a throne. Its winged back has been smashed in two, leaving a jagged row of prongs, like some macabre crown. And seated on it, glaring at you with both amusement and contempt, is Cernos. Turn to 771.

732

Congratulations, for defeating Ixion while *hexed* you have won the following rare item:

Prowler's tunic
(chest)
+1 speed +4 brawn
Ability: critical strike, prowler set
(requirement: hexed)

Once you have updated your hero sheet, return to the quest map to continue your journey.

733

You follow the sentient magic into a small, domed building. It looks to have once been a storeroom; it is now filled with broken pottery and half-rotted baskets.

A grey-haired monkey squats on the ground, trying to pull something loose from a mound of rubble. The monkey is so intent on its discovery, it doesn't notice the dark tendrils of magic winding closer and closer …

Before you can act, the magic snaps forward, driving itself inside the monkey's brain. The creature gives a surprised cry, then bolts out of the building, sending stones skittering in its wake.

You contemplate giving chase, but then you notice the object that the monkey had been trying to free. It is a thin disc of pure gold, its surface polished like a mirror. You may now take the following item:

Golden mirror
(backpack)
A circular reflector
made of pure gold

Finding little else of interest in the building, you decide to leave. Turn to 764.

734

You get the sudden feeling that you are being watched. Looking around you see a young woman standing at the lip of the crater, her skin mottled with patches of green and brown. In one hand she holds a gnarled staff, in the other a lantern glowing with a bluish light. There is an uneasy silence as her almond-shaped eyes regard you thoughtfully. Then she gestures for you to approach.

'You have done what I could not,' she states, bowing her head in reverence. 'Long has this place suffered. This was my charge and …' She looks past you, to the slime-coated remains of the cursed tree. 'I was too weak in my desire to end a life.'

'Who are you?' you ask, frowning. 'Do you live here?'

The woman gives a sad smile. 'I am a dryad. A protector of the land. You have done me a great service. And for that, I must give my thanks. Follow me.'

The dryad does not wait for your reply. Turning, she starts off across the mire, her glowing lantern lighting the way. You follow her lead, noticing that the woman's bare feet leave no mark or depression in the thick mud. Sadly, the same cannot be said for yourself as you squelch and stagger through the grasping murk.

Eventually you come to the hollow bole of a great tree. Its bark is as black and blighted as the rest of the forest that surrounds it. Inside the bole is a pedestal of stone, and resting on it is a wooden bowl.

'This is a powerful elixir,' states the dryad, walking around the pedestal. 'Sap from the elder tree, before it was tainted. It would be the elder's wish that you receive this gift, so a similar fate does not befall you also.'

As you lean closer you see that the bowl contains an amber liquid, sparkling with magic. Reaching into your pack, you take out your empty water bottle and sink it into the tree sap, filling it with the strange potion. You have now gained:

Elder sap (1 use)
(backpack)
Use any time in combat
to heal yourself to full *health*

If you are *hexed*, turn to 746. Otherwise, turn to 804.

735

As the marsh fog thickens, you feel an increasing sense that you are travelling through some peculiar dreamscape. Everything becomes slow and sluggish, from your own movements as you drag your feet through the mud to those of your companions slinking ahead, their ears pricked as they glance from side to side. You can sense their nervousness. Neither wanted to come here.

You struggle to stay focused, your limbs feeling weak and lethargic. Several times you stumble and fall into the cold, brackish waters – each time, taking a little longer to drag yourself back to your feet. Eventually, you find yourself crawling – head bowed – shivering from the wet and the cold. You cannot tell how long you have travelled or how far, but when your hands scrabble over stone, you finally look up.

Before you is a ruined building. It might have been a temple once, a grand structure surrounded by columns and decorative arches. Now it is part of the marsh, crumbling and old – most of its walls dragged down by reed-like vines. A vulture peers at you from one of the broken statues, its collar of white fur standing stark against its black feathers. An ill omen, perhaps.

You manage to stand, swaying with nausea, the grey-stone of the ruin swimming in and out of focus. There is no sign of the others. You sag against a wall, gasping for breath … then your strength gives out and you fall …

'Get up!' a voice hisses in your ear.

In the distance you hear a thunderous boom and the clatter of falling rock. You open your eyes to see Virgil standing over you. The cell door is twisted off its hinges, black roots breaking up out of the cracked stone floor.

'Where … am I?' you croak, feeling yourself being lifted up.

The witchfinder's face swings into view. 'I told you I was coming back. We're getting out of here.'

You notice three deep gashes cutting across the man's cheek, coating his neck and the collars of his coat in blood. 'This is not what happened …' you gasp, looking around at the Durnhollow cell.

'Because this is *real*,' growls the witchfinder, slapping your face with a gloved hand. 'You are drugged on Elysium. What you have experienced – what you have seen – it isn't real.'

You push him away, backing up against the wall. 'No, you're lying.' From the passageway you can hear sounds of battle – steel clamouring against steel, and fizzling cracks of magic. 'This is not what happened!' You grip your head, struggling to remember, to reorder your thoughts. 'I was in the marsh. Lost in the marsh …'

Virgil draws a curved blade from his belt. It flickers with a yellow, sickly light. 'I can't leave you here, prophet. Come with me or you die in this cell.'

Will you:

Agree to follow Virgil?	694
Attack Virgil?	707

736

Despite your best efforts, you are unable to keep up with the nimble-footed rogue. The distance continues to widen, the imp's ceaseless laughter only adding to your frustration. Eventually you slow to a halt, forced to admit defeat. After spitting several angry curses at the thief's departing back, you rejoin Virgil in the reading room. Turn to 788.

737

A lucky blow sends the staff spinning away across the stone tiles. As the monkey starts to shrink back to his normal size you deliver a firm kick to his chest, sending him flying over the edge of the platform. His shriek of rage only lasts for a short time before a loud crunch puts paid to the king's rule.

Congratulations! You have battled your way to the top of the temple and emerged victorious. You may now choose one of the following special rewards:

Wishing staff	**Hanuman's hair**	**Crown of Gandhara**
(main hand: staff)	(necklace)	(head)
+2 speed +3 magic	+1 speed +2 health	+1 speed +2 brawn
Ability: wish master	Ability: monkey mob	Ability: command

You also discover a small chest behind the throne, containing 200 gold crowns. As you prepare to leave you spot an unusual device to the south of the platform: a circular pedestal, with two golden hands set into its top stone. They are slightly cupped, facing inwards, as if they should be holding something. If you have the *golden mirror*, turn to **848**. Otherwise, turn to **587**.

738

The dwarf is sent tumbling over the platform's edge, his ghostly form exploding into sparks of light. Quickly you follow Virgil onto the adjoining pathway, only seconds before the wind demon rushes up and smashes through the green stone. You are both forced into a full-on sprint as the path shatters behind you – the cold fingers of darkness grasping at your heels.

At the top of the Abussos is an archway, leading through into another cavern. You believe you can make it ... but then your hope sinks when you see the path ahead breaking up, the green stone tumbling away into the abyss. You are fast approaching its jagged edge, with an empty space of over seven metres stretching before you.

Virgil starts to slow. 'It's too far!' he cries desperately.

You realise that you are trapped – between an impossible jump and the pursuing demon. 'Keep going!' you cry, shoving Virgil forward. 'We're going to make it!'

The pain in your back suddenly flares with intensity, driving hot knives of agony into your spine. All around you the walls shake with the force of the wind, eldritch screams pounding in your ears. As the wailing noise grows ever louder, the pain in your back reaches its own crescendo, white spots bursting before your eyes. You feel yourself lurching forward, flailing, falling ... There is a savage ripping sound as your back explodes in a bloody miasma of bone and sinew.

Virgil reaches the edge of the ledge and hurls himself into the void. He makes half the distance before he starts to plummet, legs kicking furiously. You spring into the air, hearing the crack of your wings as they unfurl for the first time.

For several seconds you are buffeted against the wall, scales scraping on the glowing rock. Then you push off from the stone, stretching out to grab the collar of Virgil's coat. The witchfinder gives a strangled gasp as he is snatched from his fall.

You are flying.

The movement is instinctive, like breathing. You fear to hesitate, to wonder how you are doing it, in case you break your concentration and fall. Instead, you focus on the archway and your bid for freedom. The wind demon howls and snaps at your heels, so close that its graven touch is frosting the stonework around you.

Then you are through the arch, gliding over a sprawling cavern filled with dark buildings. A cold, leaden light falls in columns from the cracked ceiling, illuminating paved roads and bridges, and columned towers, their ridged walls flowing into each other like melted candlewax.

'Hold on!' You feel the wind behind you batter against your wings, throwing you forward at greater speed. Unable to keep your balance, you go hurtling head-over-heels across the grey rooftops. Your shoulder catches on a rocky crenellation, flipping you again. In the spinning chaos, you lose your grip on Virgil, who slips away ...

Smooth stone flies up at you. Then you are rolling and skidding across a dusty floor. A window reels into view. You go sprawling through it, across an alleyway and straight into an opposite building.

Ashen walls streak past, then you slam into something hard, a bench or chair, breaking your momentum with an agonising smack to the ribs.

A silence. Motes of dust dance through the air.

Your eyes scan back to the open window. There, above the rooftops, you can see the wind demon streaking across the city, shadowy body rippling like some hellish battle standard. The creature is searching for you – but for now, it seems that you have eluded its gaze.

Your first thought is Virgil and his possible whereabouts – then a more immediate concern takes hold. You glance over your shoulder, flinching at the sight of your newly-formed wings. Whereas Cernos had sported cruel-looking limbs of midnight black, your own are white-boned, with pale-coloured membranes shot with silver.

You flex your shoulder blades. The wings snap rigid, sending a wave of dust sweeping across the room.

'So, the angel gets its wings ...' Virgil is standing at the window of the opposite building, his surprised expression illuminated by his glowing swords. He shakes his head in wonderment, then glances down at the intervening alleyway. 'Don't suppose I could get a lift, could I?'

(Congratulations, you have completed the Abussos challenge. You may now restore your *health* and abilities.) Turn to 810.

739

You fling open the cage, quickly leaping aside as the beast lowers its horns and charges. It thunders past in a cloud of dust, smashing and trampling through anything that gets in its way. Luckily this also includes the giant, who is far too slow to avoid the rampaging animal. The rhinosaur rams straight into him, its sharp horns puncturing through the giant's leather armour and throwing him high over its head as if he was little more than a child's doll.

There is a roar of celebration from the nearby tigris – which ends abruptly as the rhinosaur skids around and charges again, heading straight for them. Quickly the tigris break for cover, bounding and leaping across the ruined compound while the enraged rhinosaur rumbles after them. Turn to 466.

740

Benin is slumped on the ground, his face coated with blood and dust. Standing over him is Murlic, the Wiccan rogue with the half-painted face. He holds two daggers, snarling with rage as he raises them to strike.

Your foot knocks into a broken sword hilt, sending it clattering over the loose rock. Both combatants freeze, looking in your direction.

'My friend!' wheezes Benin, clutching at his wounds. 'Thank the One God – save me!'

The Wiccan rogue scowls, glaring at you with contempt. 'Do not try to stop me, bright claw.'

Will you:

Attack Murlic and save Benin?	726
Stand by and let Benin die?	680

741

The dark rune-blade slices down in a crimson arc. It would surely have cut the witchfinder in two, if not for the ground lurching suddenly. Both of you are thrown off balance, loose rock raining down from the walls.

Virgil is clinging to one of the balcony's stony fingers. A jet of lava spirals up past his shoulder, hanging in space for a single heartbeat, then dropping back to the lake in a shower of droplets. 'See, demon!' He leers. 'Even the volcano balks at your very existence.'

He would have you back in Durnhollow. In a cell. A prisoner.

The words whisper in your ear, fuelling your anger and resentment. The demon fire is already leaping from the blade, sizzling across the space and smashing into Virgil. Such is the power of the blast that it hurls him straight across the magma lake and through the wall of the crater.

Finish him.

Your wings snap open as you take to the air, rising up on the searing-hot currents.

Finish him. Finish all who stand in our way!

A dry wind whips at your face as you glide through the opening, out across the ash-strewn slope of the volcano. Below you lie the grey lava flats, pockmarked with craters. You are sweeping down towards them, following the broken body that twists through the air. *My vision. This is my vision ...* But you realise something is wrong. You were that body, falling down the mountainside. Not Virgil.

Distracted by your thoughts, you don't see the wave of ash until it is too late. It washes over you, plunging everything into darkness. You meet the ground suddenly, the impact rattling your teeth as your hooves stumble for purchase amidst the dirt and ash. The heat from your blade sears through the cloud, turning it to fiery embers.

Finish him.

Virgil lies ahead of you, dragging himself across the ground on his elbows.

'No!' he spits with rage, blood seeping from the corners of his mouth. 'You will not take me, demon. I will not be a slave to that cursed sword!' He reaches into the tattered shreds of his coat, fumbling for something.

You stride forward, aware of the roaring thunder at your back. Above you, molten fire arcs through the smoky skies, pounding mercilessly against the earth.

Yes, the world knows of my coming. It knows fear.

You shake your head, trying to rid it of the dark thoughts, but the sword has control. It pulls you forward, until you are standing over the witchfinder.

'My journey is complete!' The words bellow from your lips, yet they are not your own. 'Ragnarok is remade!'

The blade comes down. You hear a scream. Then your voice booms once again. 'One of us will change the future.'

'Indeed I will.'

The blast comes from the side, lancing into you with the force of a battering ram. You lose your grip on the sword as you are sent sprawling through the dust. Rolling back to your feet, you scan the roiling clouds, looking for your attacker. The voice had not been Virgil's, yet it was familiar ...

An arrow of purple light streaks out of the mist. It pierces your shoulder, punching straight through to the other side. Teeth gritted with pain you stagger forward, dimly aware of the flesh folding back, healing itself.

A black-cloaked stranger stands before you, a bright staff of gold resting across his shoulder. The wind tugs at his cowl, exposing his features for the briefest of moments. A bald head, gaunt face, weasel-like eyes. A scar curves along his cheek, turning his upper lip . . .

It is the librarian from Durnhollow. The man who drugged you and then questioned you. The man who brought you to the edge of ruin.

'YOU!' Fire crackles in the palms of your hands, fuelled by your memories of that dark place; of your imprisonment.

'Back off.' The librarian speaks in a commanding tone – one you have never heard him use before. 'I am Lorcan. And I am taking the sword.' Raising his hand, he points it at Ragnarok. The pale flesh of his arm reveals three branded serpents. They writhe and twist as if alive, glowing with an alien magic. 'Try and stop me, and I'll end your life in an instant.' From his fingertips the air bends and distorts, flowing outwards in a glittering current. It curls around the sword, enfolding it within an invisible prison.

'You . . . you used me . . . used Cernos . . . to get the sword.'

He looks at you with derision, his scar twisting his features. 'You wanted freedom, didn't you? Look at you, fool. You are an archdemon now.'

The sword drifts through the air to hover at his side. He then raises the golden staff, its end panels flipping open to form the petals of a flower. 'The future is yours, demon.'

There is a bright flash of golden light – then he is gone. And the sword with him.

The ground shakes violently, throwing you sideways. Only metres away the rock is torn asunder, ripping out a jagged fissure. From its depths, a bright sludge of lava spews forth in a glutinous mass.

You quickly find your feet, lurching from side to side as the world continues to shudder in its death throes. From behind you there is a thunderous crashing din, followed by a fierce wash of heat. You dare not look back, to see the scale of devastation. Instead, you simply press on. Virgil lies nearby, his crumpled body giving off a thin grey smoke.

A sudden tremor knocks you to the ground.

Forced to crawl, you scramble over the rocks to reach the witchfinder's side. 'Virgil?' The sword has left a gaping hole in his chest, the cauterised flesh gleaming with fragments of bone. He lies twisted, arms outstretched as if reaching for something. Your eyes trace the line of his body, to the golden sphere lying in the dust.

A beacon stone. Identical to the one that Virgil placed inside you, to summon himself and Avian to the volcano. He had another …

Your hand closes around the sphere, thumb resting on the switch. 'Freedom …' The word has a bitter ring to it now, tainted with lies – tainted by what you have become. An archdemon. Like the great Barahar who once waged war on the world. 'All I ever wanted was freedom ….'

Your eyes stray to the witchfinder. The man who had fought by your side. In the end, Ragnarok had taken his life. You wonder if he will ever find peace, or be forced to serve the sword's new master for all eternity …

There are many steps on the path of darkness. I pray you find deliverance before its end.

You crush the sphere in your fist – just as a violent earthquake rips open the ground. You spread your wings and take to the air, sweeping over the ravaged landscape. A thought, a desire, now spurs you on – driving you across the forested hills and sparkling turquoise ocean. A desire for revenge.

Congratulations! You have now reached the end of this adventure and have earned yourself the title *The Blood of Barahar*. You may now turn to the epilogue.

742

Clouds of blood obscure your vision as you pummel away at the beast, until you feel its grip around your limbs ease. Then you frantically kick with your last remaining strength, breaking above the surface in a fit of coughing and choking. The carcass of the dead alligator bobs up beside you – a twenty-foot long giant, its aged body scarred by hundreds of previous encounters.

With this fearsome hunter defeated, you may now help yourself to one of the following rewards:

Gator aid	**Brock's medallion**	**Creek guard**
(chest)	(necklace)	(left hand: shield)
+1 speed +2 armour	+1 brawn	+2 speed + 1 armour
Ability: second skin	Ability: fearless	Ability: retaliation
		(requirement: warrior)

You swim to the nearest bank, using the splayed roots of a tree to drag yourself up onto the sand. After taking a few minutes to attend to your wounds, you set off again – following the edge of the treeline. Turn to 703.

743

You study the complex arrangement of cogs. The system is operated by a handle, attached to a small cog on the left of the contraption. You give it a tentative push, watching as the chain of cogs starts to turn, groaning and creaking as the grime-covered teeth scrape against each other. Several cogs have come loose from the wall. Virgil places them back into the chain, looking less than certain over his choice of positioning. He stands back, scratching at his scarred cheek. 'Hope you understand this better than I do. Makes my head spin …'

To stop the lava reaching the forge, you must now solve the following puzzle:

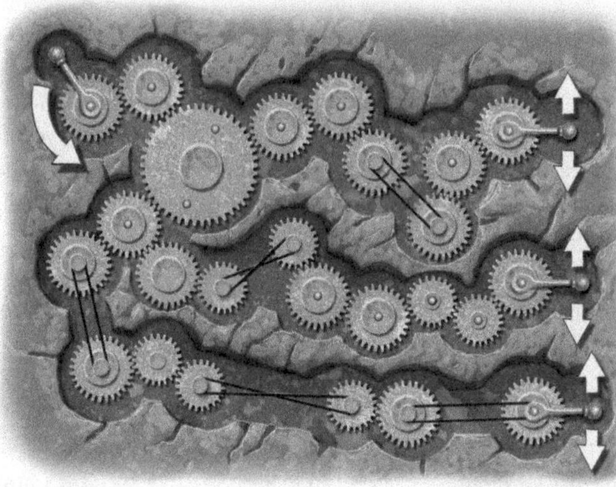

The handle turns the first cog anticlockwise (top left of diagram). Follow the three pathways of cogs to determine the direction the final switch/cog of each path will turn – clockwise (down arrow) or anti-clockwise (up arrow).

If a final switch moves down, you must count up the total number of clockwise cogs that are used in the chain, to make that switch turn. If the final switch moves up, you must count the total number of anti-clockwise cogs that are used in the chain, to make that switch turn. This will give you three numbers, one for each switch. Put them in order, from top switch to bottom switch, to arrive at a three figure number. This is your answer. Then turn to the paragraph number that matches your answer to see if you were correct. (For example, if you had 3 for the first switch, 6 for the second and 8 for the third, you would turn to 368.)

If you are unable to solve the puzzle, then you can have no choice but to leave the cogs and concentrate your efforts elsewhere. You may now examine the pipes, if you haven't already (turn to 692) or head up the stairs to the forge (turn to 601).

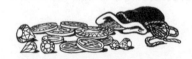

744

The hunter's camp looms out of the mist like a military fortress, with high walls of staked wood and lookout towers bristling with crossbows. As you approach there is a cry from one of the towers, then the gates swing open, admitting you inside.

A black-bearded man steps out from one of the huts, chewing on a fat cigar. He looks like an animal himself – with thick hair on his arms and chest, and a predator's guile to his steely grey eyes. He watches with interest as you set down your tigris trophy. Several of the other hunters have already hurried over, chatting excitedly and patting Jerem on the back. Your companion seems happy to take the praise, recounting a colourful version of the night's events that have little in common with what really happened.

'Welcome to the jungle,' grins the bearded man, walking over. He offers out his hand, which you take – wincing as his grip tightens like the coils of a snake. 'Survival of the fittest, my friend. And you chose the right side. Guess you'll be wanting a cut.' He releases your hand, much to your relief, and unfastens a purse of money from his belt. 'I think this is fair reward.' (You have gained 150 gold crowns.)

'I'm Buckmaster Bill,' he says. 'And this here be my camp. Make yourself at home – we got supplies if you need them, for a price of course.' He spits into the mud before stuffing his cigar back into his mouth. 'Come back here anytime – treat it like a home away from home.'

'What about him?' you ask, nodding towards a ten-foot giant who is currently performing a workout by lifting a wooden cart in each hand. A woman next to him is keeping count – 'two hundred and eleven … two hundred and twelve.'

'Ah, that's our Nelson,' grins Bill proudly. 'Not the sharpest tool, but the only one I'd choose to watch my back in this den of snakes. A good fighter, that one – I'd be willing to hire him out if you need his muscle. You look like someone that might have,' he raises an eyebrow knowingly, 'unfinished business to attend to.' (Make a note of this entry number. You may return here at any time during act 2 to make use of the hunters' services.)

Will you:

Visit the supplies tent?	824
Ask about hiring Nelson?	413
Ask what he knows of the jungle?	373
Ask about further work?	758
Leave the camp?	**Return to the map**

745

Amongst the remains of the drake, you find one of the following special rewards:

Drake's chestguard	**Drake's defender**	**Drake's scales**
(chest)	(left hand: shield)	(gloves)
+4 brawn +3 armour	+2 speed +4 armour	+1 speed +4 brawn
Ability: barbs	Ability: piercing	Ability: rake

Lorcan approaches the banks of the pool and raises the palm of his hand. Suddenly the waters of the pool start to churn and spin, as if caught in the pull of a whirlpool. Then black blood sprays up into the air as an object flies out of the water, straight into Lorcan's fist. He turns, offering out the prize. 'It's your lucky day,' he grins.

You lean away in revulsion when you realise he is holding the beast's heart, its purple flesh blackened and scorched.

'The demon's kha can make you stronger,' he insists. 'You have the gift – I can see you do. Use it to take on the drake's powers.'

If you wish, you may take the following item:

Drake spirit
(talisman)
+1 speed
Ability: drake career

By equipping this item, you automatically learn the drake career. (NOTE: As soon as the *drake spirit* is unequipped or you learn a new career, you lose the abilities associated with the drake career.)

A drake warrior has the following special abilities:

Fiery temper (pa): Keep a record of all ⚅ results that your opponent rolls for damage. For every two ⚅ results your *brawn* is increased by 2. At the end of the combat, your *brawn* returns to normal.
Searing mantle (pa): Your armour is coated in fire. This causes 1 damage to all opponents at the end of every combat round for every 4 *armour* you are wearing.

When you have made your decision, turn to 551 if you still need to choose rewards, or 844 to continue.

746

By drinking the elder sap, you may also remove your hex. This will give you access to all of your abilities once again. However, if you are carrying the *glaive of souls* this weapon will automatically shatter and you will no longer be able to use it. Turn to 804.

747

The tunnel rises steeply, its rough-hewn walls crusted with mould. Eventually, after nearly an hour of following the twisting path, you see a band of light ahead. Quickening your step you hurry out of the tunnel, to find yourself at the edge of a rocky bluff. In the distance, protruding above the jungle canopy, are the crumbling ziggurats of a Lamuri city – and beyond that an immense black volcano, its dark form brooding and ominous against the white haze. It reminds you of the black peak from your vision at Durnhollow – the mountain that rained fire.

Congratulations, you have successfully navigated the dark interior. If you have the word *explorer* on your hero sheet turn to 817. Otherwise, you may now return to the quest map to continue your adventure.

748

With the deadly succubus defeated, you may now help yourself to one of the following rewards:

Dreamcatcher	Desolation robes	Shroud of nightmares
(necklace)	(chest)	(cloak)
+1 speed	+2 speed +2 magic	+1 speed +2 brawn
Ability: immobilise	Ability: siphon	Ability: confound

When you have made your decision, turn to 636.

749

Looking back towards the tower, you are relieved to see that there is no sign of the guardians. You can only assume that they returned to their original positions within the rock.

'Seems the plan worked,' you smile.

Avian pulls himself up onto the bridge, his face ashen and beaded with sweat. When Virgil helps him to his feet, you see that the mage has removed much of his armour, leaving only leg-plates and a silver-threaded tunic and breeches.

After brushing himself down, the mage slides his staff from its harness and reignites its headpiece with a crackle of magic. Then his gaze turns to Cernos, who is limping across the final stretch of the bridge. 'Time to finish the race,' he states grimly. Turn to 762.

750

You can sense the powerful enchantments trapped within the idol – ancient magics to command both rock and earth. Perhaps this is what the dwarves used to build their breath-taking city, moulding intricate structures out of the bare volcanic rock. Such power could become a devastating weapon in the right hands . . .

If you wish, you may now take the following item:

Rock idol
(talisman)
+1 armour
Ability: geomancer career

While this item is equipped, the geomancer has the following special abilities:

Stone rain (co): Instead of rolling for damage after winning a round, you can cast *stone rain*. This will automatically inflict 1 damage die to a single opponent, ignoring *armour*. In each consecutive round, *stone rain* will double its damage on the same opponent. (In the second round, you would roll 2 damage dice, the third round 4 damage dice.) If you use another ability (of any type) or lose a round, *stone rain* ends. This ability will last up to three rounds (4 damage dice). It can only be cast once per combat.
Tremor strike (sp): Make the ground beneath your enemies' feet tremble. This lowers opponents' *speed* by 2 for two combat rounds.

Once you have made your decision, you leave the storeroom and continue your journey. Turn to 842.

751

As you contemplate changing course, to make for the river, your eyes catch on a symbol scored deep into the trunk of a tree. You move closer to inspect it, recognising it as one of the sacred symbols used to represent the One God. Assuming it is a marker of some kind, you press on into the trees, soon spotting another symbol carved onto a mossy boulder. You realise this could be a pilgrim trail – marking the route to a shrine. Either that, or a trap to bait you.

Will you:

Follow the symbols?	760
Head towards the river instead?	500

752

The ghostly dwarf sweeps down the stairs and into the hall, his whole body trembling with excitement. *'Oh yes. They're all here. The last of the books!'* He hovers over to the nearest shelf, pulling out a hardback covered in glowing black scales. *'Ah here – oh, would you look at this! Who would put the Lone Lister black series with the original Preposterous Perils? He hadn't even discovered red crystallite yet.'*

The ghost takes his books and leaves the hall, returning a few minutes later with a beaming smile. He floats over to you and takes a bow. *'Minion one-one-three-eight, at your service.'*

You look between the ghost and Virgil in confused shock. 'What's this? He wants me to suggest my favourite reads?'

The witchfinder grins. 'He has completed the last task he was given. Now he assumes you will give him his next.' He shrugs his shoulders. 'Might be useful to have your own personal porter.'

By completing the ghost's quest, you have gained the following:

Magic porter: You may use the magic porter to access your storage locker on Emerald Isle (if you purchased one during Act 2). As before, if you swap equipment (weapons, backpack items etc.), you may put the item you are replacing in your locker (space permitting). This will prevent the item from being destroyed. You can re-equip items from your locker between quests.

When you have updated your character sheet, turn to 847.

753

'How about starting now?' you grin, eyeing the craftsmanship of the thief's blades. 'That was your work, back in the courtyard, wasn't it? A dozen undead, against . . . just you.'

Quito nods hesitantly. 'You want to learn?'

You spin the daggers, testing their weight. 'Providing it doesn't end with a knife in the back.'

Quito proceeds to teach you some of his profession's tricks. If you wish, you may now learn the thief career. The thief has the following special abilities:

Backstab (co): (requires a dagger in the main or left hand) If you or an ally play an *immobilise, knockdown, stun* or *webbed* ability in combat, you may automatically *backstab* the affected opponent, inflicting 2 damage dice, ignoring *armour*. If you have won the round, you can still roll for a damage score as normal.
Cutpurse (pa): Each time you successfully complete a combat, roll a die to discover what item you find:
⚀ or ⚁ A purse containing 20 gold crowns.
⚂ or ⚃ An elixir of invisibility (1 use – backpack item. Grants the ability: *vanish*).
⚄ or ⚅ A flask of healing (1 use – backpack item. Use any time in combat to restore 6 *health*).

When you have made your decision, turn to 701.

754

Three monkeys step out from an alcove further up the stairs. They are tall and grey-haired, with a stoop to their scrawny shoulders. Their pale faces seem almost human, with grey whiskers trailing around their mouths and deep set eyes glinting beneath a low brow. As you advance they raise their blackened fingers and begin hooting in a strange language. Suddenly blue lightning crackles across their hands, spreading up their arms and coating their furred bodies in a mesh of light. Magic, you realise in surprise. One of the trio swings its glowing fists, sending bolts of lightning streaking through the air. You duck beneath the attack, feeling scorching heat rake across your back. Then you surge forward, taking the stairs two at a time as you look to close the distance with these three deadly mages. It is time to fight:

	Speed	*Magic*	*Armour*	*Health*
Macaques	10	6	4	40

Special abilities

- Shock lightning: Each time your damage score / damage dice cause health damage to the macaques, you immediately take 1 damage in return for each point of *armour* you are wearing.

(NOTE: You cannot heal after this combat. You must continue this challenge with the *health* that you have remaining. You may use potions and abilities to heal lost *health* while you are in combat.)

If you manage to defeat these mystical monkeys, turn to 517. Otherwise, you have failed to assault the temple. Restore your *health* and turn to 449.

755

You can use the forge to craft your own magical items. For each item you wish to craft, you will need two reagents (listed below). If you have these reagents, you can make the associated item – however, each reagent can only be used once. When a reagent is used, it must be removed from your hero sheet. To craft an item, simply turn to the relevant entry number next to its description:

Reagent 1	Reagent 2	Item type (entry)
Onyx blade	*Phoenix feather*	*sword* (796)
Onyx blade	*Golem core*	*dagger* (536)
Runed rod	*Energised crystal*	*staff* (649)
Runed rod	*Phoenix feather*	*wand* (474)
Energised crystal	*Phoenix feather*	*talisman* (674)

You may return to the rune forge anytime between quests, to craft new items (make a note of this entry number on your hero sheet). You can craft as many items as you wish, providing you have the correct reagents.

Virgil folds his arms, shaking his head. 'I'll have no part of this. Rune crafting is dangerous, evil.' He averts his gaze, staring out across the shimmering lake of fire. 'But if it stops Cernos ... sometimes the means justifies the end.'

With this quest now complete, you can return to the map to continue your adventure.

756

Banks of mist roll across paved stones and grinning statues. You have discovered a set of ruins and you suspect they might be Lamuri. As you step warily past the outer buildings, you feel a tingling sensation along your spine. You stop, sensing that you are not alone …

A clatter of stones.

You spin around, but catch nothing save a subtle ripple in the curtain of mist, disturbed by someone's passing. Then you hear another clink of stone followed by a sharp, hooting cry. Answering calls suddenly rise up all around you, fast becoming a din of wailing screams and chattering noise. You frantically reach for your weapons, wondering what manner of creature lurks in these ruins. Turn to 769.

757

Hidden beneath a blanket is a loose stone slab. Lifting it up, you reveal a secret hollow filled with items. If you wish, you may take any/all of the following:

Iron recluse	**Rune stone**	**Lone wolf**
(ring)	(backpack)	(main hand: dagger)
+2 magic	A tablet of stone carved	+1 speed +2 brawn
Ability: corrode	with dwarven runes	Ability: bleed
		(requirement: rogue)

If you want to return the favour and leave some of your own backpack items in the hollow, simply make a note of the items you wish to leave. You will no longer have access to these (remove the items from your backpack), but keep a record of what you choose to leave behind.

After replacing the stone, you leave the shelter and continue your journey. Turn to 689.

758

'You want work?' The hunter slaps you on the shoulder, then points past the walls of the compound. 'Then my advice is, get out there – the jungle's full of it. Bring me some trophies and then we'll talk, eh?' He glances down at your weapons and armour, nodding with admiration. 'I daresay you could take on some of the bigger game. I'm probably too old and long in the tooth to tackle those now, but there's something about you ...' His eyes narrow, as he glimpses the dark scales glistening at your neck. You quickly tug up your collar, looking away innocently. 'Well, whatever you are,' he continues guardedly, 'ain't no concern of mine. I'll trade your trophies for gold and treasure, good as any man.'

If you have all three trophies – *Gheira's paw*, *Anansi's eye* and *Kaala's fang* – turn to 439. If you have the *quetzal egg*, turn to 628. Otherwise, you may continue exploring the camp (turn to 744) or leave and return to the quest map.

759

You place the jaguar tablet into the hole. There is a sharp click as it slots into place – and for a second you believe you have made the correct choice. However, when the stepped pyramid starts to collapse back into the stone pedestal, leaving just a flat surface behind, you realise it was the wrong decision. Despite several attempts to prise open the pedestal it remains tightly closed, guarding its secrets.

If you haven't already, you can search the main chamber (turn to 508) or leave and continue your journey (turn to 563).

760

By following the markers you find yourself entering a sunlit clearing, carpeted with wildflowers. Clouds of butterflies swirl amongst the foliage, their gossamer wings catching the light streaming through the clouds. For the first time on this journey, you feel at ease – there is no sense of danger here.

At the far side of the clearing is a wedge-shaped promontory. It rises steeply, almost like a staircase, to end on a crumbling platform of stone. Another symbol is carved next to the slope – enticing you to its summit, where a white marble pedestal sparkles in the sunlight.

As you step onto the rock you feel a shock course through your body, followed by a smarting pain in your chest. You take another step – and stagger, suddenly feeling nauseous. Gritting your teeth, you slog further up the slope, each footfall bringing fresh waves of agony to your body. Eventually, you can take it no more. You drop to your knees, aware of the sulphurous smoke drifting up out of your clothes.

Then you see a vision – a woman's face, framed with soft curls of white hair. Despite her homely appearance, there is a stern anger to her cold blue eyes. 'Go back, demon!' she hisses. 'This is a holy place.'

'No!' you spit angrily, clawing forwards on your hands and knees. 'I am not a demon!'

The vision wavers and then recedes, leaving you a clear view of the pedestal. You drag yourself towards it, crying out as some invisible force beats at your body, lancing hot fire from your scars. At last, whimpering, you grab hold of the pedestal, noticing a plaque affixed to its side. The inscription reads: 'Walk in the light. And faith will heal you.'

Using the pedestal for support you pull yourself up off the ground, slumping forward over its round top-stone. A circle of inscriptions swim into view, surrounding a shallow hollow filled with rocks and pebbles.

'I am not a demon.' You scowl angrily, beating your fists against the holy inscriptions. 'I walk in the light of the One God!'

Suddenly clear water starts to gurgle out from between the rocks in the hollow, bubbling up to fill the basin. The inscribed runes flash and then begin to glow with a soft white light.

Will you:

Drink the holy waters? 368
Leave the shrine and continue your journey? 500

761

Amongst the remains of the drake, you find one of the following special rewards:

Twilight tinder	Drakeskin epaulets	Drakefire raiment
(ring)	(cloak)	(robes)
+2 magic	+2 speed +4 magic	+2 speed +3 magic
Ability: overload	Ability: backdraft	Ability: fire aura

When you have made your decision, turn to 551 if you still need to choose rewards, or 844 to continue.

762

The bridge ends in a rectangular doorway, cut into the face of one of the dwarven structures. Its black-iron doors have been torn from their bases and beaten into the rubble, leaving the portal wide open. Beyond it, a curved passageway sweeps away into the dark city.

Cernos has almost reached the doorway when he draws to a halt, having heard your footfalls ringing against the stone. He swings around with an angry snarl, the glowing orb of fire held out before him. Its brilliance is almost blinding, masking the demon behind a shimmering barrier.

'Don't you ever give up?' he rasps, breathing hard. 'I tire of this.'

The first blast from Avian's staff blows the demon off his feet. The second drives him back to the ground as he struggles to rise. 'The dwarves gave you mercy,' spits Avian, striding forward with a purposeful air. 'They imprisoned you, Cernos – that was your punishment. To consider your crimes. To learn from your mistakes. To repent!'

The demon raises his horned head. 'Two thousand years . . . that is a long time, mage.' A nasty grin creeps across his blackened features. 'Time enough to plot my revenge.'

'Revenge against whom?' snaps the mage. 'You are no Barahar. Tell me – who has wronged you so unjustly? What evil would drive you to seek a demon sword as your ally?'

Cernos lifts his arm – and the white orb answers for him. It blazes forth, intense as the sun's rays, pummelling through the stone. The sound is terrifying, like the earth itself quaking in its death throes. Your stomach gives a sickening lurch as everything drops away to nothingness ...

You are falling through stone and dust, the maelstrom stinging and nicking at your skin. Below you, the magma lake spins out of the haze. You are hurtling towards it – already huge chunks of rock are pounding into its molten surface, throwing up ember showers. The heat is tangible. It batters against your body as surely as any rock, stealing your breath and baking your flesh raw.

Smoke is everywhere.

For a second, your vision clouds. The copper-red of the lake smears to a solid grey. You are back in the stone cell at Durnhollow. Its stench fills your nostrils – the reek of filth and sweat, and the rusted iron digging into your flesh. The bald-headed librarian scratches his quill across the parchment, grinning like an eager child. For days, weeks, months, he has diligently recorded everything that has come from your lips; each word taken down as if it was of the greatest import. Prophecies, he calls them. You wonder if this fate – this terrible end – was one of those you spoke of, preserved for all eternity in neat lines of spidery writing...

A sudden jolt brings you back to consciousness. You are surprised to find yourself hanging in mid-air, the momentum taken out of your fall. You expect to see a rope or cord. But there is nothing ...

Then you are swung sideways by the same invisible force. Before you can fathom what has happened you are falling once again, towards an island of black rock rising up out of the mist. Powerless to stop yourself, you slam down at speed, the impact drawing a pained cry from your scorched lungs. Next to you, there is a similar grunt as a body thuds down onto the rock, rolling and tumbling in a blur of flapping coat tails. Virgil.

The witchfinder comes to a halt, lying on his back, only inches from the glowing magma. Its cracked surface belches a hissing torrent of steam, forcing him to instinctively shirk away. The movement elicits another groan of pain. He puts a hand to his grey scalp, finding a deep gash above his one good eye. 'Close shave ...' He winces groggily.

'Close for both of us.' You clamber to your feet, your eyes fixed on the billowing thunder cloud above your head. There is no immediate sign of Avian or the demon, save for the flashes of magic and angry explosions visible through the writhing smoke.

Virgil staggers as he stands, his gaunt face as white as the dust on his clothing. 'We have to get back,' he gasps, squinting through the smoke.

Your gaze wanders along the bridge, its black span looming two hundred metres or more above you. The nearest supports, which might be climbed, are an equal distance away, surrounded by the ever-shifting sea of magma. 'I don't see how—'

Another burst of light draws your attention skywards. A man's cry echoes around the cavern, followed by a deafening rumble as more of the bridge is wrested free from its foundations. A fresh shower of rock falls towards the lake.

Virgil clenches his fists. 'Avian's still up there. We've got to do something!'

Your eyes continue to scan the bridge. 'It's impossible . . .'

Forget me! Find the sword! Find Ragnarok!

The words are nothing more than a whisper in your ear, but they carry with a firm and commanding tone.

Virgil's startled reaction suggests that he has heard it also. 'Avian . . .?'

Find the sword! Go!

Virgil's eyes suddenly widen. He crosses to the other side of the bobbing island. 'A good omen.' You follow his gaze to the thinning dust cloud, and the dark object buffeted back and forth on its whirling currents. A grey, broad-brimmed hat. Virgil is smiling to himself as he watches it drift towards the magma lake – flipping and bouncing onto an island of rock, only a few feet from your own. The witchfinder hops the gap and snatches up his hat. He pushes out the dents as he inspects it for damage. Apart from some singed edges, it looks relatively intact. He places it back on his head.

'We've been shown the way. Look.'

You join Virgil on the floating island, discovering that it forms part of a chain leading across to the other side of the molten lake. There, through the haze, you can dimly make out an opening at the foot of one of the dwarven walls.

Virgil runs a check of his weapons, then glances your way. His expression hardens with a frown. 'By the divines, your wounds …' You stare at him confused, then look down at your body. Where there had been flesh, reddened by the heat, there are now scales. They have spread to cover your entire body – you can even feel them beneath your leggings, prickling along your thighs and calves. You touch your face, feeling cold, hard demon-skin beneath your fingers.

Gingerly, you meet the witchfinder's gaze, aware of the blood trickling down his face and congealing with the dirt and dust. Your own wounds, your own aches and pains, have gone.

You have now gained the following bonus:

Demon blood (pa): You may permanently increase your *health* by 10. (Hexed heroes may now use up to ten abilities in combat.)

'There are many steps on the path of darkness,' warns the witchfinder. 'I pray you find deliverance before its end.' His hand reaches inside his coat, settling around the grip of a pistol. 'Or else …' He waits for you to acknowledge his warning.

'I understand.' You bow your head, wincing when you hear the leathery creak of scales. 'We have to stop Cernos. With the demon's heart, I'll become human again – as I was promised.' You raise an eyebrow, the statement becoming a challenge.

Virgil shifts his gaze, his jewelled eyepatch mirroring your crimson stare. 'Modoc is a powerful healer. He will do all he can for you – if we survive this.' He nods towards the volcano's edge. 'See that?'

You look past his shoulder, to where a line of sharp boulders bank a larger island of rock. Channels of lava converge at its centre, illuminating an anvil of purest obsidian.

'A rune forge,' states the witchfinder. 'The dwarves were master runesmiths in their day, skilled in the art of spirit-forged metals. Ordinarily, I would condemn such heathen practices, but in our present predicament, we would do well to make use of any advantage.' He tugs down the brim of his hat, then flips two pistols into his hands. 'Come. Talk gains us nothing. Time to pay Tartarus a visit.'

You have now gained the following ability:

Blessed bullets (co): While Virgil is your companion, you may use this ability instead of rolling for a damage score. It automatically inflicts 3 damage dice to a single opponent, ignoring *armour*. It also reduces their *speed* by 1 for the next combat round. You can only use *blessed bullets* once per combat. If you are *hexed*, this ability does not count towards your quota.

When you have updated your hero sheet, return to the quest map to continue your journey.

763

The body of a hunter lies nearby, a large ring of keys attached to his belt. You quickly grab them, then approach the cages. Warily, you study your options. Wooden signs have been staked into the ground next to each cage. The first reads: *rhinosaur – male*, referring to the horned, bull-like creature. By the second cage, where the winged reptile is snapping and clawing at the bars, the sign reads: *drecko – female*.

Will you:	
Free the rhinosaur?	739
Free the drecko?	819
Attack the giant instead?	772

764

As you continue, a thick mist starts to roll in from the surrounding forest, settling like a shroud over the crumbling ruins. You draw your weapons, gripped by a growing sense of unease – one that has you convinced you are no longer alone …

A clatter of stones.

You spin around, but catch nothing save a subtle ripple in the curtain of mist, disturbed by someone's passing. Then you hear another clink of stone followed by a sharp, hooting cry. Answering calls suddenly rise up all around you, fast becoming a din of wailing screams and chattering noise. Turn to 769.

765

Kicking the doll from the witch's grasp you deliver a backhanded strike, knocking her to the ground. For a moment, mercy stays your hand, but as the witch starts to summon black flames to her gnarly fingers you bring your weapons down in a brutal arc – silencing her spell.

With the witch defeated, you may now help yourself to one of the following rewards:

Voodoo doll	Bone shaker	Bone bracelets
(main hand: doll)	(left hand: wand)	(gloves)
+2 speed +2 magic	+2 speed +1 magic	+1 speed +1 brawn
Ability: curse	Ability: fear	Ability: trickster
(requirement: mage)	(requirement: mage)	

Searching the rest of the caves, you find little of value save for some gold coins scattered amongst the dirt. (You have gained 30 gold crowns.) At the back of one of the smaller chambers is a tunnel that winds away into the earth. If you wish to follow this, turn to 747. If you would prefer to leave the cave and climb the canyon wall, turn to 776.

766

Avian leads the way across the bridge, his glowing staff held aloft like a beacon. Halfway across, you spot the hunched shape of Cernos limping towards the other side, the iron casket still clutched tightly to his chest. He looks back over his shoulder, baring his teeth.

'Cernos!' Avian's voice booms like thunder, amplified by his own magic. 'Barahar is dead – and Ragnarok is broken. Do you desire a similar fate, demon? You will find nothing here, but your own end.'

Cernos shifts around on his hooved feet, his appearance now a mockery of his previous grandeur. The once broad shoulders are now stooped, the broken wings hanging limp like tattered curtains. Black ichor weeps from a hundred angry wounds where the scales have been ripped away, exposing stubs of bone and withered flesh.

And yet, despite his ravaged countenance, beneath the grime-stained horns that puncture his brow, a single eye still burns bright from its dark hollow. 'I have the heart of fire, fool!'

Avian takes a sharp intake of breath as the demon lifts up the iron casket and pulls back the lid. A blinding white light explodes from the cavity, its heat rippling outwards in shimmering bands. You see the stone around the demon's feet crack and buckle. Avian draws back, covering his face – Virgil gives a cry, averting his gaze.

You can feel the searing heat, but you are able to hold your ground, narrowing your eyes against the bright assault.

'What are you doing?' cries Avian, peering between his raised gauntlets. 'That thing will kill you!'

Cernos grips the ball of light in his fist, tossing away the casket. 'I have suffered much as its bearer. But now, my journey nears its end...'

A scream pierces the air. It is followed by a chorus of wails, distant at first but rapidly gaining volume. All eyes turn to the walls of the city, where a flock of ragged shapes are sweeping down through the steamy haze. As you watch transfixed, hundreds more break away from their makeshift perches, taking to the air on bat-like wings.

Then a series of slobbering growls add to the crescendo. You spin around to see a pack of devilish hounds clambering up the struts of the bridge, their black bodies cracked with veins of molten magma.

With a triumphant snarl, Cernos breaks into a loping run, heading for the far side of the bridge. The black swarm parts around him, shrieking and squawking, then proceeds to rush toward you in a chaotic tumble of wings and claws. You glimpse human faces perched on the straggly, hairy shoulders.

'What are they?' you hiss, your hands bunched around your weapons.

'Furies!' Avian takes his staff in both hands and pulls the ends apart, revealing two bright blades. They dance with magical fire as he strides towards the fast-approaching tide. 'They're the souls of the damned, released when Ragnarok...' The rest of his words are drowned by the cacophony of shrieks.

Behind you, Virgil is facing off against the pack of hounds. Against their flaming bright bodies he is a rapier of shadow, two pistols cutting smooth silhouettes from his gloved hands. 'Evil will be purged,' he bellows. 'By the fire of justice!'

Will you:

Help Virgil to defeat the molten hounds?	564
Help Avian to defeat the furies?	538

767

You place the snake tablet into the hole. There is a sharp click as it slots into place – and for a second you believe you have made the correct choice. However, when the stepped pyramid starts to collapse back into the stone pedestal, leaving just a flat surface behind, you realise it was the wrong decision. Despite several attempts to prise open the pedestal it remains tightly closed, guarding its secrets.

If you haven't already, you can search the main chamber (turn to 508) or leave and continue your journey (turn to 563).

768

You successfully reach the ledge. After taking a moment to recover from your ordeal, you proceed to follow the path to the top of the rock face. As you near its summit, the path widens into a set of worn stairs, leading to an open doorway in the side of the building. Warily, you follow Virgil inside. Turn to 875.

769

From out of the haze a set of stone stairs swim into view, leading up the face of an immense ziggurat of black rock. Small figures are clambering over them, hooting and jabbering to each other. Monkeys. Hundreds of them. The majority are small, almost like squirrels, with large round eyes and red whiskers. Others are larger, with white bodies and coal-black faces.

You halt at the foot of this peculiar temple, looking around at the excited mob of monkeys. They settle on the stairs, their heads turning in unison to face you. Then a heavy silence descends – almost as unsettling as the earlier din – as the monkeys glare at you, their bright eyes keen with intelligence. Suddenly one of the black-faced monkeys bares its teeth, hissing. Another beats its fists against the ground, hopping and leaping in an agitated dance. A second later and its anxiety has spread to the rest of the group, who quickly resort to screeching and hollering, deafening you once again with their angry, savage noise. From somewhere above a stone comes whipping through the air, catching you on the cheek and drawing blood.

A final warning, perhaps.

The monkey temple presents a dangerous challenge – and one that is likely to be far beyond your powers to defeat. If you do not wish to battle this foe yet, make a note of this entry number and return here at any time during Act 2 when you feel up to the challenge. If you wish to take on the monkey temple, turn to **596**. Otherwise, you carefully retrace your steps and find a safer path through the ruins. Turn to **667**.

770

Amongst the remains of the drake, you find one of the following special rewards:

Black talon hood	**Death blades**	**Spark stone**
(head)	(feet)	(ring)
+2 speed +3 brawn	+2 speed +3 brawn	+2 brawn +1 armour
Ability: vanish	Ability: fatal blow	Ability: lightning

When you have made your decision, turn to **551** if you still need to choose rewards, or **844** to continue.

771

The demon has suffered since your last meeting. Half of his body is a black crust of scabs and lesions, as if it has been exposed to a monstrous heat. One eye is closed permanently, where the melted flesh has seeped down his face, twisting his features into something even more malign and hellish.

Resting on his lap is a black iron chest. You recognise it as the one from Duerdoun, which once contained the heart of fire – the white orb, encased in the runed hammer. Cernos clutches it protectively with one hand, whilst the other plays with a black stone, glimmering with runes.

There is a heavy silence as you regard each other – both changed by your experiences since the forest of thorns.

'Why?' hisses the demon at last, fixing you with his one good eye. 'Why come here? You live – is that not enough?'

You tug open your clothing, exposing the black scales covering your flesh. Since you entered the jungle, they have continued to spread. Now they cover your entire torso and arms, forming bony ridges along your spine. 'Look at me!' you scream in anger, beating your chest. 'You did this!'

Cernos seems unmoved by your plight. 'Tell me. How does it feel?'

For a moment, his question disarms you. Then the bitter fury returns. 'I am turning into a monster! Look at me!'

Cernos rises to his feet, his immense wings flexing behind his broad shoulders. 'I was once like you – exactly like you. Although …' He pauses, glancing down at the iron casket, now cradled at his side. 'I suppose I had a choice.'

'What choice?' you growl, fists clenching at your side. 'Why are you here, demon? Why come to this accursed place?'

'You and I are linked now,' replies the demon, a cruel smile twisting his features. 'So, let me show you.'

Before you can answer you feel yourself being thrown backwards, your head exploding with pain. You crash down onto your back, gurgling and crying in agony, hands scraping over broken stone. Then you hear voices – raised in anger. In the distance, you can hear screams. A horrible discordant wailing.

Blinking through the pain you open your eyes, trying to focus – colours and shapes coalescing around you. An elderly man in stately robes is shouting at a girl, not much older than sixteen. She is beautiful, with braided locks of dark hair. She is trying to get away, frightened by the man's crazed fury.

'Let me go!' she begs, pulling to break free.

The man – who must be the king – backhands her across the face, flinging her to the ground. 'I will not leave! None of us will leave! The dwarves will come! They will save us!'

'Listen to them, Father! People are dying! Everyone's dying!'

The king raises his fist.

'Nephele!'

A young man strides into the throne room, his tanned body clad in blood-soaked armour. He removes his helmet, tossing it away, revealing blond hair and a handsome face.

'You!' snarls the king, stabbing a finger at the young warrior. 'Get out of my sight! You would dare touch my daughter – dare to think she would choose you over Ixion? You! A commoner!'

'No, Father, please!' begs the girl, sobbing. 'Cernos is a good man. He was your spear – your trusted general.'

'He is exiled!' snarls the king, his eyes wide with madness. He points back down the hall, towards the sound of screaming and bloodshed. 'Leave the city – or prove your loyalty and defend your king!'

The young man hurries to the girl's side, kneeling and putting his arms protectively about her. 'Nephele. Come with me. We have to go! The demon spares no one – the city is in ruins!'

A dark shadow passes over the room, throwing everything into darkness. Hooved feet crunch through stone, ragged breaths thundering like the bellows of a forge. A demon stomps into view – huge, a towering giant of darkness – rippling with fire, its skin scoured with spiteful runes. In one hand it carries a sword as long as the demon is tall; an immense black blade, its own runes glowing with a sorcerous evil. And there, gripped tight within the sword's hilt, is the heart of fire – the glowing stone, giving off heat like the surface of the sun.

'Barahar!' The name is whispered by the king as he falls back against his throne, face aghast.

Dark spirits roil around the blade, shrieking and hollering. Behind the demon you see a whole host of the ghostly creatures crawling in its wake, filling the corridor with an endless procession of death.

'More souls for the sword!' booms the demon, his voice like that of a God, rattling every wall, every stone, every bone. 'Ragnarok still thirsts.' Turn to 782.

772

Relying on your fast reactions you throw yourself into a charge, ducking and weaving past the giant's clumsy swings. As you close with the hunter, his club comes smashing down, throwing up a thick cloud of dust. The giant pulls back his arms ready for another swing … then gives a grunt of surprise when he sees that you have vanished.

'Thanks for the lift!'

He looks up, to see you balanced precariously on the end of his club. Before he can react, you leap off your makeshift platform, weapons cutting down through the air. It is time to fight:

	Speed	*Brawn*	*Armour*	*Health*
Nelson	9	9	8	80

Special abilities

- Knockdown: If your hero takes health damage from Nelson, you must reduce your *speed* by 1 during the next combat round.

(NOTE: You cannot heal after this combat. You must continue this quest with the *health* that you have remaining. You may use potions and abilities to heal lost *health* while you are in combat.)

If you manage to defeat this burly hunter, turn to 447. Otherwise, turn to 664.

773

After ten days aboard the *Angel's Bounty* you are grateful to finally sight land. This has been your first experience of sea travel and – you hope – the last. After falling sick on the first day from the constant lurching of the high seas, you have spent most of the journey below decks, lapsing in and out of feverish dreams filled with nightmarish demons.

The air is thick and moist, almost suffocating, as you stagger onto the deck to join the captain. Below you, the glittering turquoise waters break in curls of white foam against the sculptured prow, where a grinning cherub points eagerly towards a green smudge of land. The Emerald Isle. You had been imagining an island, as the name suggested, but you discover it is actually a narrow finger of forest, linked by a hump of sandbanks to the mainland.

The helmsman turns the wheel, guiding the ship around a natural rock wall and into the harbour. Ahead, you see other ships bobbing at anchor – most are ragtag vessels, looking barely sea-worthy, while a few are more imposing, bristling with cannons and mounted crossbows. Military or mercenaries, you cannot tell.

'All hands! All hands!' barks the captain, a weather-beaten ex-soldier forever patting his rotund belly. His crew scurry across the deck, while others clamber the rigging, seizing cables and hauling the sails to the masts.

As you glide into the harbour you see a portly man in a red bandanna scuttling along the pier, shouting similar orders to his scruffy-looking team. Within moments mooring cables are hissing through the air and boat hooks are being raised, to guide and secure the ship in dock.

'Here yer go!' The captain slaps you on the back, a little more forcibly than you would have liked. You squint through the heat haze at the ramshackle buildings that form a line along the shore. They look like they were erected overnight, after a few too many drinks – and are now competing with each other to see which will stay standing the longest. 'Ah, would yer look at her,' sighs the captain wistfully. 'She's paradise – the place dreams are made of. '

You look back at the shabby hovels, competing for space against the encroaching jungle. 'Yeah, paradise,' you nod with a little less conviction.

The gangplank is lowered. After retrieving your paltry belongings you step down onto the wharf, grateful to be finally standing on a surface that isn't rearing and bucking like a wild steed. Of the other passengers on board, you note only one disembarking with you – Quito, a short man with black, straight hair and shifty eyes. He has thankfully kept to himself for most of the journey, cleaning and sharpening his endless supply of daggers.

Quito shoulders his pack, offering you one of his rare and awkward-looking grins. 'Welcome to the jungle, my friend. Just make sure it doesn't eat you.'

Laughing, he starts away down the wooden pier, towards the sorry-looking muddle of buildings. As your eyes stray across the harbour, to the forested mainland, you start to wonder exactly what you have let yourself in for. Turn to **571**.

774

Red light courses through hidden channels in the door, forming an intricate pattern of whirls and symbols. An instant later and the two panels grind inwards, opening out onto a vast circular chamber – and a cacophony of screams.

You hurry inside, squelching through a spongy carpet of red slime. It appears to cover every surface of the chamber, dripping from the ceiling in thick bands of crimson rain. Through the spattering curtain you see a circle of runes, burnt into the ground – and a stone obelisk, facing inwards towards the circle. Avian is pressed against it, his arms and legs spread to each corner. There are no visible restraints, but clearly some magic has him pinned in place. He squirms and writhes to free himself, his screams intensifying.

A white light is spreading through grooves in the obelisk, emanating from the tortured mage. They flow like liquid along the channels, branching out to meet the runed circle scoured into the ground. When the light meets the runes the circle flares with a blinding radiance, forcing you to avert your gaze.

'My magic!' screams Avian, his voice raw. 'It's taking my magic!'

When you look back at the circle, you see a creature rising up out of the murk. It appears human, but fashioned from stringy clods of muscle and bone. You stand transfixed as a skull-like head thrusts out from its broadening shoulders, whilst its torso explodes into an array of arms, all ending in serrated scythes of yellow bone.

'No!' Avian jerks violently against the stone, his eyes rolling back into his head. 'It's taking ... me ...'

A thin layer of flesh grows across the skull, forming itself into a face – Avian's face. Then the golem lets go a savage roar, blood and spittle flying from its teeth. Desperately you look back at the mage, but he now lies slumped against the stone, the bright glow having faded from the grooved depressions. Somehow this monster has used Avian's power to give itself life – and now it is up to you to end it. It is time to fight:

	Speed	*Brawn*	*Armour*	*Health*
Evin Daala	15	12	16	100

Special abilities

- Absorption: Each time you play a speed or a combat ability, Daala absorbs it – and will use it at the first available opportunity, starting from the next combat round it was absorbed. Daala will play abilities in the order that they were absorbed, subject to their description. (Note: Daala ignores all weapon and career requirements when using abilities.)
- Boiling blood: Once you have taken health damage from Daala's damage score/damage dice, you are immediately inflicted with *boiling blood*. This causes 1 damage at the end of its first combat round, ignoring *armour*. This damage increases by 1 in each subsequent combat round, up to a maximum of 4 damage a round.
- Blood 'n gore: The demon is immune to *bleed*.

If you manage to defeat this foul abomination, turn to 890.

775

The balcony has a single doorway, which takes you through into a domed chamber. This new area is devoid of furnishings or decoration, save for the mosaic floor. You twist your head to try and discern the pattern – it looks like a runed hammer, surrounded by a circle of flames.

At the opposite end of the hall are two enormous stone doors, intricately carved to mirror the same design. They stand slightly ajar, affording a glimpse of a colonnaded platform and an outdoor plaza beyond.

As you head across the room, the ground starts to tremble underfoot. You look urgently to Virgil, then down at the tiles, which are visibly vibrating.

'When was the last time this volcano erupted?' you ask with a nervous frown.

Virgil shakes his head. 'I don't think . . .'

Suddenly, there is a loud explosion. Broken tiles go sailing through the air as a spiked head pushes up through the rock. Giant mandibles snap hungrily at you then the creature falls back, leaving a gaping hole in the floor. An instant later you hear a skittering sound, moving across the room.

'Persistent, I'll give it that,' grunts Virgil, trying to follow the sound as it sweeps past.

The skittering stops. You exchange concerned glances.

Then the ground beneath your feet explodes upwards. You go tumbling away as the centipede bursts out, its plated legs scrabbling to pull its body through the hole. You manage a futile swing at the monster as it surges past, but your weapons are deflected by its thick carapace.

The bug swarms up the wall, then across the ceiling, its head swinging around to take aim with its bile-coated mandibles. You don't need a sixth sense to know what is coming next. As the first of the slime bombs splatter across the ground, you flex your demon wings then launch yourself into the air. It is time to fight:

	Speed	*Brawn*	*Armour*	*Health*
Chilopoda	13	11	13	150

Special abilities

- Bile assault: Create a 6 by 6 grid on a sheet of paper. Number the squares 1 to 6 both horizontally and vertically (see diagram). At the start of each combat round, choose a square for your hero to occupy. (You may want to use a counter or die for this.) Then roll 2 dice for a grid reference; the first result for the horizontal (x axis) and second result for the vertical (y axis). So a roll of ⚂ and ⚃ would give you grid reference 3, 4. This square has been filled with corrosive bile.

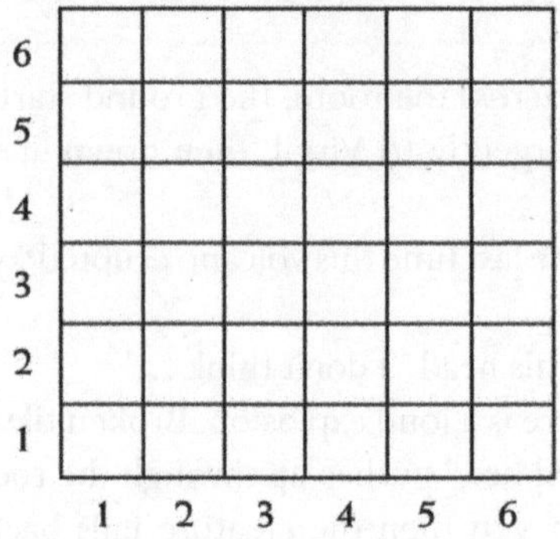

If your hero was occupying this square then they take 15 damage, ignoring *armour*. The bile remains in the square for the duration of the combat. Repeat this extra phase at the start of each round, choosing a clear spot for your hero, then rolling for where the next bile will land. If you roll the same grid reference as a previous bile, then roll again. Remember, each bile remains in play until the end of the combat.

If you manage to defeat this mucus-spitting monstrosity, turn to 781.

776

It is an arduous climb and one that frequently leaves you dangling by only your fingertips as the eroded rock crumbles and gives way beneath you. Thankfully a spattering of ledges provide a helpful respite, allowing you to gather your strength for each stage of the climb.

As you near the summit you notice that one of the ledges juts out from the wall, becoming a narrow finger of rock. At its end is a thorny-looking nest, containing three large white eggs.

Will you:

Investigate the nest?	457
Continue climbing?	472

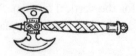

777

Searching through the vault, you find 200 gold crowns. You may also take any/all of the following:

Glyph of strength	Rune of healing	Acheron's warglaive
(special: glyph)	(special: rune)	(main hand: sword)
Use on any item to add	Use on any item to add	+2 speed +4 brawn
1 *brawn*	the special ability *heal*	Ability: cleave

When you have made your decision, you leave the vault and exit the hall through the open doorway. Turn to 797.

778

One of the rune stones is still glowing with a dim, pulsating light. You stoop down to examine it. As soon as you touch the stone's cool surface, the complex runes suddenly blossom into a crimson brilliance – their rhythm quickening like the beat of a heart.

If you wish, you may now take the following item:

Lich stone
(talisman)
+1 magic
Ability: runecaster career

The stone is imbued with ancient magics, designed to revive and energise. While this item is equipped, the runecaster has the following special abilities:

Refresh (mo): Cast this spell any time in combat to restore an ability that you or an ally has already used – allowing you to use it again. You can only cast *refresh* once per combat.
Magic tap (mo): Cast this spell any time in combat to raise your *magic* score by 2 for one combat round. If you roll a double (for attack speed or damage), then this spell is restored and can be used again.

Once you have made your decision, you leave the tomb and head up the stairs. Turn to 889.

779

You walk forward to inspect the mirror, discovering that the top stone is loose from the base and can be rotated. However, no matter in which direction you turn the mirror, nothing appears to happen. Puzzled by this, you inspect the stone doors – but once again, you are met with frustration. The doors are locked by some spell or mechanism and cannot be opened. With nothing else of interest in the room, you decide to leave and return to the main chamber, hoping that the other exit will lead to better fortune. Turn to 595.

780

The hunter is far deadlier than he appears, but his impatience is his undoing. A clumsy lunge leaves him wide open, allowing you to sweep your weapons past his guard, delivering a swift and decisive end to the combat.

Searching the hunter's body, you find 30 gold crowns and up to two of the following rewards:

Bone wild	**Rip spleen**	**Jungle runners**
(main hand: sword)	(left hand: sword)	(feet)
+1 speed +2 brawn	+2 speed +1 brawn	+1 speed +2 health
Ability: deep wound	Ability: bleed	Ability: haste

With your adversary defeated, you take a moment to inspect the crates. Sadly, they contain very little of interest – mostly arrows and crossbow bolts – but a few choice items catch your eye. You may now take any/all of the following:

Taipan poison (2 uses)
(backpack)
Use this at the start of combat to coat your weapons in snake venom. This gives you the *venom* special ability for the duration of the combat

Sharpening stone (2 uses)
(backpack)
Use this at the start of combat to sharpen your weapons. This gives you the *sure edge* special ability for the duration of the combat.

Turning back to the camp, you hear a sudden piercing shriek. Looking up, you see the sniper topple from the watch tower. A tigris follows him over the rail, her sharp claws whipping around to dig into the wood – slowing her fall. It is White Cloak. The agile tigris springs back to the ground, her eyes already scanning the battle for her next prey. Turn to 785.

781

You leap onto the centipede's back, sinking your weapons between the insect's black carapace. A shudder runs along its enormous body, then the multitude of legs give way beneath it. The centipede skids along on a film of its own bile, before finally crashing into a wall with a satisfying crunch.

You jump down from its crumpled remains. 'Always knew it had a soft spot for me . . .'

For defeating Chilopoda, you may now help yourself to one of the following rewards:

Mucus membrane
(chest)
+2 speed +2 armour
Ability: immobilise
(requirement: warrior)

Slime skimmers
(boots)
+2 speed +2 brawn
Ability: webbed

Mordant shroud
(head)
+2 speed +3 magic
Ability: acid
(requirement: mage)

When you have made your decision, turn to 884.

782

Cernos holds Nephele close, kissing her tear-soaked cheek – then he rises, drawing his sword. The girl shrieks, reaching out to stop him, clawing for his legs, but the soldier marches forward all the same, the certainty of his own death written on his face.

'Let them go!' he demands. 'Please. Take my soul instead – spare them.'

The demon snarls, its free hand whipping through the air. It catches Cernos across the chest, tearing through his armour and hurling him sideways into the wall. Then the demon surges towards the king, his rune-blade raised to strike.

'All will fall before Ragnarok!'

The demon's sword slices down, the air rippling around its edges. At the last moment the king grabs his daughter, throwing her forward. 'Take her!' he snarls. Then he turns and runs, making for the back of the chamber. The sword sweeps through the defenceless girl, her body cleaved in two by the dark blade. Its runes flare bright as a ghostly image of the girl rises up from her corpse, kicking and screaming even in death.

'NO!' Cernos struggles to rise, blood pouring from the claw marks that have raked his chest. 'Nephele!' He watches in horror as her spirit is absorbed into the blade, its malign runes growing ever brighter.

'Let me out!' The king is beating his fists against a panel at the back of the chamber. Evidently it must lead to some secret escape tunnel, but the panel has become jammed. His anguished cries become desperate whimpers.

'Do you wish revenge?' The demon points its blade at the king, who is now sobbing on his knees. 'I said, do you want revenge?' His head snaps around to glare at Cernos.

The warrior staggers to his feet, blood and dust matting his face. 'Nephele . . .' As his gaze wanders from the corpse to the whimpering king, his mouth curls into a vicious sneer. 'We are all damned!' he bellows, spitting blood. 'This is my kingdom no longer – and this is not my king.'

The demon's laughter reverberates throughout the chamber, pounding like fists against your eardrums. You watch, dumbfounded, as Cernos stalks towards the king, his body changing with each step, scales and spines punching out of his back, muscles breaking the confines of his clothing, wings unfolding like dark leaves. In a matter of heartbeats, Cernos the demon stands over the king.

'Do it!' snarls Barahar. 'And prove you are worthy of my blood.'

You look away, the king's screams turning your stomach. Then everything blurs, the room swimming and lurching once again. When you can finally see again you are lying on your stomach, coughing on dust and grit. Towering above you is the demon, Cernos, his scorched flesh disfiguring his sneer.

'So, tell me, prophet,' he spits with contempt. 'Do you really think you are worthy of *my* blood?' Turn to 584.

783

You turn to face the last of the hounds, your weapons dripping with molten ichor. The beast's eyes narrow to slivers of flame as it prepares to charge. You tense – ready for the attack. Then a crack of thunder sends you staggering sideways, the noise tearing through your skull and leaving a painful echo pounding in your ears. At that same moment, the hound's head shatters into fragments of bone as it is sent flying off the side of the bridge, its painful whine quickly lost to the mist.

Virgil lowers his smoking pistol. 'I'd cover your ears next time.'

For your victory over the hounds, you may now choose one of the following rewards:

Magma hide	**Lava pads**	**Hound hook**
(chest)	(boots)	(left hand: dagger)
+1 speed +3 brawn	+2 speed +2 magic	+2 speed +3 brawn
Ability: backdraft	Ability: fire shield	Ability: gouge
(requirement: warrior)	(requirement: mage)	(requirement: rogue)

When you have made your decision, turn to 798.

784

You take the ashes that you found in the Lamuri city and pour them into the black metal dish. The moment the ashes come in contact with the heated surface, they start to smoulder, filling the room with a strong, fragrant scent.

'So, we're making offerings to old gods now?' Virgil sniffs disapprovingly.

You watch as the smoke winds about you like an hypnotic serpent. Then, all of a sudden, there is an angry rush of heat. Green flames erupt from the consumed ashes – and with them a ghostly shape takes flight. It is a giant bird, formed of fire and brimstone, its bright plumage rippling with heat. For an instant it hovers above the flames, wings beating silently. Then it swoops down with a shrill squawk, talons raking through the air. It is time to fight:

	Speed	*Magic*	*Armour*	*Health*
Quetzal Volax	13	12	6	100

Special abilities

- Heat wave: At the start of every third combat round, the phoenix releases a surging torrent of flame. You must automatically take damage equal to its current *magic* score, ignoring *armour*.
- Healing tears: At the end of each combat round, the phoenix heals 2 *health*. This cannot take the phoenix above its starting *health* of 100.
- Body of flame: The phoenix is immune to *backdraft, fire aura, sear* and *searing mantle*.

If you manage to defeat this tempestuous fire spirit, turn to 654.

785

You stumble through the battle, eyes stinging from the smoke. It is difficult to make out who is winning, if anyone – bodies of both tigris and hunters litter the ground.

Ahead of you is a line of iron cages. Their captives are snorting and bellowing, battering against the bars to free themselves. In one you can see a squat four-legged beast, with a thickly armoured hide and a cluster of horns for a face. In another is a winged reptile, shrieking as it throws itself against the sides of the cage, desperate to escape.

Suddenly the body of a tigris goes streaking past in a tumble of arms and legs. It is closely followed by another, howling in pain. You spin around to see a giant stomping through the smoke, wielding a tree-sized club.

Will you:

Try and open the cages?	763
Attack the giant?	772

786

'This is the work of elves, not dwarves,' says Virgil, lifting up a loose cog from the ground and brushing the dust from its surface. 'Fascinating. Avian would have liked to have seen this.'

'Elves?' you frown. 'How is that possible?'

The witchfinder shrugs. 'The shroud here is thin, riven. The elven navigators could travel through it – perhaps one of their number ended up here after the city was deserted. Access to a rune forge would have been a great boon for them – particularly in their fight against the legion. ' He follows the system of cogs to a row of metal levers that appear to operate a switch mechanism.

'The lava is feeding the forge fires, look.' He leans back, pointing to the rivers of molten rock, bubbling sluggishly along their grooved channels. 'If we close them off, we can lower the heat.'

For a moment, you struggle to grasp his meaning, then you spot the stone plugs, hanging over each of the outlets. You assume they can be lowered, to shut off each individual flow of lava.

'The sprites will use the forge to heal,' says Virgil. 'I suggest we give them a little surprise.'

Will you:

Attempt to close the outlets?	743
Examine the pipes?	692
Head up the stairs to the forge?	601

787

For defeating Nephele, you may now help yourself to one of the following special items:

Nemesis shawl	**B is for Banshee**	**Azure embers**
(cloak)	(left hand: spell book)	(main hand: wand)
+2 speed +3 magic	+2 speed +4 magic	+2 speed +4 magic
Ability: wither	Ability: windblast	Ability: disrupt

If you are *hexed* then you have gained an extra reward, turn to 708. Otherwise, return to the quest map to continue your journey.

788

Back in the reading room, you may now investigate the crystal door in the north wall (turn to 809), leave via the south exit, where the echoing rumble can still be heard (turn to 854), or head east, back into the maze of aisle ways (turn to 839).

789

Thick flakes of ash rain down from the sky, glowing like embers as they burn against your weapons. You breathe in the stench of brimstone and allow yourself a smile. Whatever it was, the wind demon has now been defeated.

Amongst the deepening piles of ash, you spot a glimmer of treasure. You assume it must have been caught up inside the demon's body, but somehow managed to survive its deadly crushing forces.

If you wish, you may now help yourself to one of the following rewards:

Mourn helm	**Dark star**	**Abyssal firestone**
(head)	(left hand: mace)	(ring)
+2 speed +2 brawn	+2 speed +3 magic	+1 armour +2 health
Ability: impale	Ability: barbs	Ability: fire aura
(requirement: warrior)		

When you have updated your hero sheet, turn to 825.

790

Your weapons carve a blazing trail through the tight press of shrieking creatures, blood and severed limbs flying in all directions. The onslaught seems endless – as soon as one monster falls, there is another to take its place. Back-to-back with Avian, your attacks blur into an angered frenzy, chopping and blasting at the buzzing, shrieking swarm.

You are still swinging your weapons, snarling with anger, long after the last fury has fallen. It isn't until you hear the crack of gunfire, tearing through the silence, that you snap out of your reverie, blinking past the sweat and blood stinging your eyes.

Virgil spins his pistols, a boot resting on the corpse of the last hound. He watches you with a mix of admiration and uncertainty. 'Demons against demons,' he sniffs, holstering his guns. 'Now there's a pretty sight …'

For your victory over the furies, you may now choose one of the following rewards:

Warfists of fury	Wings of fury	Brace of fury
(gloves)	(cloak)	(chest)
+1 speed +3 brawn	+2 speed +3 magic	+2 speed +3 brawn
Ability: knockdown	Ability: surge	Ability: critical strike
(requirement: warrior)	(requirement: mage)	(requirement: rogue)

When you have made your decision, turn to **798**.

791

You search through the grisly remains of the golem, wondering if there is anything of value that can be salvaged. Amongst the charred bones and magic-imbued flesh, you find one of the following special rewards:

Gore-soaked fists	Serrated scapula	Blood soul
(gloves)	(main hand: axe)	(talisman)
+1 speed +4 brawn	+2 speed +4 brawn	+1 speed +1 brawn
Ability: slam	Ability: fallen hero	Ability: weaver

When you have updated your hero sheet, turn to **877**.

792

The last sprite is extinguished in a cloud of fizzing steam. Victorious, you advance towards the cauldron, its runed pot still shaking and bucking with violent force. Suddenly its blazing contents erupt into the air, forming a cascading column of molten fire. It sweeps up high into the shimmering haze, then comes crashing down like an angry wave. You dive for cover, shielding your face, as the sizzling droplets coalesce into an immense giant of flame, its head crowned with spines of rippling smoke.

The fiend reaches for a black-iron hammer, resting next to the hearth. With its other hand, it grabs the black anvil and rips it from its foundations. Stone and dust cascade from its underside, as the giant lifts its newfound weapons into the smoky air.

Virgil fires his pistols. The giant twists around, deflecting the shots with the iron anvil.

'It's using the anvil as a shield!' shouts Virgil, springing back as the hammer comes crashing down.

You roll under the next swing, getting as close to the fiend as you dare. Its body is a raging bonfire, scorching your scaled skin and filling your lungs with blistering-hot smoke. Virgil staggers back, the heat too much for him to bear.

'*Burn!*' snarls the demon. '*Your mortal flesh will feed my forge!*'

The demon raises its hammer once again. With an answering roar of your own, you hurl your weapons and magic against its blazing form. It is time to fight:

	Speed	*Brawn*	*Armour*	*Health*
Chard	12	(*)	8/16 (*)	60 (*)
Anvil	–	–	16	20

Special abilities

- Whirling hammer: If Chard wins a combat round, he rolls 3 damage dice for his total damage score. You may use *armour* as normal to absorb this damage.
- Anvil shield: Chard is using the anvil as a shield. While the anvil has *health*, Chard has an *armour* of 16. If the anvil is disabled (by reducing it to zero *health*), then Chard's *armour* is reduced to 8.
- Blazing inferno: For each combat round that you spent fighting the sprites, Chard may add 2 to its starting *health*.
- Body of flame: Chard is immune to *backdraft, fire aura, sear* and *searing mantle*.
- Dwarven stone: The anvil is immune to all combat abilities and passive effects, including *bleed, thorns, piercing* and *snake strike*.

In this combat you roll against Chard's *speed*. If you win a combat round, you can choose to apply your damage to Chard or the anvil.

Once Chard is reduced to zero *health*, the combat is automatically won.

If you manage to defeat this hot-headed hulk, turn to 887.

793

As the defeated giant stumbles backwards, lightning flares from the runes carved into its stonework. The crackling lines flicker across its scarred body, seconds before it smashes to the ground in an explosion of fire and rock.

You breathe a sigh of relief and are about to turn away, when Lorcan shakes his head and points with the end of his weapon.

The shattered rocks are shifting and trembling as if alive, the lightning still crackling over their misshapen forms. Suddenly they lift up, grinding and scraping together to create three squat humanoids. They look like miniature versions of the rock giant but, instead of fire, their black bodies are surrounded by lightning.

'Why don't giants ever stay dead?' You scowl, remembering the colossus in the forest of thorns.

'Clearly they enjoy the punishment.' Lorcan offers you a sly wink before charging into their midst, the purple runes on his arm pulsing with demonic power. (You must fight this next stage of the combat with the *health* and abilities you have remaining.)

	Speed	*Brawn*	*Armour*	*Health*
Elemental	14	12	10	50
Elemental	14	12	10	50
Elemental	14	12	10	50

Special abilities

- Stone dust: Once an elemental is destroyed, it creates a cloud of stone dust. This reduces both heroes' *speed* by 2 for the remainder of the combat. (NOTE: *Stone dust* is only applied once, when the first elemental is reduced to zero *health*.)
- Lightning: Each time a hero's damage score/damage dice causes health damage to an elemental, they must take 2 damage in return,

ignoring *armour*. If a hero has the *insulate* ability, they can ignore this damage.

Both heroes must choose the same elemental to attack in each combat round (unless one hero has elected to support). If successful, the winning hero strikes against the elemental as normal. If both heroes lose, the chosen elemental strikes back as a single opponent, rolling for a damage score as normal. Only one elemental will attack a round.

If you manage to finally defeat this monstrous creation, turn to **651**. If you are defeated, you must return to phase one of the combat if you wish to attempt this challenge again (turn to **610**).

794

For defeating Erkil, you may now help yourself to one of the following special items:

Rune of murder	**Grips of living stone**	**Blackthorn twister**
(special: rune)	(gloves)	(left hand: sword)
Use on any item to add	+1 speed +4 armour	+2 speed +4 brawn
the special ability *savagery*	Ability: might of stone	Ability: cruel twist

If you are *hexed* then you have gained an extra reward, turn to **878**. Otherwise, return to the quest map to continue your journey.

795

After brushing ink over the bronze plates, you lower them onto the paper. When you lift up the cross-piece, you are pleased to see that the parchment is now marked with your chosen sigils. Your book is almost complete; all that remains is to bind the loose pages. If you wish to choose a *binding of black iron*, turn to **380**. If you would prefer to choose *a binding of drake scales*, turn to **600**.

796

Using your chosen reagents you craft a black-bladed sword, its serrated edge rippling with phoenix fire. If you wish, you may now lay claim to:

Ravenos, bringer of ruin
(main hand: sword)
+2 speed +5 brawn
Ability: deep wound, sear
(requirement: warrior/rogue)

If you wish to craft another item, turn to 755. Otherwise, return to the map to continue your adventure.

797

From the hall, you enter a network of windowless passageways. They wind and twist through the black rock, constantly intersecting with other shafts and corridors to form a maddening maze. Most of the passages are blocked with rubble, others simply wind back on themselves, leading you round in an infuriating loop.

At last you sight a red glow, filtering through a crack in the wall. You squeeze through, finding yourselves at the top of a sloping ledge. Below you, through the fingers of mist, you can see the magma lake and its tiny islands, bobbing on the surface.

'There!' Virgil pats your shoulder and points. The three goblin looters are now scurrying down the rock, less than a hundred metres away. He raises his pistol to take a shot, but curses as the ledge takes them safely behind cover. 'Come on!' The witchfinder reels off in pursuit. 'We might still have a chance of catching them.' Turn to 820.

798

Avian lowers his swords, his gilt-edged armour coated with black blood. He turns and looks back at you, offering a thin smile.

'Good work.'

You step over the corpses of the furies, wondering what corruption of magic could account for such creatures. Their bodies are misshapen, no two alike, and yet all have the characteristic wings and collars of matted hair. They remind you of vultures.

'Ragnarok,' states Avian, pushing one of the bodies over with his foot. 'These were men and women once. Then the sword took their souls and turned them into this.' He lifts his chin, eyes roving across the dwarven city. 'We will encounter more of its dark work, I am sure ...'

Virgil removes his hat, poking a finger through a scorched hole in its brim. 'There's one thing I don't understand.' He kicks the hound carcass lying at his feet. 'Why did they ignore Cernos?'

'He has the heart,' replies Avian, sliding the ends of his staff back together. They lock with a faint click, sending a flicker of magic dancing along the runed shaft. 'It will afford him some protection from the guardians of Tartarus.'

You glance at Avian. 'What is this heart he carries?'

'Some would believe it a divine relic – part of the One God himself.' The mage purses his lips. 'From what I've witnessed, I'd say it's a magic anomaly. From the time of the Great Cataclysm.'

'Bad news is what it is.' Virgil flips his hat back onto his head. 'Still, look on the bright side. It is very bright.' He points to a spot further along the bridge, where you can see a white circle of light silhouetting Cernos' maimed form. The winged demon is limping beneath an arched tower.

Avian gives a sigh. 'Cernos may have safe passage, but I doubt our own crossing will be as charmed. That is a guardian tower – and it will have defences. Prepare yourselves.' Turn to 670.

799

The hat and gloves float off towards the back of the shop. They disappear through a small doorway, returning a moment later with a small black iron chest. The ghost places it on the dusty counter, then flips open the lid. Inside are several glowing stone tablets.

You may purchase any of the following for 300 gold crowns each:

Rune of winter	Glyph of the titan	Rune of shadows
(special: rune)	(special: glyph)	(special: rune)
Use on any item to add the special ability *silver frost*	Use on any item to add 1 *armour*	Use on any item to add the special ability *vanish*

If you wish to make further purchases, return to **557**. Otherwise, you thank the ghostly proprietor and resume your journey.

800

Congratulations, for defeating Ixion while *hexed* you have won an extra reward:

Blood-sworn chestguard
(chest)
+2 speed +4 brawn
Ability: unstoppable, blood-sworn set
(requirement: hexed)

Once you have updated your hero sheet, return to the quest map to continue your journey.

801

You hurry through the doorway, only to skid to a halt a second later at the edge of a vertigo-inducing drop. Arms waving at your side, you manage to stumble back, knocking into Virgil.

'Easy,' he scowls, nudging you away. 'I could have skewered you on my blade.'

'Where are we?' you gasp, catching your breath.

'The Abussos,' replies the witchfinder.

You are standing at the edge of a narrow pathway, fashioned from a translucent green stone. It winds around the insides of a gigantic stone shaft, its beginning and end lost to the darkness. Both above and below you the path hugs the walls, occasionally forming circular platforms which hang suspended over the dizzying heights.

As your eyes follow the curving walls you see that they are covered in thousands of carvings, detailing various characters and scenes. Each one glows with a soft green light.

'This is how the dwarves recorded their history,' says Virgil. 'The stone holds their memories.'

You put a hand to one of the carvings, snatching it back quickly. The stone is freezing cold, its touch sending a bone-numbing chill along your spine. When the sensation fades, you are left with a dull ache between your shoulder blades – a familiar pain that has been tormenting you since your fall from the bridge. Reaching behind your back, you feel at the bony stumps now protruding from your flesh.

Virgil gives an audible gasp.

You drop your hand quickly, concerned that you have drawn further attention to your on-going transformation.

But Virgil is staring into the shaft, a sudden gust of wind tugging at his coat. 'No ...'

You hurry to the edge. Below you, the glowing carvings of the Abussos are winking out one by one, snuffed out by a rising tide of darkness.

'We need to move!' snaps Virgil. 'Quickly!'

He starts sprinting up the pathway, his boots squeaking across the smooth stone. You follow without question, all too aware of the wailing screams that are mounting in volume.

'Can't we fight it? What is it?' You dare another glance into the shaft, horrified by the roiling, twisted shape that is fast-approaching. It looks like a black thunder-cloud, flickering with lightning.

'It's Nyx!' Virgil shouts above the screaming din. 'A greater demon from the abyss. We have to get out of this shaft – before it overtakes us!'

As you approach the first of the circular platforms, you are startled to see figures moving across its surface. They have the appearance of ghosts, glowing with the same green light as the carved walls. Sounds start to fill your ears, the cries of battle and the ring of steel.

'The magic here is tainted!' yells Virgil. 'The Abussos will turn against us, use the memories to defend itself ...'

The ghosts on the first platform fade, leaving a lone Lamuri warrior standing at its centre. He is a head taller than you, with a cloak of tiger skin draped across his broad shoulders. In one hand he holds a large bone club, banded with silver and gold.

Virgil skids to a halt, eyeing the phantom warily. 'Let us pass, we mean you no harm.'

The tiger-cloaked warrior spits at the ground. 'I am mighty Shonac! First prince of Hanuman.' He beats his chest three times. 'From the forest I come, to lay claim to the jewelled throne. Seven years of exile. Seven years I watch you grow weak. Look upon me, my people – you see Shonac, First of the Bloodied Claw – the ancestors chose me for your king!'

'It's just a ghost – a memory,' you implore, confused by the witch-finder's hesitation. 'It can't harm us.'

However, when you try and step around the warrior his face suddenly creases into a savage snarl. He springs forward, his club snapping around in a green blur. The blow smashes into your side, sending you skidding and tumbling to the very edge of the platform.

'Just a ghost.' Virgil scoffs derisively. 'I told you – the Abussos is using its magic to defend itself! If we don't get past these guardians, we're done for.'

As you scramble back to your feet, you catch sight of the wind demon hurtling up the shaft. Its black form is ripping through the jade pathways like they were nothing but paper, sucking the broken fragments into its whirling vortex. Determined not to share a similar fate, you turn back to the phantom warrior. You will have to defeat him and the many other ghosts of the Abussos, in order to outrun the demon and find a means of escape. Turn to 630.

802

Between the high-stacked shelves you see a ghostly figure pacing back and forth. It is a dwarf, a braided beard hanging down over his plain robes. His body is almost completely translucent, its outline shimmering with a faint green light. He continues to pace, muttering to himself and wringing his hands in agitation. He shows no sign of having noticed you.

Will you:

Talk to the ghost?	859
Attack the ghost?	813
Ignore it and continue?	866

803

Congratulations, for defeating Erkil while *hexed* you have won the following rare item:

Volcanist's hood
(head)
+2 speed +3 magic
Ability: overload, volcanism set
(requirement: hexed)

Once you have updated your hero sheet, return to the quest map to continue your journey.

804

You head south out of the tainted marshland, finding yourself back amongst the thick jungle and its thrumming chorus of insects. After an hour the land starts to rise, taking you through lush clearings of ferns and bright flowers into a set of fog-shrouded hills. These gradually become steeper until you are finally forced out onto a ledge of crumbling rock. Trying to ignore the vertiginous drop, you ease yourself along the narrow path, following it round to its cloud-capped summit. If you have the word *explorer* on your hero sheet, turn to 504. Otherwise, turn to 756.

805

You decide to leave the looters to their ill-gotten gains, believing that the vault will hold greater reward. There is only one problem – getting into it. After studying the strange patterns, you move closer to the wall and give one of the panels an experimental push. It gives slightly at your touch then slides forward, pivoting out of its original position. To your surprise, you discover that each panel is on some sort of grooved axle and can be rotated clockwise – all save for the middle panel, which remains locked in place.

'Dwarven thinking.' Virgil scratches his chin. 'The answer is usually a number, which needs to be spoken. Then the door opens. If you get it right …'

If you are able to solve the puzzle, then 'speak your answer' by turning to the relevant entry number. If you cannot solve the puzzle then, reluctantly, you are forced to give up – the vault's secrets remaining frustratingly hidden. Turn to 797.

806

Congratulations! You have created the following item:

Self-published tome
(left hand: spell book)
+2 speed +3 armour
Ability: trickster

If you wish to create a different spell book, you can start the process again (turn to 850). Otherwise, you may now leave the chamber and continue your journey. Turn to 866.

807

As you advance, the smell grows worse – a pungent, stagnant odour that makes you start to gag. It is accompanied by a loud crunching underfoot. You crouch down, taking a closer look at the white crispy substance that covers the ground and crushing some between your fingers.

'Bats,' sniffs Grey-hair with revulsion. His eyes flick to the ceiling, where you hear the whisper of wings.

You sniff the white goo and suddenly flinch away, realisation dawning. 'Bat guano,' you scowl, quickly wiping your hand against your chest.

'Good for earth. Bad for smell,' grins the elderly tigris, his whiskers bristling around a sly smile.

A few metres ahead the tunnel widens into another cave. At its centre is a rectangular mound, too angular to be a natural formation. Scar-face scrapes the guano from its surface, then beckons you over.

'Dwarf stone,' he says, pointing to the runes carved into the surface. You note that there are four square tiles set into the lid, each one showing a different glyph. There is an empty depression where you assume there was once a fifth tile.

If you have the *rune stone*, turn to 470. Otherwise, your attempts to break into the stone container prove in vain. You rejoin the others and continue into the opposite tunnel. Turn to 513.

808

Congratulations, for defeating Ixion while *hexed* you have won the following rare item:

Volcanist's vestment
(chest)
+2 speed +4 armour
Ability: reaper, volcanism set
(requirement: hexed)

Once you have updated your hero sheet, return to the quest map to continue your journey.

809

The smooth surface of the door suddenly ripples like water, forming itself into a pair of narrowed eyes, a hawkish nose and a wide-lipped mouth. 'Halt!' it speaks in common. 'Who goes there?'

You start to draw your weapons, but Virgil puts a hand to your arm urging restraint. 'This arratoch is harmless. A door guardian, nothing more.' He turns back to the enchanted visage, protruding from the marble. 'We seek to pass. Did your master provide a means of passage?'

The guardian takes a moment before responding. 'Answer my riddle, and you may enter.' It then proceeds to reel off a dwarven children's rhyme:

Deep, deep, seven sleep, kings under the hill.
Twenty yards and ten again,
Two hundred dwarves were marching then,
A fathom more, but four less when,
They fell into a dragon's den.
How many feet are we?

If you are able to solve the riddle, then speak your answer by turning to the relevant entry number. Otherwise, the guardian refuses to let you pass. You have no choice but to leave by the south exit (turn to **854**) or the east exit (turn to **839**).

810

You scurry from one building to the next, hugging the walls, keeping to the shadows. Somewhere in the distance, you can hear the keening wail of the wind demon. It is still searching for you, hounding your steps.

For nearly an hour you have traversed the subterranean city, its buildings all sculptured from the same black stone. A few have still held traces of their former residents – dusty animal skins on the floor, stone benches and tables, a few pots and tools, writing etched into tablets. Nothing that has proved useful or brought you any closer to finding the sword.

'How will we find anything in this place?' You glance back at Virgil. The witchfinder has resorted to one blade to light his way, fearing the brighter glow from its twin will draw unwanted attention. He scans the skies with a worried frown.

'I am starting to lose my faith, I'll admit.'

The street you are following curves around the side of a sculptured pillar, bringing you to a raised courtyard. Its centre dips away into a bowl-shaped crater, where ash has been piled into peaked mounds.

'They burnt the dead,' Virgil concludes grimly. 'A final act before the survivors fled.'

You remember back to the Lamuri ruins and the swarms of undead that had infested the temples and buildings.

'A wise choice,' you remark. 'But it hasn't erased what happened here. I can still feel it . . . the evil is everywhere.'

Across the courtyard looms a domed building of red-black granite, with a tattered banner flapping above its bronzed doors. The cloth is heavy with dust and grime, but you can still make out the faded sigils sown into the cloth: a hammer and a flame.

'The sacred union,' states Virgil. 'The dwarves always had two kings to rule, in every city. One the hammer, the other the flame.'

You glance at him, confused.

'Their society was built around two ideals. Might and strength on the one hand, learning and magic on the other. Together they believed it united them, made them strong. But those divisions . . . well, you know your history . . .'

You recall reading of the great dwarven wars, when their cities were torn apart by civil strife and bloodshed. Tartarus had been spared such an event, the city having been abandoned long before the wars. Little consolation for its former inhabitants, you reflect grimly.

'At least this building has some character about it,' says Virgil, lightening the mood. 'Let's see what's inside.' Turn to 378.

811

The dwarf's stone-hard skin turns your blades and magic, its weight adding further strength to each of his own attacks. Your second sight can barely keep up with the onslaught, his axe nicking your leg, his blade slicing across your chest. A loose stone turns beneath your foot, forcing you to stumble. In that instant, the dwarf sees his chance to finish the fight – but your misstep has given you a fortuitous opening. As the dwarf raises his weapons to strike, you thrust under his guard, piercing through his stone chest. For an instant the dwarf stands frozen in mid-step, eyes wide in astonishment. Then his stone body crumbles around your weapon, dropping to the ground into a pile of grey dust.

Virgil staggers over, nursing a shoulder wound. 'That's one way of deposing a king, I guess.' He looks back at the obsidian throne. You follow his gaze to the skeleton that is now seated there, its bones webbed with grime. 'I think the magic trapped his spirit here,' sighs Virgil. 'To keep his oath, to defend these halls. Let's hope he is finally at rest.'

If you are a warrior, turn to 834. If you are a rogue, turn to 794. If you are a mage, turn to 716.

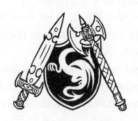

812

For defeating Ixion, you may now help yourself to one of the following special items:

Spoke of the wheel	**Crucifixion nail**	**Singed footpads**
(main hand: sword)	(ring)	(feet)
+2 speed +4 brawn	+1 brawn	+2 speed +3 brawn
Ability: deep wound	Ability: sweet spot	Ability: sidestep

If you are *hexed* then you have gained an extra reward, turn to 732. Otherwise, return to the quest map to continue your journey.

813

The dwarf gives an astonished shriek as your enchanted weapons penetrate its ghostly form. When you draw them out, its squat body collapses into wisps of green light, which go flickering away like embers on a breeze.

'Well, aren't you the mighty hero . . .'

You look back at Virgil, who is eyeing you with a smirk.

You shrug your shoulders. 'I gave it freedom – who would want to remain bound to this cursed place?'

He lifts an eyebrow. 'That was just a harmless servant, performing the same task he was given thousands of years ago.' He edges past you, glancing warily at your bared weapons. 'Perhaps not the reward for loyal service our friend was hoping for.'

He leads the way down the corridor, past more of the neatly-stacked shelves. You wonder if the ghost's task had been to keep them in order – a task that it couldn't complete for some reason. You notice several spaces on the shelves where books are missing. Turn to 866.

814

You take a bite out of one of the mushrooms, then wait tensely for any effects to become apparent. After several minutes, you grudgingly conclude that it doesn't have any special properties. Then, suddenly, you feel a tingling race along your arms and legs as your muscles start to expand with a powerful surge of strength. Eagerly you taste another of the mushrooms, discovering that this one heightens your already exceptional abilities, making you feel quick and alert. If you wish, you may now take any/all of the following:

Blood bonnet (2 uses)	**Fungal fingers (2 uses)**
(backpack)	(backpack)
Use any time in combat to raise your *brawn* by 2 for one round	Use any time in combat to raise your *speed* by 2 for one round

Pleased with your finds, you leave the cabin and continue your journey. Turn to 618.

815

With the wind demon hurtling ever closer, you draw your weapons and charge the ghostly Lamuri warrior. It is time to fight:

	Speed	*Magic*	*Armour*	*Health*
Shonac	11	8	3	40

Special abilities

- Tiger's pride: If Shonac is still alive at the end of the fourth combat round, he transforms into a spectral tiger. This raises his *speed* by 1, and his *magic* and *armour* by 4 for the remainder of the combat.
- Ghost of a victory: You cannot use *cutpurse* or *pillage* to gain gold/items from this combat.

If you manage to defeat Shonac, keep a record of your *health* and remaining abilities, and turn to 298. If you are defeated (or reach the end of your twentieth combat round), then the wind demon has outrun you. Restore your *health* and return to 630 if you wish to tackle the challenge again.

816

Congratulations! You have created the following item:

Self-published grimoire
(left hand: spell book)
+2 speed +3 magic
Ability: regrowth

If you wish to create a different spell book, you can start the process again (turn to 850). Otherwise, you may now leave the chamber and continue your journey. Turn to 866.

817

You scramble back up the rocks, to take in the view of the canyon below. While the mist obscures much of the landscape, you can still make out the course of the rivers and deltas cutting through the forest. You carefully add these details to the scholar's map. Make a note of the key word *south view* on your hero sheet. You may now return to the quest map to continue your adventure.

818

For defeating Nephele, you may now help yourself to one of the following special items:

Crystal plate	**Frostspike boots**	**Frozen heart**
(chest)	(boots)	(talisman)
+2 speed +4 brawn	+2 speed +2 armour	+1 speed
Ability: overpower	Ability: barbs	Ability: shatter

If you are *hexed* then you have gained an extra reward, turn to 679. Otherwise, return to the quest map to continue your journey.

819

The moment you open the cage door the winged creature is upon you, cawing and screeching as it seeks to rip you apart with its teeth and talons. You must fight:

	Speed	*Brawn*	*Armour*	*Health*
Drecko	8	6	8	50

Special abilities

- Winged assault: It is difficult to outmanoeuvre this agile combatant. You must lower your *speed* by 1 for the duration of this fight.
- Delirium: After the drecko makes a successful attack that causes health damage, you are immediately inflicted with delirium. If you win a combat round, roll a die. If the result is ⚀ or ⚁ then your attack misses its mark and you cannot roll for damage. If the result is ⚂ or more, you can roll for damage as normal.

(NOTE: You cannot heal after this combat. You must continue this quest with the *health* that you have remaining. You may use potions and abilities to heal lost *health* while you are in combat.)

If you manage to defeat the drecko, turn to 660. Otherwise, turn to 664.

820

The ledge curves round the dark spire of rock, widening into a bridge that spans the chasm and the shimmering magma lake below. At its opposite side, the dwarf city continues – its walls, smooth and undulating like melted tallow, rising up into a myriad of towers, columns and grey stepped terraces.

The goblins have now reached the bridge, their small hunched bodies swallowed by its vastness. You are about to pursue when a familiar wail reaches your ears. Virgil pulls you down behind a boulder.

'Our friend returns.' He sheathes his blade, extinguishing its light.

A second later and a black cloud fills the cavern, howling with the pained cries of the damned. The goblins skid to a halt, pointing and gesturing towards the looming shadow. For a second, they seem torn by indecision – to head back or continue to the other side. They choose the latter, throwing themselves into a sprint.

'They'll never make it,' remarks Virgil dryly.

You follow the wind demon as it spins across the city, its reckless momentum ripping through columns and towers, shattering walls and smashing through the sides of buildings. The broken chunks shower through the air, most of them swallowed by the demon's gaping maw to be ground to dust inside its whirling stomach.

With an ear-shattering shriek, the demon flips into a dive. As it speeds back into the chasm a clawed hand pushes out of its flanks, grabbing the side of the bridge. There is a loud echoing crunch as the claws dig deep into the stonework, halting its descent and flipping it around onto the topside of the bridge.

The demon lands on two splayed feet, staggering slightly as it finds its balance. Dust and smoke billow from its flared nostrils, laboured breathing thundering in the sudden, expectant silence.

The goblins stand frozen like statues, their necks craned back to take in the frightening visage. Then, as one, they turn and run, bawling in terror as they scramble back across the bridge. Their efforts prove futile – the demon sweeps its black fingers in a wide swathe, picking them up in one swift pass. You can hear their screams as the goblins are flipped into the air, then sucked into the hungry, crushing vortex.

Virgil shifts next to you. 'We should go back; find another route, before it's too late.'

You glance sideways at him, reading his fear.

'But we have to cross,' you state harshly, trying to sound more confident than you feel.

The witchfinder glares at you beneath his brows. 'Your demon-side makes you rash.'

'Then learn to read us better. Look.' You nod towards the bridge.

It is clear from the demon's demeanour that the creature has become weakened. Its shoulders are stooped, its body heaving with short, ragged breaths. It looks tired, drained of energy... a wind that has blown itself out.

Virgil's frown deepens. 'Even so, we can't defeat it. We should look for another way.' He twists around, taking in the sweeping walls of the canyon. Several other bridges are visible through the smoky haze, jutting out from different levels of the city.

You shake your head. 'And waste time? This demon will be forever hunting us. I'd rather face it on my terms.'

You start forward onto the bridge, ignoring Virgil's angry curses. As you get closer to the demon, you break into a run. The creature gives a blustery snort, expelling more ash from its turbulent innards. Two eyes, like orbs of lightning, flare into being amidst the darkness.

You pick up speed, your wings snapping back from your body. The leathery membranes bulge as they fill with wind. Then you kick off from the bridge, your fast-beating wings driving you towards the demon. It is time to fight:

	Speed	*Magic*	*Armour*	*Health*
Nyx	12	9	12	80

Special abilities

- Black breath: At the end of every combat round, the demon seeks to engulf you in a dust cloud. To avoid being hit, roll 3 dice. If the result is equal to or less than 10, then you have avoided it. If the result is higher, you have been hit and must take 5 damage, ignoring *armour*. You must also lower your *speed* by 1 for the next combat round.

Body of air: Nyx is immune to *bleed, disease* and *venom*.

If you manage to defeat this abyssal monster, turn to 789.

821
Quest: The Black Library

(NOTE: You must have completed the orange quest *The Abussos* before you can access this location.)

You put your shoulder to the large bronze door, pushing against the rubble that has piled up behind it. Beyond, through the whirling dust, you glimpse broken statues and more debris. You step through the doorway, clambering over the loose mounds of rock. Virgil follows, the glow from his swords spilling out to illuminate the chamber.

The atrium is high-ceilinged, its walls and vaulted roof carved with intricate scenes. In several places the carvings have melted, as if exposed to heat or some powerful magic, distorting the figures into unsettling demonic shapes.

The statues that litter the chamber all show dwarves, captured in various poises of pain and suffering. Titans, you quickly conclude – the dwarven warriors that could change their bodies to stone. Virgil walks over to one of the figures, standing at the head of the party. The portly warrior appears to be trying to pull a spear from his chest, the dark metal still lodged in the stone.

'The dwarves were fighting each other,' he states, running a finger along the shaft of the spear. 'This is runed metal.'

You notice some ragged clothing amongst the ashes, embroidered with silver runes. 'I thought their enemy was Barahar and his sword, not each other.' You pick up a dwarf helm, which has the blade of an axe lodged in its visor.

At the other side of the room, blocks of stone have been stacked together to form a makeshift barricade. Most of the stone has been scorched by magic or chipped by weapons. Beyond the barricade there is a passageway leading away into darkness. Its mouth is choked with broken stone. As you approach, you hear a bang and then a scuffling sound coming from the depths of the building. A series of wet-sounding hisses echo along the passage. They quickly grow in volume, headed in your direction.

'Looks like someone's home.' Virgil puts his back to the wall, swords raised to strike.

A moment later and a creature scampers up onto the rocks, its gruesome form illuminated by Virgil's blades. It has no skin, only muscle and sinew, glistening with a sheen of wet blood. The head is almost human, but instead of a mouth it has a trailing beard of tentacles, each one ending in a small mouth of snapping teeth.

As it stops to sniff the air, you see another pair of the creatures bounding along the passageway, running on all fours. The moment they reach the room, Virgil is upon them in a flurry of slashing blades. 'Let the shroud take you, demons!'

Blood sprays from their wounds, but the demons show no sign of pain. Instead their tentacled-teeth latch onto the witchfinder, tearing through his clothing to get at the flesh beneath. You leap to his aid, slashing frantically through muscle and tendon in an effort to draw their attention. It is time to fight:

	Speed	*Brawn*	*Armour*	*Health*
Blood demons	13	11	10	100

Special abilities

- Blood drinkers: If the demons roll a ⚅ for their damage score, then they automatically get to roll another die for damage. They also heal 4 *health*.
- Blood rage: Once the demons are reduced to 40 *health* or less, they may raise their *speed* by 1 for the remainder of the combat.

If you manage to defeat these grotesque monsters, turn to 869.

822

You hesitate, not wishing to pick a side in the fight – unsure whether anything you are witnessing is real or part of some elaborate fantasy.

'What are you waiting for?' shouts Murlic, glaring at the monk. 'This is our enemy!'

You shake your head. 'No, Murlic. Nothing is what it seems …'

'Wise move,' growls Ventus – suddenly speaking with a guttural, female voice. 'You are strong, bright claw.'

'No!' Murlic shrieks with anger, fists clenching at his side. 'You were supposed to kill her!'

Suddenly your surroundings start to blur, sweeping into ribbons of ochre light. Then you lurch forwards, as if pushed by some invisible hand, to find yourself inside a ruined building, its roof open to the misty marshland sky.

Where Ventus had been standing there is now a female tigris. She is panting heavily, looking exhausted. 'The witch,' snarls Scowler. 'We must fight her together!' Turn to 445.

823

For defeating Ixion, you may now help yourself to one of the following special items:

Ixion's wheel	Heat of ardour	Soldering iron
(left hand: shield)	(ring)	(necklace)
+2 speed +4 armour	+2 brawn	+1 speed +1 brawn
Ability: fire aura	Ability: sear	Ability: dominate

If you are *hexed* then you have gained an extra reward, turn to 800. Otherwise, return to the quest map to continue your journey.

824

Inside the tent you find two large trestle tables, covered in an array of different-sized bottles, and a crate containing netting. A young woman is stood over a smaller table, pressing the fangs of a snake to a cloth-covered jar.

'Taipan,' she says, removing the jar and holding it up. 'Deadliest venom in the jungle. Seen it bring down a tigris in under a minute. That's good going.'

You approach the table and examine the various potions and

bottles. 'How much?' you ask, picking up a healing tonic. 'I could use some of these.'

'Thirty shinies,' she replies, gently teasing the snake back into its basket. 'Uncle Bill sets the prices, so save the haggling. Where else you gonna go shopping out here?'

The following items are available for 30 gold crowns each:

Taipan poison (1 use) (backpack)	Flask of healing (1 use) (backpack)	Hunter's net (1 use) (backpack)
Use at the start of a combat to coat your weapons in snake venom. This gives you the *venom* special ability for the duration of the combat	Use any time in combat to restore 10 *health*	Use at the start of a combat round to reduce your opponent's *speed* by 2 for that round

When you have made your decision, you may explore the rest of the camp (turn to 744) or leave and return to the quest map.

825

Virgil strides through the ash cloud, his white blades resting across his shoulders. 'Seems your foolishness has paid off.' He stops to grind a chunk of stone beneath his boot heel. 'You have the luck of demons.'

You take a handful of ash, watching it spill between your clawed fingers. 'Demons die,' you reply flatly. 'And Cernos is next.'

The witchfinder grunts as he gazes up at the sprawling city. 'Easier to find a Wiccan in a wood.' He spits at the ash. 'This is a fool's errand.'

You rise to your feet, your attention drawn to an object fluttering down through the black snow. It looks like a piece of torn clothing. You reach up and snatch it out of the air, shaking it to rid it of a coat of grime. It turns out to be a square of animal hide, with a crude map drawn on one side. 'The goblins left us a memento at least.' You wave the cloth in front of Virgil before rolling it up and stuffing it into your belt.

'Is that your answer?' Virgil's tone is challenging. 'Now we resort to goblin maps?'

You meet his gaze, weighing his expression.

'Well?'

You fold your arms, drawing yourself to your full height. 'Make your point, Virgil.'

'You have a power. A link with Cernos. Why don't you use it?'

'I can't. It doesn't work like that.' Annoyance creeps into your voice. 'I don't control it – it controls me.'

Virgil shakes his head. 'At Durnhollow, your visions spoke of the future. You're a prophet.'

'So I'm told,' you reply sharply.

The witchfinder sheathes his blades, pushing them roughly into their scabbards. 'Perhaps this will help you remember . . .' He reaches inside his tattered coat, hesitating for a moment to enjoy your anxious frown. Then he lifts out a bundle of cloth. He proceeds to unravel it, revealing a small clay bottle wrapped inside. 'Know what this is?' Virgil holds it up by the tips of his fingers.

Your eyes widen. You take an involuntary step backwards, raising your hands defensively. 'No, Virgil. Don't do this.'

'Elysium. It's what they used in Durnhollow. It'll help you to see again – gain control of your power.' He extends his arm, moving the vial closer. 'What value is there in ignorance?'

Your eyes narrow. 'I don't want that poison inside me. We can find the sword, we can find Cernos, without resorting to that.'

Virgil shakes the vial. 'You fight demons well enough.' He kicks a stone off the side of the bridge. It goes spinning away into the steaming mist. 'When will you stop fighting yourself? Take the Elysium and tell me what you see.'

Will you:

Take the Elysium?	541
Refuse to use it?	639

826

Congratulations! You have created the following item:

Self-published tome
(left hand: spell book)
+2 speed +3 armour
Ability: regrowth

If you wish to create a different spell book, you can start the process again (turn to **850**). Otherwise, you may now leave the chamber and continue your journey. Turn to **866**.

827

A giant rodent swings over the side of the wall, sniffing the air with a whiskered snout. It is accompanied by a repugnant odour, like damp earth and decay. The creature grapples with the crumbling rock, splayed paws scrabbling frantically to drag its bloated, black-haired body into the corridor.

'Sorry,' hisses a voice in your ear.

A foot slams into the back of your knee, sending you lurching to the ground with a cry of pain. Angrily, you twist around to see the thief hurrying for the bronze doors. You tense, ready to follow, then a teeth-grating squeal shakes the corridor, dislodging stone and dust from the ceiling. Turning back, you see the rodent shifting to face you, its lips curling back to reveal rotting, dagger-sized teeth. Then it springs forward, intending to snap you up in its powerful jaws. It is time to fight:

	Speed	*Brawn*	*Armour*	*Health*
Terral devil	10	7	7	70

Special abilities

- Tail lash: Each time the devil rolls a double for its attack speed, you automatically lose the round, even if your attack speed was higher.

For the remainder of the round you cannot use combat or modifier abilities.

- Disease: Once the devil's damage score inflicts health damage to your hero, you must automatically lose 2 *health* at the end of each combat round.

If you manage to defeat this revolting rodent, turn to **641**.

828

Aether tugs on your arm. 'This way, the gate is near.'

You follow the spirit along the side of the building, to where a sloping track leads down to a circular platform. At its centre is an archway of black stone, carved with runic symbols. Part of the keystone has broken away, leaving a rough-toothed space at the crown of the arch.

'Dwarves did this,' hisses Aether. 'They wanted to stop Barahar from reaching the other cities. Let's see ...' The spirit passes a hand over the runes, drawing a flicker of light from their dark recesses. 'I cannot repair it fully, but I can draw on the magic that remains, craft a portal to the shroud.'

Virgil scowls. 'This is too dangerous. An open gate to the shroud will attract every demon in this place ... it is madness!'

Aether looks back at the witchfinder. 'That is why you must destroy the gate, the very moment I am gone. Break the runes and scatter their magic.'

'And the reward?' you insist.

Aether is studying the arch once again. 'Patience. Just a little more time ... yes, yes!' His shadowy hands dance across the arcane symbols. The runes flash, then brighten into a steady glow. 'Your reward is on its way.' Suddenly a sickly green light pours out of the stone, spreading out to form a glowing doorway. 'It is done,' he gasps.

A gargling roar rends the air. You spin around to see a nightmarish creature oozing between the building's chimneys. It looks to be made entirely of blood, its glutinous body sparkling with coins and treasures.

You look back at the spirit. 'Is this your doing?'

'Just honouring my word. My master's treasures are right there ...'

Aether points a smoky finger towards the advancing slime beast. 'You just need to convince Kuderas to part with them.'

Angrily you go to grab the spirit, but your hand passes straight through its vaporous body. Tittering with laughter, Aether steps into the portal and vanishes from sight.

'I told you it was a trick!' Virgil steps up to the arch, hacking furiously at the glowing runes. 'I'll destroy the portal – you take care of *that* thing!'

The giant blob is now seeping down the walls of the crematorium, its treasures scraping and clinking against the stone. You move to head it off, hoping that your weapons will prove powerful enough to break this demon's magic. It is time to fight:

	Speed	*Magic*	*Armour*	*Health*
Kuderas	14	10	11	120

Special abilities

- Blood money: Each time your damage score/damage dice cause health damage to Kuderas, roll a die. On a ⚄ or ⚅ result you have gained 100 gold crowns. If you roll ⚃ or less, then your weapons have become stuck in the creature's body. You must lower your *speed* by 2 for the next combat round, while you pull your weapons free of the sticky gloop.
- No money, no cry: If you are defeated by Kuderas, in future combats his *blood money* ability no longer applies.

If you manage to defeat the blood slime, turn to 730.

829

The imp teleports past you in a purple blur, the air popping as he reappears further along the passage. Virgil raises his pistols to take a shot, but the imp vanishes again – trailing ribbons of smoke in its wake.

The witchfinder grunts, before holstering his pistols. 'I'm done with chasing shadows.' He turns his attention to the runed bars, still glimmering with magic. 'Least we aren't alone in our dislike of thieves.' Turn to 696.

830

For defeating Krakatoa, you may now help yourself to one of the following special items:

Kraka's vengeance	Collar of correction	Rock-spine coat
(left hand: sword)	(necklace)	(chest)
+2 speed +5 brawn	+1 speed +1 brawn	+2 speed +4 brawn
Ability: piercing	Ability: sweet spot	Ability: gouge

When you have made your decision turn to **651** if you still need to choose rewards, or **545** to continue.

831

When next you awake you find yourself lying on a mattress, tangled in sweat-soaked blankets. A red-skinned man is standing over you, feathers woven into his jet-black hair. He backs away with an uncertain expression, his hand moving to the dagger at his belt.

Modoc. You recognise Virgil's healer – the man who helped you, after you were wounded by Cernos.

'You're safe here,' he nods, speaking in a thick accent. 'Modoc help you gain strength.'

You pull away the blankets, half-hoping that you might see a human body beneath – one free of the demon curse. But the black scales remain, glittering in the light from the narrow window.

'Nothing has changed.' You scowl, sliding your legs off the bed. 'Nothing will heal this.'

Modoc tilts his head to one side. 'Scars run deep, yes.'

You clench your fist, grimacing as the sharp nails draw blood. 'How far is it to Carvel?'

The healer gasps. 'No, you are not ready to leave. Need rest. Long rest.'

You glance over your shoulder, smirking when you see your newly-restored wings. You flex them, just to be sure. 'Rest?' Your eyes shift to Modoc, meeting his gaze. 'I will not rest, my friend. Not until I've had my revenge …'

Congratulations! You have now reached the end of this adventure and have earned yourself the title *The Dark Angel*. You may now turn to the epilogue.

832

Legendary monster: Nephele, Princess of the Damned

The serpentine bridge winds between a range of dark peaks, formed by the gigantic stalagmites spearing up out of the lake. As you pass round the last jagged tip, you feel a savage blast of wind against your face. Ahead, hovering above the last span of the bridge, is a pale-skinned woman clad in blue-crystal armour. A tattered cloak hangs off her shoulders, its edges lined with hoarfrost.

You advance warily, boots crunching through the slippery ice that coats the stone. The woman is watching you, eyes burning with a white fire. Her black hair has been scraped back from her brow, frozen into twisted bands.

As she floats closer, you recognise her face – it is the Lamuri princess from your vision; the one who was betrothed to Cernos and slain by the rune-sword, Ragnarok. Her dark spirit must have become trapped here after Barahar was defeated.

You raise your hands in an appeal of mercy, hoping to parlay with her – perhaps win her aid. But your movement draws an immediate scowl from her pale-blue lips. She points, and a blast of icy wind knocks you both off your feet.

'No, wait!' you implore, scrabbling across the frozen stone. 'I know what happened … Barahar took your life. I saw it!'

'You cannot reason with a demon!' growls Virgil. He pushes back his coat, drawing a pistol. Before you can stop him there is a deafening crack of gunfire. The bullet tears a bright strip through the air, but never reaches its target. A layer of ice quickly settles around it, crushing it to dust.

Virgil lowers his pistol with a disgruntled frown. 'Witchery …'

You lurch to your feet. 'Wait! Listen to me. We are looking for

Cernos!' You put deliberate emphasis on her lover's name. 'Perhaps you might help us . . .?'

'Cernos has already crossed!' she snaps icily. 'I knew he would come, to seek the broken blade. He will avenge us. He will bring this world to ruin, to suffer the pain that we have suffered!' Nephele drops to the bridge, the air around her bristling with frost. 'You will not stop us!'

The princess summons a frozen dagger to each hand then races forward, howling like a banshee. It is time to fight:

	Speed	*Magic*	*Armour*	*Health*
Nephele	14	11	11	90

Special abilities

- Aura of frost: Each time your damage score/damage dice causes health damage to Nephele, her frosty aura inflicts 2 damage to your hero, ignoring *armour*. (Note: if your blow reduces Nephele to zero *health*, you do not take damage from this ability.)
- Creeping chill: You must lose 2 *health* at the end of the first combat round. This damage increases by 1 each round. (At the end of the second round, you would lose 3 *health* and so on.) This ability ignores *armour*.

If you manage to defeat this cold-hearted sorceress, turn to **543**.

833

You dive through the archway, rolling across the uneven surface of books and broken rock. Above you the giant eel arches its long body, stretching back to reveal bloated scaly flesh glowing with arcane runes. Then it proceeds to make a disturbing series of choking sounds, the ribbed folds beneath its lower jaw bulging and contracting. The noise intensifies.

Suddenly the head jerks forward, belching a storm of pulpy missiles in your direction. You dodge out of the way, hearing the dull splatter of paper and digestive fluids break against the wall. As the creature's head rears back to take another shot, you beat your wings and take flight, aiming yourself at its scaled body. It is time to fight:

	Speed	*Brawn*	*Armour*	*Health*
Book wyrm	13	11	8	80

Special abilities

- Pulped fiction: At the end of every combat round, the wyrm spews paper bullets in your direction. Take a *speed* challenge. If the result is 19 or lower, you are hit by the pulp and must take 5 damage, ignoring *armour*. If the result is 20 or more, you dodged the pulp.

If you manage to defeat this over-sized trash compacter, turn to **554**.

834

For defeating Erkil, you may now help yourself to one of the following special items:

Runeplate pauldrons	**Erkil's hacker**	**Ironbeard band**
(cloak)	(left hand: axe)	(ring)
+2 speed +2 armour	+2 speed +4 brawn	+2 brawn
Ability: last defence	Ability: compulsion	Ability: counter

As a warrior, you may also take the following:

Titan stone
(talisman)
+1 speed
Ability: titan career

The stone is carved with powerful runes, allowing you to transform yourself into an elemental titan. While this item is equipped, the titan has the following special abilities:

Stone skin (co): Instead of rolling for a damage score, you can activate *stone skin*. This lowers your speed by 2. *Stone skin* can be removed at any time by winning a combat round, and choosing not to roll for damage. While in *stone skin*:

- If an opponent wins a combat round, roll a die. On a ⚀ or ⚁ result, their blow glances off your stone skin and they do not roll for damage.
- You cannot use any abilities other than *trample* (see below). Passive abilities that have already been applied (such as *bleed*) will continue to damage opponents.

Trample (co): Instead of rolling for a damage score, you can *trample*. Roll 3 damage dice and apply the result to each of your opponents, ignoring *armour*. You can only use *trample* once per combat.

If you are *hexed* then you have gained an extra reward, turn to 615. Otherwise, return to the quest map to continue your journey.

835

Determined not to let the imp escape you sprint after it, beating your wings to give you added momentum.

'Wait! Let it go!' shouts Virgil. 'It's a shadow scamp. You'll never catch it!'

Ignoring the witchfinder's protests, you continue your dogged pursuit of the thief. Just as you are about to finally grab a hold of it, there is a loud popping sound and it vanishes – only to reappear several metres ahead of you. The imp glances over its shoulder, giving another titter of laughter. You realise that this wily rogue will be harder to catch than you first thought.

To catch up with the thief, you will need to complete a *speed* challenge:

	Speed
To catch a thief	20

If you are successful, turn to 860. Otherwise, turn to 736.

836

Team battle (advanced): Krakatoa

(NOTE: You must have completed the team battle *Issakhar* to access this challenge.)

The ground buckles as a fist of rock punches up through the red granite. You pull Virgil away from the grasping fingers, noticing that their knuckled joints are riddled with carved runes. The hand makes another futile grab then disappears back through the hole, taking more of the ground with it. A bellowing screech comes from below, causing the hall to shake and tremble.

'Keep moving!' You stagger towards the open doorway, stone and dust showering around you. Another booming roar rattles your teeth, moments before the ground explodes once again. This time two fists break through, ripping apart the stonework and taking hold of the crumbling rock. The floor tilts, throwing you onto your stomach. The doorway – and your freedom – slope out of sight. You are sliding backwards, scrabbling for a handhold. Next to you, Virgil mutters something under his breath – a curse, or a prayer, perhaps.

Then the last of the granite breaks up and you are falling.

Directly below you is an island, dominated by some giant of a monster. You glimpse molten-glowing eyes and a body of black stone. Your wings stretch outwards, catching the thermals as you drop through the raining stone. You manage to slow your fall, wings beating furiously as you tumble down onto the island, sweat and dust stinging your eyes.

Virgil.

You look around frantically for the witchfinder. Then you catch sight of him – a pair of legs, kicking desperately from the jagged hole above you. Virgil is clinging to the edge.

You are about to go to his aid when a giant column of rock stomps down inches from your face. Bubbling lava spills from the cracks in the black rock, seeping around boulder-sized toes. You scramble backwards, eyes lifting to the colossus that towers into the haze.

The demon is nearly twenty foot tall, its open chest a raging furnace of flame. The creature lifts its huge fists above its head, preparing to bring them down and crush you. Even with your agile reflexes, you doubt you could avoid such an attack. You watch helpless as they prepare to descend, mouth still agape at the enormity of this hellish apparition.

Then something drops from above, cutting a frenzy of vivid white lines. Virgil has landed on the monster's nearest shoulder, stabbing his blades furiously into the rock. Molten liquid gushes from the wounds, venting hissing columns of steam. But his efforts appear in vain.

KRAKATOA CRUSH! With a roar like an avalanche the giant lurches back, swatting the witchfinder away as if he was nothing more than a pestering gnat.

In a tumble of coat tails, Virgil goes flailing over the magma lake, grasping for his hat as it is lifted away.

You spring to your feet, wings snapping outwards once again. Running to the edge of the island, you hurl yourself across the broiling, rock-encrusted waves. You snatch Virgil seconds before he hits the magma.

Then a huge fist comes sweeping around from out of nowhere. You feel the force of the blow against your side, smashing you and Virgil across the lake towards a curved wall of rock. You brace for impact, crashing straight through the black stone and out the other side, onto another floating island. When you finally slide to a halt you see Virgil hovering several metres away. Currents of air ripple around his body, supporting him as he floats above the lapping waves. Slowly, his body is lowered to the rock. His eyes are closed but he is still breathing.

Before you can reflect on this apparent miracle, the ground heaves and rolls. You twist around to see the giant pulling itself onto the island, its upper body dripping with rivulets of magma. You draw your weapons, wondering desperately how you can overcome such an immense adversary. Turn to 610.

837

A streak of crimson flashes through the air, blowing a fist-sized crater in the ground ahead of you. A woman's angry curse follows. You spin around, to discover a slender figure watching you from amongst the rubble, her scarlet cloak and armour dazzling against the soot-grey backdrop. Beneath the woman's raised hood you glimpse a narrow face, framed by short copper-red hair.

The woman draws back her bow, a crackling arrow of fire forming in its arch.

'Wait!'

The shaft leaps from her bow with a sizzling roar. Its aim is true and would have taken you straight in the chest – were it not for your preternatural foresight. You twist aside, letting the bolt punch another hole in the charred debris.

'Well, if that's how it's going to be!' You start forward, hands reaching for your weapons ... but then you hesitate. There is something familiar about the woman's face, the way she holds herself, the ring gleaming on the chain at her neck.

'Joss ...?'

The woman answers with a bitter scowl. 'I know you, betrayer. You're the one who murdered my Adam!'

Another bolt streaks through the air. You leap out of its path, feeling the heat of its passing against your face.

'He was not your husband,' you implore angrily, remembering back to your fight with the metal golem. 'The toymaker had taken him – turned him into a monster!'

For a moment there is silence. You realise that the woman is sobbing, her shoulders quivering. 'You left me. Left me ... if only you knew what you did, what I had to endure ...' She stops abruptly, her face hardening once again. As she raises her bow, her eyes blossom into orbs of crimson fire. 'You made me into this. YOU!'

'Joss! You have demon blood, I see it. We both do. But don't give into the rage. You can fight it.'

She throws back her head with a wild, hysterical laughter. 'Rage is all I have, fool. It's all you left me with!'

The ranger looses another arrow, then another – her hand moving blindingly fast. Left with no other choice, you throw yourself into a charge, dragging your weapons free with a sharp hiss of magic. Whatever happened to Joss in the shroud, it is clear she has now become a vessel for something darker and more powerful. It is time to fight:

	Speed	*Magic*	*Armour*	*Health*
Joss	13	11	11	80

Special abilities

- Blood hail: For each double that you roll for Joss's attack speed, you must automatically take 10 damage from the archer's arrows.
- Blood thief: Each time you take health damage from Joss (including from her *blood hail* ability), she heals 4 *health*. This ability cannot take Joss above her starting *health* of 80.

If you manage to defeat this demonic archer, turn to 598.

838

Congratulations, for defeating Nephele while *hexed* you have won the following rare item:

Prowler's handguards
(gloves)
+1 speed +4 brawn
Ability: sneak, prowler set
(requirement: hexed)

Once you have updated your hero sheet, return to the quest map to continue your journey.

839

The passage soon branches into multiple aisle ways, each crammed with shelving. As well as the customary books and carved tablets, you also spot bottles and jars, and casks filled with different-coloured crystals. Whenever you stop to take a closer look Virgil ushers you on, casting worried glances at his surroundings.

'Do not tarry,' he says. 'This place reeks with demon taint. Bad things happened here . . .'

All you can smell is musty dirt and old leather, but you decide to keep that to yourself. Eventually you come to a junction, where another aisle crosses your own. If you have the key word *barrier* on your hero sheet, turn to 619. Otherwise, turn to 868.

840

Searching the cave, you also discover one of the following rare treasures:

Widow's needle	**Carapace crest**	**Spider grips**
(left hand: sword)	(left hand: shield)	(gloves)
+2 speed +3 brawn	+2 speed +2 armour	+1 speed +2 brawn
Ability: piercing	Ability: webbed	Ability: sure grip
(requirement: rogue)	(requirement: warrior)	

Before you leave you help yourself to a trophy, to celebrate your victory over the spider. (Make a note of *Anansi's eye* on your hero sheet, it does not take up backpack space). If you have the *glaive of souls* equipped, turn to 450. Otherwise, return to the quest map to continue your adventure.

841

The ledge overlooks the main chamber of the volcano. Below you, through the sulphurous haze, you see bright tracks of lava cascading down into the lake.

The air here feels thin, as if the heat has seared it of all oxygen. You struggle for breath, putting a hand to the wall to steady yourself.

'Riven,' says Virgil, hoarsely. 'The curtain here is thin …'

You note the witchfinder's haggard demeanour, his scarred face glistening with sweat. Other than a shortness of breath, you don't seem to be suffering as badly as your companion.

'Is it your wound?' You look to his arm, where the ugly welts coil like red serpents.

He shakes his head, waiting out a dry, hacking cough. He wipes the spittle from his mouth with a shaking hand. 'The space between

… our world and the shroud …' he rasps. 'Dangerous. Possible anomaly …'

You turn your attention back to the ledge. It climbs steeply around the face of the rock, leading up to the building on its summit. Black smoke plumes from the four chimneys, jutting from its domed roof.

'What is that place?' you ask. 'We saw it from the bridge.'

'The crematorium,' Virgil wheezes. 'A sacred place to the dwarves.'

'Would they have put the sword there?'

Virgil looks doubtful. 'Ragnarok … is cursed. They'd give it greater protect—'

Suddenly the air bends and distorts above you, sending rippling waves washing against the rock. At the centre of the disturbance, a black hole rips open – rapidly getting wider and wider. A howling, freezing gale blasts you to your knees, deafening you with its dirge-like scream.

But that is nothing to the staggering roar that follows, an air-shredding landslide of elemental fury. You manage to raise your head, eyes watering from the chill wind, to see a ruined tower of black stone spinning out of the hole. Its walls and crenellations are frosted with ice, trailing white smoke as it careers straight into the side of the outcropping …

The explosion hurls you high into the air, sending you tumbling and spinning through a hailstorm of ice and rock. You try and open your wings, to slow your descent, but something slams into your stomach, flipping you over through the dust. A rock perhaps, or a body. You have lost all sense of direction, of whether you are facing up or down. There is only the wind, tearing at your body with its icy fingers, and the thunderous din of rocks breaking and smashing against each other.

The cold rapidly turns to heat, engulfing you in a stinging cloud of steam. In alarm, you realise you must be dropping towards the lake. All around you, there is a dull thud of debris hitting into something soft, viscous … like lava.

Then the mist clears and for the briefest of seconds you see an expanse of charred rubble racing up to meet you. Somehow, you manage to spread your wings, feeling the air push hard into the stretched membranes. But it is too little, too late. You slam into the ground, the sudden shock of pain dragging you straight into unconsciousness. Turn to 861.

842

You emerge in a rectangular room, piled high with rubble. A space has been cleared at its centre, where a series of runes have been marked out in congealed blood. They spiral like a coiled serpent, ending in a heap of gore and blackened bones at the centre.

'I don't need to be an expert to know this is bad,' you muse grimly.

Virgil has stopped, his one eye lifted to the ceiling. You follow his gaze, shrinking back in horror when you see the fleshy growth spread across the stonework.

'A magic anomaly,' says Virgil, dropping his voice to almost a whisper. 'Keep moving . . .'

He motions to the steps opposite, leading down into a vaulted hall. Nodding, you quickly cross the room, with one eye on the creature and the other on the strange runes. Evidently this chamber was used for some dark ritual, perhaps the one that summoned the blood demons you fought earlier.

At the foot of the stairs, a two-tiered hall stretches for several hundred metres, both levels lined with shelves of books and scrolls. Ghostly spirits are moving back and forth along the stacks, their bodies glowing with a sickly yellow light. At the far end of the hall, past heaps of rubble and several broken statues, is a large square table – and seated at it is a dwarf.

He is clad in mouldy white robes, embroidered with purple-glowing runes. The collar is flared, jutting out either side of his thin beardless face. You notice the dwarf's skin is green with rot, exposing dark hollows and bare bone.

'Yes . . . yes.' The dwarf is turning pages in a tome, his rheumy eyes roving back and forth behind a pair of iron-rimmed spectacles.

The rest of the table is a jumbled array of open books, stone tablets, bubbling potions and alchemical equipment. One of the ghosts flits over to the table, placing another book on an already teetering pile.

'Good, good! Out of my sight!' snaps the dwarf, ushering the ghost away with a rotted hand.

You notice that the only exit stands directly behind the undead librarian – a pair of obsidian doors, barred from the inside. With no other choice you make your way along the hall, wincing as your footfalls echo noisily in the chamber.

The dwarf looks up, his emaciated face cracking into a sneer. 'Silence in my library!' He slams his fists on the table, knocking over several bottles in the process. Their contents fizzle and hiss, the sound mirroring the seething snarl coming from his lips. 'They were too weak. Too stupid! But my loyal demons will succeed where they failed. You'll see!'

Virgil is at your side, his swords glowing bright with holy magic. 'A trapped spirit – undead. He probably thinks this is Tartarus, two thousand years ago.'

'I said SILENCE!' shrieks the dwarf. 'Back from whence you came, or be punished!'

Virgil takes a step forward, spinning his blades in his hands. 'We wish to leave, dwarf – but we're taking the door behind you. I suggest you comply with our wishes. Or else this will end . . . messily.'

The librarian jumps out of his seat, black magic sparking around him. 'What insolence! Spirits! To me! It seems we must rid ourselves of another nuisance from our library!'

One by one the ghostly spirits raise their arms. Motes of green light streak from their fingertips, surrounding the dwarf in a halo of swirling magic. 'Yes! YES! THE POWER!'

The dwarf rises up on the streaming currents, his frayed robes dancing about his thin body. 'The power of the Illumanti is mine!' He blurs forward, bolts of magic lancing from his rotted fingers. You leap over the deadly barrage, wings stretched taut as you sweep in to meet his attack. It is time to fight:

	Speed	*Magic*	*Armour*	*Health*
Molech	13	11	10	100
Spectres	–	–	4	40

Special abilities

- Spectral synergy: While the spectres remain alive, they boost Molech's power. At the end of each combat round, Molech heals 6 *health* (this cannot take him above his starting *health* of 100).

Also, Molech's attacks drain your strength. Each time you take health damage from Molech's damage score/damage dice, you must lower your *brawn* and *magic* by 1 for the duration of the combat.

In this combat you roll against Molech's speed. If you win a combat round, you can choose to apply your damage to Molech or the spectres. Once Molech is reduced to zero *health*, the combat is automatically won.

If you manage to defeat Molech, turn to 681. (Special achievement: If you manage to defeat Molech with the spectres still alive, turn to 880.)

843

You pull open the hinged doors, backing away as a wet mass of tubes spill out onto the ground. Covering your nose from the oily stench, you peer inside the exposed cavity. The tight space is filled with cogs and axles and grease-covered pipes. Pushing your hand deeper into the gooey innards, you discover something cold and hard at its centre. You rip it free from the wreckage, surprised to find that it is an unblemished crystal, still humming with magic.

If you wish, you may now take:

Golem core
(backpack)
A pulsing crystal filled
with dark energies

When you have updated your hero sheet, turn to 870.

844

You retrieve your pack. When you look back towards the pool, you see that Lorcan is untying the golden rod that was previously strapped to his back. He lifts it into the air, its magical radiance brightening as the flower-shaped headpiece starts to revolve.

You stare at him, baffled by the strange device.

His eyes meet your own, his scarred face attempting a semblance of a smile. 'I will see you again, prophet.'

'Wait!' You lunge forward – but you are too late. There is a bright flash of golden light, then the man is gone. Angrily, you kick at the stones where he had been standing, furious that you have been left with so many unanswered questions. But then your gaze falls on the far side of the canyon and the volcano, rising high into the hazy gloom. Thanks to Lorcan, you are now a step closer to Tartarus – and your final showdown with the demon, Cernos. (Return to the quest map to continue your adventure.)

845

Congratulations! You have created the following item:

Self-published tome
(left hand: spell book)
+2 speed +3 armour
Ability: surge

If you wish to create a different spell book, you can start the process again (turn to 850). Otherwise, you may now leave the chamber and continue your journey. Turn to 866.

846

Your eyes stray to the demonic bow. It is fashioned from lengths of wood and iron, twisted together to form a tangled arch of thorns.

Even the grip is bladed and sharp, capable of drawing blood from anyone brave enough, or foolish enough, to want to hold it.

If you wish, you may now take:

Agilax, the string of tears
(left hand: bow)
+2 speed +3 brawn
Ability: blood archer career

While this item is equipped, the *blood archer* has the following special abilities:

Blood hail (co): Instead of rolling for a damage score after winning a round, you can use *blood hail* to shower your enemies with arrows. Roll 2 damage dice and apply the result to each of your opponents, ignoring their *armour*. If any opponent is already inflicted with *bleed* from a previous round, then they take an extra 4 damage.
Blood thief (pa): For every ⚅ you roll for your damage score / damage dice, you may instantly restore 4 *health*. This cannot take you above your starting *health*.

Once you have made your decision, turn to **855**.

847

The iron doors have been barred from the inside. Together you lift the metal blocks and shove them aside, before pushing open the doors. They grate and squeal against thousands of years of grime, slowly opening out onto a narrow bridge. Across the other side you can see a projection of volcanic rock, crowned by four tower-like chimneys. Each one is belching a steady stream of smoke into the air, forming a dark pall above the nightmarish city. (Return to the quest map to continue your journey.)

848

The golden mirror rests perfectly between the two hands. The moment it clicks into place the sun's light hits the reflective disc, sending a golden beam streaking southwards through the cloudy mist. You cannot guess what purpose this device serves – perhaps some kind of signalling device. If you decide to leave the golden mirror in place, make a note of the keyword *sun seeker*. Otherwise, you may remove the mirror and take it with you again. When you have made your decision, turn to 587.

849

The hat and gloves float off towards the back of the shop. They disappear through a small doorway, returning a moment later with a silver chest. The ghost places it on the dusty counter, then flips open the lid. Inside you find several rare and unusual items.

You may purchase any of the following for 700 gold crowns each:

Runed rod	**Onyx blade**	**Golem core**
(backpack)	(backpack)	(backpack)
A splintered length of black metal	A crescent-shaped blade for a mighty weapon	A pulsing crystal filled with dark energies

If you wish to make further purchases, return to 557. Otherwise, you thank the ghostly proprietor and resume your journey (return to the map).

850

You begin by sliding the bronze plates into the metal frame. These plates contain the runes for your book. If you wish to choose the *runes of shadow*, turn to 530. If you would prefer to use the *glyphs of light*, turn to 624.

851

Virgil's sneer betrays a grim pleasure, as he drives his blades into the spirit's body. The hapless creature quickly unravels, leaving a shiny ring to drop to the ground. You crouch to retrieve it, surprised to discover that it is as light as air, its translucent bands fashioned from curls of dark smoke.

If you wish, you may now take:

Aethereal
(ring)
+1 armour +2 health
Ability: windblast

With little else of interest in the room, you decide to leave. Turn to 875.

852

You are surprised to discover that the note has been written in common, not dwarvish. Smoothing out the cracked parchment, you begin to read:

I must leave with the others. Too late now to save the city. The demons have no mercy. Trapped between two enemies. We should never have turned to them. I tried to stop it. Molech and the false whites. Blood rituals. They think it will save us.

The writing on the second part of the note has become more erratic, as if it was written in haste:

I did my duty. The demons are all around us. Tartarus will fall. No one can say I didn't do my duty. The secrets are safe. If only I was stronger. Molech and the demons have control. Barahar will fall. They will destroy the sword. But the price is too high. Too high . . .

The writing ends suddenly. You are unsure if is deliberate or if the scribe was distracted and never got to finish their message. 'Who are the false whites?' you ask Virgil, handing over the note. The witch-finder studies it with a frown.

'Possibly Illumanti. I've heard them called white robes on account of their attire. They are the high sect of mages in each dwarven city. This confirms my suspicions.' He crumples the parchment in his fist. 'They summoned demons to fight Barahar. And in doing so, they lost their city.'

Will you:

Examine the crystal ball?	659
Search the shelves?	711
Leave?	858

853

The passage slopes for several hundred metres, before levelling out into a hall of granite pillars. Between each pillar there is a statue of a dwarf, a stone urn resting at each set of feet.

'The vault of ashes,' says Virgil, his voice echoing in the still silence. 'These are the kings of Tartarus.'

You step closer to the nearest effigy. It depicts a stern-faced dwarf, dressed in thick plates of armour. In his runed gauntlets rests a two-handed hammer, almost as tall as himself.

Standing opposite is another statue – a dwarf in flowing robes patterned with intricate sigils. In place of a hammer, he holds a staff. As you continue along the hall, you pass a further four statues, arranged in pairs. When you come to the end, only a single king stands sentinel – holding a sceptre and a staff. The opposite sepulchre is empty.

'Always two kings to rule the twin thrones,' states Virgil. 'Their last was never laid to rest.' He kneels beside the vacant pedestal, studying the angular script. 'Erkil Giantsbane. King of the Hammer.'

'He must have escaped with the survivors,' you conclude.

Virgil shrugs. 'Or died somewhere in the city. Guess, we'll never know ...'

At the end of the corridor, a set of winding stairs leads you into another vaulted hall. Passages to either side stretch away into darkness, their high walls lined with hundreds of tiny alcoves.

'This must be where they kept the rest of their dead,' says Virgil, peering down one of the passages. 'The dwarves believed they were born of fire and earth. When they died their ashes were interred in vaults. This is the first I've—'

A sharp, wracking cough echoes in the chamber, making you both jump.

You turn to see a ghostly figure slouched in the corner of the hall. Its entire body is black with smoke, twisting and broiling like a thundercloud.

'Demon!' Virgil marches forward, his inscribed blades ready to strike.

Startled, the creature struggles to stand, its wispy fingers groping at the stone. 'Ah, not so hasty ... I cannot accede to such a title. I am but a rune spirit, and a minor one at that.' He gives another wheezing cough.

'An elemental of air,' scowls Virgil.

The creature blows a stream of smoke from its mouth. 'Alas, I am more a sigh than a squall.'

Virgil holds one of his blades to the spirit's throat. The ghost jerks back, shuddering in fear. 'Those ... those are words of death,' it gasps, glaring at the inscriptions. 'I have not seen their like before.'

'Then you've been here a long time,' replies the witchfinder. 'These words spell your death.'

The spirit raises a hand. 'Wait! If you help me, I will give you something. Something precious.'

'Lies!' The blade edges closer.

'Wait, Virgil.' You place a hand on his shoulder, urging restraint. 'Perhaps we should hear what it has to say?'

The spirit nods quickly. 'Wiser words, oh yes. I came here looking for the gate – the rune gate. It will take me back to the shroud.' He breaks off into a series of hacking coughs. 'My body ... so weak...'

'What happened?' you urge impatiently.

'Got caught ... by Nyx, the dark wind. Was almost scattered, lost ... but I managed to find calm, safety. But too weak ... I was so close.'

'Are you saying the dwarves have a portal?' Virgil sounds sceptical. 'Where does it lead?'

'Another dwarf city,' rasps the spirit. 'But they destroyed the gate ... when the archdemon came. To stop the evil spreading.'

'If it's destroyed, then what use is it?' you ask suspiciously.

'I can re-activate the runes, change the magic. It will take me back to the shroud, back where I belong.'

Virgil shakes his head. 'This spirit is a trickster. Do not trust its words.'

'And if we help you, what do we get in return?' you ask.

'My master's treasures are nearby – I show you where, after you help me – yes?'

Will you:

Ask the spirit why it is here in Tartarus?	857
Agree to help the spirit?	879
Allow Virgil to end its life?	851
Leave and continue your journey?	875

854

As you progress along the passageway the rumbling sound gets gradually louder, causing the tablets to rattle on their shelves. Many books lies scattered across the ground.

Eventually you pass an arched doorway in the west wall. Peering through, you are surprised to discover an immense circular shaft rising several hundred feet to a domed ceiling. Its walls are lined with row upon row of shelves, linked by a series of chain ladders.

Many of the shelves in the room are empty – and as the walls continue to tremble, more books tumble through the dusty air. The booming sound is coming from the sea of papers and bindings that now carpet the ground.

'There!' Virgil points to the far side of the chamber. He has spotted the jumbled surface bucking and shifting, as if something was moving beneath it. The shape is zigzagging towards you, the thunderous rumbling getting louder and louder . . . .

Suddenly the top layer of books is flung into the air, sending loose pages fluttering in all directions. An immense eel-like head rises out of the makeshift sea, its toothless jaws dripping with shattered rock and pulped fragments of parchment. You duck back into the passageway as it lunges forward, seeking to swallow you whole.

Will you:

Enter the chamber and fight the wyrm?	833
Continue south along the passage?	842

855

The sound of battle draws you to the edge of a wide, smoking crater. Twisted lengths of iron and steel poke out of the debris like stark winter trees, forming a tight forest with Virgil at its centre. The witchfinder is facing off against some strange metal contraption, which seems intent on slicing him to ribbons with its brutal assortment of knives and saws. With each lurching movement, lightning flashes between the crystals protruding from the golem's head, sending flickering veins of light coursing over its rusted body.

Grabbing one of the metal bars, you hurl it like a spear. The dull end bounces uselessly off the golem's thick plated armour, leaving little more than a shallow dent. But it has served its purpose – gaining the golem's attention. The contraption turns to face you, its grilled mouthpiece belching a furious cloud of steam. It is time to fight:

	Speed	*Brawn*	*Armour*	*Health*
Sparkacus	14	11	11	90

Special abilities

- Chaotic current: Each time your damage score/damage dice causes health damage to Sparkacus, your hero must take 4 damage in return, ignoring *armour*. If you have the *insulate* ability, you can ignore this damage.
- Body of metal: The automaton is immune to *bleed, disease, piercing* and *venom*.

If you manage to defeat this hulking contraption, turn to 883.

856

After brushing ink over the bronze plates, you lower them onto the paper. When you lift up the cross-piece, you are pleased to see that the parchment is now marked with your chosen sigils. Your book is almost complete; all that remains is to bind the loose pages. If you wish to choose *a binding of black iron*, turn to 845. If you would prefer to choose *a binding of drake scales*, turn to 539.

857

'Not my choice, not mine,' the spirit blusters. 'I was bound here by the dwarves – dragged from the shroud to obey their commands. But when the rune was broken, I managed to escape. Now I just want to go home. I deserve that, don't I?'

'Demons deserve only one thing,' growls Virgil. 'And that is death.'

Will you:

Agree to help the spirit?	879
Allow Virgil to end its life?	851
Leave and continue your journey?	875

858

You may leave via the south exit, where the echoing rumble can still be heard (turn to 854), or take the east passage (turn to 839).

859

The dwarf gives an impatient sigh, then starts gesturing frantically at the stacked shelves.

'Look! Look at it! Isn't it obvious? This is my section, mine, but they're missing – I can't risk it, I can't go and get them. The librarian … and the creature. The big creature. Oh, what am I to do?'

He resumes his agitated pacing.

'We could go get them,' you state hopefully, giving Virgil a sideways glance. The witchfinder rolls his eyes and looks away. 'What exactly are you looking for?'

'The shame. The shame.' The dwarf drifts over to the opposite wall, looking despondently at an empty space in the row of books. 'Pondicut's Beneficiary Substitutionary Perambulations, *volume fifty-seven! It's missing! Gone! And here ...'* He gestures to another space, then scratches furiously at his beard. 'Impractical Lyrical Alchemical Diologies, *book thirty-seven, part six. Irreplaceable. The only copy! Master will be furious!'* The dwarf continues to reel off a list of books as he floats down the aisle way.

Virgil clucks his tongue in annoyance. 'Okay, we get the picture – I think we need to clear the library of its ... resident wildlife.' He gives you a wearisome look. 'Then this ghostly servant can finish his task.' He strides past the ghost, tipping his hat.

The ghost doesn't acknowledge him, too busy rambling through another list of titles with far too many consonants. '... Episkeletal Supracostal Dichotomies of a Curmudgeon. *Gone! It's a fright!'* (Make a note of the keyword *spooks* on your hero sheet.) Turn to 866.

860

You manage to snatch one of the thief's pouches, ripping it free from its cord. (You have regained your stolen backpack item as well as 50 gold crowns.) As you tumble into a dive, you make a grab for the thief's legs. There is another popping sound ...

You crash down onto your stomach with a pained cry. Looking up, you see no sign of the imp. It has simply vanished.

Then you hear a peal of laughter, coming from behind you.

You twist around, to see the thief hurrying back down the passage. Cursing with frustration, you push off in pursuit once more. Turn to 675.

861

You awaken to dust. It billows everywhere, throwing a hazy veil over your bleak surroundings. A grim silence hangs as heavily, with only the occasional skitter of rocks to unsettle it.

Tentatively, you push yourself to your feet, surprised that you feel no pain, save for a dull ache from your ribs and shoulders. It appears the demon blood has healed you once again.

As you stagger through the fog you glimpse bright rivers of lava, lapping between the islands of debris. The strange tower must have crashed down into the lake or on one of the many rock shelves jutting from the cavern wall.

The going is slow and treacherous, the precarious mounds of rock constantly shifting beneath your weight. With patience, you manage to reach the top of one of the higher peaks, affording you a better view of the mist-shrouded wasteland. If you have the keyword *blood debt* on your hero sheet, turn to 837. Otherwise, turn to 855.

862

You scoop up a rock and charge the monk. For a split second Ventus' eyes widen in surprise, then his familiar scowl returns. He swipes his fists through the air, cutting white trails of light towards your chest. The blow would have hit you, and possibly ended your life there and then, but a blast of black magic slams into his side, blowing him back into the opposite wall.

As his smoking body slides to the ground, he fixes you with a contemptuous glare. 'Foolish cur ... it's the witch ...'

Suddenly, your surroundings start to blur, sweeping into ribbons of ochre light. You hear a woman's laughter – cold and shrill – reverberating all around you. Then you lurch forwards, as if pushed by some invisible hand, to find yourself standing in a ruined building. A female tigris lies sprawled at your feet, blood pooling around her broken body. It is Scowler. Turn to 435.

863

After brushing ink over the bronze plates, you lower them onto the paper. When you lift up the cross-piece, you are pleased to see that the parchment is now marked with your chosen sigils. Your book is almost complete; all that remains is to bind the loose pages. If you wish to choose *a binding of black iron*, turn to 826. If you would prefer to choose *a binding of drake scales*, turn to 816.

864

A crackling bolt of magic streaks overhead, smashing into Cernos and blowing him backwards. A second barrage sends him sprawling over the side of the balcony, his tattered wings flapping uselessly as his body drops from view. There is the briefest echo of a scream, then silence.

It takes a moment for you to gather your wits, so suddenly has your fortune changed. You roll onto your stomach – even this simple action eliciting a grunt of pain. Your wounds have already healed, but Cernos' magic has left knives of agony, stabbing through your chest and shoulders.

But the pain is quickly forgotten when you look upon your would-be rescuer.

A ragged, tattered shape stumbles towards you. It is drenched in blood and gore, looking more demon than man. The figure cradles an arm against its chest. It ends in a stump, bandaged with rags of cloth.

'Virgil . . .?'

Magic still courses over the fingers of his remaining hand. You have never seen him call on his witchfinder's power before. Such an act, coupled with the dark menace of his hollowed expression, suggest that he is no longer himself.

You rise cautiously. A quick glance over your shoulder confirms that Cernos has gone – consumed by the magma lake. The ground gives another shudder, the lava splashing noisily against the rocks below.

'All is lost . . .' Virgil staggers towards the blade, its runes pulsing with demonic light. 'So many … evils …'

Too late, you realise his intentions. 'No, Virgil!' You start forward to head him off, but a bolt of magic flares from his hand, punching into your stomach and lifting you off your feet. You would have gone flying over the balcony, following Cernos into the fiery maelstrom, if not for your quick reflexes. You grab a finger of rock, claws squealing across the stone as they find purchase, halting you at the very edge of the precipice. Before you can recover, Virgil has grabbed the blade, its barbed hilt sinking into his scarred hand. 'No … Virgil! Don't do this!'

The witchfinder raises the blade, his bloodied face lit by its crimson runes. His gold teeth flash in a bitter smile. 'I was weak … too weak … but now I know what I must sacrifice!'

Magic ripples along the blade, coursing up his arm and across his chest. You hear the crackle of heat, accompanied by the sickening stench of burnt flesh. Then the ground lurches violently, throwing you back against the finger of rock. As you right yourself, you look back to Virgil … and give a gasp of horror when you see a demon staring back at you. Night-black scales coat the broad, muscular body, reflecting the flames that now lick along the edge of the blade. The walls ring with laughter. Deep. Resonating.

'With Ragnarok, I will free this world … free it from the shackles of pain and torment.' A single, crimson eye burns menacingly from the shadows. Golden fangs glitter a cruel smile. 'By fire, I will purge all sin and corruption. I will cleanse these lands. In the name of Ragnarok!'

'No!' You surge forward, your weapons spinning into your hands. 'Not this day, demon!'

It is time to fight:

	Speed	*Brawn*	*Armour*	*Health*
Virgil	15	12	12	120 (*)
Damned soul	–	–	6	40
Damned soul	–	–	6	40
Damned soul	–	–	6	40

Special abilities

- Damned souls: At the start of the third combat round, Ragnarok will release three damned souls from its blade. These souls each inflict 2 damage, ignoring *armour*, at the end of each combat round.

- Dark judgement: If Virgil rolls a double for his attack speed (before or after a re-roll) and the damned souls are in play, each soul is healed for 6 *health*. This ability cannot take the damned souls above their starting *health* of 40.
- Harvest soul: If Virgil wins a round and inflicts health damage, Ragnarok will heal him for the same amount of damage (after *armour* has been taken into account). This ability cannot take Virgil above his starting *health* of 120.

In this combat you roll against Virgil's *speed*. If you win a combat round, you can choose to apply your damage to Virgil or a damned soul (if they are in play – see *Damned souls* ability). Once Virgil is reduced to 10 *health* or less, the combat is automatically won and any remaining souls are also defeated.

If you manage to survive this demonic onslaught, turn to 503.

865

'Its origins are unknown,' says Avian, his brow furrowing. 'Some say it is an imprisoned demon, others that it is a dark fragment from the very core of our world. Whatever it is, when its powers are bolstered it is capable of destruction on a scale we have not seen this age.'

'Ragnarok.' Virgil flicks a pistol into his hand and proceeds to pour a vial of powder into its casing. 'A Skard word. Means destroyer of worlds.'

Avian nods. 'Barahar was able to level entire cities with its might – and worse, those slain by the blade become damned to follow the blade-wielder and fight for their cause. Barahar's dark crusade took him south, out of Skardland and across the western regions of Valeron. By the time he reached the jungles of Terral he had an army of thousands, bound to serve his will.'

'The Lamuri ...' You grimace, thinking back to the vision that you saw in the throne room of the ruined city. 'He razed their cities, their temples ... then he came here. Why?'

Avian lifts his gaze to the dwarven city, suspended above the lakes of magma. 'I doubt there was a method to such madness. Barahar wanted to destroy – unmake this world and bring it to ruin. The dwarves just happened to be the next obstacle in his way.' Avian scratches at his stub of beard. 'Arrogance was his downfall, but I fear, when the dwarves broke the sword and shattered its power, the souls imprisoned by the blade were finally released…' You follow Avian's gaze to the shapes writhing and squirming across the walls of the city. 'Now they are tortured spirits, that will never know rest.'

Return to 590 to ask another question, or turn to 766 to continue your journey.

866

You enter what appears to be a reading room, with a dozen stone tables arranged on various levels. Each table is lit by a central cluster of crystals, glimmering with a pale-blue luminescence.

There are two corridors leading from the room, one to the east and one to the south. Both are lined with shelves, stacked full of tablets, scroll cases and books. The aisle to the south is partially blocked by rubble. A distant rumbling can be heard coming from that direction, rising and falling in undulating waves.

The north wall of the chamber is dominated by a door of blue crystal. As you approach it, you suddenly get the uneasy feeling that you are being followed. You glance down at the ground, noticing an unexplained shadow edging closer to your own. It can't be Virgil, who is several steps ahead…

You spin around, giving a cry of alarm when you catch a thief with their hands in your backpack!

The creature stands no taller than your waist, with purple skin, pointed ears and a bristly fuzz of green hair. A number of pouches and bags hang from its leather clothing, all bulging with items. The thief responds with a tittering laughter, then turns and runs – making for the east passage. You notice that one of your backpack items is clutched in the thief's hands. (You must choose one backpack item to remove from your hero sheet. Keep a note of its description as it may be returned to you at a later time.)

Will you:

Chase after the thief?	**835**
Stay and examine the crystal door?	**809**
Take the south exit?	**854**

867

Your eyes sweep the length of the cave, passing over mounds of rotting meat and animal skins, to finally rest on the far wall, where flickering candles illuminate a line of cadavers. Some are animal, but most are human, dangling from vine ropes attached to a wooden beam.

Then a wet squelch drags your attention to a side chamber, where a fresher corpse is laid out on a flat-topped boulder. An old woman in tattered hides is hunched over the body, drawing out the entrails and studying them with cackling glee.

She spins around, sensing your presence, her gnarly hand snapping forward with lightning speed. You glimpse something whip through the air, clipping the side of your head. Before you have a chance to register what has happened, you see the woman holding a hooked tooth tied to a cord. She plucks something from its end, then lifts up her other hand, revealing a bone doll. Too late – you realise she has one of your hairs and is now wrapping it around the doll. As the witch yanks it tight, you give a gargling cry as pain crushes your ribs, stealing your breath away. She tugs it again, engulfing you in a fresh wave of agony. Angrily you lope forward, your cries turning to a roar of defiance as you seek to end this witch's dark magic. It is time to fight:

	Speed	*Magic*	*Armour*	*Health*
Cave witch	7	7	4	50

Special abilities

Voodoo magic: At the end of each combat round, the witch twists the hair around her voodoo doll. This automatically inflicts 1 die of damage, ignoring *armour*.

If you manage to defeat the wicked witch, turn to 765.

868

Glancing down one of the aisles you notice a set of iron bars, blocking the doorway to another chamber. Runes have been carved into the black metal, several of which are still glowing with a soft red light.

Will you:

Take a closer look?	696
Continue on your way?	842

869

You stand over the bloody remains of the three demons. Virgil picks up a piece of tattered cloth and uses it to clean the ichor off his blades. 'This does not bode well,' he sighs, glancing down at one of the bodies. 'Those demons are the result of a blood ritual – a sacrifice.'

'Why does that surprise you? Barahar would surely stoop to such evils.' You clamber over the rocks and enter the passageway. Your sharp sight adjusts to the darkness, revealing a tight corridor that continues for thirty metres then opens out into another chamber.

'I don't think it was Barahar,' says Virgil, hopping over the stones to join you. 'Blood rituals take time, preparation. Not his style.'

'The dwarves, then?' You glance back at the witchfinder, frowning. 'Perhaps that is why they were fighting each other – to stop the rituals.'

Virgil shrugs. 'When your people are dying, your homes under threat, fear is a breeding ground for weakness – and mistrust.' He lowers one of his swords to the rubble. The bright blade picks out the decapitated head of a stone titan, its mouth hanging open in a silent scream. 'I don't think Barahar is to blame for this – some group took it on themselves to try and save Tartarus, and were willing to resort to sacrifice and magic to achieve it.'

'We can't judge them for what happened here.' You remember the cursed Lamuri city, crawling with undead.

'I'm a witchfinder,' states Virgil coldly. 'It's my duty to judge.'

He slips past you, leading the way down the corridor. You follow, eyes roving over the melted carvings along the wall. They would have once shown scholars standing at lecterns, but now the stretched, distorted stone has made them look like tormented spirits, being sucked down into some dark abyss. Their hands reach skywards, begging for absolution.

You emerge in an octagonal chamber with corridors angling to the north and south. To the north the passage ends in an arched doorway, leading through to a room dominated by a strange-looking machine. To the south the walls are lined with stone shelves, neatly stacked with runed tablets and bound tomes.

Will you:

Take the north exit?	611
Take the south exit?	802

870

The mist has started to recede, revealing the full scale of the devastation. As you suspected, there is little left of the tower save for the rubble-strewn islands dotting the lava shelf.

Above you a huge chunk has been ripped out of the rock, where the tower collided with the dwarven outcropping. Thankfully, a section of the ledge remains intact, winding up to the dark building perched on its summit. You flex your wings, hoping they are strong enough to carry you and Virgil back to the ledge.

You will need to take a *speed* test :

	Speed
Wing and a prayer	18

If you are successful, turn to 768. Otherwise, turn to 881.

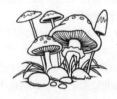

871

Boss monster: The traitors' tower

'And so they shall fall to darkness, and never rise again' Jenlar Cornelius

The walls weep with blood. It is everywhere, coating the sticky flesh that clings to every inch of stone. The air reeks with it – an overpowering metallic stench that sickens your stomach. But the grotesqueness of your surroundings pales in comparison to the demons that now assault you. Some may have been dwarves once, before they were twisted by the dark magics of this place. Others are little more than slabs of flesh, bristling with teeth and claws.

They are the only thing that stands between you and Cernos. The demon is only metres away. One hand grips the heart of fire, its heat washing out in waves. The other moves across a runed door, probing its magical defences. Avian lies crumpled at the demon's feet. It is impossible to tell if he is alive or dead – the remnants of his dented armour hang off his white tunic and breeches, now dirt-spattered like the rest of him.

So close … if not for the infuriating mass of blood-soaked creatures that stand in your way. Angrily, you hack and slash at the slick bodies. With Cernos now in sight, they seem insignificant – merely a distraction. You need to reach him … reach the heart that will give you your freedom – a cure for the curse.

But the demons' numbers seem endless. As soon as one is cut down, there is another to take its place, gibbering and clawing to reach you. An axe-shaped appendage flies out of the chaos, biting into your shoulder. Roaring with pain, you sever the demon's limb, using your return swing to scythe through its gore-soaked body, taking several more of the frenzied horde with it.

At the corner of your vision, a white hot light blazes through the sea of bodies. It is accompanied by the high-pitched screams of dying demons. The inscribed blades shred through the dark host as if they were stalks of corn, each deliberate cut and thrust sending crimson sprays showering across the hall. And at the centre of this maelstrom is Virgil. His scowling visage is bathed in the light of his holy inscriptions. It is difficult to distinguish the man from the demons, such is the vehemence etched into his face.

A hot stab of pain. A bone sword has pierced straight through your thigh, coming out the other side. Another blow knocks you sideways. Blood squelches underfoot as you struggle to keep your balance. A demon leaps onto your back, its teeth snapping at your neck. You spin, cracking open your wings to send it flailing back into the mob. The pain has gone, as it always does – your demon blood healing the wounds. But in its place comes the rage . . . overpowering. Intoxicating. Impossible to resist.

Snarling, you thrust your weapon into a demon's snapping mouth. Its body twists away, taking the weapon with it. Another creature leaps for you, but you manage to deflect them with your arm, using your spines to drive them back.

Desperately, you drag the sword from your thigh, intending to use it as a substitute – but it is so slick with gore that it slips from your fingers. Instead you are forced to use your claws and spines, slashing and raking at the gaunt, red bodies – your bestial snarls mingling with their own.

You don't remember those final minutes – or perhaps even hours – of the battle. When the blind rage subsides, drawing a sharp gasp from your lips, you find yourself surrounded by bodies. Hundreds of them, scattered in piles. You struggle to your feet, limbs dragging like leaden weights. There is something moving near the far wall – a thin, red demon. It is struggling to pull itself free from the carnage. You retrieve your weapons, then stumble towards it. Death would be a mercy, even for these abominations.

But when the head turns, you gasp as you see it is Virgil. His coat has been ripped to shreds, hanging in tatters from his sinewy body. His patch has been pulled away, exposing the dark hollow of his missing eye. Red grime covers him from head to foot, plastering his hair to his scalp.

He pulls himself to the wall and rests his back against it, his expression pained. 'It will never end,' he grunts, his voice raw and hoarse. 'This will never end.'

You look to the runed door. It stands closed, with no sign of Cernos or Avian. They must have passed through, heading deeper into the palace. When you turn back to Virgil, you see that he is weeping. Only then do you notice that his right hand is missing, the bloody stump pressed tight to his chest. 'It's over for me …. It's over.'

You start to speak, but the words die quickly. The silence lengthens.

Virgil glares up at you, scowling through his tears. 'I have hunted demons all my life. I know them better than anybody. And what good has it ever done me? I even watched my wife … my daughter …' He clenches his teeth, their bright gold darkened by blood. 'What hope is there … for this world, when there is so much … so many … evils.' He rests his head against the wall.

'There will always be good men, Virgil. Crusaders like yourself.' You crouch to retrieve his hat, brushing the flecks of demon from its brim.

'Good men,' hisses Virgil. He snorts with amusement. 'I'm no good man. I lied to you, demon. I lied to you.'

You meet his gaze.

'There is no cure for your malady. Modoc can't change what you have become. The demon blood … there is no cure. Only … death.'

The words cut deeper than any demon's blade; a wound that your blood can never heal.

'No …' Your stomach lurches, your chest tightening with a wave of panic and fear. *No cure.*

You say the words to yourself, as if struggling to understand the enormity of their meaning.

'I needed you … to track Cernos … I needed you to help me.' Virgil winces, shifting his weight to the other shoulder. 'For what's it worth … I'm sorry.'

You blink back tears. Words seem meaningless now. Hope seems meaningless now. All you have ever wanted is your freedom – to escape the past, the inquisition, this demon curse … But now you know that you can never be free. *I have become a monster.*

You glare at the witchfinder, wanting to feel anger. Hate. Betrayal. Instead, there is only a chill emptiness. *I am a demon. That is my fate.*

You offer him the hat.

'You keep it,' he smiles wanly. 'I think its luck finally wore out…'

If you wish, you may now take:

Puritan's peak
(head)
+2 speed +2 armour
Ability: charm, heal

You look back to the runed door. Ragnarok must be nearby – the dark blade that once belonged to Barahar. If Cernos takes the sword, then he will have the means of wreaking vengeance and destruction on the world – delivering the same misery and horror that has destroyed Tartarus and left the Lamuri cities forever cursed.

'Kill Cernos …' whispers Virgil, as if reading your thoughts. 'Just promise me you'll do that.' His breath rattles in the silence.

You are already headed for the door, splashing through the bloody mire. Four runes have been carved across its face, each set within a square panel. Distracted by the battle, you did not see what Cernos did to open the door. You push against the heavy stone, but it doesn't budge. Clearly, you will need to press one or more of the panels to unlock some hidden mechanism.

Will you:

Press the hammer rune? 886
Press the fire rune? 710
Press the crescent rune? 774
Press the shield rune? 894

872

As you cross the courtyard, Virgil spots something amongst the rubble. He calls a halt, crouching down next to a jagged piece of rock. Blood has been smeared across it.

'What is it?' You notice that there is a deliberate pattern to the stain. 'Another blood ritual?'

Virgil shakes his head. 'This is Avian's mark. A sign he's still alive.'

Your eyes quickly scan the rubble, half-expecting to see a body – or perhaps Cernos, lying in wait. Instead you spot a further trail of blood, winding through the ash and grime. It leads to a stepped walkway, which spirals up to the last tier of the dwarven city.

Angrily, Virgil scuffs the mark into the dirt. 'He knew this place would be the end of him. He knew and still he came …'

You turn in surprise. 'He is a prophet?'

Virgil snorts. 'Hardly. His fate was foretold by another. Jenlar Cornelius. A member of our order. Jenlar saw many deaths for Avian, but each one he has cheated. This one, I am starting to wonder...'

You frown. 'You mean the visions can be wrong?'

'Right, wrong. I don't pretend to know the way of it.'

'But Durnhollow ... what I saw ...'

He notes your look of bewilderment. 'Look, I live by my wits and my blades. If we're talking destiny now ...' He shrugs. 'Avian once told me that destiny was for fools and dreamers. I think he was right. We all have a choice.'

You look past his shoulder to the dark sprawl of the city. Dawn has started to creep over the crater's edge, steadily dressing the towers and minarets in silvery threads of light. For the briefest of moments it is as if time has flowed backwards, and you are gazing upon the true majesty of Tartarus as it once was, all of those thousands of years ago.

You lower your head with a sigh. 'I saw my own death, here – at the foot of the mountain. Cernos will take Ragnarok. We will fail to stop him.'

Virgil rises to stand at your side. 'Then we must cling to a fool's hope. One of us has to change the future.' (Return to the quest map to continue your journey.)

873

For defeating Krakatoa, you may now help yourself to one of the following special items:

Avalanche	**Stone of disillusion**	**Kraka's crown**
(main hand: staff)	(left hand: spell book)	(head)
+2 speed +6 magic	+3 speed +5 magic	+2 speed +5 magic
Ability: shatter	Ability: confound	Ability: command

When you have made your decision, turn to **651** if you still need to choose rewards, or **545** to continue.

874

Quest: The Crematorium

(NOTE: You must have completed the orange quest *The Abussos* before you can access this location.)

Bile splatters against the wall, eating through the rock in a hissing cloud of steam. You grab Virgil and push him ahead, aware that the giant centipede is closing in fast. The cavern rings with the endless tapping of its many chitinous legs.

'I need to heal.' Virgil staggers dizzily. He cradles his burnt arm to his chest, the shreds of cloth mingling with the blood and seared flesh.

'Keep going!' you urge, shoving him forward. 'We'll make it!'

Across the cave, a row of stalagmites block the face of the wall. They spear upwards to meet the stalactites hanging down from the ceiling, together forming a colonnade of crystal-glowing rock. A natural barrier.

You push Virgil between the columns. As you move to follow, you risk a look over your shoulder – and wish you hadn't. Your vision is filled with a nightmarish mishmash of spines and mandibles. The creature shows no signs of slowing, its hundreds of legs driving it forward at an alarming speed . . .

There is a loud crack.

The centipede's spiked head smashes into the columns, crumpling through the stone and filling the air with dust. You reel behind Virgil, who is already half-running and half-stumbling along the makeshift corridor. Ahead you spy a narrow opening in the wall, little more than a jagged crevice. The witchfinder has also seen it, quickening his pace. Behind you the giant monster shrieks with rage, knocking through the columns like a ball through skittles.

Just as the ensuing dust cloud is about to engulf you, your hands find the opening. Cloth and scales rip on the gnarled rock as you push yourself into the claustrophobic space. A second later and the black body of the insect hurtles past, its immensity filling your narrow view with shell and spines. Then it is gone, skittering away with an angry screech.

The crevice brings you out into another cavern, lit by pillars of multi-coloured crystals. Virgil is gasping for breath as he struggles one-handed to pull a gourd from his coat.

'Need … tonic.' He lifts the gourd to his mouth, clamping his gold teeth around the cork and yanking it free. You glance down at his burnt arm, wincing at the sight of the terrible wound. For once, the injury was not the work of demons, but Virgil's own pistol – the heated powder having exploded in its chamber.

He starts to raise the gourd to his lips, then gives a dismissive grunt. 'Ah, to Allam with it.' He tips the contents over his ravaged arm. The flesh smokes and sizzles, dragging a sobbing cry from his cracked lips. He staggers back as the skin continues to cauterise, becoming an ugly stretch of scarred tissue. 'Never did like taking medicine,' he gasps between gritted teeth.

'At least we lost the bug.' You look back towards the crevice, wondering if the creature will try and pummel its way through. Since first encountering the oversized centipede, it has proved a persistent foe, chasing you through nearly a mile of tunnels and caves.

'It will find us again, have no doubt.' Virgil rests his back against the wall, clenching and unclenching his maimed hand. 'Let's just be grateful for this reprieve.'

'I wouldn't get too settled …'

Virgil looks up, following your gaze.

Carved into the opposite wall is a colossal throne of black obsidian – and seated on it is a stone giant, its body patched with shards of bright-glowing crystal.

The witchfinder slides a pistol from his coat. When he catches your look he returns a guilty smile. 'Don't worry. It's my last one. Explosions are rare, mostly…'

Before you can deliver a reprimand, you hear a dull rumbling coming from the far wall. The throne is shaking, releasing thick curtains of stone and dust.

'That doesn't look good,' you grimace.

Through the thickening haze, you can make out movement – the giant's hands are pushing down on the throne, heaving its immense body forward. Then, with a grating sigh, the giant rises up, its gem-encrusted crown scraping the cavernous ceiling, nearly a hundred feet above you.

The witchfinder glances at his pistol. 'We're gonna need a bigger gun.'

Slowly, the giant's head tilts forward, angling its stone gaze at the floor of the cave. '*Tourmalus protect. Tourmalus obey.*' The voice seems to come from everywhere at once, amplified by the smooth, curved walls of the chamber.

Virgil moves to your side, grunting with pain as he draws his sword from its scabbard. You follow his lead, your enchanted weapons spinning into your hands. It is time to fight:

	Speed	*Brawn*	*Armour*	*Health*
Tourmalus	14/12	9	–	–
Blue agate	–	–	9	30
Red calcite	–	–	4	50
Dark citrine	–	–	9	30

Special abilities

- Blue agate: At the end of every combat round, each crystal cluster is healed for 4 *health*. This cannot take each crystal above their starting *health*. (Once a cluster is reduced to zero *health*, it can no longer heal.)
- Red calcite: Tourmalus' attacks have the *piercing* ability, ignoring your *armour*.
- Dark citrine: Tourmalus has a speed of 14 (this is reduced to 12 once the citrine is destroyed).
- Body of crystal: The crystal clusters are immune to *bleed, disease, lightning* and *venom*.

In this combat you roll against Tourmalus' speed. If you win a combat round, you can choose to apply your damage to one of the golem's crystal clusters. When a cluster is reduced to zero *health*, its ability no longer applies. You must destroy all three clusters to defeat the golem.

If you manage to overcome this ancient guardian, turn to 893.

875

You enter a vaulted hall of smooth black stone. The walls have been draped with faded banners, each one carrying a different symbol – a flame, a mountain, an axe, a hammer. You wonder if they refer to gods or spirits, or perhaps different factions that once existed within the city. A row of stone pews form a silent procession down the centre of the hall, their way illuminated by the iron braziers suspended from the ceiling.

The entire left-side of the chamber has caved in, leaving nothing but rubble. To the right, in the direction the pews are facing, there is a chimney shaft descending from the ceiling. At its base the shaft opens out into an octagonal font of glowing black coals, surrounded by magical runes. The only visible exit is a set of stairs either side of the chimney, leading up to a railed balcony.

You move to inspect the font, noticing that there is a black metal dish resting on the coals. Above it, carved into the chimney shaft, is an image of a phoenix, rising up out of a wall of flame.

If you have the *bronze urn* and wish to sprinkle the ashes onto the plate, turn to 784. Otherwise, you decide to head up the stairs, turn to 775.

876

Congratulations! You have created the following item:

Self-published grimoire
(left hand: spell book)
+2 speed +3 magic
Ability: trickster

If you wish to create a different spell book, you can start the process again (turn to 850). Otherwise, you may now leave the chamber and continue your journey. Turn to 866.

877

With Avian's grief still resounding in your ears you hurry from the chamber, following a set of stairs to a balcony of black stone. You realise that this must be the highest point of the city. Above you, the sky is blossoming into morning. Bright rays of sun rake through the thinning clouds, promising another day of stifling heat. Below, through the coiling mist, you glimpse the magma lake – its bright surface stirred with sluggish waves, as if awakening from a deep slumber.

At the edge of the balcony, where the rock curls inward like a grasping claw, a skeleton of a demon lies sprawled in the dust. Its fingers still grasp a black-bladed sword, which has been thrust straight through its ribcage.

Ragnarok.

Its size almost dwarfs the skeleton – rising a head taller than a man, its hilt a macabre fusion of bone, iron and crimson thorns. Cernos stands next to it, a broken creature – a shadow of his former strength. The enchanted stone known as the heart of fire is still gripped in his scorched hand. Smoke rises from what remains of his scaled flesh. Any ordinary mortal would have been incinerated by such power, but Cernos is a demon – like yourself. He shares the same healing blood, a gift that has allowed him to bear the burden of the heart.

He places the stone into a circular groove, where the guard of the sword meets the cold black of the blade. The moment it clicks into place the sword shudders, scraping against its bone prison.

'Yes ... yes.' Cernos moves behind it, his hands clenching, anticipating his prize.

'Cernos!' Your voice rings out, shrill and harsh. You march forward, shoulders bunched, your immense wings flaring out from your back. In each clawed fist your armaments dazzle with magic, their light catching the raised edges of your dark scales. You see it in Cernos' face, when he looks upon you with his one crimson eye. You see it written there in his scowl, in his fear.

You have become him. A mirror image. Horns curve from your skull, sweeping around to frame your reptilian face. Eyes that once shone diamond blue now burn with scarlet fires. You are Cernos as he once was. And you look upon him with contempt.

'You are too late!' Cernos raises the palm of his scorched hand, dragging a claw through the ravaged flesh. 'Ragnarok will be freed ... it is mine!' He places his palm to the hilt, letting the blood seep over the thorns and iron. 'By my blood, Barahar's blood, I free you!'

Red light surges to the tip of the blade, igniting each of its malign runes. 'Yes! Yes! Ragnarok awakens!' Cernos wrenches the hilt towards him. Bones crack as the sword comes free ...

Then you slam into his chest, your wings carrying you forward.

The sword flies from his hand as you both go tumbling over and over, towards the edge of the balcony. You come out on top, your weapons whipping down – but Cernos catches them in his hands, hissing in pain as they cut deep, spraying blood. Then he twists them from your grasp, his spiked elbow taking you across the throat.

You roll again, clawing and raking each other, snarling and hissing like pit dogs. The ground has started to tremble – you can hear rocks breaking loose. From the lake below you can hear the bubbling lava gushing up in columns of fiery spray.

Cernos reaches out for the sword. Its angular runes blaze with anger.

Take me, weakling. Take me . . . .

Its voice whispers in your ear. Getting louder, more insistent.

You grab the demon's wrist, yanking it away from the hilt. With an angry snarl he lunges forward, his fanged teeth sinking into your shoulder. You feel dizzy . . . from the pain . . . and a sudden sickening nausea. The blade. Its evil taints the very air. You can feel its runes, its words, crawling beneath your skin.

Take me. Take revenge . . .

For an instant, you see yourself wielding the blade. You are back in Durnhollow, marching through its dark halls, the warriors of the inquisition falling at your feet. You are unstoppable. A force of fury. Nothing can stop you – nothing can hold you back. *Yes. Freedom. Take me. Take revenge.*

Another blow staggers you. Cernos twists his body, pushing you onto your back. Now on top, the demon raises his arms, dark fire blossoming around his fists. Desperately you flail for something, anything . . . then your hand settles around a cold hilt, its barbs slicing into your palm. In horror, you realise it is Ragnarok. It is lying right next to you.

Take me!

You draw your hand away instinctively. The blade is cursed. A dark thing from the underworld, carried to the surface by a Skard hero who dreamt of power. A dark thing that carries a Skard name, given to it by the very people it was meant to save. Ragnarok. The destroyer of worlds.

Cernos' first blow drags a scream from your broken lips. His second almost knocks you into unconsciousness. 'Fool!' he screams, lifting his fists once again. 'The sword is mine! MINE!' Unable to summon the strength to defend yourself, you realise that you are defeated … Cernos has won. Your eyes are already starting to close as you twist to look upon the blade one more time.

Will you:

Take the sword?	892
Refuse the sword's power?	864

878

Congratulations, for defeating Erkil while *hexed* you have won the following rare item:

Prowler's cowl
(head)
+2 speed +4 brawn
Ability: vanish, prowler
(requirement: hexed)

Once you have updated your hero sheet, return to the quest map to continue your journey.

879

Virgil retracts his blade grudgingly. 'Then you're responsible for this one. I'll have no part of it.'

You watch as the spirit struggles to rise, tendrils of smoke curling about its body. 'Any hint that this is a trick and …' You nod to Virgil's blades, making your indication clear.

The spirit nods quickly. 'Yes, yes. You lead the way and Aether follows. Keep out of the way, yes?'

Aether has now joined your party. Make a note of the keyword *escort* on your hero sheet. The following rules apply:

Escort: Aether has 40 *health*. Make a note of this on your hero sheet. You must protect the spirit until you reach the rune gate. In future combats, each time you lose a round and take *health* damage, roll a die. On a ⚀ result, the spirit has also been injured and must lose 10 *health*. Once the spirit has been reduced to zero *health*, it has been destroyed. You must then remove the keyword escort from your hero sheet. A result of ⚁ or more and Aether has avoided injury. (NOTE: Aether counts as an ally. Therefore you may use abilities, such as *heal, regrowth* and *greater heal*, to restore Aether's lost *health* during combat.) The spirit cannot heal between combats.

When you have updated your hero sheet, turn to 875.

880

Your weapons and magic smash through the spectres' shield, hurling the dwarf against the stone shelves. He clutches at his wounds, black slime oozing between his rotted fingers.

'You betray me ...' spits the dwarf. 'Let Barahar take you and be damned!'

He dives past you, looking to grab one of the potion bottles from the table. But you are faster – your weapons swinging around to catch him mid-step. The dwarf gives a shriek, then his body explodes in a black shower of ash and slime. All around you the ghostly spectres flicker like candle-flames, then fade to wisps of smoke.

'A death long overdue ...' Virgil picks a string of gloop from his coat, flicking his fingers in an attempt to get rid of it. 'Told you it'd be messy.'

You walk over to the bottles, intrigued to discover what the dwarf was after. You may now take one of the following items:

Spectral syllabub (1 use)	Molech Tov's volatile cocktail (1 use)
(backpack)	(backpack)
Use any time in combat to restore your *health* to full	Use instead of rolling for a damage score to inflict 10 damage, ignoring *armour*, to all opponents

If you have the key word *clean up* on your hero sheet, turn to 752. Otherwise, turn to 847.

881

Unable to reach the ledge, you are forced to find an alternative route back into the dwarven city. This quest is now over. (Return to the map to continue your journey.)

882

'The archdemon.' Avian gives a disgruntled sigh. 'I wish more records of that time had survived. Alas, the Skards have never been renowned for their love of words.'

Virgil gives an accompanying snort of agreement.

'From what I could glean, Barahar was once a Skard hero from one of the western tribes. During the Great Cataclysm, when Skardland was torn asunder, he ventured into the underworld, looking for a means to end the incursions.'

'Incursions?' Your knowledge of Skardland history is scanty at best – mostly snatched from rowdy tavern songs, poking fun at the Skards' bloodthirsty customs and short-tempered nature.

'Caused by the cataclysm.' Avian clicks his tongue, looking irritated at being interrupted. 'It allowed the creatures of the underworld – goblins, trolls, giants – to break out onto the surface. Much of Skardland was destroyed; even today it is little more than a barren, frozen wasteland.' He pauses, studying the scrawled writing carved at his feet – you wait patiently for him to continue. 'Barahar did not return with the means to free his people. He returned a demon – one of the greatest and most powerful the realms have ever known.' His eyes stray to your glittering black scales. 'Perhaps he believed power would be his salvation. Alas, he merely became the slave to a much darker evil – the demonblade, Ragnarok.'

Return to 590 to ask another question, or turn to 766 to continue your journey.

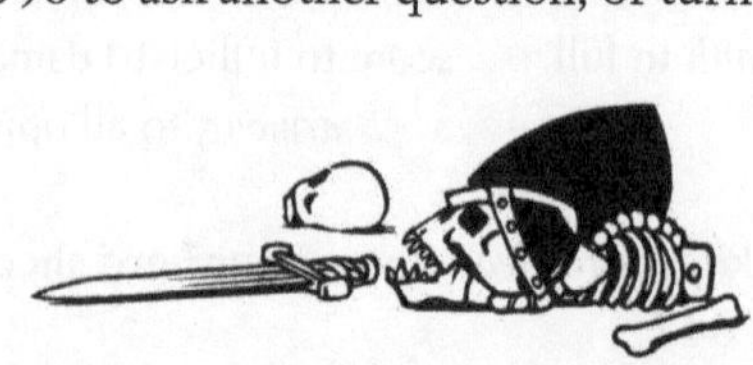

883

Your weapons shatter the golem's crystals, causing it to stagger drunkenly. Seizing his chance Virgil darts behind it, his blades crossing in a bright blur. A moment later and the golem's head hangs loose from its shoulders, bouncing up and down on a half-mangled spring. There is a dull clang from somewhere inside the rusted body, then the monster grinds to a halt, hissing jets of steam.

The witchfinder sheathes his blades, offering you a lazy half-smile. 'Battling tin pots. There's one for the ballads.'

You may now help yourself to one of the following rewards:

Golem oil (2 uses)	**Spark plugs (1 use)**	**Dull gladius**
(backpack)	(backpack)	(left hand: club)
Increase your *speed* by 4 for one combat round	Ability: shock treatment	+2 speed +3 brawn Ability: slam

You notice that the golem's belly is fashioned from two plates of hinged metal, with a large keyhole at its centre. If you have a *black iron key* or are a thief, turn to 843. Otherwise, the panels remain locked and you are unable to prise them open. Turn to 870.

884

You exit the building via the heavy stone doors. Outside you find yourselves at the top of a colonnaded platform, with wide stairs leading down to a courtyard. Several deep craters have been ripped into the ground, branched with fissures. Rubble and ash litter the space.

If you have the keyword *escort* on your hero sheet, turn to 828. Otherwise, turn to 872.

885

A sharp hiss draws your attention to the nearest pew, where the black snake is watching you from a crack in the stone. You crouch next to it, coaxing the serpent out of its den with the magic of Kaala's scale. If you wish, you may now take:

Black taipan
(left hand: snake)
+2 speed +3 brawn
Ability: convulsions

Once you have made your decision, you leave the chamber and resume your journey. Turn to 731.

886

The moment your hand touches the rune, black lightning arcs across the face of the door, sending you reeling backwards in pain. Clearly, you have chosen the incorrect rune, and have triggered some hidden trap woven into the magic of the door.

You have been inflicted with the following curse:

Curse of weakness (pa): You must lower your *brawn* and *magic* by 5 until you next roll a double in combat.

Return to 871 to choose another rune.

887

You drive your weapons into the demon's chest, watching as its immense form unravels into ribbons of black smoke. They dissipate on the air, leaving the hammer and the anvil to slam back to the ground, sending a cloud of dust billowing across the forge.

Virgil waves a hand in front of his face, choking and coughing through the smoke. 'Looks like that's the end of it.' He walks over to the anvil, moving his hand over its runed face. 'And no harm done.' He turns and glances towards the cauldron. It now rests silently atop the glowing hearth, contents steaming. 'The forge is ours, my friend.'

You are only half-listening, your attention having wandered to the charred skeleton lying spread-eagled next to the bellows. Its bones are black as coal, its clothing nothing more than tattered scraps of twisted metal. The proportions seem more human than dwarf.

'As I suspected,' says Virgil, frowning down at the corpse. 'An elf. Guess he thought he could master the forge – and got a nasty surprise. If you can't handle the heat ...' He kneels beside the burnt remains, pulling the clothing apart to reveal a metal container clutched in the skeleton's hands. He prises it loose, turning it around to examine it in the flickering firelight. The container is shaped like a pyramid, with an odd array of dials and wheels imbedded on the underside. 'An elven lock.' He tosses it to you, wiping his hands on his coat. 'See if you can get it open – might be something useful inside.'

If you have the words *fire quencher* and *wind breaker* on your hero sheet, you will have an associated number for each. Total these numbers and turn to the corresponding entry number to unlock the container. If you do not have those two keywords, then your attempts to open the container prove unsuccessful. Turn to 755.

888

You break through the demon's manacles, releasing the charred cadaver. It slumps to the ground, hoarse breath rattling from its seared lungs. 'The suffering,' it rasps. 'End the suffering ...'

You gladly oblige, watching as the demon's blackened skin starts to burn, consumed by a bright white fire. From the ashes, a wisp of smoke rises up into the steaming mist. *Peace*, whispers a voice. *I find peace.*

The wheel continues to rattle across the island, but is gradually losing speed – as if its own black spirit has now been exorcised. Reaching the edge of the rock, it finally grinds to a halt, cutting a grim silhouette against the gleaming red magma.

If you are a warrior, turn to 823. If you are a rogue, turn to 812. If you are a mage turn to 592.

889

The stairs bring you to a wide corridor. One of its walls has been completely blown away, revealing an open vista of crumbling rooftops. At the end of the corridor are a set of arched bronze doors – and hurrying towards them is a black-clothed figure. A pack and coil of rope bounce against their back.

The figure hesitates, head half-cocked – then they twist around, sending a dagger spinning through the air. Thankfully your sixth sense gives you ample warning, allowing you to dodge out of its path – leaving the blade to clatter harmlessly against the rock behind you.

With a snarl, you throw yourself into a full-on charge – looking to close the distance between you as quickly as possible. The thief looses another dagger, which you agilely avoid, your speed drawing a gasp from your would-be assassin.

Then you bowl into him, taking you both crashing down onto the ground. As you kick and struggle his hood falls back, revealing his identity.

'Quito!' There is no mistaking the short, shifty-eyed traveller who shared your journey aboard the *Angel's Bounty*.

Your surprise disarms you, giving the thief the opening he needs. Quito punches you in the ribs, sliding his knees beneath your chest and flipping you away. As you scrabble back to your feet, he moves in, ready to deliver another blow – a poisoned dagger flicking into each of his hands.

Suddenly, a piercing screech rends the air. You both turn to face the ravaged opening, sensing something large approaching, clawing its way up the outside of the building. Turn to 827.

890

Your magic blasts chunks from the demon's body, your weapons cutting crimson bands through its saggy flesh. Each blow forces the unconscious mage to jerk and twist in pain, his body still pinned to the stone. The demon is powerful, but no match for your strength. When it finally collapses into a mound of flesh and bone, you hear a horrifying peel of agony ring out across the chamber.

'No! No!' Avian has been released from his invisible restraints. He now lies at the foot of the obelisk, scrabbling like a blind man. 'My magic ... I've lost my magic.'

You hurry to his side, offering out a hand to help support him. But the mage bats you away, hissing like some rabid animal. When he finally lowers his arms, you catch sight of his face ... and draw back in dismay.

It is as if he has aged a hundred years.

His skin is now grey and wrinkled, stretched taut over crests of bone. Where once there was a shock of white hair, now there is only a bare pate, peppered with liver spots.

'No ...' Avian looks down at his hands. They are trembling uncontrollably, withered with age. He draws in a long wheezy breath, then starts sobbing. 'My magic ... my magic ...'

You rise to your feet, your eyes wandering back to the remains of the flesh golem. Both of your companions have now fallen to this cursed city. You are the only one left who can stop Cernos. Perhaps it was always meant to be this way – a demon against a demon.

If you are a warrior, turn to 791. If you are a rogue, turn to 608. If you are a mage, turn to 728.

891

'Magic isn't always a docile force that we can bend to our will. Here ...' Avian points to an island of black rock, bobbing on the surface of the magma lake. You can see some kind of fleshy growth spread out across the super-heated stone. Parts of its body are rising and falling gently with shallow breaths. 'When high levels of magic are discharged in a single place, sometimes they linger – and take on a life of their own.'

You grimace as you spot a bloodshot eye, peering back at you from between the rubbery folds of skin. 'Are they dangerous?' you ask, glancing at the mage.

Avian looks sideways at you, his fingers flexing around his staff. 'Oh yes. More dangerous than you could possibly imagine.'

Return to 590 to ask another question, or turn to 766 to continue your journey.

892

You have come too far to give up now. Snatching the hilt, you feel its cruel barbs slice deep into your hand. The pommel glistens bright with blood as you swing the mighty rune sword in a vicious swathe. For an instant the air is lit by a bright red light. You hear Cernos scream. Then the weight pinning you down is gone.

You rise, feeling power flooding through your body. It is like molten fire, racing along each and every vein, filling you with the heat of a fierce sun. Your skin cracks around your expanding muscles, exposing vivid lines of crimson. Boots split open to reveal cloven hooves while a ridged tail snaps around your thigh, narrowing to a dagger-like edge.

Cernos is on his knees, looking so small and insignificant beneath your magnificent shadow. He clutches his chest, blood pouring over his fingers. He looks up at you fearfully. Begging. Pitiful.

The sword moves of its own volition, dragging your arm with it. The blade slides into the demon, eliciting a hellish scream. The runes flare bright, greedily drinking in the last of the demon's power – his life essence. As his body starts to unravel, becoming black smoke, you place a foot to his shoulder and push, retracting the sword and sending Cernos over the edge of the balcony.

There is the briefest echo of a scream, then silence.

When you finally hear the deep laughter, resonating around the chamber, it takes a moment to realise that it is coming from your own lips. The sword tugs at your arm again, its hilt vibrating in your hand. It senses danger.

You spin around, to see a ragged, tattered shape stumbling towards you. It is drenched in blood and gore, cradling an arm against its chest.

'Virgil . . .?'

He scowls. 'You robbed Avian of his magic . . . you have undone everything. I should have killed you. Killed you when I had the chance!' He summons magic to the palm of his one remaining hand. 'I judge you, demon . . . and I find you guilty!'

The sword's rage burns within you, flowing like a furious river. It is already driving you forward, your hooved feet punching holes into the stone. You are lost to its will – unable to stop yourself. It is time fight:

	Speed	*Brawn/Magic*	*Armour*	*Health*
Virgil	15	12/10	12	120(*)

Special abilities

- Finder's fire: At the end of each combat round, you must take damage equal to Virgil's current *magic* score. This ability ignores *armour.* (If Virgil wins a combat round, he uses his *brawn* score when rolling for damage.)
- Holy light: If Virgil rolls a double for his attack speed (before or after a re-roll), he heals himself for 6 *health*. This ability cannot take Virgil above his starting *health* of 120.
- Rune reaper: Instead of rolling for a damage score after winning a round, you can absorb Virgil's magic into the rune-blade. Each time you use *rune reaper* you must pay the cost of one of your unused abilities to lower Virgil's *magic* by 2. Your sacrificed ability cannot be used again in this combat, even if you have an ability that would ordinarily let you do so. (NOTE: You can use other *magic*-lowering abilities, such as *confound* and *disrupt if you wish*, to lower Virgil's *magic*.)

Once Virgil is reduced to 10 *health* or less, the combat is automatically won. If you manage to defeat the witchfinder, turn to **741**.

893

The crystals are the key to Tourmalus' power. Once the last cluster is destroyed the giant freezes in mid-step, the sole of one enormous foot raised to stomp on Virgil. The witchfinder dashes to safety as the giant topples forward, smashing through the obsidian throne in a dusty explosion of boulders and crystal.

You may now help yourself to one of the following rewards:

Crystal hammer	**Energised crystal**	**Calcite claw**
(main hand: hammer)	(backpack)	(left hand: fist weapon)
+2 speed +5 brawn	A shard of crystal	+2 speed +4 brawn
Ability: stagger	glowing with magic	Ability: piercing
(requirement: warrior)		

Virgil removes his hat, shaking the dust from its brim. 'For once, just once, it'd be nice if something didn't want to kill us.' He plants his hat back onto his head. 'It could give a guy a complex.'

'Actually, it might have done us a favour.' You point through the swirling dust to the remains of the black throne. Part of its seat has broken away, revealing a torch-lined corridor snaking away into the rock.

'I'd rather avoid any more caves,' says Virgil. He lifts his blade, gesturing to a narrow opening in the south wall. It appears to lead out onto an exterior ledge, its edges gleaming with firelight.

Will you:

Take the secret passage?	853
Head out onto the ledge?	841

894

The moment your hand touches the rune, yellow lightning arcs across the face of the door, sending you reeling backwards in pain. Clearly you have chosen the incorrect rune, and have triggered some hidden trap woven into the magic of the door.

You have been inflicted with the following curse:

Curse of vulnerability (pa): You must lower your *armour* by 3 until you next roll a double in combat.

Return to **871** to choose another rune.

895

'Wait a second.' You discover that you can understand the strange whirls and angular markings on the bronze plate. 'These are powerful incantations.'

You turn back to the marble slab and the table covered with paper. The machine looks in perfect working order and could be used to fashion your own book of spells. If you wish to create your own spell book, turn to 850. Otherwise, you decide to leave and continue your journey. Turn to 866.

Epilogue

The guardsmen go tumbling through the door, along with its splintered remains. You step through, your bearskin cloak whipping back from your powerful shoulders. More men move to head you off, but a barking order draws them to a halt. You glare at the warriors as they move aside, making way for you.

Conall watches you from beneath his heavy brow, chin rested on his fist. A band of bronze is visible amongst the tangle of black hair, denoting his new status. King of Carvel. King of the West. He is everything you remember. A giant. A warrior. A worthy ally.

But she isn't here. The witch was always at his side ...

A raucous screeching comes from the rafters above, where a mob of crows flap in agitation. One comes wheeling down to settle on the back of the throne, glaring at you disapprovingly.

You stand before the self-made king, peering out from beneath your cowl. A shadow of a smile crosses your lips when you sense the fear from the hall. Your clawed limbs and curved horns protrude from beneath your cloak. There is no hiding what you are.

And yet, Conall does not share his men's fear. 'You will kneel,' he scowls, his face darkening.

You obey his command, dropping to one knee and bowing your head. 'Your majesty.' The words fall in a sibilant hiss.

A sharp-faced bodyguard steps forward, glaring through the teeth of his wolf-skull helm. 'Give the word, my king – and I'll make a coat of this one's scales.' An impressive show of courage, you note, but his words do not impress.

Conall waves him to silence. 'Speak, demon.'

A chill wind gusts snow through the narrow windows. It also brings the stench of death. The castle walls are lined with bodies, tarred and staked for all to see. Prince Lazlo had been one of them.

'Our paths have crossed before,' you state, pulling back your hood. There are gasps from the onlookers. 'You will not recognise me now, but I have seen your destiny. Our paths are fated to cross once more.'

Conall's eyes burn dark and fierce. 'Spit it out or you'll be hanging in a crow cage.'

'Ah, yes,' you nod. 'I saw your handiwork in the streets.' You remember the iron cages, with starving prisoners begging for water and bread. Crows wheeled over the ruins. Homes and shops burnt and plundered. 'Food for crows.'

Your eyes shift to the rafters, where the black-bodied host screech and caw.

'If that is your wish, demon.' The king beckons to his wolf-helmed guard, who starts forward, baring his teeth. You halt him with a raised hand, magic rippling around his body. He struggles to move, his limbs now heavy as lead.

You continue to regard the king, as if nothing untoward had happened. 'In truth, I come seeking your witch. Damaris. Where is she?'

'The dungeons,' replies Conall sharply, eyes flicking between you and his guard. 'Till she learns to bend the knee, as you have done.'

'She will teach me what I need to know. To master my power.' You reach into your tunic, removing a tight roll of parchment. You step past the immobilised guard and hand it to the king.

Conall spreads it open, pulling a grimace as he looks upon the image scrawled in blood.

'This means nothing,' he growls, crumpling it in his fist.

You step back, your malign shadow stretching wide across the hall. 'I am looking for a man,' you declare coldly. 'His name is Lorcan. Your witch will help me find him.'

'And what do I get in return?' Conall leans forward, his dark brows knitting together. 'What do you offer a king?'

You glance up at the wooden beams, where the crows continue to scream and caw. 'A king of crows, hmm. I can offer you more than this.' You look around at his men, each one shuffling uneasily beneath your crimson stare. 'Carvel is nothing. A faded cross on the map. You have won *nothing*.'

There are gasps and rumbles of anger. The men look to Conall, waiting for the command. The king merely watches you, his face unreadable. His silence urges you to go on.

'Damaris will give me what I need. And in return, I will give you what the fates have decreed.' You open out your arms to the screeching, cawing gallery. 'I will win you a land to call your own. I will win you a kingdom! Valeron will fall!'

Your eyes sweep around to meet Conall's.

'Words,' he grimaces scathingly. 'Tell me of these *fates*. What have you seen?'

'That victory will gift you what you desire most. The crown of kings . . . and a son.'

Conall's eyes widen for a moment. 'A son?'

Your lips part in a fanged smile. 'A boy and an heir. To the throne of Valeron.'

Conall regards you in silence. Then releases a snorting breath.

'Then war it is.' He rises to his feet to address the court. 'Our destiny is decided. The Wiccan march east – and no shield or stone, or holy words, will stop us. Valeron will fall!'

'Valeron will fall! Valeron will fall' The chant is taken up by the assembled guards, while the crows scream and flutter, voicing their own fervent approval. You bow with a flourish, your gaze shifting to the crumpled parchment.

The future is mine, Lorcan. The future is mine . . .

Glossary: Special abilities

The following is a list of all the abilities associated with special items. The letters in brackets after each name refers to the type of ability – speed (sp), combat (co), modifier (mo), passive (pa). Unless otherwise stated in the text, each ability can only be used *once* during a combat – even if you have multiple items with the same ability (i.e. if you have two items with the *piercing* ability, you can still only use *piercing* once per combat).

Acid (mo): Add 1 to the result of each die you roll for your damage score, for the duration of the combat. (Note: if you have multiple items with *acid*, you can still only add 1 to the result.)

Ashes (sp): Use at the start of combat to surround yourself with holy ashes. This increases your *armour* by 1 for the duration of the combat.

Atonement (mo): Use at the end of a combat round to heal yourself and an ally for the total passive damage inflicted on an opponent in that round, from *bleed, barbs, disease, fire aura, thorns* and *venom*. You can only use *atonement* once per combat.

Back draft (co): When your opponent's damage score causes health damage, you can immediately retaliate by inflicting 2 damage dice back to them, ignoring *armour*. You can only use *back draft* once per combat.

Backstab (co): (requires a dagger in the main or left hand) If you or an ally play an *immobilise, knockdown, stun* or *webbed* ability in combat, you may automatically *backstab* the affected opponent, inflicting 2 damage dice, ignoring *armour*. If you have won the round, you can still roll for a damage score as normal.

Barbs (pa): You automatically inflict 1 damage to all of your opponents, at the end of every combat round. This ability ignores *armour*.

Beguile (mo): You may use one of your speed abilities twice in the same combat, even if its description states it can only be used once.

Bleed (pa): If your damage dice/damage score causes health damage to your opponent, they continue to take a further point of damage at the end of each combat round. This damage ignores *armour*.

Bless (mo): This ability can be cast at any time on yourself or an ally to heal 6 *health* and increase one attribute (*magic* or *brawn*) by 1 for the remainder of the combat. *Bless* can only be used once per combat.

Blessed blades (mo): (requires a sword in the main hand and left hand.) You can heal yourself any time in a combat for the total *brawn* modifier of your two weapons. You can only use *blessed blades* once per combat.

Blind (sp): (see **Webbed**). You can only use *blind* once per combat.

Blind strike (co): If you or an ally play an *immobilise, knockdown, stun* or *webbed* ability, you can immediately inflict 2 damage dice to the affected opponent, ignoring *armour*. If you have won the round, you can still roll for a damage score as normal. This ability can only be used once per combat. (Note: a thief cannot use *backstab* and *blind strike* in the same combat round.)

Blink (co): (see **Dodge**). You can only use *blink* once per combat.

Blood hail (co): Instead of rolling for a damage score after winning a round, you can use *blood hail* to shower your enemies with arrows. Roll 2 damage dice and apply the result to each of your opponents, ignoring their *armour*. If any opponent is already inflicted with *bleed* from a previous round, then they take an extra 4 damage.

Blood-sworn set (mo): If your hero is wearing all three items from the blood-sworn set (head, gloves and chest) then you may use the *blood-sworn* ability. This allows you to sacrifice 4 *health* to use an ability that you haven't already used. This ability will not count towards your quota of hexed abilities. You can use *blood-sworn* as many times as you wish, losing 4 *health* each time.

Blood thief (mo): For every ⚅ you roll for your damage score/damage dice, you may instantly restore 4 *health*. This cannot take you above your starting *health*.

Bright spark (mo): Your powers are amplified, allowing you to re-roll any dice for your damage score for the duration of the combat. You must accept the result of the re-rolled dice.

Call of nature set (-): If your hero is equipped with both items from the *call of nature* set (ring and gloves), then you can use the *wild child* ability. (See **Wild Child**.)

Cauterise (mo): This ability can be used any time in combat to remove all *venom, bleed* and *disease* effects that your hero is currently inflicted with.

You can only use it once in combat – and once used, your hero is again susceptible to these effects.

Channel (mo): Sacrifice 2 *magic* to increase your damage score by 4 for one round. You can use this ability once for each item with the *channel* ability. At the end of the combat, your *magic* is restored to full.

Charge (sp): In the first round of combat, you may increase your *speed* by 2.

Charm (mo): You may re-roll *one* of your hero's dice any time during a combat. You must accept the result of the second roll. If you have multiple items with the *charm* ability, each one gives you a re-roll. Each *charm* can only be used once per combat.

Charm offensive (co): For each item with the *charm* ability that your hero is wearing, you can add 2 to your damage score. (If you had four items with *charm*, you could add 8 to your damage score.) You can only use *charm offensive* once per combat.

Cistene's chattels set (-): If your hero is equipped with both items from the *Cistene's chattels* set (necklace and spell book), then you can use the *miracle* ability. (See **Miracle**.)

Cleave (co): Instead of rolling for a damage score, you can use *cleave*. Roll 1 damage die and apply the result to each of your opponents, ignoring their *armour*. You can only use *cleave* once per combat.

Command (co): When an opponent wins a combat round, use *command* to instantly halt their attack, allowing you to roll for damage instead (as if you had won the combat round). This ability can only be used once per combat.

Compulsion (co): You can use *compulsion* to roll an extra die when determining your damage score. However, you must lower your *speed* by 2 for the next combat round. This ability can only be used once per combat.

Confound (co): *Use confound* to avoid taking damage from your opponent when they have won a combat round. It also inflicts 1 damage die back to them, ignoring *armour*, and lowers their *brawn* and *magic* score by 1 for the remainder of the combat. *Confound* can only be used once per combat.

Constrictor (sp): (see **Webbed**). You can only use *constrictor* once per combat.

Convulsions (pa): If your damage score causes health damage to your opponent, they automatically suffer convulsions. In all future combat rounds, the affected opponent will lose the combat round if they roll a double for attack speed – even if their result is higher.

Corrode (co): If your damage score causes health damage to your opponent, you can also cast *corrode*. This lowers the same opponent's *armour* by 2 for the remainder of the combat.

Counter (co): If your opponent wins a combat round you can use *counter* to lower your opponent's damage score by 2 and inflict 1 damage die back to them, ignoring *armour*. This ability can only be used once per combat.

Coup de grace (pa): When an opponent is reduced to 10 *health* or less, you can immediately use *coup de grace* to reduce them to zero *health*. You can only use *coup de grace* once per combat.

Crawlers (sp): Cover your opponent in creepy-crawlies, forcing them to itch and scratch their way through the combat. This lowers their *speed* by 1 for two combat rounds. *Crawlers* can only be used once per combat.

Critical strike (mo): Change the result of all dice you have rolled for damage to a ⚅. You can only use this ability once per combat.

Cruel twist (mo): If you get a ⚅ result when rolling for your damage score, you can use *cruel twist* to roll an extra die for damage. This ability can only be used once per combat.

Cunning (mo): You may raise your *brawn* score by 3 for one combat round. You can only use *cunning* once per combat.

Curse (sp): (see **Webbed**). You can only use *curse* once per combat.

Cutpurse (pa): Each time you successfully complete a combat, roll a die to discover what item you find:

⚀ or ⚁ A purse containing 20 gold crowns.

⚂ or ⚃ An elixir of invisibility (1 use – backpack item. Grants the ability: *vanish*).

⚄ or ⚅ A flask of healing (1 use – backpack item. Use any time in combat to restore 6 *health*).

Dark pact (co): Sacrifice 4 *health* to charge your strike with shadow energy, increasing your damage score by 4. This ability can only be used once per combat.

Deceive (mo): (see **Trickster**). You can only use *deceive* once per combat.

Deep wound (co): You can use this ability to roll an extra die when determining your damage score. You can only use this ability once per combat.

Defender (pa): You may use this ability any time in a team battle (as a support or attack hero), to take the damage that would normally have been inflicted to an ally and apply it to yourself (*armour* can be used as normal, if appropriate to the type of damage). *Defender* can only be used once per combat.

Deflect (co): (see **Overpower**). You can only use *deflect* once per combat.

Demon claws (pa): For every double that you roll for attack speed (before or after a re-roll), your hero automatically inflicts 4 damage to their opponent. This ability ignores *armour*.

Demon spines (co): (see **Retaliation**). You can only use *demon spines* once per combat.

Dirge (co): Use this ability to stop your opponent rolling for damage when they have won a round. You can only use *dirge* once per combat.

Disease (pa): If your damage dice/damage score causes health damage to your opponent, they continue to take 2 points of damage at the end of each combat round. This damage ignores *armour*.

Disrupt (co): If your damage score causes health damage to your opponent, you can also cast *disrupt*. This lowers your opponent's *magic* by 3 for the remainder of the combat.

Dodge (co): Use this ability when you have lost a combat round, to avoid taking damage from your opponent's damage score.

Dominate (mo): Change the result of one die you roll for damage to a ⚅. You can only use this ability once per combat.

Doom (co): If your damage score causes health damage to your opponent, you can also curse them with the sigil of doom. This lowers their *armour*, *brawn* and *magic* by 1 for the remainder of the combat.

Double punch (co): (requires a dagger in the main hand and left hand.) Use this ability instead of rolling for a damage score, to automatically inflict 2 damage dice plus the total *brawn* modifier of your two weapons to a single opponent. This ability ignores *armour*. You can only use *double punch* once per combat.

Evade (co): (see **Dodge**). You can only use *evade* once per combat.

Exploit (pa): For each ⚀ result your opponent gets when rolling for attack speed, you automatically inflict 1 damage back to them, ignoring *armour*.

Faith (mo): Each time you roll a double, you automatically heal 2 *health*. This ability cannot take you above your starting *health*.

Faith and duty set (-): If your hero is equipped with both swords from the *faith and duty* set, then you can use the *redemption* ability. (See *redemption*.)

Faithful friend (mo): Summon a faithful hound to your side, increasing your damage score by 2 for one combat round. This ability can only be used once per combat.

Fallen hero (mo): Use this ability to raise your brawn by 3 for one combat round and heal 10 *health*. This ability can only be used once per combat.

Fatal blow (co): Use *fatal blow* to ignore half of your opponent's *armour*, rounding up. This ability can only be used once per combat.

Fear (mo): Lowers your opponent's damage score by 2 for one combat round. This ability can only be used once per combat.

Fearless (sp): Use this ability to raise your *speed* by 2 for one combat round. This ability can only be used once per combat.

Feint (mo): You may reroll some or all of your dice, when rolling for attack speed. This ability can only be used once per combat.

Fiend's finest set (-): If your hero is wearing both pieces of the *night fiend* set (gloves and hood), then you can use the *exploit* ability. (See **Exploit**.)

Fiery temper (pa): Keep a record of all ⚅ results that your opponent rolls for damage. For every two ⚅ results your *brawn* is increased by 2. At the end of the combat, your *brawn* returns to normal.

Finesse (mo): Use *finesse* to re-roll one die for damage, adding 2 to the result. This ability can only be used once per combat.

Fire aura (pa): You are surrounded by magical flames. This automatically inflicts 1 damage to all of your opponents at the end of every combat round. This ability ignores *armour*.

Fire shield (pa): Your *fire shield* will protect you from some opponents' attacks. See combat descriptions for when you can use this ability.

Flurry (co): Instead of rolling for a damage score, you can use *flurry* to shower your enemies with daggers. Roll 1 damage die and apply the result to each of your opponents, ignoring their *armour*. You can only use *flurry* once per combat.

Focus (mo): Use any time in combat to raise your *magic* score by 3 for one combat round. You can only use this ability once per combat.

Focused strike (co): (requirement: fist *or* fist weapon in each hand.) Use *focused strike* to ignore your opponent's *armour* and apply your full damage score to their *health*. This ability can only be used once per combat.

Frostbite (co): If your damage score causes health damage to your opponent, you can also cast *frostbite*. This lowers your opponent's *speed* by 1 for the next two combat rounds. This ability can only be used once per combat.

Gouge (pa): Increases the damage caused by the *bleed* ability by 1.

Gorilla rage (mo): Each time you play a combat ability, roll a die. On a ⚅ result you may raise your *brawn/magic* by 1 for the duration of the combat.

Greater heal (mo): You can cast this spell any time in combat to automatically heal yourself or an ally for 8 *health*. This ability can only be used once per combat. If you have multiple items with the *greater heal* ability, each one can be used once to restore 8 *health*.

Gut ripper (mo): (see **Critical strike**). You can only use *gut ripper* once per combat.

Haste (sp): You may roll an extra die to determine your attack speed for one round of combat. You may only use this ability once per combat.

Headshot (pa): Once an opponent's *health* is reduced to 5 or less you may automatically 'headshot' them, reducing their *health* to zero. You can only use *headshot* once per combat.

Heal (mo): You can cast this spell any time in combat to automatically heal yourself or an ally for 4 *health*. This ability can only be used once per combat. If you have multiple items with the *heal* ability, each one can be used once to restore 4 *health*.

Heartless (mo): You may raise your *brawn* or *magic* score by 2 for one combat round. You can only use *heartless* once per combat.

Heavy blow (co): (see **Deep wound**). You can only use *heavy blow* once per combat.

High five (mo): Change the result of any die that you have rolled for your hero to a ⚄. This ability can only be used once per combat.

Holy protector (pa): Each undead opponent takes 1 point of damage at the end of every combat round, ignoring *armour*.

Hooked (mo): Use this ability to save one die result from your attack speed roll to use in the next combat round. You cannot change or re-roll the saved die. *Hooked* can only be used once per combat.

Hypnotise (mo): All of your opponent's ⚅ results for their damage score can be rerolled. You must accept the result of the rerolled dice.

Immobilise (sp): (see **Webbed**). You can only use *immobilise* once per combat.

Impale (co): A penetrating blow that increases your damage score by 3. In the next combat round, your opponent's *speed* is lowered by 1. You can only use *impale* once per combat.

Indomitable (pa): You are immune to any effects or abilities that would lower your *brawn* in combat.

Insight (mo): Cast any time in combat to lower your opponent's *armour* by 2 for two combat rounds. You can only use *insight* once per combat.

Insulated (pa): This ability will protect you from some opponents' lightning attacks. See combat descriptions for when you can use this ability.

Iron will (mo): (see **Might of stone**). You can only use *iron will* once per combat.

Knockdown (sp): (see **Webbed**). You can only use *knockdown* once per combat.

Last defence (mo): If your *health* is 10 or less, you may raise your *brawn* by 2.

Last rites (pa): Once an opponent has 15 or less *health*, you can instantly cast this spell to lower your opponent's *speed* and *armour* by 1 for the remainder of the combat. *Last rites* can only be used once per combat.

Leech (pa): Every time your damage score/damage dice causes health damage to your opponent, you may restore 2 *health*. This cannot take you above your maximum *health*.

Ley line infusion (co): Call on the fickle powers of nature to aid you. Instead of rolling for a damage score, roll 1 die. If the result is:

⚀ Both you and your opponent take 1 die of damage, ignoring *armour*. Roll separately for each.

⚁ or ⚂ You are healed for 5 *health* and your opponent takes 1 die of damage, ignoring *armour*.

⚃ or ⚄ You are healed for 8 *health* and your opponent takes 1 die of damage, ignoring *armour*.

⚅ You and an ally are both healed for 8 *health* and your opponent takes 1 die of damage, ignoring *armour*.

Lightning (pa): Every time you take health damage as a result of an opponent's damage score/damage dice, you automatically inflict 2 points of damage to them in return. This ability ignores *armour*. (Note: If you have multiple items with *lightning*, you still only inflict 2 damage.)

Magic tap (mo): Cast this spell any time in combat to raise your *magic* score by 2 for one combat round. If you roll a double (for attack speed or damage), then this spell is restored and can be used again.

Mangle (mo): For each ⚅ you roll for your damage score, you can add 2 to the result.

Many scales (mo): (see **Might of stone**). You can only use this ability once per combat.

Meditation (co + pa): Instead of rolling for a damage score, you can cast *meditation*. This automatically heals 1 *health* at the end of every combat round for the duration of the combat.

Melt (co): (see **Corrode**). You can only use *melt* once per combat.

Might of stone (mo): You may instantly increase your own or an ally's *armour* score by 3 for one combat round. You can only use this ability once per combat.

Miracle (pa): Your *bless* ability now increases one attribute (*magic* or *brawn*) by 2 for the remainder of the combat.

Missionary's calling set (-): If your hero is equipped with both items from the *missionary's calling* set (head and chest) then you may use the *penance* ability (see **Penance**).

Monkey mob (co): Instead of rolling for a damage score, you can summon a monkey mob to pelt a single opponent with stones. The mob cause 2 damage at the end of each combat round, ignoring *armour*, for the duration of the combat. This ability can only be used once per combat.

Near death (mo): If your *health* is 10 or less, you may raise your *magic* by 2.

Overload (co): You can use the *overload* ability to roll an extra dice when determining your damage score. You can only use this ability once per combat.

Overpower (co): This ability stops your opponent from rolling for damage after they have won a round, and automatically inflicts 2 damage dice, ignoring *armour*, to your opponent. You can only use *overpower* once per combat.

Packmaster (co): Instead of rolling for a damage score, you can summon a molten hound to attack a single opponent. The hound causes 2 damage at the end of each combat round, ignoring *armour*. As soon as you roll a double (for speed or damage), the hound leaves the combat. You can only use this ability once per combat.

Pagan's spirit set (-): If your hero is equipped with both items from the *pagan's spirit* set (dagger and boots) then you may use the *vindicator* ability (see **Vindicator**).

Parasite (mo): (see **Steal**). You can only use *parasite* once per combat.

Parry (co): Use this ability to stop your opponent rolling for damage after they have won a round. This ability can only be used once per combat.

Penance (mo): You may spend 4 *health* to add one extra die when rolling for your damage score. You may choose to use this ability before or after rolling your dice. *Penance* can only be used once per combat.

Piercing (co): Use *piercing* to ignore your opponent's *armour* and apply your full damage score to their *health*. This ability can only be used once per combat.

Pillage (pa): Each time you win a combat, roll two dice and automatically receive that amount of gold as a reward. This is in addition to any other gold or treasure you might receive.

Pound (co): A mighty blow that increases your damage score by 3. However, in the next combat round you must lower your *speed* by 1. This ability can only be used once per combat.

Primal (co): Instead of rolling for a damage score, you can cast this enchantment. It will automatically raise your own or an ally's *brawn* and *magic* score by 2 for the remainder of the battle. *Primal* can only be used once per combat.

Prowler set (pa): If your hero is wearing all three items from the *prowler* set (head, gloves and chest) then you may use the *prowler* ability. This allows you to use *evade, blind strike, backstab, sidestep* and *vanish* (if available) without counting them towards your quota of hexed abilities.

Purge (mo): You may cast this spell on yourself or an ally to automatically remove all *disease* and *venom* effects. This ability can only be used once per combat.

Quicksilver (sp): Increase your *speed* by 2 for one combat round. You can only use *quicksilver* once per combat.

Radiance (sp): Dazzle your foes, temporarily blinding them. This lowers your opponent's *speed* by 2 for one combat round. *Radiance* can only be used once per combat.

Rake (co): Instead of rolling for a damage score, you can *rake* an opponent. This inflicts 3 damage dice, ignoring *armour*. (Note: You cannot use modifiers with this ability.) You can only use *rake* once per combat.

Reaper (mo): For each 5 health damage that your damage score inflicts on an opponent, you can heal 1 *health* (rounding down). For example, if you inflicted 19 damage to an opponent, you could heal 3 *health*. You can only use *reaper* once per combat.

Reckless (sp): Use this ability to roll an extra die for your attack speed. However, if you lose the combat round, your opponent gets an extra damage die.

Redemption (mo): Use this ability to raise your *brawn* by 2 for one combat round and heal 4 *health*. This ability can only be used once per combat.

Refresh (mo): Cast this spell any time in combat to restore an ability that you or an ally has already used – allowing you to use it again. You can only cast *refresh* once per combat.

Regrowth (mo): You can cast this spell any time in combat to automatically heal yourself or an ally for 6 *health*. This ability can only be used once per combat. If you have multiple items with the *regrowth* ability, each one can be used once to restore 6 *health*.

Resolve (mo): Cast this spell any time in combat to raise your own or an ally's *armour* by 4 for one combat round.

Retaliation (co): When your opponent's damage score causes health damage, you can immediately retaliate by inflicting 1 damage dice back to them, ignoring *armour*. You can only use *retaliation* once per combat.

Roll with it (mo): If you win a round, you can use the result of one of your attack speed dice for your damage score (adding your *brawn* as normal). You can only use this ability once per combat.

Rust (co): If your damage score causes health damage to your opponent, you can also inflict *rust*. This lowers your opponent's *armour* by 2 for the remainder of the combat.

Safe path (sp): (see **Fearless**). You can only use *safe path* once per combat.

Savage arms set (-): If your hero is equipped with both items from the *savage arms* set (main hand and left hand axe) then you may use the *mangle* ability (see **Mangle**).

Savage call (co): Instead of rolling for a damage score, you can utter a *savage call*. This will automatically raise your *brawn* score by 2 for the remainder of the battle.

Savagery (mo): You may raise your *brawn* score by 2 for one combat round. You can only use *savagery* once per combat.

Sear (mo): Add 1 to the result of each die you roll for your damage score, for the duration of the combat. (Note: if you have multiple items with *sear*, you can still only add 1 to the result.)

Searing mantle (pa): Your armour is coated in fire. This causes 1 damage to all opponents at the end of every combat round for every 4 *armour* you are wearing.

Second skin (pa): You are immune to the *piercing* ability. If an opponent uses *piercing*, you may use *armour* as normal to absorb the damage.

Seraphim's symbols set (-): If your hero is equipped with both items from the *seraphim's symbols* set (necklace and ring) then you may use the *tranquillity* ability (see **Tranquillity**).

Shadow fury (co): Use this ability to add the speed of both your weapons (main hand and left hand) to your damage score. This ability can only be used once per combat.

Shadow speed (mo): When rolling for your attack speed, all results of ⚀ can be changed to a ⚂.

Shatter (co): If your damage score causes health damage to your opponent, you can also *shatter* them. This reduces their *armour* by 2 for the remainder of the combat. You can only use *shatter* once per combat.

Shock! (co): If your damage score causes health damage to your opponent, you can also electrocute them with the *shock!* ability. This inflicts 1 extra damage for every 2 points of *armour* your opponent is wearing, rounding up. You can only use *shock!* once per combat.

Shock treatment (mo): If an ally falls in battle, you can use *shock treatment* to restore them back to 10 *health*. This also removes all passive effects on that hero. This ability can only be used once per combat.

Shunt (co): If your damage score causes health damage to your opponent, you can also *shunt* them. This reduces their *speed* by 2 for the next combat round. You can only use *shunt* once per combat.

Sidestep (co): (see **Dodge**). You can only use *sidestep* once per combat.

Sideswipe (co): (see **Retaliation**). You can only use *sideswipe* once per combat.

Silver frost (mo): Use *silver frost* to 'freeze' your opponent's attack speed dice, forcing them to use the same dice result in the next combat round. You can only use *silver frost* once per combat.

Siphon (mo): All of your opponent's ⚅ results become a ⚀ when rolling for their damage score.

Skewer (co): Instead of rolling for a damage score, you can *skewer* your opponents. Roll 1 damage die and apply the result to each of your opponents, ignoring their *armour*. This also lowers their *speed* by 1 for the next combat round. You can only use *skewer* once per combat.

Slam (co): Use this ability to stop your opponent rolling for damage when they have won a round. In the next combat round only, your opponent's *speed* is reduced by 1. You can only use this ability once per combat.

Slick (co): If you win a round, you can use the total of your attack speed dice for your damage score (adding your *brawn* as normal). You can only use this ability once per combat. (Note: you cannot use modifier abilities to alter these dice results once they are used for your damage score.)

Snake strike (pa): (requires a snake in the left hand.) Before the first combat round begins you may automatically inflict 2 damage dice to a single opponent, ignoring *armour*. This will also inflict any harmful passive abilities you have, such as *bleed* and *venom*.

Sneak (mo): You may change the result of one of your opponent's speed dice to a ⚀. This ability can only be used once per combat.

Spirit mark (co + mo): When your damage score causes health damage to an opponent, you can also mark them with an ancestral rune. In subsequent combat rounds, the mark allows you to increase your damage score by 2 against this same opponent for the remainder of the battle. Allies also benefit from this modifier. *Spirit mark* can only be used once per combat.

Spirit ward (mo): Cast this spell any time in combat, on yourself or an ally, to raise *armour* by 6 for one combat round. *Spirit ward* can only be used once per combat.

Stagger (co): If your damage score causes health damage to your opponent, you can *stagger* them. This lowers their *armour* to zero for the next combat round only. You can only use *stagger* once per combat.

Steadfast (pa): You are immune to *knockdown*. If an opponent has this ability, you can ignore it.

Steal (mo): Use this ability any time in combat to automatically raise one of your attributes (*speed, brawn, magic* or *armour*) to match your opponent's. The effect wears off at the end of the combat round. You can only use *steal* once per combat.

Stone rain (co): Instead of rolling for damage after winning a round, you can cast *stone rain*. This will automatically inflict 1 damage die to a single opponent, ignoring *armour*. In each consecutive round, *stone rain* will double its damage on the same opponent. (In the second round, you would roll 2 damage dice, the third round 4 damage dice.) If you use another ability (of any type) or lose a round, *stone rain* ends. This ability will last up to three rounds (4 damage dice). It can only be cast once per combat.

Stone skin (co): Instead of rolling for a damage score, you can activate *stone skin*. This lowers your *speed* by 2. *Stone skin* can be removed at any time by winning a combat round and choosing not to roll for damage. While in stone skin:

- If an opponent wins a combat round, roll a die. On a ⚀ or ⚁ result, their blow glances off your stone skin and they do not roll for damage.
- You cannot use any abilities other than *trample*. Passive abilities that have already been applied (such as *bleed*) will continue to damage opponents.

Suppress (mo): Reduce the result of your opponent's attack speed by 2 for one combat round. *Suppress* can only be used once per combat.

Sure edge (mo): If your hero is equipped with an axe, sword, dagger or spear, you can use *sure edge*. This adds 1 to each die you roll for your damage score for the duration of the combat.

Sure grip (mo): All ⚀ results can be changed to a ⚅ result when rolling for your attack speed.

Surefooted (mo): You may re-roll all of your hero's speed dice. You must accept the result of the second roll. *Surefooted* can only be used once per combat.

Surge (co): A powerful attack that increases your *magic* score by 3. However, in the next combat round you must lower your *speed* by 1. This ability can only be used once per combat.

Stun (sp): (see **Webbed**). You can only use *stun* once per combat.

Swarm (co): Instead of rolling for a damage score, you can unleash a swarm of bugs. Roll 1 damage die and apply this to a single opponent, ignoring *armour*. In the next combat round only, their *speed* is lowered by 1. This ability can only be used once per combat.

Sweet spot (pa): Before a combat begins, choose a number 1–6. Each time your opponent rolls a die with this result when rolling for attack speed, they automatically take 2 damage.

Thorn armour (co): Use this ability to raise your *armour* by 3 for one combat round. It also inflicts 1 damage die, ignoring *armour*, to all your opponents (roll once and apply the same damage to each opponent). This ability can only be used once per combat.

Thorn cage (co + pa): Instead of rolling for a damage score, you can cast *thorn cage*. It automatically encases one opponent in a cage of thorns, inflicting 1 damage die (ignoring *armour*). It also inflicts 1 point of damage to the same opponent at the end of each combat round for the duration of the combat. *Thorn cage* can only be used once per combat.

Thorns (pa): You automatically inflict 1 damage to all of your opponents, at the end of every combat round. This ability ignores *armour*.

Time shift (sp): You may raise your *speed* to match your opponent's for three combat rounds. You cannot play another speed ability until time shift has faded. This ability can only be used once per combat.

Tome raider (pa): Using the monocle you are able to unlock the hidden secrets of the arcane. You may automatically add 2 *magic* to each spell book in your possession.

Toxicology (pa): You are immune to all *delirium, disease* and *venom* effects.

Trample (co): Instead of rolling for a damage score, you can *trample*. Roll 3 damage dice and apply the result to each of your opponents, ignoring *armour*. You can only use *trample* once per combat.

Tranquillity (pa): You may heal 2 *health* a round when you use the *meditation* ability, instead of only 1.

Tremor strike (sp): Make the ground beneath your enemies' feet tremble. This lowers opponents' *speed* by 2 for two combat rounds.

Trickster (mo): You may swap one of your opponent's speed die for your own. You can only use *trickster* once per combat.

Turn up the heat (pa): Increase the damage caused by *fire aura* by 1. Allies in team battles also benefit from this increase.

Underhand (mo): If you get a double when rolling for attack speed but your result is lower than your opponent's, you can use *underhand* to automatically win the round. *Underhand* can only be used once per combat.

Unstoppable (mo): When an opponent wins a combat round, you may spend 5 *health* to automatically win it back and roll for damage. You can only use *unstoppable* once per combat.

Vampirism (mo): When you inflict damage to your opponent you can heal yourself for half the amount of *health* your opponent has lost, rounding up. You can only use *vampirism* once per combat.

Vanish (co): (see **Dodge**). Use *vanish* to turn invisible for several seconds, avoiding your opponent's damage for one round. You can only use *vanish* once per combat.

Veil (co): Use this ability when you have lost a combat round to avoid taking damage from your opponent's damage score. You may also increase your *speed* by 1 for the duration of the next combat round. You can only use *veil* once per combat.

Venom (pa): If your damage dice/damage score causes health damage to your opponent, they lose a further 2 *health* at the end of every combat round for the remainder of the combat. This ability ignores *armour*.

Vindicator (pa): You may use your *double-punch* ability twice in the same combat and add 2 to the result each time.

Volcanism set (pa): If your hero is wearing all three items from the *volcanism* set (head, gloves and chest) then you may use the *volcanism* ability. This allows you to use *back draft, fire aura, sear* and *fire shield* (if available) without counting them towards your quota of hexed abilities.

Volley (co): Instead of rolling for a damage score, you can use *volley* to shower your enemies with arrows. Roll 1 damage die and apply the result to each of your opponents, ignoring their *armour*. You can only use *volley* once per combat.

Vortex (co): Instead of rolling for a damage score, you can cast *vortex* – a spinning whirlwind of dark energy. At the start of each subsequent combat round, roll a die. On a ⚀ or ⚁ result, you have been hit by the vortex and must lose 2 *health*. A result of ⚂ or higher, each opponent is hit instead and must lose 2 *health*. Once cast, the *vortex* stays in play for the rest of the combat. The die result cannot be modified.

War paint (mo): The runes on your body give you greater protection and strength. You may raise your *brawn* or *armour* score by 3 for one combat round. You can only use *war paint* once per combat.

Wave (co): Assault your enemies with a wave of mental energy. This does damage equal to your current *magic* score, ignoring *armour*. You can proportion this damage amongst any/all of your opponents, but no single opponent can take more than half of your *magic* score, rounding up. You can only use *wave* once per combat

Weaver (pa): Each time you play a combat ability, you may heal 2 *health*.

Webbed (sp): This ability reduces the number of dice your opponent can roll for attack speed by 1, for one combat round only. You can only use this ability once per combat.

Wild child (mo): You may add 1 to your die result, when using the *ley line infusion* ability.

Windblast (sp): (See **Webbed**.) You can only use windblast once per combat.

Wisdom (mo): Use any time in combat to raise your *magic* score by 2 for one combat round. You can only use this ability once per combat.

Wish master (sp): You can cast this spell at the start of a combat round to grow into a giant. Your *speed* is lowered by 1 but your *magic* and *armour* are increased by 2 for the remainder of the combat. *Wish master* can only be used once per combat.

Wither (co): Instead of rolling for a damage score, you can cast *wither*. This inflicts 2 damage dice to a single opponent, ignoring *armour*. It also reduces their *brawn* or *magic* score by 1 for the remainder of the combat. You can only use *wither* once per combat.

ABOUT GOLLANCZ

Gollancz is the oldest SF publishing imprint in the world. Since being founded in 1927 Gollancz has continued to publish a focused selection of bestselling and award-winning authors. The front-list includes **Ben Aaronovitch**, **Joe Abercrombie**, **Charlaine Harris**, **Joanne Harris**, **Joe Hill**, **Alastair Reynolds**, **Patrick Rothfuss**, **Nalini Singh** and **Brandon Sanderson**.

As one of the largest Science Fiction and Fantasy imprints in the UK it is no surprise we have one of the most extensive backlists in the world. Find high-quality SF on Gateway written by such authors as **Philip K. Dick**, **Ursula Le Guin**, **Connie Willis**, **Sir Arthur C. Clarke**, **Pat Cadigan**, **Michael Moorcock** and **George R.R. Martin**.

We also have a strand of publishing in translation, which includes French, Polish and Russian authors. Gollancz is home to more award-winning authors than any other imprint, with names including **Aliette de Bodard**, **M. John Harrison**, **Paul McAuley**, **Sarah Pinborough**, **Pierre Pevel**, **Justina Robson** and many more.

The SF Gateway

More than 3,000 classic, rare and previously out-of-print SF novels at your fingertips.

www.sfgateway.com

The Gollancz Blog

Bringing you news from our worlds to yours. Stories, interviews, articles and exclusive extracts just for you!

www.gollancz.co.uk

GOLLANCZ
LONDON